John Grisham

THE
BRETHREN

THE
CHAMBER

This edition published in 2001 by Cresset Editions,
an imprint of The Random House Group Ltd,
20 Vauxhall Bridge Road, London SW1V 2SA

Printed and bound in Germany

ISBN 0 09 188134 X

THE BRETHREN

ONE

For the weekly docket the court jester wore his standard garb of well-used and deeply faded maroon pajamas and lavender terry-cloth shower shoes with no socks. He wasn't the only inmate who went about his daily business in his pajamas, but no one else dared wear lavender shoes. His name was T. Karl, and he'd once owned banks in Boston.

The pajamas and shoes weren't nearly as troubling as the wig. It parted at the middle and rolled in layers downward, over his ears, with tight curls coiling off into three directions, and fell heavily onto his shoulders. It was a bright gray, almost white, and fashioned after the Old English magistrate's wigs from centuries earlier. A friend on the outside had found it at a secondhand costume store in Manhattan, in the Village.

T. Karl wore it to court with great pride, and, odd as it was, it had, with time, become part of the show. The other inmates kept their distance from T. Karl anyway, wig or not.

He stood behind his flimsy folding table in the prison cafeteria, tapped a plastic mallet that served

1

as a gavel, cleared his squeaky throat, and announced with great dignity: 'Hear ye, hear ye, hear ye. The Inferior Federal Court of North Florida is now in session. Please rise.'

No one moved, or at least no one made an effort to stand. Thirty inmates lounged in various stages of repose in plastic cafeteria chairs, some looking at the court jester, some chatting away as if he didn't exist.

T. Karl continued: 'Let all ye who search for justice draw nigh and get screwed.'

No laughs. It had been funny months earlier when T. Karl first tried it. Now it was just another part of the show. He sat down carefully, making sure the rows of curls bouncing upon his shoulders were given ample chance to be seen, then he opened a thick red leather book which served as the official record for the court. He took his work very seriously.

Three men entered the room from the kitchen. Two of them wore shoes. One was eating a saltine. The one with no shoes was also bare-legged up to his knees, so that below his robe his spindly legs could be seen. They were smooth and hairless and very brown from the sun. A large tattoo had been applied to his left calf. He was from California.

All three wore old church robes from the same choir, pale green with gold trim. They came from the same store as T. Karl's wig, and had been presented by him as gifts at Christmas. That was how he kept his job as the court's official clerk.

There were a few hisses and jeers from the spectators as the judges ambled across the tile floor, in full regalia, their robes flowing. They took

2

their places behind a long folding table, near T. Karl but not too near, and faced the weekly gathering. The short round one sat in the middle. Joe Roy Spicer was his name, and by default he acted as the Chief Justice of the tribunal. In his previous life, Judge Spicer had been a Justice of the Peace in Mississippi, duly elected by the people of his little county, and sent away when the feds caught him skimming bingo profits from a Shriners club.

'Please be seated,' he said. Not a soul was standing.

The judges adjusted their folding chairs and shook their robes until they fell properly around them. The assistant warden stood to the side, ignored by the inmates. A guard in uniform was with him. The Brethren met once a week with the prison's approval. They heard cases, mediated disputes, settled little fights among the boys, and had generally proved to be a stabilizing factor amid the population.

Spicer looked at the docket, a neat hand-printed sheet of paper prepared by T. Karl, and said, 'Court shall come to order.'

To his right was the Californian, the Honorable Finn Yarber, age sixty, in for two years now with five to go for income tax evasion. A vendetta, he still maintained to anyone who would listen. A crusade by a Republican governor who'd managed to rally the voters in a recall drive to remove Chief Justice Yarber from the California Supreme Court. The rallying point had been Yarber's opposition to the death penalty, and his high-handedness in delaying every execution. Folks wanted blood,

3

Yarber prevented it, the Republicans whipped up a frenzy, and the recall was a smashing success. They pitched him onto the street, where he floundered for a while until the IRS began asking questions. Educated at Stanford, indicted in Sacramento, sentenced in San Francisco, and now serving his time at a federal prison in Florida.

In for two years and Finn was still struggling with the bitterness. He still believed in his own innocence, still dreamed of conquering his enemies. But the dreams were fading. He spent a lot of time on the jogging track, alone, baking in the sun and dreaming of another life.

'First case is Schneiter versus Magruder,' Spicer announced as if a major antitrust trial was about to start.

'Schneiter's not here,' Beech said.

'Where is he?'

'Infirmary. Gallstones again. I just left there.'

Hatlee Beech was the third member of the tribunal. He spent most of his time in the infirmary because of hemorrhoids, or headaches, or swollen glands. Beech was fifty-six, the youngest of the three, and with nine years to go he was convinced he would die in prison. He'd been a federal judge in East Texas, a hardfisted conservative who knew lots of Scripture and liked to quote it during trials. He'd had political ambitions, a nice family, money from his wife's family's oil trust. He also had a drinking problem which no one knew about until he ran over two hikers in Yellowstone. Both died. The car Beech had been driving was owned by a young lady he was not married to. She was found naked in the front seat, too drunk to walk.

4

They sent him away for twelve years.

Joe Roy Spicer, Finn Yarber, Hatlee Beech. The Inferior Court of North Florida, better known as the Brethren around Trumble, a minimum security federal prison with no fences, no guard towers, no razor wire. If you had to do time, do it the federal way, and do it in a place like Trumble.

'Should we default him?' Spicer asked Beech.

'No, just continue it until next week.'

'Okay. I don't suppose he's going anywhere.'

'I object to a continuance,' Magruder said from the crowd.

'Too bad,' said Spicer. 'It's continued until next week.'

Magruder was on his feet. 'That's the third time it's been continued. I'm the plaintiff. I sued him. He runs to the infirmary every time we have a docket.'

'What're ya'll fightin over?' Spicer asked.

'Seventeen dollars and two magazines,' T. Karl said helpfully.

'That much, huh?' Spicer said. Seventeen dollars would get you sued every time at Trumble.

Finn Yarber was already bored. With one hand he stroked his shaggy gray beard, and with the other he raked his long fingernails across the table. Then he popped his toes, loudly, crunching them into the floor in an efficient little workout that grated on the nerves. In his other life, when he had titles – Mr. Chief Justice of the California Supreme Court – he often presided while wearing leather clogs, no socks, so that he could exercise his toes during the dull oral arguments. 'Continue it,' he said.

'Justice delayed is justice denied,' Magruder said solemnly.

'Now that's original,' said Beech. 'One more week, then we'll default Schneiter.'

'So ordered,' Spicer said, with great finality. T. Karl made a note in the docket book. Magruder sat down in a huff. He'd filed his complaint in the Inferior Court by handing to T. Karl a one-page summary of his allegations against Schneiter. Only one page. The Brethren didn't tolerate paperwork. One page and you got your day in court. Schneiter had replied with six pages of invective, all of which had been summarily stricken by T. Karl.

The rules were kept simple. Short pleadings. No discovery. Quick justice. Decisions on the spot, and all decisions were binding if both parties submitted to the jurisdiction of the court. No appeals; there was nowhere to take one. Witnesses were not given an oath to tell the truth. Lying was completely expected. It was, after all, a prison.

'What's next?' Spicer asked.

T. Karl hesitated for a second, then said, 'It's the Whiz case.'

Things were suddenly still for a moment, then the plastic cafeteria chairs rattled forward in one noisy offensive. The inmates scooted and shuffled until T. Karl announced, 'That's close enough!' They were less than twenty feet away from the bench.

'We shall maintain decorum!' he proclaimed.

The Whiz matter had been festering for months at Trumble. Whiz was a young Wall Street crook who'd bilked some rich clients. Four million dollars had never been accounted for, and legend held that Whiz had stashed it offshore and managed it from inside Trumble. He had six years left, and would be almost forty when paroled. It was widely assumed that he was quietly serving his time until one glorious day when he would walk free, still a young man, and fly off in a private jet to a beach where the money was waiting.

Inside, the legend only grew, partly because Whiz kept to himself and spent long hours every day studying financials and technical charts and reading impenetrable economic publications. Even the warden had tried to cajole him into sharing market tips.

An ex-lawyer known as Rook had somehow got next to Whiz, and had somehow convinced him to share a small morsel of advice with an investment club that met once a week in the prison chapel. On behalf of the club, Rook was now suing the Whiz for fraud.

Rook took the witness chair, and began his narrative. The usual rules of procedure and evidence were dispensed with so that the truth could be arrived at quickly, whatever form it might take.

'So I go to the Whiz and I ask him what he thinks about ValueNow, a new online company I read about in *Forbes*,' Rook explained. 'It was about to go public, and I liked the idea behind the company. Whiz said he'd check it out for me. I heard nothing. So I went back to him and said, "Hey, Whiz, what about ValueNow?" And he said he thought it was a solid company and the stock would go through the roof.'

'I did not say that,' the Whiz inserted quickly.

He was seated across the room, by himself, his arms folded over the chair in front.

'Yes you did.'

'I did not.'

'Anyway, I go back to the club and tell them that Whiz is high on the deal, so we decide we want to buy some stock in ValueNow. But little guys can't buy because the offering is closed. I go back to Whiz over there and I say, "Look, Whiz, you think you could pull some strings with your buddies on Wall Street and get us a few shares of ValueNow?" And Whiz said he thought he could do that.'

'That's a lie,' said Whiz.

'Quiet,' said Justice Spicer. 'You'll get your chance.'

'He's lying,' Whiz said, as if there was a rule against it.

If Whiz had money, you'd never know it, at least not on the inside. His eight-by-twelve cell was bare except for stacks of financial publications. No stereo, fan, books, cigarettes, none of the usual assets acquired by almost everyone else. This only added to the legend. He was considered a miser, a weird little man who saved every penny and was no doubt stashing everything offshore.

'Anyway,' Rook continued, 'we decided to gamble by taking a big position in ValueNow. Our strategy was to liquidate our holdings and consolidate.'

'Consolidate?' asked Justice Beech. Rook sounded like a portfolio manager who handled billions.

'Right, consolidate. We borrowed all we could

from friends and family, and had close to a thousand bucks.'

'A thousand bucks,' repeated Justice Spicer. Not bad for an inside job. 'Then what happened?'

'I told Whiz over there that we were ready to move. Could he get us the stock? This was on a Tuesday. The offering was on a Friday. Whiz said no problem. Said he had a buddy at Goldman Sux or some such place that could take care of us.'

'That's a lie,' Whiz shot from across the room.

'Anyway, on Wednesday I saw Whiz in the east yard, and I asked him about the stock. He said no problem.'

'That's a lie.'

'I got a witness.'

'Who?' asked Justice Spicer.

'Picasso.'

Picasso was sitting behind Rook, as were the other six members of the investment club. Picasso reluctantly waved his hand.

'Is that true?' Spicer asked.

'Yep,' Picasso answered. 'Rook asked about the stock. Whiz said he would get it. No problem.'

Picasso testified in a lot of cases, and had been caught lying more than most inmates.

'Continue,' Spicer said.

'Anyway, Thursday I couldn't find Whiz anywhere. He was hiding from me.'

'I was not.'

'Friday, the stock goes public. It was offered at twenty a share, the price we could've bought it for if Mr. Wall Street over there had done what he promised. It opened at sixty, spent most of the day at eighty, then closed at seventy. Our plans were to sell it as soon as possible. We could've bought fifty shares at twenty, sold them at eighty, and walked away from the deal with three thousand dollars in profits.'

Violence was very rare at Trumble. Three thousand dollars would not get you killed, but some bones might be broken. Whiz had been lucky so far. There'd been no ambush.

'And you think the Whiz owes you these lost profits?' asked ex-Chief Justice Finn Yarber, now plucking his eyebrows.

'Damned right we do. Look, what makes the deal stink even worse is that Whiz bought Value-Now for himself.'

'That's a damned lie,' Whiz said.

'Language, please,' Justice Beech said. If you wanted to lose a case before the Brethren, just offend Beech with your language.

The rumors that Whiz had bought the stock for himself had been started by Rook and his gang. There was no proof of it, but the story had proved irresistible and had been repeated by most inmates so often that it was now established as fact. It fit so nicely.

'Is that all?' Spicer asked Rook.

Rook had other points he wanted to elaborate on, but the Brethren had no patience with windy litigants. Especially ex-lawyers still reliving their glory days. There were at least five of them at Trumble, and they seemed to be on the docket all the time.

'I guess so,' Rook said.

'What do you have to say?' Spicer asked the Whiz.

Whiz stood and took a few steps toward their table. He glared at his accusers, Rook and his gang of losers. Then he addressed the court. 'What's the burden of proof here?'

Justice Spicer immediately lowered his eyes and waited for help. As a Justice of the Peace, he'd had no legal training. He'd never finished high school, then worked for twenty years in his father's country store. That's where the votes came from. Spicer relied on common sense, which was often at odds with the law. Any questions dealing with legal theory would be handled by his two colleagues.

'It's whatever we say it is,' Justice Beech said, relishing a debate with a stockbroker on the court's rules of procedure.

'Clear and convincing proof?' asked the Whiz.

'Could be, but not in this case.'

'Beyond a reasonable doubt?'

'Probably not.'

'Preponderance of the evidence?'

'Now you're getting close.'

'Then, they have no proof,' the Whiz said, waving his hands like a bad actor in a bad TV drama.

'Why don't you just tell us your side of the story?' said Beech.

'I'd love to. ValueNow was a typical online offering, lots of hype, lots of red ink on the books. Sure Rook came to me, but by the time I could make my calls, the offering was closed. I called a friend who told me you couldn't get near the stock. Even the big boys were shut out.'

'Now, how does that happen?' asked Justice Yarber.

The room was quiet. The Whiz was talking money, and everyone was listening.

'Happens all the time in IPOs. That's initial public offerings.'

'We know what an IPO is,' Beech said.

Spicer certainly did not. Didn't have many of those back in rural Mississippi.

The Whiz relaxed, just a little. He could dazzle them for a moment, win this nuisance of a case, then go back to his cave and ignore them.

'The ValueNow IPO was handled by the investment banking firm of Bakin-Kline, a small outfit in San Francisco. Five million shares were offered. Bakin-Kline basically presold the stock to its preferred customers and friends, so that most big investment firms never had a shot at the stock. Happens all the time.'

The judges and the inmates, even the court jester, hung on every word.

He continued. 'It's silly to think that some disbarred yahoo sitting in prison, reading an old copy of *Forbes*, can somehow buy a thousand dollars' worth of ValueNow.'

And at that very moment it did indeed seem very silly. Rook fumed while his club members began quietly blaming him.

'Did you buy any of it?' asked Beech.

'Of course not. I couldn't get near it. And besides, most of the high-tech and online companies are built with funny money. I stay away from them.'

'What do you prefer?' Beech asked quickly, his curiosity getting the better of him.

'Value. The long haul. I'm in no hurry. Look,

12

this is a bogus case brought by some boys looking for an easy buck.' He waved toward Rook, who was sinking in his chair. The Whiz sounded perfectly believable and legitimate.

Rook's case was built on hearsay, speculation, and the corroboration of Picasso, a notorious liar.

'You got any witnesses?' Spicer asked.

'I don't need any,' the Whiz said and took his seat.

Each of the three justices scribbled something on a slip of paper. Deliberations were quick, verdicts instantaneous. Yarber and Beech slid theirs to Spicer, who announced, 'By a vote of two to one, we find for the defendant. Case dismissed. Who's next?'

The vote was actually unanimous, but every verdict was officially two to one. That allowed each of the three a little wiggle room if later confronted.

But the Brethren were well regarded around Trumble. Their decisions were quick and as fair as they could make them. In fact, they were remarkably accurate in light of the shaky testimony they often heard. Spicer had presided over small cases for years, in the back of his family's country store. He could spot a liar at fifty feet. Beech and Yarber had spent their careers in courtrooms, and had no tolerance for lengthy arguments and delays, the usual tactics.

'That's all today,' T. Karl reported. 'End of docket.'

'Very well. Court is adjourned until next week.'

T. Karl jumped to his feet, his curls again vibrating across his shoulders, and declared, 'Court's adjourned. All rise.'

13

No one stood, no one moved as the Brethren left the room. Rook and his gang were huddled, no doubt planning their next lawsuit. The Whiz left quickly.

The assistant warden and the guard eased away without being seen. The weekly docket was one of the better shows at Trumble.

TWO

Though he'd served in Congress for fourteen years, Aaron Lake still drove his own car around Washington. He didn't need or want a chauffeur, or an aide, or a bodyguard. Sometimes an intern would ride with him and take notes, but for the most part Lake enjoyed the tranquillity of sitting in D.C. traffic while listening to classical guitar on the stereo. Many of his friends, especially those who'd achieved the status of a Mr. Chairman or a Mr. Vice Chairman, had larger cars with drivers. Some even had limos.

Not Lake. It was a waste of time and money and privacy. If he ever sought higher office, he certainly didn't want the baggage of a chauffeur wrapped around his neck. Besides, he enjoyed being alone. His office was a madhouse. He had fifteen people bouncing off the walls, answering phones, opening files, serving the folks back in Arizona who'd sent him to Washington. Two more did nothing but raise money. Three interns managed to further clog his narrow corridors and take up more time than they deserved.

He was single, a widower, with a quaint little

townhouse in Georgetown that he was very fond of. He lived quietly, occasionally stepping into the social scene that had attracted him and his late wife in the early years.

He followed the Beltway, the traffic slow and cautious because of a light snow. He was quickly cleared through CIA security at Langley, and was very pleased to see a preferred parking space waiting for him, along with two plainclothes security personnel.

'Mr. Maynard is waiting,' one of them said gravely, opening his car door while the other took his briefcase. Power did have its perks.

Lake had never met with the CIA director at Langley. They'd conferred twice on the Hill, years earlier, back when the poor guy could get around. Teddy Maynard was in a wheelchair and in constant pain, and even senators got themselves driven out to Langley anytime he needed them. He'd called Lake a half-dozen times in fourteen years, but Maynard was a busy man. His light-lifting was usually handled by associates.

Security barriers collapsed all around the congressman as he and his escorts worked their way into the depths of the CIA headquarters. By the time Lake arrived at Mr. Maynard's suite, he was walking a bit taller, with just a trace of a swagger. He couldn't help it. Power was intoxicating.

Teddy Maynard had sent for him.

Inside the room, a large, square, windowless place known unofficially as the bunker, the Director was sitting alone, looking blankly at a large screen upon which the face of Congressman Aaron Lake was

16

frozen. It was a recent photo, one taken at a black-tie fund-raiser three months earlier where Lake had half a glass of wine, ate baked chicken, no dessert, drove himself home, alone, and went to bed before eleven. The photo was appealing because Lake was so attractive – light red hair with almost no gray, hair that was not colored or tinted, a full hairline, dark blue eyes, square chin, really nice teeth. He was fifty-three years old and aging superbly. He did thirty minutes a day on a rowing machine and his cholesterol was 160. They hadn't found a single bad habit. He enjoyed the company of women, especially when it was important to be seen with one. His steady squeeze was a sixty-year-old widow in Bethesda whose late husband had made a fortune as a lobbyist.

Both his parents were dead. His only child was a schoolteacher in Santa Fe. His wife of twenty-nine years had died in 1996 of ovarian cancer. A year later, his thirteen-year-old spaniel died too, and Congressman Aaron Lake of Arizona truly lived alone. He was Catholic, not that that mattered anymore, and he attended Mass at least once a week. Teddy pushed the button and the face disappeared.

Lake was unknown outside the Beltway, primarily because he'd kept his ego in check. If he had aspirations to higher office, they were closely guarded. His name had been mentioned once as a potential candidate for governor of Arizona, but he enjoyed Washington too much. He loved George-town – the crowds, the anonymity, the city life – good restaurants and cramped bookstores and espresso bars. He liked theater and music, and he and his late wife had never missed an event at the Kennedy Center.

On the Hill, Lake was known as a bright and hardworking congressman who was articulate, fiercely honest, and loyal, conscientious to a fault. Because his district was the home of four large defense contractors, he had become an expert on military hard-ware and readiness. He was Chairman of the House Committee on Armed Services, and it was in that capacity that he had come to know Teddy Maynard.

Teddy pushed the button again, and there was Lake's face. For a fifty-year veteran of intelligence wars, Teddy seldom had a knot in his stomach. He'd dodged bullets, hidden under bridges, frozen in mountains, poisoned two Czech spies, shot a traitor in Bonn, learned seven languages, fought the cold war, tried to prevent the next one, had more adventures than any ten agents combined, yet looking at the innocent face of Congressman Aaron Lake he felt a knot.

He – the CIA – was about to do something the agency had never done before.

They'd started with a hundred senators, fifty governors, four hundred and thirty-five congressmen, all the likely suspects, and now there was only one. Representative Aaron Lake of Arizona.

Teddy flicked a button and the wall went blank. His legs were covered with a quilt. He wore the same thing every day – a V-necked navy sweater, white shirt, subdued bow tie. He rolled his wheelchair to a spot near the door, and prepared to meet his candidate.

*

18

During the eight minutes Lake was kept waiting, he was served coffee and offered a pastry, which he declined. He was six feet tall, weighed one-seventy, was fastidious about his appearance, and had he taken the pastry Teddy would've been surprised. As far as they could tell, Lake never ate sugar. Never.

His coffee was strong, though, and as he sipped it he reviewed a little research of his own. The purpose of the meeting was to discuss the alarming flow of black market artillery into the Balkans. Lake had two memos, eighty pages of double-spaced data he'd crunched until two in the morning. He wasn't sure why Mr. Maynard wanted him to appear at Langley to discuss such a matter, but he was determined to be prepared.

A soft buzzer sounded, the door opened, and the Director of the CIA rolled out, wrapped in a quilt and looking every day of his seventy-four years. His handshake was firm, though, probably because of the strain of pushing himself around. Lake followed him back into the room, leaving the two college-educated pit bulls to guard the door.

They sat opposite each other, across a very long table that ran to the end of the room where a large white wall served as a screen. After brief preliminaries, Teddy pushed a button and another face appeared. Another button, and the lights grew dim. Lake loved it – push little buttons, high-tech images flash instantly. No doubt the room was wired with enough electronic junk to monitor his pulse from thirty feet.

'Recognize him?' Teddy asked.

'Maybe. I think I've seen the face before.'

'He's Natli Chenkov. A former general. Now a member of what's left of the Russian parliament.'

'Also known as Natty,' Lake said proudly.

'That's him. Hard-line Communist, close ties to the military, brilliant mind, huge ego, very ambitious, ruthless, and right now the most dangerous man in the world.'

'Didn't know that.'

A flick, another face, this one of stone under a gaudy military parade hat. 'This is Yuri Goltsin, second in command of what's left of the Russian army. Chenkov and Goltsin have big plans.' Another flick, a map of a section of Russia north of Moscow. 'They're stockpiling arms in this region,' Teddy said. 'They're actually stealing them from themselves, looting the Russian army, but, and more important, they're buying them on the black market.'

'Where's their money coming from?'

'Everywhere. They're swapping oil for Israeli radar. They're trafficking in drugs and buying Chinese tanks through Pakistan. Chenkov has close ties with some mobsters, one of whom recently bought a factory in Malaysia where they make nothing but assault rifles. It's very elaborate. Chenkov has a brain, a very high IQ. He's probably a genius.'

Teddy Maynard was a genius, and if he bestowed that title on another, then Congressman Lake certainly believed it. 'So who gets attacked?'

Teddy dismissed the question because he wasn't ready to answer it. 'See the town of Vologda. It's about five hundred miles east of Moscow. Last week we tracked sixty Vetrov to a warehouse there. As you know, the Vetrov –'

'Is equivalent to our Tomahawk Cruise, but two feet longer.'

'Exactly. That makes three hundred they've moved in during the last ninety days. See the town of Rybinsk, just southwest of Vologda?'

'Known for its plutonium.'

'Yes, tons of it. Enough to make ten thousand nuclear warheads. Chenkov and Goltsin and their people control the entire area.'

'Control?'

'Yes, through a web of regional mobsters and local army units. Chenkov has his people in place.'

'In place for what?'

Teddy squeezed a button and the wall was blank. But the lights stayed dim, so that when he spoke across the table he did so almost from the shadows. 'The coup is right around the corner, Mr. Lake. Our worst fears are coming true. Every aspect of Russian society and culture is cracking and crumbling. Democracy is a joke. Capitalism is a nightmare. We thought we could McDonaldize the damned place, and it's been a disaster. Workers are not getting paid, and they're the lucky ones because they have jobs. Twenty percent do not. Children are dying because there are no medicines. So are many adults. Ten percent of the population are homeless. Twenty percent are hungry. Each day things get worse. The country has been looted by the mobsters. We think at least five hundred billion dollars has been stolen and taken out of the country. There's no relief in sight. The time is perfect for a new strongman, a new

21

dictator who'll promise to lead the people back to stability. The country is crying for leadership, and Mr. Chenkov has decided it's up to him.'

'And he has the army.'

'He has the army, and that's all it takes. The coup will be bloodless because the people are ready for it. They'll embrace Chenkov. He'll lead the parade into Red Square and dare us, the United States, to stand in his way. We'll be the bad guys again.'

'So the cold war is back,' Lake said, his words fading at the end.

'There'll be nothing cold about it. Chenkov wants to expand, to recapture the old Soviet Union. He desperately needs cash, so he'll simply take it in the form of land, factories, oil, crops. He'll start little regional wars, which he'll easily win.' Another map appeared. Phase One of the new world order was presented to Lake. Teddy didn't miss a word. 'I suspect he'll roll through the Baltic States, toppling governments in Estonia, Latvia, Lithuania, etc. Then he'll go to the old Eastern bloc and strike a deal with some of the Communists there.'

The congressman was speechless as he watched Russia expand. Teddy's predictions were so certain, so precise.

'What about the Chinese?' Lake asked.

But Teddy wasn't finished with Eastern Europe. He flicked; the map changed. 'Here's where we get sucked in.'

'Poland?'

'Yep. Happens every time. Poland is now a member of NATO, for some damned reason.

22

Imagine that. Poland signing on to help protect us and Europe. Chenkov solidifies Russia's old turf, and casts a longing eye westward. Same as Hitler, except he was looking to the east.'

'Why would he want Poland?'

'Why did Hitler want Poland? It was between him and Russia. He hated the Poles, and he was ready to start a war. Chenkov doesn't give a damn about Poland, he just wants to control it. And he wants to destroy NATO.'

'He's willing to risk a third world war?'

Buttons were pushed; the screen became a wall again; lights came on. The audiovisuals were over and it was time for an even more serious conversation. Pain shot through Teddy's legs, and he couldn't keep from frowning.

'I can't answer that,' he said. 'We know a lot, but we don't know what the man's thinking. He's moving very quietly, putting people in place, setting things up. It's not completely unexpected, you know.'

'Of course not. We've had these scenarios for the last eight years, but there's always been hope that it wouldn't happen.'

'It's happening, Congressman. Chenkov and Goltsin are eliminating their opponents as we speak.'

'What's the timetable?'

Teddy shifted again under the quilt, tried another position to stop the pain. 'It's difficult to say. If he's smart, which he certainly is, he'll wait until there's rioting in the streets. I think that a year from now Natty Chenkov will be the most famous man in the world.'

'A year,' Lake said to himself, as if he'd just been given his own death sentence.

There was a long pause as he contemplated the end of the world. Teddy certainly let him. The knot in Teddy's stomach was significantly smaller now. He liked Lake a lot. He was indeed very handsome, and articulate, and smart. They'd made the right choice.

He was electable.

After a round of coffee and a phone call Teddy had to take – it was the Vice President – they reconvened their little conference and moved forward. The congressman was pleased that Teddy had so much time for him. The Russians were coming, yet Teddy seemed so calm.

'I don't have to tell you how unprepared our military is,' he said gravely.

'Unprepared for what? For war?'

'Perhaps. If we are unprepared, then we could well have a war. If we are strong, we avoid war. Right now the Pentagon could not do what it did in the Gulf War in 1991.'

'We're at seventy percent,' Lake said with authority. This was his turf.

'Seventy percent will get us a war, Mr. Lake. A war we cannot win. Chenkov is spending every dime he can steal on new hardware. We're cutting budgets and depleting our military. We want to push buttons and launch smart bombs so that no American blood is shed. Chenkov will have two million hungry soldiers, anxious to fight and die if necessary.'

For a brief moment Lake felt proud. He'd had

the guts to vote against the last budget deal because it decreased military spending. The folks back home were upset about it. 'Can't you expose Chenkov now?' he asked.

'No. Absolutely not. We have excellent intelligence. If we react to him, then he'll know that we know. It's the spy game, Mr. Lake. It's too early to make him a monster.'

'So what's your plan?' Lake asked boldly. It was quite presumptuous to ask Teddy about his plans. The meeting had accomplished its purpose. One more congressman had been sufficiently briefed. At any moment Lake could be asked to leave so that another committee chairman of some variety could be shown in.

But Teddy had big plans, and he was anxious to share them. 'The New Hampshire primary is two weeks away. We have four Republicans and three Democrats all saying the same thing. Not a single candidate wants to increase defense spending. We have a budget surplus, miracle of all miracles, and everyone has a hundred ideas about how to spend it. A bunch of imbeciles. Just a few years ago we had huge budget deficits, and Congress spent money faster than it could be printed. Now there's a surplus. They're gorging themselves on the pork.'

Congressman Lake looked away for a second, then decided to let it pass.

'Sorry about that,' Teddy said, catching himself. 'Congress as a whole is irresponsible, but we have many fine congressmen.'

'You don't have to tell me.'

'Anyway, the field is crowded with a bunch of

clones. Two weeks ago we had different front-runners. They're slinging mud and knifing each other, all for the benefit of the country's forty-fourth largest state. It's silly.' Teddy paused and grimaced and tried to reshift his useless legs. 'We need someone new, Mr. Lake, and we think that someone is you.'

Lake's first reaction was to suppress a laugh, which he did by smiling, then coughing. He tried to compose himself, and said, 'You must be kidding.'

'You know I'm not kidding, Mr. Lake,' Teddy said sternly, and there was no doubt that Aaron Lake had walked into a well-laid trap.

Lake cleared his throat and completed the job of composing himself. 'All right, I'm listening.'

'It's very simple. In fact, its simplicity makes it beautiful. You're too late to file for New Hampshire, and it doesn't matter anyway. Let the rest of the pack slug it out there. Wait until it's over, then startle everyone by announcing your candidacy for President. Many will ask, "Who the hell is Aaron Lake?" And that's fine. That's what we want. They'll find out soon enough.

'Initially, your platform will have only one plank. It's all about military spending. You're a doom-sayer, with all sorts of dire predictions about how weak our military is becoming. You'll get every-body's attention when you call for doubling our military spending.'

'Doubling?'

'It works, doesn't it? It got your attention. Double it during your four-year term.'

'But why? We need more military spending, but a twofold increase would be excessive.'

'Not if we're facing another war, Mr. Lake. A war in which we push buttons and launch Tomahawk missiles by the thousands, at a million bucks a pop. Hell, we almost ran out of them last year in that Balkan mess. We can't find enough soldiers and sailors and pilots, Mr. Lake. You know this. The military needs tons of cash to recruit young men. We're low on everything – soldiers, missiles, tanks, planes, carriers. Chenkov is building now. We're not. We're still downsizing, and if we keep it up through another Administration, then we're dead.'

Teddy's voice rose, almost in anger, and when he stopped with 'we're dead,' Aaron Lake could almost feel the earth shake from the bombing.

'Where does the money come from?' he asked.

'Money for what?'

'The military.'

Teddy snorted in disgust, then said, 'Same place it always comes from. Need I remind you, sir, that we have a surplus?'

'We're busy spending the surplus.'

'Of course you are. Listen, Mr. Lake, don't worry about the money. Shortly after you announce, we'll scare the hell out of the American people. They'll think you're half-crazy at first, some kind of wacko from Arizona who wants to build even more bombs. But we'll jolt them. We'll create a crisis on the other side of the world, and suddenly Aaron Lake will be called a visionary. Timing is everything. You make a speech about how weak we are in Asia, few people listen. Then we'll create a situation over there that stops the world, and suddenly everyone wants to talk to you. It will go on like that, throughout the campaign. We'll build the tension on this end. We'll release reports, create situations, manipulate the media, embarrass your opponents. Frankly, Mr. Lake, I don't expect it to be that difficult.'

'You sound like you've been here before.'

'No. We've done some unusual things, all in an effort to protect this country. But we've never tried to swing a presidential election.' Teddy said this with an air of regret.

Lake slowly pushed his chair back, stood, stretched his arms and legs, and walked along the table to the end of the room. His feet were heavier. His pulse was racing. The trap had been sprung; he'd been caught.

He returned to his seat. 'I don't have enough money,' he offered across the table. He knew it was received by someone who'd already thought about it.

Teddy smiled and nodded and pretended to give this some thought. Lake's Georgetown home was worth $400,000. He kept about half that much in mutual funds and another $100,000 in municipal bonds. There were no significant debts. He had $40,000 in his reelection account.

'A rich candidate would not be attractive,' Teddy said, then reached for yet another button. Images returned to the wall, sharp and in color. 'Money will not be a problem, Mr. Lake,' he said, his voice much lighter. 'We'll get the defense contractors to pay for it. Look at that,' he said, waving with his right hand as if Lake wasn't sure what to look at. 'Last year the aerospace and defense industry did almost two hundred billion in business. We'll take just a fraction of that.'

'How much of a fraction?'

'As much as you need. We can realistically collect a hundred million dollars from them.'

'You also can't hide a hundred million dollars.'

'Don't bet on it, Mr. Lake. And don't worry about it. We'll take care of the money. You make the speeches, do the ads, run the campaign. The money will pour in. By the time November gets here, the American voters will be so terrified of Armageddon they won't care how much you've spent. It'll be a landslide.'

So Teddy Maynard was offering a landslide. Lake sat in a stunned but giddy silence and gawked at all that money up there on the wall – $194 billion, defense and aerospace. Last year's military budget was $270 billion. Double that to $540 billion in four years, and the contractors would get fat again. And the workers! Wages soaring through the roof! Jobs for everyone!

Candidate Lake would be embraced by executives with the cash and unions with the votes. The initial shock began to fade, and the simplicity of Teddy's plan became clear. Collect the cash from those who will profit. Scare the voters into racing to the polls. Win in a landslide. And in doing so save the world.

Teddy let him think for a moment, then said, 'We'll do most of it through PACs. The unions, engineers, executives, business coalitions – there's no shortage of political groups already on the books. And we'll form some others.'

Lake was already forming them. Hundreds of PACs, all flush with more cash than any election had ever seen. The shock was now completely gone, replaced by the sheer excitement of the idea. A thousand questions raced through his mind: Who'll be my Vice President? Who'll run the campaign? Chief of staff? Where to announce? 'It might work,' he said, under control.

'Oh yes. It'll work, Mr. Lake. Trust me. We've been planning this for some time.'

'How many people know about it?'

'Just a few. You've been carefully chosen, Mr. Lake. We examined many potential candidates, and your name kept rising to the top. We've checked your background.'

'Pretty dull, huh?'

'I suppose. Although your relationship with Ms. Valotti concerns me. She's been divorced twice and likes painkillers.'

'Didn't know I had a relationship with Ms. Valotti.'

'You've been seen with her recently.'

'You guys are watching, aren't you?'

'You expect something less?'

'I guess not.'

'You took her to a black-tie cry-a-thon for oppressed women in Afghanistan. Gimme a break.' Teddy's words were suddenly short and dripping with sarcasm.

'I didn't want to go.'

'Then don't. Stay away from that crap. Leave it for Hollywood. Valotti's nothing but trouble.'

'Anybody else?' Lake asked, more than a little defensive. His private life had been pretty dull since he'd become a widower. He was suddenly proud of it.

'Not really,' Teddy said. 'Ms. Benchly seems to be quite stable and makes a lovely escort.'

'Oh, thank you very much.'

'You'll get hammered on abortion, but you won't be the first.'

'It's a tired issue,' Lake said. And he was tired of grappling with it. He'd been for abortions, against abortions, soft on reproductive rights, tough on reproductive rights, pro-choice, pro-child, anti-women, embraced by the feminists. In his fourteen years on Capitol Hill he'd been chased all over the abortion minefield, getting bloodied with each new strategic move.

Abortion didn't scare him anymore, at least not at the moment. He was much more concerned with the CIA sniffing through his background.

'What about GreenTree?' he asked.

Teddy waved his right hand as if it was nothing. 'Twenty-two years ago. Nobody got convicted. Your partner went bankrupt and got himself indicted, but the jury let him walk. It'll come up; everything will come up. But frankly, Mr. Lake, we'll keep the attention diverted elsewhere. There's an advantage in jumping in at the last minute. The press won't have too much time to dig up dirt.'

'I'm single. We've elected an unmarried president only once.'

'You're a widower, the husband of a very lovely lady who was well respected both here and back home. It won't be an issue. Trust me.'

'So what worries you?'

'Nothing, Mr. Lake. Not a thing. You're a solid candidate, very electable. We'll create the issues and the fear, and we'll raise the money.'

Lake stood again, walked around the room rubbing his hair, scratching his chin, trying to clear his head. 'I have a lot of questions,' he said.

'Maybe I can answer some of them. Let's talk again tomorrow, right here, same time. Sleep on it, Mr. Lake. Time is crucial, but I suppose a man should have twenty-four hours before making such a decision.' Teddy actually smiled when he said this.

'That's a wonderful idea. Let me think about it. I'll have an answer tomorrow.'

'No one knows we've had this little chat.'

'Of course not.'

THREE

In terms of space, the law library occupied exactly one fourth of the square footage of the entire Trumble library. It was in a corner, partitioned off by a wall of red brick and glass, tastefully done at taxpayer expense. Inside the law library, shelves of well-used books stood packed together with barely enough room for an inmate to squeeze between them. Around the walls were desks covered with typewriters and computers and sufficient research clutter to resemble any big-firm library.

The Brethren ruled the law library. All inmates were allowed to use it, of course, but there was an unwritten policy that one needed permission to stay there for any length of time. Maybe not permission, but at least notice.

Justice Joe Roy Spicer of Mississippi earned forty cents an hour sweeping the floors and straightening the desks and shelves. He also emptied the trash, and was generally considered to be a pig when it came to his menial tasks. Justice Hatlee Beech of Texas was the official law librarian, and at fifty cents an hour was the highest paid. He was fastidious about 'his volumes,' and often bickered with Spicer about their care. Justice Finn Yarber, once of the California Supreme Court, was paid twenty cents an hour as a computer technician. His pay was at the bottom of the scale because he knew so little about computers.

On a typical day, the three spent between six and eight hours in the law library. If a Trumble inmate had a legal problem, he simply made an appointment with one of the Brethren and visited their little suite. Hatlee Beech was an expert on sentencing and appeals. Finn Yarber did bankruptcies, divorces, and child support cases. Joe Roy Spicer, with no formal legal training, had no real specialty. Nor did he want one. He ran the scams.

Strict rules prohibited the Brethren from charging fees for their legal work, but the strict rules meant little. They were, after all, convicted felons, and if they could quietly pick up some cash on the outside then everyone would be happy. Sentencing was a moneymaker. About a fourth of the inmates who arrived at Trumble had been improperly sentenced. Beech could review the records overnight and find the loopholes. A month earlier, he had knocked four years off the sentence of a young man who'd been given fifteen. The family had agreed to pay, and the Brethren earned $5,000, their biggest fee to date. Spicer arranged the secret deposit through their lawyer in Neptune Beach.

There was a cramped conference room in the back of the law library, behind the shelves and barely visible from the main room. The door to it had a large glass window, but no one bothered to look in. The Brethren retired there for quiet business. They called it their chamber.

34

Spicer had just met with their lawyer and he had mail, some really good letters. He closed the door and removed an envelope from a file. He waved it for Beech and Yarber to see. 'It's yellow,' he said. 'Ain't that sweet? It's for Ricky.'

'Who's it from?' Yarber asked.

'Curtis from Dallas.'

'The banker?' Beech asked excitedly.

'No, Curtis owns the jewelry stores. Listen.' Spicer unfolded the letter, also on soft yellow stationery. He smiled and cleared his throat and began to read: ' "Dear Ricky: Your letter of January eighth made me cry. I read it three times before I put it down. You poor boy. Why are they keeping you there?" '

'Where is he?' asked Yarber.

'Ricky's locked down in a fancy drug rehab unit his rich uncle is paying for. He's been in for a year, is clean and fully rehabbed, but the terrible people who run the place won't release him until April because they've been collecting twenty thousand dollars a month from his rich uncle, who just wants him locked away and won't send any spending money. Do you remember any of this?'

'Now I do.'

'You helped with the fiction. May I proceed?'

'Please do.'

Spicer continued reading: ' "I'm tempted to fly down there and confront those evil people myself. And your uncle, what a loser! Rich people like him think they can just send money and not get involved. As I told you, my father was quite wealthy, and he was the most miserable person I've ever known. Sure he bought me things – objects that were temporary and meant nothing when they were gone. But he never had time for me. He was a sick man, just like your uncle. I've enclosed a check for a thousand dollars if you need anything from the commissary.

' "Ricky, I can't wait to see you in April. I've already told my wife that there is an international diamond show in Orlando that month, and she has no interest in going with me." '

'April?' asked Beech.

'Yep. Ricky is certain he will be released in April.'

'Ain't that sweet,' Yarber said with a smile. 'And Curtis has a wife and kids?'

'Curtis is fifty-eight, three adult children, two grandchildren.'

'Where's the check?' asked Beech.

Spicer flipped the sheets of stationery and went to page two. ' "We have to make certain you can meet me in Orlando," ' he read. ' "Are you sure you'll finally be released in April? Please tell me you will. I think about you every hour. I keep your photo hidden in my desk drawer, and when I look into your eyes I know that we should be together." '

'Sick, sick, sick,' Beech said, still smiling. 'And he's from Texas.'

'I'm sure there are a lot of sweet boys in Texas,' Yarber said.

'And none in California?'

'The rest of it is just mush,' Spicer said, scanning quickly. There would be plenty of time to read it later. He held up the $1,000 check for his colleagues to see. In due course, it would be

36

smuggled out to their attorney and he would deposit it in their hidden account.

'When are we gonna bust him?' Yarber asked.

'Let's swap a few more letters. Ricky needs to share some more misery.'

'Maybe one of the guards could beat him up, or something like that,' Beech said.

'They don't have guards,' replied Spicer. 'It's a designer rehab clinic, remember? They have counselors.'

'But it's a lockdown facility, right? That means gates and fences, so surely there's a guard or two around. What if Ricky got attacked in the shower or the locker room by some goon who wanted his body?'

'It can't be a sexual attack,' Yarber said. 'That might scare Curtis. He might think Ricky caught a disease or something.'

And so the fiction went for a few minutes as they created more misery for poor Ricky. His picture had been lifted from the bulletin board of a fellow inmate, copied at a quick print by their lawyer, and had now been sent to more than a dozen pen pals across North America. The photo was of a smiling college grad, in a navy robe with a cap and gown, holding a diploma, a very handsome young man.

It was decided that Beech would work on the new story for a few days, then write a rough draft of the next letter to Curtis. Beech was Ricky, and at that moment their little tormented fictional boy was writing his tales of misery to eight different caring souls. Justice Yarber was Percy, also a young man locked away for drugs but now clean and nearing release and looking for an older sugar daddy with whom to spend meaningful time. Percy had five hooks in the water, and was slowly reeling them in.

Joe Roy Spicer didn't write very well. He coordinated the scam, helped with the fiction, kept the stories straight, and met with the lawyer who brought the mail. And he handled the money.

He pulled out another letter and announced, 'This, Your Honors, is from Quince.'

Everything stopped as Beech and Yarber stared at the letter. Quince was a wealthy banker in a small town in Iowa, according to the six letters he and Ricky had swapped. Like the rest, they'd found him through the personals of a gay magazine now hidden in the law library. He'd been their second catch, the first having become suspicious and disappearing. Quince's photo of himself was a snapshot taken at a lake, with the shirt off, the potbelly, the skinny arms, the receding hairline of a fifty-one-year-old – his family all around him. It was a bad photo, no doubt selected by Quince because it might be difficult to identify him, if anyone ever tried.

'Would you like to read it, Ricky boy?' Spicer asked, handing the letter to Beech, who took it and looked at the envelope. Plain white, no return address, typed lettering.

'Have you read it?' Beech asked.

'No. Go ahead.'

Beech slowly removed the letter, a plain sheet of white paper with tight single-spaced paragraphs produced by an old typewriter. He cleared his voice, and read: ' "Dear Ricky: It's done. I can't believe I did it, but I pulled it off. I used a pay phone and a money order so nothing could be traced – I think my trail is clean. The company you suggested in New York was superb, very discreet and helpful. I have to be honest, Ricky, it scared the hell out of me. Booking a gay cruise is something I never dreamed of doing. And you know what? It was exhilarating. I am so proud of myself. We have a cabin suite, a thousand bucks a night, and I can't wait." '

Beech stopped and glanced above his reading glasses halfway down his nose. Both of his colleagues were smiling, savoring the words.

He continued: ' "We set sail on March tenth, and I have a wonderful idea. I will arrive in Miami on the ninth, so we won't have much time to get together and introduce ourselves. Let's meet on the boat, in our suite. I'll get there first, check in, get the champagne on ice, then wait for you. Won't that be fun, Ricky? We'll have three days to ourselves. I say we don't leave the room." '

Beech couldn't help but smile, and he somehow managed to do so while shaking his head in disgust.

He continued: ' "I am so excited about our little trip. I have finally decided to discover who I really am, and you've given me the courage to take the first step. Though we haven't met, Ricky, I can never thank you enough.

' "Please write me back immediately and confirm. Take care, my Ricky. Love, Quince." '

'I think I'm gonna vomit,' Spicer said, but he wasn't convincing. There was too much to do.

'Let's bust him,' Beech said. The others quickly agreed.

'How much?' asked Yarber.

'At least a hundred thousand,' said Spicer. 'His family has owned banks for two generations. We know his father is still active in the business, so you have to figure the old man might go nuts if his boy gets outed. Quince can't afford to get booted from the family gravy train, so he'll pay whatever we demand. It's a perfect situation.'

Beech was already taking notes. So was Yarber. Spicer began pacing around the small room like a bear stalking prey. The ideas came slowly, the language, the opinions, the strategy, but before long the letter took shape.

In rough draft, Beech read it: '"Dear Quince: So nice to get your letter of January fourteenth. I'm so happy you got the gay cruise booked. It sounds delightful. One problem, though. I won't be able to make it, and there are a couple of reasons for this. One is that I won't be released for a few more years. I'm in a prison, not a drug treatment clinic. And I'm not gay, far from it. I have a wife and two kids, and right now they're having a difficult time financially because I'm sitting here in prison, unable to support them. That's where you come in, Quince. I need some of your money. I want a hundred thousand dollars. We can call it hush money. You send it, and I'll forget the Ricky business and the gay cruise and no one in Bakers, Iowa, will ever know anything about it. Your wife and your children and your father and the rest of your rich family will never know about Ricky. If you don't send the money, then I'll flood your little town with copies of our letters.

' "It's called extortion, Quince, and you're

caught. It's cruel and mean and criminal, and I don't care. I need money, and you have it."'

Beech stopped and looked around the room for approval.

'It's beautiful,' said Spicer, already spending the loot.

'It's nasty,' said Yarber. 'But what if he kills himself?'

'That's a long shot,' said Beech.

They read the letter again, then debated whether the timing was right. They did not mention the illegality of their scam, or the punishment if they got caught. Those discussions had been laid to rest months earlier when Joe Roy Spicer had convinced the other two to join him. The risks were insignificant when weighed against the potential returns. The Quinces who got themselves snared were not likely to run to the police and complain of extortion.

But they hadn't busted anyone yet. They were corresponding with a dozen or so potential victims, all middle-aged men who'd made the mistake of answering this simple ad:

> SWM in 20s looking for kind and
> discreet gentleman in 40s or 50s
> to pen pal with.

One little personal in small print in the back of a gay magazine had yielded sixty responses, and Spicer had the chore of sifting through the rubbish and identifying rich targets. At first he'd found the work disgusting, then he became amused by it. Now it was a business because they were about to

41

extort a hundred thousand bucks from a perfectly innocent man.

Their lawyer would take a third, the usual cut but a frustrating percentage nonetheless. They had no choice. He was a critical player in their crimes.

They worked on the letter to Quince for an hour, then agreed to sleep on it and do a final draft the next day. There was another letter from a man using the pseudonym of Hoover. It was his second, written to Percy, and rambled on for four paragraphs about bird-watching. Yarber would be forced to study birds before writing back as Percy and professing a great interest in the subject. Evidently, Hoover was afraid of his shadow. He revealed nothing personal, and there was no indication of money.

Give him some more rope, the Brethren decided. Talk about birds, then try to nudge him to the subject of physical companionship. If Hoover didn't take the hint, and if he didn't reveal something about his financial situation, then they'd drop him.

Within the Bureau of Prisons, Trumble was officially referred to as a camp. Such a designation meant there were no fences around the grounds, no razor wire, no watchtowers, no guards with rifles waiting to nail escapees. A camp meant minimum security, so that any inmate could simply walk away if he chose. There were a thousand at Trumble, but few walked away.

It was nicer than most public schools. Air-conditioned dorms, clean cafeteria serving three squares a day, a weight room, billiards, cards, racquetball, basketball, volleyball, jogging track, library, chapel, ministers on duty, counselors, caseworkers, unlimited visiting hours.

Trumble was as good as it could get for prisoners, all of whom were classified as low risk. Eighty percent were there for drug crimes. About forty had robbed banks without hurting or really scaring anyone. The rest were white-collar types whose crimes ranged from small-time scams to Dr. Floyd, a surgeon whose office had bilked Medicare out of $6 million over two decades.

Violence was not tolerated at Trumble. Threats were rare. There were plenty of rules and the administration had little trouble enforcing them. If you screwed up, they sent you away, to a medium-security prison, one with razor wire and rough guards.

Trumble's prisoners were content to behave themselves and count their days, the federal way.

Pursuing serious criminal activity on the inside was unheard of, until the arrival of Joe Roy Spicer. Before his fall, Spicer had heard stories about the Angola scam, named for the infamous Louisiana state penitentiary. Some inmates there had perfected the gay-extortion scheme, and before they were caught they had fleeced their victims of $700,000.

Spicer was from a rural county near the Louisiana line, and the Angola scam was a notorious affair in his part of the state. He never dreamed he'd copy it. But he woke up one morning in a federal pen, and decided to shaft every living soul he could get close enough to.

He walked the track every day at 1 P.M., usually

alone, always with a pack of Marlboros. He hadn't smoked for ten years before his incarceration; now he was up to two packs a day. So he walked to negate the damage to his lungs. In thirty-four months he'd walked 1,242 miles. And he'd lost twenty pounds, though probably not from exercise, as he liked to claim. The prohibition against beer was more responsible for the weight loss.

Thirty-four months of walking and smoking, twenty-one months to go.

Ninety thousand dollars of the stolen bingo money was literally buried in his backyard, a half a mile behind his house next to a toolshed – entombed in a homemade concrete vault his wife knew nothing about. She'd helped him spend the rest of the loot, $180,000 altogether, though the feds had traced only half of it. They'd bought Cadillacs and flown to Las Vegas, first class out of New Orleans, and they'd been driven around by casino limos and put up in suites.

If he had any dreams left, one was to be a professional gambler, headquartered out of Vegas but known and feared by casinos everywhere. Blackjack was his game, and though he'd lost a ton, he was still convinced he could beat any house. There were casinos in the Caribbean he'd never seen. Asia was heating up. He'd travel the world, first class, with or without his wife, stay in fancy suites, order room service, and terrorize any blackjack dealer dumb enough to deal him cards.

He'd take the $90,000 from his backyard, add it to his share of the Angola scam, and move to Vegas. With or without her. She hadn't been to Trumble in four months, although she used to

44

come every three weeks. He had nightmares of her plowing up the backyard looking for his buried treasure. He was almost convinced she didn't know about the money, but there was room for doubt. He'd been drinking two nights before being shipped off to prison, and had said something about the $90,000. He couldn't remember his exact words. Try as he might, he simply could not recall what he'd told her.

He lit another Marlboro at mile one. Maybe she had a boyfriend now. Rita Spicer was an attractive woman, a little chunky in places but nothing $90,000 couldn't hide. What if she and a new squeeze had found the money and were already spending it? One of Joe Roy's worst recurring nightmares was a scene from a bad movie – Rita and some unknown male with shovels digging like idiots in the rain. Why the rain, he didn't know. But it was always at night, in the middle of a thunderstorm, and the lightning would flash and he would see them slogging their way through the backyard, each time getting nearer and nearer to the toolshed.

In one dream the new mystery boyfriend was on a bulldozer, pushing piles of dirt all over the Spicer farm while Rita stood nearby, pointing here and there with her shovel.

Joe Roy craved the money. He could feel the cash in his hands. He would steal and extort all he could while he counted his days at Trumble, then he would rescue his buried loot and head for Vegas. No one in his hometown would have the pleasure of pointing and whispering and saying,

'There's old Joe Roy. Guess he's out of the pen now.' No sir.

He'd be living the high life. With or without her.

FOUR

Teddy looked at his pill bottles lined along the edge of his table, like little executioners ready to take away his misery. York was seated across from him, reading from his notes.

York said, 'He was on the phone until three this morning, talking to friends in Arizona.'

'Who?'

'Bobby Lander, Jim Gallison, Richard Hassel, the usual gang. His money people.'

'Dale Winer?'

'Yes, him too,' York said, amazed at Teddy's recall. Teddy had his eyes closed now, and was rubbing his temples. Somewhere between them, somewhere deep in his brain, he knew the names of Lake's friends, his contributors, his confidants, his poll workers, and his old high school teachers. All of it neatly tucked away, ready to be used if necessary.

'Anything unusual?'

'No, not really. Just the typical questions you'd expect from a man contemplating such an unexpected move. His friends were surprised, even

47

shocked, and somewhat reluctant, but they'll come around.'

'Did they ask about money?'

'Of course. He was vague, said it would not be a problem, though. They are skeptical.'

'Did he keep our secrets?'

'He certainly did.'

'Was he worried about us listening?'

'I don't think so. He made eleven calls from his office and eight from his home. None from his cell phones.'

'Faxes? E-mail?'

'None. He spent two hours with Schiara, his –'

'Chief of staff.'

'Right. They basically planned the campaign. Schiara wants to run it. They like Nance of Michigan as VP.'

'Not a bad choice.'

'He looks fine. We're already checking him. Had a divorce when he was twenty-three, but that was thirty years ago.'

'Not a problem. Is Lake ready to commit?'

'Oh yes. He's a politician, isn't he? He's been promised the keys to the kingdom. He's already writing speeches.'

Teddy removed a pill from a bottle and swallowed it without the aid of anything liquid. He frowned as if it was bitter. He squeezed the wrinkles in his forehead and said, 'York, tell me we're not missing anything on this guy. No skeletons.'

'No skeletons, Chief. We've examined his dirty underwear for six months. There's nothing that can hurt us.'

'He's not going to marry some fool, is he?'

'No. He dates several women, but nothing serious.'

'No sex with his interns?'

'None. He's clean.'

They were repeating a dialogue they'd had many times. Once more wouldn't hurt.

'No shady financial deals from another lifetime?'

'This is his life, Chief. There's nothing back there.'

'Booze, drugs, prescription pills, gambling on the Internet?'

'No sir. He's very clean, sober, straight, bright, pretty remarkable.'

'Let's talk to him.'

Aaron Lake was once again escorted to the same room deep inside Langley, this time with three handsome young men guarding him as if danger lurked at every corner. He walked even quicker than the day before, his head even taller, his back without the slightest curve. His stature was rising by the hour.

Once again he said hello to Teddy and shook his calloused hand, then followed the quilt-laden wheelchair into the bunker and sat across the table. Pleasantries were exchanged. York watched from a room down the hall where three monitors hooked to hidden cameras relayed every word, every movement. Next to York were two men who spent their time studying tapes of people as they talked and breathed and moved their hands and eyes and heads and feet, in an effort to determine what the speakers really meant.

'Did you sleep much last night?' Teddy asked, managing a smile.

'Yes, actually,' Lake lied.

'Good. I take it you're willing to accept our deal.'

'Deal? I didn't know it was exactly a deal.'

'Oh yes, Mr. Lake, it's exactly a deal. We promise to get you elected, and you promise to double defense spending and get ready for the Russians.'

'Then you have a deal.'

'That's good, Mr. Lake. I'm very pleased. You'll make an excellent candidate and a fine President.'

The words rang through Lake's ears, and he couldn't believe them. President Lake. President Aaron Lake. He'd paced the floor until five that morning trying to convince himself that the White House was being offered to him. It seemed too easy.

And as hard as he tried, he couldn't ignore the trappings. The Oval Office. All those jets and helicopters. The world to be traveled. A hundred aides at his beck and call. State dinners with the most powerful people in the world.

And, above all, a place in history.

Oh yes, Teddy had himself a deal.

'Let's talk about the campaign itself,' Teddy said. 'I think you should announce two days after New Hampshire. Let the dust settle. Let the winners get their fifteen minutes and let the losers sling more mud, then announce.'

'That's pretty fast,' Lake said.

'We don't have a lot of time. We ignore New

Hampshire and get ready for Arizona and Michigan on February twenty-second. It's imperative that you win those two states. When you do, you establish yourself as a serious candidate, and you're set for the month of March.'

'I was thinking of announcing back home, somewhere in Phoenix.'

'Michigan's better. It's a bigger state, fifty-eight delegates, compared to twenty-four for Arizona. You'll be expected to win at home. If you win in Michigan on the same day, then you're a candidate to be reckoned with. Announce in Michigan first, then do it again hours later in your home district.'

'An excellent idea.'

'There's a helicopter plant in Flint, D-L Trilling. They have a large hangar, four thousand workers. The CEO is a man I can talk to.'

'Book it,' Lake said, certain that Teddy had already chatted with the CEO.

'Can you start filming ads day after tomorrow?'

'I can do anything,' Lake said, settling into the passenger's seat. It was becoming obvious who was driving the bus.

'With your approval, we'll hire an outside consulting group to front the ads and publicity. But we have better people here, and they won't cost you anything. Not that money will be a problem, you understand.'

'I think a hundred million should cover things.'

'It should. Anyway, we'll start working on the TV ads today. I think you'll like them. They're total gloom and doom – the miserable shape of our military, all sorts of threats from abroad. Armageddon, that sort of stuff. They'll scare the hell out of people. We'll plug in your name and face and a few brief words, and in no time you'll be the most famous politician in the country.'

'Fame won't win the election.'

'No, it won't. But money will. Money buys television and polls, and that's all it takes.'

'I'd like to think the message is important.'

'Oh, it is, Mr. Lake, and our message is far more important than tax cuts and affirmative action and abortion and trust and family values and all the other silliness we're hearing. Our message is life and death. Our message will change the world and protect our affluence. That's all we really care about.'

Lake was nodding his agreement. Protect the economy, keep the peace, and American voters would elect anyone. 'I have a good man to run the campaign,' Lake said, anxious to offer something.

'Who?'

'Mike Schiara, my chief of staff. He's my closest adviser, a man I trust implicitly.'

'Any experience on the national level?' Teddy asked, knowing full well there was none.

'No, but he's quite capable.'

'That's fine. It's your campaign.'

Lake smiled and nodded at the same time. That was good to hear. He was beginning to wonder.

'What about Vice President?' Teddy asked.

'I have a couple of names. Senator Nance of Michigan is an old friend. There's also Governor Guyce from Texas.'

Teddy received the names with careful deliberation. Not bad selections, really, though Guyce would never work. He was a rich boy who'd skated through college and golfed through his thirties, then spent a fortune of his father's money to purchase the governor's mansion for four years. Besides, they wouldn't have to worry about Texas.

'I like Nance,' Teddy said.

Then Nance it would be, Lake almost said.

They talked about money for an hour, the first wave from the PACs and how to accept instant millions without creating too much suspicion. Then the second wave from the defense contractors. Then the third wave of cash and other untraceables.

There'd be a fourth wave Lake would never know about. Depending on the polls, Teddy Maynard and his organization would be prepared to literally haul boxes filled with cash into union halls and black churches and white VFWs in places like Chicago and Detroit and Memphis and throughout the Deep South. Working with locals they were already identifying, they would be prepared to buy every vote they could find.

The more Teddy pondered his plan, the more convinced he became that the election would be won by Mr. Aaron Lake.

Trevor's little law office was in Neptune Beach, several blocks from Atlantic Beach, though no one could tell where one beach stopped and the other started. Jacksonville was several miles to the west and creeping toward the sea every minute. The office was a converted summer rental, and from his sagging back porch Trevor could see the beach and the ocean and hear the seagulls. Hard to believe he'd been renting the place for twelve years now.

Early in the lease he'd enjoyed hiding on the porch, away from the phone and the clients, staring endlessly at the gentle waters of the Atlantic two blocks away.

He was from Scranton, and like all snowbirds, he'd finally grown weary of gazing at the sea, roaming the beaches barefoot, and throwing bread crumbs to the birds. Now he preferred to waste time locked in his office.

Trevor was terrified of courtrooms and judges. While this was unusual and even somewhat honorable, it made for a different style of lawyering. It relegated Trevor to paperwork – real estate closings, wills, leases, zoning – all the mundane, nondazzling, smalltime areas of the profession no one told him about in law school. Occasionally he handled a drug case, never one involving a trial, and it was one of his unfortunate clients at Trumble who'd connected him with the Honorable Joe Roy Spicer. In short order he'd become the official attorney for all three – Spicer, Beech, and Yarber. The Brethren, as even Trevor referred to them.

He was a courier, nothing more or less. He smuggled them letters disguised as official legal documents and thus protected by the lawyer-client privilege. And he sneaked their letters out. He gave them no advice, and they sought none. He ran their bank account offshore and handled phone calls from the families of their clients inside Trumble. He fronted their dirty little deals, and in doing so avoided courtrooms and judges and other lawyers, and this suited Trevor just fine.

He was also a member of their conspiracy, easily

54

indictable should they ever be exposed, but he wasn't worried. The Angola scam was absolutely brilliant because its victims couldn't complain. For an easy fee with potential rewards, he'd gamble with the Brethren.

He eased from his office without seeing his secretary, then sneaked away in his restored 1970 VW Beetle, no air-conditioning. He drove down First Street toward Atlantic Boulevard, the ocean visible through homes and cottages and rentals. He wore old khakis, a white cotton shirt, a yellow bow tie, a blue seersucker jacket, all of it heavily wrinkled. He passed Pete's Bar and Grill, the oldest watering hole along the beaches and his personal favorite even though the college kids had discovered the place. He had an outstanding and very past-due bar tab there of $361, almost all for Coors longnecks and lemon daiquiris, and he really wanted to clear the debt.

He turned west on Atlantic Boulevard, and began fighting the traffic into Jacksonville. He cursed the sprawl and the congestion and the cars with Canadian plates. Then he was on the bypass, north past the airport and soon deep into the flat Florida countryside.

Fifty minutes later he parked at Trumble. You gotta love the federal system, he told himself again. Lots of parking close to the front entrance, nicely landscaped grounds tended daily by the inmates, and modern, well-kept buildings.

He said, 'Hello, Mackey,' to the white guard at the door, and 'Hello, Vince,' to the black one. Rufus at the front desk X-rayed the briefcase while

Nadine did the paperwork for his visit. 'How're the bass?' he asked Rufus.

'Ain't biting,' Rufus said.

No lawyer in the brief history of Trumble had visited as much as Trevor. They took his picture again, stamped the back of his hand with invisible ink, and led him through two doors and a short hallway. 'Hello, Link,' he said to the next guard.

'Mornin, Trevor,' Link said. Link ran the visitors' area, a large open space with lots of padded chairs and vending machines against one wall, a playground for youngsters, and a small outdoor patio where two people could sit at a picnic table and share a moment. It was cleaned and shined and completely empty. It was a weekday. Traffic picked up on Saturdays and Sundays, but for the rest of the time Link observed an empty area.

They went to the lawyers' room, one of several private cubbyholes with doors that shut and windows through which Link could do his observing, if he were so inclined. Joe Roy Spicer was waiting and reading the daily sports section where he played the odds on college basketball. Trevor and Link stepped into the room together, and very quickly Trevor removed two twenty-dollar bills and handed them to Link. The closed-circuit cameras couldn't see them if they did this just inside the door. As part of the routine, Spicer pretended not to see the transaction.

Then the briefcase was opened and Link made a pretense of looking through it. He did this without touching a thing. Trevor removed a large manila envelope which was sealed and marked in bold

'Legal Papers.' Link took it and squeezed it to make sure it held only papers and not a gun or a bottle of pills, then he gave it back. They'd done this dozens of times.

Trumble regulations required a guard to be present in the room when all papers were removed and all envelopes were opened. But the two twenties got Link outside where he posted himself at the door because there was simply nothing else to guard at the moment. He knew letters were being passed back and forth, and he didn't care. As long as Trevor didn't traffic in weapons or drugs, Link wouldn't get involved. The place had so many silly regulations anyway. He leaned on the door, with his back to it, and before long was drifting into one of his many horse naps, one leg stiff, the other bent at the knee.

In the lawyers' room, little legal work was being done. Spicer was still absorbed in point spreads. Most inmates welcomed their guests. Spicer only tolerated his.

'Got a call last night from the brother of Jeff Daggett,' Trevor said. 'The kid from Coral Gables.'

'I know him,' Spicer said, finally lowering his newspaper because money was on the horizon. 'He got twelve years in a drug conspiracy.'

'Yep. His brother says that there's this ex-federal judge inside Trumble who's looked over his papers and thinks he might be able to knock off a few years. This judge wants a fee, so Daggett calls his brother, who calls me.' Trevor removed his rumpled blue seersucker jacket and flung it on a chair. Spicer hated his bow tie.

'How much can they pay?'

'Have you guys quoted a fee?' Trevor asked.

'Beech may have, I don't know. We try to get five thousand for a two-two-five-five reduction.' Spicer said this as if he had practiced criminal law in the federal courts for years. Truth was, the only time he'd actually seen a federal courtroom was the day he was sentenced.

'I know,' Trevor said. 'I'm not sure they can pay five thousand. The kid had a public defender for a lawyer.'

'Then squeeze whatever you can, but get at least a thousand up front. He's not a bad kid.'

'You're getting soft, Joe Roy.'

'No. I'm getting meaner.'

And in fact he was. Joe Roy was the managing partner of the Brethren. Yarber and Beech had the talent and the training, but they'd been too humiliated by their fall to have any ambition. Spicer, with no training and little talent, possessed enough manipulative skills to keep his colleagues on track. While they brooded, he dreamed of his comeback.

Joe Roy opened a file and withdrew a check. 'Here's a thousand bucks to deposit. Came from a pen pal in Texas named Curtis.'

'What's his potential?'

'Very good, I think. We're ready to bust Quince in Iowa.' Joe Roy withdrew a pretty lavender envelope, tightly sealed and addressed to Quince Garbe in Bakers, Iowa.

'How much?' Trevor asked, taking the envelope.

'A hundred thousand.'

'Wow.'

'He's got it, and he'll pay it. I've given him the wiring instructions. Alert the bank.'

In twenty-three years of practicing law, Trevor had never earned a fee anywhere close to $33,000. Suddenly, he could see it, touch it, and, though he tried not to, he began spending it – $33,000 for doing nothing but shuttling mail.

'You really think this will work?' he asked, mentally paying off the tab at Pete's Bar and telling MasterCard to take this check and shove it. He'd keep the same car, his beloved Beetle, but he might spring for an air conditioner.

'Of course it will,' Spicer said, without a trace of doubt.

He had two more letters, both written by Justice Yarber posing as young Percy in rehab. Trevor took them with anticipation.

'Arkansas is at Kentucky tonight,' Spicer said, returning to his newspaper. 'The line is fourteen. Whatta you think?'

'Much closer than that. Kentucky is very tough at home.'

'Are you in?'

'Are you?'

Trevor had a bookie at Pete's Bar, and though he gambled little he had learned to follow the lead of Justice Spicer.

'I'll put a hundred on Arkansas,' Spicer said.

'I think I will too.'

They played blackjack for half an hour, with Link occasionally glancing in and frowning his disapproval. Cards were prohibited during visitation, but who cared? Joe Roy played the game hard because he was training for his next career. Poker and gin rummy were the favorites in the rec room, and Spicer often had trouble finding a blackjack opponent.

Trevor wasn't particularly good, but he was always willing to play. It was, in Spicer's opinion, his only redeeming quality.

FIVE

The announcement had the festive air of a victory party, with red, white, and blue banners and bunting draped from the ceiling and parade music blasting through the hangar. Every D-L Trilling employee was required to be present, all four thousand of them, and to heighten their spirits they had been promised a full day of extra vacation. Eight hours paid, at an average wage of $22.40, but management didn't care because they had found their man. The hastily built stage was also covered in banners and packed with every suit in the company, all smiling broadly and clapping wildly as the music whipped the crowd into a frenzy. Three days earlier no one had heard of Aaron Lake. Now he was their savior.

He certainly looked like a candidate, with a new slightly trimmer haircut suggested by one consultant and a dark brown suit suggested by another. Only Reagan had been able to wear brown suits, and he'd won two landslides.

When Lake finally appeared, and strode purposefully across the stage, shaking vigorously the hands of corporate honchos he'd never see again, the laborers went wild. The music was carefully ratcheted up a couple of notches by a sound consultant who was a member of a sound team Lake's people had hired for $24,000 for the event. Money was of little concern.

Balloons fell like manna. Some were popped by workers who'd been asked to pop them, so for a few seconds the hangar sounded like the first wave of a ground attack. Get ready for it. Get ready for war. Lake Before It's Too Late.

The Trilling CEO clutched him as if they were fraternity brothers, when in fact they'd met two hours earlier. The CEO then took the podium and waited for the noise to subside. Working with notes he'd been faxed the day before, he began a long-winded and quite generous introduction of Aaron Lake, future President. On cue, the applause interrupted him five times before he finished.

Lake waved like a conquering hero and waited behind the microphone, then with perfect timing stepped forward and said, 'My name is Aaron Lake, and I am now running for President.' More roaring applause. More piped-in parade music. More balloons drifting downward.

When he'd had enough, he launched into his speech. The theme, the platform, the only reason for running was national security, and Lake hammered out the appalling statistics proving just how thoroughly the current Administration had depleted our military. No other issues were really that important, he said bluntly. Lure us into a war we can't win, and we'll forget about the tired old quarrels over abortion, race, guns, affirmative action, taxes. Concerned about family values? Start losing our sons and daughters in combat and you'd see some families with real problems.

Lake was very good. The speech had been written by him, edited by consultants, polished by other professionals, and the night before he'd delivered it to Teddy Maynard, alone, deep inside Langley. Teddy had approved, with minor changes.

Teddy was tucked under his quilts and watching the show with great pride. York was with him, silent as usual. The two often sat alone, staring at screens, watching the world grow more dangerous.

'He's good,' York said quietly at one point.

Teddy nodded, even managing a slight smile.

Halfway through his speech, Lake became wonderfully angry at the Chinese. 'Over a twenty-year period, we allowed them to steal forty percent of our nuclear secrets!' he said, and the laborers hissed.

'Forty percent!' he shouted.

It was closer to fifty, but Teddy chose to downplay it just a little. The CIA had received its share of blame for the Chinese thievery.

For five minutes Aaron Lake blistered the Chinese, and their looting and their unprecedented military buildup. The strategy was Teddy's. Use the Chinese to scare the American voters, not the Russians. Don't tip them. Protect the real threat until later in the campaign.

Lake's timing was near-perfect. His punch line brought down the house. When he promised to double the defense budget in the first four years of his Administration, the four thousand D-L Trilling employees who built military helicopters exploded in a frenzy.

Teddy watched it quietly, very proud of his creation. They had managed to upstage the spectacle in New Hampshire by simply snubbing it. Lake's name had not been on the ballot, and he was the first candidate in decades to be proud of that fact. 'Who needs New Hampshire?' he'd been quoted as saying. 'I'll take the rest of the country.'

Lake signed off amid thunderous applause, and reshook all the hands on the stage. CNN returned to its studio where the talking heads would spend fifteen minutes telling the viewers what they had just witnessed.

On his table, Teddy pushed buttons and the screen changed. 'Here's the finished product,' he said. 'The first installment.'

It was a television ad for candidate Lake, and it began with a brief glimpse of a row of grim Chinese generals standing rigidly at a military parade, watching massive hardware roll by. 'You think the world's a safer place?' a deep, rich ominous voice asked off-camera. Then, glimpses of the world's current madmen, all watching their armies parade by – Hussein, Qaddafi, Milosevic, Kim in North Korea. Even poor Castro, with the last of his ragtag army lumbering through Havana, got a split second of airtime. 'Our military could not now do what it did in 1991 during the Gulf War,' the voice said as gravely as if another war had already been declared. Then a blast, an atomic mushroom, followed by thousands of Indians dancing in the streets. Another blast, and the Pakistanis were dancing next door.

'China wants to invade Taiwan,' the voice continued as a million Chinese soldiers marched in perfect step.'North Korea wants South Korea,' the voice said, as tanks rolled through the DMZ. 'And the United States is always an easy target.'

The voice changed quickly into one with a high pitch, and the ad shifted to a congressional hearing of some sort, with a heavily bemedaled general lecturing some subcommittee. 'You, the Congress,' he was saying, 'spend less on the military each year. This defense budget is smaller than it was fifteen years ago. You expect us to be ready for war in Korea, the Middle East, and now Eastern Europe, yet our budget keeps shrinking. The situation is critical.' The ad went blank, nothing but a dark screen, then the first voice said, 'Twelve years ago there were two superpowers. Now there are none.' The handsome face of Aaron Lake appeared, and the ad finished with the voice saying, 'Lake, Before It's Too Late.'

'I'm not sure I like it,' York said after a pause.

'Why not?'

'It's so negative.'

'Good. Makes you feel uncomfortable, doesn't it?'

'Very much so.'

'Good. We're going to flood television for a week, and I suspect Lake's soft numbers will get even softer. The ads will make people squirm, and they won't like them.'

York knew what was coming. The people would indeed squirm and dislike the ads, then get the hell

65

scared out of them, and Lake would suddenly become a visionary. Teddy was working on the terror.

There were two TV rooms on each wing at Trumble; two small bare rooms where you could smoke and watch whatever the guards wanted you to watch. No remote – they'd tried that at first but it had caused too much trouble. By far the nastiest disagreements occurred when the boys couldn't agree on what to watch. So the guards made the selections.

Rules prohibited inmates from having their own TVs.

The guard on duty happened to like basketball. There was a college game on ESPN, and the room was packed with inmates. Hatlee Beech hated sports, and he sat alone in the other TV room and watched one banal sitcom after another. When he was on the bench and working twelve hours a day, he had never watched television. Who had the time? He'd had an office in his home where he dictated opinions until late while everyone else was glued to prime time. Now, watching the mindless crap, he realized how lucky he'd been. In so many ways.

He lit a cigarette. He hadn't smoked since college, and for the first two months at Trumble he'd resisted the temptation. Now it helped with the boredom, but only a pack a day. His blood pressure was up and down. Heart disease ran in the family. At fifty-six with nine years to go, he would leave in a box, he was certain.

Three years, one month, one week, and Beech

was still counting the days in as opposed to the days to go. Just four years ago he'd been building his reputation as a tough young federal judge who was going places. Four rotten years. When he traveled from one courthouse to the next in East Texas, he did so with a driver, a secretary, a clerk, and a U.S. Marshal. When he walked into a courtroom people stood out of respect. Lawyers gave him high marks for his fairness and hard work. His wife had been an unpleasant woman, but with her family's oil trust he'd managed to live peacefully with her. The marriage was stable, not exactly warm, but with three fine kids in college they had reason to be proud. They had weathered some rough times and were determined to grow old together. She had the money. He had the status. Together they'd raised a family. Where was there to go?

Certainly not to prison.

Four miserable years.

The drinking came from nowhere. Maybe it was pressure from work, maybe it was to escape his wife's bickering. For years, after law school, he'd been a light social drinker, nothing serious. Certainly not a habit. Once when the kids were small, his wife took them to Italy for two weeks. Beech was left alone, which suited him fine. For some reason he could never determine, or remember, he turned to bourbon. Lots of it, and he never stopped. The bourbon became important. He kept it in his study and sneaked it late at night. They had separate beds so he seldom got caught.

The trip to Yellowstone had been a three-day judicial conference. He'd met the young lady in a

67

bar in Jackson Hole. After hours of drinking they made the sad decision to take a ride. While Hatlee drove she took off her clothes, but for no other reason than to just do it. Sex had not been discussed, and at that point he was completely harmless.

The two hikers were from D.C., just college kids returning from the trails. Both died at the scene, slaughtered on the shoulder of a narrow road by a drunken driver who never saw them. The young lady's car was found in a ditch with Beech hugging the steering wheel, unable to remove himself. She was naked and knocked out.

He remembered nothing. When he awoke hours later he saw for the first time the inside of a cell. 'Better get used to it,' the sheriff had said with a sneer.

Beech called in every favor and pulled every string imaginable, all to no avail. Two young people were dead. He'd been caught with a naked woman. His wife had the oil money so his friends ran like scared dogs. In the end, no one stood up for the Honorable Hatlee Beech.

He was lucky to get twelve years. MADD mothers and SADD students protested outside the courthouse when he made his first official appearance. They wanted a life sentence. Life!

He himself, the Honorable Hatlee Beech, was charged with two counts of manslaughter, and there was no defense. There was enough alcohol in his blood to kill the next guy. A witness said he'd been speeding on the wrong side of the road.

Looking back, he'd been lucky his crime was on federal lands. Otherwise he would have been shipped away to some state pen where things were much tougher. Say what you want, but the feds knew how to run a prison.

He smoked alone in the semidarkness, watching prime-time comedy written by twelve-year-olds, and there was a political ad, one of many those days. It was one Beech had never seen, a menacing little segment with a somber voice predicting doom if we didn't hurry and build more bombs. It was very well done, ran for a minute and a half, cost a bundle, and delivered a message no one wanted to hear. Lake Before It's Too Late.

Who the hell's Aaron Lake?

Beech knew his politics. It had been his passion in another life, and at Trumble he was known as a fellow who watched Washington. He was one of the few who cared what happened there.

Aaron Lake? Beech had missed the guy. What an odd strategy, to enter the race as an unknown after New Hampshire. Never a shortage of clowns who want to be President.

Beech's wife kicked him out before he pled guilty to two counts of manslaughter. Quite naturally, she was angrier over the naked woman than the dead hikers. The kids sided with her because she had the money and because he'd screwed up so badly. It was an easy decision on their part. The divorce was final a week after he arrived at Trumble.

His youngest had been to see him twice in three years, one month, and one week. Both visits were on the sly, lest the mother find out about them. She had prohibited the kids from going to Trumble.

Then he got sued, two wrongful death cases brought by the families. With no friends willing to step forward, he'd tried to defend himself from prison. But there wasn't much to defend. A judgment of $5 million had been entered against him by the trial court. He appealed from Trumble, lost from Trumble, and appealed again.

In the chair beside him, next to his cigarettes, was an envelope brought earlier by Trevor, the lawyer. The court had rejected his final appeal. The judgment was now written in stone.

Didn't really matter, because he'd also filed for bankruptcy. He'd typed the papers himself in the law library and filed them with a pauper's oath, sent them to the same courthouse in Texas where he was once a god.

Convicted, divorced, disbarred, imprisoned, sued, bankrupt.

Most of the losers at Trumble handled their time because their falls had been so short. Most were repeat offenders who'd blown third and fourth chances. Most liked the damned place because it was better than any other prison they'd visited.

But Beech had lost so much, had fallen so far. Just four years ago he'd had a wife with millions and three kids who loved him and a big home in a small town. He was a federal judge, appointed by the President for life, making $140,000 a year, which was a lot less than her oil royalties but still not a bad salary. He got himself called to Washington twice a year for meetings at Justice. Beech had been important.

An old lawyer friend had been to see him twice,

on his way to Miami where he had kids, and he stayed long enough to deliver the gossip. Most of it was worthless, but there was a strong rumor that the ex-Mrs. Beech was now seeing someone else. With a few million bucks and slender hips it was only a matter of time.

Another ad. Lake Before It's Too Late again. This one began with a grainy video of men with guns slithering through the desert, dodging and shooting and undergoing some type of training. Then the sinister face of a terrorist – dark eyes and hair and features, obviously some manner of Islamic radical – and he said in Arabic with English subtitles, 'We will kill Americans wherever we find them. We will die in our holy war against the great Satan.' After that, quick videos of burning buildings. Embassy bombings. A busload of tourists. The remains of a jetliner scattered through a pasture.

A handsome face appeared, Mr. Aaron Lake himself. He looked directly at Hatlee Beech and said, 'I'm Aaron Lake, and you probably don't know me. I'm running for President because I'm scared. Scared of China and Eastern Europe and the Middle East. Scared of a dangerous world. Scared of what's happened to our military. Last year the federal government had a huge surplus, yet spent less on defense than we did fifteen years ago. We're complacent because our economy is strong, but the world today is far more dangerous than we realize. Our enemies are legion, and we cannot protect ourselves. If elected, I will double defense spending during my term of office.'

No smiles, no warmth. Just plain talk from a

71

man who meant what he said. A voice over said, 'Lake, Before It's Too Late.'

Not bad, thought Beech.

He lit another cigarette, his last of the night, and stared at the envelope on the empty chair – $5 million lodged against him by the two families. He'd pay the money if he could. Never saw the kids, not before he killed them. The paper the next day had their happy photos, a boy and a girl. Just college kids, enjoying the summer.

He missed the bourbon.

He could bankrupt half the judgment. The other half was for punitive damages, nonbankruptable. So it would follow wherever he went, which he assumed was nowhere. He'd be sixty-five when his sentence was over, but he'd be dead before then. They'd carry him out of Trumble in a box, send him home to Texas, where they'd bury him behind the little country church where he'd been baptized. Maybe one of the kids would spring for a head-stone.

Beech left the room without turning off the TV. It was almost ten, time for lights-out. He bunked with Robbie, a kid from Kentucky who'd broken into 240 houses before they caught him. He sold the guns and microwaves and stereos for cocaine. Robbie was a four-year veteran of Trumble, and because of his seniority he had chosen the bottom bunk. Beech crawled into the top one, said, 'Good night, Robbie,' and turned off the light.

'Night, Hatlee,' came the soft response.

Sometimes they chatted in the dark. The walls were cinderblock, the door was metal, their words were confined to their little room. Robbie was

72

twenty-five and would be forty-five before he left Trumble. Twenty-four years – one for every ten houses.

The time between bed and sleep was the worst of the day. The past came back with a vengeance – the mistakes, the misery, the could-haves and should-haves. Try as he might, Hatlee could not simply close his eyes and go to sleep. He had to punish himself first. There was a grandchild he'd never seen, and he always started with her. Then his three kids. Forget the wife. But he always thought about her money. And the friends. Ah, the friends. Where were they now?

Three years in, and with no future there was only the past. Even poor Robbie below dreamed of a new beginning at the age of forty-five. Not Beech. At times he almost longed for the warm Texas soil, layered upon his body, behind the little church.

Surely someone would buy him a headstone.

SIX

For Quince Garbe, February 3 would be the worst
day of his life. It was almost the last, and it
would've been had his doctor been in town. He
couldn't get a prescription for sleeping pills, and he
didn't have the courage to use a gun on himself.

It began pleasantly enough with a late breakfast,
a bowl of oatmeal by the fire in the den, alone. His
wife of twenty-six years had already left for town,
for another day of charity teas and fund-raising
and frantic small-town volunteerism that kept her
busy and away from him.

It was snowing when he left their large and
pretentious banker's home on the edge of Bakers,
Iowa, and drove ten minutes to work in his long
black Mercedes, eleven years old. He was an
important man about town, a Garbe, a member of
a family that had owned the bank for generations.
He parked in his reserved spot behind the bank,
which faced Main Street, and made a quick detour
to the post office, something he did twice a week.
For years he'd had a private box there, away from
his wife and especially away from his secretary.

Because he was rich and few others were in

Bakers, Iowa, he seldom spoke to people on the street. He didn't care what they thought. They worshiped his father and that was enough to keep their business.

But when the old man died, would he have to change his personality? Would he be forced to smile on the sidewalks of Bakers and join the Rotary Club, the one founded by his grandfather?

Quince was tired of being dependent on the whims of the public for his security. He was tired of relying on his father to keep their customers happy. He was tired of banking and tired of Iowa and tired of snow and tired of his wife, and what Quince wanted more than anything that morning in February was a letter from his beloved Ricky. A nice, brief little note confirming their rendezvous.

What Quince really wanted was three warm days on a love boat with Ricky. He might never come back.

Bakers had eighteen thousand people, so the central post office on Main was usually busy. And there was always a different clerk behind the counter. That's how he'd rented the box – he'd waited until a new postal worker was on duty. CMT Investments was the official lessee. He went straight to the box, around a corner to a wall with a hundred others.

There were three letters, and as he snatched them and stuffed them in his coat pocket his heart froze as he saw that one was from Ricky. He hurried onto Main, and minutes later entered his bank, at exactly 10 A.M. His father had been there for four hours, but they had long since stopped bickering over Quince's work schedule. As always, he stopped at his secretary's desk to hurriedly remove his gloves as if important matters were waiting. She handed him his mail, his two phone messages, and reminded him that he had lunch in two hours with a local real estate agent.

He locked his door behind him, flung his gloves one way and his coat the other, and ripped open the letter from Ricky. He sat on his sofa and put on his reading glasses, breathing heavily not from the walk but from anticipation. He was on the verge of arousal when he started reading.

The words hit like bullets. After the second paragraph, he emitted a strange, painful 'Awwww.' Then a couple of 'Oh my gods.' Then a low, hissing 'Sonofabitch.'

Quiet, he told himself, the secretary is always listening. The first reading brought shock, the second disbelief. Reality began settling in with the third reading, and Quince's lip started to quiver. Don't cry, dammit, he told himself.

He threw the letter on the floor and paced around his desk, ignoring as best he could the cheerful faces of his wife and children. Twenty years' worth of class photos and family portraits were lined along his credenza, just under the window. He looked out and watched the snow, now heavier and accumulating on the sidewalks. God how he hated Bakers, Iowa. He'd thought he might leave and escape to the beach, where he could frolic with a handsome young pal and maybe never come home.

Now he would leave under different circumstances.

It was a joke, a hoax, he told himself, but he

instantly knew better. The scam was too tight. The punch line was too perfect. He'd been set up by a professional.

All his life he'd fought his desires. Somehow he'd finally found the nerve to crack the closet door, and now he got shot between the eyes by a con man. Stupid, stupid, stupid. How could this be so difficult?

Random thoughts hit from every direction as he watched the snow. Suicide was the easy answer, but his doctor was gone and he really didn't want to die. At least not at the moment. He wasn't sure where he'd find a hundred thousand bucks he could send off without raising suspicions. The old bastard next door paid him a pittance and kept his thumb on every dime. His wife insisted on balancing their checkbook. There was some money in mutuals, but he couldn't move it without her knowing. The life of a rich banker in Bakers, Iowa, meant a title and a Mercedes and a large mortgaged house and a wife with social activities. Oh how he wanted to escape!

He'd go to Florida anyway, and track the letter somehow, and confront this con man, expose his extortion attempt, find some justice. He, Quince Garbe, had done nothing wrong. Surely a crime was being perpetrated here. Perhaps he could hire an investigator, and maybe a lawyer, and they'd protect him. They'd get to the bottom of this scam.

Even if he found the money, and wired it as instructed, the gate would be opened and Ricky, whoever in hell Ricky was, might want more. What would stop Ricky from extorting again, and again?

If he had guts he'd run off anyway, run to Key

West or some hot spot where it never snowed and live any damn way he wanted to live, and let the pitiful little people of Bakers, Iowa, gossip about him for the next half-century. But he didn't have the guts, and that's what made Quince so sad.

His children were staring at him, freckled smiles with teeth wrapped in silver braces. His heart sank, and he knew he'd find the money and wire it precisely as directed. He had to protect them. They had done nothing wrong.

The bank's stock was worth about $10 million, all of it still tightly controlled by the old man, who at the moment was barking in the hallway. The old man was eighty-one, very much alive but still eighty-one. When he was gone, Quince would have to contend with a sister in Chicago, but the bank would be his. He'd sell the damned thing as fast as he could and leave Bakers with a few million in his pocket. Until then, though, he'd be forced to do what he'd always done, keep the old man content.

Quince's getting yanked out of the closet by some con man would devastate his father, and pretty much take care of the stock. Sister in Chicago would get all of it.

When the barking stopped outside, he eased through the door and passed his secretary for a cup of coffee. He ignored her as he returned to his room, locked his door, read the letter for the fourth time, and collected his thoughts. He'd find the money, and he'd wire it just as instructed, and he'd hope and pray with a fury that Ricky would go away. If not, if he came back for more, Quince would call his doctor and get some pills.

The real estate agent he was meeting for lunch was a high-roller who took chances and cut corners, probably a crook. Quince began to make plans. The two of them would arrange a few shady loans; overappraise some land, lend the money, sell to a strawman, etc. He would know how to do it.

Quince would find the money.

The Lake campaign's doomsday ads landed with a thud, at least in public opinion. Massive polling through the first week showed a dramatic increase in name recognition, from 2 to 20 percent, but the ads were universally disliked. They were frightening and people just didn't want to think about wars and terrorism and old nukes getting hauled across mountains in the dark. People saw the ads (they were impossible to miss), and they heard the message, but most voters simply didn't want to be bothered. They were too busy making money and spending it. When issues were confronted in the midst of a roaring economy, they were limited to the old standbys of family values and tax cuts.

Candidate Lake's early interviewers treated him as just another flake until he announced, live on the air, that his campaign had received in excess of $11 million in less than a week.

'We expect to have twenty million in two weeks,' he said without boasting, and real news started to happen. Teddy Maynard had assured him the money would be there.

Twenty million in two weeks had never been done before, and by the end of that day Washington was consumed with the story. The frenzy reached its peak when Lake was interviewed, live yet again, by two of the three networks on the evening news. He looked great; big smile, smooth words, nice suit and hair. The man was electable.

Final confirmation that Aaron Lake was a serious candidate came late in the day, when one of his opponents took a shot at him. Senator Britt of Maryland had been running for a year and had finished a strong second in New Hampshire. He'd raised $9 million, spent a lot more than that, and was forced to waste half of his time soliciting money rather than campaigning. He was tired of begging, tired of cutting staff, tired of worrying about TV ads, and when a reporter asked him about Lake and his $20 million Britt shot back, 'It's dirty money. No honest candidate can raise that much that fast.' Britt was shaking hands in the rain at the entrance to a chemical plant in Michigan.

The dirty money comment was seized with great gusto by the press and soon splattered all over the place.

Aaron Lake had arrived.

Senator Britt of Maryland had other problems, though he'd tried to forget them.

Nine years earlier he'd toured Southeast Asia to find some facts. As always, he and his colleagues from the Congress flew first class, stayed in nice hotels, and ate lobster, all in an effort to study poverty in the region and to get to the bottom of the raging controversy brought about by Nike and its use of cheap foreign labor. Early in the journey, Britt met a girl in Bangkok, and, feigning illness, decided to stay behind while his buddies continued their fact-finding into Laos and Vietnam.

Her name was Payka, and she was not a prostitute. She was a twenty-year-old secretary in the U.S. embassy in Bangkok, and because she was on his country's payroll Britt felt a slight proprietary interest. He was far away from Maryland, from his wife and five kids and his constituents. Payka was stunning and shapely, and anxious to study in the United States.

What began as a fling quickly turned into a romance, and Senator Britt had to force himself to return to Washington. Two months later he was back in Bangkok on, as he told his wife, pressing but secret business.

In nine months he made four trips to Thailand, all first class, all at taxpayer expense, and even the globe-trotters in the Senate were beginning to whisper. Britt pulled strings with the State Department and Payka appeared to be headed for the United States.

She never made it. During the fourth and final rendezvous, Payka confessed that she was pregnant. She was Catholic and abortion was not an option. Britt stiff-armed her, said he needed time to think, then fled Bangkok in the middle of the night. The fact-finding was over.

Early in his Senate career, Britt, a fiscal hardliner, had grabbed a headline or two by criticizing CIA wastefulness. Teddy Maynard said not a word, but certainly didn't appreciate the grandstanding. The rather thin file on Senator Britt was dusted off and given priority, and when he went to Bangkok for the second time the CIA went with him. Of course he didn't know it, but they sat near him on the flight, first class also, and they had people on the ground in Bangkok. They watched the hotel where the two lovebirds spent three days. They took pictures of them eating in fine restaurants. They saw everything. Britt was oblivious and stupid.

Later, when the child was born, the CIA obtained the hospital records, then the medical records to link the blood and DNA. Payka kept her job at the embassy, so she was easy to find.

When the child was a year old, he was photographed sitting on Payka's knee in a downtown park. More photos followed, and by the time he was four he was beginning to remotely favor Senator Dan Britt of Maryland.

His daddy was long gone. Britt's zeal for finding facts in Southeast Asia had faded dramatically, and he'd turned his attention to other critical areas of the world. In due course he was seized with presidential ambitions, the old senatorial affliction that sooner or later gets them all. He'd never heard from Payka, and that nightmare had been easy to forget.

Britt had five legitimate children, and a wife with a big mouth. They were a team, Senator and Mrs. Britt, both leading the juggernaut of family values and 'We've Got to Save Our Kids!' Together they wrote a book on how to raise children in a sick American culture, though their oldest was only thirteen. When the President was embarrassed by sexual misadventures, Senator Britt became the biggest virgin in Washington.

He and his wife struck a nerve, and the money

rolled in from conservatives. He did well in the Iowa caucuses, ran a close second in New Hampshire, but was running out of money and sinking in the polls.

He would sink even more. After a brutal day of campaigning, his entourage settled into a motel in Dearborn, Michigan, for a short night. It was there that the senator finally came face to face with child number six, though not in person.

The agent's name was McCord, and he'd been following Britt with phony press credentials for a week. He said he worked for a newspaper in Tallahassee, but in fact he'd been a CIA agent for eleven years. There were so many reporters swarming around Britt that no one thought to check.

McCord befriended a senior aide, and over a late drink in the Holiday Inn bar he confessed that he had something in his possession that would destroy candidate Britt. He said it was given to him by a rival camp, Governor Tarry's. It was a notebook, with a bomb on every page: an affidavit from Payka setting forth the broad details of their affair; two photos of the child, the last of which had been taken a month earlier and the child, now seven, looking more and more like his dad; blood and DNA summaries indelibly linking father and son; and travel records which showed in black and white that Senator Britt had burned $38,600 in taxpayers' money to carry on his affair on the other side of the world.

The deal was simple and straightforward: Withdraw from the race immediately, and the story would never be told. McCord, the journalist, was ethical and didn't have the stomach for such trash. Governor Tarry would keep it quiet if Britt disappeared. Quit, and not even Mrs. Britt would know.

Shortly after 1 A.M., in Washington, Teddy Maynard took the call from McCord. The package had been delivered. Britt was planning a press conference for noon the next day.

Teddy had dirt files on hundreds of politicians, past and present. As a group they were an easy bunch to trap. Place a beautiful young woman in their path, and you generally gathered something for the file. If women didn't work, money always did. Watch them travel, watch them crawl in bed with the lobbyists, watch them pander to any foreign government smart enough to send lots of cash to Washington, watch them set up their campaigns and committees to raise funds. Just watch them, and the files always grew thicker. He wished the Russians were so easy.

Though he despised politicians as a group, he did respect a handful of them. Aaron Lake was one. He'd never chased women, never drank much or picked up habits, never seemed preoccupied with cash, never had been inclined to grandstand. The more he watched Lake, the more he liked him.

He took his last pill of the night and rolled himself to bed. So Britt was gone. Good riddance. Too bad he couldn't leak the story anyway. The pious hypocrite deserved a good thrashing. Save it, he told himself. And use it again. President Lake might need Britt one day, and that little boy over in Thailand might come in handy.

SEVEN

Picasso was suing Sherlock and other unnamed defendants for injunctive relief in an effort to stop them from urinating on his roses. A little misdirected urine was not going to upset the balance of life at Trumble, but Picasso also wanted damages in the amount of five hundred dollars. Five hundred dollars was a serious matter.

The dispute had been festering since the past summer, when Picasso caught Sherlock in the act, and the assistant warden had finally intervened. He asked the Brethren to settle the matter. Suit was filed, then Sherlock hired an ex-lawyer named Ratliff, yet another tax evader, to stall, delay, postpone, and file frivolous pleadings, the usual routine for those practicing the art of law on the outside. But Ratliff's tactics didn't sit well with the Brethren, and neither Sherlock nor his lawyer was held in high esteem by the panel.

Picasso's rose garden was a carefully tended patch of dirt next to the gym. It had taken him three years of bureaucratic wars to convince some mid-level paper-pusher in Washington that such a hobby was and always had been therapeutic, since

Picasso suffered from several disorders. Once the garden was approved, the warden quickly signed off, and Picasso dug in with both hands. He got his roses from a supplier in Jacksonville, which in itself took another box of paperwork.

His real job was that of a dishwasher in the cafeteria, for which he earned thirty cents an hour. The warden refused his request to be classified as a gardener, so the roses were deemed a hobby. During the season, Picasso could be seen early and late in his little patch, on all fours, tilling and digging and watering. He even talked to his flowers.

The roses in question were Belinda's Dream, a pale pink rose, not particularly beautiful, but loved by Picasso nonetheless. When they arrived from the supplier everybody at Trumble knew that the Belindas were there. He lovingly planted them in the front and center of his garden.

Sherlock began urinating on them just for the sheer hell of it. He wasn't fond of Picasso anyway because he was a notorious liar, and peeing on the man's roses just seemed appropriate for some reason. Others caught on. Sherlock encouraged them by assuring that they were in fact helping the roses by adding fertilizer.

The Belindas lost their pinkness and began to fade, and Picasso was horrified. An informant left a note under his door, and the secret was out. His beloved garden had become a favorite watering hole. Two days later, he ambushed Sherlock, caught him in the act, and the two chubby middle-aged white men had an ugly wrestling match on the sidewalk.

The plants turned a dull yellow, and Picasso filed suit.

When it finally reached trial, after months of delays by Ratliff, the Brethren were already tired of it. They had quietly preassigned the case to Justice Finn Yarber, whose mother had once raised roses, and after a few hours of research he had informed the other two that urine would, in fact, not change the color of the plants. So two days before the hearing they reached their decision: They would grant the injunction to keep Sherlock and the other pigs from spraying Picasso's roses, but they would not award damages.

For three hours they listened to grown men bicker about who peed where and when, and how often. At times, Picasso, acting as his own attorney, was near tears as he begged his witnesses to squeal on their friends. Ratliff, counsel for the defense, was cruel and abrasive and redundant, and after an hour it was obvious he deserved his disbarment, whatever his crimes may have been.

Justice Spicer passed the time by studying the point spreads on college basketball games. When he couldn't contact Trevor he placed make-believe bets, every game. He was up $3,600 in two months, on paper. He was on a roll, winning at cards, winning at sports, and he had trouble sleeping at night dreaming about his next life, in Vegas or in the Bahamas, doing it as a pro. With or without his wife.

Justice Beech frowned with deep judicial deliberation and appeared to be taking exhaustive notes, when in fact he was drafting another letter to Curtis in Dallas. The Brethren had decided to bait him again. Writing as Ricky, Beech explained that a cruel guard at the rehab unit was threatening all sorts of vile physical attacks unless Ricky could produce some 'protection money.' Ricky needed $5,000 to secure his safety from the beast, and could Curtis lend it to him?

'Could we move this along?' Beech said loudly, interrupting ex-lawyer Ratliff once again. When he was a real judge, Beech had mastered the practice of reading magazines while half-listening to lawyers drone on before juries. A blaring and well-timed admonition from the bench kept everyone sharp.

He wrote: 'It is such a vicious game they play here. We arrive broken into tiny pieces. Slowly, they clean us up, dry us out, put us back together, piece by piece. They clear our heads, teach us discipline and confidence, and prepare us for our return to society. They do a good job of this, yet they allow these ignorant thugs who guard the grounds to threaten us, fragile as we still are, and in doing so break down what we've worked so hard to produce. I am so scared of this man. I hide in my room when I'm supposed to be tanning and lifting weights. I cannot sleep. I long for booze and drugs as a means of escape. Please, Curtis, loan me the $5,000 so I can buy this guy off, so I can complete my rehab and leave here in one piece. When we meet, I want to be healthy and in great shape.'

What would his friends think? The Honorable Hatlee Beech, federal judge, writing prose like a faggot, extorting money out of innocent people.

He had no friends. He had no rules. The law he

once worshiped had placed him where he was, which, at the moment, was in a prison cafeteria wearing a faded green choir robe from a black church, listening to a bunch of angry convicts argue over urine.

'You've already asked that question eight times,' he barked at Ratliff, who'd obviously been watching too many bad lawyer shows on television.

Since the case was Justice Yarber's, he was expected to at least appear as if he were paying attention. He was not, nor was he concerned about appearances. As usual, he was naked under his robe, and he sat with his legs crossed wide, cleaning his long toenails with a plastic fork.

'You think they'd turn brown if I crapped on them?' Sherlock yelled at Picasso, and the cafeteria erupted with laughter.

'Language, please,' Justice Beech admonished.

'Order in the court,' said T. Karl, the court jester, under his bright gray wig. It was not his role in the courtroom to demand order, but it was something he did well and the Brethren let it slide. He rapped his gavel, said, 'Order, gentlemen.'

Beech wrote: 'Please help me, Curtis. I have no one else to turn to. I'm breaking again. I fear another collapse. I fear I will never leave this place. Hurry.'

Spicer put a hundred dollars on Indiana over Purdue, Duke over Clemson, Alabama over Vandy, Wisconsin over Illinois. What did he know about Wisconsin basketball? he asked himself. Didn't matter. He was a professional gambler, and a damned good one. If the $90,000 was still buried behind the toolshed he'd parlay it into a million within a year.

'That's enough,' Beech said, holding up his hands.

'I've heard enough too,' Yarber said, forgetting his toenails and leaning on the table.

The Brethren huddled and deliberated as if the outcome might set a serious precedent, or at least have some profound impact on the future of American jurisprudence. They frowned and scratched their heads and appeared to even argue over the merits of the case. Meanwhile, poor Picasso sat by himself, ready to cry, thoroughly exhausted by Ratliff's tactics.

Justice Yarber cleared his throat and said, 'By a vote of two to one, we have reached a decision. We are issuing an injunction against all inmates urinating on the damned roses. Anyone caught doing so will be fined fifty dollars. No damages will be assessed at this time.'

With perfect timing T. Karl slammed his gavel and yelled, 'Court's adjourned until further notice. All rise.'

Of course, no one moved.

'I want to appeal,' Picasso yelled.

'So do I,' said Sherlock.

'Must be a good decision,' Yarber said, collecting his robe and standing. 'Both sides are unhappy.'

Beech and Spicer stood too, and the Brethren paraded out of the cafeteria. A guard walked into the middle of the litigants and witnesses and said, 'Court's over, boys. Get back to work.'

★

The CEO of Hummand, a company in Seattle which made missiles and radar-jamming machinery, had once been a congressman who'd been quite close to the CIA. Teddy Maynard knew him well. When the CEO announced at a press conference that his company had raised $5 million for the Lake campaign, CNN interrupted a liposuction segment to carry the story Live! Five thousand Hummand workers had written checks for $1,000 each, the maximum allowed under federal law. The CEO had the checks in a box that he showed to the cameras, then he flew with them on a Hummand jet to Washington, where he took them to the Lake headquarters.

Follow the money, and you'll find your winner. Since Lake's announcement, over eleven thousand defense and aerospace workers from thirty states had contributed just over $8 million. The Postal Service was delivering their checks in boxes. Their unions had sent almost that much, with another $2 million promised. Lake's people hired a D.C. accounting firm just to process and count the money.

The Hummand CEO arrived in Washington amid as much fanfare as could be generated. Candidate Lake was on another private jet, a Challenger freshly leased at $400,000 a month. When he landed in Detroit he was met by two black Suburbans, both brand new, both just leased at $1,000 a month each. Lake now had an escort, a group of people moving in sync with him wherever he went, and though he was certain he'd soon get used to it, it was unnerving at first. Strangers around him all the time. Grave young men in dark suits with little microphones in their ears, guns strapped to their bodies. Two Secret Service agents were on the flight with him, and three more waited with the Suburbans.

And he had Floyd from his congressional office. Floyd was a dull-witted young man from a prominent family back in Arizona who was good for nothing but running errands. Now Floyd was a driver. Floyd took the wheel of one Suburban, Lake in the front seat, two agents and a secretary sitting behind. Two aides and three agents piled into the other, and away they went, headed for downtown Detroit where serious local TV journalists were waiting.

Lake had no time for stumping or walking neighborhoods or eating catfish or standing in the rain outside busy factories. He couldn't hike for the cameras or stage town meetings or stand amid rubble in ghettos and decry failed policies. There wasn't enough time to do all the things candidates were expected to do. He was entering late, with no groundwork in place, no grass roots, no local support of any kind. Lake had a handsome face, a pleasant voice, nice suits, an urgent message, and lots of cash.

If buying TV could buy an election, Aaron Lake was about to get himself a new job.

He called Washington, talked to his moneyman, and was given the news about the $5 million announcement. He'd never heard of Hummand. 'Is it a public company?' he asked. No, came the answer. Very private. Just under a billion in annual sales. An innovator in radar jamming. Could make billions if the right man took charge of the military and started spending again.

Nineteen million dollars was now in hand, a record, of course. And they were revising their projections. The Lake campaign would collect thirty million in its first two weeks.

There was no way to spend money that fast.

He folded the cell phone, handed it back to Floyd, who appeared to be lost in traffic. 'From now on we use helicopters,' Lake announced over his shoulder to the secretary, who actually wrote down the directive: Find helicopters.

Lake hid behind his sunglasses and tried to analyze thirty million bucks. The transition from a fiscal conservative to a freewheeling candidate was awkward, but the money had to be spent. It wasn't squeezed from the taxpayers; rather, it was freely given. He could rationalize. Once elected, he'd continue his fight for the workingman.

He thought again about Teddy Maynard, sitting in some dark room deep inside Langley, legs wrapped in a quilt, face squinting from pain, pulling strings only he could pull, making money fall from trees. Lake would never know the things Teddy was doing on his behalf, nor did he want to.

The Director of Middle East Operations was named Lufkin, a twenty-year man Teddy trusted implicitly. Fourteen hours earlier he'd been in Tel Aviv. Now he was in Teddy's war room, somehow looking fresh and alert. His message had to be delivered in person, mouth to mouth, no wires or signals or satellites. And what was said between them would never be repeated. It had been that way for many years.

'An attack on our embassy in Cairo is now imminent,' Lufkin said. No reaction from Teddy; no frown, no surprise, no cutting of the eyes, nothing. He'd gotten such news many times before.

'Yidal?'

'Yes. His top lieutenant was seen in Cairo last week.'

'Seen by whom?'

'The Israelis. They've also followed two truck-loads of explosives from Tripoli. Everything seems to be in place.'

'When?'

'Imminent.'

'How imminent?'

'Within a week, I'd guess.'

Teddy pulled an earlobe and closed his eyes. Lufkin tried not to stare, and he knew better than to ask questions. He would leave soon, and return to the Middle East. And he would wait. The attack on the embassy might proceed with no warning. Dozens would be killed and maimed. A crater in the city would smolder for days, and in Washington fingers would point and accusations would fly. The CIA would be blamed again.

None of it would faze Teddy Maynard. As Lufkin had learned, sometimes Teddy needed the terror to accomplish what he wanted.

Or maybe the embassy would be spared, the attack thwarted by Egyptian commandos working with the United States. The CIA would be praised for its excellent intelligence. That wouldn't faze Teddy either.

'And you're certain?' he asked.

'Yes, as certain as one can be in these situations.'

Lufkin, of course, had no clue that the Director was now plotting to elect a President. Lufkin had barely heard of Aaron Lake. Frankly, he didn't care who won the election. He'd been in the Middle East long enough to know it didn't really matter who set American policy there.

He'd leave in three hours, on the Concorde to Paris, where he'd spend a day before going to Jerusalem.

'Go to Cairo,' Teddy said without opening his eyes.

'Sure. And do what?'

'Wait.'

'Wait for what?'

'Wait for the ground to shake. Stay away from the embassy.'

York's initial reaction was one of horror. 'You can't run this damned ad, Teddy,' he said. 'It's R-rated. I've never seen so much blood.'

'I like that,' Teddy said, pushing a button on the remote. 'An R-rated campaign ad. It's never been done before.'

They watched it again. It began with the sound of a bomb, then footage of the Marine barracks in Beirut; smoke, rubble, chaos, Marines being pulled from debris, mangled bodies, Marines lying dead in a neat row. President Reagan addressing the press and vowing revenge. But the threat sounded hollow. Then the photo of an American soldier standing between two masked gunmen. A heavy, ominous voiceover said, 'Since 1980, hundreds of Americans have been murdered by terrorists around the world.' Another bomb scene, more bloody and dazed survivors, more smoke and chaos. 'We always vow revenge. We always threaten to find and punish those responsible.' Quick clips of President Bush on two separate occasions angrily promising retaliation – another attack, more bodies. Then footage of a terrorist standing in the door of a jetliner, dragging off the body of an American soldier. President Clinton, near tears, his voice ready to crack, saying, 'We will not rest until we find those responsible.' Next the handsome but serious face of Aaron Lake, looking sincerely at the camera, coming into our homes, saying, 'The fact is, we don't retaliate. We react with words, we swagger and threaten, but in reality we bury our dead, then forget about them. The terrorists are winning the war because we have lacked the guts to fight back. When I'm your President, we will use our new military to fight terrorism wherever we find it. No American death will go unanswered. I promise. We will not be humiliated by ragtag little armies hiding in mountains. We will destroy them.'

The ad ran for exactly sixty seconds, cost very little to make because Teddy already had the footage, and would start running during prime time in forty-eight hours.

'I don't know, Teddy,' York said. 'It's gruesome.'

'It's a gruesome world.'

96

Teddy liked the ad and that's all that mattered. Lake had objected to the blood, but came around quickly. His name recognition was up to 30 percent, but his ads were still disliked.

Just wait, Teddy kept telling himself. Wait until there are more bodies.

EIGHT

Trevor was sipping a carry-out double latte from Beach Java and debating whether to add a generous shot or two of Amaretto to help soothe away the morning's cobwebs when the call came. His cramped suite had no intercom system; one was not needed. Jan could simply yell any message down the hall, and he could yell back if he wanted. For eight years he and this particular secretary had been barking at each other.

'It's some bank in the Bahamas!' she announced. He almost spilled the coffee as he lunged for the phone.

It was a Brit whose accent had been softened by the islands. A substantial wire had been received, from a bank in Iowa.

How substantial, he wanted to know, covering his mouth so Jan couldn't hear.

A hundred thousand dollars.

Trevor hung up and added the Amaretto, three shots of it, and sipped the delightful brew while smiling goofily at the wall. In his career he'd never come close to a fee of $33,000. He'd settled a car wreck once for $25,000, taken a fee of $7,500, and within two months had spent all of it.

Jan knew nothing about the offshore account and the scam that diverted money to it, so he was forced to wait an hour, make a bunch of useless phone calls, and try to look busy before announcing he had to take care of some crucial business in downtown Jacksonville, then he was needed at Trumble. She didn't care. He disappeared all the time and she had some reading to keep her occupied.

He raced to the airport, almost missed his shuttle, and drank two beers during the thirty-minute flight to Fort Lauderdale, then two more on the way to Nassau. On the ground, he fell into the back of a cab, a 1974 Cadillac painted gold, without air-conditioning and with a driver who'd also been drinking. The air was hot and wet, the traffic slow, and Trevor's shirt was sticking to his back by the time they stopped downtown near the Geneva Trust Bank Building.

Inside, Mr. Brayshears came forward eventually and led Trevor to his small office. He presented a sheet of paper which gave the bare details: a $100,000 wire originating from the First Iowa Bank in Des Moines, remitter being a faceless entity named CMT Investments. The payee was another generic entity named Boomer Realty, Ltd. Boomer was the name of Joe Roy Spicer's favorite bird dog.

Trevor signed the forms to transfer $25,000 to his own, separate account with Geneva Trust, money he kept hidden from his secretary and from the IRS. The remaining $8,000 was handed to him in a thick envelope, cash. He stuffed it deep into his khaki pants pocket, shook Brayshears' soft little hand, and raced out of the building. He was tempted to stay a couple of days, find a room on the beach, get a chair by the pool, and drink rum until they stopped bringing it to him. The temptation grew to the point that he almost bolted from the gate at the airport and raced to get another cab. But he reached deep, determined not to squander his money this time.

Two hours later he was in the Jacksonville airport, drinking strong coffee, without liquor, and making his plans. He drove to Trumble, arriving at four-thirty, and he waited for Spicer for almost half an hour.

'A pleasant surprise,' Spicer said dryly as he stepped into the attorney-conference room. Trevor had no briefcase to inspect, so the guard patted his pockets and stepped outside. His cash was hidden under the floor mat of his Beetle.

'We received a hundred thousand dollars from Iowa,' Trevor said, glancing at the door.

Spicer was suddenly happy to see his lawyer. He resented the 'we' in Trevor's announcement, and he resented the healthy cut he raked off the top. But the scam wouldn't work without help from the outside, and, as usual, the lawyer was a necessary evil. So far, Trevor could be trusted.

'It's in the Bahamas?'

'Yes. I just left there. The money's tucked away, all sixty-seven thousand of it.'

Spicer breathed deeply and savored the victory. A third of the loot gave him $22,000 and change. It was time to write some more letters!

He reached into the pocket of his olive prison shirt and removed a folded newspaper clipping. He stretched his arms, studied it for a second, then said, 'Duke's at Tech tonight. The line is eleven. Put five thousand bucks on Tech.'

'Five thousand?'

'Yep.'

'I've never put five thousand on a game before.'

'What kinda bookie you got?'

'Small time.'

'Look, if he's a bookie, he can handle the numbers. Call him as soon as you can. He may have to make a few calls, but he can do it.'

'All right, all right.'

'Can you come back tomorrow?'

'Probably.'

'How many other clients have ever paid you thirty-three thousand bucks?'

'None.'

'Right, so be here at four tomorrow. I'll have some mail for you.'

Spicer left him and walked quickly from the administration building with only a nod at a guard in a window. He walked with a purpose across the finely manicured lawn, the Florida sun heating the sidewalk even in February. His colleagues were deep in their unhurried labors in their little library, alone as always, so Spicer did not hesitate to announce: 'We got the hundred thousand from ole Quince in Iowa!'

Beech's hands froze on his keyboard. He peered over his reading glasses, his jaw dropping, and managed to say, 'You're kidding.'

'Nope. Just talked to Trevor. The money was

wired in exactly as instructed, arrived in the Bahamas this morning. Quincy baby came through.'

'Let's hit him again,' Yarber said, before the others could think of it.

'Quince?'

'Sure. The first hundred was easy, let's squeeze him one more time. What could we lose?'

'Not a damned thing,' Spicer said with a smile. He wished he'd said it first.

'How much?' asked Beech.

'Let's try fifty,' Yarber said, pulling numbers from the air as if anything was possible.

The other two nodded and pondered the next fifty thousand, then Spicer took charge and said, 'Look, let's evaluate where we are now. I think Curtis in Dallas is ripe. We'll hit Quince again. This thing is working, and I think we should shift gears, get more aggressive, know what I mean? Let's take each pen pal, analyze them one by one, and step up the pressure.'

Beech turned off his computer and reached for a file. Yarber cleared his small desk. Their little Angola scam had just received a fresh infusion of capital, and the smell of ill-gotten cash was intoxicating.

They began reading all the old letters, and drafting new ones. More victims were needed, they quickly decided. More ads would be placed in the back pages of those magazines.

Trevor made it as far as Pete's Bar and Grill, arriving there just in time for happy hour, which at Pete's began at 5 P.M. and ran until the first fistfight. He found Prep, a thirty-two-year-old sophomore at North Florida, shooting nine-ball for twenty bucks a game. Prep's dwindling trust fund required the family lawyer to pay him $2,000 a month as long as he was enrolled as a full-time student. He'd been a sophomore for eleven years.

Prep was also the busiest bookie at Pete's, and when Trevor whispered that he had serious money to place on the Duke-Tech game, Prep asked, 'How much?'

'Fifteen thousand,' Trevor said, then gulped his longneck beer.

'You serious?' Prep asked, chalking his cue stick and glancing around the smoky table. Trevor had never bet more than a hundred bucks on any game.

'Yep.' Another long pull on the bottle. He was feeling lucky. If Spicer had the guts to lay $5,000 on the game, Trevor would double it. He'd just earned 33,000 tax-free dollars. So what if he lost ten? That much belonged to the IRS anyway.

'I'll have to make a call,' Prep said, pulling out a cell phone.

'Hurry. The game starts in thirty minutes.'

The bartender was a local who'd never left the state of Florida but had somehow developed an intense passion for Australian Rules Football. A game was on from Down Under, and it took a $20 bribe from Trevor to get the channel changed to ACC basketball.

With $15,000 riding on Georgia Tech, there was no way Duke could miss a shot, at least not in the first half. Trevor ate french fries, drank one bottle after another, and tried to ignore Prep, who was standing near a pool table in a dark corner, watching.

In the second half, Trevor almost bribed the bartender to switch back to the Aussie game. He was getting drunker, and with ten minutes to go was openly cursing Joe Roy Spicer to anyone who would listen. What did that redneck know about ACC basketball? Duke led by twenty with nine minutes to go, when Tech's point guard got hot and nailed four straight threes. Trevor had Tech and eleven.

The game was tied with a minute to go. Trevor didn't care who won. He'd beat the spread. He paid his tab, tipped the bartender another $100, then flashed a smart-ass salute to Prep as he walked out the door. Prep flipped him the bird.

In the cool darkness, Trevor skipped along Atlantic Boulevard, away from the lights, past the cheap summer rentals packed tightly together, past the neat little retirement homes with their fresh paint and perfect lawns, down the old wooden steps to the sand, where he took off his shoes and strolled along the edge of the water. The temperature was in the forties, not unusual for Jacksonville in February, and before long his feet were cold and wet.

Not that he felt much – $43,000 in one day, tax-free, all hidden from the government. Last year after expenses he'd cleared $28,000, and that was working practically full time – haggling with clients too poor or too cheap to pay, avoiding courtrooms, dealing with penny-ante real estate agents and bankers, bickering with his secretary, cutting corners on taxes.

Ah, the joy of quick cash. He'd been suspicious of the Brethren's little scam, but now it seemed so brilliant. Extort from those who can't complain. How thoroughly clever.

And since it was working so well, he knew Spicer would turn up the heat. The mail would get heavier, the visits to Trumble more frequent. Hell, he'd be there every day if necessary, hauling letters in and out, bribing guards.

He splashed his feet in the water as the wind picked up and the waves roared in.

Even more clever would be to steal from the extortionists, court-certified crooks who certainly couldn't complain. It was a nasty thought, one he was almost ashamed of, but a valid one nonetheless. All options would be kept open. Since when were thieves known for their loyalty?

He needed a million dollars, nothing more or less. He'd done the math many times, driving to Trumble, drinking at Pete's, sitting at his desk with the door locked. A lousy million bucks, and he could close his sad little office, surrender his law license, buy a sailboat, and spend eternity drifting with the winds around the Caribbean.

He was closer than he would ever be.

Justice Spicer rolled over again on the bottom bunk. Sleep was a rare gift in his tiny room, on his tiny bed with a small, smelly roommate named Alvin snoring above him. Alvin had roamed North America as a hobo for decades, but late in life had grown weary and hungry. His crime had been the robbery of a rural mail carrier in Oklahoma. His apprehension had been aided mightily when Alvin walked into the FBI office in Tulsa and declared, 'I did it.' The FBI scrambled for six hours to find the crime. Even the judge knew Alvin planned it all. He wanted a federal bed, certainly not one provided by the state.

Sleep was even more difficult than usual because Spicer was worried about the lawyer. Now that the scam had hit its stride, there was serious cash lying around. And more on the way. The more Boomer Realty collected in the Bahamas, the more tempting it would become for Trevor. He and he alone could steal their ill-gotten loot and get away with it.

But the scam worked only with an outside conspirator. Someone had to sneak the mail back and forth. Someone had to collect the money.

There had to be a way to bypass the lawyer, and Joe Roy was determined to find it. If he didn't sleep for a month, he didn't care. No slimy lawyer would take a third of his money, then steal the rest.

NINE

Defensepac, or D-PAC as it would quickly and widely become known, made a roaring entry onto the loose and murky field of political finance. No political-action committee in recent history had appeared with as much muscle behind it.

Its seed money came from a Chicago financier named Mitzger, an American with dual Israeli citizenship. He put up the first $1 million, which lasted about a week. Other Jewish high-rollers were quickly brought into the fold, though their identities were shielded by corporations and offshore accounts. Teddy Maynard knew the dangers of having a bunch of rich Jews contribute openly and in an organized fashion to Lake's campaign. He relied on old friends in Tel Aviv to organize the money in New York.

Mitzger was a liberal when it came to politics, but no issue was as dear as the security of Israel. Aaron Lake was much too moderate on social matters, but he was also dead serious about a new military. Middle East stability depended on a strong America, at least in Mitzger's opinion.

He rented a suite at the Willard in D.C. one day,

and by noon the next he had leased an entire floor of an office building near Dulles. His staff from Chicago worked around the clock plowing through the myriad details required to instantly outfit forty thousand square feet with the latest technology. He had a 6 A.M. breakfast with Elaine Tyner, a lawyer/lobbyist from a gigantic Washington firm, one she'd built with her own iron will and lots of oil clients. Tyner was sixty years old and currently regarded as the most powerful lobbyist in town. Over bagels and juice she agreed to represent D-PAC for an initial retainer of $500,000. Her firm would immediately dispatch twenty associates and that many clerks to the new D-PAC offices where one of her partners would take charge. One section would do nothing but raise money. One would analyze congressional support for Lake and begin, gently at first, the delicate process of lining up endorsements from senators and representatives and even governors. It would not be easy; most were already committed to other candidates. Yet another section would do nothing but research – military hardware, its costs, new gadgets, futuristic weapons, Russian and Chinese innovations – anything that candidate Lake might need to know.

Tyner herself would work on raising money from foreign governments, one of her specialties. She was very close to the South Koreans, having been their presence in Washington for the past decade. She knew the diplomats, the businessmen, the big shots. Few countries would sleep easier with a beefed-up United States military than South Korea.

'I feel sure they'll be good for at least five million,' she said confidently. 'Initially, anyway.'

From memory, she made a list of twenty French and British companies that derived at least a fourth of their annual sales from the Pentagon. She'd start working on them immediately.

Tyner was very much the Washington lawyer these days. She hadn't seen a courtroom in fifteen years, and every meaningful world event originated within the Beltway and somehow affected her.

The challenge at hand was unprecedented – electing an unknown, last-minute candidate who, at the moment, enjoyed 30 percent name recognition and 12 percent positives. What their candidate had, though, unlike the other flakes who dropped in and out of the presidential derby, was seemingly unlimited cash. Tyner had been well paid to elect and defeat scores of politicians, and she held the unwavering belief that money would always win. Give her the money, and she could elect or beat anybody.

During the first week of its existence, D-PAC buzzed with unbridled energy. The offices were open twenty-four hours a day as Tyner's people set up shop and charged forward. Those raising money produced an exhaustive computerized list of 310,000 hourly workers in defense and related industries, then hit them hard with a slick mail-out pleading for money. Another list had the names of twenty-eight thousand white-collar defense workers who earned in excess of $50,000 a year. They were mailed a different type of solicitation.

The D-PAC consultants looking for endorsements found the fifty members of Congress with the most defense jobs in their districts. Thirty-seven were up for reelection, which would make the arm-twisting that much easier. D-PAC would go to the grassroots, to the defense workers and their bosses, and orchestrate a massive phone campaign in support of Aaron Lake and more military spending. Six senators from defense-heavy states had tough opponents in November, and Elaine Tyner planned a lunch with each of them.

Unlimited cash cannot go unnoticed for long in Washington. A rookie congressman from Kentucky, one of the lowest of the 435, desperately needed money to fight what appeared to be a losing campaign back home. No one had heard of the poor boy. He hadn't said a word during his first two years, and now his rivals back home had found an attractive opponent. No one would give him money. He heard rumors, tracked down Elaine Tyner, and their conversation went something like this:

'How much money do you need?' she asked.

'A hundred thousand dollars.' He flinched, she did not.

'Can you endorse Aaron Lake for President?'

'I'll endorse anybody if the price is right.'

'Good. We'll give you two hundred thousand and run your campaign.'

'It's all yours.'

Most were not that easy, but D-PAC managed to buy eight endorsements in the first ten days of its existence. All were insignificant congressmen who'd served with Lake and liked him well enough. The strategy was to line them up before the cameras a week or two before big Super Tuesday, March 7. The more the merrier.

Most, however, had already committed to other candidates.

Tyner hurriedly made the rounds, sometimes eating three power meals a day, all happily covered by D-PAC. Her goal was to let the town know that her brand-new client had arrived, had plenty of money, and was backing a dark horse soon to break from the pack. In a city where talk was an industry in itself, she had no trouble spreading her message.

Finn Yarber's wife arrived unannounced at Trumble, her first visit in ten months. She wore fraying leather sandals, a soiled denim skirt, a baggy blouse adorned with beads and feathers, and all sorts of old hippie crap around her neck and wrists and head. She had a gray butch cut and hair under her arms, and looked very much like the tired, worn-out refugee from the sixties that she really was. Finn was less than thrilled when word got to him that his wife was waiting up front.

Her name was Carmen Topolski-Yocoby, a mouthful that she had used as a weapon all of her adult life. She was a radical feminist lawyer in Oakland whose speciality was representing lesbians suing for sexual harassment at work. So every single client was an angry woman battling an angry employer. Work was a bitch.

She had been married to Finn for thirty years – married, but not always living together. He'd lived with other women; she'd lived with other men.

111

Once when they were newlyweds, they lived with an entire houseful of others, different combinations each week. Both came and went. For one six-year stretch they lived together in chaotic monogamy, and produced two children, neither of whom had amounted to much.

They'd met on the battlefields of Berkeley in 1965, both protesting the war and all other evils, both law students, both committed to the high moral ground of social change. They worked diligently to register voters. They fought for the dignity of migrant workers. They got arrested during the Tet Offensive. They chained themselves to redwoods. They fought the Christians in the schools. They sued on behalf of the whales. They marched the streets of San Francisco in every parade, for any and every cause.

And they drank heavily, partied with great enthusiasm, and relished the drug culture; they moved in and out and slept around, and this was okay because they defined their own morality. They were fighting for the Mexicans and the redwoods, dammit! They had to be good people!

Now they were just tired.

She was embarrassed that her husband, a brilliant man who'd somehow stumbled his way onto the California Supreme Court, was now locked away in a federal prison. He was quite relieved that the prison was in Florida and not California; otherwise she might visit more often. His first digs had been near Bakersfield, but he managed to get himself transferred away.

They never wrote each other, never called. She

was passing through because she had a sister in Miami.

'Nice tan,' she said. 'You're looking good.'

And you're shriveling like an old prune, he thought. Damn, she looked ancient and tired.

'How's life?' he asked, not really caring.

'Busy. I'm working too hard.'

'That's good.' Good that she was working and making a living, something she'd done off and on for many years. Finn had five years to go before he could shake Trumble's dust from his gnarled and bare feet. He had no intention of returning to her, or to California. If he survived, something he doubted every day, he'd leave at the age of sixty-five, and his dream was to find a land where the IRS and the FBI and all the rest of those alphabetized government thugs had no jurisdiction. Finn hated his own government so much he planned to renounce his citizenship and find another nationality.

'Are you still drinking?' he asked. He, of course, was not, though he did manage a little pot occasionally from one of the guards.

'I'm still sober, thanks for asking.'

Every question was a barb, every reply a retort. He honestly wondered why she had stopped by. Then he found out.

'I've decided to get a divorce,' she said.

He shrugged as if to say, 'Why bother?' Instead he said, 'Probably not a bad idea.'

'I've found someone else,' she said.

'Male or female?' he asked, more curious than anything else. Nothing would surprise him.

'A younger man.'

113

He shrugged again and almost said, 'Go for it, old girl.'

'He's not the first,' Finn said.

'Let's not go there,' she said.

Fine with Finn. He had always admired her exuberant sexuality, her stamina, but it was difficult to imagine this old woman doing it with any regularity. 'Show me the papers,' he said. 'I'll sign them.'

'They'll be here in a week. It's a clean break, since we own so little these days.'

At the height of his rise to power, Justice Yarber and Ms. Topolski-Yocoby had jointly applied for a mortgage on a home in the marina district of San Francisco. The application, properly sanitized to remove any hint of chauvinism or sexism or racism or ageism, blandly worded by spooked California lawyers terrified of being sued by some offended soul, showed a gap between assets and liabilities of almost a million dollars.

Not that a million dollars had mattered to either one of them. They were too busy fighting timber interests and ruthless farmers, etc. In fact, they'd taken pride in the scantness of their assets.

California was a community property state, which roughly meant an equal split. The divorce papers would be easy to sign, for many reasons.

And there was one reason Finn would never mention. The Angola scam was producing money, hidden and dirty, and off-limits to any and every greedy agency. Ms. Carmen would damned sure never know about it.

Finn wasn't certain how the tentacles of community property might reach a secret bank account in the Bahamas, but he had no plans to find out. Show him the papers, he'd be happy to sign.

They managed to chat a few minutes about old friends, a brief conversation indeed because most friends were gone. When they said good-bye, there was no sadness, no remorse. The marriage had been dead for a long time. They were relieved at its passing.

He wished her well, without so much as a hug, then went to the track, where he stripped to his boxers and walked an hour in the sun.

TEN

Lufkin was finishing his second day in Cairo with dinner at a sidewalk café on Shari' el-Corniche, in the Garden City section of the city. He sipped strong black coffee and watched the merchants close their shops – sellers of rugs and brass pots and leather bags and linens from Pakistan, all for the tourists. Less than twenty feet away, an ancient vendor meticulously folded his tent, then left his spot without a trace.

Lufkin looked very much the part of a modern Arab – white slacks, light khaki jacket, a white vented fedora with the bill down close to his eyes. He watched the world from behind a hat and a pair of sunshades. He kept his face and arms tanned and his dark hair cut very short. He spoke perfect Arabic and moved with ease from Beirut to Damascus to Cairo.

His room was at the Hotel El-Nil on the edge of the Nile River, six crowded blocks away, and as he drifted through the city he was suddenly joined by a tall thin foreigner of some breed with only passable English. They knew each other well enough to trust each other, and continued their walk.

'We think tonight is the night,' the contact said, his eyes also hidden.

'Go on.'

'There's a party at the embassy.'

'I know.'

'Yes, a nice setting. Lots of traffic. The bomb will be in a van.'

'What kind of van?'

'We don't know.'

'Anything else?'

'No,' he said, then vanished in a swarming crowd.

Lufkin drank a Pepsi in a hotel bar, alone, and thought about calling Teddy. But it had been four days since he'd seen him at Langley, and Teddy had made no contact. They'd been through this before. Teddy was not going to intervene. Cairo was a dangerous place for Westerners these days, and no one could effectively blame the CIA for not stopping an attack. There would be the usual grandstanding and finger pointing, but the terror would quickly be shoved into the recesses of the national memory, then forgotten. There was a campaign at hand, and the world moved fast anyway. With so many attacks, and assaults, and mindless violence both at home and abroad, the American people had become hardened. Twenty-four-hour news, nonstop flash points, the world always with a crisis somewhere. Late-breaking stories, a shock here and a shock there, and before long you couldn't keep up with events.

Lufkin left the bar and went to his room. From

his window on the fourth floor the city rambled forever, built helter-skelter over the centuries. The roof of the American embassy was directly in front of him, a mile away.

He opened a paperback Louis L'Amour, and waited for the fireworks.

The truck was a two-ton Volvo panel van, loaded from floor to ceiling with three thousand pounds of plastic explosives made in Romania. Its door happily advertised the services of a well-known caterer in the city, a company which made frequent visits to most of the Western embassies. It was parked near the service entrance, in the basement.

The driver of the truck had been a large, friendly Egyptian called Shake by the Marines who guarded the embassy. Shake passed through often, hauling food and supplies to and from social events. Shake was now dead on the floor of his truck, a bullet in his brain.

At twenty minutes after ten, the bomb was detonated by a remote device, operated by a terrorist hiding across the street. As soon as he pushed the right buttons, he ducked behind a car, afraid to look.

The explosion ripped out supporting columns deep in the basement, so the embassy fell to one side. Debris rained for blocks. Most of the nearby buildings suffered structural damage. Windows within a quarter of a mile were cracked.

Lufkin was napping in his chair when the quake came. He jumped to his feet, walked onto his narrow balcony, and watched the cloud of dust.

The roof of the embassy was no longer visible. Within minutes flames were seen and the interminable sirens began. He propped his chair against the railing of the balcony, and settled in for the duration. There would be no sleep. Six minutes after the explosion, the electricity in Garden City went out, and Cairo was dark except for the orange glow of the American embassy.

He called Teddy.

When the technician, Teddy's sanitizer, assured Lufkin the line was secure, the old man's voice came through as clearly as if they were chatting from New York to Boston. 'Yes, Maynard here.'

'I'm in Cairo, Teddy. Watching our embassy go up in smoke.'

'When did it happen?'

'Less than ten minutes ago.'

'How big –'

'Hard to tell. I'm in a hotel a mile away. Massive, I'd say.'

'Call me in an hour. I'll stay here at the office tonight.'

'Done.'

Teddy rolled himself to a computer, punched a few buttons, and within seconds found Aaron Lake. The candidate was en route from Philadelphia to Atlanta, aboard his shiny new airplane. There was a phone in Lake's pocket, a secure digital unit as slim as a cigarette lighter.

Teddy punched more numbers, the phone was summoned, and Teddy spoke to his monitor. 'Mr. Lake, it's Teddy Maynard.'

Who else could it be? Lake thought. No one else could use the phone.

'Are you alone?' Teddy asked.

'Just a minute.'

Teddy waited, then the voice returned. 'I'm in the kitchen now,' Lake said.

'Your plane has a kitchen?'

'A small one, yes. It's a very nice plane, Mr. Maynard.'

'Good. Listen, sorry to bother you, but I have some news. They bombed the American embassy in Cairo fifteen minutes ago.'

'Who?'

'Don't ask that.'

'Sorry.'

'The press will be all over you. Take a moment, prepare some remarks. It will be a good time to express concern for the victims and their families. Keep the politics to a minimum, but also keep the hard line. Your ads are prophetic now, so your words will be repeated many times.'

'I'll do it right now.'

'Call me when you get to Atlanta.'

'Yes, I will.'

Forty minutes later, Lake and his group landed in Atlanta. The press had been duly notified of his arrival, and with the dust just settling in Cairo, there was a crowd waiting. No live pictures had yet emerged of the embassy, yet several agencies were already reporting that 'hundreds' had been killed.

In the small terminal for private aircraft, Lake stood before an eager group of reporters, some with cameras and mikes, others with slim recorders, others still with just plain old notepads. He spoke solemnly, without notes: 'At this moment, we should be in prayer for those who've been injured and killed by this act of war. Our thoughts and prayers are with them and their families, and also with the rescue people. I am not going to politicize this event, but I will say that it is absurd for this country to once again suffer at the hands of terrorists. When I am President, no American life will go unaccounted for. I will use our new military to track down and annihilate any terrorist group that preys upon innocent Americans. That's all I have to say.'

He walked off, ignoring the shouts and questions from the pack of shaggy dogs.

Brilliant, thought Teddy, watching live from his bunker. Quick, compassionate, yet tough as hell. Superb! He once again patted himself on the back for choosing such a wonderful candidate.

When Lufkin called again it was past midnight in Cairo. The fires had been extinguished and they were hauling out bodies as fast as they could. Many were buried in the rubble. He was a block away, behind an army barricade, watching with thousands of others. The scene was chaos, smoke and dust thick in the air. Lufkin had been to several bomb sites in his career, and this was a bad one, he reported.

Teddy rolled around his room and poured another decaf coffee. The Lake terror ads would begin at prime time. On this very night the campaign would spend $3 million in a coast-to-coast deluge of fear and doom. They'd pull the ads tomorrow, and announce it beforehand. Out of respect for the dead and their families, the Lake campaign would temporarily suspend its little prophecies. And they'd start polling at noon tomorrow, massive polling.

High time candidate Lake's positives shot upward. The Arizona and Michigan primaries were less than a week away.

The first pictures from Cairo were of a harried reporter with his back to an army barricade, soldiers watching him fiercely, as he might get shot if he tried once more to charge forward. Sirens wailed all around; lights flashed. But the reporter knew little. A massive bomb had exploded deep in the embassy at ten-twenty when a party was breaking up; no idea of the casualties, but there'd be plenty, he promised. The area was cordoned off by the army, and for good measure they'd sealed the airspace so, dammit, there'd be no helicopter shots. As of yet, no one had claimed responsibility, but for good measure he gave the names of three radical groups as the usual suspects.

'Could be one of these, could be someone else,' he said helpfully. With no carnage to film, the camera was forced to stay with the reporter, and since he had nothing to say he prattled on about how dangerous the Middle East had become, as if this were breaking news and he was there to report it!

Lufkin called around 8 P.M. D.C. time to tell Teddy that the American ambassador to Egypt could not be located, and they were beginning to fear he might be in the rubble. At least that was the word on the street. While talking to Lufkin on the

122

phone, Teddy watched the muted reporter; a Lake terror ad appeared on another screen. It showed the rubble, the carnage, the bodies, the radicals from some other attack, then the smooth but earnest voice of Aaron Lake promising revenge.

How perfect the timing, Teddy thought.

An aide woke Teddy at midnight with lemon tea and a vegetable sandwich. As he so often did, he'd napped in his wheelchair, the wall of TV screens alive with images but no sound. When the aide left, he pushed a button and listened.

The sun was well up in Cairo. The ambassador had not been found, and it was now being assumed he was somewhere in the rubble.

Teddy had never met the ambassador to Egypt, an absolute unknown anyway, who was now being idolized by the chattering reporters as a great American. His death didn't particularly bother Teddy, though it would increase the criticism of the CIA. It would also add gravity to the attack, which, in the scheme of things, would benefit Aaron Lake.

Sixty-one bodies had been recovered so far. The Egyptian authorities were blaming Yidal, the likeliest of suspects because his little army had bombed three Western embassies in the past sixteen months, and because he was openly calling for war against the United States. The current CIA dossier on Yidal gave him thirty soldiers and an annual budget of around $5 million, almost all originating from Libya and Saudi Arabia. But to the press, the leaks suggested an army of a thousand with unlimited funds with which to terrorize innocent Americans.

The Israelis knew what Yidal had for breakfast and where he ate it. They could've taken him out a dozen times, but so far he'd kept his little war away from them. As long as he killed Americans and Westerners, the Israelis really didn't care. It was to their benefit for the West to loathe the Islamic radicals.

Teddy ate slowly, then napped some more. Lufkin called before noon Cairo time with the news that the bodies of the ambassador and his wife had been found. The count was now at eighty-four; all but eleven were Americans.

The cameras caught up with Aaron Lake outside a plant in Marietta, Georgia, shaking hands in the dark as the shift changed, and when asked about events in Cairo, he said: 'Sixteen months ago these same criminals bombed two of our embassies, killing thirty Americans, and we've done nothing to stop them. They're operating with impunity because we lack the commitment to fight. When I'm President, we'll declare war on these terrorists and stop the killing.'

The tough talk was contagious, and as America woke up to the terrible news in Cairo, the country was also treated to a brash chorus of threats and ultimatums from the other seven candidates. Even the more passive among them now sounded like gunslingers.

ELEVEN

It was snowing again in Iowa, a steady swirl of snow and wind that turned to slush on the streets and sidewalks and made Quince Garbe once again long for a beach. He covered his face on Main Street as if to protect himself, but the truth was he didn't want to speak to anyone. Didn't want anyone to see him darting yet again into the post office.

There was a letter in the box. One of those letters. His jaw fell and his hands froze when he saw it, just lying there with some junk mail, innocent, like a note from an old friend. He glanced over both shoulders – a thief racked with guilt – then yanked it out and thrust it into his coat.

His wife was at the hospital planning a ball for crippled children, so the house was empty except for a maid who spent her day napping down in the laundry room. He hadn't given her a raise in eight years. He took his time driving there, fighting the snow and the drifts, cursing the con man who'd entered his life under the ruse of love, anticipating

125

the letter, which grew heavier near his heart with each passing minute.

No sign of the maid as he entered the front door, making as much noise as possible. He went upstairs to his bedroom, where he locked the door. There was a pistol under the mattress. He flung his overcoat and his gloves onto an armchair, then his jacket, and he sat on the edge of his bed and examined the envelope. Same lavender paper, same handwriting, same everything with a Jacksonville postmark, two days old. He ripped it open and removed a single page.

Dear Quince:
Thanks so much for the money. So that you won't think I'm a total thug, I think you should know the money went to my wife and children. They are suffering so. My incarceration has left them destitute. My wife is clinically depressed and cannot work. My four children are fed by welfare and food stamps.
(A hundred thousand bucks should certainly fatten them up, Quince thought.)
They live in government housing and have no dependable transportation. So, thanks again for your help. Another $50,000 should get them out of debt and start a nice college fund.
Same rules as before; same wiring instructions; same promises to expose your secret life if the money is not received quickly. Do it now, Quince, and I swear this is my last letter.

Thanks again, Quince.

Love, Ricky

He went to the bathroom, to the medicine cabinet, where he found his wife's Valium. He took two, but thought about eating all of them. He needed to lie down but he couldn't use the bed because it would be wrinkled and someone would ask questions. So he stretched himself out on the floor, on the worn but clean carpet, and waited for the pills to work.

He'd begged and scraped and even lied a little to borrow the first installment for Ricky. There was no way he could squeeze another $50,000 from a personal balance sheet already heavily padded and still teetering on the edge of insolvency. His nice large house was choked with a fat mortgage held by his father. His father signed his paychecks. His cars were large and imported, but they had a million miles on them and little value. Who in Bakers, Iowa, would want to buy an eleven-year-old Mercedes?

And what if he managed to somehow steal the money? The criminal otherwise known as Ricky would simply thank him again, then demand more.

It was over.

Time for the pills. Time for the gun.

The phone startled him. Without thinking, he scrambled to his feet and grabbed the receiver. 'Hello,' he grunted.

'Where the hell are you?' It was his father, with a tone he knew so well.

'I'm, uh, not feeling well,' he managed to say,

staring at his watch and now remembering the ten-thirty meeting with a very important inspector from the FDIC.

'I don't give a damn how you feel. Mr. Colthurst from the FDIC has been waiting in my office for fifteen minutes.'

'I'm vomiting, Dad,' he said, and cringed again with the word Dad. Fifty-one years old, still using the word Dad.

'You're lying. Why didn't you call if you're sick? Gladys told me she saw you just before ten walking toward the post office. What the hell's going on here?'

'Excuse me. I gotta go to the toilet. I'll call you later.' He hung up.

The Valium rolled in like a pleasant fog, and he sat on the edge of his bed staring at the lavender squares scattered on the floor. Ideas were slow in coming, hampered by the pills.

He could hide the letters, then kill himself. His suicide note would place the bulk of the blame on his father. Death was not an altogether unpleasant prospect; no more marriage, no more bank, no more Dad, no more Bakers, Iowa, no more hiding in the closet.

But he would miss his children and grandchildren.

And what if this Ricky monster didn't learn of the suicide, and sent another letter, and they found it, and somehow Quince got himself outed anyway, long after his funeral?

The next lousy idea involved a conspiracy with his secretary, a woman he trusted marginally to begin with. He would tell her the truth, then ask her to write a letter to Ricky and break the news of Quince Garbe's suicide. Together, Quince and his secretary could scheme and fake their way through a suicide, and in the process take some measure of revenge against Ricky.

But he'd rather be dead than tell his secretary.

The third idea occurred after the Valium had settled in at full throttle, and it made him smile. Why not try a little honesty? Write a letter to Ricky and plead poverty. Offer another $10,000 and tell him that's all. If Ricky was determined to destroy him, then he, Quince, would have no choice but to come after Ricky. He'd inform the FBI, let them track the letters and the wire transfers, and both men would go down in flames.

He slept on the floor for thirty minutes, then gathered his jacket, gloves, and overcoat. He left the house without seeing the maid. As he drove to town, flush with the desire to confront the truth, he admitted aloud that only the money mattered. His father was eighty-one. The bank's stock was worth about $10 million. Someday it would be his. Stay in the closet until the cash was in hand, then live any way he damned well pleased.

Don't screw up the money.

Coleman Lee owned a taco hut in a strip mall on the outskirts of Gary, Indiana, in a section of town now ruled by the Mexicans. Coleman was forty-eight, with two bad divorces decades earlier, no children, thank God. Because of all the tacos, he was thick and slow, with a drooping stomach and large fleshy cheeks. Coleman was not pretty, but he was certainly lonely.

His employees were mainly young Mexican boys, illegal immigrants, all of whom he, sooner or later, tried to molest, or seduce, or whatever you'd call his clumsy efforts. Rarely was he successful, and his turnover was high. Business was slow too because people talked and Coleman was not well regarded. Who wanted to buy tacos from a pervert?

He rented two small boxes at the post office at the other end of the strip mall – one for his business, the other for his pleasure. He collected porno and gathered it almost daily from the post office. The mail carrier at his apartment was a curious type, and it was best to keep some things as quiet as possible.

He strolled along the dirty sidewalk at the edge of the parking lot, past the discount stores for shoes and cosmetics, past a XXX video dive he'd been banned from, past a welfare office, one brought to the suburbs by a desperate politician looking for votes. The post office was crowded with Mexicans taking their time because it was cold out.

His daily haul was two hard-core magazines sent to him in plain brown wrappers, and a letter which looked vaguely familiar. It was a square yellow envelope, no return address, postmarked in Atlantic Beach, Florida. Ah, yes, he remembered as he held it. Young Percy in rehab.

Back in his cramped little office between the kitchen and the utility room, he quickly flipped through the magazines, saw nothing new, then stacked them in a pile with a hundred others. He opened the letter from Percy. Like the two before, it was handprinted, and addressed to Walt, a name he used to collect all his porn. Walt Lee.

Dear Walt:

I really enjoyed your last letter. I've read it many times. You have a nice way with words. As I told you, I've been here for almost eighteen months, and it gets very lonely. I keep your letters under my mattress, and when I feel really isolated I read them over and over. Where did you learn to write like that? Please send another one as soon as possible.

With a little luck, I'll be released in April. I'm not sure where I'll go or what I'll do. It's frightening, really, to think that I'll just walk out of here after almost two years, and have no one to be with. I hope we're still pen pals by then.

I was wondering, and I really hate to ask this, but since I have no one else I'll do it anyway, and please feel free to say no, it won't hurt our friendship, but could you loan me a thousand bucks? They have this little book and music shop here at the clinic, and they let us buy paperbacks and CDs on credit, and, well, I've been here so long that I've run up quite a tab.

If you can make the loan, I'd really appreciate it. If not, I completely understand.

Thanks for being there, Walt. Please write me soon. I treasure your letters.

Love, Percy

A thousand bucks? What kinda little creep was this? Coleman smelled a con. He ripped the letter into pieces and threw them in the trash.

'A thousand bucks,' he mumbled to himself, reaching for the magazines again.

Curtis was not the real name of the jeweler in Dallas. Curtis worked fine when corresponding with Ricky in rehab, but the real name was Vann Gates.

Mr. Gates was fifty-eight years old, on the surface happily married, the father of three and the grandfather of two, and he and his wife owned six jewelry stores in the Dallas area, all located in malls. On paper they had $2 million, and they'd made it themselves. They had a very nice new home in Highland Park, with separate bedrooms at opposite ends. They met in the kitchen for coffee and in the den for TV and grandkids.

Mr. Gates ventured from the closet now and then, always with excruciating caution. No one had a clue. His correspondence with Ricky was his first attempt at finding love through the want ads, and so far he'd been thrilled with the results. He rented a small box in a post office near one of the malls, and used the name Curtis V. Cates.

The lavender envelope was addressed to Curtis Cates, and as he sat in his car and carefully opened it, he at first had no clue anything was wrong. Just another sweet letter from his beloved Ricky. Lightning hit, though, with the first words:

Dear Vann Gates:
The party's over, pal. My name ain't Ricky,

and you're not Curtis. I'm not a gay boy looking for love. You, however, have an awful secret, which I'm sure you want to keep. I want to help.

Here's the deal: Wire $100,000 to Geneva Trust Bank, Nassau, Bahamas, account number 144-DXN-9593, for Boomer Realty, Ltd., routing number 392844–22.

Do so immediately! This is not a joke. It's a scam, and you've been hooked. If the money is not received within ten days, I will send to your wife, Ms. Glenda Gates, a little packet filled with copies of all letters, photos, etc.

Wire the money, and I'll simply go away.

Love, Ricky

With time, Vann found the Dallas I-635 loop, and before long he was on the I-820 loop around Fort Worth, then back to Dallas, driving at exactly fifty-five, in the right-hand lane, oblivious to the traffic stacked up behind him. If crying would help, then he would've certainly had a good one. He had no qualms about weeping, especially in the privacy of his Jaguar.

But he was too angry to cry, too bitter to be wounded. And he was too frightened to waste time yearning for someone who did not exist. Action was needed – quick, decisive, secretive.

Heartache, though, overcame him, and he finally pulled onto the shoulder and parked with the engine running. All those wonderful dreams of Ricky, those countless hours staring at his hand-some face with his crooked little smile, and reading his letters – sad, funny, desperate, hopeful – how could so many emotions be conveyed with the written word? He'd practically memorized the letters.

And he was just a boy, so young and virile, yet lonely and in need of mature companionship. The Ricky he'd come to love needed the loving embrace of an older man, and Curtis/Vann had been making plans for months. The ploy of a diamond show in Orlando while his wife was in El Paso at her sister's. He'd sweated the details and left no tracks.

He did, finally, cry. Poor Vann shed tears without shame or embarrassment. No one could see him; the other cars were flying past at eighty miles per hour.

He vowed revenge, like any jilted lover. He'd track down this beast, this monster who'd posed as Ricky and broken his heart.

When the sobbing began to subside, he thought of his wife and family and that helped greatly in drying up the tears. She'd get all six stores and the $2 million and the new house with separate bedrooms, and he would get nothing but ridicule and scorn and gossip in a town that loved it so. His children would follow the money, and for the rest of their lives his grandchildren would hear the whispers about their grandfather.

Back in the right lane at fifty-five, back through Mesquite for the second time, reading the letter again as eighteen-wheelers roared past.

There was no one to call, no banker he could trust to check out the account in the Bahamas, no lawyer to run to for advice, no friend to hear his sorry tale.

For a man who'd carefully lived a double life, the money would not be insurmountable. His wife watched every dime, both at home and at the stores, and for that reason Vann had long since mastered the scheme of hiding money. He did it with gems, rubies and pearls and sometimes small diamonds he placed aside and later sold to other dealers for cash. It was common in the business. He had boxes of cash – shoe boxes neatly stacked in a fireproof safe in a mini-storage out in Plano. Post-divorce cash. Cash for the afterlife when he and Ricky would sail the world and spend it all in one endless voyage.

'Sonofabitch!' he said through gritted teeth. And again and again.

Why not write this con man and plead poverty? Or threaten to expose his little extortion scheme? Why not fight back?

Because the sonofabitch knew exactly what he was doing. He'd tracked Vann well enough to learn his real name, and the name of his wife. He knew Vann had the money.

He pulled into his driveway and there was Glenda sweeping the sidewalk. 'Where have you been, honey?' she asked pleasantly.

'Running errands,' he said with a smile.

'Took a long time,' she said, still sweeping.

He was so sick of it. She timed his movements! For thirty years he'd been under her thumb, with a stopwatch clicking in the palm of her hand.

He pecked her on the cheek out of habit, then went to the basement where he locked a door and

135

began to cry again. The house was his prison (with a mortgage of $7,800 a month, it certainly felt like it). She was the guard, the keeper of the keys. His sole means of escape had just collapsed, replaced by a cold-blooded extortionist.

TWELVE

Eighty coffins required a lot of space. They were laid in perfect rows, all neatly wrapped in red, white, and blue, all the same length and width. They'd arrived thirty minutes earlier aboard an Air Force cargo plane, and were removed with great pomp and ceremony. Almost a thousand friends and relatives sat on folding chairs, on the concrete floor of the hangar, and stared in shock at the sea of flags arranged before them. They were outnumbered only by the shaggy dogs, all quarantined behind barricades and military police.

Even for a country well accustomed to foreign policy boondoggles, it was an impressive body count. Eighty Americans, eight Brits, eight Germans – no French because they'd been boycotting Western diplomatic functions in Cairo. Why were eighty Americans still in the embassy after 10 P.M.? That was the question of the hour, and so far no good answer had surfaced. So many of those who made such decisions were now lying in their coffins. The best theory buzzing around D.C. was that the caterer had been late, and the band even later.

But the terrorists had proved all too well that they would strike at any hour, so what difference did it make how late the ambassador and his wife and their staff and colleagues and guests wanted to party?

The second great question of the hour was just exactly why did we have eighty people in our embassy in Cairo to begin with? The State Department had yet to acknowledge the question.

After some mournful music from an Air Force band, the President spoke. His voice broke and he managed to summon a tear or two, but after eight years of such theatrics the act had worn thin. He'd already promised revenge many times, so he dwelt on comfort and sacrifice and the promise of a better life in the hereafter.

The Secretary of State called the names of the dead, a morbid recitation designed to capture the gravity of the moment. The sobbing increased. Then some more music. The longest speech was delivered by the Vice President, fresh from the campaign trail and filled with a newly discovered commitment to eradicate terrorism from the face of the earth. Though he'd never worn a military uniform, he seemed eager to start tossing grenades.

Lake had them all on the run.

Lake watched the grim ceremony while flying from Tucson to Detroit, late for another round of interviews. On board was his pollster, a newly acquired magician who now traveled with him. While Lake and his staff watched the news, the pollster worked feverishly at the small conference table upon which he had two laptops, three phones, and more printouts than any ten people could digest.

The Arizona and Michigan primaries were three days away, and Lake's numbers were climbing, especially in his home state, where he was in a dead heat with the long-established front-runner, Governor Tarry of Indiana. In Michigan, Lake was ten points down, but people were listening. The fiasco in Cairo was working beautifully in his favor.

Governor Tarry was suddenly scrambling for money. Aaron Lake was not. It was coming in faster than he could spend it.

When the Vice President finally finished, Lake left the screen and returned to his leather swivel recliner and picked up a newspaper. A staff member brought him coffee, which he sipped while watching the flatlands of Kansas eight miles below him. Another staff member handed him a message – one that was supposed to require an urgent call from the candidate. Lake glanced around the plane, and counted thirteen people, pilots not included.

For a private man who still missed his wife, Lake was not adjusting well to the complete lack of privacy. He moved with a group, every half hour slotted by someone, every action coordinated by a committee, every interview preceded by written guesses about the questions and suggested responses. He got six hours each night alone, in his hotel room, and damned if the Secret Service wouldn't sleep on the floor if he'd allow it. Because of the fatigue, he slept like an infant. His only true moments of quiet reflection occurred in the bathroom, either in the shower or on the toilet.

But he wasn't kidding himself. He, Aaron Lake, quiet congressman from Arizona, had become an overnight sensation. He was charging while the rest were faltering. Big money was aimed at him. The press followed like bloodhounds. His words got repeated. He had very powerful friends, and as the pieces were falling in place the nomination looked realistic. He hadn't dreamed of such things a month earlier.

Lake was savoring the moment. The campaign was madness, but he could control the tempo of the job itself. Reagan was a nine-to-five President, and he'd been far more effective than Carter, an avid workaholic. Just get to the White House, he told himself over and over, suffer these fools, gut it through the primaries, endure with a smile and a quick wit, and one day very soon he'd sit in the Oval Office, alone, with the world at his feet.

And he would have his privacy.

Teddy sat with York in his bunker, watching the live scene from Andrews Air Force Base. He preferred York's company when things were rough. The accusations had been brutal. Scapegoats were in demand, and many of the idiots chasing the cameras blamed the CIA because that's who they always blamed.

If they only knew.

He'd finally told York of Lufkin's warnings, and York understood completely. Unfortunately, they'd been through this before. When you police the world you lose a lot of cops, and Teddy and

York had shared many sad moments watching the flag-covered coffins roll off the C-130s, evidence of another debacle abroad. The Lake campaign would be Teddy's final effort at saving American lives.

Failure seemed unlikely. D-PAC had collected more than $20 million in two weeks, and was in the process of hauling the money around Washington. Twenty-one congressmen had been recruited for Lake endorsements, at a total cost of $6 million. But the biggest prize so far was Senator Britt, the ex-candidate, the father of a little Thai boy. When he abandoned his quest for the White House he owed close to $4 million, with no viable plan to cover his deficit. Money tends not to follow those who pack up and go home. Elaine Tyner, the lawyer running D-PAC, met with Senator Britt. It took her less than an hour to cut the deal. D-PAC would pay off all his campaign debts, over a three-year period, and he would make a noisy endorsement of Aaron Lake.

'Did we have a projection of casualties?' York asked.

After a while Teddy said, 'No.'

Their conversations were never hurried.

'Why so many?'

'Lots of booze. Happens all the time in the Arab countries. Different culture, life is dull, so when our diplomats throw a party, they throw a good one. Many of the dead were quite drunk.'

Minutes passed. 'Where's Yidal?' asked York.

'Right now he's in Iraq. Yesterday, Tunisia.'

'We really should stop him.'

'We will, next year. It'll be a great moment for President Lake.'

Twelve of the sixteen congressmen endorsing Lake wore blue shirts, a fact that was not lost on Elaine Tyner. She counted such things. When a D.C. politician got near a camera, odds were he'd put on his best blue cotton shirt. The other four wore white.

She arranged them before the reporters in a ballroom of the Willard Hotel. The senior member, Representative Thurman of Florida, opened things up by welcoming the press to this very important occasion. Working from prepared notes, he offered his opinions on the current state of world events, commented on things in Cairo and China and Russia, and said that the world was a lot more dangerous than it looked. He rattled off the usual statistics about our reduced military. Then he launched into a long soliloquy about his close friend Aaron Lake, a man he'd served with for ten years and whom he knew better than most. Lake was a man with a message, one we didn't particularly want to hear, but a very important one nonetheless.

Thurman was breaking ranks with Governor Tarry, and though he did so with great reluctance and no small feeling of betrayal, he had become convinced through painful soul-searching that Aaron Lake was needed for the safety of our nation. What Thurman didn't say was that a recent poll showed Lake becoming very popular back in Tampa-St. Pete.

The mike was then passed to a congressman

from California. He covered no new territory, but rambled for ten minutes anyway. In his district north of San Diego were forty-five thousand defense and aerospace workers, and all of them, it seemed, had written or called. He'd been an easy convert; the pressure from home plus $250,000 from Ms. Tyner and D-PAC, and he had his marching orders.

When the questions started, the sixteen bunched together in a tight little pack, all anxious to answer and say something, all afraid their faces might not get wedged into the picture.

Though there were no committee chairmen, the group was not unimpressive. They managed to convey the image that Aaron Lake was a legitimate candidate, a man they knew and trusted. A man the nation needed. A man who could be elected.

The event was well staged and well covered, and instantly made news. Elaine Tyner would trot out five more the following day, then save Senator Britt for the day before big Super Tuesday.

The letter in Ned's glove box was from Percy, young Percy in rehab who got his mail through Laurel Ridge, Post Office Box 4585, Atlantic Beach, FL 32233.

Ned was in Atlantic Beach, had been for two days, with the letter and with the determination to track down young Percy because he smelled a hoax. He had nothing better to do. He was retired with plenty of money, no family to speak of, and besides, it was snowing in Cincinnati. He had a room at the Sea Turtle Inn, on the beach, and at night he hit the bars along Atlantic Boulevard.

He'd found two excellent restaurants, crowded little places with lots of young pretty girls and boys. He'd discovered Pete's Bar and Grill a block away, and for the last two nights he'd staggered from the place, drunk on cold drafts. The Sea Turtle was just around the corner.

During the day Ned watched the post office, a modern brick and glass government job on First Street, parallel to the beach. A small, windowless box midway from the floor, 4585 was on a wall with eighty others, in an area of medium traffic. Ned had inspected the box, tried to open it with keys and wire, and had even asked questions at the front desk. The postal workers had been most unhelpful. Before leaving the first day, he had stuck a two-inch strand of thin black thread to the bottom of the box's door. It was imperceptible to anyone else, but Ned would know if the mail was checked.

He had a letter in there, in a bright red envelope, one he'd mailed three days earlier from Cincinnati, then raced south. In it he'd sent Percy a check for $1,000, money the boy needed for a set of artist's supplies. In an earlier letter, Ned had revealed that he had once owned a modern art gallery in Greenwich Village. It was a lie, he had not, but he doubted everything Percy said too.

Ned had been suspicious from the beginning. Before he answered the solicitation, he had tried to verify Laurel Ridge, the fancy detox unit supposedly holding Percy. There was a telephone, a private number he'd been unable to pry out of directory assistance. There was no street address. Percy had explained in his first letter that the place was top-secret because many of its patients were high-powered corporate executives and top-level government officials, all of whom had, in one way or another, succumbed to chemicals. It sounded good. The boy had a way with words.

And a very pretty face. That's why Ned kept writing. The photo was something he admired every day.

The request for money had caught him by surprise, and since he was bored he decided to make the drive to Jacksonville.

From his spot in the parking lot, low behind the steering wheel of his car, with his back to First Street, he could watch the wall of boxes and the postal customers as they came and went. It was a long shot, but what the hell. He used a small pair of foldable binoculars, and on occasion caught a stare from someone walking by. The task grew monotonous after two days, but as the time passed he became more and more convinced that his letter would be retrieved. Surely someone checked the box at least once every three days. A rehab clinic with patients would get plenty of mail, wouldn't it? Or was it simply a front for a con man who dropped by once a week to check his traps?

The con man showed up late in the afternoon of the third day. He parked a Beetle next to Ned, then ambled into the post office. He wore wrinkled khakis, white shirt, straw hat, bow tie, and had the disheveled air of a would-be beach Bohemian.

Trevor had enjoyed a long midday break at Pete's, then slept off his liquid lunch with an hour nap at his desk, and was just stirring about, making his rounds. He put the key in Box 4585 and removed a handful of correspondence, most of it junk mail, which he threw away as he flipped through the letters on his way out of the building.

Ned watched every move. After three days of tedium, he was thrilled that his surveillance had paid off. He followed the Beetle, and when it parked and the driver walked into a small, run-down law office, Ned drove away, scratching his temple, repeating out loud, 'A lawyer?'

He kept driving, down Highway A1A, along the shore, away from the sprawl of Jacksonville, south through Vilano Beach and Crescent Beach and Beverly Beach and Flagler Beach and finally to a Holiday Inn outside Port Orange. He went to the bar before he went to his room.

It wasn't the first scam he'd flirted with. In fact, it was the second. He'd sniffed the other one out too before any damage was done. Over his third martini he swore it would be his last.

THIRTEEN

The day before the Arizona and Michigan primaries, the Lake campaign unleashed a media blitz, the likes of which had never been seen before in presidential politics. For eighteen hours, the two states were bombarded with one ad after another. Some were fifteen seconds, little softies with not much more than his handsome face and the promises of decisive leadership and a safer world. Others were one-minute documentaries on the dangers of the post-cold war. Still others were macho, in-your-face promises to the terrorists of the world – kill people simply because they are Americans, and you will pay a very dear price. Cairo was still very fresh, and the assurances hit their mark.

The ads were bold, put together by high-powered consultants, and the only downside was oversaturation. But Lake was too new to the scene to bore anyone, not now anyway. His campaign spent $10 million on television in the two states, a staggering amount.

They ran at a slower clip during voting hours on Tuesday, February 22, and when the polls closed the exit analysts predicted Lake would win his home state and run a close second in Michigan. Governor Tarry, after all, was from Indiana, another midwestern state, and he'd spent weeks in Michigan during the previous three months.

Evidently, he hadn't spent enough time there. The voters in Arizona opted for their native son, and those in Michigan liked the new fellow too. Lake got 60 percent at home, and 55 percent in Michigan where Governor Tarry got a paltry 31 percent. The balance was divided among the noncontenders.

It was a devastating loss for Governor Tarry, just two weeks before big Super Tuesday and three weeks before the little one.

Lake watched the vote counting from on board his airplane, en route from Phoenix, where'd he'd voted for himself. An hour from Washington, CNN declared him the surprise winner in Michigan, and his staff opened the champagne. He savored the moment, even allowed himself two glasses.

History was not lost on Lake. No one had ever started so late, and come so far so fast. In the darkened cabin, they watched the analysts on four screens, the experts all marveling at this man Lake and what he'd done. Governor Tarry was gracious, but also worried about the enormous sums of money being spent by his heretofore unknown opponent.

Lake chatted politely with the small group of reporters waiting for him at Reagan National Airport, then rode in yet another black Suburban to his national campaign headquarters where he thanked his highly paid staff and told them to go home and get some sleep.

It was almost midnight when he got to Georgetown, to his quaint little rowhouse on Thirty-fourth, near Wisconsin. Two Secret Service agents got out of the car behind Lake, and two more were waiting on the front steps. He had adamantly refused an official request to put guards inside his home.

'I do not want to see you people lurking around here,' he said harshly at his front door. He resented their presence, didn't know their names, and didn't care if they disliked him. They had no names, as far as he was concerned. They were simply 'You people,' said with as much contempt as possible.

Once he was locked inside, he went upstairs to his bedroom and changed clothes. He turned out the lights as if he were asleep, waited fifteen minutes, then eased downstairs to the den to see if anyone was looking in, then down another flight to the small basement. He climbed through a window, and stepped into the cold night near his tiny patio. He paused, listened, heard nothing, then quietly opened a wooden gate and darted between the two buildings behind his. He surfaced on Thirty-fifth Street, alone, in the dark, dressed like a jogger with a running cap pulled low to his brow. Three minutes later he was on M Street, in the crowds. He found a taxi and disappeared into the night.

Teddy Maynard had gone to sleep reasonably

content with his candidate's first two victories, but he was awakened by the news that something had gone wrong. When he rolled himself into the bunker at ten minutes after 6 A.M., he was more frightened than angry, though his emotions had run the gamut in the past hour. York was waiting, along with a supervisor named Deville, a tiny nervous man who'd obviously been wired for many hours.

'Let's hear it,' Teddy growled, still rolling and looking for coffee.

Deville did the talking. 'At twelve-o-two this morning he said good-bye to the Secret Service and entered his house. At twelve-seventeen he exited through a small window in the basement. We, of course, have wires and timers on every door and window. We've leased a rowhouse across the street, and we were on alert anyway. He hasn't been home in six days.' Deville waved a small pill, the size of an aspirin. 'This is a little device known as a T-Dec. They're in the soles of all of his shoes, including his jogging shoes. So if he's not barefoot we know where he is. Once pressure is applied from the foot, the bug emits a signal that is broadcast for two hundred yards without a transmitter. When pressure is relaxed, it will continue to provide a signal for fifteen minutes. We scrambled and picked him up on M Street. He was dressed in sweats with a cap over his eyes. We had two cars in place when he jumped in a cab. We followed him to Chevy Chase, to a suburban shopping center. While the cab waited, he darted into a place called Mailbox America, one of these new places where you can send and receive mail outside the Postal Service. Some, including this one, are open twenty-four hours for mail pickup. He was inside for less than a minute, just long enough to open his box with a key, remove several pieces of mail, throw it all away, then return to the cab. One of our cars followed him back to M Street, where he got out and sneaked back home. The other car stayed at the mailbox place. We went through the waste can just inside the door, and found six pieces of junk mail, evidently his. The address is A1 Konyers, Box 455, Mailbox America, 39380 Western Avenue, Chevy Chase.'

'So he didn't find what he was looking for?' Teddy asked.

'It looks as though he tossed everything he took from his box. Here's the video.'

A screen dropped from the ceiling as the lights faded. Footage from a video camera zoomed across a parking lot, past the cab, and onto the figure of Aaron Lake in his baggy sweats as he disappeared around a corner inside Mailbox America. Seconds later he reappeared, flipping through letters and papers in his right hand. He stopped briefly at the door and then dumped everything in a tall wastebasket.

'What the hell's he looking for?' Teddy mumbled to himself.

Lake left the building and quickly ducked inside the cab. The video stopped; the lights became brighter.

Deville resumed his narrative. 'We're confident we found the right papers in the trash can. We were there within seconds, and no one else entered the premises while we waited. The time was twelve fifty-eight. An hour later, we entered again and keyed the lock to Box 455, so we'll have access anytime we need it.'

'Check it every day,' Teddy said. 'Inventory every piece of mail. Leave the junk, but when something arrives I want to know it.'

'You got it. Mr. Lake reentered the basement window at one twenty-two and stayed at home for the rest of the night. He's there now.'

'That's all,' Teddy said, and Deville left the room.

A minute passed as Teddy stirred his coffee. 'How many addresses does he have?'

York knew the question was coming. He glanced at some notes. 'He gets most of his personal mail at his home in Georgetown. He has at least two addresses on Capitol Hill, one at his office, the other at the Armed Services Committee. He has three offices back home in Arizona. That's six that we know about.'

'Why would he need a seventh?'

'I don't know the reason, but it can't be good. A man who has nothing to hide does not use an alias or a secret address.'

'When did he rent the box?'

'We're still working on that.'

'Maybe he rented the box after he decided to enter the race. He's got the CIA doing his thinking for him, so maybe he figures we're watching everything too. And he figures he might need a little privacy, thus the box. Maybe it's a girlfriend we missed somehow. Maybe he likes dirty magazines or videos, something that is shipped through the mail.'

After a long pause, York said, 'Could be. What

if the box was rented months ago, long before he entered the race?'

'Then he's not hiding from us. He's hiding from the world, and his secret is truly dreadful.'

They silently contemplated the dreadfulness of Lake's secret, neither wanting to venture a guess. They decided to step up surveillance even more, and to check the mailbox twice a day. Lake would be leaving town in a matter of hours, off to do battle in other primaries, and they would have the box to themselves.

Unless someone else was also checking it for him.

Aaron Lake was the man of the hour in Washington. From his office on Capitol Hill he graciously granted live interviews to the early morning news programs. He received senators and other members of Congress, friends and former enemies alike, all bearing tidings of great joy and congratulations. He had lunch with his campaign staff, and followed it with long meetings on strategy. After a quick dinner with Elaine Tyner, who brought wonderful news of tons of new cash over at D-PAC, he left the city and flew to Syracuse to make plans for the New York primary.

A large crowd welcomed him. He was, after all, now the front-runner.

FOURTEEN

The hangovers were becoming more frequent, and as Trevor opened his eyes for another day he told himself that he simply had to get a grip. You can't lay out at Pete's every night, drinking cheap longnecks with coeds, watching meaningless basketball games just because you've got a thousand bucks on them. Last night it had been Logan State and somebody, some team with green uniforms. Who the hell cared about Logan State?

Joe Roy Spicer, that's who. Spicer put $500 on them, Trevor backed it up with a thousand of his own, and Logan won it for them. In the past week, Spicer had picked ten out of twelve winners. He was up $3,000 in real cash, and Trevor, happily following along, was up $5,500 for himself. His gambling was proving to be much more profitable than his lawyering. And someone else was picking the winners!

He went to the bathroom and splashed water on his face without looking at the mirror. The toilet was still clogged from the day before, and as he stomped around his dirty little house looking for a plunger the phone rang. It was a wife from a

154

previous life, a woman he loathed and one who loathed him, and when he heard her voice he knew she needed money. He said no angrily and got in the shower.

Things were worse at the office. A divorcing couple had arrived in separate cars to finish the negotiations for their property settlement. The assets they were fighting over were of no consequence to anyone else – pots, pans, a toaster – but since they had nothing, they had to fight over something. The fights are nastiest when the stakes are smallest.

Their lawyer was an hour late, and they had used the time to simmer and boil until finally Jan had separated them. The wife was parked in Trevor's office when he stumbled in from the back door.

'Where the hell you been?' she demanded loud enough for husband to hear up front. Husband charged down the hall, past Jan, who did not give chase, and burst into Trevor's small office.

'We've been waiting for an hour!' he announced.

'Shut up, both of you!' Trevor screamed, and Jan left the building. His clients were stunned at the volume.

'Sit down!' he screamed again, and they fell into the only empty chairs. 'You people pay five hundred bucks for a lousy divorce and you think you own the place!'

They looked at his red eyes and red face and decided this was not a man to mess with. The phone started ringing and no one answered it. Nausea hit again, and Trevor bolted out of his office and across the hall to the bathroom, where he puked, as quietly as possible. The toilet failed to flush, the little metal chain clinking harmlessly inside the tank.

The phone was still ringing. He staggered down the hall to fire Jan, and when he couldn't find her he left the building too. He walked to the beach, took off his shoes and socks, and splashed his feet in the cool salt water.

Two hours later, Trevor sat motionless at his desk, door locked to keep out clients, bare feet on the desk, with sand still wedged between the toes. He needed a nap and he needed a drink, and he stared at the ceiling trying to organize his priorities. The phone rang, this time duly answered by Jan, who was still employed but secretly checking want ads.

It was Brayshears, in the Bahamas. 'We have a wire, sir,' he said.

Trevor was instantly on his feet. 'How much?'

'A hundred thousand, sir.'

Trevor glanced at his watch. He had about an hour to catch a flight. 'Can you see me at three-thirty?' he asked.

'Certainly, sir.'

He hung up and yelled toward the front, 'Cancel my appointments for today and tomorrow. I'm leaving.'

'You don't have any appointments,' Jan yelled back. 'You're losing money faster than ever.'

He wouldn't bicker. He slammed the back door and drove away.

The flight to Nassau stopped first in Fort Lauderdale, though Trevor hardly knew it. After

156

two quick beers he was sound asleep. Two more over the Atlantic, and a flight attendant had to wake him when the plane was empty.

The wire was from Curtis in Dallas, as expected. It was remitted by a Texas bank, payable to Boomer Realty, care of Geneva Trust Bank, Nassau. Trevor raked his one third off the top, again hiding $25,000 in his own secret account, and taking $8,000 in cash. He thanked Mr. Brayshears, said he hoped to see him soon, and staggered out of the building.

The thought of going home had not crossed his mind. He headed for the shopping district, where packs of heavy American tourists choked the sidewalks. He needed shorts and a straw hat and a bottle of sunscreen.

Trevor eventually made it to the beach, where he found a room in a nice hotel, $200 a night but what did he care? He lathered himself in oil and stretched out by the pool, close enough to the bar. A waitress in a thong fetched him drinks.

He woke up after dark, sufficiently cooked but not burned. A security guard escorted him to his room, where he fell on the bed and returned to his coma. The sun was up again before he moved.

After such a long period of rest, he awoke surprisingly clear-headed, and very hungry. He ate some fruit and went looking for sailboats, not exactly shopping for one, but paying close attention to the details. A thirty-footer would be sufficient, just large enough to live on yet manageable by a crew of one. There would be no passengers; just the lonely skipper hopping from island to island. The cheapest one he found was $90,000 and it needed some work.

Noon found him back at the pool with a cell phone trying to placate a client or two, but his heart wasn't in it. The same waitress brought another drink. Off the phone, he hid behind dark sunshades and tried to crunch the numbers. But things were wonderfully dull between his ears.

In the past month he'd earned about $80,000 in tax-free graft. Could the pace continue? If so, he'd have his million bucks in a year, and he could abandon his office and what was left of his career, and he could buy his little boat and hit the sea.

For the first time ever, the dream almost seemed real. He could see himself at the wheel, shirtless, shoeless, cold beer at the ready, gliding across the water from St. Barts to St. Kitts, from Nevis to St. Lucia, from one island to a thousand others, wind popping his mainsail, not a damned thing in the world to worry about. He closed his eyes and longed even harder for an escape.

His snoring woke him. The thong was nearby. He ordered some rum and checked his watch.

Two days later Trevor finally made it back to Trumble. He arrived with mixed feelings. First, he was quite anxious to pick up the mail and facilitate the scam, anxious to keep the extortion going and the money rolling in. On the other hand, he was tardy and Judge Spicer would not be happy.

'Where the hell you been?' Spicer growled at him as soon as the guard left the attorney-conference room. It seemed to be the standard question these days. 'I've missed three games because of you, and I picked nothing but winners.'

'The Bahamas. We got a hundred thousand from Curtis in Dallas.'

Spicer's mood changed dramatically. 'It took three days to check on a wire in the Bahamas?' he asked.

'I needed a little rest. Didn't know I was supposed to visit this place every day.'

Spicer was mellowing by the second. He'd just picked up another $22,000. It was safely tucked away with his other loot, in a place no one could find, and as he handed the lawyer yet another stack of pretty envelopes he was thinking of ways to spend the money.

'Aren't we busy,' Trevor said, taking the letters.

'Any complaints? You're making more than we are.'

'I have more to lose than you do.'

Spicer handed over a sheet of paper. 'I've picked ten games here. Five hundred bucks on each.'

Great, thought Trevor. Another long weekend at Pete's, watching one game after another. Oh well, there could be worse things. They played blackjack at a dollar a hand until the guard broke up the meeting.

Trevor's increased visits had been discussed by the warden and the higher-ups at the Bureau of Prisons in Washington. Paperwork had been created on the subject. Restrictions had been contemplated, but then abandoned. The visits were useless, and besides, the warden didn't want to alienate the Brethren. Why pick a fight?

The lawyer was harmless. After a few phone

calls around Jacksonville they decided that Trevor was basically unknown and probably had nothing better to do than hang out in the attorney-conference room of a prison.

The money gave new life to Beech and Yarber. Spending it would necessarily entail getting to it, and that would require they one day walk away as free men, free to do whatever they wanted with their growing fortunes.

With $50,000 or so now in the bank, Yarber was busy plotting an investment portfolio. No sense letting it sit there at 5 percent per annum, even if it was tax-free. One day very soon he'd roll it over into aggressive growth funds, with emphasis on the Far East. Asia would boom again, and his little pile of dirty money would be there to share in the wealth. He had five years to go, and if he earned between 12 and 15 percent on his money until then the $50,000 would grow to roughly $100,000 by the time he left Trumble. Not a bad start for a man who would be sixty-five, and hopefully still in good health.

But if he (and Percy and Ricky) could keep adding to the principal, he might indeed be rich when they turned him loose. Five lousy years – months and weeks he'd been dreading. Now he was suddenly wondering if he had enough time to extort all he needed. As Percy, he was writing letters to over twenty pen pals across North America. No two were in the same town. It was Spicer's job to keep the victims separated. Maps were being used in the law library to make certain neither Percy nor Ricky was corresponding with men who appeared to live near one another.

When he wasn't writing letters, Yarber caught himself thinking about the money. Thankfully, the divorce papers from his wife had come and gone. He'd be officially single in a few months, and by the time he was paroled she'd have long since forgotten about him. Nothing would be shared. He'd be free to walk away without a single string attached.

Five years, and he had so much work to do. He'd cut out the sugar and walk an extra mile each day.

In the darkness of his top bunk, during sleepless nights, Hatlee Beech had done the same math as his colleagues. Fifty thousand dollars in hand, a healthy rate of return somewhere, add to the principal by squeezing from as many victims as they could catch, and one day there'd be a fortune. Beech had nine years, a marathon that once seemed endless. Now there was a flicker of hope. The death sentence they'd handed him was slowly becoming a time of harvest. Conservatively, if the scam netted him only $100,000 a year for the next nine years, plus a healthy rate of return, then he'd be a multimillionaire when he danced through the gates, also at the age of sixty-five.

Two, three, four million was not out of the question.

He knew exactly what he'd do. Since he loved Texas, he'd go to Galveston and buy one of those ancient Victorians near the sea, and he'd invite old friends to stop by and see how rich he was. Forget the law, he'd put in twelve-hour days working the money, nothing but work, nothing but money, so that by the time he was seventy he'd have more than his ex-wife.

For the first time in years, Hatlee Beech thought he might live to see sixty-five, maybe seventy.

He, too, gave up sugar, and butter, and he cut his cigarettes in half with the goal of going cold turkey real soon. He vowed to stay away from the infirmary and stop taking pills. He began walking a mile every day, in the sun, like his colleague from California. And he wrote his letters, he and Ricky.

And Justice Spicer, already equipped with sufficient motivation, was finding it difficult to sleep. He wasn't plagued by guilt or loneliness or humiliation, nor was he depressed by the indignity of prison. He was simply counting money, and juggling rates of return, and analyzing point spreads. With twenty-one months to go, he could see the end.

His lovely wife Rita had passed through the week before, and they'd spent four hours together over two days. She'd cut her hair, stopped drinking, and lost eighteen pounds, and she promised to be even skinnier when she picked him up at the front gate in less than two years. After four hours with her, Joe Roy was convinced the $90,000 was still buried behind the toolshed.

They'd move to Vegas, buy a new condo, and say to hell with the rest of the world.

With the Percy-and-Ricky scam working so well, Spicer had found a new worry. He'd leave Trumble first, happily, gladly, without looking back. But what about the money to be made after he was gone? If the scam was still printing money, what would happen to his share of the future earnings, money he was clearly entitled to? It had been, after all, his idea, one he'd borrowed from the prison in Louisiana. Beech and Yarber had been reluctant conspirators at first.

He had time to devise an exit strategy, just as he had time to contrive a way to get rid of the lawyer. But it would cost him some sleep.

The letter from Quince Garbe in Iowa was read by Beech: "'Dear Ricky (or whoever the hell you are): I don't have any more money. The first $100,000 was borrowed from a bank using a bogus financial statement. I'm not sure how I'll pay it back. My father owns our bank and all its money. Why don't you write him some letters, you thug! I can possibly scrape together $10,000 if we can agree that the extortion will stop there. I'm on the verge of suicide, so don't push. You're scum, you know that. I hope you get caught. Sincerely, Quince Garbe.'"

'Sounds pretty desperate,' Yarber said, looking up from his own pile of mail.

Spicer said, toothpick hanging from his bottom lip, 'Tell him we'll take twenty-five thousand.'

'I'll write him and tell him to wire it,' Beech said, opening another envelope addressed to Ricky.

FIFTEEN

During lunch, when experience had shown that traffic picked up somewhat at Mailbox America, an agent nonchalantly entered the place behind two other customers, and for the second time that day placed a key in Box 455. Lying on top of three pieces of junk mail – one from a pizza carryout, one from a car wash, one from the U.S. Postal Service – he noticed something new. It was an envelope, light orange in color, five by eight. With a pair of tweezers he kept on his key ring, he clamped the end of the envelope, slid it quickly from the box, and dropped it in a small leather briefcase. The junk mail was left undisturbed.

At Langley, it was carefully opened by experts. Two handwritten pages were removed, and copied.

An hour later, Deville entered Teddy's bunker, holding a file. Deville was in charge of what was commonly referred to, deep inside Langley, as the 'Lake mess.' He gave copies of the letter to Teddy and York, then scanned it to a large screen, where Teddy and York at first just stared at it. The printing was bold, in block form, easily readable, as if the author had labored over each word. It read:

Dear Al:

Where you been? Did you get my last letter? I wrote three weeks ago and I haven't heard a word. I guess you're busy, but please don't forget about me. I get very lonely here, and your letters have always inspired me to keep going. They give me strength and hope because I know somebody out there cares. Please don't give up on me, Al.

My counselor says that I might be released in two months. There's a halfway house in Baltimore, actually a few miles from where I grew up, and the people here are trying to get me a spot there. It would be for ninety days, enough time for me to find a job, some friends, etc., you know, get used to society again. It's a lockdown place at night, but I'd be free during the day.

There aren't many good memories, Al. Every person who ever loved me is now dead, and my uncle, the guy who's paying for this rehab, is very rich but very cruel.

I need friends so desperately, Al.

By the way, I've lost another five pounds, and my waist is now a thirty-two. The photo I sent you is getting outdated. I've never liked the way my face looks in it – too much flesh on the cheeks.

I'm much leaner now, and tanned. They let us tan for up to two hours a day here, weather permitting. It's Florida, but some days are too cool. I'll send you another photo, maybe one from the chest up. I'm lifting weights like crazy. I think you'll like the next photo.

You said you would send me one of you. I'm still waiting. Please don't forget me, Al. I need one of your letters.

Love, Ricky

Since York had had the responsibility of investigating every aspect of Lake's life, he felt compelled to try and speak first. But he could think of nothing to say. They read the letter in silence again, and again.

Finally, Deville broke the ice by saying, 'Here's the envelope.' He flashed it on the wall. It was addressed to Mr. Al Konyers, at Mailbox America. The return address was: Ricky, Aladdin North, P.O. Box 44683, Neptune Beach, FL 32233.

'It's a front,' Deville said. 'There's no such place as Aladdin North. There's a telephone number, and you get an answering service. We've called ten times with questions, but the operators know nothing. We've called every rehab and treatment clinic in North Florida, and no one's heard of this place.'

Teddy was silent, still staring at the wall.

'Where's Neptune Beach?' York grunted.

'Jacksonville.'

Deville was excused, but told to stand by. Teddy began making notes on a green legal pad. 'There are other letters, and at least one photo,' he said, as if the problem were just part of the routine. Panic was a state unknown to Teddy Maynard.

'We have to find them,' he said.

'We've done two thorough searches of his home,' York said.

'Then do a third. I doubt if he would keep such stuff at his office.'

'How soon – '

'Do it now. Lake is in California looking for votes. We have no time on this, York. There may be other secret boxes, other men writing letters and bragging about their tans and waistlines.'

'Do you confront him?'

'Not yet.'

Since they had no sample of Mr. Konyers' handwriting, Deville made a suggestion that Teddy eventually liked. They would use the ruse of a new laptop, one with a built-in printer. The first draft was composed by Deville and York, and after an hour or so the fourth draft read as follows:

Dear Ricky:

I got your letter of the twenty-second; forgive me for not writing sooner. I've been on the road a lot lately, and I'm behind on everything. In fact, I'm writing this letter at thirty-five thousand feet, somewhere over the Gulf, en route to Tampa. And I'm using a new laptop, one so small it almost fits in my pocket. Amazing technology. The printer leaves something to be desired. I hope you can read it okay.

Wonderful news about your release, and the halfway house in Baltimore. I have some business interests there, and I'm sure I can help you find a job.

Keep your head up, only two months to go. You're a much stronger person now, and you're ready to live life to its fullest. Don't be discouraged.

I'll help in any way possible. When you get to Baltimore, I'll be happy to spend some time with you, show you around, you know.

I promise I'll write sooner. I can't wait to hear from you.

Love, Al

They decided Al was in a hurry and forgot to sign his name. The letter was marked up, revised, redrafted, pored over with more care than a treaty. The final version was printed on a piece of stationery from the Royal Sonesta Hotel in New Orleans, and placed in a thick, plain brown envelope with optic wiring hidden along the bottom edge. In the lower right-hand corner, in a spot that looked as if it had been slightly damaged and knotted in transit, a tiny transmitter the size of a pinhead was installed. When activated, it would send a signal a hundred yards for up to three days.

Since Al was traveling to Tampa, the envelope was stamped with a Tampa postmark, dated that day. This was done in less than half an hour by a team of very strange people down in Documents on the second floor.

At 4 P.M., a green van with many miles on it stopped at the curb in front of Aaron Lake's townhouse, near one of the many shade trees on Thirty-fourth, in a lovely section of Georgetown.

Its door advertised a plumbing company in the District. Four plumbers got out and began removing tools and equipment.

After a few minutes, the only neighbor who'd noticed grew bored and returned to her television. With Lake in California, the Secret Service was with him, and his home had yet to qualify for round-the-clock surveillance, at least by the Secret Service. That scrutiny would come quickly, though.

The ploy was a clogged sewer line in the small front lawn, something that could be done without entering the home. An outside job, one that would pacify the Secret Service in case they happened to drop by.

But two of the plumbers did indeed enter the home, with their own keys. Another van stopped by to check on progress, and to drop off a tool. Two plumbers from the second van mixed with those already there, and a regular unit began to form.

Inside the house, four of the agents began their tedious search for hidden files. They moved from room to room, inspecting the obvious, prying for the secrets.

The second van left, and a third one came from the other direction and parked with its tires on the sidewalk, as service vans often do. Four more plumbers joined the sewer cleaning, and two eventually drifted inside. After dark, a spotlight was rigged in the front yard, over the sewer cover, and directed into the home so the lights inside would not be noticed. The four men left outside sipped coffee and told jokes and tried to stay warm. Neighbors hurried by on foot.

After six hours the sewer was clean, as was the home. Nothing unusual was found, certainly no hidden file with correspondence from one Ricky in rehab. No sign of a photo. The plumbers turned off their lights, packed their tools, and disappeared without a trace.

At eight-thirty the next morning, when the doors opened at the Neptune Beach post office, an agent named Barr walked hurriedly in as if he were late for something. Barr was an expert on locks and keys, and he'd spent five hours the previous afternoon at Langley studying various boxes used by the Postal Service. He had four master keys, one of which he was certain would open number 44683. If not, he'd be forced to key it, which might take sixty seconds or so and could possibly draw attention. The third key worked, and Barr placed the brown envelope, postmarked the day before from Tampa, addressed to Ricky with no last name, care of Aladdin North, inside the box. There were two other letters already there. For good measure, he removed a piece of junk mail, then closed the door to the box, wadded up the mail, and threw it in the wastebasket.

Barr and two others waited patiently in a van in the parking lot, sipping coffee and videoing every postal customer. They were seventy yards away from the box. Their handheld receiver beeped with the faint signal from the envelope. A diverse group came and went with the flow – a black female in a short brown dress, a white male with a beard and

170

leather jacket, a white female in a jogging suit, a black male in jeans – all agents of the CIA, all watching the box without a clue about who wrote the letter or where it was going. Their job was simply to find the person who'd rented the box.

They found him after lunch.

Trevor drank his lunch at Pete's, but only two beers. Cold drafts with salty peanuts from the community bowl, consumed while losing fifty bucks on a dogsled race in Calgary. Back at the office, he napped for an hour, snoring so loudly his long-suffering secretary finally had to close his door. She slammed it actually, but not loud enough to wake him.

Dreaming of sailboats, he made his trek to the post office, this time choosing to walk because the day was beautiful, he had nothing better to do, and his head needed clearing. He was delighted to find four of the little treasures angled neatly in Aladdin North's box. He placed them carefully in the pocket of his well-worn seersucker jacket, straightened his bow tie, and ambled forth, certain that another payday was fast approaching.

He'd never been tempted to read the letters. Let the Brethren do the dirty work. He could keep his hands clean, shuttle the mail, rake his third off the top. And besides, Spicer would kill him if he delivered mail that had been tampered with.

Seven agents watched him stroll back to his office.

Teddy was napping in his wheelchair when Deville

entered. York had gone home; it was after 10 P.M. York had a wife, Teddy did not.

Deville delivered his narrative while referring to pages of scribbled notes: 'The letter was removed from the box at one-fifty P.M. by a local lawyer named Trevor Carson. We followed him to his office in Neptune Beach, where he stayed for eighty minutes. It's a small one-man office, one secretary, not a lot of clients. Carson is a small-timer along the beaches, does divorces, real estate, two-bit stuff. He's forty-eight, divorced at least twice, native of Pennsylvania, college at Furman, law school at Florida State, got his license suspended eleven years ago for commingling client funds, then got it back.'

'All right, all right,' Teddy said.

'At three-thirty, he left his office, drove an hour to the federal prison at Trumble, Florida. Took the letters with him. We followed but lost the signal when he entered the prison. Since then, we've gathered some information about Trumble. It's a minimum-security prison, commonly referred to as a camp. No walls or fences, very low risk inmates. A thousand of them at Trumble. According to a source within the Bureau of Prisons here in Washington, Carson visits all the time. No other lawyer, no other person visits as much as Carson. Up until a month ago he went once a week, now it's at least three times a week. Sometimes four. All visits are official attorney-client conferences.'

'Who is his client?'

'It's not Ricky. He is the attorney of record for three judges.'

'Three judges?'

'Yes.'

'Three judges in prison?'

'That's right. They call themselves the Brethren.'

Teddy closed his eyes and rubbed his temples. Deville let things sink in for a moment, then continued: 'Carson was in the prison for fifty-four minutes, and when he exited we could not pick up the signal from the envelope. By this time, we were parked next to his car. He walked within five feet of our receiver, and we're certain he did not have the letter. We followed him back to Jacksonville, back to the beaches. He parked near a place called Pete's Bar and Grill, where he stayed for three hours. We searched his car, found his briefcase, and inside there were eight letters addressed to various men all over the country. All letters were outbound from the prison, none were inbound. Evidently, Carson shuttles mail back and forth to his clients. As of thirty minutes ago, he was still in the bar, quite drunk, betting on college basketball games.'

'A loser.'

'Very much so.'

The loser staggered out of Pete's after the second overtime of a game on the West Coast. Spicer had picked three out of four winners. Trevor had dutifully followed suit, and was up a thousand bucks for the night.

Drunk as he was, he was smart enough not to drive. His DUI three years earlier was still a painful memory, and besides the damned cops were all over the place. The restaurants and bars around

173

the Sea Turtle Inn attracted the young and restless, thus the cops.

Walking was a challenge, though. He made it well enough to his office, a straight shot south, past the quiet little summer rentals and retirement cottages, all dark and tucked in for the night. He carried his briefcase with the letters from Trumble.

He pressed onward, searching for his house. He crossed the street for no reason, and half a block later recrossed it. There was no traffic. When he began to circle back, he came within twenty yards of an agent who'd ducked behind a parked car. The silent army watched him, suddenly fearful that the drunken fool might stumble into one of them.

At some point he gave up, and managed to find his office again. He rattled keys on the front steps, dropped his briefcase and forgot about it, and less than a minute after opening the door he was at his desk, sprawled in his swivel rocker, fast asleep, the front door half open.

The back door had been unlocked throughout the night. Following orders from Langley, Barr and company had entered the office and wired everything. There was no alarm system, no locks on the windows, nothing of value to attract thievery in the first place. Tapping the phones and bugging the walls had been an easy task, made so by the obvious fact that no one on the outside observed anything inside the offices of L. Trevor Carson, Attorney and Counselor-at-Law.

The briefcase was emptied, its contents cataloged at Langley's instructions. Langley wanted a precise record of the letters the lawyer had taken

174

from Trumble. When everything had been inspected and photographed, the briefcase was placed in the hallway near his office. The snoring was impressive, and uninterrupted.

Shortly before 2, Barr managed to start the Beetle parked near Pete's. He drove it down the empty street and left it innocently on the curb in front of the law office, so that the drunk would rub his eyes in a few hours and pat himself on the back for such a nice job of driving. Or maybe he would shrink in horror at the thought of having driven while intoxicated once again. Either way, they'd be listening.

SIXTEEN

Thirty-seven hours before the polls opened in Virginia and Washington, the President appeared live on national television to announce that he had ordered an air attack in and around the Tunisian city of Talah. The Yidal terrorist unit was believed to train there, in a well-stocked compound on the edge of town.

And so the country became glued to yet another mini-war, one of pushbuttons and smart bombs and retired generals on CNN prattling on about this strategy or that. It was dark in Tunisia, thus no footage. The retired generals and their clueless interviewers did a lot of guessing. And waiting. Waiting for sunlight so the smoke and rubble could be broadcast to a jaded nation.

But Yidal had its sources, most likely the Israelis. The compound was empty when the smart bombs dropped in from nowhere. They hit their targets, shook the desert, destroyed the compound, but killed not a single terrorist. A couple strayed, however, one venturing into the center of Talah, where it hit a hospital. Another hit a small house where a family of seven was fast asleep. Fortunately, they never knew what happened.

Tunisian television was quick to cover the burning hospital, and at daybreak on the East Coast the country learned that the smart bombs weren't so smart after all. At least fifty bodies had been recovered, all very innocent civilians.

At some point during the early morning, the President developed a sudden uncharacteristic aversion to reporters, and could not be reached for comment. The Vice President, a man who'd said plenty when the attack started, was in seclusion with his staff somewhere in Washington.

The bodies piled up, the cameras kept rolling, and by midmorning world reaction was swift, brutal, and unanimous. The Chinese were threatening war. The French seemed inclined to join them. Even the Brits said the United States was trigger-happy.

Since the dead were nothing more than Tunisian peasants, certainly not Americans, the politicians were quick to politicize the debacle. The usual finger-pointing and grandstanding and calls for investigations happened before noon in Washington. And on the campaign circuit, those still in the race took a few moments to reflect on just how ill-fated the mission had been. None of them would have engaged in such desperate retaliation without better intelligence. None but the Vice President, who was still in seclusion. As the bodies were being counted, not a single candidate thought the raid was worthy of the risks. All condemned the President.

But it was Aaron Lake who attracted the most

attention. He found it difficult to move without tripping over cameramen. In a carefully worded statement, he said, without notes, 'We are inept. We are helpless. We are feeble. We should be ashamed of our inability to wipe out a ragtag little army of less than fifty cowards. You cannot simply push buttons and run for cover. It takes guts to fight wars on the ground. I have the guts. When I am President, no terrorist with American blood on his hands will be safe. That is my solemn promise.'

In the fury and chaos of the morning, Lake's words found their mark. Here was a man who meant what he said, who knew precisely what he would do. We wouldn't slaughter innocent peasants if a man with guts were making the decisions. Lake was the man.

In the bunker, Teddy weathered another storm. Bad intelligence was blamed for every disaster. When the raids were successful, the pilots and the brave boys on the ground and their commanders and the politicians who sent them into battle got the credit. But when the raids went wrong, as they usually did, the CIA got the blame.

He had advised against the attack. The Israelis had a tenuous and very secret agreement with Yidal – don't kill us, and we won't kill you. As long as the targets were Americans and an occasional European, then the Israelis would not get involved. Teddy knew this, but it was information he had not shared. Twenty-four hours before the attack, he had advised the President, in writing, that he doubted the terrorists would be in the compound when the bombs arrived. And, because of the target's proximity to Talah, there was an excellent chance of collateral damage.

Hatlee Beech opened the brown envelope without noticing that the right lower corner was somewhat wadded and slightly damaged. He was opening so many personal envelopes these days, he looked only at the return address to see who and where they came from. Nor did he notice the Tampa postmark.

He hadn't heard from Al Konyers in several weeks. He read the letter through without stopping, and found little if no interest in the fact that Al was using a new laptop. It was perfectly believable that Ricky's pen pal had taken a sheet of stationery from the Royal Sonesta in New Orleans, and was pecking out the letter at thirty-five thousand feet.

Wonder if he was flying first class? he asked himself. Probably so. They wouldn't have computer hookups back in coach, would they? Al had been in New Orleans on business, stayed at a very nice hotel, then flew first class to his next destination. The Brethren were interested in the financial conditions of all their pen pals. Nothing else mattered.

After he read the letter, he handed it to Finn Yarber, who was in the process of writing another one as poor Percy. They were working in the small conference room in the corner of the law library, their table littered with files and mail and a pretty assortment of soft pastel correspondence cards. Spicer was outside, at his table, guarding the door and studying point spreads.

179

'Who's Konyers?' Finn asked.

Beech was flipping through some files. They kept a neat folder on every pen pal, complete with the letters they received and copies of all letters they'd sent.

'Don't know much,' Beech said. 'Lives in the D.C. area, fake name, I'm sure. Uses one of those mailbox services. That's his third letter, I think.'

From the Konyers file Beech pulled out the first two letters. The one from December 11 read:

Dear Ricky:

Hello. My name is Al Konyers. I'm in my fifties. I like jazz, old movies, Humphrey Bogart, and I like to read biographies. I don't smoke and don't like people who do. Fun is Chinese take-out, a little wine, a black-and-white western with a good friend. Drop me a line.

Al Konyers

It was typewritten on plain white paper, the way most of them were at first. Fear was stamped between every line – fear of getting caught, fear of starting a long-distance relationship with a complete stranger. Every letter of every word was typewritten. He didn't even sign his name.

Ricky's first response was the standard letter Beech had written a hundred times now: Ricky's twenty-eight, in rehab, bad family, rich uncle, etc. And dozens of the same enthusiastic questions: What kind of work do you do? How about your family? Do you like to travel? If Ricky could bare his soul, then he needed something in return. Two

180

pages of the same crap Beech had been writing for five months. He wanted so desperately to simply Xerox the damned thing. But he couldn't. He was forced to personalize each one, on nice pretty paper. And he sent Al the same handsome photo he'd sent to the others. The picture was the bait that hooked almost all of them.

Three weeks passed. On January 9, Trevor had delivered a second letter from Al Konyers. It was as clean and sterile as the first, probably typed with rubber gloves.

Dear Ricky:

I enjoyed your letter. I have to admit I felt sorry for you at first, but you seem to have adjusted well to rehab and know where you're going. I've never had problems with drugs and alcohol, so it's difficult for me to understand. It sounds as though you're getting the best treatment money can buy. You shouldn't be so harsh on your uncle. Think of where you might be if not for him.

You ask many questions about me. I'm not ready to discuss a lot of personal matters, but I understand your curiosity. I was married for thirty years, but not anymore. I live in D.C., and work for the government. My job is challenging and fulfilling.

I live alone. I have few close friends and prefer it that way. When I travel, it's usually to Asia. I adore Tokyo.

I'll keep you in my thoughts in the days to come.

Al Konyers

Just above the typewritten name, he'd scribbled the name 'Al,' with a black-felt pen, fine point.

The letter was most unimpressive for three reasons. First, Konyers did not have a wife, or at least he said he didn't. A wife was crucial for extortion. Threaten to tell the wife, to send her copies of all the letters from the gay pen pal, and the money rolled in.

Second, Al worked for the government, so he probably didn't have a lot of money.

Third, Al was much too scared to waste time with. Getting information was like pulling teeth. The Quince Garbes and Curtis Cateses were much more fun because they'd spent their lives in the closet and were now anxious to escape. Their letters were long and windy and filled with all the damning little facts an extortionist might need. Not Al. Al was boring. Al wasn't sure what he wanted.

So Ricky raised the stakes with his second letter, another piece of boilerplate Beech had perfected with practice. Ricky had just learned that he would be released in a few months! And he was from Baltimore. What a coincidence! And he might need some help getting a job. His rich uncle was refusing to help anymore, he was afraid of life on the outside without the help of friends, and he really couldn't trust his old friends because they were still on drugs, etc., etc.

The letter went unanswered, and Beech assumed that Al Konyers was frightened by it. Ricky was on his way to Baltimore, just an hour from Washington, and that was too close for Al.

While waiting for an answer from Al, the Quince

Garbe money landed, followed by the wire from Curtis in Dallas, and the Brethren found renewed energy in their scam. Ricky wrote Al the letter that was intercepted and analyzed at Langley.

Now, suddenly, Al's third letter had a very different tone. Finn Yarber read it twice, then reread the second letter from Al. 'Sounds like a different person, doesn't it?' he said.

'Yes, it does,' Beech said, looking at both letters. 'I think the old boy is finally excited about meeting Ricky.'

'I thought he worked for the government.'

'Says he does.'

'Then what's this about having business interests in Baltimore?'

'We worked for the government, didn't we?'

'Sure.'

'What was your highest salary on the bench?'

'When I was chief justice I made a hundred and fifty thousand.'

'I made a hundred and forty. Some of those professional bureaucrats make more than that. Plus, he's not married.'

'That's a problem.'

'Yeah, but let's keep pushing. He's got a big job, which means he's got a big boss, lots of colleagues, typical Washington hotshot. We'll find a pressure point somewhere.'

'What the hell,' Finn said.

What the hell, indeed. What was there to lose? So what if they pushed a little too hard, and Mr. Al got scared or got mad and decided to throw the letters away? You can't lose what you don't have.

Serious money was being made here. It was not

a time to be timid. Their aggressive tactics were producing spectacular results. The mail was growing each week, as was their offshore account. Their scam was foolproof because their pen pals lived double lives. Their victims had no one to complain to.

Negotiations were quick because the market was ripe. It was still winter in Jacksonville, and because the nights were chilly and the ocean was too cool to swim in, the busy season was a month away. There were hundreds of small rentals available along Neptune Beach and Atlantic Beach, including one almost directly across the street from Trevor. A man from Boston offered $600 cash for two months, and the real estate agent snatched it. The place was furnished with odds and ends no flea market would handle. The old shag carpet was well worn and emitted a permanent musty smell. It was perfect.

The renter's first chore was to cover the windows. Three of them faced the street and looked across to Trevor's, and during the first few hours of surveillance it became obvious how few clients came and went. There was so little business over there! When work surfaced it was usually done by the secretary, Jan, who also read a lot of magazines.

Others quietly moved into the rental, men and women with old suitcases and large duffel bags filled with electronic wizardry. The fragile furnishings were shoved to the rear of the cottage, and the front rooms were quickly filled with screens and monitors and listening devices of a dozen varieties.

Trevor himself would make an interesting case study for third-year law students. He arrived around 9 A.M., and spent the first hour reading newspapers. His morning client seemed to always arrive at ten-thirty, and after an exhaustive half-hour conference he was ready for lunch, always at Pete's Bar and Grill. He carried a phone with him, to prove his importance to the bartenders there, and he usually made two or three unnecessary calls to other lawyers. He called his bookie a lot.

Then he walked back to his office, past the rental where the CIA monitored every step, back to his desk where it was time for a nap. He came to life around three, and hit it hard for two hours. By then he needed another longneck from Pete's.

The second time they followed him to Trumble, he left the prison after an hour and returned to his office about 6 P.M. While he was having dinner in an oyster bar on Atlantic Boulevard, alone, an agent entered his office and found his old briefcase. In it were five letters from Percy and Ricky.

The commander of the silent army in and around Neptune Beach was a man named Klockner, the best Teddy had in the field of domestic street spying. Klockner had been instructed to intercept all mail flowing through the law office.

When Trevor went straight home after leaving the oyster bar, the five letters were taken across the street to the rental, where they were opened, copied, then resealed and replaced in Trevor's briefcase. None of the five was for Al Konyers.

At Langley, Deville read the five letters as they came off the fax. They were examined by two handwriting experts who agreed that Percy and

Ricky were not the same people. Using samples taken from their court files, it was determined, without much effort, that Percy was really former Justice Finn Yarber, and that Ricky was former U.S. District Judge Hatlee Beech.

Ricky's address was the Aladdin North box at the Neptune Beach post office. Percy, to their surprise, used a postal box in Atlantic Beach, one rented to an outfit called Laurel Ridge.

SEVENTEEN

For his next visit to Langley, the first in three weeks, the candidate arrived in a caravan of shiny black vans, all going too fast but who would complain. They were cleared and waved onward, deeper into the complex, until they roared to a collective stop near a very convenient door where all sorts of grim-faced, thick-necked young men were waiting. Lake rode the wave into the building, losing escorts as he went until finally he arrived not at the usual bunker but in Mr. Maynard's formal office, with a view of a small forest. Everyone else was left at the door. Alone, the two great men shook hands warmly and actually appeared happy to see one another.

Important things first. 'Congratulations on Virginia,' Teddy said.

Lake shrugged as if he wasn't sure. 'Thank you, in more ways than one.'

'It's a very impressive win, Mr. Lake,' Teddy said. 'Governor Tarry worked hard there for a year. Two months ago he had commitments from every precinct captain in the state. He looked unbeatable. Now, I think he's fading fast. It's often a disadvantage to be the front-runner early in the race.'

'Momentum is a strange animal in politics,' Lake observed wisely.

'Cash is even stranger. Right now, Governor Tarry can't find a dime because you've got it all. Money follows momentum.'

'I'm sure I'll say this many times, Mr. Maynard, but, well, thanks. You've given me an opportunity I'd hardly dreamed of.'

'Are you having any fun?'

'Not yet. If we win, the fun will come later.'

'The fun starts next Tuesday, Mr. Lake, with big Super Tuesday. New York, California, Massachusetts, Ohio, Georgia, Missouri, Maryland, Maine, Connecticut, all in one day. Almost six hundred delegates!' Teddy's eyes were dancing as if he could almost count the votes. 'And you're ahead in every state, Mr. Lake. Can you believe it?'

'No, I cannot.'

'It's true. You're neck and neck in Maine, for some damned reason, and it's close in California, but you're going to win big next Tuesday.'

'If you believe the polls,' Lake said, as if he didn't trust them himself. Fact was, like every candidate, Lake was addicted to the polls. He was actually gaining in California, a state with 140,000 defense workers.

'Oh, I believe them. And I believe that a landslide is coming on little Super Tuesday. They love you down South, Mr. Lake. They love guns and tough talk and such, and right now they're falling in love with Aaron Lake. Next Tuesday will be fun, but the following Tuesday will be a romp.'

188

Teddy Maynard was predicting a romp, and Lake couldn't help but smile. His polls showed the same trends, but it just sounded better coming from Teddy. He lifted a sheet of paper and read the latest polling data from around the country. Lake was ahead by at least five points in every state.

They reveled in their momentum for a few minutes, then Teddy turned serious. 'There's something you should know,' he said, and the smile was gone. He flipped a page and glanced at some notes. 'Two nights ago, in the Khyber Pass in the mountains of Afghanistan, a Russian long-range missile with nuclear warheads was moved by truck into Pakistan. It is now en route to Iran, where it will be used for God knows what. The missile has a range of three thousand miles, and the capability of delivering four nuclear bombs. The price was about thirty million dollars U.S., cash up front paid by the Iranians through a bank in Luxembourg. It's still there, in an account believed to be controlled by Natty Chenkov's people.'

'I thought he was stockpiling, not selling.'

'He needs cash, and he's getting it. In fact, he's probably the only man we know who's collecting it faster than you.'

Teddy didn't do humor well, but Lake laughed out of politeness anyway.

'Is the missile operational?' Lake asked.

'We think so. It originated from a collection of silos near Kiev, and we believe it's of a recent make and model. With so many lying around, why would the Iranians buy an old one? Yes, it's safe to assume it's fully operational.'

'Is it the first?'

'There've been some spare parts and plutonium, to Iran and Iraq and India and others, but I think this is the first fully assembled, ready-to-shoot missile.'

'Are they anxious to use it?'

'We don't think so. It appears as if the transaction was instigated by Chenkov. He needs the money to buy other kinds of weapons. He's shopping his wares, things he doesn't need.'

'Do the Israelis know it?'

'No. Not yet. You have to be careful with them. Everything is give and take. Someday, if we need something from them, then we might tell them about this transaction.'

For a moment, Lake longed to be President, and immediately. He wanted to know everything Teddy knew, then he realized he probably never would. There was, after all, a sitting President right then, at that moment, albeit a lame duck, and Teddy wasn't chatting with him about Chenkov and his missiles.

'What do the Russians think about my campaign?' he asked.

'At first, they weren't concerned. Now they're watching closely. But you have to remember, there is no such thing as a Russian voice anymore. The free marketers speak favorably of you because they fear the Communists. The hard-liners are scared of you. It's very complex.'

'And Chenkov?'

'I'm ashamed to say we're not that close to him,

yet. But we're working on it. We should have some ears in the vicinity soon.'

Teddy tossed his papers onto his desk, and rolled himself closer to Lake. The many wrinkles in his forehead pinched closer together, downward. His bushy eyebrows fell hard on his sad eyes. 'Listen to me, Mr. Lake,' he said, his voice much more somber. 'You have this thing won. There will be a bump or two in the road, things we cannot foresee, and even if we could we'd be powerless to prevent them. We'll ride them out together. The damage will be slight. You're something brand new and the people like you. You're doing a marvelous job and communicating. Keep the message simple – our security is at risk, the world is not as safe as it looks. I'll take care of the money, and I'll certainly keep the country frightened. That missile in the Khyber Pass, we could've detonated it. Five thousand people would've been killed, five thousand Pakistanis. Nuclear bombs exploding in the mountains. You think we'd wake up and worry about the stock market? Not a chance. I'll take care of the fear, Mr. Lake. You keep your nose clean and run hard.'

'I'm running as hard as I can.'

'Run harder, and no surprises, okay?'

'Certainly not.'

Lake wasn't sure what he meant by surprises, but he let it pass. Just a bit of grandfatherly wisdom, perhaps.

Teddy rolled away again. He found his buttons and a screen dropped from the ceiling. They spent twenty minutes viewing rough cuts of the next series of Lake ads, then said their goodbyes.

Lake sped away from Langley, two vans in front and one behind, all racing to Reagan National Airport, where the jet was waiting. He wanted a quiet night in Georgetown, at home where the world was held at bay, where he could read a book in solitude, with no one watching or listening. He longed for the anonymity of the streets, the nameless faces, the Arab baker on M Street who made a perfect bagel, the used-book dealer on Wisconsin, the coffeehouse where they roasted beans from Africa. Would he ever be able to walk the streets again, like a normal person, doing whatever he pleased? Something told him no, that those days were gone, probably forever.

When Lake was airborne, Deville entered the bunker and announced to Teddy that Lake had come and gone without trying to check the mailbox. It was time for the daily briefing on the Lake mess. Teddy was spending more time than he'd planned worrying about what his candidate might do next.

The five letters Klockner and his group intercepted from Trevor had been thoroughly researched. Two had been written by Yarber as Percy; the other three by Beech as Ricky. The five pen pals were in different states. Four were using fictitious names; one was bold enough not to hide behind an alias. The letters were basically the same: Percy and Ricky were troubled young men in rehab, trying desperately to pull their lives together, both talented and still able to dream big dreams, but in need of moral and physical support from new friends because the old ones were dangerous. They freely divulged their sins and foibles, their weaknesses and heartaches. They rambled about their lives after rehab, their hopes and dreams of all the things they wanted to do. They were proud of their tans and their muscles, and seemed anxious to show their new hardened bodies to their pen pals.

Only one letter asked for money. Ricky wanted a loan of $1,000 from a correspondent named Peter in Spokane, Washington. He said the money was needed to cover some expenses his uncle was refusing to pay.

Teddy had read the letters more than once. The request for money was important because it began to shed light on the Brethren's little game. Perhaps it was just a two-bit enterprise someone taught them, some other con who'd finished his time at Trumble and was now roaming at large stealing anew.

But the size of the stakes was not the issue. It was a flesh game – thinner waists and bronze skin and firm biceps – and their candidate was in the middle of it.

There were still questions, but Teddy was patient. They would watch the mail. The pieces would fall into place.

With Spicer guarding the door to the conference room, and daring anyone to use the law library, Beech and Yarber labored away with their mail. To Al Konyers, Beech wrote:

Dear Al:
Thanks for your last letter. It means so much to me to hear from you. I feel like I've

193

been living in a cage for months, and I'm slowly seeing daylight. Your letters help to open the door. Please don't stop writing.

I'm sorry if I've bored you with too much personal stuff. I respect your privacy and hope I haven't asked too many questions. You seem like a very sensitive man who enjoys solitude and the finer things of life. I thought about you last night when I watched *Key Largo*, the old Bogart and Bacall film. I could almost taste the Chinese carry-out. The food here is pretty good, I guess, but they simply can't do Chinese.

I have a great idea. In two months when I get out of here, let's rent *Casablanca and African Queen*, get the carry-out, get a bottle of nonalcoholic wine, and spend a quiet evening on the sofa. God, I get excited just thinking about life on the outside and doing real things again.

Forgive me if I'm going too fast, Al. It's just that I've done without a lot of things here, and not just booze and good food. Know what I mean?

The halfway house in Baltimore is willing to take me if I can find a part-time job of some type. You said you had some interests there. I know I'm asking a lot because you don't know me, but can you arrange this? I will be forever grateful.

Please write me soon, Al. Your letters, and the hopes and dreams of leaving here in two months with a job on the outside, sustain me in my darkest hours.

Thanks, friend.

Love, Ricky

The one to Quince Garbe had a very different tone. Beech and Yarber had kicked it around for several days. The final draft read:

Dear Quince:

Your father owns a bank, yet you say you can only raise another $10,000. I think you're lying, Quince, and it really ticks me off. I'm tempted to send the file to your father and wife anyway.

I'll settle for $25,000, immediately, same wiring instructions.

And don't threaten suicide. I really don't care what you do. We'll never meet, and I think you're a sicko anyway.

Wire the damned money, Quince, and now!

Love, Ricky

Klockner worried that Trevor might visit Trumble one day before noon, then drop off the mail at some point along the way before returning to his office or his home. There was no way to intercept it while en route. It was imperative that he haul it back, and leave it overnight so they could get their hands on it.

He worried, but at the same time Trevor was proving to be a late starter. He showed few signs of life until after his two o'clock nap.

So when he informed his secretary that he was about to leave for Trumble at 11 A.M., the rental across the street sprang into action. A call was

195

immediately placed to Trevor's office by a middle-aged woman claiming to be a Mrs. Beltrone, who explained to Jan that she and her rich husband were in dire need of a quick divorce. The secretary put her on hold, and yelled down the hallway for Trevor to wait a second. Trevor was gathering papers from his desk and placing them in his briefcase. The camera in the ceiling above him caught his look of displeasure at having been interrupted by a new client.

'She says she's rich!' Jan yelled, and Trevor's frown disappeared. He sat down and waited.

Mrs. Beltrone unloaded on the secretary. She was wife number three, the husband was much older, they had a home in Jacksonville but spent most of their time at their home in Bermuda. Also had a home in Vail. They'd been planning the divorce for some time, everything had been agreed upon, no fighting at all, very amicable, just needed a good lawyer to handle the paperwork. Mr. Carson had come highly recommended, but they had to act fast for some undisclosed reason.

Trevor took over and listened to the same story. Mrs. Beltrone was sitting across the street in the rental, working from a script the team had put together just for this occasion.

'I really need to see you,' she said after fifteen minutes of baring her soul.

'Well, I'm awfully busy,' Trevor said, as if he were flipping pages in half a dozen daily appointment books. Mrs. Beltrone was watching him on the monitor. His feet were on the desk, his eyes closed, his bow tie crooked. The life of an awfully busy lawyer.

'Please,' she begged. 'We need to get this over with. I must see you today.'

'Where's your husband?'

'He's in France, but he'll be here tomorrow.'

'Well, uh, let's see,' Trevor mumbled, playing with his bow tie.

'What's your fee?' she asked, and his eyes flew open.

'Well, this is obviously more complicated than your simple no-fault. I'd have to charge a fee of ten thousand dollars.' He grimaced when he said it, holding his breath for the response.

'I'll bring it today,' she said. 'Can I see you at one?'

He was on his feet, hovering over the phone. 'How about one-thirty?' he managed to say.

'I'll be there.'

'Do you know where my office is?'

'My driver can find it. Thanks, Mr. Carson.'

Just call me Trevor, he almost said. But she was gone.

They watched as he wrung his hands together, then pumped his fists, gritted his teeth, said, 'Yes!' He'd hooked a big one.

Jan appeared from the hall and said, 'Well?'

'She'll be here at one-thirty. Get this place cleaned up a little.'

'I'm not a maid. Can you get some money up front? I need to pay bills.'

'I'll get the damned money.'

Trevor attacked his bookshelves, straightening volumes he hadn't touched in years, dusting the planks with a paper towel, stuffing files in drawers.

When he charged his desk, Jan finally felt a twinge of guilt and began vacuuming the reception area.

They labored through lunch, their bitching and straining making for great amusement across the street.

No sign of Mrs. Beltrone at one-thirty.

'Where the hell is she?' Trevor barked down the hall just after two.

'Maybe she checked around, got some more references,' Jan said.

'What did you say?' he yelled.

'Nothing, boss.'

'Call her,' he demanded at two-thirty.

'She didn't leave a number.'

'You didn't get a number?'

'That's not what I said. I said she didn't leave a number.'

At three-thirty, Trevor stormed out of his office, still trying desperately to uphold his end of a raging argument with a woman he'd fired at least ten times in the past eight years.

They followed him straight to Trumble. He was in the prison for fifty-three minutes, and when he left it was after five, too late to drop off mail in either Neptune Beach or Atlantic Beach. He returned to his office and left his briefcase on his desk. Then, predictably, he went to Pete's for drinks and dinner.

EIGHTEEN

The unit from Langley flew to Des Moines, where the agents rented two cars and a van, then drove forty minutes to Bakers, Iowa. They arrived in the quiet, snowbound little town two days before the letter. By the time Quince picked it up at the post office, they knew the names of the postmaster, the mayor, the chief of police, and the short-order cook at the pancake house next to the hardware store. But no one in Bakers knew them.

They watched Quince hurry to the bank after leaving the post office. Thirty minutes later, two agents known only as Chap and Wes found the corner of the bank where Mr. Garbe, Jr., did business, and they presented themselves to his secretary as inspectors from the Federal Reserve. They certainly looked official – dark suits, black shoes, short hair, long overcoats, clipped speech, efficient manners.

Quince was locked inside, and at first seemed unwilling to come out. They impressed upon his secretary the urgency of their visit, and after almost forty minutes the door opened slightly. Mr. Garbe looked as though he'd been crying. He was pale, shaken, unhappy with the prospect of entertaining anyone. But he showed them in anyway, too unnerved to ask for identification. He didn't even catch their names.

He sat across the massive desk, and looked at the twins facing him. 'What can we do for you?' he asked, with a very faint smile.

'Is the door locked?' Chap asked.

'Why yes, it is.' The twins got the impression that most of Mr. Garbe's day was spent behind locked doors.

'Can anyone hear us?' Wes asked.

'No.' Quince was even more rattled now.

'We're not reserve officials,' Chap said. 'We lied.'

Quince wasn't sure if he should be angry or relieved or even more frightened, so he just sat there for a second, mouth open, frozen, waiting to be shot.

'It's a long story,' Wes said.

'You've got five minutes.'

'Actually, we have as long as we want.'

'This is my office. Get out.'

'Not so fast. We know some things.'

'I'll call security.'

'No you won't.'

'We've seen the letter,' Chap said. 'The one you just got from the post office.'

'I picked up several.'

'But only one from Ricky.'

Quince's shoulders sagged, his eyes closed slowly. Then they opened again and looked at the tormentors in total, absolute defeat. 'Who are you?' he mumbled.

'We're not enemies.'

'You're working for him, aren't you?'

'Him?'

'Ricky, or whoever the hell he is.'

'No,' Wes said. 'He's our enemy too. Let's just say that we have a client who's in the same boat you're in, more or less. We've been hired to protect him.'

Chap pulled a thick envelope from his coat pocket and tossed it on the desk. 'There's twenty-five thousand cash. Send it to Ricky.'

Quince stared at the envelope, his mouth open wide. His poor brain was choked with so many thoughts he was dizzy. So he closed his eyes again, and squinted fiercely in a vain effort to organize things. Forget the question of who they were. How did they read the letter? Why were they offering him money? How much did they know?

He sure as hell couldn't trust them.

'The money's yours,' Wes said. 'In return, we need some information.'

'Who is Ricky?' Quince asked, his eyes barely open.

'What do you know about him?' Chap asked.

'His name's not Ricky.'

'True.'

'He's in prison.'

'True,' Chap said again.

'Says he has a wife and children.'

'Partially true. The wife is now an ex-wife. The children are still his.'

'Says they're destitute, and that's why he's scamming people.'

'Not exactly. His wife is quite wealthy, and his

201

children have followed the money. We're not sure why he's scamming people.'

'But we'd like to stop him,' Chap added. 'We need your help.'

Quince suddenly realized that for the first time in his life, in all of his fifty-one years, he was sitting in the presence of two living, breathing people who knew he was a homosexual. The knowledge terrified him. For a second he wanted to deny it, to concoct some story of how he came to know Ricky, but invention failed him. He was too scared to be inspired.

Then he realized that these two, whoever they were, could ruin him. They knew his little secret, and they had the power to wreck his life.

And they were offering $25,000 cash?

Poor Quince covered his eyes with his knuckles and said, 'What do you want?'

Chap and Wes thought he was about to cry. They didn't particularly care, but there was no need for it. 'Here's the deal, Mr. Garbe,' said Chap. 'You take the money lying there on your desk, and you tell us everything about Ricky. Show us your letters. Show us everything. If you have a file or a box or some secret place where you've hidden everything, we'd like to see it. Once we've gathered all we need, then we'll leave. We'll disappear as quickly as we've come, and you'll never know who we are or who we're protecting.'

'And you'll keep the secrets?'

'Absolutely.'

'There's no reason for us to tell anyone about you,' Wes added.

'Can you make him stop?' Quince asked, staring at them.

Chap and Wes paused and glanced at each other. Their responses had been perfect so far, but this question had no clear answer. 'We can't promise, Mr. Garbe,' Wes said. 'But we'll try our best to put this Ricky character out of business. As we said, he's upsetting our client too.'

'You've got to protect me on this.'

'We'll do all we can.'

Suddenly Quince stood and leaned forward with his palms flat on the desk. 'Then I have no choice,' he announced. He didn't touch the money, but walked a few steps to an ancient glass bookcase filled with weathered and peeling volumes. With one key he unlocked the case, and with another he opened a small, hidden safe on the second shelf from the floor. Carefully, he withdrew a thin, letter-sized folder, which he delicately placed next to the envelope filled with cash.

Just as he opened the file, an offensive, high-pitched voice squawked through the intercom, 'Mr. Garbe, your father would like to see you immediately.'

Quince bolted upright in horror, his cheeks instantly pale, his face contorted in panic. 'Uh, tell him I'm in a meeting,' he said, trying to sound reassuring but coming off as a hopeless liar.

'You tell him,' she said, and the intercom clicked.

'Excuse me,' he said, actually trying to smile. He picked up the receiver, punched three numbers, and turned his back on Wes and Chap so that maybe they wouldn't hear.

'Dad, it's me. What's up?' he said, head low.

A long pause as the old man filled his ear.

Then, 'No, no, they're not from the Federal Reserve. They're, uh, they're lawyers from Des Moines. They represent the family of an old college buddy of mine. That's all.'

A shorter pause.

'Uh, Franklin Delaney, you wouldn't remember him. He died four months ago, without a will, a big mess. No, Dad, uh, it has nothing to do with the bank.'

He hung up. Not a bad piece of lying. The door was locked. That's all that mattered.

Wes and Chap stood and moved in tandem to the edge of the desk, where they leaned forward together as Quince opened the file. The first thing they noticed was the photo, paper-clipped to the inside flap. Wes gently removed it, and said, 'Is this supposed to be Ricky?'

'That's him,' Quince said, ashamed but determined to get through it.

'A nice-looking young man,' Chap said, as if they were staring at a *Playboy* centerfold. All three were immediately uncomfortable.

'You know who Ricky is, don't you?' Quince asked.

'Yes.'

'Then tell me.'

'No, it's not part of the deal.'

'Why can't you tell me? I'm giving you everything you want.'

'That's not what we agreed on.'

'I want to kill the bastard.'

'Relax, Mr. Garbe. We have a deal. You get the money, we get the file, nobody gets hurt.'

'Let's go back to the beginning,' Chap said, looking down at the fragile and suffering little man in the oversized chair. 'How did it all start?'

Quince moved some papers around in the file and produced a thin magazine. 'I bought this at a bookstore in Chicago,' he said, sliding it around so they could read it. The title was *Out and About*, and it described itself as a publication for mature men with alternative lifestyles. He let them take in the cover, then flipped to the back pages. Wes and Chap didn't try to touch it, but their eyes took in as much as possible. Very few pictures, lots of small print. It wasn't pornography by any means.

On page forty-six was a small section of personals. One was circled with a red pen. It read:

> SWM in 20s looking for kind and
> discreet gentleman in 40s or 50s
> to pen pal with.

Wes and Chap leaned lower to read it, then came back up together. 'So you answered this ad?' Chap said.

'I did. I sent a little note, and about two weeks later I heard from Ricky.'

'Do you have a copy of your note?'

'No. I didn't copy my letters. Nothing left this office. I was afraid to make copies around here.'

Wes and Chap frowned in disbelief, then great disappointment. What kind of dumb ass were they dealing with here?

'Sorry,' Quince said, tempted to grab the cash before they changed their minds.

Moving things along, he removed the first letter from Ricky and thrust it at them. 'Just lay it down,' Wes said, and they leaned in again, inspecting without touching. They were very slow readers, Quince noticed, and they read with incredible concentration. His mind was beginning to clear, and a glimmer of hope emerged. How sweet it was to have the money and not have to worry about another crooked loan, another pack of lies to cover his trail. And now he had allies, Wes and Chap here, and God knows who else working against Ricky. His heart slowed a little and his breathing was not as labored.

'The next letter please,' Chap said.

Quince laid them out in sequence, one beside the other, three lavender in color, one a soft blue, one yellow, all written in the tedious block handwriting of a person with plenty of time. When they finished one page, Chap would carefully arrange the next one with a pair of tweezers. Their fingers touched nothing.

The odd thing about the letters, as Chap and Wes would whisper to each other much later, was that they were so thoroughly believable. Ricky was wounded and tortured and in dire need of someone to talk to. He was pitiful and sympathetic. And there was hope because the worst was over for him and he would soon be free to pursue new friendships. The writing was superb!

After a deafening silence, Quince said, 'I need to make a phone call.'

'To whom?'

'It's business.'

Wes and Chap looked at each other with uncertainty, then nodded. Quince walked with the phone to his credenza and watched Main Street below while talking to another banker.

At some point, Wes began making notes, no doubt in preparation for the cross-examination to come. Quince loitered by the bookcase, trying to read a newspaper, trying to ignore the note-taking. He was calm now, thinking as clearly as possible, plotting his next move, the one after these goons left him.

'Did you send a check for a hundred thousand dollars?' Chap asked.

'I did.'

Wes, the grimmer-faced of the two, glared at him with contempt, as if to say, 'What a fool.'

They read some more, took a few notes, whispered and mumbled between themselves.

'How much money has your client sent?' Quince asked, just for the hell of it.

Wes got even grimmer and said, 'We can't say.'

No surprise to Quince. The boys had no sense of humor.

They sat down after an hour, and Quince took his seat in his banker's chair.

'Just a couple of questions,' Chap said, and Quince knew they'd be talking for another hour.

'How'd you book the gay cruise?'

'It's in the letter there. This thug gave me the name and number of a travel agency in New York. I called, then sent a money order. It was easy.'

'Easy? Have you done it before?'

'Are we here to talk about my sex life?'

'No.'

'So let's stick to the issues,' Quince said like a real ass, and he felt good again. The banker in him boiled for a moment. Then he thought of something he simply couldn't resist. With a straight face, he said, 'The cruise is still paid for. You guys wanna go?'

Fortunately, they laughed. It was a quick flash of humor, then back to business. Chap said, 'Did you consider using a pseudonym?'

'Yes, of course. It was stupid not to. But I'd never done this before. I thought the guy was legitimate. He's in Florida, I'm in Podunk, Iowa. It never crossed my mind the guy was a fraud.'

'We'll need copies of all this,' Wes said.

'That could be a problem.'

'Why?'

'Where would you copy it?'

'The bank doesn't have a copier?'

'It does, but you're not copying that file in this bank.'

'Then we'll take it to a quick print somewhere.'

'This is Bakers. We don't have a quick print.'

'Do you have an office supply store?'

'Yes, and the owner owes my bank eighty thousand dollars. He sits next to me at the Rotary Club. You're not copying it there. I'm not going to be seen with that file.'

Chap and Wes looked at each other, then at Quince. Wes said, 'Okay, look. I'll stay here with you. Chap will take the file and find a copier.'

'Where?'

'The drugstore,' Wes said.

'You've found the drugstore?'

'Sure, we needed some tweezers.'

'That copier's twenty years old.'

'No, they have a new one.'

'You must be careful, okay? The pharmacist is my secretary's second cousin. This is a very small town.'

Chap took the file and walked to the door. It clicked loudly when he unlocked it, and when he stepped through he was immediately under scrutiny. The secretary's desk was crowded with older women, all busy doing nothing until Chap emerged and they froze and gawked. Old Mr. Garbe was not far away, holding a ledger, pretending to be busy but himself consumed with curiosity. Chap nodded to them all and eased away, passing as he went virtually every employee of the bank.

The door clicked loudly again as Quince locked the damned thing before anyone could barge in. He and Wes chatted awkwardly about this and that for a few minutes, the conversation almost dying at times for lack of common ground. Forbidden sex had brought them together, and they certainly had to avoid that subject. Life in Bakers was of little interest. Quince could ask nothing about Wes' background.

Finally, he said, 'What should I say in my letter to Ricky?'

Wes warmed to the idea immediately. 'Well, I would wait, first of all. Wait a month. Let him sweat. If you hurry back with a response, and with the money, he might think it's too easy.'

'What if he gets mad?'

'He won't. He has plenty of time, and he wants the money.'

'Do you see all his mail?'

'We think we have access to most of it.'

Quince was overcome with curiosity. Sitting with a man who now knew his deepest secret, he felt as though he could prod. 'How will you stop him?'

And Wes, for no reason he would ever understand, said simply, 'We'll probably just kill him.'

A radiant peace broke out around the eyes of Quince Garbe, a warm calming glow that spread through his tortured countenance. His wrinkles softened. His lips spread into a tiny smile. His inheritance would be safe after all, and when the old man was gone and the money was his he'd flee this life and live as he pleased.

'How nice,' he said softly. 'How very nice.'

Chap took the file to a motel room where a leased color copier was waiting with other members of the unit. Three sets were made, and thirty minutes later he was back at the bank. Quince inspected his originals; everything was in order. He carefully relocked the file, then said to his guests, 'I think it's time for you to go.'

They left without shaking hands or the usual good-byes. What was there to say?

A private jet was waiting at the local airport, whose runway was barely long enough. Three hours after leaving Quince, Chap and Wes reported to Langley. Their mission was a resounding success.

★

210

A summary of the account in the Geneva Trust Bank was procured with a bribe of $40,000 to a Bahamian banking official, a man they'd used before. Boomer Realty had a balance of $189,000. Its lawyer had about $68,000 in his account. The summary listed all the transactions – money wired in, money taken out. Deville's people were trying desperately to track down the originators of the wires. They knew about Mr. Garbe's remitting bank in Des Moines, and they knew that another wire of $100,000 had been sent from a bank in Dallas. They could not, however, find out who'd originated that wire.

They were scrambling on many fronts when Teddy summoned Deville to the bunker. York was with him. The table was covered with copies of Garbe's file and copies of the bank summaries.

Deville had never seen his boss so dejected. York too had little to say. York was bearing the brunt of the Lake screwup, though Teddy was blaming himself.

'The latest,' Teddy said softly.

Deville never sat while in the bunker. 'We're still tracking the money. We've made contact with the magazine *Out and About*. It's published in New Haven, a very small outfit, and I'm not sure if we'll be able to penetrate. Our contact in the Bahamas is on retainer and we'll know if and when any wires are received. We have a unit ready to search Lake's offices on Capitol Hill, but that's a long shot. I'm not optimistic. We have twenty people on the ground in Jacksonville.'

'How many of our people are shadowing Lake?'

'We've just gone from thirty to fifty.'

'He must be watched. We cannot turn our backs. He is not the person we thought he was, and if we lose sight of him for one hour he might mail a letter, or buy another magazine.'

'We know. We're doing the best we can.'

'This is our highest domestic priority.'

'I know.'

'What about planting someone inside the prison?' Teddy asked. It was a new idea, one hatched by York within the past hour.

Deville rubbed his eyes and chewed his nails for a moment, then said, 'I'll go to work on it. We'll have to pull strings we've never pulled before.'

'How many prisoners are in the federal system?' York asked.

'One hundred thirty-five thousand, give or take,' Deville said.

'Surely we could slip in another, couldn't we?'

'I'll give it a look.'

'Do we have contacts at the Bureau of Prisons?'

'It's new territory, but we're working on it. We're using an old friend at Justice. I'm optimistic.'

Deville left them for a while. He'd get called back in an hour or so. York and Teddy would have another checklist of questions and thoughts and errands for him to tend to.

'I don't like the idea of searching his office on Capitol Hill,' York said. 'It's too risky. And besides, it would take a week. Those guys have a million files.'

'I don't like it either,' Teddy said softly.

'Let's get our guys in Documents to write a

letter from Ricky to Lake. We'll wire the envelope, track it, maybe it will lead us to his file.'

'That's an excellent idea. Tell Deville.'

York made a note on a pad filled with many other notes, most of which had been scratched through. He scribbled to pass the time, then asked the question he'd been saving. 'Will you confront him?'

'Not yet.'

'When?'

'Maybe never. Let's gather the intelligence, learn all we can. He seems to be very quiet about his other life, perhaps it came about after his wife died. Who knows? Maybe he can keep it quiet.'

'But he has to know that you know. Otherwise, he might take another chance. If he knows we're always watching, he'll behave himself. Maybe.'

'Meanwhile the world's going to hell. Nuclear arms are bought and sold and sneaked across borders. We're tracking seven small wars with three more on the brink. A dozen new terrorist groups last month alone. Maniacs in the Middle East building armies and hoarding oil. And we sit here hour after hour plotting against three felonious judges who are at this very moment probably playing gin rummy.'

'They're not stupid,' York said.

'No, but they're clumsy. Their nets have snared the wrong person.'

'I guess we picked the wrong person.'

'No, they did.'

NINETEEN

The memo arrived by fax from the Regional Supervisor, Bureau of Prisons, Washington. It was directed to M. Emmitt Broon, the warden of Trumble. In terse but standard language the supervisor said he'd reviewed the logs from Trumble and was bothered by the number of visits by one Trevor Carson, attorney for three of the inmates. Lawyer Carson had reached the point of logging in almost every day.

While every inmate certainly had a constitutional right to meet with his attorney, the prison likewise had the power to regulate the traffic. Beginning immediately, attorney-client visits would be restricted to Tuesdays, Thursdays, and Saturdays, between the hours of 3 and 6 P.M. Exceptions would be granted liberally for good cause shown.

The new policy would be utilized for a period of ninety days, after which time it would be reviewed.

Fine with the warden. He too had grown suspicious of Trevor's almost daily appearances. He'd questioned the front desk and the guards in a vain effort to determine what, exactly, was the

214

nature of all this legal work. Link, the guard who usually escorted Trevor to the conference room, and who usually pocketed a couple of twenties on each visit, told the warden that the lawyer and Mr. Spicer talked about cases and appeals and such. 'Just a bunch of law crap,' Link said.

'And you always search his briefcase?' the warden had asked.

'Always,' Link had replied.

Out of courtesy, the warden dialed the number of Mr. Trevor Carson in Neptune Beach. The phone was answered by a woman who said rudely, 'Law office.'

'Mr. Trevor Carson, please.'

'Who's calling?'

'This is Emmitt Broon.'

'Well, Mr. Broon, he's taking a nap right now.'

'I see. Could you possibly wake him? I'm the warden at the federal prison at Trumble, and I need to speak with him.'

'Just a minute.'

He waited for a long time, and when she returned she said, 'I'm sorry. I couldn't wake him up. Could I have him return your call?'

'No, thank you. I'll just fax him a note.'

The idea of a reverse scam was hatched by York, while playing golf on a Sunday, and as his game progressed, occasionally on the fairways but more often in the sand and trees, the scheme grew and grew and became brilliant. He abandoned his pals after fourteen holes and called Teddy.

They would learn the tactics of their adversaries.

And they could divert attention away from Al Konyers. There was nothing to lose.

The letter was created by York, and assigned to one of the top forgers in Documents. The pen pal was christened Brant White, and the first note was handwritten on a plain, white, but expensive correspondence card.

Dear Ricky:

Saw your ad, liked it. I'm fifty-five, in great shape, and looking for more than a pen pal. My wife and I just bought a home in Palm Valley, not far from Neptune Beach. We'll be down in three weeks, with plans to stay for two months.

If interested, send photo. If I like what I see, then I'll give more details.

Brant

The return address was from Brant, P.O. Box 88645, Upper Darby, PA 19082.

To save two or three days, a Philadelphia postmark was applied in Documents, and the letter was flown to Jacksonville where agent Klockner himself delivered it to Aladdin North's little box in the Neptune Beach post office. It was a Monday.

After his nap the following day, Trevor picked up the mail and headed west, out of Jacksonville, along the familiar route to Trumble. He was greeted by the same guards, Mackey and Vince, at the front door, and he signed the same logbook Rufus shoved in front of him. He followed Link into the visitors' area and to a corner where Spicer

216

was waiting in one of the small attorney-conference rooms.

'I'm catchin some heat,' Link said as they stepped into the room. Spicer did not look up. Trevor handed two twenties to Link, who took them in a flash.

'From who?' Trevor asked, opening his briefcase. Spicer was reading a newspaper.

'The warden.'

'Hell, he's cut back on my visits. What else does he want?'

'Don't you understand?' Spicer said, without lowering the newspaper. 'Link here is upset because he's not collecting as much. Right, Link?'

'You got that right. I don't know what kinda funny business you boys are runnin here, but if I tightened up on my inspections you'd be in trouble, wouldn't you?'

'You're being paid well,' Trevor said.

'That's what you think.'

'How much do you want?' Spicer said, staring at him now.

'A thousand a month, cash,' he said, looking at Trevor. 'I'll pick it up at your office.'

'A thousand bucks and the mail doesn't get checked,' Spicer said.

'Yep.'

'And not a word to anybody.'

'Yep.'

'It's a deal. Now get outta here.'

Link smiled at both of them and left the room. He positioned himself outside the door, and for the benefit of the closed-circuit cameras looked through the window occasionally.

Inside, the routine varied little. The exchange of mail happened first and took only a second. From a worn manila folder, the same one every time, Joe Roy Spicer removed the outgoing letters and handed them to Trevor, who took the incoming mail from his briefcase and gave it to his client.

There were six letters to be mailed. Some days there were as many as ten, seldom less than five. Though Trevor didn't keep records, or copies, or documents in a file that would serve as proof that he had anything whatsoever to do with the Brethren's little scam, he knew there had to be twenty or thirty potential victims currently being set up. He recognized some of the names and addresses.

Twenty-one to be exact, according to Spicer's precise records. Twenty-one serious prospects, with another eighteen who were marginal. Almost forty pen pals currently hiding in their various closets, some terrified of their shadows, others getting bolder by the week, still others on the verge of kicking down the door and dashing off to meet Ricky or Percy.

The difficult part was being patient. The scam was working, money was changing hands, the temptation was to squeeze them too quickly. Beech and Yarber were proving to be workhorses, laboring over their letters for hours at a time while Spicer directed operations. It took discipline to hook a new pen pal, one with money, then ply him with enough pretty words to earn his trust.

'Aren't we due for a bust?' Trevor said.

Spicer was flipping through the new letters. 'Don't tell me you're broke,' he said. 'You're making more than we are.'

'My money's tucked away just like yours. I'd just like to have some more of it.'

'So would I.' Spicer looked at the envelope from Brant in Upper Darby, Pa. 'Ah, a new one,' he mumbled to himself, then opened it. He read it quickly, and was surprised by its tone. No fear, no wasted words, no peeking around corners. This man was ready for action.

'Where's Palm Valley?' he asked.

'Ten miles south of the beaches. Why?'

'What kinda place is it?'

'It's one of the gated golf communities for rich retirees, almost all from up North.'

'How much are the houses?'

'Well, I've never been there, okay. They keep the damned gate locked, guards everywhere like somebody might break in and steal their golf carts, but —'

'How much are the houses?'

'Nothing less than a million. I've seen a couple advertised for three million.'

'Wait here,' Spicer said, gathering his file and walking to the door.

'Where you going?' Trevor asked.

'To the library. I'll be back in half an hour.'

'I got things to do.'

'No you don't. Read the newspaper.'

Spicer said something to Link, who escorted him through the visitors' area and out of the administration building. He walked quickly along the manicured grounds. The sun was warm, and the gardeners were earning their fifty cents an hour.

So were the keepers of the law library. Beech

and Yarber were hiding in their little conference room, taking a break from their writings with a game of chess, when Spicer entered in a rush, with an uncharacteristic smile. 'Boys, we've finally hooked the big one,' he said, and tossed Brant's letter on the table. Beech read it aloud.

'Palm Valley is one of the golf communities for rich folks,' Spicer explained proudly. 'Houses go for about three million. The boy's got plenty of dough and he ain't much for letters.'

'He does seem anxious,' Yarber observed.

'We need to move fast,' Spicer said. 'He wants to come down in three weeks.'

'What's the upside potential?' Beech asked. He loved the jargon of those who invested millions.

'At least a half a million,' Spicer said. 'Let's do the letter now. Trevor is waiting.'

Beech opened one of his many files and displayed his wares; sheets of paper in soft pastels. 'I think I'll try the peach,' he said.

'Oh definitely,' Spicer said. 'Gotta do peach.'

Ricky wrote a scaled-down version of the initial contact letter. Twenty-eight years old, college graduate, locked down in rehab but on the verge of release, probably in ten days, very lonely, looking for a mature man to start a relationship. How convenient that Brant would be living nearby, because Ricky had a sister in Jacksonville and he'd be staying with her. There were no obstacles, no hurdles to cross. He'd be ready for Brant when he came South. But he'd like a photo first. Was Brant really married? Would his wife be living at Palm Valley too? Or would she stay up there in Pennsylvania? Wouldn't it be great if she did?

They enclosed the same color photo they'd used a hundred times. It had proved to be irresistible.

The peach envelope was taken by Spicer back to the attorney-conference room where Trevor was napping. 'Mail this immediately,' Spicer barked at him.

They spent ten minutes on their basketball bets, then said goodbye without a handshake.

Driving back to Jacksonville, Trevor called his bookie, a new one, a bigger bookie, now that he was a player. The digital line was indeed more secure, but the phone wasn't. Agent Klockner and his band of operatives were listening as usual, and tracking Trevor's bets. He wasn't doing badly, up $4,500 in the past two weeks. By contrast, his law firm had put $800 on the books during the same period.

In addition to the phone, there were four mikes in the Beetle, most of them of little value but operational nonetheless. And under each bumper was a transmitter, both wired to the car's electrical system and checked every other night when Trevor was either drinking or sleeping. A powerful receiver in the rental across the street tracked the Beetle wherever it went. As Trevor puttered down the highway, talking on his phone like a big shot, tossing money around like a Vegas high roller, sipping scalded coffee from a quick-stop grocery, he was emitting more signals than most private jets.

March 7. Big Super Tuesday. Aaron Lake bounced triumphantly across the stage in a large banquet room of a Manhattan hotel, while thousands cheered and music roared and balloons fell from above. He'd taken New York with 43 percent of the vote. Governor Tarry had a rather weak 29 percent, and the other also-rans got the rest. Lake hugged people he'd never seen before and waved to people he'd never see again, and he delivered without notes a stirring victory speech.

Then he was off, on his way to L.A. for another victory celebration. For four hours, in his new Boeing jet that would hold a hundred and leased for $1 million a month and flew at a speed of five hundred miles per hour, thirty-eight thousand feet above the country, he and his staff monitored the returns from the twelve states participating in big Super Tuesday. Along the East Coast, where the polls had already closed, Lake barely won in Maine and Connecticut, but put up big margins in New York, Massachusetts, Maryland, and Georgia. He lost Rhode Island by eight hundred votes, and won Vermont by a thousand. As he was flying over Missouri, CNN declared him the winner of that state by four percentage points over Governor Tarry. Ohio was just as close.

By the time Lake reached California, the rout was over. Of the 591 delegates at stake, he'd captured 390. He'd also solidified the momentum. And most important, Aaron Lake now had the money. Governor Tarry was falling hard and fast, and all bets were on Lake.

TWENTY

Six hours after claiming victory in California, Lake awoke to a frenzied morning of live interviews. He suffered through eighteen in two hours, then flew to Washington.

He went straight to his new campaign headquarters, on the ground floor of a large office building on H Street, a stone's throw from the White House. He thanked his workers, almost none of whom were volunteers. He worked his crowd, shook their hands, all the while asking himself, 'Where did these people come from?'

We're gonna win, he said over and over, and everybody believed it. Why not?

He met for an hour with his top people. He had $65 million, no debt. Tarry had less than $1 million on hand and he was still trying to count the money he owed. In fact, the Tarry campaign had missed a federal filing deadline because its books were in such a mess. All cash had vanished. Contributions had stopped. Lake was getting all the money.

The names of three potential Vice Presidents were debated with great enthusiasm. It was an exhilarating exercise because it meant the nomination was in the bag. Lake's first choice, Senator Nance from Michigan, was drawing fire because he'd had some shady business deals in another life. His partners had been of Italian extraction, from Detroit, and Lake could close his eyes and see the press peeling skin off Nance. A committee was appointed to explore the issue further.

And a committee was appointed to begin planning Lake's presence at the convention in Denver. Lake wanted a new speech-writer, now, and he wanted him working on the acceptance speech.

Lake secretly marveled at his own overhead. His campaign chairman was getting $150,000 for the year, not for twelve months, but until Christmas. There was a chairman of finance, of policy, of media relations, of operations, and of strategic planning, and all had contracts for $120,000 for about ten months of work. Each chairman had two or three immediate underlings, people Lake hardly knew, and they earned $90,000 apiece. Then there were the campaign assistants, or CAs, not the volunteers that most candidates attracted, but real employees who earned $50,000 each and kept the offices in a frenzy. There were dozens of them. And dozens of clerks and secretaries and, hell, nobody made less than $40,000.

And on top of all this waste, Lake kept telling himself, if I make it to the White House then I'll have to find jobs for them there. Every damned one of them. Kids now running around with Lake buttons on every lapel will expect to have West Wing clearances and jobs paying $80,000 a year.

It's a drop in the bucket, he kept reminding

himself. Don't get hung up on the small stuff when so much more is at stake.

Negatives were pushed to the end of the meeting and given short shrift. A reporter for the *Post* had been digging into Lake's early business career. Without too much effort he'd stumbled upon the GreenTree mess, a failed land development, twenty-two years in the past. Lake and a partner had bankrupted GreenTree, legally shafting creditors out of $800,000. The partner had been indicted for bankruptcy fraud, but a jury let him walk. No one laid a glove on Lake, and seven times after that the people of Arizona elected him to Congress.

'I'll answer any question about GreenTree,' Lake said. 'It was just a bad business deal.'

'The press is about to shift gears,' said the chairman of media relations. 'You're new and you haven't been subjected to enough scrutiny. It's time for them to get nasty.'

'It's already started,' Lake said. 'I have no skeletons.'

For an early dinner he was whisked away to Mortimer's, the current power place to be seen, just down Pennsylvania, where he met Elaine Tyner, the lawyer running D-PAC. Over fruit and cottage cheese she laid out the current financials of the newest PAC on the block. Cash in hand of $29 million, no significant debt, money being churned around the clock, coming in from all directions, from everywhere in the world.

Spending it was the challenge. Since it was considered 'soft money,' or money that couldn't go directly to the Lake campaign, it had to be used elsewhere. Tyner had several targets. The first was a series of generic ads similar to the doomsday ads Teddy had put together. D-PAC was already buying prime-time spots for the fall. The second, and by far the most enjoyable, were the Senate and congressional races. 'They're lining up like ants,' she said with great amusement. 'It's amazing what a few million bucks can do.'

She told the story of a House race in a district in Northern California where the incumbent, a twenty-year veteran Lake knew and despised, started the year with a forty-point lead against an unknown challenger. The unknown found his way to D-PAC and surrendered his soul to Aaron Lake. 'We've basically taken over his campaign,' she said. 'We're writing speeches, polling, doing all his print and TV ads, we even hired a new staff for him. So far we've spent one-point-five million, and our boy has cut the lead to ten points. And we have seven months to go.'

In all, Tyner and D-PAC were meddling in thirty House races and ten in the Senate. She expected to raise a total of $60 million, and spend every dime of it by November.

Her third area of 'focus' was taking the pulse of the country. D-PAC was polling nonstop, every day, fifteen hours a day. If labor in western Pennsylvania was bothered by an issue, D-PAC would know it. If the Hispanics in Houston were pleased with a new welfare policy, D-PAC would know it. If the women in greater Chicago liked or disliked a Lake ad, D-PAC knew yes or no and by what percentage. 'We know everything,' she boasted. 'We're like Big Brother, always watching.'

The polling cost $60,000 a day, a bargain. No one could touch it. For the important matters, Lake was nine points ahead of Tarry in Texas, even in Florida, a state Lake had yet to visit, and very close in Indiana, Tarry's home state.

'Tarry's tired,' she said. 'Morale is low because he won in New Hampshire and the money was rolling in. Then you came from nowhere, a fresh face, no baggage, new message, you start winning, and suddenly the money finds you. Tarry can't raise fifty bucks at a church bake sale. He's losing key people because he can't pay them, and because they smell another winner.'

Lake chewed a piece of pineapple and savored the words. They weren't new; he'd heard them from his own people. But coming from a seasoned insider like Tyner, they were even more reassuring.

'What are the Vice President's numbers?' Lake asked. He had his own set, but for some reason trusted her more.

'He'll squeak out the nomination,' she said, offering nothing new. 'But the convention will be bloody. Right now, you're only a few points behind him on the big question: Who will you vote for in November?'

'November is far away.'

'It is and it isn't.'

'A lot can change,' Lake said, thinking of Teddy, and wondering what sort of crisis he'd create to terrify the American people.

The dinner was more of a snack, and from Mortimer's Lake he was driven to a small dining room at the Hay-Adams Hotel. It was a long, late dinner with friends, two dozen of his colleagues from the House. Few of them had rushed to endorse him when he'd entered the race, but now they were all wildly enthusiastic about their man. Most had their own pollsters. The bandwagon was rolling down the mountain.

Lake had never seen his old pals so happy to be around him.

The letter was prepared in Documents by a woman named Bruce, one of the agency's three best counterfeiters. Tacked to the corkboard just above the worktable in her small lab were letters written by Ricky. Excellent samples, much more than she needed. She had no idea who Ricky was, but there was no doubt his handwriting was contrived. It was fairly consistent, with the more recent samples clearly showing an ease that came only with practice. His vocabulary was not remarkable, but then she suspected he was trying to downplay it. His sentence structure showed few mistakes. Bruce guessed him to be between the ages of forty and sixty, with at least a college education.

But it wasn't her job to make such inferences, at least not in this case. With the same pen and paper as Ricky, she wrote a nice little note to Al. The text had been prepared by someone else, she did not know who. Nor did she care.

It was, 'Hey, Al, where have you been? Why haven't you written? Don't forget about me.' That kind of letter, but with a nice little surprise. Since Ricky couldn't use the phone, he was sending Al a cassette tape with a brief message from deep inside rehab.

Bruce fit the letter onto one page, then worked

228

for an hour on the envelope. The postmark she applied was from Neptune Beach, Florida.

She didn't seal the envelope. Her little project was inspected, then taken to another lab. The tape was recorded by a young agent who'd studied drama at Northwestern. In a soft, accentless voice he said, 'Hey, Al, this is Ricky. Hope you're surprised to hear my voice. They won't let us use the phones around here, I don't know why, but for some reason we can send tapes back and forth. I can't wait to get out of this place.' Then he rambled for five minutes about his rehab and how much he hated his uncle and the people who ran Aladdin North. But he did concede that they had rid him of his addictions. He was certain he would look back and not judge the place too harshly.

His entire narrative was nothing but babble. No plans were discussed for his release, no hint of where he might go or what he might do, only a vague reference about seeing Al one day.

They were not yet ready to bait Al Konyers. The sole purpose of the tape was to hide within its casing a transmitter strong enough to lead them to Lake's hidden file. A tiny bug in the envelope was too risky. Al might be smart enough to find it.

At Mailbox America in Chevy Chase, the CIA now controlled eight boxes, duly rented for one year by eight different people, each of whom had the same twenty-four-hour access that Mr. Konyers had. They came and went at all hours, checking their little boxes, picking up mail they'd sent themselves, occasionally taking a peek at Al's box if no one was looking.

Since they knew his schedule better than he

229

knew it himself, they waited patiently until he'd made his rounds. They felt certain he'd sneak out as before, dressed like a jogger, so they held the envelope with the tape until almost ten one night. Then they placed it in his box.

Four hours later, with a dozen agents watching every move, Lake the jogger jumped from a cab in front of Mailbox America, darted inside, his face hidden by the long bill of a running cap, went to his box, pulled out the mail, and hurried back into the cab.

Six hours later he left Georgetown for a prayer breakfast at the Hilton, and they waited. He addressed an association of police chiefs at nine, and a thousand high school principals at eleven. He lunched with the Speaker of the House. He taped a stressful Q&A session with some talking heads at three, then returned home to pack. His itinerary called for him to depart Reagan National at eight and fly to Dallas.

They followed him to the airport, watched the Boeing 707 take off, then called Langley. When the two Secret Service agents arrived to check the perimeter of Lake's townhouse, the CIA was already inside.

The search ended in the kitchen ten minutes after it began. A handheld receptor caught the signal from the cassette tape. They found it in the wastebasket, along with an empty half-gallon milk jug, two torn packages of oatmeal, some soiled paper towels, and that morning's edition of the *Washington Post*. A maid came twice a week. Lake had simply left the garbage for her to take care of.

They couldn't find Lake's file because he didn't have one. Smart man, he tossed away the evidence.

Teddy was almost relieved when he got word. The team was still in the townhouse, hiding and waiting for the Secret Service to leave. Whatever Lake did in his secret life, he worked hard not to leave a trail.

The tape unnerved Aaron Lake. Reading Ricky's letters and looking at his handsome face had given him a nervous thrill. The young man was far away and odds were they'd never meet. They could be pen pals and play tag at a distance and move slowly, at least that's what Lake had contemplated initially.

But hearing Ricky's voice had brought him much closer, and Lake was rattled. What had begun a few months earlier as a curious little game now held horrible possibilities. It was much too risky. Lake trembled at the thought of getting caught.

It still seemed impossible, though. He was well hidden behind the mask of Al Konyers. Ricky had not a clue. It was 'Al this' and 'Al that' on the tape. The post office box was his shield.

But he had to end it. At least for now.

The Boeing was packed with Lake's well-paid people. They didn't make an airplane big enough to haul his entire entourage. If he leased a 747, within two days it would be filled with CAs and advisers and consultants and pollsters, not to mention his own growing army of bodyguards from the Secret Service.

The more primaries he won, the heavier his

plane became. It might be wise to lose a couple of states so he could jettison some of the baggage.

In the darkness of the plane, Lake sipped tomato juice and decided to write a final letter to Ricky. Al would wish him the best, and simply terminate the correspondence. What could the boy do?

He was tempted to write the note right then, sitting in his deep recliner, his feet in the air. But at any moment an assistant of some variety would emerge with another breathless report that the candidate had to hear immediately. He had no privacy. He had no time to think or loaf or daydream. Every pleasant thought was interrupted by a new poll or a late-breaking story or an urgent need to make a decision.

Surely he'd be able to hide in the White House. Loners had lived there before.

TWENTY-ONE

The case of the stolen cell phone had fascinated the inmates at Trumble for the past month. Mr. T-Bone, a wiry street kid from Miami serving twenty for drugs, had taken original possession of the phone by means that were still unclear. Cell phones were strictly prohibited at Trumble, and the method by which he got one had created more rumors than T. Karl's sex life. The few who'd actually seen it had described it, not in court, but around the camp, as being no larger than a stopwatch. Mr. T-Bone had been seen lurking in the shadows, hunched at the waist, chin to his chest, back to the world, mumbling into the phone. No doubt he was still directing street operations in Miami.

Then it disappeared. Mr. T-Bone let it be known that he might kill whoever took it, and when the threats of violence didn't work he offered a reward of $1,000 cash. Suspicion soon fell upon another young drug dealer, Zorro, from a section of Atlanta just as rough as Mr. T-Bone's. A killing seemed likely, so the guards and the suits up front intervened and convinced the two that they'd be shipped away if things got out of hand. Violence was not tolerated at Trumble. The punishment was a trip to a medium-security pen with inmates who understood violence.

Someone told Mr. T-Bone about the weekly dockets the Brethren held, and in due course he found T. Karl and filed suit. He wanted his phone back, plus a million bucks in punitive damages.

When it was first set for trial, an assistant warden appeared in the cafeteria to observe the proceedings, and the matter was quickly postponed by the Brethren. The same thing happened just before the second trial. Allegations of who did or did not have possession of an outlawed cell phone could not be heard by anyone in administration. The guards who watched the weekly shows wouldn't repeat a word.

Justice Spicer finally convinced a prison counselor that the boys had a private matter to reconcile, without interference from the front. 'We're trying to settle a little matter,' he whispered. 'And we need to do it in private.'

The request worked its way upward, and at the third trial date the cafeteria was packed with spectators, most of whom were hoping to see bloodshed. The only prison official in the room was a solitary guard, sitting in the back, half asleep.

Neither of the litigants was a stranger to courtrooms, so it was no surprise that Mr. T-Bone and Zorro acted as their own attorneys. Justice Beech spent most of the first hour trying to keep the language out of the gutter. He finally gave up. Wild accusations spewed forth from the plaintiff, charges that couldn't have been proved with the aid of a thousand FBI agents. The denials were just as loud and preposterous from the defense. Mr. T-Bone scored heavy blows with two affidavits, signed by inmates whose names were revealed only to the Brethren, which contained eyewitness accounts of seeing Zorro trying to hide while talking on a tiny phone.

Zorro's angry response described the affidavits in language the Brethren had never before encountered.

The knockout punch came from nowhere. Mr. T-Bone, in a move that even the slickest lawyer would admire, produced documentation. His phone records had been smuggled in, and he showed the court in black and white that exactly fifty-four calls had been made to numbers in southeast Atlanta. His supporters, by far the majority but whose loyalty could vanish in an instant, whooped and hollered until T. Karl slammed his plastic gavel and got them quiet.

Zorro had trouble regrouping, and his hesitation killed him. He was ordered to immediately turn over the phone to the Brethren within twenty-four hours, and to reimburse Mr. T-Bone $450 for long-distance charges. If twenty-four hours passed with no phone, the matter would be referred to the warden, along with a finding of fact from the Brethren that Zorro did indeed possess an illegal cell phone.

The Brethren further ordered the two to maintain a distance of at least fifty feet from one another at all times, even when eating.

T. Karl rapped a gavel and the crowd began a

noisy exit. He called the next case, another petty gambling dispute, and waited for the spectators to leave. 'Quiet!' he shouted, and the racket only grew louder. The Brethren went back to their newspapers and magazines.

'Quiet!' he barked again, slamming his gavel.

'Shut up,' Spicer yelled at T. Karl. 'You're making more noise than they are.'

'It's my job,' T. Karl snapped back, the curls of his wig bouncing in all directions.

When the cafeteria was empty, only one inmate remained. T. Karl looked around and finally asked him, 'Are you Mr. Hooten?'

'No sir,' the young man said.

'Are you Mr.Jenkins?'

'No sir.'

'I didn't think so. The case of Hooten versus Jenkins is hereby dismissed for failure to show,' T. Karl said, and made a dramatic entry into his docket book.

'Who are you?' Spicer asked the young man, who was sitting alone and glancing around as if he wasn't sure he was welcome. The three men in the pale green robes were now looking at him, as was the clown with the gray wig and the old maroon pajamas and the lavender shower shoes, no socks. Who were these people!

He slowly got to his feet and moved forward with great apprehension until he stood before the three. 'I'm looking for some help,' he said, almost afraid to speak.

'Do you have business before the court?' T.Karl growled from the side.

'No sir.'

'Then you'll have to –'

'Shut up!' Spicer said. 'Court's adjourned. Leave.'

T.Karl slammed his docket book, kicked back his folding chair, and stormed out of the room, his shower shoes sliding on the tile, his wig bouncing behind him.

The young man appeared ready to cry. 'What can we do for you?' Yarber asked.

He was holding a small cardboard box, and the Brethren knew from experience that it was filled with the papers that had brought him to Trumble. 'I need some help,' he said again. 'I got here last week, and my roommate said you guys could help with my appeals.'

'Don't you have a lawyer?' Beech asked.

'I did. He wasn't very good. He's one reason I'm here.'

'Why are you here?' asked Spicer.

'I don't know. I really don't know.'

'Did you have a trial?'

'Yes. A long one.'

'And you were found guilty by a jury?'

'Yes. Me and a bunch of others. They said we were part of a conspiracy.'

'A conspiracy to do what?'

'Import cocaine.'

Another druggie. They were suddenly anxious to get back to their letter writing. 'How long is your sentence?' asked Yarber.

'Forty-eight years.'

'Forty-eight years! How old are you?'

'Twenty-three.'

The letter writing was momentarily forgotten.

They looked at his sad young face and tried to picture it fifty years later. Released at the age of seventy-one; it was impossible to imagine. Each of the Brethren would leave Trumble a younger man than this kid.

'Pull up a chair,' Yarber said, and the kid grabbed the nearest one and placed it in front of their table. Even Spicer felt a little sympathy for him.

'What's your name?' Yarber asked.

'I go by Buster.'

'Okay, Buster, what'd you do to get yourself forty-eight years?'

The story came in torrents. Balancing his box on his knees, and staring at the floor, he began by saying he'd never been in trouble with the law, nor had his father. They owned a small boat dock together in Pensacola. They fished and sailed and loved the sea, and running the dock was the perfect life for them. They sold a used fishing boat, a fifty-footer, to a man from Fort Lauderdale, an American who paid them in cash – $95,000. The money went in the bank, or at least Buster thought it did. A few months later the man was back for another boat, a thirty-eight-footer for which he paid $80,000. Cash for boats was not unusual in Florida. A third and fourth boat followed. Buster and his dad knew where to find good used fishing boats, which they overhauled and renovated. They enjoyed doing the work themselves. After the fifth boat, the narcs came calling. They asked questions, made vague threats, wanted to see the books and records. Buster's dad refused initially, then they hired a lawyer who advised them not to cooperate. Nothing happened for months.

Buster and his father were arrested at 3 A.M. on a Sunday morning by a pack of goons wearing vests and enough guns to hold Pensacola hostage. They were dragged half-dressed from their small home near the bay, lights flashing all over the place. The indictment was an inch thick, 160 pages, eighty-one counts of conspiracy to smuggle cocaine. He had a copy of it in his box. Buster and his dad were barely mentioned in the 160 pages, but they were nonetheless named as defendants and lumped together with the man they'd sold the boats to, along with twenty-five other people they'd never heard of. Eleven were Colombians. Three were lawyers. Everybody else was from South Florida.

The U.S. Attorney offered them a deal – two years each in return for guilty pleas and cooperation against the other codefendants. Pleading guilty to what? They'd done nothing wrong. They knew exactly one of their twenty-six coconspirators. They'd never seen cocaine.

Buster's father remortgaged their home to raise $20,000 for a lawyer, and they made a bad selection. At trial, they were alarmed to find themselves sitting at the same table with the Colombians and the real drug traffickers. They were on one side of the courtroom, all the coconspirators, sitting together as if they'd once been a well-oiled drug machine. On the other side, near the jury, were the government lawyers, groups of pompous little bastards in dark suits, taking notes, glaring at them as if they were child molesters. The jury glared at them too.

During seven weeks of trial, Buster and his father were practically ignored. Three times their names were mentioned. The government's principal charge against them was that they had conspired to procure and rebuild fishing boats with souped-up engines to transport drugs from Mexico to various drop-offs along the Florida panhandle. Their lawyer, who complained that he wasn't getting paid enough to handle a seven-week trial, proved ineffective at rebutting these loose charges. Still, the government lawyers did little damage and were much more concerned with nailing the Colombians.

But they didn't have to prove much. They had done a superior job of picking the jury. After eight days of deliberation, the jurors, obviously tired and frustrated, found every conspirator guilty of all charges. A month after they were sentenced, Buster's father killed himself.

As the narrative wound down, the kid looked as if he might cry. But he stuck out his jaw, gritted his teeth, and said, 'I did nothing wrong.'

He certainly wasn't the first inmate at Trumble to declare his innocence. Beech watched and listened and remembered a young man he'd sentenced once to forty years for drug trafficking back in Texas. The defendant had a rotten childhood, no education, a long record as a juvenile offender, not much of a chance in life. Beech had lectured him from the bench, high and lordly from above, and had felt good about himself for handing down such a brutal sentence. Gotta get these damned drug dealers off the streets!

A liberal is a conservative who's been arrested.

After three years on the inside of a prison Hatlee Beech agonized over many of the people he'd thrown the book at. People far guiltier than Buster here. Kids who just needed a break.

Finn Yarber watched and listened and felt immense pity for the young man. Everybody at Trumble had a sad story, and after a month or so of hearing them he'd learned to believe almost nothing. But Buster was believable. For the next forty-eight years he would wither and decline, all at taxpayer expense. Three meals a day. A warm bed at night – $31,000 a year was the latest guess of what a federal inmate cost the government. Such a waste. Half the inmates at Trumble had no business being there. They were non-violent men who should've been punished with stiff fines and community service.

Joe Roy Spicer listened to Buster's compelling story, and he sized the boy up for future use. There were two possibilities. First, in Spicer's opinion, the telephones were not being properly utilized in the Angola scam. The Brethren were old men writing letters as if they were young. It would be too risky to call Quince Garbe in Iowa, for example, and pretend to be Ricky, a robust twenty-eight-year-old. But with a kid like Buster working for them, they could convince any potential victim. There were plenty of young guys at Trumble, and Spicer had considered several of them. But they were criminals, and he didn't trust them. Buster was fresh off the streets, seemingly innocent, and he was coming to them for help. The boy could be manipulated.

The second possibility was an offshoot of the

241

first. If Buster joined their conspiracy, he would be in place when Joe Roy was released. The scam was proving too profitable to simply walk away from. Beech and Yarber were splendid at writing the letters, but they had no business sense. Perhaps Spicer could train young Buster here to fill his shoes, and to divert his share to the outside.

Just a thought.

'Do you have any money?' Spicer asked.

'No sir. We lost everything.'

'No family, no uncles, aunts, cousins, friends who could help you with your legal fees?'

'No sir. What kinda legal fees?'

'We usually charge for reviewing cases and helping with the appeals.'

'I'm dead broke, sir.'

'I think we can help,' Beech said. Spicer didn't work on the appeals anyway. The man never finished high school.

'Sort of a pro bono case, wouldn't you say?' Yarber said to Beech.

'A pro what?' Spicer asked.

'Pro bono.'

'What's that?'

'Free legal work,' Beech said.

'Free legal work. Done by whom?'

'By lawyers,' Yarber explained. 'Every lawyer is expected to donate a few hours of his time to help people who can't afford to hire him.'

'It's part of the Old English common law,' Beech added, further clouding the issue.

'It never caught on over here, did it?' Spicer said.

'We'll review your case,' Yarber said to Buster. 'But please do not be optimistic.'

'Thank you.'

They left the cafeteria in a group, three ex-judges in green choir robes followed by a scared young inmate. Frightened, but also quite curious.

TWENTY-TWO

Brant's reply from Upper Darby, Pa., had an urgent tone to it:

Dear Ricky:
  Wow! What a photo! I'm coming down even sooner. I'll be there on April 20. Are you available? If so, we'll have the house to ourselves because my wife will stay here for another two weeks. Poor woman. We've been married for twenty-two years and she doesn't have a clue.
  Here's a picture of me. That's my Learjet in the background, one of my favorite toys. We'll buzz around in it if you want.
  Write me immediately, please.
                              Sincerely, Brant

There was still no last name, not that that was a problem. They would dig for it soon enough.

Spicer inspected the postmark, and for a passing moment thought about how quickly the mail was running between Jacksonville and Philadelphia. But the photo kept his attention. It was a four-by-six candid shot, very similar to an ad for a get-rich-quick scheme where the huckster is pictured with a proud smile, flanked by his jet, his Rolls, and possibly his latest wife. Brant was standing beside a plane, smiling, dressed neatly in tennis shorts and a sweater, with no Rolls in sight but with an attractive middle-aged woman next to him.

It was the first photo, in their growing collection, in which one of their pen pals had included his wife. Odd, thought Spicer, but then Brant had mentioned her in both letters. Nothing surprised him anymore. The scam would work forever because there was an endless supply of potential victims willing to ignore the risks.

Brant himself was fit and tanned, short dark hair with shades of gray, and a mustache. He was not particularly handsome, but what did Spicer care?

Why would a man with so much be so careless? Because he'd always taken chances and never been caught. Because it was a way of life. And after they squeezed him and took his money, Brant would slow down for a while. He'd avoid the personal ads, and the anonymous lovers. But an aggressive type like Brant would soon return to his old ways.

Spicer figured the thrill of finding random partners overshadowed the risks. He was still bothered by the fact that he, of all people, spent time each day trying to think like a homosexual.

Beech and Yarber read the letter and studied the photo. The small cramped room was completely silent. Could this be the big one?

'Reckon how much that jet cost,' Spicer said, and all three laughed. It was nervous laughter, as if they weren't sure they could believe it.

'A couple of million,' Beech said. Since he was from Texas, and had been married to a rich woman, the other two assumed he knew more about jets than they. 'It's a small Lear.'

Spicer would settle for a small Cessna, anything that would lift him off the ground and take him away. Yarber didn't want a plane. He wanted tickets, in first class where they brought you champagne and two menus and you had your choice of movies. First class over the ocean, far away from this country.

'Let's bust him,' Yarber said.

'How much?' asked Beech, still staring at the photo.

'At least a half a million,' Spicer said. 'And if we get that, we'll go back for more.'

They sat in silence, each playing with his portion of half a million dollars. Trevor's third was suddenly getting in the way. He'd take $167,000 off the top, leaving each of them $111,000. Not bad for prisoners, but it should be a helluva lot more. Why was the lawyer making so much?

'We're going to cut Trevor's fee,' Spicer announced. 'I've been thinking about this for some time. Beginning now, the money will be split four ways. He takes an equal share.'

'He won't do it,' Yarber said.

'He has no choice.'

'It's only fair,' Beech said. 'We're doing the work, and he's getting more than each of us. I say we cut it.'

'I'll do it Thursday.'

Two days later, Trevor arrived at Trumble just

246

after four with a particularly bad hangover, one deadened by neither the two-hour lunch nor the one-hour nap.

Joe Roy seemed particularly edgy. He passed across the outgoing mail, but held a large, red, oversized envelope. 'We're getting ready to bust this guy,' he said, tapping it on the table.

'Who is he?'

'Brant somebody, near Philadelphia. He's hiding behind the post office, so you need to flush him out.'

'How much?'

'A half a million bucks.'

Trevor's red eyes narrowed and his dry lips fell open. He did the math – $167,000 in his pocket. His sailing career was suddenly drawing closer. Perhaps he didn't need a full million bucks before he slammed his office door and left for the Caribbean. Maybe half that would do it. And he was getting so close.

'You're kidding,' he said, knowing that Spicer was not. Spicer had no sense of humor, and he certainly took his money seriously.

'No. And we're changing your percentage.'

'I'll be damned if we are. A deal's a deal.'

'Deals can always be changed. From now on you get the same piece we do. One fourth.'

'No way.'

'Then you're fired.'

'You can't fire me.'

'I just did. What, you think we can't find another crooked lawyer to run mail for us?'

'I know too much,' Trevor said, his cheeks flashing pink and his tongue suddenly parched.

'Don't overestimate yourself. You're not that valuable.'

'Yes I am. I know everything that's going on here.'

'And so do we, hotshot. Difference is, we're already in jail. You're the one with the most to lose. You play hardball with me and you'll be sittin on this side of the table.'

Bolts of pain shot through Trevor's forehead and he closed his eyes. He was in no condition to argue. Why had he stayed at Pete's so late last night? He had to be sharp when he met with Spicer. Instead, he was tired and half-drunk.

His head spun and he thought he might be sick again. He did the math. They were arguing over the difference between $167,000 and $125,000. Frankly, both sounded good to Trevor. He couldn't run the risk of being fired because he'd managed to alienate what few clients he had. He spent less time in the office; he wouldn't return their calls. He'd found a far richer source of income, so to hell with the small-time foot traffic along the beaches.

And he was no match for Spicer. The man had no conscience. He was mean and conniving and desperate to stash away as much money as possible.

'Are Beech and Yarber in favor of this?' he asked, knowing damned well they were, and knowing that even if they weren't he'd never know the difference.

'Sure. They're doing all the work. Why should you make more than them?'

It did seem a little unfair. 'Okay, okay,' Trevor said, still in pain. 'There's a good reason you're in prison.'

'Are you drinking too much?'

'No! Why do you ask?'

'I've known drunks. Lots of them. You look like hell.'

'Thanks. You take care of your business, I'll take care of mine.'

'It's a deal. But nobody wants a drunk for a lawyer. You're handling all our money, in an enterprise that's very illegal. A little loose talk in a bar and somebody starts asking questions.'

'I can handle myself.'

'Good. Watch your back too. We're squeezing people, making them hurt. If I were on the other end of our little sting, I'd be tempted to come down and try to get some answers before I coughed up the money.'

'They're too scared.'

'Keep your eyes open anyway. It's important for you to stay sober and alert.'

'Thank you very much. Anything else?'

'Yeah, I got some games for you.' On to the important stuff. Spicer opened a newspaper and they began making their bets.

Trevor bought a quart of beer at a country store on the edge of Trumble, and sipped it slowly as he puttered back to Jacksonville. He tried his best not to think of their money, but his thoughts were out of control. Between his account and their account, there was just over $250,000 sitting offshore, money he could take anytime he wanted. Add a half a million bucks to it, and, well, he just couldn't stop adding – $750,000!

He'd never get caught stealing dirty money; that was the beauty of it. The victims of the Brethren weren't complaining now because they were too ashamed. They weren't breaking any laws. They were just scared. The Brethren, on the other hand, were committing crimes. So who would they run to if their money disappeared?

He had to stop thinking such thoughts.

But how could they, the Brethren, catch him? He'd be on a sailboat drifting between islands they'd never heard of. And when they were finally released, would they have the energy and money and willpower to track him down? Of course not. They were old men. Beech would probably die at Trumble.

'Stop it,' he yelled at himself.

He walked to Beach Java for a triple-shot latte, and returned to his office determined to do something productive. He went online and found the names of several private investigators in Philadelphia. It was almost six when he began calling. The first two went to answering machines.

The third, to the offices of Ed Pagnozzi, was answered by the investigator himself. Trevor explained that he was a lawyer in Florida and needed a quick job in Upper Darby.

'Okay. What kinda job?'

'I'm trying to track some mail here,' Trevor said glibly. He'd done this enough to have it well rehearsed. 'Pretty big divorce case. I got the wife, and I think the husband's hiding money. Anyway,

250

I need somebody up there to find out who's renting a certain post office box.'

'You gotta be kiddin.'

'Well, no, I'm pretty serious about this.'

'You want me to go snoopin around a post office?'

'It's just basic detective work.'

'Look, pal, I'm very busy. Call somebody else.' Pagnozzi was gone, off to more important matters. Trevor cursed him under his breath and punched the next number. He tried two more, and hung up on both when the machines answered. He'd try again tomorrow.

Across the street, Klockner listened to the brief chat with Pagnozzi one more time, then called Langley. The final piece of the puzzle had just fallen into place, and Mr. Deville would want to know it immediately.

While dependent on fancy words and smooth talk and compelling photos, the scam was basic in its operation. It preyed on human desire and it paid off by sheer terror. Its mechanics had been solved by Mr. Garbe's file, and by the Brant White reverse scam, and by the other letters they'd intercepted.

Only one question had gone unanswered: When aliases were used to rent post office boxes, how did the Brethren find the real names of their victims? The phone calls to Philadelphia had just given them their answer. Trevor simply hired a local private detective, evidently one with less business than Mr. Pagnozzi.

It was almost ten when Deville was finally

cleared to see Teddy. The North Koreans had shot another American soldier in the DMZ, and Teddy had been dealing with the fallout since noon. He was eating cheese and crackers and sipping a Diet Coke when Deville entered the bunker.

After a quick briefing, Teddy said, 'That's what I thought.'

His instincts were uncanny, especially with hindsight.

'This means, of course, that the lawyer could hire a local here to somehow uncover the real identity of Al Konyers,' Deville said.

'But how?'

'We can think of several ways. First is surveillance, the same way we caught Lake sneaking to his box. Watch the post office. That's somewhat risky because there's a good chance you'll get noticed. Second is bribery. Five hundred bucks cash to a postal clerk will work in a lot of places. Third is computer records. This is not highly classified material. One of our guys just hacked his way into the central post office in Evansville, Indiana, and got the list of all box leases. It was a random test, took him about an hour. That's high tech. Low tech is to simply break into the post office at night and have a look around.'

'How much does he pay for this?'

'Don't know, but we'll find out soon when he hires an investigator.'

'He has to be neutralized.'

'Eliminated?'

'Not yet. I'd rather buy him first. He is our window. If he's working for us, then we know everything and we keep him away from Konyers. Put together a plan.'

'And for his removal?'

'Go ahead and plan it, but we're in no hurry. Not yet anyway.'

TWENTY-THREE

The South did indeed like Aaron Lake, with his love of guns and bombs and tough talk and military readiness. He flooded Florida, Mississippi, Tennessee, Oklahoma, and Texas with ads that were even bolder than his first ones. And Teddy's people flooded the same states with more cash than had ever changed hands the night before an election.

The result was another rout, with Lake getting 260 of the 312 delegates at stake on little Super Tuesday. After the votes were counted on March 14, 1,301 of the 2,066 total delegates had been decided. Lake held a commanding lead over Governor Tarry – 801 to 390.

The race was over, barring an unforeseen catastrophe.

Buster's first job at Trumble was running a Weed Eater, for which he earned a starting wage of twenty cents an hour. It was either that or mopping floors in the cafeteria. He chose the weed eating because he liked the sun and vowed that his skin would not turn as pale as some of the bleached-out inmates he'd seen. Nor would he get fat like some of them. This is prison, he kept telling himself, how can they be so fat?

He worked hard in the bright sun, kept his tan, vowed to keep his flat stomach, and tried gamely to go through the motions. But after ten days Buster knew he would not last for forty-eight years.

Forty-eight years! He couldn't begin to comprehend such time. Who could?

He'd cried for the first forty-eight hours.

Thirteen months earlier he and his father were running their dock, working on boats, fishing twice a week in the Gulf.

He worked slowly around the concrete edge of the basketball court where a rowdy game was in progress. Then to the big sandbox where they sometimes played volleyball. In the distance, a solitary figure was walking around the track, an old-looking man with his long gray hair in a ponytail and with no shirt. He looked vaguely familiar. Buster worked both edges of a sidewalk, making his way to the track.

The lone walker was Finn Yarber, one of the judges who was trying to help him. He moved around the oval at a steady pace, head level, back and shoulders stiff and erect, not a picture of athleticism but not bad for a sixty-year-old man. He was barefoot and barebacked, sweat rolling off his leathery skin.

Buster turned off the Weed Eater and placed it on the ground. When Yarber drew near, he saw the kid and said, 'Hello, Buster. How's it goin?'

'I'm still here,' the kid said. 'Mind if I walk with you?'

'Not at all,' Finn said without breaking stride.

They did an eighth of a mile before Buster could find the courage to say, 'So how about my appeals?'

'Judge Beech is lookin at it. The sentencing appears to be in order, which is not good news. A lot of guys get here with flaws in their sentencing, and we can usually file a couple of motions and knock off a few years. Not so with you. I'm sorry.'

'That's okay. What's a few when you have forty-eight? Twenty-eight, thirty-eight, forty-eight, what does it matter?'

'You still have your appeals. There's a chance the decision can be overturned.'

'A slim chance.'

'You can't give up hope, Buster,' Yarber said, without the slightest trace of conviction. Keeping some measure of hope meant keeping some faith in the system. Yarber certainly had none. He'd been framed and railroaded by the same law he'd once defended.

But at least Yarber had enemies, and he could almost understand why they came after him.

This poor boy had done nothing wrong. Yarber had read enough of his file to believe Buster was completely innocent, another victim of an over-zealous prosecutor.

It appeared, at least from the record, that the kid's father may have been hiding some cash, but nothing serious. Nothing to warrant a 160-page conspiracy indictment.

Hope. He felt like a hypocrite for even thinking the word. The appeals courts were now packed with right-wing law and order types, and it was a rare drug case that got reversed. They'd slamdunk the kid's appeal with a rubber stamp, and tell themselves they were making the streets safer.

The biggest coward had been the trial judge. Prosecutors are expected to indict the world, but the judges are supposed to weed out the fringe defendants. Buster and his father should've been separated from the Colombians and their cohorts, and sent home before the trial began.

Now one was dead. The other was ruined. And nobody in the federal criminal system gave a damn. It was just another drug conspiracy.

At the first curve of the oval, Yarber slowed, then stopped. He looked off in the distance, beyond a grassy field to the edge of a treeline. Buster looked too. For ten days he'd been looking at the perimeter of Trumble, and seeing what wasn't there – fences, razor wire, guard towers.

'Last guy who left here,' Yarber said, gazing at nothing, 'left through those trees. They're thick for a few miles, then you come to a country road.'

'Who was he?'

'A guy named Tommy Adkins. He was a banker in North Carolina, got caught with his hand in the cookie jar.'

'What happened to him?'

'He went crazy and walked away one day. He was gone six hours before anybody knew it. A month later they found him in a motel room in Cocoa Beach, not the cops but the maids. He was curled in the fetal position on the floor, naked, suckin his thumb, his mind completely gone. They put him in some mental joint.'

'Six hours, huh?'

'Yeah, it happens about once a year. Somebody just walks away. They notify the cops in your hometown, put your name in the national computers, the usual drill.'

'How many get caught?'

'Almost all.'

'Almost.'

'Yeah, but they get caught because they do dumb things. Get drunk in bars. Drive cars with no taillights. Go see their girlfriends.'

'So if you had a brain you could pull it off?'

'Sure. Careful planning, a little cash, it would be easy.'

They began walking again, a bit slower. 'Tell me something, Mr. Yarber,' Buster said. 'If you were facing forty-eight years, would you take a walk?'

'Yes.'

'But I don't have a dime.'

'I do.'

'Then you'll help me.'

'We'll see. Give it some time. Settle in here. They're watchin you a bit closer because you're new, but with time they'll forget about you.'

Buster actually smiled. His sentence had just been reduced dramatically.

'You know what happens if you get caught?' Yarber said.

'Yeah, they add some more years. Big deal. Maybe I'll get fifty-eight. No sir, if I get caught, I blow my brains out.'

'That's what I'd do. You have to be prepared to leave the country.'

'And go where?'

'Go someplace where you look like the locals, and where they don't extradite to the U.S.'

'Anyplace in particular?'

'Argentina or Chile. You speak any Spanish?'

'No.'

'Start learnin. We have Spanish lessons here, you know. Some of the Miami boys teach them.'

They walked a lap in silence as Buster reconsidered his future. His feet were lighter, his shoulders straighter, and he couldn't keep a grin off his face.

'Why are you helping me?' he asked.

'Because you're twenty-three years old. Too young and too innocent. You've been screwed by the system, Buster. You have the right to fight back any way you can. Do you have a girlfriend?'

'Sort of.'

'Forget about her. She'll only get you in trouble. Besides, you think she'll wait forty-eight years?'

'She said she would.'

'She's lyin. She's already playin the field. Forget about her, unless you want to get caught.'

Yeah, he's probably right, thought Buster. He'd yet to get a letter from her, and though she lived only four hours away she hadn't made it to Trumble. They'd talked twice on the phone, and all she seemed to care about was whether he'd been attacked.

'Any kids?' asked Yarber.

'No. Not that I know of.'

'What about your mother?'

'She died when I was very young. My dad raised me. It was just the two of us.'

'Then you're the perfect guy to walk away.'

'I'd like to leave now.'

259

'Be patient. Let's plan it carefully.'

Another lap, and Buster wanted to sprint. He couldn't think of a damned thing he'd miss in Pensacola. He'd made As and Bs in Spanish in high school, and while he couldn't remember any of it, he hadn't struggled with the material. He'd pick it up fast. He'd take the courses and hang out with the Latins.

The more he walked the more he wanted his conviction to be affirmed. And the quicker the better. If it got reversed, he'd be forced to have another trial, and he had no confidence in the next jury.

Buster wanted to run, starting over there in the grassy field, to the treeline, through the woods to the country road where he wasn't sure what to do next. But if an insane banker could walk away and make it to Cocoa Beach, so could he.

'Why haven't you walked away?' he asked Yarber.

'I've thought about it. But in five years they'll let me go. I can last that long. I'll be sixty-five, in good health, with a life expectancy of sixteen years. That's what I'm livin for, Buster, the last sixteen years. I don't wanna be lookin over my shoulder.'

'Where will you go?'

'Don't know yet. Maybe a little village in the Italian countryside. Maybe the mountains of Peru. I've got the whole world to choose from, and I spend hours every day just dreamin about it.'

'So you have plenty of money?'

'No, but I'm gettin there.'

That raised a number of questions, but Buster

let them pass. He was learning that in prison you kept most of your questions to yourself.

When Buster was tired of walking, he stopped near his Weed Eater. 'Thanks, Mr. Yarber,' he said.

'No problem. Just keep it between the two of us.'

'Sure. I'm ready whenever you are.'

Finn was off, pacing another lap, his shorts now soaked with sweat, his gray ponytail dripping with moisture. Buster watched him go, then for a second looked across the grassy field, into the trees.

At that moment, he could see all the way to South America.

TWENTY-FOUR

For two long, hard months Aaron Lake and Governor Tarry had gone head to head, toe to toe, coast to coast, in twenty-six states with almost 25 million votes cast. They'd pushed themselves with eighteen-hour days, brutal schedules, relentless travel, the typical madness of a presidential race.

Yet they'd worked just as hard to avoid a face-to-face debate. Tarry didn't want one in the early primaries because he was the front-runner. He had the organization, the cash, the favorable polls. Why legitimize the opposition? Lake didn't want one because he was a newcomer to the national scene, a novice at highstakes campaigning, and besides it was much easier to hide behind a script and a friendly camera and make ads whenever needed. The risks of a live debate were simply too high.

Teddy didn't like the thought of one either.

But campaigns change. Front-runners fade, small issues become big ones, the press can create a crisis simply out of boredom.

Tarry decided he needed a debate because he was broke, and losing one primary after another. 'Aaron Lake is trying to buy this election,' he said over and over. 'And I want to confront him, man to man.' It sounded good, and the press had beaten it to death.

'He's running from a debate,' Tarry declared, and the pack liked that too.

'The governor's been dodging a debate since Michigan' was Lake's standard response.

And so for three weeks they played the he's-running-from-me game until their people quietly worked out the details.

Lake was reluctant, but he also needed a forum. Though he was winning week after week, he was rolling over an opponent who'd been fading for a long time. His polls and D-PAC's polls showed a great deal of voter interest in him, but mainly because he was new and handsome and seemingly electable.

Unknown to outsiders, the polls also showed some very soft areas. The first was on the question of Lake's single-issue campaign. Defense spending can excite the voters for only so long, and there was great concern, in the polls, about where Lake stood on other issues.

Second, Lake was still five points behind the Vice President in their hypothetical November matchup. The voters were tired of the Vice President, but at least they knew who he was. Lake remained a mystery to many. Also, the two would debate several times prior to November. Lake, who had the nomination in hand, needed the experience.

Tarry didn't help matters with his constant query, 'Who is Aaron Lake?' With some of his few remaining funds, he authorized the printing of

bumper stickers with the now famous question –
Who is Aaron Lake?

(It was a question Teddy asked himself almost
every hour, but for a different reason.)

The setting of the debate was in Pennsylvania at
a small Lutheran college with a cozy auditorium,
good acoustics and light, a controllable crowd.
Even the smallest of details were haggled over by
the two camps, but because both sides now needed
a debate agreements were eventually reached. The
precise format had nearly caused fistfights, but
once ironed out it gave everybody something. The
media got three reporters on the stage to ask direct
questions during one segment. The spectators got
twenty minutes to ask about anything, with nothing screened. Tarry, a lawyer, wanted five minutes
for opening remarks and a ten-minute closing
statement. Lake wanted thirty minutes of one-on-
one debate with Tarry, no holds barred, no one to
referee, just the two of them slugging it out
without rules. This had terrified the Tarry camp,
and had almost broken the deal.

The moderator was a local public radio figure,
and when he said, 'Good evening, and welcome to
the first and only debate between Governor Wen-
dell Tarry and Congressman Aaron Lake,' an
estimated 18 million people were watching.

Tarry wore a navy suit his wife had selected,
with the standard blue shirt and the standard red
and blue tie. Lake wore a dashing light brown suit,
a white shirt with a spread collar, and a tie of red
and maroon and a half-dozen other colors. The
entire ensemble had been put together by a fashion
consultant, and was designed to complement the

colors of the set. Lake's hair had received a tinting. His teeth had been bleached. He'd spent four hours in a tanning bed. He looked thin and fresh, and anxious to be onstage.

Governor Tarry was himself a handsome man. Though he was only four years older than Lake, the campaign was taking a heavy toll. His eyes were tired and red. He'd gained a few pounds, especially in his face. When he began his opening remarks, beads of sweat popped up along his forehead and glistened in the lights.

Conventional wisdom held that Tarry had more to lose because he'd already lost so much. Early in January, he'd been declared, by prophets as prescient as *Time* magazine, to have the nomination within his grasp. He'd been running for three years. His campaign was built on grassroots support and shoe leather. Every precinct captain and poll worker in Iowa and New Hampshire had drunk coffee with him. His organization was impeccable.

Then came Lake with his slick ads and single-issue magic.

Tarry badly needed either a stunning performance by himself, or a major gaffe by Lake.

He got neither. By a flip of the coin, he was chosen to go first. He stumbled badly in his opening remarks as he moved stiffly around the stage, trying desperately to look at ease but forgetting what his notes said. Sure he'd once been a lawyer, but his specialty had been securities. As he forgot one point after another, he returned to his common theme – Mr. Lake here is trying to buy this election because he has nothing to say. A nasty tone developed quickly. Lake smiled hand-somely; water off a duck's back.

Tarry's weak beginning emboldened Lake, gave him a shot of confidence, and convinced him to stay behind the podium where it was safe and where his notes were. He began by saying that he wasn't there to throw mud, that he had respect for Governor Tarry, but they had just listened to him speak for five minutes and eleven seconds and he'd said nothing positive.

He then ignored his opponent, and briefly covered three issues that needed to be discussed. Tax relief, welfare reform, and the trade deficit. Not a word about defense.

The first question from the panel of reporters was directed at Lake, and it dealt with the budget surplus. What should be done with the money? It was a soft pitch, lobbed by a friendly reporter, and Lake was all over it. Save Social Security, he answered, then in an impressive display of finan-cial straight talk he outlined precisely how the money should be used. He gave figures and percentages and projections, all from memory.

Governor Tarry's response was simply to cut taxes. Give the money back to the people who'd earned it.

Few points were scored during the questioning. Both candidates were well prepared. The surprise was that Lake, the man who wanted to own the Pentagon, was so well versed in all other issues.

The debate settled into the usual give and take. The questions from the spectators were thoroughly predictable. The fireworks began when the candi-dates were allowed to quiz one another. Tarry went first, and, as expected, asked Lake if he was trying to buy the election.

'You weren't concerned about money when you had more than everybody else,' Lake shot back, and the audience came to life.

'I didn't have fifty million dollars,' Tarry said.

'Neither do I,' Lake said. 'It's more like sixty million, and it's coming in faster than we can count it. It's coming from working people and middle-income folks. Eighty-one percent of our contributors are people earning less than forty thousand dollars a year. Something wrong with those people, Governor Tarry?'

'There should be a limit on how much a candidate should spend.'

'I agree. And I've voted for limits eight different times in Congress. You, on the other hand, never mentioned limits until you ran out of money.'

Governor Tarry looked Quayle-like at the camera, the frozen stare of a deer in headlights. A few of Lake's people in the audience laughed just loud enough to be heard.

The beads of sweat returned to the governor's forehead as he shuffled his oversized notecards. He wasn't actually a sitting governor, but he still preferred the title. In fact, it had been nine years since the voters of Indiana sent him packing, after only one term. Lake saved this ammo for a few minutes.

Tarry then asked why Lake had voted for fifty-four new taxes during his fourteen years in Congress.

'I don't recall fifty-four taxes,' Lake said. 'But a lot of them were on tobacco and alcohol and

267

gambling. I also voted against increases in personal income taxes, corporate income taxes, federal withholding taxes, and Social Security taxes. I'm not ashamed of that record. And speaking of taxes, Governor, during your four years in Indiana, how do you explain the fact that individual tax rates increased by an average of six percent?'

No quick response was forthcoming, so Lake plowed ahead. 'You want to cut federal spending, yet in your four years in Indiana state spending increased eighteen percent. You want to cut corporate income taxes, yet during your four years in Indiana, corporate income taxes went up three percent. You want to end welfare, yet when you were governor forty thousand people were added to the welfare rolls in Indiana. How do you explain this?'

Each blow from Indiana drew blood, and Tarry was on the ropes. 'I disagree with your figures, sir,' he managed to say. 'We created jobs in Indiana.'

'Is that so?' Lake said sardonically. He pulled up a sheet of paper from his podium as if it were a federal indictment against Governor Tarry. 'Maybe you did, but during your four years almost sixty thousand ex-workers signed up for unemployment,' he announced without looking at the paper.

Sure Tarry had had a bad four years as governor, but the economy had gone south on him. He had explained all this before and he'd love to do it again, but, gosh, he had only a few short minutes on national television. Surely he shouldn't waste it splitting hairs about the past. 'This race is not about Indiana,' he said, managing a smile. 'It's about all fifty states. It's about working people everywhere who'll be expected to pay more taxes to finance your gold-plated defense projects, Mr. Lake. You can't be serious about doubling the Pentagon's budget.'

Lake looked hard at his opponent. 'I'm very serious about it. And if you wanted a strong military, you'd be serious too.' He then rattled off a string of statistics that went on and on, each building on the other. It was conclusive proof of our military unreadiness, and when he finally finished our armed forces would've been hard-pressed to invade Bermuda.

But Tarry had a study to the contrary, a thick glossy manuscript produced by a think tank run by ex-admirals. He waved it for the cameras and argued such a buildup was unnecessary. The world was at peace, with the exception of a few civil and regional wars, disputes in which we had no national interest, and the United States was by far the only superpower left standing. The cold war was history. The Chinese were decades away from achieving anything remotely resembling parity. Why burden the taxpayers with tens of billions in new hardware?

They argued for a while about how to pay for it, and Tarry scored minor points. But they were on Lake's turf, and as the issue dragged on it became evident that Lake knew far more than the governor.

Lake saved his best for last. During his ten-minute recap, he returned to Indiana and continued the miserable list of Tarry's failures there during his sole term. The theme was simple, and very effective: If he can't run Indiana, how can he run the entire nation?

'I'm not knocking the people of Indiana,' Lake said at one point. 'In fact, they had the wisdom to return Mr. Tarry to private life after only one term. They knew he was doing a terrible job. That's why only thirty-eight percent of them voted for him when he asked for four more years. Thirty-eight percent! We should trust the people of Indiana. They know this man. They've seen him govern. They made a mistake, and they got rid of him. It would be sad if the rest of the country now made the same mistake.'

The instant polls gave a solid win to Lake. D-PAC called a thousand voters immediately after the debate. Almost 70 percent thought Lake was the better of the two.

On a late flight from Pittsburgh to Wichita, several bottles of champagne were opened on Air Lake and a small party began. The debate poll results were flowing in, each better than the last, and the mood was victorious.

Lake hadn't banned alcohol on his Boeing, but he had discouraged it. If and when a member of his staff took a drink, it was always a quick one, and always on the sly. But some moments called for a little celebration. He enjoyed two glasses of champagne himself. Only his closest people were present. He thanked them and congratulated them, and just for fun they watched the highlights of the debate while another bottle was opened. They paused the video each time Governor Tarry looked particularly puzzled, and the laughs grew louder.

But the party was brief; fatigue hit hard. These were people who'd been sleeping five hours a night for weeks. Most had slept even less the night before the debate. Lake himself was exhausted. He finished a third glass, the first time in many years he'd drunk that much, and settled into his massive leather recliner with a heavy quilt. Bodies sprawled everywhere in the darkness of the cabin.

He couldn't sleep; he seldom did on airplanes. There were too many things to think and worry about. It was impossible not to savor the victory in the debate, and as he kicked around under the quilt Lake repeated his best lines of the night. He had been brilliant, something he'd never admit to anyone else.

The nomination was his. He would be showcased at the convention, then for four months he and the Vice President would slug it out in the grandest of American traditions.

He turned on the small overhead reading light. Someone else was reading down the aisle, near the flight deck. Another insomniac, with the only other light on in the cabin. People were actually snoring under their blankets, the sleep of hurried young people running on fumes.

Lake opened his briefcase and pulled out a small leather folder filled with his personal correspondence cards. They were four by six, heavy stock, off-white in color, and in light black Old English print had the name of 'Aaron Lake' printed at the top. With a thick, antique Mont Blanc pen, Lake scribbled a brief word to his college roommate, now a professor of Latin at a small college in Texas. He wrote a thank-you to the moderator of the debate, and one to his Oregon coordinator. Lake loved Clancy novels. He'd just finished the latest one, the thickest yet, and he wrote the author a complimentary note.

Sometimes his notes ran long, and for this reason he had plain cards, same size and color but without his name. He looked around to make sure everyone was sound asleep, and he quickly wrote:

Dear Ricky:
I think it's best if we end our correspondence. I wish you well with your rehab.

Sincerely, Al

He addressed an unmarked envelope. The address of Aladdin North came from memory. Then he returned to his personalized cards and wrote a series of thank-you notes to serious contributors. He wrote twenty of them before fatigue finally settled in. With the cards still in front of him, and his reading light still on, he yielded to exhaustion and within minutes was napping.

He'd slept less than an hour when panicked voices awakened him. Lights were on, people were moving, and there was smoke in the cabin. A buzzer of some sort was ringing loudly from the cockpit, and once he got his bearings Lake realized the nose of the Boeing was pointed downward. Total panic set in quickly as the air masks dropped from above. After years of half-watching flight attendants give their routine demonstrations before takeoff, the damned masks were actually going to be used. Lake snapped his into place and inhaled mightily.

The pilot announced they were making an emergency landing in St. Louis. The lights flickered, and someone actually screamed. Lake wanted to move about the cabin and reassure everyone, but the mask wouldn't move with him. In the section behind him were two dozen reporters and about that many Secret Service people.

Maybe the air masks didn't drop back there, he thought, then felt guilty.

The smoke got thicker, and the lights faded. After the onset of panic, Lake managed a rational thought or two, if only for a brief second. He quickly gathered the correspondence cards and envelopes. The one to Ricky got his attention just long enough to place it in the envelope to Aladdin North. He sealed it, and stuffed the folder back into his briefcase. The lights flickered again, then went out for good.

The smoke burned their eyes and warmed their faces. The plane was descending at a rapid pace. Warning bells and sirens shrieked from the flight deck.

This can't be happening, Lake told himself as he gripped his armrests. I'm about to be elected President of the United States. He thought of Rocky Marciano, Buddy Holly, Otis Redding, Thurman Munson, Senator Tower of Texas, Mickey Leland from Houston, a friend of his. And JFK, Jr., and Ron Brown.

The air suddenly turned cold and the smoke

dissipated rapidly. They were below ten thousand feet, and the pilot had somehow managed to vent the cabin. The plane leveled and from the windows they could see lights on the ground.

'Please continue to use the oxygen masks,' the pilot said in the darkness. 'We'll be on the ground in a few minutes. The landing should be uneventful.'

Uneventful? He must be kidding, thought Lake. He needed to find the nearest toilet.

Relief settled uneasily through the plane. Just before it touched down, Lake saw the flashing lights of a hundred emergency vehicles. They bounced a little, a typical landing, and when they stopped at the end of the runway the emergency doors flew open.

A controlled stampede occurred, and within minutes they were grabbed by rescue personnel and rushed to ambulances. The fire, in the luggage area of the Boeing, was still spreading when they landed. As Lake jogged away from the plane, firemen rushed toward it. Smoke boiled from under the wings.

Just a few more minutes, Lake said to himself, and we would be dead.

'That was a close one, sir,' a paramedic said as they raced away. Lake clutched his briefcase, with his little letters inside, and for the first time went rigid with horror.

The near miss, and the obligatory nonstop media barrage after it, probably did little to boost Lake's popularity. But the publicity certainly didn't hurt. He was everywhere on the morning news, one

274

moment talking about his decisive victory over Governor Tarry in the debate, and the next giving details of what could've been his last flight.

'I think I'll take the bus for a while,' he said with a laugh. He used as much humor as he could muster, and took the high road of aw-shucks-it-was-nothing. His staff members had different stories, of breathing oxygen in the dark while the smoke grew thicker and hotter. And the reporters on board were eager sources of information, providing detailed narratives of the terror.

Teddy Maynard watched it all from his bunker. Three of his men were on the plane, and one had called him from the hospital in St. Louis.

It was a perplexing event. On the one hand, he still believed in the importance of a Lake presidency. The security of the nation depended on it.

On the other hand, a crash wouldn't have been a catastrophe. Lake and his double life would be gone. A huge headache wiped out. Governor Tarry had learned firsthand the power of unlimited cash. Teddy could cut a deal with him in time to win in November.

But Lake was still standing, taller than ever now. His tanned face was on the front of every newspaper and close to every camera. His campaign had progressed far faster than Teddy had dreamed.

So why was there so much angst in the bunker? Why was Teddy not celebrating?

Because he had yet to solve the puzzle of the Brethren. And he couldn't simply start killing people.

TWENTY-FIVE

The team in Documents used the same laptop they'd used to write the last letter to Ricky. This letter was composed by Deville himself, and approved by Mr. Maynard. It read:

Dear Ricky:
   Good news about your release to the halfway house in Baltimore. Give me a few days and I think I'll have a full-time job lined up for you there. It's a clerical position, not a lot of money, but a pretty good place to start.
   I suggest we go a bit slower than you want. Maybe a nice lunch at first, then we'll see where things go. I'm not the type to rush in.
   Hope you're doing well. I'll write you next week with the details of the job. Hang in there.

                                        Best Wishes, Al

Only the 'Al' was handwritten. A D.C. postmark was applied, and the letter was flown and hand-delivered to Klockner in Neptune Beach.
   Trevor happened to be in Fort Lauderdale,

oddly enough tending to legitimate legal business, and so the letter sat in the Aladdin North box for two days. When he returned, exhausted, he stopped by his office just long enough to commence a nasty argument with Jan, then stormed out, got back in his car, and went straight to the post office. To his delight, the box was full. He sorted out the junk mail, then drove a half mile to the Atlantic Beach post office and checked the box for Laurel Ridge, Percy's fancy rehab spa.

Once all the mail was collected, and much to the dismay of Klockner, Trevor left for Trumble. He made one call en route, to his bookie. He'd lost $2,500 in three days on hockey, a sport Spicer knew nothing about and refused to bet on. Trevor was picking his own favorites, with predictable results.

Spicer didn't answer the page at the courtyard at Trumble, so Beech met with Trevor in the attorney-conference room. They did their mail swap – eight letters going out, fourteen coming in.

'What about Brant in Upper Darby?' Beech asked, flipping through the envelopes.

'What about him?'

'Who is he? We're ready to bust him.'

'I'm still searching. I've been out of town for a few days.'

'Get it done, okay. This guy could be the biggest fish yet.'

'I'll do it tomorrow.'

Beech had no Vegas lines to ponder and he didn't want to play cards. Trevor left after twenty minutes.

★

Long after they should've eaten dinner, and long after the library should've been closed, the Brethren remained locked in their little room, saying little, avoiding eye contact with one another, each staring at the walls, deep in thought.

On the table were three letters. One was from Al's laptop, postmarked two days earlier in D.C. One was Al's handwritten note ending his correspondence with Ricky, postmarked from St. Louis, three days earlier. These two conflicted sharply, and were obviously written by different people. Someone was tampering with their mail.

The third letter had stopped them cold. They'd read it over and over, one by one, collectively, in silence, in unison. They'd picked at its corners, held it up to the light, even smelled it. There was a very faint smoky odor, same as the envelope and the note from Al to Ricky.

Handwritten in ink, it was dated April 18, at 1:20 A.M., and addressed to a woman named Carol.

> Dear Carol:
>   What a great night! The debate couldn't have gone better, thanks in part to you and the Pennsylvania volunteers. Many thanks! Let's push harder and win this thing. We're ahead in Pennsylvania, let's stay there. See you next week.

It was signed by Aaron Lake. The card had his name personalized across the top. The handwriting was identical to that on the terse note Al had sent Ricky.

The envelope was addressed to Ricky at Aladdin North, and when Beech opened it he did not notice the second card stuck behind the first. Then it fell on the table, and when he picked it up he saw the name 'Aaron' Lake engraved in black.

That had happened sometime around 4 P.M., not long after Trevor had left. For almost five hours they'd studied the mail, and they were now almost certain that (a) the laptop letter was a fake, with the name 'Al' signed by someone who was quite good at forging; (b) the forged 'Al' signature was virtually identical to the original 'Al,' so the forger at some point had gained access to Ricky's correspondence with Al; (c) the notes to Ricky and Carol were handwritten by Aaron Lake; and (d) the one to Carol had obviously been sent to them by mistake.

Above all, Al Konyers was really Aaron Lake.

Their little scam had snared the most famous politician in the country.

Other, less important pieces of evidence also pointed toward Lake. His front was a mailbox service in the D.C. area, a place where Congressman Lake spent almost all of his time. Being a high-profile elected official, subject to the whims of voters every so often, he would certainly hide behind an alias. And he'd use a machine with a printer to hide his handwriting. Al had not sent a photograph, another sign that he had a lot to conceal.

They'd checked recent newspapers in the library to get the dates straight. The handwritten notes had been mailed from St. Louis the day after the debate, when Lake was there because his airplane had caught fire.

The timing seemed perfect for Lake to call off the letters. He'd started the correspondence before he entered the race. In three months he'd taken the country by storm and become very famous. Now, he had so much to lose.

Slowly, with no concern for time, they built their case against Aaron Lake. And when it looked airtight, they tried to break it down. The most compelling counterpoint came from Finn Yarber.

Suppose, he said, someone on Lake's staff had access to his stationery? Not a bad question, and one they'd kicked around for an hour. Wouldn't Al Konyers do such a thing in order to hide himself? What if he lived in the D.C. area and worked for Lake? Suppose Lake, a very busy man, trusted this assistant to write personal notes for him. Yarber couldn't remember allowing an assistant such authority back when he was Chief Justice. Beech had never let anyone write his personal notes. Spicer had never fooled with such nonsense. That's what phones were for.

But Yarber and Beech had never known the stress and fury of anything remotely similar to a presidential campaign. They'd been busy men in their times, they reflected with sadness, but nothing like Lake.

Say it was an assistant to Lake. So far he had a perfect cover because he'd told them almost nothing. No photo. Only the vaguest details about career and family. He liked old movies and Chinese food, and that was about all they'd extracted. Konyers was on their list of pen pals to soon dispose of because he was too timid. Why, then, would he call off the relationship at this moment?

There was no ready answer.

And the argument was a long shot anyway. Beech and Yarber concluded that no man in Lake's position, someone with a good chance of becoming President of the United States, would allow anyone else to write and sign personal notes. Lake had a hundred staff members to type letters and memos, all of which could be signed by him at a rapid clip.

Spicer had posed a more serious question. Why would Lake run the risk of a handwritten note? His prior letters had been typed on plain white paper, and mailed in a plain white envelope. They could spot a coward by his choice of stationery, and Lake was as fainthearted as anyone who'd answered their ad. The campaign, rich as it was, had plenty of word processors and typewriters and laptops, no doubt the latest in technology.

To find the answer, they went back to the little evidence they had. The letter to Carol had been written at 1:20 A.M. According to a newspaper, the emergency landing happened around 2:15, less than an hour later.

'He wrote it on the plane,' Yarber said. 'It was late, the plane was filled with people, almost sixty according to the paper, these people were exhausted, and maybe he couldn't get his hands on a computer.'

'Then why not wait?' asked Spicer. He'd proved to be excellent at asking questions no one, especially him, could answer.

'He made a mistake. He thought he was being smart, and he probably was. Somehow the mail got mixed.'

'Look at the big picture,' Beech said. 'The nomination is in the bag. He's just wiped out his only opponent, before a national audience, and he's finally convinced that his name will be on the ballot in November. But he's got this secret. He's got Ricky, and he's been thinking for weeks about what to do with Ricky. The boy's going to be released, he wants to have a rendezvous, etc. Lake feels the pressure on both fronts – from Ricky, and from the realization that he might just be elected President. So he decides to stiff Ricky. He writes a note that has one chance in a billion of getting screwed up, then the plane catches on fire. He makes a small mistake, but it turns into a monster.'

'And he doesn't know it,' Yarber added. 'Yet.'

Beech's theory settled in. They absorbed it in the heavy stillness of their little room. The gravity of their discovery weighed down their words and thoughts. The hours passed, and it slowly sank in.

For the next great question they grappled with the baffling reality that someone was meddling with their mail. Who? And why would anyone want to? How had they intercepted the letters? The puzzle seemed hopeless.

Again, they argued the scenario that the culprit was someone very close to Lake, perhaps an assistant with access who'd stumbled across the letters. And maybe he was trying to protect Lake from Ricky by commandeering the correspondence, with the goal of somehow, someday ending the relationship.

But there were too many unknowns to build any evidence. They scratched their heads and bit their nails, and finally admitted they would have to sleep on it. They couldn't plot the next move because the situation before them had more riddles than answers.

They slept little, and they were red-eyed and unshaved when they reconvened just after 6 A.M. with black coffee steaming from Styrofoam cups. They locked the door, pulled out the letters, placed them exactly where they'd been the night before, and began thinking.

'I think we should scope out the box in Chevy Chase,' said Spicer. 'It's easy, safe, usually quick. Trevor's been able to do it almost everywhere. If we know who's renting it, then a lot of questions will be answered.'

'It's hard to believe a man like Aaron Lake would be renting a box so he could hide letters like these,' Beech said.

'It's not the same Aaron Lake,' Yarber said. 'When he rented the box and began writing to Ricky, he was just a simple congressman, one of four hundred and thirty-five. You'd never heard of him. Now, things have changed dramatically.'

'And that's exactly why he's trying to end the relationship,' Spicer said. 'Things are very different now. He has much more to lose.'

The first step would be to get Trevor to investigate the post office box in Chevy Chase.

The second step was not as clear. They were concerned that Lake, and they assumed that Lake was Al and Al was Lake, might realize his screwup with the letters. He had tens of millions of dollars (a fact they had certainly not overlooked), and he could easily use some of it to track down Ricky. Given the enormity of the stakes, Lake, if he did realize his mistake, would do almost anything to neutralize Ricky.

So they debated whether to write him a note, in which Ricky would beg Al not to slam the door like this. Ricky needed his friendship, nothing more, etc. The purpose would be to give the impression that everything was fine, nothing out of the ordinary. They hoped Lake would read it and scratch his head and wonder to himself just where, exactly, did that damned card to Carol get off to.

Such a note was unwise, they decided, because someone else was also reading the letters. Until they knew who, they couldn't risk any more contact with Al.

They finished their coffee and walked to the cafeteria. They ate alone, cereal and fruit and yogurt, healthy stuff because they would now live again on the outside. They walked four smoke-free laps together, at a leisurely pace, then returned to their chamber to finish the morning deep in thought.

Poor Lake. He was scrambling from one state to the next with fifty people in tow, late for three engagements at once, a dozen aides whispering in both ears. He had no time to think for himself.

And the Brethren had all day, hours upon hours to sit with their thoughts and their schemes. It was not an equal match.

TWENTY-SIX

There were two types of phones at Trumble; secured and unsecured. In theory, all calls made on unsecured lines were taped and subject to review by little elves in a booth somewhere who did nothing but listen to a million hours of useless chatter. In reality, about half the calls were actually taped, at random, and only about 5 percent were ever heard by anybody working for the prison. Not even the federal government could hire enough elves to handle all the listening.

Drug dealers had been known to direct their gangs from unsecured lines. Mafia bosses had been known to order hits on their rivals. The odds were very high against getting caught.

The secured lines were fewer in number, and by law could not be wired for surveillance. The secured calls went only to lawyers, and always with a guard posted nearby.

When Spicer's turn finally came to make a secured call, the guard had drifted away.

'Law office,' came the rude hello from the free world.

'Yes, this is Joe Roy Spicer, calling from the Trumble prison, and I need to speak with Trevor.'

'He's asleep.'

It was 1:30 P.M. 'Then wake the sonofabitch up,' Spicer growled.

'Hang on.'

'Would you please hurry? I'm on a prison phone.'

Joe Roy glanced around and wondered, not for the first time, what kind of lawyer they'd crawled in bed with.

'Why are you calling?' were Trevor's first words.

'Never mind. Wake your ass up and get to work. We need something done quickly.'

By now, the rental across from Trevor's office was buzzing. This was the first call from Trumble.

'What is it?'

'We need a box checked out. Quickly. And we want you to go supervise it. Don't leave until it's finished.'

'Why me?'

'Just do it, dammit, okay? This could be the biggest one yet.'

'Where is it?'

'Chevy Chase, Maryland. Write this down. Al Konyers, Box 455, Mailbox America, 39380 Western Avenue, Chevy Chase. Be very careful because this guy could have some friends, and there's a good chance someone else is already watching the box. Take some cash and hire a couple of good investigators.'

'I'm pretty busy around here.'

'Yeah, sorry I woke you up. Do it now, Trevor.

Leave today. And don't come back until you know who rented the box.'

'All right, all right.'

Spicer hung up, and Trevor put his feet back on his desk and appeared to return to his nap. But he was just contemplating matters. A moment later he yelled for Jan to check the flights to Washington.

In fourteen years as a field supervisor, Klockner had never seen so many people watch one person do so little. He made a quick call to Deville at Langley, and the rental sprang into action. It was time for the Wes and Chap show.

Wes walked across the street and entered the creaking and peeling door of Mr. L. Trevor Carson, Attorney and Counselor-at-Law. Wes was dressed in khakis and a pullover knit, loafers, no socks, and when Jan offered him her customary sneer she couldn't tell if he was a native or a tourist. 'What can I do for you?' she asked.

'I really need to see Mr. Carson,' Wes said with an air of desperation.

'Do you have an appointment?' she asked, as if her boss was so busy she couldn't keep track of his meetings.

'Well, no, it's sort of an emergency.'

'He's very busy,' she said, and Wes could almost hear the laughter from the rental.

'Please, I've got to talk to him.'

She rolled her eyes and didn't budge. 'What kind of matter is it?'

'I've just buried my wife,' he said, on the verge of tears, and Jan finally cracked a bit. 'I'm very sorry,' she said. Poor guy.

'She was killed in a car wreck on I–95, just north of Jacksonville.'

Jan was standing now and wishing she'd made fresh coffee. 'I'm so sorry,' she said. 'When did this happen?'

'Twelve days ago. A friend recommended Mr. Carson.'

Not much of a friend, she wanted to say. 'Would you like some coffee?' she asked, putting the top on her nail polish. Twelve days ago, she thought. Like all good legal secretaries, she read the newspapers with a keen eye on the accidents. Who knows, one might walk in the door.

Never Trevor's door. Until now.

'No, thanks,' Wes said. 'She was hit by a Texaco truck. The driver was drunk.'

'Oh my god!' she exclaimed, hand over her mouth. Even Trevor could handle this one.

Serious money, big fees, right here in the reception area, and that fool back there snoring off his lunch.

'He's in a deposition,' she said. 'Let me see if I can disturb him. Please have a seat.' She wanted to lock the front door so he couldn't escape.

'The name's Yates. Yates Newman,' he said, trying to help her.

'Oh yes,' she said, racing down the hall. She knocked politely on Trevor's door, then stepped inside. 'Wake up, asshole!' she hissed through clenched teeth, loud enough for Wes to hear up front.

'What is it?' Trevor said, standing, ready for a fistfight. He wasn't sleeping after all. He'd been reading an old *People*.

288

'Surprise! You have a client.'

'Who is it?'

'A man whose wife got run over by a Texaco truck twelve days ago. He wants to see you right now.'

'He's here?'

'Yep. Hard to believe, isn't it? Three thousand lawyers in Jacksonville and this poor guy falls through the cracks. Said a friend recommended you.'

'What'd you tell him?'

'I told him he needed to find new friends.'

'No, really, what did you tell him?'

'That you're in a deposition.'

'I haven't had a deposition in eight years. Send him back.'

'Be cool. I'll make him some coffee. Act like you're finishing some important stuff back here. Why don't you straighten this place up?'

'You just make sure he can't get out.'

'The Texaco driver was drunk,' she said, opening the door. 'Don't screw this up.'

Trevor froze, slack-jawed, glassy-eyed, his deadened mind suddenly springing to life. One third of $2 million, $4 million, hell, $10 million if he was really drunk and punitive damages kicked in. He wanted to at least straighten his desk, but he couldn't move.

Wes stared out the front window, stared at the rental, where his buddies were staring at him. He kept his back to the ruckus down the hall because he was struggling to keep a straight face. Footsteps, then Jan said, 'Mr. Carson will see you in just a moment.'

'Thanks,' he said softly, without turning around.

Poor guy's still grieving, she thought, then walked to the dirty kitchen to make coffee.

The deposition was over in a flash, and the other participants miraculously vanished without a trace. Wes followed her down the hall to Mr. Carson's cluttered office. Introductions were made. She brought them fresh coffee, and when she was finally gone, Wes made an unusual request.

'Is there any place to get a strong latte around here?'

'Why, certainly, yes, of course,' Trevor said, the words jumping across the desk. 'There's a place called Beach Java just a few blocks away.'

'Could you send her to get me one?'

Absolutely. Anything!

'Yes, of course. Tall or grande?'

'Tall's fine.'

Trevor bounced out of his office, and a few seconds later Jan hit the front door and practically ran down the street. When she was out of sight, Chap left the rental and walked to Trevor's. The front door was locked, so he opened it with a key of his own. Inside, he latched the chain, so poor Jan would be stuck on the porch with a cup of scalding latte.

Chap eased down the hall and made a sudden entrance into the lawyer's office.

'Excuse me,' Trevor said.

'It's okay,' Wes said. 'He's with me.'

Chap closed and locked the door, then he yanked a 9-millimeter pistol from his jacket and almost pointed it at poor Trevor, whose eyes bulged and heart froze.

'What –' he managed to emit in a high-pitched painful voice.

'Just shut up, okay,' said Chap, handing the pistol to Wes, who was sitting. Trevor's wild eyes followed it from one to the other, then it disappeared. What have I done? Who are these thugs? All my gambling debts are paid.

He was very happy to shut up. Whatever they wanted.

Chap leaned on the wall, pretty damned close to Trevor, as if he might lunge at any moment. 'We have a client,' he began. 'A wealthy man, who has been snagged in the little scam run by you and Ricky.'

'Oh my god,' Trevor mumbled. His worst nightmare.

'It's a wonderful idea,' Wes said. 'Extorting from rich gay men who are still hiding in the closet. They can't complain. Ricky's already in prison, so what does he have to lose?'

'Almost perfect,' Chap said. 'Until you hook the wrong fish, which is exactly what you've done.'

'It's not my scam,' Trevor said, his voice still two octaves above normal, his eyes still searching for the pistol.

'Yes, but it wouldn't work without you, would it?' Wes asked. 'There has to be a crooked lawyer on the outside to shuttle mail. And Ricky needs someone to direct the money and do a little investigative work.'

'You're not cops, are you?' Trevor asked.

'No. We're private thugs,' Chap said.

'Because if you're cops then I'm not sure I wanna talk anymore.'

291

'We're not cops, okay.'

Trevor was breathing and thinking again, the breathing going much faster than the thinking, but his training kicked in. 'I think I'll record this,' he said. 'Just in case you're cops.'

'I said we're not cops.'

'I don't trust cops, especially the FBI. The fibbies would walk in here just like the two of you, wave a gun around, and swear that they weren't fibbies. I just don't like cops. I think I'll get this on tape.'

Don't worry, pal, they wanted to say. It was all being recorded, live and in high-density digital color from a tiny camera in the ceiling a few feet behind where they were sitting. And there were mikes planted all around Trevor's littered desk so that when he snored or burped or even cracked his knuckles somebody across the street heard it.

The pistol was back. Wes held it with both hands and examined it carefully.

'You're not recording anything,' Chap said. 'As I told you, we're private boys. And we're calling the shots right now.' He took a step closer along the wall. Trevor watched him with one eye, and with the other helped Wes examine the pistol.

'In fact, we come in peace,' Chap said.

'We have some money for you,' Wes said, and put the damned thing away again.

'Money for what?' Trevor asked.

'We want you on our side. We want to retain your services.'

'To do what?'

'To help us protect our client,' Chap said. 'Here's the way we see it. You're a conspirator in

292

an extortion scheme operating from inside a federal prison, and you've been discovered by us. We could go to the feds, get you and your client busted, you'd be sent away for thirty months, probably to Trumble, where you'd fit right in. You'd be automatically disbarred, which means you'd lose all this.' Chap casually waved his right hand, dismissing the clutter and dust and heaps of old files untouched in years.

Wes jumped right in. 'We're prepared to go to the feds right now, and we could probably stop the mail out of Trumble. Our client would probably be spared any embarrassment. But there's an element of risk our client is not willing to take. What if Ricky has another cohort, either inside or out of Trumble, somebody we haven't found yet, and he somehow manages to expose our client in retaliation?'

Chap was already shaking his head. 'It's too risky. We'd rather work with you, Trevor. We'd rather buy you off, and kill the scam from this office.'

'I cannot be bought,' Trevor said with only a trace of conviction.

'Then we'll lease you for a while, how about that?' Wes said. 'Aren't all lawyers leased by the hour anyway?'

'I suppose, but you're asking me to sell out a client.'

'Your client is a felon who's committing crimes every day from inside a federal prison. And you're just as guilty as he is. Let's not get too sanctimonious here.'

'When you become a criminal, Trevor,' Chap

said gravely, 'you lose the privilege of being self-righteous. Don't preach to us. We know it's just a question of how much money.'

Trevor forgot about the gun for a moment, and he forgot about his law license hanging on the wall behind him, slightly crooked. As he so often did these days when faced with yet another unpleasantry from the practice of law, he closed his eyes and dreamed of his forty-foot schooner, anchored in the warm, still waters of a secluded bay, topless girls on the beach a hundred yards away, and himself barely clad, sipping a beverage on the deck. He could smell the salt water, feel the gentle breeze, taste the rum, hear the girls.

He opened his eyes and tried to focus on Wes across the desk. 'Who is your client?' he asked.

'Not so fast,' Chap said. 'Let's cut the deal first.'

'What deal?'

'We give you some money, and you work as a double agent. We get access to everything. We wire you when you talk to Ricky. We see all the mail. You don't make a move until we discuss it.'

'Why don't you just pay the extortion money?' Trevor asked. 'It'd be a whole lot easier.'

'We've thought of that,' Wes said. 'But Ricky doesn't play fair. If we paid him, then he'd come back for more. And more.'

'No, he wouldn't.'

'Really? What about Quince Garbe in Bakers, Iowa?'

Oh my god, thought Trevor, and he almost said it aloud. How much do they know? All he could manage was a very weak 'Who's he?'

'Come on, Trevor,' Chap said. 'We know where

the money is hidden in the Bahamas. We know about Boomer Realty, and about your little account, currently with a balance of almost seventy thousand bucks.'

'We've dug as far as we can dig, Trevor,' Wes said, jumping in with perfect timing. Trevor was watching tennis, back and forth, back and forth. 'But we've finally hit a rock. That's why we need you.'

Truthfully, Trevor had never liked Spicer. He was a cold, ruthless, nasty little man who'd had the gall to cut Trevor's percentage. Beech and Yarber were okay, but what the hell. It wasn't as if Trevor had a lot of choices here. 'How much?' he asked.

'Our client is prepared to pay a hundred thousand dollars, cash,' Chap said.

'Of course it's cash,' Trevor replied. 'A hundred thousand is a joke. That would be Ricky's first installment. My self-respect is worth a helluva lot more than a hundred thousand.'

'Two hundred thousand,' Wes said.

'Let's do it this way,' Trevor said, trying to willfully suppress his racing heart. 'How much is it worth to your client to have his little secret buried?'

'And you're willing to bury it?' Wes asked.

'Yep.'

'Give me a second,' Chap said, yanking a tiny phone from his pocket. He punched numbers as he opened the door and stepped into the hallway, then mumbled several sentences Trevor could barely hear. Wes stared at a wall, the gun lying peacefully beside his chair. Trevor couldn't see it, though he tried.

Chap returned and stared hard at Wes, as if his

295

eyebrows and wrinkles could somehow deliver a crucial message. In the brief hesitation, Trevor rushed in. 'I think it's worth a million bucks,' he said. 'It could be my last case. You're asking me to divulge confidential client information, a rather egregious act for a lawyer. It would get me disbarred in an instant.'

Disbarment would be a step up for old Trevor, but Wes and Chap let it pass. Nothing good could come from an argument about how valuable his law license might be.

'Our client will pay a million dollars,' Chap said.

And Trevor laughed. He couldn't help it. He cackled as if he'd just heard the perfect punch line, and across the street in the rental they laughed because Trevor was laughing.

Trevor managed to control himself. He stopped chuckling but couldn't wipe off the smile. A million bucks. Cash. Tax-free. Hidden offshore, in another bank, of course, away from the clutches of the IRS and every other branch of the government.

Then he managed to arrange a lawyerly frown, a little embarrassed that he'd reacted so unprofessionally. He was about to say something important when three sharp raps on glass came from the front. 'Oh yes,' he said. 'That would be the coffee.'

'She's gotta go,' Chap said.

'I'll send her home,' Trevor said, standing for the first time, a little light-headed.

'No. Permanently. Get her out of the office.'

'How much does she know?' Wes asked.

'She's dumb as a rock,' Trevor said happily.

'It's part of the deal,' Chap said. 'She goes, and

now. We have a lot to discuss, and we don't want her around.'

The knocking grew louder. Jan had unlocked the door but was caught by the security chain. 'Trevor! It's me!' she shouted through the two-inch crack.

Trevor walked slowly down the hall, scratching his head, searching for words. He came face to face with her through the window of the front door, and he looked very confused.

'Open up,' she growled. 'This coffee is hot.'

'I want you to go home,' he said.

'Why?'

'Why?'

'Yes, why?'

'Because, well, uh –' Words failed him for a second, then he thought of the money. Her exit was part of the deal. 'Because you're fired,' he said.

'What?'

'I said you're fired!' he yelled, loud enough for his new pals in the back to hear.

'You can't fire me! You owe me too much money.'

'I don't owe you a damned thing!'

'How about a thousand bucks in back salary!'

The windows of the rental were crowded with faces hidden by one-way shading. The voices echoed down the quiet street.

'You're crazy!' Trevor screamed. 'I don't owe you a dime!'

'One thousand forty bucks, to be exact!'

'You're nuts.'

'You sonofabitch! I stick with you for eight years, making minimum wage, then you finally get the big case, and you fire me. Is that what you're doing, Trevor!?'

'Something like that! Now leave!'

'Open the door, you little coward!'

'Leave, Jan!'

'Not until I get my things!'

'Come back tomorrow. I'm meeting with Mr. Newman.' With that, Trevor took a step back. When she saw he wasn't opening the door, she lost it. 'You sonofabitch!' she screamed even louder, then hurled the tall latte at the door. The thin, rickety window shook but didn't break, and was instantly covered with creamy brown liquid.

Trevor, safe on the inside, flinched anyway and watched in horror as this woman he knew so well lost her mind. She stormed away, red-faced and cursing, and took a few steps until a rock caught her attention. It was a remnant of a long-forgotten, low-budget landscaping project he'd once okayed at her insistence. She grabbed it, gritted her teeth, cursed some more, then launched it toward the door.

Wes and Chap had done a masterful job of playing it straight, but when the rock crashed through the door window, they couldn't help but laugh. Trevor yelled, 'You crazy bitch!' They laughed again and looked away from each other, trying gamely to tighten up.

Silence followed. Peace had broken out in and around the reception area.

Trevor appeared in the doorway of his office, unscathed, no visible injuries. 'Sorry about that,' he said softly, and went to his chair.

'You okay?' Chap asked.

'Sure. No problem. How about plain coffee?' he asked Wes.

'Forget about it.'

The details were hammered out during lunch, which Trevor insisted they enjoy at Pete's. They found a table in the back, near the pinball machines. Wes and Chap were concerned with privacy, but they soon realized that nobody listened because nobody conducted business at Pete's.

Trevor knocked down three longnecks with his french fries. They had soft drinks and burgers.

Trevor wanted all the money in hand before he betrayed his client. They agreed to deliver a hundred thousand cash that afternoon, and immediately start a wire transfer for the balance. Trevor demanded a different bank, but they insisted on keeping Geneva Trust in Nassau. They assured him their access was limited only to observing the account; they could not tamper with the funds. Besides, the money would arrive there by late afternoon. If they changed banks, then it might take a day or two. Both sides were anxious to complete the deal. Wes and Chap wanted full, immediate protection for their client. Trevor wanted his fortune. After three beers he was already spending it.

Chap left early to fetch the money. Trevor ordered a longneck to go, and they got into Wes' car for a ride around town. The plan was to meet Chap at some spot and take possession of the cash. As they rode south on Highway A1A, along the beach, Trevor began talking.

'Isn't it amazing,' he said, his eyes hidden behind cheap sunglasses, his head back on the headrest.

'What's amazing?'

'The risks people are willing to take. Your client, for example. A rich man. He could hire all the young boys he wanted, yet he answers an ad in a gay magazine and starts writing letters to a complete stranger.'

'I don't understand it,' Wes said, and the two straight boys bonded for a second. 'It's not my job to ask questions.'

'I suppose the thrill is in the unknown,' Trevor said and took a small sip.

'Yeah, probably so. Who's Ricky?'

'I'll tell you when I get the money. Which one's your client?'

'Which one? How many victims are you working on right now?'

'Ricky's been busy lately. Probably twenty or so in the works.'

'How many have you extorted?'

'Two or three. It's a nasty business.'

'How'd you get involved?'

'I'm Ricky's lawyer. He's very bright, very bored, somehow he cooked up this scheme to put the squeeze on gays still in the closet. Against my better judgment, I signed on.'

'Is he gay?' Wes asked. Wes knew the names of Beech's grandchildren. He knew Yarber's blood type. He knew who Spicer's wife was dating back in Mississippi.

'No,' said Trevor.

'He's a sicko then.'

'No, he's a nice guy. So who's your client?'

'Al Konyers.'

Trevor nodded and tried to remember how many letters he'd handled between Ricky and Al. 'What a coincidence. I was making plans to go to Washington to do some background work on Mr. Konyers. Not his real name, of course.'

'Of course not.'

'Do you know his real name?'

'No. We were hired by some of his people.'

'How interesting. So none of us knows the real Al Konyers?'

'That's correct. And I'm sure it'll stay that way.'

Trevor pointed to a convenience store and said, 'Pull in there. I need a beer.'

Wes waited near the gas pumps. It had been determined that they would not say anything about his drinking until the money changed hands and he'd told them everything. They would build some trust, then gently try to nudge him closer to sobriety. The last thing they needed was Trevor at Pete's every night, drinking and talking too much.

Chap was waiting in a matching rental car, in front of a Laundromat five miles south of Ponte Vedra Beach. He handed Trevor a thin, cheap briefcase and said, 'It's all there. A hundred thousand. I'll meet you guys back at the office.'

Trevor didn't hear him. He opened the briefcase and began counting the money. Wes turned around and headed north. Ten stacks of $10,000, all in $100 bills.

Trevor closed it, and crossed over to the other side.

301

TWENTY-SEVEN

Chap's first task as Trevor's new paralegal was to organize the front desk and rid it of anything remotely female. He put Jan's things in a cardboard box, everything from lipstick tubes and nail files to peanut candy and several X-rated romance novels. There was an envelope with eighty dollars and change. The boss claimed it for himself, said it was petty cash.

Chap wrapped her photos in old newspapers and placed them carefully in another box, along with the breakable knickknacks you find on most front desks. He copied her appointment books so they would know who was scheduled to appear in the future. The traffic would be light, he saw with little surprise. Not a single court date anywhere on the horizon. Two office appointments this week, two the next, then nothing. As Chap studied the calendars, it was obvious that Trevor had shifted to a slower gear at about the time the money arrived from Quince Garbe.

They knew Trevor's gambling had picked up in recent weeks, and probably his drinking. Several times Jan had told friends on the phone that

Trevor was spending more time at Pete's than at the office.

As Chap busied himself in the front room, packing her junk, rearranging her desk, dusting and vacuuming and throwing away old magazines, the phone rang occasionally. His job description covered the phone, and he stayed close to it. Most of the calls were for Jan, and he politely explained that she no longer worked there. 'Good for her' seemed to be the general feeling.

An agent dressed as a carpenter arrived early to replace the front door. Trevor marveled at Chap's efficiency. 'How'd you find one so quick?' he asked.

'You just have to work the yellow pages,' Chap said.

Another agent posing as a locksmith followed the carpenter and changed every lock in the building.

Their agreement included the provision that Trevor would see no new clients for at least the next thirty days. He'd argued long and hard against this, as if he had a stellar reputation to protect. Think of all the people who might need him, he'd complained. But they knew how slow the last thirty days had been, and they pressed him until he conceded. They wanted the place to themselves. Chap called those clients with scheduled appointments and told them that Mr. Carson would be tied up in court on the day they were supposed to stop by. Rescheduling would be difficult, Chap explained, but he'd give them a call when there was a break in the action.

'I didn't think he went to court,' one of them said.

'Oh yes,' Chap said. 'It's a really big case.'

When the client list was pared to the core, only one case required an office visit. It was an ongoing child support matter, and Trevor had represented the woman for three years. He couldn't simply give her the boot.

Jan stopped by to cause trouble, and brought with her a boyfriend of sorts. He was a wiry young man with a goatee, polyester pants, white shirt, and tie, and Chap figured he probably sold used cars. No doubt he could have easily thrashed Trevor, but he wanted no part of Chap.

'I'd like to speak to Trevor,' Jan said, her eyes darting around her newly organized desk.

'Sorry. He's in a meeting.'

'And who the hell are you?'

'I'm a paralegal.'

'Yeah, well get your money up front.'

'Thank you. Your things are in those two boxes over there,' Chap said, pointing.

She noticed the magazine racks were purged and neat, the wastebasket was empty, the furniture had been polished. There was a smell of antiseptic, as if they'd fumigated the place where she'd once sat. She was no longer needed.

'Tell Trevor he owes me a thousand dollars in unpaid salary,' she said.

'I will,' Chap replied. 'Anything else?'

'Yeah, that new client yesterday, Yates Newman. Tell Trevor I checked the newspapers. In the past two weeks there's been no accident deaths on

I-95. No record of a female named Newman getting killed either. Something's up.'

'Thank you. I'll tell him.'

She looked around for the last time, and smirked again when she saw the new door. Her boyfriend glared at Chap as if he might just step over and break his neck anyway, but the glaring was done as he headed for the door. They left without breaking anything, both of them carrying a box as they lumbered down the sidewalk.

Chap watched them leave, then began preparing for the challenge of lunch.

Dinner the night before had been nearby, at a crowded new seafood place two blocks from the Sea Turtle Inn. Given the size of the portions, the prices were outrageous, and that was exactly why Trevor, the newest millionaire in Jacksonville, had insisted they eat there. Of course the evening was on him and he spared no expense. He was drunk after the first martini, and didn't remember what he ate. Wes and Chap had explained that their client did not allow them to drink. They sipped designer water and kept his wineglass full.

'I'd find me another client,' Trevor said, laughing at his own humor.

'Guess I'll have to drink for all three of us,' he said halfway through dinner, then proceeded to do just that.

Much to their relief, they learned that he was a docile drunk. They kept pouring, in an effort to see how far he would go. He got quieter and lower in his seat, and long after dessert he tipped the waiter

$300 in cash. They helped him to their car and drove him home.

He slept with the new briefcase across his chest. When Wes turned off his light, Trevor was lying on his bed in his rumpled pants and white cotton shirt, bow tie undone, shoes still on, snoring, and clutching the briefcase tightly with both arms.

The wire had arrived just before five. The money was in place. Klockner had told them to get him drunk, see how he behaved in that condition, then start working in the morning.

At 7:30 A.M. they returned to his house, unlocked the door with their key, and found him pretty much as they'd left him. One shoe was off, and he was curled on his side with the briefcase tucked away like a football.

'Let's go! Let's go!' Chap had yelled while Wes turned on lights and raised shades and made as much noise as possible. Trevor, to his credit, scrambled from bed, raced to the bathroom, took a quick shower, and twenty minutes later walked into his den with a fresh bow tie and not a wrinkle anywhere. His eyes were slightly swollen, but he was smiling and determined to tackle the day.

The million dollars helped. In fact, he'd never conquered a hangover as quickly.

They had a quick muffin and strong coffee at Beach Java, then attacked his little office with vigor. While Chap took care of the front, Wes kept Trevor in his office.

Some of the pieces had fallen into place over dinner. The names of the Brethren had finally been extracted from Trevor, and Wes and Chap had done a splendid job of being surprised.

306

'Three judges?' they'd both repeated, in apparent disbelief.

Trevor had smiled and nodded with great pride, as if he and he alone had been the architect of this masterful scheme. He wanted them to believe that he'd had the brains and skill to convince three former judges that they should spend their time writing letters to lonely gay men so he, Trevor, could rake off a third of their extortion. Hell, he was practically a genius.

Other pieces of the puzzle remained unclear, and Wes was determined to keep Trevor locked away until he had answers.

'Let's talk about Quince Garbe,' he said. 'His post office box was rented to a fake corporation. How'd you learn his true identity?'

'It was easy,' Trevor said, very proud of himself. Not only was he a genius now, but he was a very rich one. He had awakened yesterday morning with a headache, and had spent the first half hour in bed, worrying about his gambling losses, worrying about his dwindling law practice, worrying about his increasing reliance on the Brethren and their scam. Twenty-four hours later, he'd awakened with a worse headache, but one soothed with the balm of a million bucks.

He was euphoric, giddy, and anxious to finish the task at hand so he could get on with life.

'I found a private investigator in Des Moines,' he said, sipping coffee, his feet on his desk, where they belonged. 'Sent him a check for a thousand bucks. He spent two days in Bakers – you been to Bakers?'

'Yep.'

'I was afraid I'd have to go. The scam works best if you can snare some prominent guy with money. He'll pay anything to keep you quiet. Anyway, this investigator found a postal clerk who needed some money. She was a single mother, houseful of kids, old car, small apartment, you get the picture. He called her at night and said he'd give her five hundred dollars cash if she could tell him who was renting Box 788 in the name of CMT Investments. Next morning he called her at the post office. They met in a parking lot during her lunch break. She gave him a piece of paper with the name of Quince Garbe, and he gave her an envelope with five one-hundred-dollar bills. She never asked who he was.'

'Is that a typical method?'

'It worked with Garbe. Curtis Cates, the guy in Dallas, the second one we scammed, was a little more complicated. The investigator we hired there couldn't find anyone on the inside, so he had to watch the post office for three days. Cost eighteen hundred dollars, but he finally saw him and got his license number.'

'Who's next?'

'Probably this guy in Upper Darby, Pennsylvania. His alias is Brant White, and he appears to be a hot prospect.'

'Do you ever read the letters?'

'Never. I don't know what's being said back and forth; don't wanna know. When they're ready to bust somebody, they'll tell me to scope out the box and get a real name. That's if their pen pal is using a front, like your client Mr. Konyers. You'd be amazed how many men use their real names. Unbelievable.'

'Do you know when they send the extortion letters?'

'Oh yeah. They tell me so I can alert the bank in the Bahamas that a wire might be on the way. The bank calls me as soon as the money hits.'

'Tell me about this Brant White in Upper Darby,' Wes said. He was taking pages of notes, as if something might be missed. Every word was being recorded on four different machines across the street.

'They're ready to bust him, that's all I know. He seems hot to trot because they've just swapped a couple of letters. Some of these guys, it's like pulling teeth, judging by the number of letters.'

'But you don't keep track of the letters?'

'There are no records here. I was afraid the feds would show up one day with a search warrant, and I wanted no evidence of my involvement.'

'Smart, very smart.'

Trevor smiled and savored his shrewdness. 'Yeah, well, I've done a lot of criminal law. After a while, you start thinking like a criminal. Anyway, I've been unable to find the right investigator in the Philadelphia area. Still working on it though.'

Brant White was a Langley creation. Trevor could hire every investigator in the Northeast and they'd never find a real person behind the post office box.

'In fact,' he continued, 'I was preparing to go up there myself when I got the call from Spicer telling me to go to Washington and track down Al Konyers. Then you guys showed up, and, well, the rest is history.' His words trailed away as he once again thought of the money. Sure it was a coincidence that Wes and Chap entered his life just hours after he was supposed to go searching for their client. But he didn't care. He could hear the seagulls and feel the hot sand. He could hear the reggae from the island bands, and feel the wind pushing his little boat.

'Is there another contact on the outside?' Wes asked.

'Oh no,' he said vainly. 'I don't need any help. The fewer people involved, the easier the operation works.'

'Very smart,' Wes said.

Trevor leaned back even deeper in his chair. The ceiling above him was cracked and peeling and in need of a fresh coat of enamel. A couple of days ago that might have worried him. Now he knew it would never get painted, not if they expected him to foot the bill. He'd walk out of the place one day very soon, once Wes and Chap here had finished with the Brethren. He'd spend a day or two boxing up his files to store for what reason he was not certain, and he'd give away his outdated and unused law books. He'd find some broke rookie fresh out of law school and looking for a few crumbs around city court, and he'd sell him the furniture and computer for a very reasonable price. And when all the loose ends were covered, he, L. Trevor Carson, Attorney and Counselor-at-Law, would walk out of the office and never look back.

What a glorious day that would be.

Chap interrupted the brief daydream with a sack

of tacos and soft drinks. Lunch had not been discussed among the three, but Trevor had already been checking his watch in anticipation of another long meal at Pete's. He grudgingly took a taco and seethed for a moment. He needed a drink.

'I think it's a good idea to lay off the booze during lunch,' Chap said as they huddled around Trevor's desk and tried not to spill black beans and ground beef.

'Do as you please,' Trevor said.

'I was talking to you,' Chap said. 'At least for the next thirty days.'

'That wasn't part of our deal.'

'It is now. You need to be sober and alert.'

'Why, exactly?'

'Because our client wants you that way. And he's paying you a million dollars.'

'Does he want me to floss twice a day and eat my spinach?'

'I'll ask him.'

'Tell him to kiss my ass while you're at it.'

'Don't overreact, Trevor,' Wes said. 'Just cut back on the drinking for a few days. It'll be good for you.'

If the money had set him free, these two were beginning to choke him. They'd now spent twenty-four hours together, and they showed no signs of leaving. In fact, the opposite was happening. They were moving in.

Chap left early to collect the mail. They'd convinced Trevor that he'd been very sloppy in his habits, and that's how they'd tracked him so easily. Suppose other victims were lurking out there? Trevor'd had little trouble in finding the real names of their victims. Why couldn't the victims do the same to the person behind Aladdin North and Laurel Ridge? From now on, Wes and Chap would take turns collecting the mail. They'd mix things up, visit the post offices at different times, use disguises, real cloak-and-dagger stuff.

Trevor eventually agreed. They seemed to know what they were doing.

There were four letters for Ricky waiting in the Neptune Beach post office, and two for Percy in Atlantic Beach. Chap quickly made the rounds, with a team behind him, watching anyone who might be watching him. The letters were taken to the rental, where they were quickly opened, and copied, then put back together.

The copies were read and analyzed by agents anxious to have something to do. Klockner read them too. Of the six, they'd seen five of the names before. All were lonely middle-aged men trying to muster the nerve to take the next step with Ricky or Percy. None seemed particularly aggressive.

One wall in a converted bedroom of the rental had been painted white and a large map of the fifty states had been stenciled on it. Red pushpins were used to mark Ricky's pen pals. Green for Percy. The names and hometowns of the correspondents were printed in black under the pins.

The nets were getting wider. Ricky had twenty-three men actively writing him; Percy, eighteen. Thirty states were represented. The Brethren were fine-tuning their venture with each passing week. They were now running ads in three magazines, as far as Klockner could tell. They held firm to their profile, and by the third letter they usually knew if a new guy had any money. Or a wife.

It was a fascinating game to watch, and now that they had complete access to Trevor they wouldn't miss a letter.

The day's mail was summarized in two pages, then given to an agent who took off to Langley. Deville had it in hand by 7 P.M.

The first call of the afternoon, at three-ten, came when Chap was washing windows. Wes was still in Trevor's office, grilling him with one question after another. Trevor was weary. He'd missed his nap and he desperately needed a drink.

'Law office,' Chap answered.

'Is this Trevor's office?' the caller asked.

'It is. Who's calling?'

'Who are you?'

'I'm Chap, the new paralegal.'

'What happened to the girl?'

'She no longer works here. What can I do for you?'

'This is Joe Roy Spicer. I'm a client of Trevor's, and I'm calling from Trumble.'

'Calling from where?'

'Trumble. It's a federal prison. Is Trevor there?'

'No sir. He's in Washington, and he should be back here in a couple of hours.'

'Okay. Tell him I'll call back at five.'

'Yes sir.'

Chap hung up and took a deep breath, as did Klockner across the street. The CIA had just had its first live contact with one of the Brethren.

★

313

The second call came at exactly five. Chap answered the phone and recognized the voice. Trevor was waiting in his office. 'Hello.'

'Trevor, this is Joe Roy Spicer.'

'Hello, Judge.'

'What'd you find in Washington?'

'We're still working on it. It's gonna be a tough one, but we'll find him.'

There was a long pause, as if Spicer didn't like this news and was uncertain about how much to say. 'Are you comin tomorrow?'

'I'll be there at three.'

'Bring five thousand dollars cash.'

'Five thousand dollars?'

'That's what I said. Get the money and bring it here. All in twenties and fifties.'

'What are you gonna do –'

'Don't ask stupid questions, Trevor. Bring the damned money. Put it in an envelope with the other mail. You've done it before.'

'All right.'

Spicer hung up without another word. Then Trevor spent an hour discussing the economics of Trumble. Cash was prohibited. Every inmate had a job and his wages were credited to his account. Expenditures, such as long-distance calls, commissary charges, copying expenses, stamps, were all debited against his account.

But cash was present, though seldom seen. It was smuggled in and hidden, and it was used to pay gambling debts and bribe guards for small favors. Trevor was afraid of it. If he, as the attorney, got caught sneaking it in, his visiting privileges would be permanently eliminated. He'd

314

smuggled on two previous occasions, both times $500, in tens and twenties.

He couldn't imagine what they wanted with $5,000.

TWENTY-EIGHT

After three days of stepping over and around Wes and Chap, Trevor needed a break. They wanted breakfast, lunch, and dinner together. They wanted to drive him home and pick him up for work, very early in the morning. They were running what was left of his practice – Chap the paralegal, Wes the office manager, both of them drilling him with endless questions because there was precious little lawyering to be done.

So it was no surprise when they announced they would drive him to Trumble. He didn't need a driver, he explained. He'd made the trip many times, in his trusty little Beetle, and he'd go it alone. This upset them, and they threatened to call their client for guidance.

'Call the damned client, for all I care,' Trevor yelled at them, and they backed down. 'Your client is not running my life.'

But the client was, and they all knew it. Only the money mattered now. Trevor had already performed his Judas act.

He left Neptune Beach in his Beetle, alone, followed by Wes and Chap in their rental car, and behind them was a white van occupied by people Trevor would never see. Nor did he want to see them. Just for the hell of it, he made a sudden turn into a convenience store for a six-pack, and laughed when the rest of the caravan slammed on brakes and barely avoided a wreck. Once out of town, he drove painfully slow, sipping his beer, savoring his privacy, telling himself he could suffer through the next thirty days. He could suffer through anything for a million bucks.

As he neared the village of Trumble, he had the first pangs of guilt. Could he pull this off? He was about to face Spicer, a client who trusted him, a prisoner who needed him, a partner in crime. Could he keep a straight face and act as if things were fine, while every word was being captured by a high-frequency mike in his briefcase? Could he swap letters with Spicer as if nothing had changed, knowing that the mail was being monitored? Plus, he was throwing away his law career, something he'd worked hard to attain and had once been proud of.

He was selling his ethics, his standards, even his morals for money. Was his soul worth a million bucks? Too late now. The money was in the bank. He took a sip of beer and washed away the fading twinges of guilt.

Spicer was a crook, and so were Beech and Yarber, and he, Trevor Carson, was just as culpable. There's no honor among thieves, he kept repeating silently.

Link got a whiff of the beer wafting off Trevor as they walked down the hall and into the visitors' area. At the lawyers' room Trevor looked inside.

He saw Spicer, partially hidden by a newspaper, and was suddenly nervous. What kind of low-life lawyer carries an electronic listening device into a confidential meeting with a client? The guilt hit Trevor like a brick, but there was no turning back.

The mike was almost as big as a golf ball, and had been meticulously installed by Wes in the bottom of Trevor's beaten-up and scruffy black leather briefcase. It was extremely powerful, and would easily transmit everything to the faceless boys in the white van. Wes and Chap were there too, ready with their earphones, anxious to hear it all.

'Afternoon, Joe Roy,' Trevor said.

'Same to you,' Spicer said.

'Lemme see the briefcase,' Link said. He gave a cursory look, then said, 'It looks fine.' Trevor had warned Wes and Chap that Link sometimes took a peek into the briefcase. The mike was covered by a pile of papers.

'Here's the mail,' Trevor said.

'How many?' Link asked.

'Eight.'

'You got any?' Link asked Spicer.

'No. None today,' Spicer replied.

'I'll be outside,' Link said.

The door closed; feet shuffled, and suddenly there was silence. A very long silence. Nothing. Not a word between lawyer and client. They waited in the white van for an eternity, until it was obvious something had gone wrong.

As Link stepped from the small room, Trevor quickly and deftly set the briefcase outside the

318

door, on the floor, where it rested benignly during the remainder of the attorney-client conference. Link noticed it, and thought nothing about it.

'What'd you do that for?' Spicer asked.

'It's empty,' Trevor said, shrugging. 'Let the closed-circuit see it. We have nothing to hide.' Trevor had had one final, brief attack of ethics. Maybe he'd bug the next chat with his client, but not this one. He'd simply tell Wes and Chap that the guard took his briefcase, something that happened occasionally.

'Whatever,' Spicer said, riffling through the mail until he came to two envelopes that were slightly thicker. 'Is this the money?'

'It is. I had to use some hundreds.'

'Why? I plainly said twenties and fifties.'

'That's all I could find, okay. I didn't anticipate needing that much cash.'

Joe Roy studied the addresses on the other letters. Then he asked, rather caustically, 'So what happened in Washington?'

'It's a tough one. One of those rent-a-box outfits in the suburbs, open twenty-four hours, seven days a week, always somebody on duty, lots of traffic. Security is tight. We'll figure it out.'

'Who are you using?'

'Some outfit in Chevy Chase.'

'Gimme a name.'

'Whatta you mean, gimme a name?'

'Give me the name of the investigator in Chevy Chase.'

Trevor drew a blank; invention failed him. Spicer was on to something, his dark liquid eyes glowing with intensity. 'I can't remember,' Trevor said.

'Where'd you stay?'

'What is this, Joe Roy?'

'Give me the name of your hotel.'

'Why?'

'I have the right to know. I'm the client. I'm paying for your expenses. Where did you stay?'

'Ritz-Carlton.'

'Which one?'

'I don't know. The Ritz-Carlton.'

'There are two. Which one was it?'

'I don't know. Not downtown.'

'What flight did you take?'

'Come on, Joe Roy. What is this?'

'What airline?'

'Delta.'

'The flight number?'

'I don't remember.'

'You got back yesterday. Less than twenty-four hours ago. What was your flight number?'

'I don't recall.'

'Are you sure you went to Washington?'

'Of course I went,' Trevor said, but his voice broke a little from a lack of sincerity. He had not planned his lies, and they were breaking down as fast as he put them up.

'You don't know your flight number, which hotel you stayed in, or the name of the investigator you spent the last two days with. You must think I'm stupid.'

Trevor didn't answer. He could only think of the mike in the briefcase and how lucky he was to have it outside. Getting flogged like this was something he'd rather Wes and Chap not hear.

'You've been drinking, haven't you?' Spicer asked, on the attack.

'Yes,' Trevor said, a temporary pause in the lying. 'I stopped and bought a beer.'

'Or two.'

'Yes, two.'

Spicer leaned on his elbows, his face halfway across the table. 'I got some bad news for you, Trevor. You're fired.'

'What?'

'Terminated. Sacked. Gone for good.'

'You can't fire me.'

'I just did. Effective immediately. By unanimous vote of the Brethren. We're notifying the warden so your name will be removed from the list of attorneys. When you leave today, Trevor, don't come back.'

'Why?'

'Lying, drinking too much, sloppy habits, a general lack of trust on behalf of your clients.'

It sounded true enough, but Trevor nevertheless took it hard. It had never crossed his mind that they'd have the guts to fire him. He clenched his teeth and asked, 'What about our little enterprise?'

'It's a clean break. You keep your money, we'll keep ours.'

'Who'll run it on the outside?'

'We'll worry about that. You can pursue an honest living, if you're able.'

'What would you know about an honest living?'

'Why don't you just leave, Trevor? Get up, walk out, it's been lovely.'

'Sure,' he mumbled, his thoughts a blur but two coming to the forefront. First, Spicer had brought no letters, the first time that had happened in many weeks. Second, the cash. What did they need the five grand for? Probably to bribe their new lawyer. They'd planned their ambush well, which was always an advantage they held because they had so much time on their hands. Three very bright men, with lots of idle time. It wasn't fair.

Pride made him stand. He extended a hand and said, 'Sorry it had to happen.'

Spicer shook it reluctantly. Just get out of here, he wanted to say.

When they made eye contact for the last time, Trevor said, almost in a whisper, 'Konyers is the man. Very rich. Very powerful. He knows about you.'

Spicer leapt up like a cat. With their faces just inches apart, he said, also in a whisper, 'Is he watching you?'

Trevor nodded and winked. Then he grabbed the door. He picked up his briefcase without a word to Link. What was he supposed to say to the guard? Sorry, old boy, but the thousand bucks a month in cash you were getting under the table just got cut off. Sad about it? Then ask Judge Spicer here why it happened.

But he let it pass. He was reeling and almost dizzy, and the alcohol didn't help. What would he tell Wes and Chap? That was the question of the moment. They would hammer him as soon as they could catch him.

He said good-bye to Link, and Vince, Mackey,

and Rufus up front, same as always but now for the last time, and walked into the hot sun.

Wes and Chap were parked three cars down. They wanted to talk but played it safe. Trevor ignored them as he tossed his briefcase into the passenger's seat and got in the Beetle. The caravan followed him away from the prison, and slowly down the highway toward Jacksonville.

Their decision to dispose of Trevor had been reached with a maximum of judicial deliberation. They'd spent hours hiding in their little room, studying the Konyers file until every word of every letter was memorized. They'd walked miles around the track, just the three of them, playing one scenario against another. They ate together, played cards together, all the while whispering new theories of who might be watching their mail.

Trevor was the nearest culprit, and the only one they could control. If their victims got sloppy, they could do nothing about it. But if their lawyer had failed to watch his trail, then he had to be fired. He was not the type to evoke a lot of trust in the first place. How many good, busy lawyers would be willing to risk their careers in a gay extortion scheme?

The only hesitation in ridding themselves of Trevor was the fear of what he might do with their money. They expected him to steal it, frankly, and they couldn't stop him. But they were willing to run that risk in return for a bigger score with Mr. Aaron Lake. To get to Lake, they felt they had to eliminate Trevor.

Spicer gave them the details of their meeting,

word for word. Trevor's muted message at the end stunned them. Konyers was watching Trevor. Konyers knew about the Brethren. Did that mean Lake knew about the Brethren? Who was really Konyers now? Why did Trevor whisper this and why did he leave his briefcase outside the door?

With the scrutiny that only a team of bored judges could generate, the questions poured forth. And then the strategies.

Trevor was making coffee in his newly cleaned and shined kitchen when Wes and Chap made their quiet entry and came straight at him.

'What happened?' Wes asked. They were frowning and gave the impression they'd been fretting for some time.

'What do you mean?' Trevor asked, as if things were splendid.

'What happened to the mike?'

'Oh that. The guard took the briefcase and kept it outside.'

They frowned at each other some more. Trevor poured the water into his coffee machine. The fact that it was almost five and he was making coffee was duly noted by the agents.

'Why did he do that?'

'It's routine. About once a month the guard will keep the briefcase during the visit.'

'Did he search it?'

Trevor busied himself by watching the coffee drip. Absolutely nothing was wrong. 'He made his usual quick exam, which I think he does with his eyes closed. He removed the ingoing letters, then took it. The mike was safe.'

'Did he notice the thick envelopes?'

'Of course not. Relax.'

'And the meeting went well?'

'It was routine, except that Spicer had no outgoing mail, which is a bit unusual these days, but it happens. I'll go back in two days and he'll have a stack of letters, and the guard will not even touch the briefcase. You'll get to hear every word. Want some coffee?'

They relaxed in unison. 'Thanks, but we'd better go,' Chap said. There were reports to make, questions to answer. They started for the door, but Trevor stopped them.

'Look, fellas,' he said very politely. 'I'm perfectly capable of getting dressed by myself, and of having a quick bowl of cereal, alone, the way I've done it for many years. And I like to open my office here no earlier than nine. Since it's my office, we'll open at nine, and not a minute sooner. You're welcome to be here at that unholy hour, but not at eight fifty-nine. Stay away from my house, and stay away from this office until nine. Understood?'

'Sure,' one of them said, and they were gone. It didn't really matter to them. They had bugs crawling all over the office, the house, the car, even the briefcase now. They knew where he bought his toothpaste.

Trevor drank the entire pot of coffee and sobered up. Then he began his movements, all carefully planned. He'd started preparing the moment he left Trumble. He assumed they were watching, back there with the boys from the white van. They had the gadgets and the toys, the mikes and the bugs, and Wes and Chap certainly knew

325

how to use them. Money was no object. He told himself to believe they knew everything, just let his imagination run wild and assume they heard every word, followed every turn, and knew exactly where he was at all times.

The more paranoid he was, the better his chances of escape.

He drove to a mall sixteen miles away near Orange Park, in the sprawl south of Jacksonville. He roamed and window-shopped and ate pizza in a near-empty food court. It was difficult not to dart behind a rack of clothes in a store and wait for the shadows to walk by. But he resisted. In a Radio Shack, he bought a small cell phone. One month of long distance with a local service came with the package, and Trevor had what he needed.

He returned home after nine, certain that they were watching. He turned the television on full volume, and made more coffee. In the bathroom he stuffed his cash into pockets.

At midnight, with the house dark and quiet and Trevor evidently asleep, he slipped out the back door and into the night. The air was brisk, the moon full, and he tried his best to look as though he was simply going for a walk on the beach. He wore baggy cargo pants with pockets from the waist down, two denim shirts, and an oversized windbreaker with money stuffed inside the liner. In all, Trevor had $80,000 hidden on himself as he wandered aimlessly south, along the edge of the water, just another beachcomber out for a midnight stroll.

After a mile his pace quickened. When he'd

gone three miles he was exhausted, but he was in a desperate hurry. Sleep and rest would have to wait.

He left the beach and walked into the grungy lobby of a rundown motel. There was no traffic along Highway A1A; nothing was open except for the motel and a convenience store in the distance.

The door rattled enough for the clerk to come to life. A television was on somewhere in the back. A chubby young man of no more than twenty emerged and said, 'Good evening. Need a room?'

'No sir,' Trevor said, as he slowly drew a hand from a pocket and produced a thick roll of bills. He began peeling them off and placing them in a neat row on the counter. 'I need a favor.'

The clerk stared at the money, then rolled his eyes. The beach attracted all kinds. 'These rooms ain't that expensive,' he said.

'What's your name?' Trevor asked.

'Oh, I don't know. Let's say it's Sammy Sosa.'

'All right, Sammy. There's a thousand bucks. It's yours if you'll drive me to Daytona Beach. Take you ninety minutes.'

'It'll take me three hours because I have to drive back.'

'Whatever. That's more than three hundred bucks an hour. When's the last time you made three hundred bucks an hour?'

'It's been a while. I can't do it. I run the night shift, you see. My job is to be on duty from ten until eight.'

'Who's the boss?'

'He's in Atlanta.'

'When's the last time he stopped by?'

'I've never met him.'

'Of course you haven't. If you owned a dump like this, would you stop by?'

'It's not that bad. We have free color TVs and most of the air-conditioning works.'

'It's a dump, Sammy. You can lock that door, drive away, and come back three hours later, and no one will ever know it.'

Sammy looked at the money again. 'You runnin from the law or something?'

'No. And I'm not armed. I'm just in a hurry.'

'So what's up?'

'A bad divorce, Sammy. I have a little money. My wife wants it all and she has some pretty nasty lawyers. I gotta get out of town.'

'You got money, but no car?'

'Look, Sammy. You want the deal or not? If you say no, then I'll walk down the street to the convenience store and find somebody smart enough to take my cash.'

'Two thousand.'

'You'll do it for two thousand?'

'Yep.'

The car was worse than Trevor had expected. It was an old Honda, uncleaned by Sammy or any of the previous five owners. But A1A was deserted, and the trip to Daytona Beach took exactly ninety-eight minutes.

At 3:20 A.M., the Honda stopped in front of an all-night waffle grill, and Trevor got out. He thanked Sammy, said good-bye, and watched him drive away. Inside, he drank coffee and chatted with the waitress long enough to persuade her to go fetch a local phone directory. He ordered pancakes and used his new Radio Shack cell phone to find his way around town.

The nearest airport was Daytona Beach International. A few minutes after four, his cab stopped at the general aviation terminal. Dozens of small planes sat in neat rows on the tarmac. He stared at them as the cab drove away. Surely, he told himself, one of them was available for a quick charter. He just needed one, preferably a twin-engine.

TWENTY-NINE

The back bedroom of the rental had been converted into the meeting room, with four folding tables pushed together to make one large one. It was covered with newspapers, magazines, and doughnut boxes. Every morning at seven-thirty Klockner and his team met over coffee and pastries to review the night and plan the day. Wes and Chap were always there, and six or seven others joined them, depending on who was in town from Langley. The technicians from the front room sometimes sat in, though Klockner did not require their attendance. Now that Trevor was on their side, they needed fewer people to track him.

Or so they thought. Surveillance detected no movement inside his home before seven-thirty, which was not altogether unusual for a man who often went to bed drunk and woke up late. At eight, while Klockner was still meeting in the back, a technician called the house under the ruse of a wrong number. After three rings, the recorder came on and Trevor announced he was not in, please leave a message. This happened occasionally when he was trying to sleep late, but it usually worked well enough to roust him from bed.

Klockner was notified at eight-thirty that the house was completely still; no shower, no radio, no television, no stereo, not a sound from the normal routine.

It was entirely possible he'd gotten drunk at home, by himself, but they knew he had not spent last night at Pete's. He'd gone to a mall and arrived home apparently sober.

'He could be sleeping,' Klockner said, unconcerned. 'Where's his car?'

'In his driveway.'

At nine, Wes and Chap knocked on Trevor's door, then opened it when there was no answer. The rental sprang to life when they reported there was no sign of him, and that his car was still there. Without panic, Klockner sent people to the beach, to the coffee shops near the Sea Turtle, even to Pete's, which was not yet open. They canvassed the area around his house and office, by foot and by car, and saw nothing.

At ten, Klockner called Deville at Langley. The lawyer's missing, was the message.

Every flight to Nassau was checked; nothing turned up, no sign of a Trevor Carson. Deville's contact in Bahamian customs could not be located, nor could he find the banking supervisor they'd been bribing.

Teddy Maynard was in the middle of a briefing on North Korean troop movements when he was interrupted by an urgent message that Trevor Carson, their drunken lawyer in Neptune Beach, Florida, was missing.

331

'How can you lose a fool like him?' Teddy growled at Deville, in a rare display of anger.

'I don't know.'

'I don't believe this!'

'Sorry, Teddy.'

Teddy shifted his weight and grimaced from the pain. 'Find him, dammit!' he hissed.

The plane was a Beech Baron, a twin-engine owned by some doctors and chartered by Eddie, the pilot Trevor had coaxed out of bed at six in the morning with the promise of cash on the spot and more under the table. The official quote was $2,200 for a round-trip between Daytona Beach and Nassau – two hours each way, total of four at $400 an hour, plus some fees for landing and immigration and pilot downtime. Trevor kicked in another $2,000 for Eddie's pocket if the trip took place immediately.

The Geneva Trust Bank in downtown Nassau opened at 9 EST, and Trevor was waiting when the doors were unlocked. He barged into the office of Mr. Brayshears and demanded immediate assistance. He had almost a million dollars in his account – $900,000 from Mr. Al Konyers, through Wes and Chap; about $68,000 from his dealings with the Brethren.

With one eye on the door, he pressed Brayshears to help him move the money, and quickly. The money was owned by Trevor Carson, and no one else. Brayshears had no choice. There was a bank in Bermuda managed by a friend of his, which suited Trevor just fine. He didn't trust Brayshears, and he planned to keep moving the money until he felt safe.

For a moment, Trevor cast a lustful eye at the account of Boomer Realty, currently with a balance of $189,000 and change. It was within his power, during that fleeting moment, to snatch their money too. They were nothing but felons – Beech, Yarber, the odious Spicer, all crooks. And they'd had the arrogance to fire him. They had forced him to run. He tried to hate them enough to take their money, but as he wavered back and forth he felt a soft spot for them. Three old men wasting away in prison.

A million was enough. Besides, he was in a hurry. If Wes and Chap suddenly charged in with guns, it wouldn't have surprised him. He thanked Brayshears and ran from the building.

When the Beech Baron lifted off the runway at Nassau International, Trevor couldn't help but laugh. He laughed at the heist, at the getaway, at his luck, at Wes and Chap and their rich client now minus a million, at his shabby little law office now mercifully idle. He laughed at his past and at his glorious future.

At three thousand feet he gazed downward at the still blue waters of the Caribbean. A lonely sailboat rocked along, its captain at the wheel, a scantily clad lady nearby. That would be him down there in just a few short days.

He found a beer in a carry-on cooler. He drank it and fell sound asleep. They landed on the island of Eleuthera, a place Trevor had seen in a travel magazine he'd bought the night before. There were beaches and hotels and all the water sports.

He paid Eddie in cash, then waited an hour at the small airport for a taxi to happen by.

He bought clothes at a tourist shop in Governor's Harbour, then walked to a hotel on the beach. He was amused at how quickly he stopped watching the shadows. Sure Mr. Konyers had plenty of money, but no one could afford a secret army big enough to track someone through the Bahamas. His future would be one of sheer delight. He would not ruin it by looking over his shoulder.

He drank rum by the pool as fast as the bar maid could bring it. At the age of forty-eight, Trevor Carson welcomed his new life in pretty much the same condition he'd left his old one.

The law office of Trevor Carson opened on time and things proceeded as if nothing was amiss. Its owner had fled, but its paralegal and office manager were on duty to take care of any business that might unexpectedly develop. They listened in all the right places, and heard nothing. The phone rang twice before noon, two misguided inquiries from souls lost in the yellow pages. Not a single client needed Trevor. Not a single friend called to say hello. Wes and Chap busied themselves by going through the few drawers and files they had not yet inspected. Nothing of consequence was found.

Another crew combed every inch of Trevor's house, primarily looking for the cash he'd been paid. Not surprisingly, they didn't find it. The cheap briefcase was in a closet, empty. There was no trail. Trevor had just walked away, with his cash.

The Bahamian banking official was tracked to New York, where he was visiting on government business. He was reluctant to get involved from such a long distance, but he eventually made his calls. Around 1 P.M. it was confirmed that the money had been moved. Its owner had done so in person, and the official would divulge nothing else.

Where did the money go? It was moved by wire, and that's all he would tell Deville. His country's banking reputation depended upon secrecy, and he could reveal only so much. He was corrupt, but he did have his limits.

U.S. Customs cooperated after some initial reluctance. Trevor's passport had been scanned at Nassau International early that morning, and so far he had not left the Bahamas, at least not officially. His passport was red-listed. If he used it to enter another country, U.S. Customs would know it within two hours.

Deville delivered a quick update to Teddy and York, his fourth of the day, then hung around for further instructions.

'He'll make a mistake,' York said. 'He'll use his passport somewhere, and we'll catch him. He doesn't know who's chasing him.'

Teddy seethed but said nothing. His agency had toppled governments and killed kings, yet he was constantly amazed at how the little things often got botched. One bumbling and witless lawyer from Neptune Beach slipped through their net while a dozen people were supposed to be watching. He thought he was beyond surprises.

The lawyer was to be their link, their bridge to the inside of Trumble. For a million dollars they thought they could trust him. There'd been no contingency plan for his sudden flight. Now they were scrambling to develop one.

'We need someone inside the prison,' Teddy said.

'We're close,' Deville answered. 'We're working with Justice and the Bureau of Prisons.'

'How close?'

'Well, in light of what's happened today, I think we can have a man there, inside Trumble, within forty-eight hours.'

'Who is he?'

'His name is Argrow, eleven years with the agency, age thirty-nine, solid credentials.'

'His story?'

'He'll transfer into Trumble from a federal prison in the Virgin Islands. His paperwork will be cleared by the Bureau here in Washington so the warden down there won't ask any questions. He's just another federal prisoner who requested a transfer.'

'And he's ready to go?'

'Almost. Forty-eight hours.'

'Do it now.'

Deville left, again with the burden of a difficult task that suddenly had to be done overnight.

'We have to find out how much they know,' Teddy said, almost in a mumble.

'Yes, but we have no reason to believe they suspect anything,' York said. 'I've read all their mail. There's nothing to indicate they are particularly excited about Konyers. He's just one of their potential victims. We bought the lawyer to stop him from snooping around behind Konyers' post office box. He's off in the Bahamas now, drunk with his money, so he's not a threat.'

'But we still dispose of him,' Teddy said. It was not a question.

'Of course.'

'I'll feel better when he's gone,' Teddy said.

A guard with a uniform but no gun entered the law library in mid-afternoon. He first encountered Joe Roy Spicer, who was by the door to the chamber.

'The warden would like to see you,' the guard said. 'You and Yarber and Beech.'

'What's this about?' Spicer asked. He was reading an old copy of *Field & Stream*.

'None of my business. He wants you now. Up front.'

'Tell him we're busy.'

'I ain't tellin him nothin. Let's go.'

They followed him to the administration building, picking up other guards along the way until a regular entourage emerged from the elevator and stood before the warden's secretary. She and she alone somehow managed to escort the Brethren into the big office where Emmitt Broon was waiting. When she was gone, he said abruptly, 'I have been notified by the FBI that your lawyer is missing.'

No visible response from the three, but each instantly thought about the money hidden offshore.

He continued, 'He disappeared this morning,

and there's some money missing. I don't have the details.'

Whose money? they wanted to ask. No one knew about their hidden funds. Had Trevor stolen from someone else?

'Why are you telling us?' Beech asked.

The real reason was that the Justice Department in Washington had asked Broon to inform the three of the latest news. But the reason he gave was 'Just thought you'd want to know in case you needed to call him.'

They'd fired Trevor the day before, and had not yet informed the administration that he was no longer their attorney of record.

'What're we gonna do for a lawyer?' Spicer asked, as if life couldn't go on.

'That's your problem. Frankly, I'd say you gentlemen have had enough legal counsel to last you many years.'

'What if he contacts us?' Yarber asked, knowing full well they'd never hear from Trevor again.

'You are to notify me immediately.'

They agreed to do so. Whatever the warden wanted. He excused them.

Buster's escape was less complicated than a trip to the grocery. They waited until the next morning, until breakfast was over and most of the inmates were busy with their menial jobs. Yarber and Beech were on the track, walking an eighth of a mile apart so that one was always watching the prison while the other watched the woods in the distance. Spicer loitered near the basketball court, on the lookout for guards.

With no fences or towers or pressing security concerns, guards were not that critical at Trumble. Spicer saw none.

Buster was lost in the whining noise of his Weed Eater, which he slowly worked toward the track. He took a break to wipe his face and look around. Spicer, from fifty yards away, heard the engine die. He turned and quickly gave a thumbs-up, the sign to do it quickly. Buster stepped onto the track, caught up with Yarber, and for a few steps they walked together.

'Are you sure you want to do this?' Yarber asked.

'Yes. I'm positive.' The kid appeared calm and ready.

'Then do it now. Pace yourself. Be cool.'

'Thanks, Finn.'

'Don't get caught, son.'

'No way.'

At the turn, Buster kept walking, off the track, across the freshly cut grass, a hundred yards to some brush, then he was gone. Beech and Yarber saw him go, then turned to watch the prison. Spicer was calmly walking toward them. There was no sign of alarm around the courtyards or dorms or any of the other buildings on the prison grounds. Not a guard in sight.

They walked three miles, twelve laps, at the leisurely pace of fifteen minutes per mile, and when they'd had enough they retired to the coolness of the chamber to relax and listen for news of the escape. It would be hours before they heard a word.

Buster's pace was much faster. Once into the

woods, he began to jog without looking back. Watching the sun, he moved due south for half an hour. The woods were not thick; the undergrowth was thin and did not slow him. He passed a deer stand twenty feet up in an oak tree, and soon found a trail that ran to the southwest.

In his left front pants pocket he had $2,000 cash, given to him by Finn Yarber. In his other front pocket he had a map Beech had drawn by hand. And in his rear pocket he had a yellow envelope addressed to a man named Al Konyers in Chevy Chase, Maryland. All three were important, but the envelope had received the most attention from the Brethren.

After an hour, he stopped to rest, and to listen. Highway 30 was his first landmark. It ran east and west and Beech figured he would find it within two hours. He heard nothing, and started running again.

He had to pace himself. There was a chance his absence would be noticed just after lunch, when the guards sometimes walked the grounds in a very casual inspection. If one of them thought to look for Buster, then other questions might follow. But after two weeks of watching the guards, neither Buster nor any of the Brethren thought this was a possibility.

So he had at least four hours. And probably a lot more because his workday ended at five when he turned in his Weed Eater. When he didn't show, they'd start looking around the prison. After two hours of that, they'd notify the surrounding police agencies that another one had walked away from Trumble. They were never armed and dangerous, and no one got too excited. No search parties. No bloodhounds. No helicopters hovering over the woods. The county sheriff and his deputies would patrol the main roads and warn the citizens to lock their doors.

The escapee's name went into a national computer. They watched his home and watched his girlfriend, and they waited for him to do something stupid.

After ninety minutes of freedom, Buster stopped for a moment and heard the whine of an eighteen-wheeler not far away. The woods stopped abruptly at a right-of-way ditch, and there was the highway. According to Beech's map, the nearest town was several miles to the west. The plan was to hike along the highway, dodging traffic by using ditches and bridges, until civilization in some form was found.

Buster wore the standard prison issue of khaki pants and an olive-colored short-sleeve shirt, both darkened with sweat. The locals knew what the prisoners wore, and if he were spotted walking down Highway 30 someone would call the sheriff. Get to town, Beech and Spicer had told him, and find different clothes. Then pay cash for a bus ticket, and never stop running.

It took him three hours of ducking behind trees and jumping over roadside ditches before he saw the first buildings. He moved away from the highway, and cut through a hay field. A dog growled at him as he stepped onto a street lined with house trailers. Behind one of them he noticed a clothesline with someone's laundry hanging in the windless air. He took a red and white pullover and threw away his olive shirt.

Downtown was nothing more than two blocks of stores, a couple of gas stations, a bank, some sort of town hall, and a post office. He bought denim shorts, a tee shirt, and a pair of boots at a discount store, and changed in the employee restroom. He found the post office inside the town hall. He smiled and thanked his friends at Trumble as he dropped their precious envelope into the Out-of-Town slot.

Buster caught a bus to Gainesville, where he purchased, for $480, the right to ride a bus anywhere in the United States for sixty days. He headed west. He wanted to get lost in Mexico.

THIRTY

The Pennsylvania primary on April 25 was to be Governor Tarry's last mighty effort. Undaunted by his dismal showing in the debate there two weeks earlier, he campaigned with great enthusiasm, but with very little money. 'Lake has it all,' he proclaimed at every stop, feigning pride at being the pauper. He did not leave the state for eleven straight days. Reduced to traveling in a large Winnebago camper, he ate his meals in the homes of supporters, stayed in cheap motels, and worked himself ragged shaking hands and walking neighborhoods.

'Let's talk about the issues,' he pleaded. 'Not about money.'

Lake, too, worked very hard in Pennsylvania. His jet traveled ten times faster than Tarry's RV. Lake shook more hands, made more speeches, and he certainly spent more money.

The result was predictable. Lake received 71 percent of the vote, a landslide so embarrassing to Tarry that he openly talked about quitting. But he vowed to hang on for at least another week, until the Indiana primary. His staff had left him. He was

343

$11 million in debt. He'd been evicted from his campaign headquarters in Arlington.

Yet, he wanted the good people of Indiana to have the opportunity to see his name on the ballot.

And who knew, Lake's shiny new jet might catch on fire, just like the previous one.

Tarry licked his rather deep wounds, and the day after the primary he promised to fight on.

Lake almost felt sorry for him, and he sort of admired his determination to endure until the convention. But Lake, along with everybody else, could do the math. Lake needed just forty more delegates to lock up the nomination, and there were almost five hundred still out there. The race was over.

After Pennsylvania, newspapers across the country confirmed his nomination. His happy handsome face was everywhere, a political miracle. He was praised by many as a symbol of why the system works – an unknown with a message who came from nowhere and captured the attention of the people. Lake's campaign gave hope to every person who dreamed of running for President. It didn't take months of pounding the back roads of Iowa. Skip New Hampshire, it was such a small state anyway.

And he was condemned for buying his nomination. Before Pennsylvania, it was estimated he'd spent $40 million. A more precise number was difficult because the money was being burned on so many fronts. Another $20 million had been spent by D-PAC and half a dozen other high-powered lobbying groups, all working on Lake's behalf.

No other candidate in history had spent anything close.

The criticism stung Lake, and it dogged him day and night. But he'd rather have the money and the nomination than suffer the alternative.

Big money was hardly taboo. Online entrepreneurs were making billions. The federal government, of all bumbling entities, was showing a surplus! Nearly everybody had a job, and an affordable mortgage, and a couple of cars. Lake's nonstop polling led him to believe that the big money was not yet an issue with the voters. In a November matchup against the Vice President, Lake was now practically even.

He once again returned to Washington, from the wars of the West, as a triumphant hero. Aaron Lake, lowly congressman from Arizona, was now the man of the hour.

Over a quiet and very long breakfast, the Brethren read the Jacksonville morning paper, the only one allowed inside Trumble. They were very happy for Aaron Lake. In fact, they were thrilled with his nomination. They were now among his most ardent supporters. Run, Aaron, run.

The news of Buster's walk to freedom had created hardly a stir. Good for him, the inmates were saying. He was just a kid with a long sentence. Run, Buster, run.

The escape wasn't mentioned in the morning paper. They passed it around, reading every word but the want ads and the obituaries. They were waiting now. No more letters would be written; none would be brought in because they'd lost their courier. Their little scam was on hold until they heard from Mr. Lake.

Wilson Argrow arrived at Trumble in an unmarked green van, handcuffed, with two marshals pulling at his elbows. He'd flown with his escorts from Miami to Jacksonville, of course at the expense of the taxpayers.

According to his paperwork, he had served four months of a sixty-month sentence for bank fraud. He had requested a transfer for reasons that were not clear, but his reasons were of no concern to anyone at Trumble. He was just another low-security prisoner in the federal system. They moved around all the time.

He was thirty-nine years old, divorced, college-educated, and his home address, for prison records, was in Coral Gables, Florida. His real name was Kenny Sands, an eleven-year veteran of the CIA, and though he'd never seen the inside of a prison, he'd had much tougher assignments than Trumble. He'd be there a month or two, then request another transfer.

Argrow maintained the cool facade of an old prison hand as he was processed, but his stomach churned. He'd been assured that violence was not tolerated at Trumble, and he could certainly take care of himself. But prison was prison. He suffered through a one-hour orientation by an assistant warden, then was given a quick tour of the grounds. He began to relax when he saw Trumble for himself. The guards had no guns, and most of the inmates looked rather harmless.

His cell mate was an old man with a spotty white

beard, a career criminal who'd seen many prisons and loved Trumble. He told Argrow he planned to die there. The man took Argrow to lunch and explained the vagaries of the menu. He showed him the game room, where groups of thick men bunched around folding tables studying their cards, every one with a cigarette stuck to the lips. 'Gambling's illegal,' his cell mate said with a wink.

They walked to the lifting area outdoors where the younger men sweated in the sun, polishing their tans while their muscles expanded. He pointed to the track in the distance and said, 'You gotta love the federal government.'

He showed Argrow the library, a place he never visited, and he pointed to a corner and said, 'That's the law library.'

'Who uses it?' Argrow asked.

'We usually have some lawyers here. Right now we have some judges too.'

'Judges?'

'Three of 'em.'

The old man had no interest in the library. Argrow followed him to the chapel, then around the grounds again.

Argrow thanked him for the tour, then excused himself and returned to the library, which was empty except for an inmate mopping a floor. Argrow went to the corner, and opened a door to the law library.

Joe Roy Spicer glanced up from his magazine and saw a man he'd never seen before. 'Lookin for something?' he asked, with no effort at being helpful.

Argrow recognized the face from the file. An ex-

347

Justice of the Peace caught stealing bingo profits. What a low-life.

'I'm new,' he said, forcing a smile. 'Just got here. This is the law library?'

'It is.'

'I guess anybody can use it, huh?'

'I guess,' Spicer said. 'You a lawyer?'

'Nope, a banker.'

A few months earlier, Spicer would've hustled him for some legal work, under the table, of course. But not now. They no longer needed the nickel-and-dime stuff. Argrow looked around and did not see Beech and Yarber. He excused himself and returned to his room.

Contact was made.

Lake's plan to rid himself of any memories of Ricky and their ill-fated correspondence depended upon someone else. He, Lake, was simply too scared and too famous to sneak away again in the middle of the night, in a disguise, in the back of a taxi, dashing through the suburbs to an all-night mailbox. The risks were too great; plus he seriously doubted if he could shake the Secret Service anymore. He couldn't count the number of agents now assigned to protect him. Count, hell, he couldn't see them all.

The young lady's name was Jayne. She'd joined the campaign in Wisconsin and had quickly worked her way into the inner circle. A volunteer at first, she now earned $55,000 a year as a personal aide to Mr. Lake, who trusted her completely. She seldom left his side, and they'd already had two little chats about Jayne's future job in the White House.

At the right moment, Lake would give Jayne the key to the box rented by Mr. Al Konyers, and instruct her to get the mail, close out the rental, and leave no forwarding address. He would tell her it was a box he'd rented in an effort to monitor the sale of classified defense contracts, back when he was convinced the Iranians were buying data they should never see. Or some such tale. She would believe him because she wanted to believe him.

If he were incredibly lucky, there would be no letter from Ricky. The box would be forever closed. And if a letter was waiting for Jayne, and if she was the least bit curious, Lake would simply tell her he had no idea who the person was. She would ask nothing further. Blind allegiance was her strong suit.

He waited for the right moment. He waited too long.

THIRTY-ONE

It arrived safely with a million other letters, tons of paperwork shipped into the capital to sustain the government for one more day. It was sorted by zip code, then by street. Three days after Buster dropped it off, Ricky's last letter to Al Konyers made it to Chevy Chase. A routine check of Mailbox America by a surveillance team found it. The envelope was examined, then quickly taken to Langley.

Teddy was between briefings, alone for a moment in his office, when Deville rushed in, holding a thin file. 'We got this thirty minutes ago,' he said as he handed over three sheets of paper. 'It's a copy. The original is in the file.'

The Director adjusted his bifocals and looked at the copies before he began reading. There was the Florida postmark, same as always. The handwriting was too familiar. He knew it was serious trouble before he began reading.

Dear Al:
  In your last letter you tried to end our correspondence. Sorry, it won't be that easy.

I'll get right to the point. I'm not Ricky, and you're not Al. I'm in a prison, not some fancy drug rehab clinic.

I know who you are, Mr. Lake. I know you're having a great year, just wrapped up the nomination and all, and you have all that money pouring in. They give us newspapers here at Trumble, and we've been following your success with great pride.

Now that I know who Al Konyers really is, I'm sure you'd like for me to keep quiet about our little secret. I'll be happy to remain silent, but it will cost you dearly.

I need money, and I want out of prison. I can keep secrets and I know how to negotiate.

The money is the easy part, because you have so much of it. My release will be more complicated, but you're collecting all sorts of very powerful friends. I'm sure you'll think of something.

I have nothing to lose, and I'm willing to ruin you if you don't negotiate with me.

My name is Joe Roy Spicer. I'm an inmate at Trumble Federal Prison. You figure out a way to contact me, and do it quickly.

I will not go away.

Sincerely,
Joe Roy Spicer

The next briefing was canceled. Deville found York, and ten minutes later they were locked away in the bunker.

Killing them was the first option discussed.

Argrow could do it with the right tools; pills and poisons and such. Yarber could die in his sleep. Spicer could drop dead on the track. Beech the hypochondriac could get a bad prescription from the prison pharmacy. They were not particularly fit or healthy, and certainly no match for Argrow. A nasty fall, a broken neck. There were many ways to make it look natural or accidental.

It would have to be done quickly, while they were still waiting for a reply from Lake.

But it would be messy, and unduly complicated. Three dead bodies all at once, in a harmless little prison like Trumble. And the three were close friends who spent most of their time together, and they would each die in different ways within a very short period of time. It would create an avalanche of suspicion. What if Argrow became a suspect? His background was hidden to begin with.

And the Trevor factor frightened them. Wherever he was, there was the chance he would hear of their deaths. The news would scare him even more, but it might also make him unpredictable. There was a chance he knew more than they thought.

Deville would work on plans to take them out, but Teddy was very reluctant. He had no qualms about killing the three, but he was not convinced it would protect Lake.

What if the Brethren had told someone else?

There were too many unknowns. Make the plans, Deville was told, but they would be used only when every other option was gone.

All scenarios were on the table. York suggested, for the sake of argument, that the letter be returned to the box so Lake could find it. It was his screwup to begin with.

'He wouldn't know what to do,' Teddy said.

'Do we?'

'Not yet.'

The thought of Aaron Lake reacting to this ambush and somehow trying to silence the Brethren was almost amusing, but there was a strong element of justice to it. Lake had created this mess; let him handle it.

'Actually, we created this mess,' Teddy said, 'and we'll deal with it.'

They couldn't predict, and thus they couldn't control, what Lake would do. Somehow the fool had avoided their net long enough to drop something in the mail to Ricky. And he'd been so stupid that the Brethren now knew who he was.

Not to mention the obvious: Lake was the type of person who secretly swapped letters with a gay pen pal. He was living a double life, and didn't deserve a lot of confidence.

Confronting Lake was discussed for a moment. York had been advocating a showdown since the first letter from Trumble, but Teddy wasn't convinced. The sleep he'd lost fretting over Lake was always filled with thoughts and hopes of stopping the mail long before now. Quietly take care of the problem, then have a chat with the candidate.

Oh, how he'd love to confront Lake. He'd love to sit him in a chair over there and start flashing copies of all those damned letters up on a screen. And a copy of the ad from *Out and About*. He'd tell him about Mr. Quince Garbe in Bakers, Iowa, another idiot who fell for the scam, and Curtis

Vann Gates in Dallas. 'How could you be so stupid!?' he wanted to scream at Aaron Lake.

But Teddy kept his eye on the bigger picture. The problems with Lake were small when compared to the urgency of national defense. The Russians were coming, and when Natty Chenkov and the new regime seized power the world would change forever.

Teddy had neutralized men far more powerful than three felonious judges rotting away in a federal prison. Meticulous planning was his strong suit. Patient, tedious planning.

The meeting was interrupted by a message from Deville's office. Trevor Carson's passport had been scanned at a departure checkpoint at the airport in Hamilton, Bermuda. He left on a flight to San Juan, Puerto Rico, that was scheduled to land in about fifty minutes.

'Did we know he was in Bermuda?' York asked.

'No, we did not,' Deville answered. 'Evidently he entered without using his passport.'

'Maybe he's not as drunk as we thought.'

'Do we have someone in Puerto Rico?' Teddy asked, his voice only a shade more excited.

'Of course,' said York.

'Let's pick up the scent.'

'Have the plans changed for ole Trevor?' Deville asked.

'No, not at all,' Teddy said. 'Not at all.'

Deville left to deal with the latest Trevor crisis. Teddy called an assistant and ordered mint tea. York was reading the letter again. When they were alone, he asked, 'What if we separate them?'

'Yes, I was thinking of that. Do it quickly, before

354

they have time to confer. Send them to three prisons far apart, put them in isolation for a period of time, make sure they have no phone privileges, no mail. Then what? They still have their secret. Any one of them could conceivably ruin Lake.'

'I'm not sure we have the contacts within the Bureau of Prisons.'

'It can be done. If necessary, I'll have a chat with the Attorney General.'

'Since when did you become friends with the Attorney General?'

'It's a matter of national security.'

'Three crooked judges sitting in a federal prison in Florida can somehow affect national security? I'd like to hear that conversation.'

Teddy sipped his tea with his eyes closed, all ten fingers on the cup. 'It's too risky,' he whispered. 'We make them mad, they become even more erratic. We can't take chances here.'

'Suppose Argrow can find their records,' York said. 'Think about it – these are con men, convicted criminals. No one will believe their story about Lake unless they have proof. The proof is documentation, pieces of paper, originals and copies of the correspondence. The proof exists somewhere. We find it, take it from them, then who will listen?'

Another small sip with his eyes closed, another long pause. Teddy shifted slightly in his chair and grimaced from the pain. 'True,' he said softly. 'But I'm worried about somebody on the outside, somebody we know nothing about. These guys are a step ahead of us, and they always will be. We're trying to figure out what they've known for some time. I'm not sure we'll ever catch up. Maybe they've thought about losing their little files. I'm sure the prison has rules against maintaining such paperwork, so they're already hiding things. The Lake letters are much too valuable not to copy again and stash on the outside.'

'Trevor was their mailman. We've seen every letter he's carried out of Trumble for the past month.'

'We think we have. But we don't know for certain.'

'But who?'

'Spicer has a wife. She's been to see him. Yarber's getting a divorce, but who knows what they're doing. She's visited in the past three months. Or maybe they're bribing guards to run mail for them. These people are bored and they're smart and they're very creative. We can't just assume we know everything they're up to. And if we make a mistake here, if we assume too much, then Mr. Aaron Lake gets himself shoved out of the closet.'

'How? How would they do it?'

'Probably contact a reporter, feed him one letter at a time until he was convinced. It would work.'

'The press would go insane.'

'It can't happen, York. We simply cannot allow it to happen.'

Deville returned in a rush. U.S. Customs had been notified by the authorities in Bermuda ten minutes after the flight departed for San Juan. Trevor would be landing in eighteen minutes.

Trevor was just following his money. He had

quickly grasped the fundamentals of wire transfers, and was now perfecting the art. In Bermuda, he had sent half of it to a bank in Switzerland, and the other half to a bank in Grand Cayman. East or west? That had been the great question. The quickest flight out of Bermuda went to London, but the idea of sneaking through Heathrow scared him. He was not a wanted man, at least not by the government. No charges were filed or pending. But the Brits were so efficient at customs. He'd go west and take his chances in the Caribbean.

He landed in San Juan and went straight to a bar where he ordered a tall draft and studied the flights. No hurry, no pressure, a pocket full of cash. He could go anywhere, do anything, and take as long as he wanted. He had another draft and decided to spend a few days in Grand Cayman, with his money. He went to the Air Jamaica counter and bought a ticket, then back to the bar because it was almost five and he had thirty minutes before boarding.

Of course he flew first class. He boarded early so he could get another drink, and as he watched the other passengers file by he saw a face he'd seen before.

Where was it now? Just moments ago, somewhere in the airport. A long thin face, with a salt-and-pepper goatee, and little narrow slits for eyes behind square glasses. The eyes glanced at him just long enough to meet Trevor's, then looked away, down the aisle, as if nothing had been seen.

It had been near the airline counter, as Trevor was turning to leave after buying his ticket. The face was watching him. The man was standing nearby, studying the departure notices.

When you're on the run, the stray glances and second looks and drifting eyes all seem more suspicious. See a face once, and you don't even know it. See it again a half hour later, and somebody is watching every move you make.

Stop drinking, Trevor ordered himself. He asked for coffee after takeoff, and drank it quickly. He was the first passenger off the plane in Kingston, and he walked quickly through the terminal, through immigration. No sign of the man behind him.

He grabbed his two small bags and raced for the taxi stand.

THIRTY-TWO

The Jacksonville paper arrived at Trumble each morning around seven. Four copies were taken to the game room where they were to be read and left behind for any of the inmates who cared about life on the outside. Most of the time Joe Roy Spicer was the only one waiting at seven, and he usually took one paper for himself because he needed to study the Vegas lines throughout the day. The scene rarely changed: Spicer with a tall Styrofoam cup of coffee, feet on a card table, waiting for Roderick the guard to bring the papers.

So Spicer saw the story first, at the bottom of the front page. Trevor Carson, a local lawyer who'd been missing for some vague reason, found dead outside a hotel in Kingston, Jamaica, shot twice in the head last night, just after dark. The story had no picture of Trevor, Spicer noticed. Why would the paper have one on file? Why would anyone care if Trevor died?

According to Jamaican officials, Carson was a tourist who'd apparently been robbed. An unidentified source close to the scene had tipped the police as to the identity of Mr. Carson, since his wallet was missing. The source seemed to know a lot.

The paragraph recapping Trevor's legal career was quite brief. A former secretary, Jan something or other, had no comment. The story had been thrown together, and placed on the front page only because the victim was a murdered lawyer.

Finn was at the far end of the track, rounding the turn, walking at a rapid clip in the damp early morning air, his shirt already off. Spicer waited at the homestretch, and handed him the paper without a word.

They found Beech waiting in line in the cafeteria, holding his plastic tray and staring forlornly at the crude piles of freshly scrambled eggs. They sat together in a corner, away from everyone else, picking at their food, talking in muted voices.

'If he was running, who the hell was he running from?'

'Maybe Lake was after him.'

'He didn't know it was Lake. He didn't have a clue, did he?'

'Okay, then he was running from Konyers. The last time he was here he said Konyers was the big one. He said Konyers knew about us, then he disappeared the next day.'

'Maybe he was just scared. Konyers confronted him, threatened to expose his role in our scam, and so Trevor, who wasn't the most stable guy to begin with, decided to steal all he could and disappear.'

'Whose money was missing, that's what I want to know.'

'Nobody knows about our money. How could it be missing?'

'Trevor probably stole from everybody he could, then vanished. Happens all the time. Lawyers get in trouble, crack up. They raid their clients' trust funds and bolt.'

'Really?' asked Spicer.

Beech could think of three examples, and Yarber added a couple more for good measure.

'So who killed him?'

'There's a good chance he was just in the wrong part of town.'

'Outside the Sheraton Hotel? I don't think so.'

'Okay, what if Konyers iced him?'

'That's possible. Konyers somehow smoked out Trevor, learned he was the outside contact for Ricky. He put pressure on Trevor, threatened to nail him or whatever, and Trevor ran off to the Caribbean. Trevor didn't know Konyers was Aaron Lake.'

'And Lake certainly has the money and power to track down a drunken lawyer.'

'What about us? By now, Lake knows Ricky ain't Ricky, that Joe Roy here is the man, and that he has friends with him in prison.'

'Question is, can he get to us?'

'I guess I'll find out first,' Spicer said with a nervous laugh.

'And there's always the chance that Trevor was down there in Jamaica hanging around in the wrong part of town, probably drunk and trying to pick up a woman, and he got himself shot.'

They all agreed on this, that Trevor was perfectly capable of getting himself killed.

May he rest in peace. But only if he didn't steal their money.

They scattered for an hour or so. Beech went to the track, to walk and think. Yarber was on the clock, twenty cents an hour trying to fix a computer in the chaplain's office. Spicer went to the library, where he found Mr. Argrow reading law books.

The law library was open, no appointments were necessary, but the unwritten rule was that you should at least ask one of the Brethren before using their books. Argrow was new, and obviously had not yet learned the rules. Spicer decided to give him a break.

They acknowledged each other with a nod, then Spicer got busy clearing tables and straightening books.

'Rumor has it you guys do legal work,' Argrow said from across the room. No one else was present.

'You hear a lot of rumors around here.'

'My case is on appeal.'

'What happened at trial?'

'Jury nailed me on three counts of bank fraud, hiding money offshore, in the Bahamas. The judge gave me sixty months. I've served four. I'm not sure I'm gonna last for fifty-six more. I need some help with my appeals.'

'What court?'

'Virgin Islands. I worked for a big bank in Miami. Lots of drug money.'

Argrow was glib and fast and very anxious to talk, and this irritated Spicer, but only slightly. The reference to the Bahamas had his attention.

'For some reason, I developed a fascination for money laundering. I dealt with tens of millions

362

every day, and it was intoxicating. I could move dirty money quicker than any banker in South Florida. Still can. But I made some bad friends, and bad choices.'

'You admit you're guilty?'

'Sure.'

'That puts you in the distinct minority around here.'

'No, I was wrong, but I think the sentence was too harsh. Somebody said you guys can get some time knocked off.'

Spicer was no longer concerned with the untidy tables and disorganized books. He took a chair nearby and had time to talk. 'We can take a look at your papers,' he said, as if he'd handled a thousand appeals.

You idiot, Argrow wanted to say. You dropped out of high school in the tenth grade, and stole a car when you were nineteen. Your father pulled some strings and got the charges dropped. You got yourself elected Justice of the Peace by voting dead people and stuffing absentee ballots, and now you're stuck in a federal pen and trying to play the big shot.

And, Argrow conceded, you, Mr. Spicer, now have the power to bring down the next President of the United States.

'What will it cost?' Argrow asked.

'How much do you have?' Spicer asked, just like a real lawyer.

'Not much.'

'I thought you knew how to hide money off-shore.'

363

'Oh, I do, believe me. And at one point I had a nice bundle, but I let it get away.'

'So you can't pay anything?'

'Not much. Maybe a couple of thousand or so.'

'What about your lawyer?'

'He got me convicted. I don't have enough to hire a new one.'

Spicer pondered the situation for a moment. He realized he did indeed miss Trevor. Things had been much simpler when they had him on the outside collecting money. 'You still got contacts in the Bahamas?'

'I have contacts all over the Caribbean. Why?'

'Because you'll have to wire the money. Cash is forbidden around here.'

'You want me to wire two thousand dollars?'

'No. I want you to wire five thousand dollars. That's our minimum fee.'

'Where's your bank?'

'In the Bahamas.'

Argrow's eyes narrowed. His eyebrows pushed together, and while he was deep in thought so was Spicer. The minds were in the process of meeting.

'Why the Bahamas?' Argrow asked.

'Same reason you used the Bahamas.'

Thoughts rattled around in both heads. 'Lemme ask you something,' Spicer said. 'You said you could move dirty money quicker than anybody else.'

Argrow nodded and said, 'No problem.'

'Can you still do it?'

'You mean, from in here?'

'Yes. From here.'

Argrow laughed and shrugged as if nothing could be easier. 'Sure. I still have some friends.'

'Meet me here in an hour. I might have a deal for you.'

An hour later, Argrow returned to the law library and found the three judges already in position, behind a table with papers and law books scattered about as if the Supreme Court of Florida were in session. Spicer introduced him to Beech and Yarber, and he took a seat across the table. No one else was present.

They talked for a moment about his appeal, and he was sufficiently vague on the details. His file was en route from the other prison, and they couldn't do much without it.

The appeal was a preliminary topic of conversation, and both sides of the table knew it.

'Mr. Spicer tells us you're an expert on moving dirty money,' Beech said.

'I was until I got caught,' Argrow said modestly. 'I take it you have some.'

'We have a little account offshore, money we've earned doing legal work and a few other things we can't be too open about. As you know, we can't charge for legal work.'

'But we do anyway,' added Yarber. 'And we get paid for it.'

'How much is in the account?' Argrow asked, knowing yesterday's closing balance to the exact penny.

'Let's wait on that,' Spicer said. 'There's a good chance the money may have disappeared.'

Argrow let the words hang for a second, and managed to appear confused. 'I'm sorry?' he said.

'We had a lawyer,' Beech said slowly, each word measured. 'He disappeared and he may have taken the money.'

'I see. And this account is in a bank in the Bahamas?'

'It was. We're not sure if it still is.'

'We doubt the money is still there,' Yarber added.

'But we'd like to know for sure,' Beech added.

'Which bank?' Argrow asked.

'Geneva Trust, in Nassau,' Spicer answered, glancing at his colleagues.

Argrow nodded smugly, as if he knew dark little dirty secrets about the bank.

'You know the bank?' Beech asked.

'Sure,' he said, and let them hang for a long second.

'And?' Spicer said.

Argrow was overcome with smugness and insider knowledge, so he stood rather dramatically and walked around the small library for a moment, deep in thought, then moved closer to the table again. 'Look, what do you guys want me to do? Let's cut to the chase.'

The three looked at him, then at each other, and it was obvious they weren't sure of two things: (a) how much they trusted this man they'd just met, and (b) what they really wanted from him.

But they figured the money was gone anyway, so what was there to lose. Yarber said, 'We're not too sophisticated when it comes to moving dirty money. That was not our original calling, you understand. Forgive our lack of knowledge, but is there any way to verify if the money is still where it once was?'

'We're just not sure if the lawyer stole it,' Beech added.

'You want me to verify the balance of a secret account?' Argrow asked.

'Yes, that's it,' said Yarber.

'We figure that maybe you still have some friends in the business,' Spicer said, treading water. 'And we're just curious as to whether there's any way to do this.'

'You're lucky,' Argrow said, and allowed the words to settle.

'How's that?' Beech asked.

'You picked the Bahamas.'

'Actually, the lawyer picked the Bahamas,' Spicer said.

'Anyway, the banks are pretty loose there. Lots of secrets get told. Lots of officials get bribed. Most of the serious money launderers stay away from the Bahamas. Panama is the current hot spot, and, of course, Grand Cayman is still rock solid.'

Of course, of course, they all three nodded. Offshore was offshore, wasn't it? Just another example of trusting an idiot like Trevor.

Argrow watched them with their puzzled faces and thought how truly clueless they were. For three men with the ability to totally wreck the American electoral process, they seemed awfully naive.

'You haven't answered our question,' Spicer said.

'Anything's possible in the Bahamas.'

'So you can do it?'

'I can try. No guarantees.'

'Here's the deal,' Spicer said. 'You verify the account, and we'll do your appeals for free.'

'That's not a bad deal,' Argrow said.

'We didn't think so. Agreed?'

'Agreed.'

For an awkward second they just looked at one another, proud of their mutual agreement but not sure who moved next. Finally, Argrow said, 'I'll need to know something about the account.'

'Such as?' Beech asked.

'Such as a name or a number.'

'The account name is Boomer Realty, Ltd. The account number is 144-DXN-9593.'

Argrow scribbled some notes on a sheet of scrap paper.

'Just curious,' Spicer said as they watched him closely. 'How do you plan to communicate with your contacts outside?'

'Phone,' Argrow said without looking up.

'Not these phones,' Beech said.

'These phones are not secure,' Yarber said.

'You can't use these phones,' Spicer said with an edge.

Argrow smiled and acknowledged their concerns, then he glanced over his shoulder and removed from his pants pocket an instrument of some sort, not much larger than a pocketknife. He held it between his thumb and index finger, and said, 'This is a phone, gentlemen.'

They stared in disbelief, then watched as he quickly unfolded it from the top and the bottom and from one side so that when properly opened it still looked much too small for any meaningful conversation. 'It's digital,' he said. 'Very secure.'

'Who gets the monthly bill?' asked Beech.

'I have a brother in Boca Raton. The phone and the service were gifts from him.' He snapped it back smartly, and it vanished before their eyes. Then he pointed to the small conference room behind them, to their chamber. 'What's in there?' he asked.

'Just a conference room,' Spicer said.

'It has no windows, right?'

'None, except for that small one in the door.'

'All right. What if I go in there, get on the phone, and go to work. You three stay here and watch out for me. If anyone enters the library, come knock on the door.'

The Brethren readily agreed, though they did not believe Argrow could pull it off.

The call went to the white van, parked a mile and a half from Trumble, on a gravel road sometimes maintained by the county. The road was next to a hay field, farmed by a man they'd yet to meet. The property line for the acreage owned by the federal government was a quarter of a mile away, but from where the van was sitting there was no sign of a prison.

Only two technicians were in the van, one fully asleep in the front seat, the other half asleep in the back with a headset on. When Argrow pressed the Send button on his fancy little gadget, a receiver in the van was activated, and both men came to life.

'Hello,' he said. 'This is Argrow.'

'Yes, Argrow, Chevy One here, go ahead,' said the technician in the back.

'I'm near the three stooges, going through the motions, supposedly making calls to friends on the outside to verify the existence of their account offshore. So far things are progressing even faster than I'd hoped.'

'Sounds like it.'

'Roger. I'll check in later.' He pushed the End button, but kept the phone at his head and appeared to be deep in conversation. He sat on the edge of the table, then he walked around some, glancing occasionally at the Brethren and beyond.

Spicer couldn't help but sneak a look through the window of the door. 'He's making calls,' he said excitedly.

'What do you expect him to be doing?' asked Yarber, who was actually reading recent court decisions.

'Relax, Joe Roy,' Beech said. 'The money disappeared with Trevor.'

Twenty minutes passed, and things became dull as usual. While Argrow worked the phones, the judges killed time, waiting at first, then returning to more pressing business. It had been six days since Buster had left with their letter. No word from Buster meant he'd walked away clean, dropped off the note to Mr. Konyers, and was now somewhere far away. Give it three days to travel to Chevy Chase, and the way they had it figured Mr. Aaron Lake should now be scrambling with a plan to deal with them.

Prison had taught them patience. Only one deadline worried them. Lake had the nomination, which meant he would be vulnerable to their blackmail until November. If he won, they would have four years in which to torment him. But if he lost he would fade quickly away, like all the losers. 'Where's Dukakis now?' Beech had asked.

They had no plans to wait until November. Patience was one thing, release was another. Lake was their one fleeting opportunity to walk away with enough money to coast forever.

They intended to give it a week, then write another letter to Mr. Al Konyers in Chevy Chase. They weren't sure how to smuggle it out, but they would think of something. Link, the guard up front whom Trevor had been bribing for months, was their first prospect.

Argrow's phone presented an option. 'If he'll let us use it,' Spicer said, 'then we can call Lake, call his campaign office, his congressional office, call every damned number we can get from directory assistance. Leave the message that Ricky in rehab really needs to see Mr. Lake. That'll scare the hell out of him.'

'But Argrow will have a record of our calls, or at least his brother will,' Yarber said.

'So? We'll pay him for the calls, and so what if they know we're trying to call Aaron Lake. Right now, half the country is trying to call him. Argrow won't have a clue why we're doing it.'

A brilliant idea, one they pondered for a long time. Ricky in rehab could make the calls and leave the messages. Spicer in Trumble could do the same. Poor Lake would get hounded.

Poor Lake. The man had money pouring in so fast he couldn't count it.

After an hour, Argrow emerged from the chamber and announced he was making progress. 'I need to wait an hour, then make a few more calls,' he said. 'What about lunch?'

They were anxious to continue their discussion, and they did so over sloppy joes and coleslaw.

THIRTY-THREE

Pursuant to Mr. Lake's precise instructions, Jayne drove alone to Chevy Chase. She found the shopping center on Western Avenue, and parked in front of Mailbox America. With Mr. Lake's key, she opened the box, removed eight pieces of junk mail, and placed them in a folder. There were no personal letters. She walked to the counter and informed the clerk that she wished to close the box on behalf of her employer, Mr. Al Konyers.

The clerk pecked a few times on a keyboard. The records indicated that a man named Aaron L. Lake had rented the box in the name of Al Konyers about seven months earlier. The rental had been paid for twelve months, so nothing was owed.

'That guy running for President?' the clerk asked as she slid a form across the counter.

'Yes,' Jayne said, signing where indicated.

'No forwarding address?'

'No.'

She left with the folder and headed south, back into the city. She had not stopped to question Lake's story about renting the box in a clandestine effort to expose fraud at the Pentagon. It didn't matter to her, nor did she have time to ask a lot of questions. Lake had them sprinting eighteen hours a day, and she had far more important things to worry about.

He was waiting in his campaign office, alone for the moment. The offices and hallways around him were choked with assistants of a dozen varieties, all running back and forth as if war were imminent. But Lake was enjoying a lull in the action. She gave him the folder and left.

Lake counted eight pieces of junk mail – taco delivery, long-distance service, a car wash, coupons for this and for that. And nothing from Ricky. The box was closed, there was no forwarding address. The poor boy would have to find someone else to help him through his new life. Lake fed the junk mail and the cancellation agreement through a small shredder under his desk, then paused a moment to count his blessings. He carried little baggage in life, and he'd made few mistakes. Writing to Ricky had been a stupid thing to do, yet he was walking away unscathed. What a lucky man!

He smiled and almost giggled to himself, then he bounced from his chair, grabbed his jacket, and rounded up his entourage. The candidate had meetings to attend, then a lunch with defense contractors.

Oh what a lucky man!

Back in the corner of the law library, with his three new friends guarding the perimeter like sleepy sentries, Argrow fiddled with the phone long enough to convince them he'd pulled strings all through the dark and murky world of offshore banking. Two hours of pacing and mumbling and holding the phone to his head like a frantic stockbroker, and he finally came out of the room.

'Good news, gentlemen,' he said with a tired smile.

They huddled around, eager for the results.

'It's still there,' he said.

Then the great question, the one they'd been planning, the one that would verify whether Argrow was a fraud or a player.

'How much?' asked Spicer.

'A hundred and ninety thousand, and small change,' he said, and they exhaled in unison. Spicer smiled. Beech looked away. Yarber looked at Argrow with a quizzical frown, but a rather pleasant one.

According to their figures, the balance was $189,000, plus whatever paltry rate of interest the bank was paying.

'He didn't steal it,' Beech mumbled, and they shared a pleasant memory of their dead lawyer, who suddenly was not the devil they'd made him out to be.

'I wonder why not,' Spicer mused, almost to himself.

'Well, it's still there,' Argrow said. 'That's a lot of legal work.'

It certainly appeared to be, and since neither of the three could think of a quick fib, they just let it pass.

'I suggest you move it, if you don't mind my

saying so,' Argrow said. 'This bank is known for its leaks.'

'Move it where?' Beech asked.

'If the money were mine, I'd move it to Panama immediately.'

This was a new issue, a train of thought they had not pursued because they had been obsessed with Trevor and his certain theft. But they weighed it carefully anyway, as if the matter had been discussed many times.

'Why would you move it?' Beech asked. 'It's safe, isn't it?'

'I guess,' Argrow answered, quick with a response. He knew where he was going, they did not. 'But you see how loose the confidentiality can be. I wouldn't use banks in the Bahamas these days, especially this one.'

'And we don't know if Trevor told anyone about it,' Spicer said, always anxious to nail the lawyer.

'If you want the money protected, move it,' Argrow said. 'It takes less than a day and you won't have to worry about it. And put the money to work. This account is just sitting there, drawing a few pennies in interest. Put it with a fund manager and let it earn fifteen or twenty percent. You're not gonna be using it any time soon.'

That's what you think, pal, they thought. But he made perfect sense.

'And I assume you can move it?' Yarber said.

'Of course I can. Do you doubt me now?'

All three shook their heads. No sir, they did not doubt him.

'I have some nice contacts in Panama. Think about it.' Argrow glanced at his watch as if he had lost interest in their account and had a hundred pressing matters elsewhere. A punch line was coming, and he didn't want to push.

'We've thought about it,' Spicer said. 'Let's move it now.'

He looked at three sets of eyes, all looking back at him. 'There's a fee involved,' he said, like a seasoned money launderer.

'What kinda fee?' Spicer asked.

'Ten percent, for the transfer.'

'Who gets ten percent?'

'I do.'

'That's rather steep,' said Beech.

'It's a sliding scale. Anything under a million pays ten percent. Anything over a hundred million pays one percent. It's pretty common in the business, and it's exactly the reason I'm wearing an olive prison shirt and not a thousand-dollar suit.'

'That's pretty sleazy,' said Spicer, the man who'd skimmed bingo profits from a charity.

'Let's not preach, okay. We're talking about a small cut from money that's already tainted, both here and there. Take it or leave it.' His tone was aloof, an icy veteran who'd cut much larger deals.

It was only $19,000, and this from a stash they'd been certain was gone. After his 10 percent, they still had $170,000, roughly $60,000 each, and it would've been more if treacherous Trevor hadn't raked so much off the top. And, besides, they were confident of greener pastures just around the corner. The loot in the Bahamas was pocket change.

'It's a deal,' Spicer said as he looked at the other two for approval. They both nodded slowly. All three were thinking the same thing now. If the shakedown of Aaron Lake proceeded as they dreamed it would, then serious money was coming their way. They would need a place to hide it, and maybe someone to help them. They wanted to trust this new guy Argrow. Let's give him the chance.

'Plus, you do my appeals,' Argrow said.

'Yes, we'll do the appeals.'

Argrow smiled and said, 'Not a bad deal. Lemme make some more calls.'

'There's one thing you should know,' Beech said.

'Okay.'

'The lawyer's name was Trevor Carson. He set up the account, directed the deposits, did everything really. And he was murdered night before last in Kingston, Jamaica.'

Argrow searched their faces for more. Yarber handed him a copy of the newspaper, which he read very deliberately. 'Why was he missing?' he asked after a long silence.

'We don't know,' Beech said. 'He left town, and we got word through the FBI that he was missing. We just assumed that he'd stolen our money.'

Argrow handed the paper back to Yarber, and crossed his arms over his chest. He cocked his head, narrowed his eyes, and managed to look suspicious. Let them sweat.

'How dirty is this money?' he asked, as if he might not want to get involved with it after all.

'It's not drug money,' Spicer said quickly, on the defensive, as if all other money was clean.

'We really can't say,' Beech replied.

'You've got a deal,' Yarber said. 'Take it or leave it.'

Good move, old boy, Argrow said to himself. 'The FBI is involved?' he asked.

'Only with the lawyer's disappearance,' Beech said. 'The feds know nothing about the offshore account.'

'Let me get this straight. You got a dead lawyer, the FBI, an offshore account hiding dirty money, right? What've you boys been up to?'

'You don't wanna know,' Beech said.

'I think you're right.'

'No one's forcing you to get involved,' Yarber said.

So a decision had to be made. For Argrow, the red flags were up, the minefield was marked. If he went forward, then he did so armed with sufficient warnings that his three new friends could be dangerous. This, of course, meant nothing to Argrow. But to Beech, Spicer, and Yarber, the opening in their tight little partnership, however slight it might be, meant they were admitting another conspirator. They would never tell him about their scam, and certainly not about Aaron Lake, nor would he share in any more of their loot, unless he earned it with his wiring prowess. But he already knew more than he should. They had no choice.

Desperation played no small role in their decision. With Trevor, they'd had access to the outside, something they'd taken for granted. Now that he was gone, their world had shrunk considerably.

Though they had yet to admit it, firing him had

been a mistake. With perfect hindsight, they should've warned him, and told him everything about Lake and the tampered mail. He'd been far from perfect, but they needed all the help they could get.

Perhaps they would've hired him back a day or two later, but they never had the chance. Trevor bolted, and now he was gone forever.

Argrow had access. He had a phone and friends; he had guts and he knew how to get things done. Perhaps they might need him, but they would take it slowly.

He scratched his head and frowned as if a headache was coming. 'Don't tell me anything else,' he said. 'I don't wanna know.'

He returned to the conference room and closed the door behind him, then perched on the edge of the table and once again seemed to be firing calls all over the Caribbean.

They heard him laugh twice, probably a joke with an old friend surprised to hear his voice. They heard him swear once, but had no idea at whom or for what reason. His voice rose and fell, and try as they might to read court decisions and dust off old books and study Vegas odds, they couldn't ignore the noise from the room.

Argrow put on quite a show, and after an hour of useless chatter he came out and said, 'I think I can finish it tomorrow, but we need an affidavit signed by one of you stating that you are the sole owners of Boomer Realty.'

'Who sees the affidavit?' Beech asked.

'Only the bank in the Bahamas. They're getting a copy of the story about Mr. Carson, and they want verification about the ownership of the account.'

The idea of actually signing any type of document in which they admitted they had anything to do with the dirty money terrified them. But the request made sense.

'Is there a fax machine around here?' Argrow asked.

'No, not for us,' Beech replied.

'I'm sure the warden has one,' Spicer said. 'Just trot up there and tell him you need to send a document to your offshore bank.'

It was unnecessarily sarcastic. Argrow glared at him, then let it pass. 'Okay, tell me how to get the affidavit from here to the Bahamas. How does the mail run?'

'The lawyer was our mail runner,' Yarber said. 'Everything else is subject to inspection.'

'How close do they inspect the legal mail?'

'They glance at it,' Spicer said. 'But they can't open it.'

Argrow paced around a bit, deep in thought. Then, for the benefit of his audience he stepped between two racks of books, so that he could not be seen from outside the law library. He deftly unfolded his gadget, punched numbers, and stuck it to his ear. He said, 'Yes, Wilson Argrow here. Is Jack in? Yes, tell him it's important.' He waited.

'Who the hell's Jack?' Spicer asked from across the room. Beech and Yarber listened but watched for passersby.

'My brother in Boca,' Argrow said. 'He's a real estate lawyer. He's visiting me tomorrow.' Then, into the phone, he said, 'Hey, Jack, it's me. You comin tomorrow? Good, can you come in the morning? Good. Around ten. I'll have some mail going out. Good. How's Mom? Good. I'll see you in the morning.'

The prospect of the resumption of mail intrigued the Brethren. Argrow had a brother who was a lawyer. And he had a phone, and brains, and guts.

He slid the gadget back into his pocket and walked from the racks. 'I'll give the affidavit to my brother in the morning. He'll fax it to the bank. By noon the next day the money will be in Panama, safe and sound and earning fifteen percent. Piece of cake.'

'We're assuming we can trust your brother?' Yarber said.

'With your life,' Argrow said, almost offended by the question. He was walking to the door. 'I'll see you guys later. I need some fresh air.'

THIRTY-FOUR

Trevor's mother arrived from Scranton. She was with her sister, Trevor's aunt Helen. They were both in their seventies and in reasonably good health. They got lost four times between the airport and Neptune Beach, then meandered through the streets for an hour before stumbling on Trevor's house, a place his mother hadn't seen in six years. She hadn't seen Trevor in two years. Aunt Helen hadn't seen him in at least ten, not that she particularly missed him.

His mother parked the rental car behind his little Beetle, and had a good cry before getting out.

What a dump, Aunt Helen said to herself.

The front door was unlocked. The place had been abandoned, but long before its owner fled the dishes had collected in the sink, the garbage had gone unattended, the vacuum hadn't left the closet.

The odor drove Aunt Helen out first, and Trevor's mother soon followed. They had no clue what to do. His body was still in Jamaica, in a crowded morgue, and according to the unfriendly young man she'd talked to at the State Department it would cost $600 to ship him home. The airlines would cooperate, but the paperwork was tied up in Kingston.

It took a half hour of bad driving to find his office. By then, word was out. Chap the paralegal was waiting at the reception desk, trying to look sad and busy at the same time. Wes the office manager was in a back room, just to listen and observe. The phone had rung constantly the day the news broke, but after a round of condolences from fellow lawyers and a client or two it went silent again.

On the front door was a cheap wreath, paid for by the CIA. 'Ain't that nice,' his mother said as they waddled up the sidewalk.

Another dump, thought Aunt Helen.

Chap greeted them and introduced himself as Trevor's paralegal. He was in the process of trying to close the office, a most difficult task.

'Where's the girl?' his mother asked, her eyes red from grieving.

'She left some time back. Trevor caught her stealing.'

'Oh dear.'

'Would you like some coffee?' he asked.

'That would be nice, yes.' They sat on the dusty and uneven sofa, while Chap fetched three coffees from a pot that just happened to be fresh. He sat across from them in an unstable wicker chair. The mother was bewildered. The aunt was curious, her eyes darting around the office, looking for any sign of prosperity. They were not poor, but at their ages affluence would never be attained.

'I'm very sorry about Trevor,' Chap said.

'It's just awful,' Mrs. Carson said, her lip quivering. Her cup shook and coffee splashed onto her dress. She didn't notice it.

'Did he have a lot of clients?' Aunt Helen asked.

'Yes, he was very busy. A good lawyer. One of the best I've ever worked with.'

'And you're a secretary?' Mrs. Carson asked.

'No, I'm a paralegal. I go to law school at night.'

'Are you handling his affairs?' Aunt Helen asked.

'Well, not really,' Chap said. 'I was hoping that's why the two of you were here.'

'Oh, we're too old,' his mother said.

'How much money did he leave?' asked the aunt.

Chap stepped it up a notch. This old bitch was a bloodhound. 'I have no idea. I didn't handle his money.'

'Who did?'

'I guess his accountant.'

'Who's his accountant?'

'I don't know. Trevor was very private about most things.'

'He certainly was,' his mother said sadly. 'Even as a boy.' She splashed her coffee again, this time on the sofa.

'You pay the bills around here, don't you?' asked the aunt.

'No. Trevor took care of his money.'

'Well, listen, young man, they want six hundred dollars to fly him home from down in Jamaica.'

'Why was he down there?' his mother interrupted.

'It was a short vacation,' Chap said.

'And she doesn't have six hundred dollars,' Helen finished.

'Yes I do.'

'Oh, there's some cash here,' Chap said, and Aunt Helen looked satisfied.

'How much?' she asked.

'A little over nine hundred dollars. Trevor liked to keep plenty of petty cash.'

'Give it to me,' Aunt Helen demanded.

'Do you think we should?' asked his mother.

'You'd better take it,' Chap said gravely. 'If not, it will just go into his estate and the IRS will get it all.'

'What else will go into his estate?' asked the aunt.

'All this,' Chap said, waving his arms at the office while he walked to the desk. He removed a wrinkled envelope stuffed with bills of all denominations, money they'd just transferred from the rental across the street. He gave it to Helen, who snatched it and counted the money.

'Nine twenty, and some change,' Chap said.

'Which bank did he use?' Helen asked.

'I have no idea. Like I said, he was very private about his money.' And in one respect, Chap was telling the truth. Trevor had wired the $900,000 from the Bahamas to Bermuda, and from there the trail had disappeared. The money was now hidden in a bank somewhere, in a numbered account accessible only by Trevor Carson. They knew he was headed for Grand Cayman, but the bankers there were famous for their secrecy. Two days of intense digging had revealed nothing. The man who shot him took his wallet and room key, and while the police were inspecting the crime scene the gunman searched the hotel room. There was about $8,000 in cash hidden in a drawer, and nothing else of any significance. Not a clue as to where Trevor had parked his money.

It was the collected wisdom at Langley that Trevor, for some reason, suspected he was being followed closely. The bulk of the cash was missing, though he could have deposited it in a bank in Bermuda. His hotel room had been secured without a reservation – he simply walked in from the street and paid cash for one night.

A person on the run, chasing $900,000 from one island to the next, would have, somewhere on his body or in his effects, evidence of banking activities. Trevor had none.

While Aunt Helen riffled through what would surely be the only cash they'd net from the estate, Wes thought about the fortune lost somewhere in the Caribbean.

'What do we do now?' Trevor's mother asked.

Chap shrugged and said, 'I guess you need to bury him.'

'Can you help us?'

'That's not really something I do. I –'

'Should we take him back to Scranton?' Helen asked.

'That's up to you.'

'How much would that cost?' Helen asked.

'I have no idea. I've never had to do anything like this.'

'But all his friends are here,' his mother said, touching her eyes with a tissue.

'He left Scranton a long time ago,' Helen said, her eyes cutting in all directions, as if there was a long story behind Trevor's leaving Scranton. No doubt, thought Chap.

'I'm sure his friends here will want a memorial service,' Mrs. Carson said.

'Actually, one is already planned,' Chap said.

'It is!' she said, thrilled.

'Yes, it's tomorrow at four o'clock.'

'Where?'

'A place called Pete's, just down the street a few blocks.'

'Pete's?' Helen said.

'It's, well, it's sort of a restaurant.'

'A restaurant. What about a church?'

'I don't think he went.'

'He did when he was a boy,' his mother said in defense.

In memory of Trevor, the five o'clock happy hour would begin at four, and run until midnight. Fifty-cent longnecks, Trevor's favorite.

'Should we go?' asked Helen, sensing trouble.

'I wouldn't think so.'

'Why not?' asked Mrs. Carson.

'It could be a rough crowd. A bunch of lawyers and judges, you know the scene.' He frowned at Helen, and she got the message.

They asked about funeral parlors and cemetery lots, and Chap felt himself getting dragged deeper and deeper into their problems. The CIA killed Trevor. Was it expected to send him off with a proper burial?

Klockner thought not.

After the ladies left, Wes and Chap finished the

removal of the cameras, wires, mikes, and phone taps. They tidied up the place, and when they locked the doors for the last time Trevor's office had never been so orderly.

Half of Klockner's team had already left town. The other half monitored Wilson Argrow inside Trumble. And they waited.

When the forgers at Langley finished with Argrow's court file it fit in a cardboard box, and was flown to Jacksonville on a small jet along with three agents. It contained, among many other things, a fifty-one-page indictment handed down by a grand jury in Dade County, a correspondence file filled with letters from Argrow's defense lawyer and the U.S. Attorney's office, a thick file of motions and other pretrial maneuverings, research memos, a list of witnesses and summaries of their testimonies, a trial brief, jury analysis, an abstract of the trial, presentencing reports, and the final sentence itself. It was reasonably well organized, though not too neat to arouse suspicion. Copies were smudged, and pages were missing, and staples were hanging off, little touches of reality carefully added by the good folks in Documents to create authenticity. Ninety percent of it would not be needed by Beech and Yarber, but its sheer heft made it impressive. Even the cardboard box had some age on it.

The box was delivered to Trumble by Jack Argrow, a semiretired real estate lawyer in Boca Raton, Florida, and brother of the inmate. Lawyer Argrow's state bar certification had been faxed to the proper bureaucrat at Trumble, and his name was on the approved list of attorneys.

Jack Argrow was Roger Lyter, a thirteen-year man with a law degree from Texas. He'd never met Kenny Sands, who was Wilson Argrow. The two shook hands and said hello while Link looked suspiciously at the cardboard box sitting on the table.

'What's in there?' he asked.

'It's my court records,' Wilson said.

'Just paperwork,' Jack said.

Link stuck a hand in the box and moved some files around, and in a few seconds the search was over and he stepped out of the room.

Wilson slid a paper across the desk, and said, 'This is the affidavit. Wire the money to the bank in Panama, then get me written verification so I'll have something to show them.'

'Less ten percent.'

'Yes, that's what they think.'

The Geneva Trust Bank in Nassau had not been contacted. To do so would've been futile and risky. No bank would release funds under the circumstances Argrow was creating. And questions would be raised if he tried.

The wire transfer going to Panama was new money.

'Langley is quite anxious,' the lawyer said.

'I'm ahead of schedule,' the banker replied.

The box was emptied on a table in the law library. Beech and Yarber began sifting through its contents while Argrow, their new client, watched with

390

feigned interest. Spicer had better things to do. He was in the middle of his weekly poker game.

'Where's the sentencing report?' Beech asked, scratching through the pile.

'I want to see the indictment,' Yarber mumbled to himself.

They found what they wanted, and both settled into their chairs for a long afternoon of reading. Beech's choice was quite dull. Yarber's, however, was not.

The indictment read like a crime narrative. Argrow, along with seven other bankers, five accountants, five securities brokers, two lawyers, eleven men identified only as drug traffickers, and six gentlemen from Colombia, had organized and run an elaborate enterprise designed to take drug proceeds in the form of cash and turn them into respectable deposits. At least $400 million had been laundered before the ring was infiltrated, and it appeared as though their man Argrow was right in the thick of things. Yarber admired him. If half the allegations were true, then Argrow was a very smart and talented financier.

Argrow became bored with the silence, and left to stroll around the prison. When Yarber finished reading the indictment, he interrupted Beech and made him read it. Beech enjoyed it too. 'Surely,' he said, 'he's got some of the loot buried somewhere.'

'You know he does,' Yarber agreed. 'Four hundred million bucks, and that's just what they could find. What about his appeal?'

'Doesn't look good. The judge followed the guidelines. I see no error.'

'Poor guy.'

'Poor guy, my ass. He'll be out four years before me.'

'I don't think so, Mr. Beech. We've spent our last Christmas in prison.'

'Do you really believe that?' Hatlee asked.

'Indeed I do.'

Beech placed the indictment back on the table, then stood and stretched and paced around the room 'We should've heard something by now,' he said, very softly though no one else was there.

'Patience.'

'But the primaries are almost over. He's back in Washington most of the time. He's had the letter for a week.'

'He can't ignore it, Hatlee. He's trying to figure out what to do. That's all.'

The latest memo from the Bureau of Prisons in Washington baffled the warden. Who in hell's name up there had nothing better to do than to stare at a map of the federal prisons and decide which one to meddle with that day? He had a brother making $150,000 selling used cars, and there he was making half that much running a prison and reading idiotic memos from pencil-pushers making $100,000 and not doing a productive damned thing. He was so sick of it!

RE: Attorney Visitation, Trumble Federal Prison

Disregard prior order, said order restricting attorney visitation to Tuesdays, Thursdays, and Saturdays, from 3 to 6 P.M.

Attorneys are now permitted to visit seven days a week, from 9 to 7 P.M.

'It takes a dead lawyer to get the rules changed,' he mumbled to himself.

THIRTY-FIVE

Deep in a basement garage, they rolled Teddy Maynard into his van and locked the doors. York and Deville sat with him. A driver and a bodyguard handled the van, which had a television, a stereo, and a small bar with bottled water and sodas, all of which were ignored by Teddy. He was subdued, and dreading the next hour. He was tired – tired of his work, tired of the fight, tired of forcing himself through another day, then another. Fight it six more months, he kept telling himself, then give it up and let someone else worry about saving the world. He'd go quietly to his small farm in West Virginia where he'd sit by the pond, watch the leaves fall into the water, and wait for the end. He was so tired of the pain.

There was a black car in front of them and a gray one behind, and the little convoy made its way around the Beltway, then east across the Roosevelt Bridge and onto Constitution Avenue.

Teddy was silent, so therefore York and Deville were too. They knew how much he loathed what he was about to do.

He talked to the President once a week, usually

on Wednesday morning, always by phone if Teddy had his way. They last saw each other nine months earlier when Teddy was in the hospital and the President needed to be briefed.

The favors usually fell to an equal level, but Teddy hated to be on the same footing with any President. He'd get the favor he wanted, but it was the asking that humiliated him.

In thirty years he'd survived six Presidents, and his secret weapon had been the favors. Gather the intelligence, hoard it, rarely tell the President everything, and occasionally gift-wrap a small miracle and deliver it to the White House.

This President was still pouting over the humiliating defeat of a nuclear test ban treaty Teddy had helped sabotage. The day before the Senate killed it, the CIA leaked a classified report raising legitimate concerns about the treaty, and the President got flattened in the stampede. He was leaving office, a lame duck more concerned with his legacy than with the pressing matters of the country.

Teddy had dealt with lame ducks before, and they were impossible. Since they wouldn't face the voters again, they dwelt on the big picture. In their waning days, they liked to travel, with lots of their friends, to foreign lands where they held summits with other lame ducks. They worried about their presidential libraries. And their portraits. And their biographies, so they spent time with historians. As the clock ticked they became wiser and more philosophical, and their speeches became grander. They talked of the future, of the challenges and the way things ought to be, conveniently ignoring the fact that they'd had eight years to do all the things that needed to be done.

There was nothing worse than a lame duck. And Lake would be just as bad if and when he had the chance.

Lake. The very reason Teddy was trekking to the White House, hat in hand, to grovel for a while.

They were cleared through the West Wing, where Teddy suffered the indignity of having his wheelchair examined by a Secret Service agent. Then they rolled him to a small office next to the cabinet room. A busy appointment secretary explained with no apology that the President was running late. Teddy smiled and waved her off and mumbled something to the effect that this President had never been on time for anything. He'd suffered a dozen fussy secretaries just like her, in the same position she was now in, and the others were long gone. She led York and Deville and the others away, down to the dining room where they would eat by themselves.

Teddy waited, as he knew he would. He read a thick report as if time meant nothing. Ten minutes passed. They brought him coffee. Two years ago the President had visited Langley, and Teddy had made him wait for twenty-one minutes. He needed a favor then, the President did, needed a little matter kept quiet.

The only advantage to being crippled was that he didn't have to jump to his feet when the President entered the room. He finally arrived in a rush, with aides scrambling behind him, as if this would impress Teddy Maynard. They shook hands and made the required greetings as the aides got rid of themselves. A waiter appeared and placed small green salads before them.

'It's good to see you,' the President said with a soft voice and drippy smile. Save it for television, Teddy thought, and he couldn't bring himself to return the lie. 'You're looking well,' he said, only because it was partially true. The President had a new tint to his hair, and he looked younger. They ate their salads, and a quietness settled around them.

Neither wanted a long lunch. 'The French are selling toys to the North Koreans again,' Teddy said, offering a crumb.

'What kinds of toys?' the President asked, though he knew precisely about the trafficking. And Teddy knew he knew.

'It's their version of stealth radar, which is quite stupid because they haven't perfected it yet. But the North Koreans are even dumber because they're paying for it. They'll buy anything from France, especially if the French try to hide it. The French, of course, know this, so it's all cloak and dagger and the North Koreans pay top dollar.'

The President pushed a button and the waiter appeared to remove their plates. Another brought chicken and pasta.

'How's your health?' the President asked.

'About the same. I'll probably leave when you do.'

This pleased them both, the prospect of the other leaving. For no apparent reason, the President then launched into a windy narrative about his Vice President, and what a wonderful job he would do in the Oval Office. He ignored his lunch and became very earnest in his opinions of what a fine human being and brilliant thinker and capable leader the man was. Teddy played with his chicken.

'How do you see the race?' the President asked.

'I honestly don't care,' Teddy said, lying again. 'As I told you, I'm leaving Washington when you do, Mr. President. I'm retiring to my little farm where there's no television, no newspapers, nothing but a little fishing and a lot of rest. I'm tired, sir.'

'Aaron Lake scares me,' the President said.

You don't know the half of it, Teddy thought. 'Why?' he asked, taking a bite. Eat, and let him talk.

'A single issue. Nothing but defense. You give the Pentagon unlimited resources and they'll waste enough to feed the third world. And all this money worries me.'

It never worried you before. The last thing Teddy wanted was a long, useless conversation about politics. They were wasting time. The sooner he finished his business, the sooner he could return to the safety of Langley. 'I'm here to ask a favor,' he said slowly.

'Yes, I know. What can I do for you?' The President was smiling and chewing, enjoying both the chicken and the rare moment of having the upper hand.

'It's a little out of the ordinary. I'd like clemency for three federal prisoners.'

The chewing and smiling stopped, not out of shock but out of confusion. Clemency was usually a simple matter, unless it involved spies or terrorists or infamous politicians. 'Spies?' the President asked.

'No. Judges. One from California, one from Texas, one from Mississippi. They're serving their time together in a federal prison in Florida.'

'Judges?'

'Yes, Mr. President.'

'Do I know these people?'

'I doubt it. The one from California was once the Chief Justice of the Supreme Court out there. He got himself recalled, then had a little trouble with the IRS.'

'I think I remember that.'

'He was convicted of tax evasion and sentenced to seven years. He's served two. The one from Texas was a trial judge, a Reagan appointee. He got drunk and killed a couple of hikers in Yellowstone.'

'I do remember that, but vaguely.'

'It was several years ago. The one from Mississippi was a Justice of the Peace who got caught embezzling bingo profits.'

'I must've missed that one.'

There was a long pause as they considered the questions. The President was bewildered and not certain where to start. Teddy wasn't sure what was coming, so they finished eating in silence. Neither wanted dessert.

The request was an easy one, at least for the President. The felons were virtually unknown, as were their victims. Any fallout would be quick and painless, especially for a politician whose career was less than seven months from being over. He'd been pressured to grant far more difficult pardons. The Russians always had a few spies they lobbied to get back. There were two Mexican businessmen locked away in Idaho for drug trafficking, and every time a treaty of some sort was on the table their clemency became an issue. There was a Canadian Jew serving a life sentence for spying, and the Israelis were determined to get him out.

Three unknown judges? The President could sign his name three times and the matter would be over. Teddy would owe him.

It would be a simple matter, but that was no reason to make things easy for Teddy.

'I'm sure there's a good reason for this request,' he said.

'Of course.'

'A matter of grave national security?'

'Not really. Just a few favors for old friends.'

'Old friends? Do you know these men?'

'No. But I know their friends.'

The lie was so obvious the President almost jumped at it. How could Teddy know the friends of three judges who just happened to be serving time together?

Nothing would come from grilling Teddy Maynard, nothing but frustration. And the President would not stoop that low. He would not beg for information he'd never get. Whatever Teddy's motives were, he would take them to his grave.

'This is a bit confusing,' the President said with a shrug.

'I know. Let's leave it at that.'

'What's the fallout?'

'Not much. The families of the two kids who

were killed in Yellowstone might squawk, and I wouldn't blame them.'

'How long ago was it?'

'Three and a half years.'

'You want me to pardon a Republican federal judge?'

'He's not a Republican now, Mr. President. They have to swear off politics once they take the bench. Now that he's been convicted, he can't even vote. I'm sure if you granted clemency he'd become a big fan of yours.'

'I'm sure he would.'

'If it'll make matters easier, these gentlemen will agree to leave the country for at least two years.'

'Why?'

'It might look bad if they return home. Folks will know that they somehow got out early. This can be kept very quiet.'

'Did the judge from California pay the taxes he tried to evade?'

'He did.'

'And did the guy from Mississippi repay the money he stole?'

'Yes sir.'

All the questions were superficial. He had to ask something.

The last favor had dealt with nuclear spying. The CIA had a report documenting widespread infiltration of Chinese spies in and through virtually all levels of the U.S. nuclear arms program. The President learned of the report just days before he was scheduled to visit China for a highly touted summit. He asked Teddy to come have lunch, and over the same chicken and pasta he asked that the report be held for a few weeks. Teddy agreed. Later, he wanted the report modified to place more blame on prior administrations. Teddy rewrote it himself. When it was finally released, the President deflected most of the blame.

Chinese spying and national security, versus three obscure ex-judges. Teddy knew he would get the pardons.

'If they leave the country, where will they go?' the President asked.

'We're not sure yet.'

The waiter brought coffee. When he was gone, the President asked, 'Will this in any way hurt the Vice President?'

And with the same expressionless face, Teddy said, 'No. How could it?'

'You tell me. I have no clue what you're doing.'

'There's nothing to worry about, Mr. President. I'm asking for a small favor. With a little luck, this will not be reported anywhere.'

They sipped their coffee and both wanted to leave. The President had a full afternoon with more pleasant matters. Teddy needed a nap. The President was relieved it was such a benign request. Teddy was thinking, If you only knew.

'Give me a few days to do the background,' the President said. 'These requests are pouring in, as you might guess. Seems everybody wants something now that my days are numbered.'

'Your last month here will be your happiest,' Teddy said with a rare grin. 'I've seen enough Presidents to know.'

After forty minutes together, they shook hands and promised to talk in a few days.

There were five ex-lawyers at Trumble, and the newest one was using the library when Argrow entered. Poor guy was up to his elbows in briefs and legal pads, working feverishly, no doubt pursuing his last feeble appeal.

Spicer was rearranging law books and managing to look sufficiently busy. Beech was in the chamber, writing something. Yarber was absent.

Argrow removed a folded sheet of white paper from his pocket, and gave it to Spicer. 'I just saw my lawyer,' he whispered.

'What is it?' Spicer asked, holding the paper.

'It's a wire confirmation. Your money is now in Panama.'

Spicer looked at the lawyer across the room, but he was oblivious to everything except his legal pad. 'Thanks,' he whispered. Argrow left the room, and Spicer took the paper to Beech, who examined it carefully.

Their loot was now safely guarded by the First Coast Bank of Panama.

THIRTY-SIX

Joe Roy had dropped eight more pounds, was down to ten cigarettes a day and averaging twenty-five miles a week around the track. Argrow found him there, walking and pacing in the late afternoon heat.

'Mr. Spicer, we need to talk,' Argrow said.

'Two more laps,' Joe Roy said without breaking stride.

Argrow watched him for a few seconds, then jogged fifty yards until he caught up. 'Mind if I join?' he asked.

'Not at all.'

They went into the first turn, stride for stride. 'I just met with my lawyer again,' Argrow said.

'Your brother?' Spicer asked, breathing heavily. His paces were not nearly as graceful as Argrow's, a man twenty years younger.

'Yes. He's talked to Aaron Lake.'

Spicer stopped as if he'd hit a wall. He glared at Argrow, then looked at something in the distance.

'Like I said, we need to talk.'

'I suppose we do,' Spicer said.

'I'll meet you in the law library in half an hour,'

404

Argrow said, and walked away. Spicer watched him until he disappeared.

There was no Jack Argrow, Attorney-at-Law, in the Boca Raton yellow pages, and this initially caused concern. Finn Yarber frantically worked the unsecured phone, seeking directory assistance all over South Florida. When he asked for Pompano Beach, the operator said, 'One moment, please,' and Finn actually smiled. He scribbled down the number, then dialed it. A recorded voice said, 'You've reached the law offices of Jack Argrow. Mr. Argrow keeps hours by appointment only, so please leave your name and number and a brief description of the real estate you're interested in, and we'll get in touch with you.' Finn hung up and walked quickly across the lawn to the law library, where his colleagues were waiting. Argrow was already ten minutes late.

A moment before he arrived, the same ex-lawyer entered the room carrying a bulky file, evidently ready to spend hours trying to save himself. To ask him to leave would cause a fight and create suspicion, and besides he wasn't the type who respected judges anyway. One by one they retired to the small conference room, where Argrow joined them. The room was cramped when Beech and Yarber worked there, writing their letters. With Argrow as the fourth man in, and bringing no small amount of pressure, the room had never felt so crowded. They sat around the small table, each able to reach and touch the other three.

'I know only what I've been told,' Argrow began. 'My brother is a semiretired lawyer in Boca

Raton. He has some money, and for years he's been active in Republican politics in South Florida. Yesterday he was approached by some people who work for Aaron Lake. They had investigated matters and knew that I was his brother, and that I was here in Trumble along with Mr. Spicer. They made promises, swore him to secrecy, and now he's sworn me to secrecy. Now that everything is nice and confidential, I think you can connect the dots.'

Spicer had not showered. His shirt and face were still wet, but his breathing had slowed. Not the slightest sound from either Beech or Yarber. The Brethren were in a collective trance. Keep going, they said with their eyes.

Argrow looked at the three faces, and pushed onward. He reached into his pocket and removed a sheet of paper, which he unfolded and laid before them. It was a copy of their last letter to Al Konyers, the outing letter, the extortion demand, signed by Joe Roy Spicer, current address of Trumble Federal Prison. They had the words memorized, so there was no need to read it again. They recognized the handwriting, that of poor little Ricky, and they realized that it had now come full circle. From the Brethren to Mr. Lake, from Mr. Lake to Argrow's brother, from Argrow's brother back to Trumble, all in thirteen days.

Spicer finally picked it up, and glanced at the words. 'I guess you know everything, don't you?' he asked.

'I don't know how much I know.'

'Tell us what they've told you.'

'You're running a scam, the three of you. You

advertise in gay magazines, you develop relationships with older men, by mail, you somehow learn their true identities, then you extort money from them.'

'That's a pretty fair summary of the game,' Beech said.

'And Mr. Lake made the mistake of answering one of your ads. I don't know when he did this, and I don't know how you found out who he was. There are some gaps in the plot, as far as I'm concerned.'

'It's best to keep it that way,' Yarber said.

'Fair enough. I didn't volunteer for this job.'

'What will you get out of it?' Spicer asked.

'Early release. I'll spend a few more weeks around here, then they'll move me again. I'll walk by the end of the year, and if Mr. Lake gets elected then I'll get a full pardon. Not a bad deal. My brother gets a huge favor from the next President.'

'So you're the negotiator?' Beech said.

'No, I'm the messenger.'

'Then shall we begin?'

'The first move belongs to you.'

'You've got the letter. We want some money and we want out of this place.'

'How much money?'

'Two million each,' Spicer said, and it was obvious this had been discussed many times already. All six eyes watched Argrow, waiting for the twitch, the frown, the shock. But there was no reaction, just a pause as he returned their stares. 'I have no authority here, okay? I can't say yes or no to your demands. All I do is relay the details to my brother.'

'We read the newspaper every day,' Beech said. 'Mr. Lake has more money than he can spend right now. Six million is a drop in the bucket.'

'He has seventy-eight million on hand, with no debt,' Yarber added.

'Whatever,' Argrow said. 'I'm just the courier, the mail runner, sort of like Trevor.'

They froze again, with the mention of their dead lawyer. They glared at Argrow, whose fingernails had caught his attention, and they wondered if the Trevor comment had been laid across the table as some sort of warning. How deadly had their game become? They were giddy with thoughts of money and freedom, but how safe were they now? How safe would they be in the future?

They would always know Lake's secret.

'And the terms of the money?' Argrow asked.

'Very simple,' Spicer said. 'All of it up front, all of it wired to some delightful little place, probably Panama.'

'Okay. Now what about your release?' Argrow asked.

'What about it?' asked Beech.

'Any suggestions?'

'Not really. We thought Mr. Lake could take care of that. He has lots of friends these days.'

'Yes, but he's not the President yet. He can't lean on the right people yet.'

'We're not waiting until January when he's inaugurated,' Yarber said. 'In fact, we're not waiting until November to see if he wins.'

'So you want to be released now?'

'Pretty damned quick,' Spicer said.

'Does it matter how you're released?'

They thought for a moment, then Beech said, 'It has to be clean. We're not running for the rest of our lives. We're not looking over our shoulders.'

'Do you leave together?'

'Yes,' Yarber said. 'And we have some definite plans on how we want to do it. First, though, we need to agree on the important things – money, and exactly when we walk out of here.'

'Fair enough. From this side of the table, they'll want your files, all of the letters and notes and records from your scam. Obviously, Mr. Lake has to receive assurances that the secrets will be buried.'

'If we get what we want,' Beech said, 'he has nothing to worry about. We'll gladly forget we ever heard of Aaron Lake. But we must warn you, so you can warn Mr. Lake, that if anything happens to us, his story will be told anyway.'

'We have an outside contact,' Yarber said.

'It's a delayed reaction,' Spicer added, as if he were helping explain the unexplainable. 'Something happens to us, like, for instance, the same thing that happened to Trevor, and a few days later a little delay bomb goes off. Mr. Lake gets himself outed anyway.'

'That won't happen,' Argrow said.

'You're the messenger. You don't know what will or will not happen,' Beech said, lecturing. 'These are the same people who killed Trevor.'

'You're not sure of that.'

'No, but we have our opinions.'

'Let's not argue something we can't prove, gentlemen,' Argrow said, ending the session. 'I'll see my brother at nine in the morning. Let's meet here at ten.'

Argrow left the room, left them sitting trance-like, deep in thought, counting their money but afraid to start spending it. He headed for the track, but turned away when he saw a group of inmates jogging. He roamed the grounds until he found a secluded spot behind the cafeteria, then he called Klockner.

Within an hour, Teddy was briefed.

THIRTY-SEVEN

The 6 A.M. bell shrieked through Trumble, through the corridors of the dorms, across the lawns, around the buildings, into the surrounding woods. It lasted for exactly thirty-five seconds, most inmates could tell you, and by the time it quit no one was left asleep. It jolted them to life, as if important events were planned that day, and they had to hurry and get ready. But the only pressing matter was breakfast.

The bell startled Beech, Spicer, and Yarber, but it didn't wake them. Sleep had been elusive, the reasons obvious. They lived in different dorms, but not surprisingly they met in line for coffee, at ten minutes after six. With their tall cups, and without a word, they walked to the basketball court where they sat on a bench and sipped in the early dawn. They watched the prison grounds; the track was behind them.

How many more days would they wear their olive shirts and sit in the Florida heat, getting paid pennies by the hour for doing nothing, just waiting, dreaming, drinking endless cups of coffee? Would it be a month, or two? Were they talking

411

days now? The possibilities had robbed them of sleep.

'There are only two possible ways,' Beech was saying. He was the federal judge, and they listened carefully, though it was familiar ground. 'The first is to go back to the sentencing jurisdiction and file a motion for reduced time. Under very narrow circumstances, the trial judge has the authority to release an inmate. It's rarely done, though.'

'Did you ever do it?' Spicer asked.

'No.'

'Asshole.'

'For what reasons?' Yarber asked.

'Only when the prisoner has provided new information about old crimes. If the prisoner provides substantial assistance to the authorities, then he might get a few years off.'

'That's not encouraging,' Yarber said.

'What's number two?' Spicer asked.

'We're shipped out to a halfway house, a really nice one where they don't expect us to live by the rules. The Bureau of Prisons has sole authority in placing inmates. If the right pressure is applied by our new friends in Washington, then the Bureau could move us out and basically forget about us.'

'Don't you have to live in a halfway house?' Spicer asked.

'Yes, in most of them. But they're all different. Some are locked down at night, with strict rules. Others are very laid back. You can phone in once a day, or once a week. It's all up to the Bureau.'

'But we'll still be convicted felons,' Spicer said.

'Doesn't bother me,' Yarber said. 'I'll never vote again.'

412

'I have an idea,' Beech said. 'It came to me last night. As part of our negotiations, we make Lake agree to pardon us if he's elected.'

'I thought of that too,' Spicer said.

'So did I,' said Yarber. 'But who cares if we have a record? The only thing that matters is that we get out.'

'It won't hurt to ask,' Beech replied. They concentrated on their coffee for a few minutes.

'Argrow's making me nervous,' Finn finally said.

'How's that?'

'Well, he drops in here from nowhere, and suddenly becomes our best friend. He does a magic trick with our money, gets it wired to a safer bank. Now he's the point man for Aaron Lake. Keep in mind, somebody out there was reading our mail. And it wasn't Lake.'

'He doesn't bother me,' Spicer said. 'Lake had to find somebody to talk to us. He pulled some strings, did some research, found out that Argrow was here and that he had a brother they could talk to.'

'That's awfully convenient, don't you think?' Beech asked.

'You too, huh?'

'Maybe. Finn's got a point. We know for a fact that somebody else got involved.'

'Who?'

'That's the big question,' Finn said. 'That's why I haven't slept in a week. There's somebody else out there.'

'Do we really care?' Spicer asked. 'If Lake can get us outta here, fine. If somebody else can get us outta here, what's wrong with that?'

'Don't forget Trevor,' Beech said. 'Two bullets in the back of the head.'

'This place might be safer than we think.'

Spicer was not convinced. He finished a drink and said, 'Do you really think that Aaron Lake, a man about to be elected President of the United States, would order a hit on a worthless lawyer like Trevor?'

'No,' replied Yarber. 'He would not. It's much too risky. And he wouldn't kill us. But the mystery man would. The guy who killed Trevor is the same guy who read our mail.'

'I'm not convinced.'

They were together where Argrow expected to find them, in the law library, and they seemed to be waiting. He entered in a rush, and when he was sure they were alone, he said, 'I just met with my brother again. Let's talk.'

They scurried into their little conference room, closed the door, and crowded around the table.

'Things are about to happen very fast,' Argrow said nervously. 'Lake will pay the money. It'll be wired anywhere you want it. I can help if you want; otherwise you can handle it any way you wish.'

Spicer cleared his throat. 'That's two million each?'

'That's what you asked for. I don't know Mr. Lake, but evidently he moves fast.' Argrow glanced at his watch, then looked over his shoulder at the door. 'There are some people from Washington here to meet with you. Big shots.' He yanked some papers from his pocket, unfolded them, and laid a single sheet before each of the three. 'These are presidential pardons, signed yesterday.'

With great reserve, they reached forward, took the papers, and tried to read them. The copies certainly looked official. They gawked at the bold letters across the top, the paragraphs of fussy prose, the compact signature of the President of the United States, and not a single word could be summoned. They were just stunned.

'We've been pardoned?' Yarber finally managed to ask, his voice dry.

'Yes. By the President of the United States.'

They kept reading. They fidgeted and chewed their lips and clenched their jaws, and tried to quietly hide their shock.

'They're gonna come get you, take you to the warden's office where the big shots from Washington will deliver the good news. Act surprised, okay?'

'No problem.'

'That should be easy.'

'How did you get these copies?' Yarber asked.

'They were given to my brother. I have no idea how. Lake has powerful friends. Anyway, here's the deal. You'll be released within the hour. A van will take you to Jacksonville, to a hotel where my brother will meet you. You will wait there until the wire transfers are confirmed, then you will hand over all of your dirty little files. Everything. Understood?'

They nodded in unison. For two million bucks, they could have it all.

'You will agree to leave the country immediately, and not to return for at least two years.'

'How can we leave the country?' Beech asked. 'We have no passports, no papers.'

'My brother will have all of that. You will be given new identities, with a complete set of papers, including credit cards. It's all waiting for you.'

'Two years?' Spicer asked, and Yarber looked at him as if he'd lost his mind.

'That's right. Two years. It's part of the deal. Agreed?'

'I don't know,' Spicer said, his voice shaking. Spicer had never left the United States.

'Don't be foolish,' Yarber snapped at him. 'A complete pardon, a million bucks a year for two years to live abroad. Hell, yes, we'll take the deal.'

A sudden knock on the door terrified them. Two guards were looking in. Argrow grabbed the copies of the pardons and stuffed them in his pocket. 'Do we have a deal, gentlemen?'

They nodded yes, and all three shook hands with him.

'Good,' he said. 'Remember, act surprised.'

They followed the guards to the warden's office where they were introduced to two very stern-faced men from Washington, one from Justice, one from the Bureau of Prisons. The warden completed the stiff introductions without getting any of the names confused, then he handed each of the three a legal-sized document. They were the originals of what Argrow had just shown them.

'Gentlemen,' the warden announced with as much drama as he could muster, 'you've just been pardoned by the President of the United States.' He smiled warmly as if he were responsible for this good news.

They stared at their pardons, still in shock, still dizzy with a thousand questions, the biggest of which was, How in the world did Argrow scoop the warden and show them the documents first?

'I don't know what to say,' Spicer managed to mumble, then the other two mumbled something else.

The man from Justice said, 'The President reviewed your cases, and he felt that you have served enough time. He feels very strongly that you have more to offer your country and your communities by once again becoming productive citizens.'

They stared blankly at him. This fool didn't know they were about to assume new names and flee their country and their communities for at least two years? Who was on which side here?

And why was the President granting them clemency when they had enough dirt to destroy Aaron Lake, the man who was primed to defeat the Vice President? It was Lake who wanted them silenced, not the President? Right?

How could Lake convince the President to pardon them?

How could Lake convince the President to do anything, at this stage of the campaign?

They clutched their pardons and sat speechless, their faces drawn tight as the questions hammered away inside.

The man from the Bureau said, 'You should feel honored. Clemency is very rare.'

Yarber managed to acknowledge him with a quick nod, but even then he was thinking, Who's waiting for us on the outside?

'I think we're in shock,' Beech said.

It was a first for Trumble, inmates so important that the President decided to pardon them. The warden was quite proud of the three, but uncertain as to how the moment should be commemorated. 'When would you like to leave?' he asked, as if they might want to stick around for a party.

'Immediately,' Spicer said.

'Very well. We'll drive you to Jacksonville.'

'No thanks. We'll have someone pick us up.'

'Okay, then, well, there's some paperwork.'

'Make it quick,' Spicer said.

They were each given a duffel bag to collect their things in. As they walked rather briskly across the grounds, all still very close together and in perfect step, with a guard trailing behind, Beech said, under his breath, 'So who got us the damned pardons?'

'It wasn't Lake,' Yarber said, just barely loud enough to be heard.

'Of course it wasn't Lake,' Beech said. 'The President wouldn't do a damned thing Aaron Lake asked him to.'

They walked faster.

'What difference does it make?' Spicer asked.

'It doesn't make any sense,' Yarber said.

'So what're you gonna do, Finn?' Spicer asked without looking. 'Stay here for a few days and ponder the situation? And then if you figure out who's responsible for the pardon, then maybe you won't accept it? Gimme a break.'

'Somebody else is behind this,' Beech said.

'Then I love this somebody else, okay?' Spicer said. 'I'm not sticking around to ask questions.'

They ransacked their rooms in a mad rush, never slowing to say good-bye to anyone. Most of their friends were scattered around the camp anyway.

They had to hurry before the dream was over, or before the President changed his mind.

At eleven-fifteen, they walked through the front door of the administration building, the same door they'd each entered years ago, and waited on the hot sidewalk for their ride. None of the three looked back.

The van was driven by Wes and Chap, though they gave other names. They used so many.

Joe Roy Spicer lay down on the backseat, and covered his eyes with a forearm, determined not to see anything until he was far away. He wanted to cry and he wanted to scream, but he was numb with euphoria – sheer, uncut, unabashed euphoria. He hid his eyes and smiled a goofy smile. He wanted a beer and he wanted a woman, preferably his wife. He'd call her soon. The van was rolling now.

The suddenness of the release had them rattled. Most inmates count the days, and in doing so know with some measure of accuracy when the moment will come. And they know where they're going, and who's waiting for them there.

But the Brethren knew so little. And the few things they knew, they didn't really believe. The pardons were a hoax. The money was nothing but bait. They were being taken away to be slaughtered, same as poor Trevor. The van would stop any minute, and the two goons up front would search their bags, find their dirty files, then murder them in a roadside ditch.

Maybe. But, at the moment, they did not miss the safety of Trumble.

Finn Yarber sat behind the driver and watched the road ahead. He held his pardon, ready to present it to anyone who might stop them and tell them the dream was over. Next to him was Hatlee Beech, who after a few minutes on the road began to cry, not loud, but with his eyes tightly closed and his lips quivering.

Beech had reason to cry. With almost eight and a half years to go, clemency meant more to him than to his two colleagues combined.

Not a word was uttered between Trumble and Jacksonville. As they approached the city, and the roads became wider and the traffic heavier, the three watched the scenery with great curiosity. People were driving, moving about. Planes overhead. Boats on the rivers. Things were normal again.

They inched through the traffic on Atlantic Boulevard, thoroughly enjoying every moment of the congestion. The weather was hot, the tourists were out, ladies with long bronze legs. They saw the seafood restaurants and bars with signs advertising cold beer and cheap oysters. When the street ended, the beach began, and they pulled under the veranda of the Sea Turtle. They followed one of their escorts through the lobby, where they caught a look or two because they were still dressed alike. Up to the fifth floor, and off the elevator before Chap said, 'Your rooms are right here, these three.' He was pointing down the hall. 'Mr. Argrow would like to see you as soon as possible.'

'Where is he?' Spicer asked.

Chap pointed again. 'Over there, in the corner suite. He's waiting.'

'Let's go,' Spicer said, and they followed Chap into the corner, their duffel bags bouncing against one another.

Jack Argrow looked nothing like his brother. He was much shorter, and his hair was blond and wavy where his brother's was dark and thinning. It was just a casual observation, but the three noticed it and mentioned it later. He shook their hands quickly, but only to be polite. He was edgy and talked very fast. 'How's my brother?' he askéd.

'He's doing well,' Beech said.

'We saw him this morning,' Yarber added.

'I want him out of prison,' Jack snapped, as if they'd put him there in the first place. 'That's what I'll get outta this deal, you know. I'll get my brother out of prison.'

They glanced at each other; nothing could be said.

'Have a seat,' Argrow said. 'Look, I don't know how or why I'm in the middle of this, you understand. It makes me very nervous. I'm here on behalf of Mr. Aaron Lake, a man I believe will be elected, and make a great President. I suppose I can then get my brother outta prison. But anyway, I've never met Mr. Lake. Some of his people approached me about a week ago, and asked me to get involved in a very secret and delicate matter. That's why I'm here. It's a favor, okay? I don't know everything, you understand?' The sentences were clipped and rapid. He talked with his hands and his mouth, and he couldn't be still.

The Brethren offered no response, none was really expected.

Two hidden cameras captured the scene and sent it immediately to Langley, where Teddy, York, and Deville watched it on a wide screen in the bunker. The ex-judges, now ex-inmates, looked like freshly released POWs, dazed and subdued, still in uniform, still in disbelief. They sat close together, watching Agent Lyter give a splendid performance.

After trying to outthink and outmaneuver them for three months, it was fascinating to finally see them. Teddy studied their faces, and grudgingly admitted a little admiration. They'd been shrewd and lucky enough to hook the right victim; now they were free and about to be well compensated for their ingenuity.

'Okay, look, the first thing is the money,' Argrow barked. 'Two million each. Where do you want it?'

It was not the sort of question they'd had much experience with. 'What are the options?' asked Spicer.

'You have to wire it somewhere,' Argrow snapped back.

'How about London?' Yarber asked.

'London?'

'We'd like the money, all of it, all six million, to be wired at one time, to one account, to a bank in London,' Yarber said.

'We can wire it anywhere. Which bank?'

'Can you help us with the details?' Yarber asked.

422

'I'm told we can do anything you want. I'll have to make a few calls. Why don't you go to your rooms, take a shower, change clothes. Give me fifteen minutes.'

'We don't have any clothes,' Beech said.

'There are some things in your rooms.'

Chap led them down the hall and gave them their keys.

Spicer stretched out on his king-sized bed and stared at the ceiling. Beech stood in the window of his room and looked north, for miles along the beach, the blue water gently rolling onto the white sand. Children played near their mothers. Couples strolled hand in hand. A fishing boat inched along on the horizon. Free at last, he said to himself. Free at last.

Yarber took a long hot shower – complete privacy, no time limit, plenty of soap, thick towels. Someone had placed a selection of toiletries on the vanity – deodorant, shaving cream, razors, toothpaste, toothbrush, floss. He took his time, then changed into a pair of Bermuda shorts, sandals, and a white tee shirt. He'd be the first to leave, and he needed to find a clothing store.

Twenty minutes later they reconvened in Argrow's suite, and they brought with them their collection of files wrapped neatly in a pillowcase. Argrow was just as anxious as before. 'There's a large bank in London called Metropolitan Trust. We can send the money there, then you can do with it whatever you want.'

'That's fine,' Yarber said. 'The account will be in my name only.'

Argrow looked at Beech and Spicer, and they

nodded their approval. 'Very well. I assume you have a plan of some sort.'

'We do,' Spicer said. 'Mr. Yarber here will leave for London this afternoon, and when he gets there he'll go to the bank and take care of the money. If all goes well, then we'll leave soon afterward.'

'I assure you things will go well.'

'And we believe you. We're just being careful.'

Argrow handed two sheets of paper to Finn. 'I need your signature to start the wire and open the account.' Yarber scribbled his name.

'Have you had lunch?' he asked.

They shook their heads. Lunch was certainly on their minds, but they weren't sure how to proceed.

'You're free men now. There are some nice restaurants just a few blocks from here. Go enjoy yourselves. Give me an hour to start the wire. Let's meet here at two-thirty.'

Spicer was holding the pillowcase. He sort of waved it at Argrow and said, 'Here are the files.'

'Right. Just throw them on the sofa there.'

THIRTY-EIGHT

They left the hotel on foot, without escorts, without restrictions, but with their pardons in their pockets, just in case. And though the sun was warmer near the beach, the air was certainly lighter. The sky was clearer. The world was pretty again. Hope filled the air. They smiled and laughed at almost anything. They strolled along Atlantic Boulevard, and mixed easily with the tourists.

Lunch was steak and beer at a sidewalk café, under an umbrella, so they could watch the foot traffic. Little was said as they ate and drank. Everything was seen, though, especially the younger ladies in shorts and skimpy tops. Prison had turned them into old men. Now they felt the urge to party.

Especially Hatlee Beech. He'd had wealth and status and ambition, and as a federal judge he'd had what was all but impossible to lose – a lifetime appointment. He'd fallen hard, lost everything, and during his first two years at Trumble he'd existed in a state of depression. He had accepted the fact that he would die there, and he'd seriously considered suicide. Now, at the age of fifty-six, he was emerging from the darkness in a rather splendid fashion. He was fifteen pounds lighter, nicely tanned, in good health, divorced from a woman who had money but not much else to offer, and about to collect a fortune. Not a bad middle-aged rally, he told himself. He missed his children, but they'd followed the money and forgotten about him.

Hatlee Beech was ready for some fun.

Spicer was also looking for a party, preferably one at a casino. His wife had no passport, so it would be a few weeks before she could join him in London, or wherever he might land. Did they have casinos in Europe? Beech thought so. Yarber had no idea, and didn't care.

Finn was the most reserved of the three. He drank a soda instead of beer, and he wasn't as interested in the flesh passing by. Finn was already in Europe. He'd never leave, never return to his native land. He was sixty, very fit, now with lots of money, and was about to bum around Italy and Greece for the next ten years.

Across the street, they found a small bookstore and bought several travel books. In a shop specializing in beachwear, they found just the right sunglasses. Then it was time to see Jack Argrow again, and finish the deal.

Klockner and company watched them stroll back to the Sea Turtle. Klockner and company were weary of Neptune Beach and Pete's and the Sea Turtle and the crowded rental. Six agents, including Chap and Wes, were still there, all very anxious

426

for another assignment. The unit had discovered the Brethren, plucked them from inside Trumble, brought them to the beach, and now they just wanted them to leave the country.

Jack Argrow had not touched the files, or at least they appeared untouched. They were still wrapped in the pillowcase, on the sofa, in the exact spot Spicer had left them.

'The wire is under way,' Argrow said as they settled into his suite.

Teddy was still watching from Langley. The three were now wearing all manner of beach garb. Yarber had a fishing cap with a six-inch bill. Spicer had a straw hat and a yellow tee shirt of some variety. Beech, the Republican, wore khaki shorts, a knit pullover, and a golf cap.

There were three large envelopes on the dining table. Argrow handed one to each of the Brethren. 'Inside, you'll find your new identities. Birth certificates, credit cards, Social Security cards.'

'What about passports?' asked Yarber.

'We have a camera set up in the next room. The passports and driver's licenses will need photos. It'll take thirty minutes. There's also five thousand dollars cash in those small envelopes there.'

'I'm Harvey Moss?' Spicer asked, looking at his birth certificate.

'Yes. You don't like Harvey?'

'I guess I do now.'

'You look like a Harvey,' Beech said.

'And who are you?'

'Well, I'm James Nunley.'

'Nice to meet you, James.'

Argrow never cracked a smile, never relaxed for

a second. 'I need to know your travel plans. The people in Washington really want you out of the country.'

'I need to check flights to London,' Yarber said.

'We've already done that. A flight to Atlanta leaves Jacksonville in two hours. At seven-ten tonight, there's a flight leaving Atlanta for London Heathrow that arrives early tomorrow morning.'

'Can you get me a seat?'

'It's already done. First class.'

Finn closed his eyes and smiled.

'And what about you?' Argrow asked, looking at the other two.'

'I kinda like it here,' Spicer said.

'Sorry. We have a deal.'

'We'll take the same flights tomorrow afternoon,' Beech said. 'Assuming all goes well with Mr. Yarber.'

'Do you want us to handle the reservations?'

'Yes, please.'

Chap eased into the room without making a sound, and took the pillowcase from the sofa. He left with the files.

'Let's do the photos,' Argrow said.

Finn Yarber, now traveling as a Mr. William McCoy of San Jose, California, flew to Atlanta without incident. For an hour he walked the concourses of the airport, rode the underground shuttles, and thoroughly enjoyed the frenzy and chaos of being in the midst of a million people in a hurry.

His first-class seat was a massive leather recliner. After two glasses of champagne, he began to drift, and to dream. He was afraid to sleep because he was afraid to wake up. He was certain he would be back on his top bunk, staring at the ceiling, counting off another day at Trumble.

From a pay phone next to Beach Java, Joe Roy finally caught his wife. At first, she thought the call was a hoax and refused to accept the collect charges. 'Who is this?' she asked.

'It's me, dear. I'm no longer in prison.'

'Joe Roy?'

'Yes, now listen. I'm out of prison, okay. Are you there?'

'I think so. Where are you?'

'I'm staying at a hotel near Jacksonville, Florida. I was released from prison this morning.'

'Released? But how –'

'Don't ask, okay. I'll explain everything later. I'm leaving tomorrow for London. I want you to go to the post office first thing in the morning, and get an application for a passport.'

'London? Did you say London?'

'Yes.'

'England?'

'That's it, yes. I have to go there for a while. It's part of the deal.'

'For how long?'

'A couple of years. Listen, I know it's hard to believe, but I'm free and we're gonna live abroad for a couple of years.'

'What kinda deal? Have you escaped, Joe Roy? You said it'd be easy to do.'

'No. I have been released.'

'But you got more than twenty months to go.'

'Not anymore. Listen, get the application for a passport and follow the instructions.'

'Why do I need a passport?'

'So we can meet in Europe.'

'For two years?'

'Yes, that's it.'

'But Mother's sick. I can't just run off and leave Mother.'

He thought of all the things he'd like to say about her mother, then let it pass. A deep breath, a glance down the street. 'I'm going away,' he said. 'I have no choice.'

'Just come home,' she said.

'I can't. I'll explain it later.'

'An explanation would be nice.'

'I'll call you tomorrow.'

Beech and Spicer ate seafood in a restaurant crowded with people much younger. They roamed the sidewalks and eventually found their way to Pete's Bar and Grill, where they watched the Braves and enjoyed the noise.

Finn was somewhere over the Atlantic, following their money.

The customs agent at Heathrow barely glanced at Finn's passport, which was a marvel of forgery. It was well used and had accompanied Mr. William McCoy around the world. Aaron Lake did indeed have powerful friends.

Finn took a taxi to the Basil Street Hotel in Knightsbridge, and paid cash for the smallest room available. He and Beech had selected the hotel at random from a travel guide. It was an old-fashioned place, filled with antiques, and it rambled

430

from floor to floor. At the small restaurant upstairs, he had breakfast of coffee, eggs, and black sausage, then went for a walk. At ten, his taxi stopped in front of the Metropolitan Trust in the City. The receptionist didn't care for his attire – jeans and a pullover – but when she realized he was an American she shrugged and seemed to tolerate it.

They made him wait for an hour, but he didn't mind it at all. Finn was nervous, but didn't show it. He'd wait for days, weeks, months to get the money. He'd learned how to be patient. The Mr. MacGregor who was in charge of the wire finally came for him. The money had just arrived, sorry for the delay. All six million bucks had crossed the Atlantic safely, and was now on British soil.

But not for long. 'I'd like to wire it to Switzerland,' Finn said, with the proper dose of confidence and experience.

That afternoon, Beech and Spicer flew to Atlanta. Like Yarber, they roamed the airport with unrestrained freedom while waiting for their London flight. They sat together in first class, ate and drank for hours, watched movies, tried to sleep as they crossed the ocean.

Much to their surprise, Yarber was waiting when they cleared customs at Heathrow. He delivered the wonderful news that the money had come and gone. It was hidden in Switzerland. He surprised them again with the idea of leaving immediately.

'They know we're here,' he said over coffee in an airport bar. 'Let's shake them.'

'You think they're following us?' Beech asked.

'Let's assume they are.'

'But why?' Spicer asked.

They discussed it for half an hour, then began looking for flights. Alitalia to Rome caught their attention. First class, of course.

'Do they speak English in Rome?' Spicer asked as they were boarding.

'Actually, they speak Italian,' Yarber said.

'You think the Pope will see us?'

'He's probably busy.'

THIRTY-NINE

Buster zigzagged westward for days until he made his final bus stop in San Diego. The ocean attracted him, the first water he'd seen in months. He hung around the docks looking for odd jobs and chatting with the regulars. A charter boat captain hired him as a gopher, and he jumped ship in Los Cabos, Mexico, at the southern tip of the Baja. The harbor there was filled with expensive fishing boats, much nicer than the ones he and his father once traded. He met a few of the captains, and within two days had a job as a deckhand. The customers were wealthy Americans from Texas and California, and they spent more time drinking than fishing. He earned no wages or salary, but worked for tips, which invariably got larger the more the clients drank. A slow day would net him $200; a good day, $500, all cash. He lived in an inexpensive motel, and after a few days stopped looking over his shoulder. Los Cabos quickly became his home.

Wilson Argrow was suddenly transferred out of

Trumble and sent to a halfway house in Milwaukee, where he stayed exactly one night before walking away. Since he didn't exist he couldn't be found. Jack Argrow met him at the airport with tickets, and they flew together to D.C. Two days after leaving Florida, the Argrow brothers, Kenny Sands and Roger Lyter, reported to Langley for their next assignment.

Three days before he was scheduled to depart D.C. for the convention in Denver, Aaron Lake arrived at Langley for lunch with the Director. It was to be a joyful occasion, the conquering candidate once again thanking the genius who'd asked him to run. His acceptance speech had been written for a month, but Teddy had a few suggestions he wanted to discuss.

He was escorted to Teddy's office, where the old man was waiting under his quilt, as always. He looked so pale and tired, Lake thought. The aides vanished, the door was closed, and Lake noticed that no table had been prepared. They sat away from the desk, face to face, very close together.

Teddy liked the speech and made just a few comments. 'Your speeches are getting too long,' he said quietly. But Lake had so much to say these days.

'We're still editing,' he said.

'This election belongs to you, Mr. Lake,' Teddy said, quite feebly.

'I feel good, but it will be a brawl.'

'You'll win by fifteen points.'

Lake stopped smiling and listened hard. 'That's, uh, quite a margin.'

'You're up slightly in the polls. Next month the Vice President will be up. It will go back and forth until the middle of October. Then, there will be a nuclear situation that will terrify the world. And you, Mr. Lake, will become the messiah.'

The prospect frightened even the messiah. 'A war?' Lake asked quietly.

'No. There will be casualties, but they won't be Americans. Natty Chenkov will get the blame, and the good voters of this republic will flock to the polls. You could win by as much as twenty points.'

Lake breathed deeply. He wanted to ask more questions, even perhaps object to the bloodshed. But it would be futile. Whatever terror Teddy had planned for October was already in the works. There was nothing Lake could say or do to stop it.

'Keep beating the same drum, Mr. Lake. The same message. The world is about to become a lot crazier, and we have to be strong to protect our way of life.'

'The message has worked so far.'

'Your opponent will become desperate. He'll attack you for the single issue, and he'll whine about the money. He'll beat you up and score some points. Don't panic. The world will be turned upside down in October, trust me.'

'I do.'

'You've got this thing won, Mr. Lake. Keep preaching the same message.'

'Oh, I will.'

'Good,' Teddy said, and closed his eyes for a moment as if he needed a quick nap. Then he opened them and said, 'Now, on an entirely different topic, I'm a little curious about your plans once you get to the White House.'

Lake was puzzled, and his face showed it.

Teddy continued the ambush: 'You need a partner, Mr. Lake, a First Lady, someone to grace the White House with her presence. Someone to entertain and decorate, a pretty woman, one young enough to have children. It's been a long time since we had children in the White House, Mr. Lake.'

'You must be kidding.' Lake was flabbergasted.

'I like this Jayne Cordell on your staff. She's thirty-eight, smart, articulate, quite pretty though she needs to drop fifteen pounds. Her divorce was twelve years ago, and it's forgotten. I think she'd make a fine First Lady.'

Lake cocked his head to one side, and was suddenly angry. He wanted to lash out at Teddy, but for the moment words failed him. He managed to mumble, 'Have you lost your mind?'

'We know about Ricky,' Teddy said, very coolly, with his eyes penetrating Lake's.

The wind was sucked out of Lake's lungs, and as he exhaled he said, 'Oh my god.' He studied his feet for a moment, his entire body frozen in shock.

To make matters worse, Teddy handed over a sheet of paper. Lake took it, and instantly recognized it as a copy of his last note to Ricky.

Dear Ricky:
   I think it's best if we end our correspondence. I wish you well with your rehab.

Sincerely, Al

436

Lake almost said that he could explain things; they were not as they seemed. But he decided to say nothing, at least not for a while. The questions flooded his thoughts – How much do they know? How in hell did they intercept the mail? Who else knows?

Teddy let him suffer in silence. There was no hurry.

When his thoughts cleared somewhat, the politician in Lake came to the surface. Teddy was offering a way out. Teddy was saying, 'Just play ball with me, son, and things will be fine. Do it my way.'

And so Lake swallowed hard and said, 'I actually like her.'

'Of course you do. She's perfect for the job.'

'Yes. She's very loyal.'

'Are you sleeping with her?'

'No. Not yet.'

'Start soon. Hold hands with her during the convention. Let the gossip start, let nature take its course. A week before the election, announce a Christmas wedding.'

'Big or small?'

'Huge. The social event of the year in Washington.'

'I like that.'

'Get her pregnant quickly. Just before your inauguration, announce that the First Lady is expecting. It'll make a marvelous story. And it will be so nice to see young children in the White House again.'

Lake smiled and nodded and appeared to like

the thought, then he suddenly frowned. 'Will anyone ever know about Ricky?' he asked.

'No. He's been neutralized.'

'Neutralized?'

'He'll never write another letter, Mr. Lake. And you'll be so busy playing with all your little children that you won't have time to think about people like Ricky.'

'Ricky who?'

'Atta boy, Lake. Atta boy.'

'I'm very sorry, Mr. Maynard. Very sorry. It won't happen again.'

'Of course it won't. I've got the file, Mr. Lake. Always remember that.' Teddy began rolling himself backward, as if the meeting was over.

'It was an isolated moment of weakness,' Lake said.

'Never mind, Lake. Take care of Jayne. Get her a new wardrobe. She works too hard and she looks tired. Ease up on her. She's going to make a wonderful First Lady.'

'Yes sir.'

Teddy was at the door. 'No more surprises, Lake.'

'No sir.'

Teddy opened the door and rolled himself away.

By late November, they had settled in Monte Carlo, primarily because of its beauty and warm weather, but also because so much English was spoken there. And there were casinos, a must for Spicer. Neither Beech nor Yarber could tell if he was winning or losing, but he was certainly enjoying himself. His wife was still tending to her mother, who'd yet to die. Things were tense because Joe Roy wouldn't go home, and she wouldn't leave Mississippi.

They lived in the same small but handsome hotel on the edge of town, and they usually had breakfast together twice a week before scattering. As the months passed and they settled into their new lives, they saw less and less of each other. They had differing interests. Spicer wanted to gamble and drink and spend time with the ladies. Beech preferred the sea and enjoyed fishing. Yarber traveled and studied the history of southern France and northern Italy.

But each always knew where the others were. If one disappeared, the other two wanted to know it.

They'd read nothing about their pardons. Beech and Yarber had spent hours in a library in Rome, reading American newspapers just after they fled. Not a word about them. They'd had no contact with anyone from home. Spicer's wife claimed to have told no one that he was out of prison. She still thought he'd escaped.

On Thanksgiving Day, Finn Yarber was enjoying an espresso at a sidewalk café in downtown Monte Carlo. It was warm and sunny, and he was only vaguely aware that it was an important holiday back home. He didn't care because he would never go back. Beech was asleep in his hotel room. Spicer was in a casino three blocks away.

A vaguely familiar face appeared from nowhere. In a flash, the man sat across from Yarber and said, 'Hello, Finn. Remember me?'

Yarber calmly took a sip of coffee and studied the face. He'd last seen it at Trumble.

'Wilson Argrow, from prison,' the man said, and Yarber put down his cup before he dropped it.

'Good morning, Mr. Argrow,' Finn said slowly, calmly, though there were many other things he wanted to say.

'I guess you're surprised to see me.'

'Yes, as a matter of fact.'

'Wasn't that exciting news about Aaron Lake's landslide?'

'I suppose. What can I do for you?'

'I just want you to know that we're always close by, just in case you need us.'

Finn actually chuckled, then said, 'That doesn't seem likely.' It had been five months since their release. They had moved from country to country, from Greece to Sweden, from Poland to Portugal, slowly heading south as the weather changed. How on earth could Argrow track them down?

It was impossible.

Argrow pulled a magazine from inside his jacket. 'I ran across this last week,' he said, handing it over. The magazine was turned to a page in the back where a personal ad was circled with a red marker:

> SWM in 20s looking for kind and discreet American gentleman in 40s or 50s to pen pal with.

Yarber had certainly seen it before, but he shrugged as if he hadn't a clue.

'Looks familiar, doesn't it?' Argrow asked.

'They all look the same to me,' Finn said. He

440

tossed the magazine on the table. It was the European edition of *Out and About*.

'We traced the address to the post office here in Monte Carlo,' Argrow said. 'A brand-new box rental, with a fake name and everything. What a coincidence.'

'Look, I don't know who you work for, but I have a very strong hunch that we're not in your jurisdiction. We haven't broken a single law. Why don't you bug off?'

'Sure, Finn, but two million bucks isn't enough?'

Finn smiled and looked around the lovely café. He took a sip of coffee and said, 'You gotta keep busy.'

'I'll see you around,' Argrow said, then jumped to his feet and vanished.

Yarber finished his coffee as if nothing had happened. He watched the street and the traffic for a while, then left to gather his colleagues.

THE CHAMBER

ACKNOWLEDGEMENTS

I was a lawyer once, and represented people charged with all sorts of crimes. Fortunately, I never had a client convicted of capital murder and sentenced to death. I never had to go to death row, never had to do the things the lawyers do in this story.

Since I despise research, I did what I normally do when writing a novel. I found lawyers with expertise, and I befriended them. I called them at all hours and picked their brains. And it is here that I thank them.

Leonard Vincent has been the attorney for the Mississippi Department of Corrections for many years, and he opened his office to me. He helped me with the law, showed me his files, took me to death row, and toured me around the vast state penitentiary known simply as Parchman. He told me many stories that somehow found their way into this one. Leonard and I are still struggling with the moral perplexities of the death penalty, and I suspect we always will. Thanks also to his staff, and to the guards and personnel at Parchman.

Jim Craig is a man of great compassion and a fine lawyer. As the Executive Director of the Mississippi Capital Defense Resource Center, he's the official attorney for most of the inmates on death row. He deftly steered me through the impenetrable maze of postconviction appeals and habeas corpus warfare. The inevitable mistakes are mine, not his.

I went to law school with Tom Freeland and Guy Gillespie, and I thank them for their ready assistance. Marc Smirnoff is a friend and the editor of *The Oxford American*, and, as usual, worked on the manuscript before I sent it to New York.

Thanks also to Robert Warren and William Ballard for their help. And, as always, a very special thanks to my best friend, Renee, who still reads each chapter over my shoulder.

ONE

THE DECISION to bomb the office of the radical Jew lawyer was reached with relative ease. Only three people were involved in the process. The first was the man with the money. The second was a local operative who knew the territory. And the third was a young patriot and zealot with a talent for explosives and an astonishing knack for disappearing without a trail. After the bombing, he fled the country and hid in Northern Ireland for six years.

The lawyer's name was Marvin Kramer, a fourth-generation Mississippi Jew whose family had prospered as merchants in the Delta. He lived in an antebellum home in Greenville, a river town with a small but strong Jewish community, a pleasant place with a history of little racial discord. He practiced law because commerce bored him. Like most Jews of German descent, his family had assimilated nicely into the culture of the Deep South, and viewed themselves as nothing but typical Southerners who happened to have a different religion. Anti-Semitism rarely surfaced. For the most part, they blended with the rest of established society and went about their business.

Marvin was different. His father sent him up North to Brandeis in the late fifties. He spent four years there, then three years in law school at Columbia, and when he returned to Greenville in 1964 the civil rights movement had center stage in Mississippi. Marvin got in the thick of it. Less than a month after opening his little law office, he was arrested along with two of his Brandeis classmates for

1

attempting to register black voters. His father was furious. His family was embarrassed, but Marvin couldn't have cared less. He received his first death threat at the age of twenty-five, and started carrying a gun. He bought a pistol for his wife, a Memphis girl, and instructed their black maid to keep one in her purse. The Kramers had twin two-year-old sons.

The first civil rights lawsuit filed in 1965 by the law offices of Marvin B. Kramer and Associates (there were no associates yet) alleged a multitude of discriminatory voting practices by local officials. It made headlines around the state, and Marvin got his picture in the papers. He also got his name on a Klan list of Jews to harass. Here was a radical Jew lawyer with a beard and a bleeding heart, educated by Jews up North and now marching with and representing Negroes in the Mississippi Delta. It would not be tolerated.

Later, there were rumors of Lawyer Kramer using his own money to post bail for Freedom Riders and civil rights workers. He filed lawsuits attacking whites-only facilities. He paid for the reconstruction of a black church bombed by the Klan. He was actually seen welcoming Negroes into his home. He made speeches before Jewish groups up North and urged them to get involved in the struggle. He wrote sweeping letters to newspapers, few of which were printed. Lawyer Kramer was marching bravely toward his doom.

The presence of a nighttime guard patrolling benignly around the flower beds prevented an attack upon the Kramer home. Marvin had been paying the guard for two years. He was a former cop and he was heavily armed, and the Kramers let it be known to all of Greenville that they were protected by an expert marksman. Of course, the Klan knew about the guard, and the Klan knew to leave him alone. Thus, the decision was made to bomb Marvin Kramer's office, and not his home.

The actual planning of the operation took very little time, and this was principally because so few people were involved in it. The man with the money, a flamboyant redneck prophet named Jeremiah Dogan, was at the time

2

the Imperial Wizard for the Klan in Mississippi. His predecessor had been loaded off to prison, and Jerry Dogan was having a wonderful time orchestrating the bombings. He was not stupid. In fact, the FBI later admitted Dogan was quite effective as a terrorist because he delegated the dirty work to small, autonomous groups of hit men who worked completely independent of one another. The FBI had become expert at infiltrating the Klan with informants, and Dogan trusted no one but family and a handful of accomplices. He owned the largest used car lot in Meridian, Mississippi, and had made plenty of money on all sorts of shady deals. He sometimes preached in rural churches.

The second member of the team was a Klansman by the name of Sam Cayhall from Clanton, Mississippi, in Ford County, three hours north of Meridian and an hour south of Memphis. Cayhall was known to the FBI, but his connection to Dogan was not. The FBI considered him to be harmless because he lived in an area of the state with almost no Klan activity. A few crosses had been burned in Ford County recently, but no bombings, no killings. The FBI knew that Cayhall's father had been a Klansman, but on the whole the family appeared to be rather passive. Dogan's recruitment of Sam Cayhall was a brilliant move.

The bombing of Kramer's office began with a phone call on the night of April 17, 1967. Suspecting, with good reason, that his phones were tapped, Jeremiah Dogan waited until midnight and drove to a pay phone at a gas station south of Meridian. He also suspected he was being followed by the FBI, and he was correct. They watched him, but they had no idea where the call was going.

Sam Cayhall listened quietly on the other end, asked a question or two, then hung up. He returned to his bed, and told his wife nothing. She knew better than to ask. The next morning he left the house early and drove into the town of Clanton. He ate his daily breakfast at The Coffee Shop, then placed a call on a pay phone inside the Ford County Courthouse.

Two days later, on April 20, Cayhall left Clanton at dusk

3

and drove two hours to Cleveland, Mississippi, a Delta college town an hour from Greenville. He waited for forty minutes in he parking lot of a busy shopping center, but saw no sign of a green Pontiac. He ate fried chicken in a cheap diner, then drove to Greenville to scout the law offices of Marvin B. Kramer and Associates. Cayhall had spent a day in Greenville two weeks earlier, and knew the city fairly well. He found Kramer's office, then drove by his stately home, then found the synagogue again. Dogan said the synagogue might be next, but first they needed to hit the Jew lawyer. By eleven, Cayhall was back in Cleveland, and the green Pontiac was parked not at the shopping center but at a truck stop on Highway 61, a secondary site. He found the ignition key under the driver's floor mat, and took the car for a drive through the rich farm fields of the Delta. He turned onto a farm road and opened the trunk. In a cardboard box covered with newspapers, he found fifteen sticks of dynamite, three blasting caps, and a fuse. He drove into town and waited in an all-night café.

At precisely 2 A.M., the third member of the team walked into the crowded truck stop and sat across from Sam Cayhall. His name was Rollie Wedge, a young man of no more than twenty-two, but a trusted veteran of the civil rights war. He said he was from Louisiana, now lived somewhere in the mountains where no one could find him, and though he never boasted, he had told Sam Cayhall several times that he fully expected to be killed in the struggle for white supremacy. His father was a Klansman and a demolition contractor, and from him Rollie had learned how to use explosives.

Sam knew little about Rollie Wedge, and didn't believe much of what he said. He never asked Dogan where he found the kid.

They sipped coffee and made small talk for half an hour. Cayhall's cup shook occasionally from the jitters, but Rollie's was calm and steady. His eyes never blinked. They had done this together several times now, and Cayhall marveled at the coolness of one so young. He had reported

4

to Jeremiah Dogan that the kid never got excited, not even when they neared their targets and he handled the dynamite.

Wedge's car was a rental from the Memphis airport. He retrieved a small bag from the backseat, locked the car, and left it at the truck stop. The green Pontiac with Cayhall behind the wheel left Cleveland and headed south on Highway 61. It was almost 3 A.M., and there was no traffic. A few miles south of the village of Shaw, Cayhall turned onto a dark, gravel road and stopped. Rollie instructed him to stay in the car while he inspected the explosives. Sam did as he was told. Rollie took his bag with him to the trunk where he inventoried the dynamite, the blasting caps, and the fuse. He left his bag in the trunk, closed it, and told Sam to head to Greenville.

They drove by Kramer's office for the first time around 4 A.M. The street was deserted, and dark, and Rollie said something to the effect that this would be their easiest job yet.

'Too bad we can't bomb his house,' Rollie said softly as they drove by the Kramer home.

'Yeah. Too bad,' Sam said nervously. 'But he's got a guard, you know.'

'Yeah, I know. But the guard would be easy.'

'Yeah, I guess. But he's got kids in there, you know.'

'Kill 'em while they're young,' Rollie said. 'Little Jew bastards grow up to be big Jew bastards.'

Cayhall parked the car in an alley behind Kramer's office. He turned off the ignition, and both men quietly opened the trunk, removed the box and the bag, and slid along a row of hedges leading to the rear door.

Sam Cayhall jimmied the rear door of the office and they were inside within seconds. Two weeks earlier, Sam had presented himself to the receptionist under the ruse of asking for directions, then asked to use the rest room. In the main hallway, between the rest room and what appeared to be Kramer's office, was a narrow closet filled with stacks of old files and other legal rubbish.

5

'Stay by the door and watch the alley,' Wedge whispered coolly, and Sam did exactly as he was told. He preferred to serve as the watchman and avoid handling the explosives.

Rollie quickly sat the box on the floor in the closet, and wired the dynamite. It was a delicate exercise, and Sam's heart raced each time as he waited. His back was always to the explosives, just in case something went wrong.

They were in the office less than five minutes. Then they were back in the alley strolling nonchalantly to the green Pontiac. They were becoming invincible. It was all so easy. They had bombed a real estate office in Jackson because the realtor had sold a house to a black couple. A Jewish realtor. They had bombed a small newspaper office because the editor had uttered something neutral on segregation. They had demolished a Jackson synagogue, the largest in the state.

They drove through the alley in the darkness, and as the green Pontiac entered a side street its headlights came on.

In each of the prior bombings, Wedge had used a fifteen-minute fuse, one simply lit with a match, very similar to a firecracker. And as part of the exercise, the team of bombers enjoyed cruising with the windows down at a point always on the outskirts of town just as the explosion ripped through the target. They had heard and felt each of the prior hits, at a nice distance, as they made their leisurely getaways.

But tonight would be different. Sam made a wrong turn somewhere, and suddenly they were stopped at a railroad crossing staring at flashing lights as a freighter clicked by in front of them. A rather long freight train. Sam checked his watch more than once. Rollie said nothing. The train passed, and Sam took another wrong turn. They were near the river, with a bridge in the distance, and the street was lined with rundown houses. Sam checked his watch again. The ground would shake in less than five minutes, and he preferred to be easing into the darkness of a lonely highway when that happened. Rollie fidgeted once as if he was becoming irritated with his driver, but he said nothing.

6

Another turn, another new street. Greenville was not that big a city, and if he kept turning Sam figured he could work his way back to a familiar street. The next wrong turn proved to be the last. Sam hit the brakes as soon as he realized he had turned the wrong way on a one-way street. And when he hit the brakes, the engine quit. He yanked the gearshift into park, and turned the ignition. The engine turned perfectly, but it just wouldn't start. Then, the smell of gasoline.

'Dammit!' Sam said through clenched teeth. 'Dammit!'

Rollie sat low in his seat and stared through the window.

'Dammit! It's flooded!' He turned the key again, same result.

'Don't run the battery down,' Rollie said slowly, calmly.

Sam was near panic. Though he was lost, he was reasonably sure they were not far from downtown. He breathed deeply, and studied the street. He glanced at his watch. There were no other cars in sight. All was quiet. It was the perfect setting for a bomb blast. He could see the fuse burning along the wooden floor. He could feel the jarring of the ground. He could hear the roar of ripping wood and sheetrock, brick and glass. Hell, Sam thought as he tried to calm himself, we might get hit with debris.

'You'd think Dogan would send a decent car,' he mumbled to himself. Rollie did not respond, just kept his gaze on something outside his window.

At least fifteen minutes had passed since they had left Kramer's office, and it was time for the fireworks. Sam wiped rows of sweat from his forehead, and once again tried the ignition. Mercifully, the engine started. He grinned at Rollie, who seemed completely indifferent. He backed the car a few feet, then sped away. The first street looked familiar, and two blocks later they were on Main Street. 'What kind of fuse did you use?' Sam finally asked, as they turned onto Highway 82, less than ten blocks from Kramer's office.

Rollie shrugged as if it was his business and Sam shouldn't ask. They slowed as they passed a parked police

7

car, then gained speed on the edge of town. Within minutes, Greenville was behind them.

'What kind of fuse did you use?' Sam asked again with an edge to his voice.

'I tried something new,' Rollie answered without looking.

'What?'

'You wouldn't understand,' Rollie said, and Sam did a slow burn.

'A timing device?' he asked a few miles down the road.

'Something like that.'

THEY DROVE to Cleveland in complete silence. For a few miles, as the lights of Greenville slowly disappeared across the flat land, Sam half-expected to see a fireball or hear a distant rumble. Nothing happened. Wedge even managed to catch a little nap.

The truck stop café was crowded when they arrived. As always, Rollie eased from his seat and closed the passenger door. 'Until we meet again,' he said with a smile through the open window, then walked to his rental car. Sam watched him swagger away, and marveled once more at the coolness of Rollie Wedge.

It was by now a few minutes after five-thirty, and a hint of orange was peeking through the darkness to the east. Sam pulled the green Pontiac onto Highway 61, and headed south.

THE HORROR of the Kramer bombing actually began about the time Rollie Wedge and Sam Cayhall parted ways in Cleveland. It started with the alarm clock on a nightstand not far from Ruth Kramer's pillow. When it erupted at five-thirty, the usual hour, Ruth knew instantly that she was a very sick woman. She had a slight fever, a vicious pain in her temples, and she was quite nauseous. Marvin helped her to the bathroom not far away where she stayed for thirty minutes. A nasty flu bug had been circulating through Greenville for a month, and had now found its way into the Kramer home.

8

The maid woke the twins, Josh and John, now five years old, at six-thirty, and quickly had them bathed, dressed, and fed. Marvin thought it best to take them to nursery school as planned and get them out of the house and, he hoped, away from the virus. He called a doctor friend for a prescription, and left the maid twenty dollars to pick up the medication at the pharmacy in an hour. He said good-bye to Ruth, who was lying on the floor of the bathroom with a pillow under her head and an icepack over her face, and left the house with the boys.

Not all of his practice was devoted to civil rights litigation; there was not enough of that to survive on in Mississippi in 1967. He handled a few criminal cases and other generic civil matters: divorces, zoning, bankruptcy, real estate. And despite the fact that his father barely spoke to him, and the rest of the Kramers barely uttered his name, Marvin spent a third of his time at the office working on family business. On this particular morning, he was scheduled to appear in court at 9 A.M. to argue a motion in a lawsuit involving his uncle's real estate.

The twins loved his law office. They were not due at nursery school until eight, so Marvin could work a little before delivering the boys and heading on to court. This happened perhaps once a month. In fact, hardly a day passed without one of the twins begging Marvin to take them to his office first and then to nursery school.

They arrived at the office around seven-thirty, and once inside, the twins went straight for the secretary's desk and the thick stack of typing paper, all waiting to be cut and copied and stapled and folded into envelopes. The office was a sprawling structure, built over time with additions here and there. The front door opened into a small foyer where the receptionist's desk sat almost under a stairway. Four chairs for waiting clients hugged the wall. Magazines were scattered under the chairs. To the right and left of the foyer were small offices for lawyers – Marvin now had three associates working for him. A hallway ran directly from the foyer through the center of the downstairs, so from the

9

front door the rear of the building could be seen some eighty feet away. Marvin's office was the largest room downstairs, and it was the last door on the left, next to the cluttered closet. Just across the hall from the closet was Marvin's secretary's office. Her name was Helen, a shapely young woman Marvin had been dreaming about for eighteen months.

Upstairs on the second floor were the cramped offices of another lawyer and two secretaries. The third floor had no heat or air conditioning, and was used for storage.

He normally arrived at the office between seven-thirty and eight because he enjoyed a quiet hour before the rest of the firm arrived and the phone started ringing. As usual, he was the first to arrive on Friday, April 21.

He unlocked the front door, turned on the light switch, and stopped in the foyer. He lectured the twins about making a mess on Helen's desk, but they were off down the hallway and didn't hear a word. Josh already had the scissors and John the stapler by the time Marvin stuck his head in for the first time and warned them. He smiled to himself, then went to his office where he was soon deep in research.

At about a quarter to eight, he would recall later from the hospital, Marvin climbed the stairs to the third floor to retrieve an old file which, he thought at the time, had some relevance to the case he was preparing. He mumbled something to himself as he bounced up the steps. As things evolved, the old file saved his life. The boys were laughing somewhere down the hall.

The blast shot upward and horizontally at several thousand feet per second. Fifteen sticks of dynamite in the center of a wooden framed building will reduce it to splinters and rubble in a matter of seconds. It took a full minute for the jagged slivers of wood and other debris to return to earth. The ground seemed to shake like a small earthquake, and, as witnesses would later describe, bits of glass sprinkled downtown Greenville for what seemed like an eternity.

Josh and John Kramer were less than fifteen feet from the epicenter of the blast, and fortunately never knew what hit them. They did not suffer. Their mangled bodies were found under eight feet of rubble by local firemen. Marvin Kramer was thrown first against the ceiling of the third floor, then, unconscious, fell along with the remnants of the roof into the smoking crater in the center of the building. He was found twenty minutes later and rushed to the hospital. Within three hours, both legs were amputated at the knees.

The time of the blast was exactly seven forty-six, and this in itself was somewhat fortunate. Helen, Marvin's secretary, was leaving the post office four blocks away and felt the blast. Another ten minutes, and she would have been inside making coffee. David Lukland, a young associate in the law firm, lived three blocks away, and had just locked his apartment door when he heard and felt the blast. Another ten minutes, and he would've been picking through his mail in his second-floor office.

A small fire was ignited in the office building next door, and though it was quickly contained it added greatly to the excitement. The smoke was heavy for a few moments, and this sent people scurrying.

There were two injuries to pedestrians. A three-foot section of a two-by-four landed on a sidewalk a hundred yards away, bounced once, then hit Mrs Mildred Talton square in the face as she stepped away from her parked car and looked in the direction of the explosion. She received a broken nose and a nasty laceration, but recovered in due course.

The second injury was very minor but very significant. A stranger by the name of Sam Cayhall was walking slowly toward the Kramer office when the ground shook so hard he lost his footing and tripped on a street curb. As he struggled to his feet, he was hit once in the neck and once in the left cheek by flying glass. He ducked behind a tree as shards and pieces rained around him. He gaped at the devastation before him, then ran away.

Blood dripped from his cheek and puddled on his shirt.

11

He was in shock and did not remember much of this later. Driving the same green Pontiac, he sped away from downtown, and would most likely have made it safely from Greenville for the second time had he been thinking and paying attention. Two cops in a patrol car were speeding into the business district to respond to the bombing call when they met a green Pontiac which, for some reason, refused to move to the shoulder and yield. The patrol car had sirens blaring, lights flashing, horns blowing, and cops cursing, but the green Pontiac just froze in its lane of traffic and wouldn't budge. The cops stopped, ran to it, yanked open the door, and found a man with blood all over him. Handcuffs were slapped around Sam's wrists. He was shoved roughly into the rear seat of the police car, and taken to jail. The Pontiac was impounded.

THE BOMB that killed the Kramer twins was the crudest of sorts. Fifteen sticks of dynamite wrapped tightly together with gray duct tape. But there was no fuse. Rollie Wedge had used instead a detonating device, a timer, a cheap windup alarm clock. He had removed the minute hand from the clock, and drilled a small hole between the numbers seven and eight. Into the small hole he had inserted a metal pin which, when touched by the sweeping hour hand, would complete the circuit and detonate the bomb. Rollie wanted more time than a fifteen-minute fuse could provide. Plus, he considered himself an expert and wanted to experiment with new devices.

Perhaps the hour hand was warped a bit. Perhaps the dial of the clock was not perfectly flat. Perhaps Rollie in his enthusiasm had wound it too tight, or not tight enough. Perhaps the metal pin was not flush with the dial. It was, after all, Rollie's first effort with a timer. Or perhaps the timing device worked precisely as planned.

But whatever the reason or whatever the excuse, the bombing campaign of Jeremiah Dogan and the Ku Klux Klan had now spilled Jewish blood in Mississippi. And, for all practical purposes, the campaign was over.

TWO

ONCE THE BODIES were removed, the Greenville police sealed off the area around the ruins and kept the crowd away. Within hours, the premises were given to an FBI team from Jackson, and before dark a demolition unit was sifting through the rubble. Dozens of FBI agents solemnly began the tedious task of picking up every tiny piece, examining it, showing it to someone else, then packing it away to be fitted together on another day. An empty cotton warehouse on the edge of town was leased and became the repository for the Kramer rubble.

With time, the FBI would confirm what it initially assumed. Dynamite, a timer, and a few wires. Just a basic bomb hooked together by a hack lucky enough not to have killed himself.

Marvin Kramer was quickly flown to a fancier hospital in Memphis, and listed as critical but stable for three days. Ruth Kramer was hospitalized for shock, first in Greenville, then driven in an ambulance to the same hospital in Memphis. They shared a room, Mr and Mrs Kramer, and also shared a sufficient quantity of sedatives. Countless doctors and relatives stood vigil. Ruth was born and raised in Memphis, so there were plenty of friends to watch her.

AS THE DUST WAS SETTLING around Marvin's office, the neighbors, some of them storekeepers and others office clerks, swept glass from the sidewalks and whispered to one another as they watched the police and rescue people start

13

the digging. A mighty rumor swept downtown Greenville that a suspect was already in custody. By noon on the day of the bombing, it was common knowledge among the clusters of onlookers that the man's name was Sam Cayhall, from Clanton, Mississippi, that he was a member of the Klan, and that he was somehow injured in the attack. One report provided ghastly details of other Cayhall bombings with all sorts of gruesome injuries and disfigured corpses, all involving poor Negroes, though. Another report told of the brilliant heroics of the Greenville police in tracking down this madman within seconds of the blast. On the news at noon, the Greenville TV station confirmed what was already known, that the two little boys were dead, their father was severely injured, and that Sam Cayhall was in custody.

Sam Cayhall came within moments of being released on thirty dollars' bond. By the time he was rushed to the police station, he had regained his senses and had apologized sufficiently to the angry cops for not yielding as they wished. He was booked on a very minor charge, and sent to a holding room to be further processed and released. The two arresting officers sped away to inspect the blast.

A janitor who doubled as the jail medic approached Sam with a battered first aid kit, and washed the dried blood from his face. The bleeding had stopped. Sam repeated again that he'd been in a fight in a bar. Rough night. The medic left, and an hour later an assistant jailer appeared in the sliding window of the holding room with more papers. The charge was failure to yield to an emergency vehicle, the maximum fine was thirty dollars, and if Sam could post this sum in cash then he would be free to go as soon as the paperwork cleared and the car was released. Sam paced nervously around the room, glancing at his watch, softly rubbing the wound to his cheek.

He would be forced to disappear. There was a record of this arrest, and it wouldn't be long before these yokels put his name and the bombing together, and then, well, he needed to run away. He'd leave Mississippi, maybe team up

14

with Rollie Wedge and leave for Brazil or some place. Dogan would give them the money. He'd call Dogan as soon as he left Greenville. His car was sitting at the truck stop in Cleveland. He would swap vehicles there, then head on to Memphis and catch a Greyhound bus.

That's what he would do. He was an idiot for returning to the scene, but, he thought, if he just kept his cool these clowns would release him.

Half an hour passed before the assistant jailer arrived with another form. Sam handed him thirty dollars cash, and received a receipt. He followed the man through a narrow hallway to the front desk of the jail where he was given a summons to appear in Greenville Municipal Court in two weeks. 'Where's the car?' he asked as he folded the summons.

'They're bringing it. Just wait here.'

Sam checked his watch and waited for fifteen minutes. Through a small window in a metal door he watched cars come and go in the parking lot in front of the jail. Two drunks were dragged to the desk by a husky cop. Sam fidgeted, and waited.

From somewhere behind him a new voice called slowly, 'Mr Cayhall.' He turned and came face-to-face with a short man in a badly faded suit. A badge was waved under Sam's nose.

'I'm Detective Ivy, Greenville P.D. Need to ask you a few questions.' Ivy waved at a row of wooden doors along a hallway, and Sam obediently followed.

FROM THE MOMENT he first sat across the dirty desk from Detective Ivy, Sam Cayhall had little to say. Ivy was in his early forties but gray and heavily wrinkled around the eyes. He lit an unfiltered Camel, offered one to Sam, then asked how his face got cut. Sam played with the cigarette but did not light it. He'd given up smoking years earlier, and though he felt the urge to start puffing at this critical moment, he just thumped it gently on the table. Without looking at Ivy, he said that maybe he'd been in a fight.

15

Ivy sort of grunted with a short smile as if he expected this type of reply, and Sam knew he was facing a pro. He was scared now, and his hands began shaking. Ivy, of course, noticed all this. Where was the fight? Who were you fighting with? When did it happen? Why were you fighting here in Greenville when you live three hours away? Where did you get the car?

Sam said nothing. Ivy peppered him with questions, all unanswerable by Sam because the lies would lead to more lies and Ivy would have him tied in knots in seconds.

'I'd like to talk to an attorney,' Sam finally said.

'That's just wonderful, Sam. I think that's exactly what you should do.' Ivy lit another Camel and blew thick smoke at the ceiling.

'We had a little bomb blast this morning, Sam. Do you know that?' Ivy asked, his voice rising slightly in a mocking tone.

'No.'

'Tragic. A local lawyer by the name of Kramer got his office blown to bits. Happened about two hours ago. Probably the work of Kluckers, you know. We don't have any Kluckers around here, but Mr Kramer is a Jewish fellow. Let me guess – you know nothing about it, right?'

'That's right.'

'Really, really sad, Sam. You see, Mr Kramer had two little boys, Josh and John, and, as fate would have it, they were in the office with their daddy when the bomb went off.'

Sam breathed deeply and looked at Ivy. Tell me the rest of it, his eyes said.

'And these two little boys, twins, five years old, just cute as can be, got blown to bits, Sam. Deader than hell, Sam.'

Sam slowly lowered his head until his chin was an inch off his chest. He was beaten. Murder, two counts. Lawyers, trials, judges, juries, prison, everything hit at once and he closed his eyes.

'Their daddy might get lucky. He's at the hospital now in surgery. The little boys are at the funeral home. A real

16

tragedy, Sam. Don't suppose you know anything about the bomb, do you, Sam?'

'No. I'd like to see a lawyer.'

'Of course.' Ivy slowly stood and left the room.

THE PIECE OF GLASS in Sam's face was extracted by a physician and sent to an FBI lab. The report contained no surprises – same glass as the front windows of the office building. The green Pontiac was quickly traced to Jeremiah Dogan in Meridian. A fifteen-minute fuse was found in the trunk. A deliveryman came forward and explained to the police that he had seen the car near Mr Kramer's office around 4 A.M.

The FBI made sure the press immediately knew Mr Sam Cayhall was a longtime member of the Klan, and that he was the prime suspect in several more bombings. The case was cracked, they felt, and they heaped accolades upon the Greenville police. J. Edgar Hoover himself issued a statement.

Two days after the bombing, the Kramer twins were laid to rest in a small cemetery. At the time, 146 Jews lived in Greenville, and with the exception of Marvin Kramer and six others, every one attended the service. And they were outnumbered two to one by reporters and photographers from all over the country.

SAM SAW THE PICTURES and read the stories in his tiny cell the next morning. The assistant jailer, Larry Jack Polk, was a simpleton who by now was a friend because, as he had whispered to Sam early on, he had cousins who were Klansmen and he'd always wanted to join but his wife wouldn't stand for it. He brought Sam fresh coffee and newspapers each morning. Larry Jack had already confessed his admiration for Sam's bombing skills.

Other than the few bare words needed to keep Larry Jack manipulated, Sam said virtually nothing. The day after the bombing he had been charged with two counts of capital murder, so the gas chamber scenario occupied his thoughts. He refused to say a word to Ivy and the other police; same for the FBI. The reporters asked, of course, but didn't make it past Larry Jack. Sam phoned his wife and told her to stay in Clanton with the doors locked. He sat alone in his cinder-block cell and began a diary.

If Rollie Wedge was to be discovered and linked to the bombing, then he would have to be found by the cops. Sam Cayhall had taken an oath as a Klansman, and to him the oath was sacred. He would never, never squeal on a Klansman. He fervently hoped Jeremiah Dogan felt the same about his oath.

Two days after the bombing, a shady lawyer with a swirling hairdo named Clovis Brazelton made his first appearance in Greenville. He was a secret member of the Klan, and had become quite notorious around Jackson representing all sorts of thugs. He wanted to run for governor, said his platform would stand for the preservation of the white race, that the FBI was satanic, that blacks should be protected but not mixed with whites, and so on. He was sent by Jeremiah Dogan to defend Sam Cayhall, and more importantly, to make sure Cayhall kept his mouth shut. The FBI was all over Dogan because of the green Pontiac, and he feared an indictment as a co-conspirator.

Co-conspirators, Clovis explained to his new client right off the bat, are just as guilty as the ones who actually pull the trigger. Sam listened, but said little. He had heard of Brazelton, and did not yet trust him.

'Look, Sam,' Clovis said as if explaining things to a first grader, 'I know who planted the bomb. Dogan told me. If I count correctly, that makes four of us – me, you, Dogan, and Wedge. Now, at this point, Dogan is almost certain that Wedge will never be found. They haven't talked, but the kid's brilliant and he's probably in another country by now. That leaves you and Dogan. Frankly, I expect Dogan to be charged anytime now. But the cops'll have a hard time nailing him unless they can prove that ya'll conspired to blow up the Jew's office. And the only way they can prove this is if you tell them.'

'So I take the fall?' Sam asked.

18

'No. You just keep quiet about Dogan. Deny everything. We'll fabricate a story about the car. Let me worry about that. I'll get the trial moved to another county, maybe up in the hills or some place where they don't have Jews. Get us an all-white jury, and I'll hang it up so fast it'll make heroes out of both of us. Just let me handle it.'

'You don't think I'll be convicted?'

'Hell no. Listen, Sam, take my word for it. We'll get us a jury full of patriots, your kind of people, Sam. All white. All worried about their little children being forced to go to schools with little nigger kids. Good people, Sam. We'll pick twelve of 'em, put 'em in the jury box, and explain to 'em how these stinkin' Jews have encouraged all this civil rights nonsense. Trust me, Sam, it'll be easy.' With that, Clovis leaned across the shaky table, patted Sam on the arm, and said, 'Trust me, Sam, I've done it before.'

Later that day, Sam was handcuffed, surrounded by Greenville city policemen, and led to a waiting patrol car. Between the jail and the car, he had his picture taken by a small army of photographers. Another group of these assertive people were waiting at the courthouse when Sam arrived with his entourage.

He appeared before the municipal judge with his new lawyer, the Honorable Clovis Brazelton, who waived the preliminary hearing and performed a couple of other quiet and routine legal maneuvers. Twenty minutes after he'd left the jail, Sam was back. Clovis promised to return in a few days to start plotting strategy, then he wandered outside and performed admirably for the reporters.

IT TOOK A FULL MONTH for the media frenzy to subside in Greenville. Both Sam Cayhall and Jeremiah Dogan were indicted for capital murder on May 5, 1967. The local district attorney proclaimed loudly that he would seek the death penalty. The name of Rollie Wedge was never mentioned. The police and FBI had no idea he existed.

Clovis, now representing both defendants, successfully argued for a change of venue, and on September 4, 1967,

19

the trial began in Nettles County, two hundred miles from Greenville. It turned into a circus. The Klan set up camp on the front lawn of the courthouse and staged noisy rallies almost on the hour. They shipped in Klansmen from other states, even had a list of guest speakers. Sam Cayhall and Jeremiah Dogan were seized as symbols of white supremacy, and their beloved names were called a thousand times by their hooded admirers.

The press watched and waited. The courtroom was filled with reporters and journalists, so the less fortunate were forced to wait under the shade trees on the front lawn. They watched the Klansmen and listened to the speeches, and the more they watched and photographed the longer the speeches became.

Inside the courtroom, things were going smoothly for Cayhall and Dogan. Brazelton worked his magic and seated twelve white patriots, as he preferred to call them, on the jury, then began poking rather significant holes in the prosecution's case. Most importantly, the evidence was circumstantial – no one actually saw Sam Cayhall plant the bomb. Clovis preached this loudly in his opening statement, and it found its mark. Cayhall was actually employed by Dogan, who'd sent him to Greenville on an errand, and he just happened to be near the Kramer building at a most unfortunate moment. Clovis almost cried when he thought of those two precious little boys.

The dynamite fuse in the trunk had probably been left there by its previous owner, a Mr Carson Jenkins, a dirt contractor from Meridian. Mr Carson Jenkins testified that he handled dynamite all the time in his line of work, and that he evidently had simply left the fuse in the trunk when he sold the car to Dogan. Mr Carson Jenkins was a Sunday school teacher, a quiet, hardworking salt-of-the-earth little man who was completely believable. He was also a member of the Ku Klux Klan, but the FBI didn't know it. Clovis orchestrated this testimony without a flaw.

The fact that Cayhall's car had been left at the truck stop in Cleveland was never discovered by the police or FBI.

20

During his first phone call from jail, he had instructed his wife to get his son, Eddie Cayhall, and drive to Cleveland immediately for the car. This was a significant piece of luck for the defense.

But the strongest argument presented by Clovis Brazelton was simply that no one could prove that his clients conspired to do anything, and how in the world can you, the jurors of Nettles County, send these two men to their deaths?

After four days of trial, the jury retired to deliberate. Clovis guaranteed his clients an acquittal. The prosecution was almost certain of one. The Kluckers smelled victory, and increased the tempo on the front lawn.

There were no acquittals, and there were no convictions. Remarkably, two of the jurors boldly dug in their heels and pressed to convict. After a day and a half of deliberations, the jury reported to the judge that it was hoplessly deadlocked. A mistrial was declared, and Sam Cayhall went home for the first time in five months.

THE RETRIAL took place six months later in Wilson County, another rural area four hours from Greenville and a hundred miles from the site of the first trial. There were complaints of Klan harassment of prospective jurors in the first trial, so the judge, for reasons that were never made clear, changed venue to an area crawling with Kluckers and their sympathizers. The jury again was all-white and certainly non-Jewish. Clovis told the same stories with the same punch lines. Mr Carson Jenkins told the same lies.

The prosecution changed strategy a bit, to no avail. The district attorney dropped the capital charges and pressed for a conviction for murder only. No death penalty, and the jury could, if it so chose, find Cayhall and Dogan guilty of manslaughter, a much lighter charge but a conviction nonetheless.

The second trial had something new. Marvin Kramer sat in a wheelchair by the front row and glared at the jurors for three days. Ruth had tried to watch the first trial, but went

21

home to Greenville where she was hospitalized again for emotional problems. Marvin had been in and out of surgery since the bombing, and his doctors would not allow him to watch the show in Nettles County.

For the most part, the jurors could not stand to look at him. They kept their eyes away from the spectators, and, for jurors, paid remarkable attention to the witnesses. However, one young lady, Sharon Culpepper, mother of twin boys, could not help herself. She glanced at Marvin repeatedly, and many times their eyes locked. He pleaded with her for justice.

Sharon Culpepper was the only one of the twelve who initially voted to convict. For two days she was verbally abused and harangued by her peers. They called her names and made her cry, but she doggedly held on.

The second trial ended with a jury hung eleven to one. The judge declared a mistrial, and sent everybody home. Marvin Kramer returned to Greenville, then to Memphis for more surgery. Clovis Brazelton made a spectacle of himself with the press. The district attorney made no promises of a new trial. Sam Cayhall went quietly to Clanton with a solemn vow to avoid any more dealings with Jeremiah Dogan. And the Imperial Wizard himself made a triumphant return to Meridian where he boasted to his people that the battle for white supremacy had just begun, good had defeated evil, and on and on.

The name of Rollie Wedge had been uttered only once. During a lunch break in the second trial, Dogan whispered to Cayhall that a message had been received from the kid. The messenger was a stranger who spoke to Dogan's wife in a hallway outside the courtroom. And the message was quite clear and simple. Wedge was nearby, in the woods, watching the trial, and if Dogan or Cayhall mentioned his name, their homes and families would be bombed to hell and back.

THREE

RUTH AND MARVIN KRAMER separated in 1970. He was admitted to a mental hospital later that year, and committed suicide in 1971. Ruth returned to Memphis and lived with her parents. In spite of their problems, they had pressed hard for a third trial. In fact, the Jewish community in Greenville was highly agitated and vocal when it became apparent that the district attorney was tired of losing and had lost his enthusiasm for prosecuting Cayhall and Dogan.

Marvin was buried next to his sons. A new park was dedicated to the memory of Josh and John Kramer, and scholarships were established. With time, the tragedy of their deaths lost some of its horror. Years passed, and Greenville talked less and less about the bombing.

Despite pressure from the FBI, a third trial did not materialize. There was no new evidence. The judge would no doubt change venue again. A prosecution looked hopeless, but still the FBI did not quit.

With Cayhall unwilling and Wedge unavailable, Dogan's bombing campaign fizzled. He continued to wear his robe and make his speeches, and began to fancy himself as a major political force. Journalists up North were intrigued by his blatant race-baiting, and he was always willing to put on his hood and give outrageous interviews. He was mildly famous for a brief period, and he enjoyed it immensely.

But by the late 1970s, Jeremiah Dogan was just another thug with a robe in a rapidly declining organization. Blacks were voting. The public schools were desegregated. Racial

23

barriers were being struck down by federal judges throughout the South. Civil rights had arrived in Mississippi, and the Klan had proven pitifully inept in keeping Negroes where they belonged. Dogan couldn't draw flies to a cross-burning.

In 1979, two significant events occurred in the open but inactive Kramer bombing case. The first was the election of David McAllister as the district attorney in Greenville. At twenty-seven he became the youngest D.A. in the state's history. As a teenager he had stood in the crowd and watched the FBI pick through the rubble of Marvin Kramer's office. Shortly after his election, he vowed to bring the terrorists to justice.

The second event was the indictment of Jeremiah Dogan for income tax evasion. After years of successfully dodging the FBI, Dogan got sloppy and ran afoul of the IRS. The investigation took eight months and resulted in an indictment that ran for thirty pages. According to it, Dogan had failed to report over a hundred thousand dollars between 1974 and 1978. It contained eighty-six counts, and carried a maximum of twenty-eight years in prison.

Dogan was dead guilty, and his lawyer (not Clovis Brazelton) immediately began exploring the possibility of a plea bargain. Enter the FBI.

Through a series of heated and angry meetings with Dogan and his lawyer, a deal was offered by the government whereby Dogan would testify against Sam Cayhall in the Kramer case, and in return he would serve no time in jail for tax evasion. Zero days behind bars. Heavy probation and fines, but no jail. Dogan had not spoken to Cayhall in over ten years. Dogan was not active in the Klan anymore. There were lots of reasons to consider the deal, not the least of which was the issue of remaining a free man or spending a decade or so in prison.

To prod him along, the IRS attached all of his assets, and planned a nice little fire sale. And to help with his decision, David McAllister convinced a grand jury in Greenville to indict him and his pal Cayhall once again for the Kramer bombing.

Dogan caved in and jumped at the deal.

AFTER TWELVE YEARS of living quietly in Ford County, Sam Cayhall once again found himself indicted, arrested, and facing the certainty of a trial and the possibility of the gas chamber. He was forced to mortgage his house and small farm to hire a lawyer. Clovis Brazelton had gone on to bigger things, and Dogan was no longer an ally.

Much had changed in Mississippi since the first two trials. Blacks had registered to vote in record numbers, and these new voters had elected black officials. All-white juries were rare. The state had two black trial judges, two black sheriffs, and black lawyers could be spotted with their white brethren roaming the courthouse hallways. Officially, segregation was over. And many white Mississippians were beginning to look back and wonder what all the fuss was about. Why had there been such resistance to basic rights for all people? Though it had a long way to go, Mississippi was a far different place in 1980 than in 1967. And Sam Cayhall understood this.

He hired a skilled trial advocate from Memphis named Benjamin Keyes. Their first tactic was to move to dismiss the indictment on the grounds that it was unfair to try him again after such a delay. This proved to be a persuasive argument, and it took a decision by the Mississippi Supreme Court to settle the matter. By a vote of six to three, the court ruled the prosecution could proceed.

And proceed it did. The third and final trial of Sam Cayhall began in February of 1981, in a chilly little courthouse in Lakehead County, a hill county in the northeastern corner of the state. Much could be said about the trial. There was a young district attorney, David McAllister, who performed brilliantly but had the obnoxious habit of spending all his spare time with the press. He was handsome and articulate and compassionate, and it became very clear that this trial had a purpose. Mr McAllister had political ambitions on a grand scale.

There was a jury of eight whites and four blacks. There

were the glass sample, the fuse, the FBI reports, and all the other photos and exhibits from the first two trials.

And then, there was the testimony of Jeremiah Dogan, who took the stand in a denim workshirt and with a humble countenance solemnly explained to the jury how he conspired with Sam Cayhall sitting over there to bomb the office of Mr Kramer. Sam glared at him intensely and absorbed every word, but Dogan looked away. Sam's lawyer berated Dogan for half a day, and forced him to admit that he'd cut a deal with the government. But the damage was done.

It was of no benefit to the defense of Sam Cayhall to raise the issue of Rollie Wedge. Because to do so would be to admit that Sam in fact had been in Greenville with the bomb. Sam would be forced to admit that he was a co-conspirator, and under the law he would be just as guilty as the man who planted the dynamite. And to present this scenario to the jury, Sam would be forced to testify, something neither he nor his attorney wanted. Sam could not withstand a rigorous cross-examination, because Sam would be forced to tell one lie to cover the last.

And, at this point, no one would believe a sudden tale of a mysterious new terrorist who'd never been mentioned before, and who came and went without being seen. Sam knew the Rollie Wedge angle was futile, and he never mentioned the man's name to his own lawyer.

AT THE CLOSE of the trial, David McAllister stood before the jury in a packed courtroom and presented his closing argument. He talked of being a youngster in Greenville and having Jewish friends. He didn't know they were different. He knew some of the Kramers, fine folks who worked hard and gave back to the town. He also played with little black kids, and learned they made wonderful friends. He never understood why they went to one school and he went to another. He told a gripping story of feeling the earth shake on the morning of April 21, 1967, and running in the direction of downtown where smoke was drifting upward. For three hours, he stood behind the police barricades and waited. He saw the firemen scurry about when they found Marvin Kramer. He saw them huddle in the debris when they found the boys. Tears dripped down his cheeks when the little bodies, covered in white sheets, were carried slowly to an ambulance.

It was a splendid performance, and when McAllister finished the courtroom was silent. Several of the jurors dabbed at their eyes.

ON FEBRUARY 12, 1981, Sam Cayhall was convicted on two counts of capital murder and one count of attempted murder. Two days later, the same jury in the same courtroom returned with a sentencing verdict of death.

He was transported to the state penitentiary at Parchman to begin waiting for his appointment with the gas chamber. On February 19, 1981, he first set foot on death row.

27

FOUR

THE LAW FIRM of Kravitz & Bane had almost three hundred lawyers peacefully coexisting under the same roof in Chicago. Two hundred and eighty-six to be exact, though it was difficult for anyone to keep score because at any given moment there were a dozen or so leaving for a multitude of reasons, and there were always two dozen or so shiny, fresh new recruits trained and polished and just itching for combat. And though it was huge, Kravitz & Bane had failed to play the expansion game as quickly as others, had failed to gobble up weaker firms in other cities, had been slow to raid clients from its competitors, and thus had to suffer the distinction of being only the third-largest firm in Chicago. It had offices in six cities, but, much to the embarrassment of the younger partners, there was no London address on the letterhead.

Though it had mellowed some, Kravitz & Bane was still known as a vicious litigation firm. It had tamer departments for real estate, tax, and antitrust, but its money was made in litigation. When the firm recruited it sought the brightest third-year students with the highest marks in mock trials and debate. It wanted young men (a token female here and there) who could be instantly trained in the slash-and-attack style perfected long ago by Kravitz & Bane litigators.

There was a nice though small unit for plaintiffs' personal injury work, good stuff from which they took 50 percent and allowed their clients the remainder. There was a sizable section for a white-collar criminal defense, but the white-collar defendant needed a sizable net worth to strap on Kravitz & Bane. Then there were the two largest sections, one for commercial litigation and one for insurance defense. With the exception of the plaintiffs' work, and as a percentage of gross it was almost insignificant, the firm's money was earned by billable hours. Two hundred bucks per hour for insurance work; more if the traffic could stand it. Three hundred bucks for criminal defense. Four hundred for a big bank. Even five hundred dollars an hour for a rich corporate client with lazy in-house lawyers who were asleep at the wheel.

Kravitz & Bane printed money by the hour and built a dynasty in Chicago. Its offices were fashionable but not plush. They filled the top floors of, fittingly, the third-tallest building downtown.

Like most large firms, it made so much money it felt obligated to establish a small pro bono section to fulfill its moral responsibility to society. It was quite proud of the fact that it had a full-time pro bono partner, an eccentric do-gooder named E. Garner Goodman, who had a spacious office with two secretaries on the sixty-first floor. He shared a paralegal with a litigation partner. The firm's gold-embossed brochure made much of the fact that its lawyers were encouraged to pursue pro bono projects. The brochure proclaimed that last year, 1989, Kravitz & Bane lawyers donated almost sixty thousand hours of their precious time to clients who couldn't pay. Housing project kids, death row inmates, illegal aliens, drug addicts, and, of course, the firm was deeply concerned with the plight of the homeless. The brochure even had a photograph of two young lawyers, jackets off, sleeves rolled up, ties loosened about the neck, sweat in the armpits, eyes filled with compassion, as they performed some menial chore in the midst of a group of minority children in what appeared to be an urban landfill. Lawyers saving society.

Adam Hall had one of the brochures in his thin file as he eased slowly along the hallway on floor sixty-one, headed in

29

the general direction of the office of E. Garner Goodman. He nodded and spoke to another young lawyer, one he'd never seen before. At the firm Christmas party name tags were distributed at the door. Some of the partners barely knew each other. Some of the associates saw each other once or twice a year. He opened a door and entered a small room where a secretary stopped typing and almost smiled. He asked for Mr Goodman, and she nodded properly to a row of chairs where he was to wait. He was five minutes early for a 10 A.M. appointment, as if it mattered. This was pro bono now. Forget the clock. Forget billable hours. Forget performance bonuses. In defiance of the rest of the firm, Goodman allowed no clocks on his walls.

Adam flipped through his file. He chuckled at the brochure. He read again his own little résumé – college at Pepperdine, law school at Michigan, editor of the law review, case note on cruel and unusual punishment, comments on recent death penalty cases. A rather short résumé, but then he was only twenty-six. He'd been employed at Kravitz & Bane for all of nine months now.

He read and made notes from two lengthy U.S. Supreme Court decisions dealing with executions in California. He checked his watch, and read some more. The secretary eventually offered coffee, which he politely declined.

THE OFFICE of E. Garner Goodman was a stunning study in disorganization. It was large but cramped, with sagging bookshelves on every wall and stacks of dusty files covering the floor. Little piles of papers of all sorts and sizes covered the desk in the center of the office. Refuse, rubbish, and lost letters covered the rug under the desk. If not for the closed wooden blinds, the large window could have provided a splendid view of Lake Michigan, but it was obvious Mr Goodman spent no time at his window.

He was an old man with a neat gray beard and bushy gray hair. His white shirt was painfully starched. A green paisley bow tie, his trademark, was tied precisely under his chin. Adam entered the room and cautiously weaved around the

30

piles of papers. Goodman did not stand but offered his hand with a cold greeting.

Adam handed the file to Goodman, and sat in the only empty chair in the room. He waited nervously while the file was studied, the beard was gently stroked, the bow tie was tinkered with.

'Why do you want to do pro bono work?' Goodman mumbled after a long silence. He did not look up from the file. Classical guitar music drifted softly from recessed speakers in the ceiling.

Adam shifted uncomfortably. 'Uh, different reasons.'

'Let me guess. You want to serve humanity, give something back to your community, or, perhaps, you feel guilty because you spend so much time here in this sweatshop billing by the hour that you want to cleanse your soul, get your hands dirty, do some honest work, and help other people.' Goodman's beady blue eyes darted at Adam from above the black-framed reading spectacles perched on the tip of his rather pointed nose. 'Any of the above?'

'Not really.'

Goodman continued scanning the file. 'So you've been assigned to Emmitt Wycoff?' He was reading a letter from Wycoff, Adam's supervising partner.

'Yes, sir.'

'He's a fine lawyer. I don't particularly care for him, but he's got a great criminal mind, you know. Probably one of our top three white-collar boys. Pretty abrasive, though, don't you think?'

'He's okay.'

'How long have you been under him?'

'Since I started. Nine months ago.'

'So you've been here for nine months?'

'Yes sir.'

'What do you think of it?' Goodman closed the file and stared at Adam. He slowly removed the reading glasses and stuck one stem in his mouth.

'I like it, so far. It's challenging.'

'Of course. Why did you pick Kravitz & Bane? I mean,

31

surely with your credentials you could've gone anywhere. Why here?'

'Criminal litigation. That's what I want, and this firm has a reputation.'

'How many offers did you have? Come on, I'm just being curious.'

'Several.'

'And where were they?'

'D.C. mainly. One in Denver. I didn't interview with New York firms.'

'How much money did we offer you?'

Adam shifted again. Goodman was, after all, a partner. Surely he knew what the firm was paying new associates. 'Sixty or so. What are we paying you?'

This amused the old man, and he smiled for the first time. 'They pay me four hundred thousand dollars a year to give away their time so they can pat themselves on the back and preach about lawyers and about social responsibility. Four hundred thousand, can you believe it?'

Adam had heard the rumors. 'You're not complaining, are you?'

'No. I'm the luckiest lawyer in town, Mr Hall. I get paid a truckload of money for doing work I enjoy, and I punch no clock and don't worry about billing. It's a lawyer's dream. That's why I still bust my ass sixty hours a week. I'm almost seventy, you know.'

The legend around the firm was that Goodman, as a younger man, succumbed to the pressure and almost killed himself with liquor and pills. He dried out for a year while his wife took the kids and left him, then he convinced the partners he was worth saving. He just needed an office where life did not revolve around a clock.

'What kind of work are you doing for Emmitt Wycoff?' Goodman asked.

'Lot of research. Right now he's defending a bunch of defense contractors, and that takes most of my time. I argued a motion in court last week.' Adam said this with a touch of pride. Rookies were usually kept chained to their desks for the first twelve months.

'A real motion?' Goodman asked, in awe.

'Yes sir.'

'In a real courtroom?'

'Yes sir.'

'Before a real judge?'

'You got it.'

'Who won?'

'Judge ruled for the prosecution, but it was close. I really tied him in knots.' Goodman smiled at this, but the game was quickly over. He opened the file again.

'Wycoff sends along a pretty strong letter of recommendation. That's out of character for him.'

'He recognizes talent,' Adam said with a smile.

'I assume this is a rather significant request, Mr Hall. Just what is it you have in mind?'

Adam stopped smiling and cleared his throat. He was suddenly nervous, and decided to recross his legs. 'It's, uh, well, it's a death penalty case.'

'A death penalty case?' Goodman repeated.

'Yes sir.'

'Why?'

'I'm opposed to the death penalty.'

'Aren't we all, Mr Hall? I've written books about it. I've handled two dozen of these damned things. Why do you want to get involved?'

'I've read your books. I just want to help.'

Goodman closed the file again and leaned on his desk. Two pieces of paper slid off and fluttered to the floor. 'You're too young and you're too green.'

'You might be surprised.'

'Look, Mr Hall, this is not the same as counseling winos at a soup kitchen. This is life and death. This is high pressure stuff, son. It's not a lot of fun.'

Adam nodded but said nothing. His eyes were locked onto Goodman's, and he refused to blink. A phone rang somewhere in the distance, but they both ignored it.

33

'Any particular case, or do you have a new client for Kravitz & Bane?' Goodman asked.

'The Cayhall case,' Adam said slowly.

Goodman shook his head and tugged at the edges of his bow tie. 'Sam Cayhall just fired us. The Fifth Circuit ruled last week that he does indeed have the right to terminate our representation.'

'I've read the opinion. I know what the Fifth Circuit said. The man needs a lawyer.'

'No he doesn't. He'll be dead in three months with or without one. Frankly, I'm relieved to have him out of my life.'

'He needs a lawyer,' Adam repeated.

'He's representing himself, and he's pretty damned good, to be perfectly honest. Types his own motions and briefs, handles his own research. I hear he's been giving advice to some of his buddies on death row, just the white ones though.'

'I've studied his entire file.'

E. Garner Goodman twirled his spectacles slowly and thought about this. 'That's a half a ton of paper. Why'd you do it?'

'I'm intrigued by the case. I've watched it for years, read everything written about the man. You asked me earlier why I chose Kravitz & Bane. Well, the truth is that I wanted to work on the Cayhall case, and I think this firm has handled it pro bono for, what, eight years now?'

'Seven, but it seems like twenty. Mr Cayhall is not the most pleasant man to deal with.'

'Understandable, isn't it? I mean, he's been in solitary for almost ten years.'

'Don't lecture me about prison life, Mr Hall. Have you ever seen the inside of a prison?'

'No.'

'Well I have. I've been to death row in six states. I've been cursed by Sam Cayhall when he was chained to his chair. He's not a nice man. He's an incorrigible racist who hates just about everybody, and he'd hate you if you met him.'

34

'I don't think so.'

'You're a lawyer, Mr Hall. He hates lawyers worse than he hates blacks and Jews. He's been facing death for almost ten years, and he's convinced he's the victim of a lawyer conspiracy. Hell, he tried to fire us for two years. This firm spent in excess of two million dollars in billable time trying to keep him alive, and he was more concerned with firing us. I lost count of the number of times he refused to meet with us after we traveled all the way to Parchman. He's crazy, Mr Hall. Find yourself another project. How about abused kids or something?'

'No thanks. My interest is in death penalty cases, and I'm somewhat obsessed with the story of Sam Cayhall.'

Goodman carefully returned the spectacles to the tip of his nose, then slowly swung his feet onto the corner of the desk. He folded his hands across the starched shirt. 'Why, may I ask, are you so obsessed with Sam Cayhall?'

'Well, it's a fascinating case, don't you think? The Klan, the civil rights movement, the bombings, the tortured locale. The backdrop is such a rich period in American history. Seems ancient, but it was only twenty-five years ago. It's a riveting story.'

A ceiling fan spun slowly above him. A minute passed.

Goodman lowered his feet to the floor and rested on his elbows. 'Mr Hall, I appreciate your interest in pro bono, and I assure you there's much to do. But you need to find another project. This is not a mock trial competition.'

'And I'm not a law student.'

'Sam Cayhall has effectively terminated our services, Mr Hall. You don't seem to realize this.'

'I want the chance to meet with him.'

'For what?'

'I think I can convince him to allow me to represent him.'

'Oh really.'

Adam took a deep breath, then stood and walked deftly around the stacks of files to the window. Another deep breath. Goodman watched, and waited.

'I have a secret for you, Mr Goodman. No one else knows

35

but Emmitt Wycoff, and I was sort of forced to tell him. You must keep it confidential, okay?'

'I'm listening.'

'Do I have your word?'

'Yes, you have my word,' Goodman said slowly, biting a stem.

Adam peeked through a slit in the blinds and watched a sailboat on Lake Michigan. He spoke quietly. 'I'm related to Sam Cayhall.'

Goodman did not flinch. 'I see. Related how?'

'He had a son, Eddie Cayhall. And Eddie Cayhall left Mississippi in disgrace after his father was arrested for the bombing. He fled to California, changed his name, and tried to forget his past. But he was tormented by his family's legacy. He committed suicide shortly after his father was convicted in 1981.'

Goodman now sat with his rear on the edge of his chair.

'Eddie Cayhall was my father.'

Goodman hesitated slightly. 'Sam Cayhall is your grandfather?'

'Yes. I didn't know it until I was almost seventeen. My aunt told me after we buried my father.'

'Wow.'

'You promised not to tell.'

'Of course.' Goodman moved his butt to the edge of his desk, and placed his feet in the chair. He stared at the blinds. 'Does Sam know –'

'No. I was born in Ford County, Mississippi, a town called Clanton, not Memphis. I was always told I was born in Memphis. My name then was Alan Cayhall, but I didn't know this until much later. I was three years old when we left Mississippi, and my parents never talked about the place. My mother believes that there was no contact between Eddie and Sam from the day we left until she wrote him in prison and told him his son was dead. He did not write back.'

'Damn, damn, damn,' Goodman mumbled to himself.

'There's a lot to it, Mr Goodman. It's a pretty sick family.'

36

'Not your fault.'

'According to my mother, Sam's father was an active Klansman, took part in lynchings and all that. So I come from pretty weak stock.'

'Your father was different.'

'My father killed himself. I'll spare you the details, but I found his body, and I cleaned up the mess before my mother and sister returned home.'

'And you were seventeen?'

'Almost seventeen. It was 1981. Nine years ago. After my aunt, Eddie's sister, told me the truth, I became fascinated with the sordid history of Sam Cayhall. I've spent hours in libraries digging up old newspaper and magazine stories; there are quite a lot of materials. I've read the transcripts of all three trials. I've studied the appellate decisions. In law school I began studying this firm's representation of Sam Cayhall. You and Wallace Tyner have done exemplary work.'

'I'm glad you approve.'

'I've read hundreds of books and thousands of articles on the Eighth Amendment and death penalty litigation. You've written four books, I believe. And a number of articles. I know I'm just a rookie, but my research is impeccable.'

'And you think Sam will trust you as his lawyer?'

'I don't know. But he's my grandfather, like it or not, and I have to go see him.'

'There's been no contact –'

'None. I was three when we left, and I certainly don't remember him. I've started a thousand times to write him, but it never happened. I can't tell you why.'

'It's understandable.'

'Nothing's understandable, Mr Goodman. I do not understand how or why I'm standing here in this office at this moment. I always wanted to be a pilot, but I went to law school because I felt a vague calling to help society. Someone needed me, and I suppose I felt that someone was my demented grandfather. I had four job offers, and I

37

picked this firm because it had the guts to represent him for free.'

'You should've told someone up front about this, before we hired you.'

'I know. But nobody asked if my grandfather was a client of this firm.'

'You should've said something.'

'They won't fire me, will they?'

'I doubt it. Where have you been for the past nine months?'

'Here, working ninety hours a week, sleeping on my desk, eating in the library, cramming for the bar exam, you know, the usual rookie boot camp you guys designed for us.'

'Silly, isn't it?'

'I'm tough.' Adam opened a slit in the blinds for a better view of the lake. Goodman watched him.

'Why don't you open these blinds?' Adam asked. 'It's a great view.'

'I've seen it before.'

'I'd kill for a view like this. My little cubbyhole is a mile from any window.'

'Work hard, bill even harder, and one day this will all be yours.'

'Not me.'

'Leaving us, Mr Hall?'

'Probably, eventually. But that's another secret, okay? I plan to hit it hard for a couple of years, then move on. Maybe open my own office, one where life does not revolve around a clock. I want to do public interest work, you know, sort of like you.'

'So after nine months you're already disillusioned with Kravitz & Bane.'

'No. But I can see it coming. I don't want to spend my career representing wealthy crooks and wayward corporations.'

'Then you're certainly in the wrong place.'

Adam left the window and walked to the edge of the desk.

38

He looked down at Goodman. 'I am in the wrong place, and I want a transfer. Wycoff will agree to send me to our little office in Memphis for the next few months so I can work on the Cayhall case. Sort of a leave of absence, with full pay of course.'

'Anything else?'

'That's about it. It'll work. I'm just a lowly rookie, expendable around here. No one will miss me. Hell, there are plenty of young cutthroats just eager to work eighteen hours a day and bill twenty.'

Goodman's face relaxed, and a warm smile appeared. He shook his head as if this impressed him. 'You planned this, didn't you? I mean, you picked this firm because it represented Sam Cayhall, and because it has an office in Memphis.'

Adam nodded without a smile. 'Things have worked out. I didn't know how or when this moment would arrive, but, yes, I sort of planned it. Don't ask me what happens next.'

'He'll be dead in three months, if not sooner.'

'But I have to do something, Mr Goodman. If the firm won't allow me to handle the case, then I'll probably resign and try it on my own.'

Goodman shook his head and jumped to his feet. 'Don't do that, Mr Hall. We'll work something out. I'll need to present this to Daniel Rosen, the managing partner. I think he'll approve.'

'He has a horrible reputation.'

'Well deserved. But I can talk to him.'

'He'll do it if you and Wycoff recommend it, won't he?'

'Of course. Are you hungry?' Goodman was reaching for his jacket.

'A little.'

'Let's go out for a sandwich.'

THE LUNCH CROWD at the corner deli had not arrived. The partner and the rookie took a small table in the front window overlooking the sidewalk. Traffic was slow and hundreds of pedestrians scurried along, just a few feet away. The waiter delivered a greasy Reuben for Goodman and a bowl of chicken soup for Adam.

'How many inmates are on death row in Mississippi?' Goodman asked.

'Forty-eight, as of last month. Twenty-five black, twenty-three white. The last execution was two years ago, Willie Parris. Sam Cayhall will probably be next, barring a small miracle.'

Goodman chewed quickly on a large bite. He wiped his mouth with the paper napkin. 'A large miracle, I would say. There's not much left to do legally.'

'There are the usual assortment of last ditch motions.'

'Let's save the strategy talks for later. I don't suppose you've ever been to Parchman.'

'No. Since I learned the truth, I've been tempted to return to Mississippi, but it hasn't happened.'

'It's a massive farm in the middle of the Mississippi Delta, not too far from Greenville, ironically. Something like seventeen thousand acres. Probably the hottest place in the world. It sits on Highway 49, just like a little hamlet off to the west. Lots of buildings and houses. The front part is all administration, and it's not enclosed by fencing. There are about thirty different camps scattered around the farm, all fenced and secured. Each camp is completely separate. Some are miles apart. You drive past various camps, all enclosed by chain link and barbed wire, all with hundreds of prisoners hanging around, doing nothing. They wear different colors, depending on their classification. It seemed as if they were all young black kids, just loitering about, some playing basketball, some just sitting on the porches of the buildings. An occasional white face. You drive in your car, alone and very slowly, down a gravel road, past the camps and the barbed wire until you come to a seemingly innocuous little building with a flat roof. It has tall fences around it with guards watching from the towers. It's a fairly modern facility. It has an official name of some sort, but everyone refers to it simply as the Row.'

'Sounds like a wonderful place.'

'I thought it would be a dungeon, you know, dark and cold with water dripping from above. But it's just a little flat building out in the middle of a cotton field. Actually, it's not as bad as death rows in other states.'

'I'd like to see the Row.'

'You're not ready to see it. It's a horrible place filled with depressing people waiting to die. I was sixty years old before I saw it, and I didn't sleep for a week afterward.' He took a sip of coffee. 'I can't imagine how you'll feel when you go there. The Row is bad enough when you're representing a complete stranger.'

'He is a complete stranger.'

'How do you intend to tell him –'

'I don't know. I'll think of something. I'm sure it'll just happen.'

Goodman shook his head. 'This is bizarre.'

'The whole family is bizarre.'

'I remember now that Sam had two children, seems like one is a daughter. It's been a long time. Tyner did most of the work, you know.'

'His daughter is my aunt, Lee Cayhall Booth, but she tries to forget her maiden name. She married into old Memphis money. Her husband owns a bank or two, and they tell no one about her father.'

'Where's your mother?'

'Portland. She remarried a few years ago, and we talk about twice a year. Dysfunctional would be a mild term.'

'How'd you afford Pepperdine?'

'Life insurance. My father had trouble keeping a job, but he was wise enough to carry life insurance. The waiting period had expired years before he killed himself.'

'Sam never talked about his family.'

'And his family never talks about him. His wife, my grandmother, died a few years before he was convicted. I didn't know this, of course. Most of my genealogical research has been extracted from my mother, who's done a great job of forgetting the past. I don't know how it works in normal families, Mr Goodman, but my family seldom gets

41

together, and when two or more of us happen to meet the last thing we discuss is the past. There are many dark secrets.'

Goodman was nibbling on a chip and listening closely. 'You mentioned a sister.'

'Yes, I have a sister, Carmen. She's twenty-three, a bright and beautiful girl, in graduate school at Berkeley. She was born in L.A., so she didn't go through the name change like the rest of us. We keep in touch.'

'She knows?'

'Yes, she knows. My aunt Lee told me first, just after my father's funeral, then, typically, my mother asked me to tell Carmen. She was only fourteen at the time. She's never expressed any interest in Sam Cayhall. Frankly, the rest of the family wishes he would quietly just go away.'

'They're about to get their wish.'

'But it won't be quietly, will it, Mr Goodman?'

'No. It never is. For one brief terrible moment, Sam Cayhall will be the most talked about man in the country. We'll see the same old footage from the bomb blast, and the trials with the Klan marching around the courthouses. The same old debate about the death penalty will erupt. The press will descend upon Parchman. Then, they'll kill him, and two days later it'll all be forgotten. Happens every time.'

Adam stirred his soup and carefully picked out a sliver of chicken. He examined it for a second, then returned it to the broth. He was not hungry. Goodman finished another chip, and touched the corners of his mouth with the napkin.

'I don't suppose, Mr Hall, that you're thinking you can keep this quiet.'

'I had given it some thought.'

'Forget it.'

'My mother begged me not to do it. My sister wouldn't discuss it. And my aunt in Memphis is rigid with the remote possibility that we'll all be identified as Cayhalls and forever ruined.'

'The possibility is not remote. When the press finishes

42

with you, they'll have old black-and-whites of you sitting on your granddaddy's knee. It'll make great print, Mr Hall. Just think of it. The forgotten grandson charging in at the last moment, making a heroic effort to save his wretched old grandfather as the clock ticks down.'

'I sort of like it myself.'

'Not bad, really. It'll bring a lot of attention to our beloved little law firm.'

'Which brings up another unpleasant issue.'

'I don't think so. There are no cowards at Kravitz & Bane, Adam. We have survived and prospered in the rough and tumble world of Chicago law. We're known as the meanest bastards in town. We have the thickest skins. Don't worry about the firm.'

'So you'll agree to it.'

Goodman placed his napkin on the table and took another sip of coffee. 'Oh, it's a wonderful idea, assuming your gramps will agree to it. If you can sign him up, or re-sign him I should say, then we're back in business. You'll be the front man. We can feed you what you need from up here. I'll always be in your shadow. It'll work. Then, they'll kill him and you'll never get over it. I've watched three of my clients die, Mr Hall, including one in Mississippi. You'll never be the same.'

Adam nodded and smiled and looked at the pedestrians on the sidewalk.

Goodman continued. 'We'll be around to support you when they kill him. You won't have to bear it alone.'

'It's not hopeless, is it?'

'Almost. We'll talk strategy later. First, I'll meet with Daniel Rosen. He'll probably want a long conference with you. Second, you'll have to see Sam and have a little reunion, so to speak. That's the hard part. Third, if he agrees to it, then we'll get to work.'

'Thanks.'

'Don't thank me, Adam. I doubt if we'll be on speaking terms when this is over.'

'Thanks anyway.'

FIVE

THE MEETING was organized quickly. E. Garner Goodman made the first phone call, and within an hour the necessary participants had been summoned. Within four hours they were present in a small, seldom used conference room next to Daniel Rosen's office. It was Rosen's turf, and this disturbed Adam more than a little.

By legend, Daniel Rosen was a monster, though two heart attacks had knocked off some of the edge and mellowed him a bit. For thirty years he had been a ruthless litigator, the meanest, nastiest, and without a doubt one of the most effective courtroom brawlers in Chicago. Before the heart attacks, he was known for his brutal work schedule – ninety-hour weeks, midnight orgies of work with clerks and paralegals digging and fetching. Several wives had left him. As many as four secretaries at a time labored furiously to keep pace. Daniel Rosen had been the heart and soul of Kravitz & Bane, but no longer. His doctor restricted him to fifty hours a week, in the office, and prohibited any trial work.

Now, Rosen, at the age of sixty-five and getting heavy, had been unanimously selected by his beloved colleagues to graze the gentler pastures of law office management. He had the responsibility of overseeing the rather cumbersome bureaucracy that ran Kravitz & Bane. It was an honor, the other partners had explained feebly when they bestowed it upon him.

So far the honor had been a disaster. Banished from the

battlefield he desperately loved and needed, Rosen went about the business of managing the firm in a manner very similar to the preparation of an expensive lawsuit. He cross-examined secretaries and clerks over the most trivial of matters. He confronted other partners and harangued them for hours over vague issues of firm policy. Confined to the prison of his office, he called for young associates to come visit him, then picked fights to gauge their mettle under pressure.

He deliberately took the seat directly across the small conference table from Adam, and held a thin file as if it possessed a deadly secret. E. Garner Goodman sat low in the seat next to Adam, twiddling his bow tie and scratching his beard. When he telephoned Rosen with Adam's request, and broke the news of Adam's lineage, Rosen had reacted with predictable foolishness.

Emmitt Wycoff stood at one end of the room with a matchbox-sized cellular phone stuck to his ear. He was almost fifty, looked much older, and lived each day in a fixed state of panic and telephones.

Rosen carefully opened the file in front of Adam and removed a yellow legal pad. 'Why didn't you tell us about your grandfather when we interviewed you last year?' he began with clipped words and a fierce stare.

'Because you didn't ask me,' Adam answered. Goodman had advised him the meeting might get rough, but he and Wycoff would prevail.

'Don't be a wise ass,' Rosen growled.

'Come on, Daniel,' Goodman said, and rolled his eyes at Wycoff who shook his head and glanced at the ceiling.

'You don't think, Mr Hall, that you should've informed us that you were related to one of our clients? Certainly you believe we have a right to know this, don't you, Mr Hall?' His mocking tone was one usually reserved for witnesses who were lying and trapped.

'You guys asked me about everything else,' Adam replied, very much under control. 'Remember the security check? The fingerprints? There was even talk of a polygraph.'

'Yes, Mr Hall, but you knew things we didn't. And your grandfather was a client of this firm when you applied for employment, and you damned sure should've told us.' Rosen's voice was rich, and moved high and low with the dramatic flair of a fine actor. His eyes never left Adam.

'Not your typical grandfather,' Adam said quietly.

'He's still your grandfather, and you knew he was a client when you applied for a job here.'

'Then I apologize,' Adam said. 'This firm has thousands of clients, all well heeled and paying through the nose for our services. I never dreamed one insignificant little pro bono case would cause any grief.'

'You're deceitful, Mr Hall. You deliberately selected this firm because it, at the time, represented your grandfather. And now, suddenly, here you are begging for the file. It puts us in an awkward position.'

'What awkward position?' Emmitt Wycoff asked, folding the phone and stuffing it in a pocket. 'Look, Daniel, we're talking about a man on death row. He needs a lawyer, dammit!'

'His own grandson?' Rosen asked.

'Who cares if it's his own grandson? The man has one foot in the grave, and he needs a lawyer.'

'He fired us, remember?' Rosen shot back.

'Yeah, and he can always rehire us. It's worth a try. Lighten up.'

'Listen, Emmitt, it's my job to worry about the image of this firm, and the idea of sending one of our new associates down to Mississippi to have his ass kicked and his client executed does not appeal to me. Frankly, I think Mr Hall should be terminated by Kravitz & Bane.'

'Oh wonderful, Daniel,' Wycoff said. 'Typical hard-nose response to a delicate issue. Then who'll represent Cayhall? Think about him for a moment. The man needs a lawyer! Adam may be his only chance.'

'God help him,' Rosen mumbled.

E. Garner Goodman decided to speak. He locked his hands together on the table and glared at Rosen. 'The image

46

of this firm? Do you honestly think we're viewed as a bunch of underpaid social workers dedicated to helping people?'

'Or how about a bunch of nuns working in the projects?' Wycoff added helpfully, with a sneer.

'How could this possibly hurt the image of our firm?' Goodman asked.

The concept of retreat had never entered Rosen's mind. 'Very simple, Garner. We do not send our rookies to death row. We may abuse them, try to kill them, expect them to work twenty hours a day, but we do not send them into battle until they are ready. You know how dense death penalty litigation is. Hell, you wrote the books. How can you expect Mr Hall here to be effective?'

'I'll supervise everything he does,' Goodman answered.

'He's really quite good,' Wycoff added again. 'He's memorized the entire file, you know, Daniel.'

'It'll work,' Goodman said. 'Trust me, Daniel, I've been through enough of these things. I'll keep my finger on it.'

'And I'll set aside a few hours to help,' Wycoff added. 'I'll even fly down if necessary.'

Goodman jerked and stared at Wycoff. 'You! Pro bono?'

'Sure. I have a conscience.'

Adam ignored the banter and stared at Daniel Rosen. Go ahead and fire me, he wanted to say. Go ahead, Mr Rosen, terminate me so I can go bury my grandfather, then get on with the rest of my life.

'And if he's executed?' Rosen asked in the direction of Goodman.

'We've lost them before, Daniel, you know that. Three, since I've run pro bono.'

'What are his chances?'

'Quite slim. Right now he's holding on by virtue of a stay granted by the Fifth Circuit. The stay should be lifted any day now, and a new execution date will be set. Probably late summer.'

'Not long then.'

'Right. We've handled his appeals for seven years, and they've run their course.'

'Of all the people on death row, how'd we come to represent this asshole?' Rosen demanded.

'It's a very long story, and at this moment it's completely irrelevant.'

Rosen made what appeared to be serious notes on his legal pad. 'You don't think for a moment you'll keep this quiet, do you?'

'Maybe.'

'Maybe hell. Just before they kill him, they'll make him a celebrity. The media will surround him like a pack of wolves. You'll be discovered, Mr Hall.'

'So?'

'So, it'll make great copy, Mr Hall. Can't you see the headlines – LONG-LOST GRANDSON RETURNS TO SAVE GRAMPS.'

'Knock it off, Daniel,' Goodman said.

But he continued. 'The press will eat it up, don't you see, Mr Hall? They'll expose you and talk about how crazy your family is.'

'But we love the press, don't we, Mr Rosen?' Adam asked coolly. 'We're trial lawyers. Aren't we supposed to perform for the cameras? You've never –'

'A very good point,' Goodman interrupted. 'Daniel, perhaps you shouldn't advise this young man to ignore the press. We can tell stories about some of your stunts.'

'Yes, please, Daniel, lecture the kid about everything else, but lay off the media crap,' Wycoff said with a nasty grin. 'You wrote the book.'

For a brief moment, Rosen appeared to be embarrassed. Adam watched him closely.

'I rather like the scenario myself,' Goodman said, twirling his bow tie and studying the bookshelves behind Rosen. 'There's a lot to be said for it, actually. Could be great for us poor little pro bono folks. Think of it. This young lawyer down there fighting like crazy to save a rather famous death row killer. And he's our lawyer – Kravitz & Bane. Sure there'll be a ton of press, but what will it hurt?'

'It's a wonderful idea, if you ask me,' Wycoff added just

as his mini-phone buzzed somewhere deep in a pocket. He stuck it to his jaw and turned away from the meeting.

'What if he dies? Don't we look bad?' Rosen asked Goodman.

'He's supposed to die, okay? That's why he's on death row,' Goodman explained.

Wycoff stopped his mumbling and slid the phone into a pocket. 'I gotta go,' he said, moving toward the door, nervous now, in a hurry. 'Where are we?'

'I still don't like it,' Rosen said.

'Daniel, Daniel, always a hard ass,' Wycoff said as he stopped at the end of the table and leaned on it with both hands. 'You know it's a good idea, you're just pissed because he didn't tell us up front.'

'That's true. He deceived us, and now he's using us.'

Adam took a deep breath and shook his head.

'Get a grip, Daniel. His interview was a year ago, in the past. It's gone, man. Forget about it. We have more pressing matters at hand. He's bright. He works very hard. Smooth on his feet. Meticulous research. We're lucky to have him. So his family's messed up. Surely we're not going to terminate every lawyer here with a dysfunctional family.' Wycoff grinned at Adam. 'Plus, all the secretaries think he's cute. I say we send him south for a few months, then get him back here as soon as possible. I need him. Gotta run.' He disappeared and closed the door behind him.

The room was silent as Rosen scribbled on his pad, then gave it up and closed the file. Adam almost felt sorry for him. Here was this great warrior, the legendary Charlie Hustle of Chicago law, a great barrister who for thirty years swayed juries and terrified opponents and intimidated judges, now sitting here as a pencil pusher, trying desperately to agonize over the question of assigning a rookie to a pro bono project. Adam saw the humor, the irony, and the pity.

'I'll agree to it, Mr Hall,' Rosen said with much drama in his low voice, almost a whisper, as if terribly frustrated by all this. 'But I promise you this: when the Cayhall matter is

49

over, and you return to Chicago, I'll recommend your termination from Kravitz & Bane.'

'Probably won't be necessary,' Adam said quickly.

'You presented yourself to us under false pretenses,' Rosen continued.

'I said I was sorry. Won't happen again.'

'Plus, you're a smart ass.'

'So are you, Mr Rosen. Show me a trial lawyer who's not a smart ass.'

'Real cute. Enjoy the Cayhall case, Mr Hall, because it'll be your last bit of work for this firm.'

'You want me to enjoy an execution?'

'Relax, Daniel,' Goodman said softly. 'Just relax. No one's getting fired around here.'

Rosen pointed an angry finger at Goodman. 'I swear I'll recommend his termination.'

'Fine. All you can do is recommend, Daniel. I'll take it to the committee, and we'll just have a huge brawl. Okay?'

'I can't wait,' Rosen snarled as he jumped to his feet. 'I'll start lobbying now. I'll have my votes by the end of the week. Good day!' He stormed from the room and slammed the door.

They sat in silence next to each other, just staring across the table over the backs of the empty chairs to the rows of thick law books lined neatly on the wall, listening to the echo of the slamming door.

'Thanks,' Adam finally said.

'He's not a bad guy, really,' Goodman said.

'Charming. A real prince.'

'I've known him a long time. He's suffering now, really frustrated and depressed. We're not sure what to do with him.'

'What about retirement?'

'It's been considered, but no partner has ever been forced into retirement. For obvious reasons, it's a precedent we'd like to avoid.'

'Is he serious about firing me?'

'Don't worry, Adam. It won't happen. I promise. You

50

were wrong in not disclosing it, but it's a minor sin. And a perfectly understandable one. You're young, scared, naive, and you want to help. Don't worry about Rosen. I doubt if he'll be in this position three months from now.'

'Deep down, I think he adores me.'

'It's quite obvious.'

Adam took a deep breath and walked around the table. Goodman uncapped his pen and began making notes. 'There's not much time, Adam,' he said.

'I know.'

'When can you leave?'

'Tomorrow. I'll pack tonight. It's a ten-hour drive.'

'The file weighs a hundred pounds. It's down in printing right now. I'll ship it tomorrow.'

'Tell me about our office in Memphis.'

'I talked to them about an hour ago. Managing partner is Baker Cooley, and he's expecting you. They'll have a small office and a secretary for you, and they'll help if they can. They're not much when it comes to litigation.'

'How many lawyers?'

'Twelve. It's a little boutique firm we swallowed ten years ago, and no one remembers exactly why. Good boys, though. Good lawyers. It's the remnants of an old firm that prospered with the cotton and grain traders down there, and I think that's the connection to Chicago. Anyway, it looks nice on the letterhead. Have you been to Memphis?'

'I was born there, remember?'

'Oh yes.'

'I've been once. I visited my aunt there a few years ago.'

'It's an old river town, pretty laid back. You'll enjoy it.'

Adam sat across the table from Goodman. 'How can I possibly enjoy the next few months?'

'Good point. You should go to the Row as quickly as possible.'

'I'll be there the day after tomorrow.'

'Good. I'll call the warden. His name is Philip Naifeh, Lebanese oddly enough. There are quite a few of them in

51

the Mississippi Delta. Anyway, he's an old friend, and I'll tell him you're coming.'

'The warden is your friend?'

'Yes. We go back several years, to Maynard Tole, a nasty little boy who was my first casualty in this war. He was executed in 1986, I believe, and the warden and I became friends. He's opposed to the death penalty, if you can believe it.'

'I don't believe it.'

'He hates executions. You're about to learn something, Adam – the death penalty may be very popular in our country, but the people who are forced to impose it are not supporters. You're about to meet these people: the guards who get close to the inmates; the administrators who must plan for an efficient killing; the prison employees who rehearse for a month beforehand. It's a strange little corner of the world, and a very depressing one.'

'I can't wait.'

'I'll talk to the warden, and get permission for the visit. They'll usually give you a couple of hours. Of couse, it may take five minutes if Sam doesn't want a lawyer.'

'He'll talk to me, don't you think?'

'I believe so. I cannot imagine how the man will react, but he'll talk. It may take a couple of visits to sign him up, but you can do it.'

'When did you last see him?'

'Couple of years ago. Wallace Tyner and I went down. You'll need to touch base with Tyner. He was the point man on this case for the past six years.'

Adam nodded and moved to the next thought. He'd been picking Tyner's brain for the past nine months.

'What do we file first?'

'We'll talk about it later. Tyner and I are meeting early in the morning to review the case. Everything's on hold, though, until we hear from you. We can't move if we don't represent him.'

Adam was thinking of the newspaper photos, the black and whites from 1967 when Sam was arrested, and the

52

magazine photos, in color, from the third trial in 1981, and the footage he'd pieced together into a thirty-minute video about Sam Cayhall. 'What does he look like?'

Goodman left his pen on the table and fiddled with his bow tie. 'Average height. Thin – but then you seldom see a fat one on the Row – nerves and lean food. He chain-smokes, which is common because there's not much else to do, and they're dying anyway. Some weird brand, Montclair, I believe, in a blue pack. His hair is gray and oily, as I recall. These guys don't get a shower every day. Sort of long in the back, but that was two years ago. He hasn't lost much of it. Gray beard. He's fairly wrinkled, but then he's pushing seventy. Plus, the heavy smoking. You'll notice the white guys on the Row look worse than the black ones. They're confined for twenty-three hours a day, so they sort of bleach out. Real pale, fair, almost sickly-looking. Sam has blue eyes, nice features. I suspect that at óne time Sam Cayhall was a handsome fellow.'

'After my father died, and I learned the truth about Sam, I had a lot of questions for my mother. She didn't have many answers, but she did tell me once that there was little physical resemblance between Sam and my father.'

'Nor between you and Sam, if that's what you're getting at.'

'Yeah, I guess.'

'He hasn't seen you since you were a toddler, Adam. He will not recognize you. It won't be that easy. You'll have to tell him.'

Adam stared blankly at the table. 'You're right. What will he say?'

'Beats me. I expect he'll be too shocked to say much. But he's a very intelligent man, not educated, but well read and articulate. He'll think of something to say. It may take a few minutes.'

'You sound as if you almost like him.'

'I don't. He's a horrible racist and bigot, and he's shown no remorse for his actions.'

'You're convinced he's guilty.'

Goodman grunted and smiled to himself, then thought of a response. Three trials had been held to determine the guilt or innocence of Sam Cayhall. For nine years now the case had been batted around the appellate courts and reviewed by many judges. Countless newspaper and magazine articles had investigated the bombing and those behind it. 'The jury thought so. I guess that's all that matters.'

'But what about you? What do you think?'

'You've read the file, Adam. You've researched the case for a long time. There's no doubt Sam took part in the bombing.'

'But?'

'There are a lot of buts. There always are.'

'He had no history of handling explosives.'

'True. But he was a Klan terrorist, and they were bombing like hell. Sam gets arrested, and the bombing stops.'

'But in one of the bombings before Kramer, a witness claims he saw two people in the green Pontiac.'

'True. But the witness was not allowed to testify at trial. And the witness had just left a bar at three in the morning.'

'But another witness, a truck driver, claims he saw Sam and another man talking in a coffee shop in Cleveland a few hours before the Kramer bombing.'

'True. But the truck driver said nothing for three years, and was not allowed to testify at the last trial. Too remote.'

'So who was Sam's accomplice?'

'I doubt if we'll ever know. Keep in mind, Adam, this is a man who went to trial three times, yet never testified. He said virtually nothing to the police, very little to his defense lawyers, not a word to his juries, and he's told us nothing new in the past seven years.'

'Do you think he acted alone?'

'No. He had help. Sam's carrying dark secrets, Adam. He'll never tell. He took an oath as a Klansman, and he has this really warped, romantic notion of a sacred vow he can never violate. His father was a Klansman too, you know?'

'Yeah, I know. Don't remind me.'

54

'Sorry. Anyway, it's too late in the game to fish around for new evidence. If he in fact had an accomplice, he should've talked long ago. Maybe he should've talked to the FBI. Maybe he should've cut a deal with the district attorney. I don't know, but when you're indicted on two counts of capital murder and facing death, you start talking. You talk, Adam. You save your ass and let your buddy worry about his.'

'And if there was no accomplice?'

'There was.' Goodman took his pen and wrote a name on a piece of paper. He slid it across the table to Adam, who looked at it and said, 'Wyn Lettner. The name is familiar.'

'Lettner was the FBI agent in charge of the Kramer case. He's now retired and living on a trout river in the Ozarks. He loves to tell war stories about the Klan and the civil rights days in Mississippi.'

'And he'll talk to me?'

'Oh sure. He's a big beer drinker, and he gets about half loaded and tells these incredible stories. He won't divulge anything confidential, but he knows more about the Kramer bombing than anyone. I've always suspected he knows more than he's told.'

Adam folded the paper and placed it in his pocket. He glanced at his watch. It was almost 6 P.M. 'I need to run. I have to pack and all.'

'I'll ship the file down tomorrow. You need to call me as soon as you talk to Sam.'

'I will. Can I say something?'

'Sure.'

'On behalf of my family, such as it is – my mother who refuses to discuss Sam; my sister who only whispers his name; my aunt in Memphis who has disowned the name Cayhall – and on behalf of my late father, I would like to say thanks to you and to this firm for what you've done. I admire you greatly.'

'You're welcome. And I admire you. Now get your ass down to Mississippi.'

55

SIX

THE APARTMENT was a one-bedroom loft somewhere above the third floor of a turn-of-the-century warehouse just off the Loop, in a section of downtown known for crime but said to be safe until dark. The warehouse had been purchased in the mid-eighties by an S&L swinger who spent a bundle sanitizing and modernizing. He chopped it into sixty units, hired a slick realtor, and marketed it as yuppie starter condos. He made money as the place filled overnight with eager young bankers and brokers.

Adam hated the place. He had three weeks left on a six-month lease, but there was no place to go. He would be forced to renew for another six months because Kravitz & Bane expected eighteen hours a day, and there'd been no time to search for another apartment.

Nor had there been much time to purchase furniture, evidently. A fine leather sofa without arms of any kind sat alone on the wooden floor and faced an ancient brick wall. Two bean bags – yellow and blue – were nearby in the unlikely event a crowd materialized. To the left was a tiny kitchen area with a snack bar and three wicker stools, and to the right of the sofa was the bedroom with the unmade bed and clothes on the floor. Seven hundred square feet, for thirteen hundred bucks a month. Adam's salary, as a blue chip prospect nine months earlier, had begun at sixty thousand a year, and was now at sixty-two. From his gross pay of slightly over five thousand a month, fifteen hundred was withheld for state and federal income taxes. Another six hundred never reached his fingers but went instead into a Kravitz & Bane retirement fund guaranteed to relieve the pressure at age fifty-five, if they didn't kill him first. After rent, utilities, four hundred a month for a leased Saab, and incidentals such as frozen food and some nice clothes, Adam found himself with about seven hundred dollars to play with. Some of this remainder was spent on women, but the ones he knew were also fresh from college with new jobs and credit cards and generally insistent on paying their own way. This was fine with Adam. Thanks to his father's faith in life insurance, he had no student loans. Even though there were things he wanted to buy, he doggedly plowed five hundred a month into mutual funds. With no immediate prospect of a wife and family, his goal was to work hard, save hard, and retire at forty.

Against the brick wall was an aluminum table with a television on it. Adam sat on the sofa, nude except for boxer shorts, holding the remote control. But for the colorless radiation from the screen, the loft was dark. It was after midnight. The video was one he'd pieced together over the years – *The Adventures of a Klan Bomber*, he called it. It started with a brief news report filed by a local crew in Jackson, Mississippi, on March 3, 1967, the morning after a synagogue was leveled by a bomb blast. It was the fourth known attack against Jewish targets in the past two months, the reporter said as a backhoe roared behind her with a bucket full of debris. The FBI had few clues, she said, and even fewer words for the press. The Klan's campaign of terror continues, she declared gravely, and signed off.

The Kramer bombing was next, and the story started with sirens screaming and police pushing people away from the scene. A local reporter and his cameraman were on the spot quickly enough to capture the initial bedlam. People were seen running to the remains of Marvin's office. A heavy cloud of gray dust hung above the small oak trees on the front lawn. The trees were battered and leafless, but standing. The cloud was still and showed no signs of dissipating. Off camera, voices yelled about a fire, and the

57

camera rocked along and stopped in front of the building next door where thick smoke poured from a damaged wall. The reporter, breathless and panting into the microphone, jabbered incoherently about the entire shocking scene. He pointed over here, then over there as the camera jerked in belated response. The police pushed him away, but he was too excited to care. Glorious pandemonium had erupted in the sleepy town of Greenville, and this was his grand moment.

Thirty minutes later, from a different angle, his voice was somewhat calmer as he described the frantic removal of Marvin Kramer from the rubble. The police extended their barricades and inched the crowd backward as the fire and rescue people lifted his body and worked the stretcher through the wreckage. The camera followed the ambulance as it sped away. Then, an hour later and from still another angle, the reporter was quite composed and somber as the two stretchers with the covered little bodies were delicately handled by the firemen.

The video cut from the footage of the bombing scene to the front of the jail, and for the first time there was a glimpse of Sam Cayhall. He was handcuffed and ushered quickly into a waiting car.

As always, Adam pushed a button and replayed the brief scene with the shot of Sam. It was 1967, twenty-three years ago. Sam was forty-six years old. His hair was dark and cut close, the fashion of the times. There was a small bandage under his left eye, away from the camera. He walked quickly, stride for stride with the deputies because people were watching and taking pictures and yelling questions. He turned only once to their voices, and, as always, Adam froze the tape and stared for the millionth time into the face of his grandfather. The picture was black and white and not clear, but their eyes always met.

Nineteen sixty-seven. If Sam was forty-six, then Eddie was twenty-four, and Adam was almost three. He was known as Alan then. Alan Cayhall, soon to be a resident of a distant state where a judge would sign a decree giving him a new name. He had often watched this video and wondered where he was at the precise moment the Kramer boys were killed: 7:46 A.M., April 21, 1967. His family lived at that time in a small house in the town of Clanton, and he was probably still asleep not far from his mother's watch. He was almost three, and the Kramer twins were only five.

The video continued with more quick shots of Sam being led to and from various cars, jails, and courthouses. He was always handcuffed, and he developed the habit of staring at the ground just a few feet in front of him. His face bore no expression. He never looked at the reporters, never acknowledged their inquiries, never said a word. He moved quickly, darting out of doors and into waiting cars.

The spectacle of his first two trials was amply recorded by daily television news reports. Over the years, Adam had been able to retrieve most of the footage, and had carefully edited the material. There was the loud and blustering face of Clovis Brazelton, Sam's lawyer, holding forth for the press at every opportunity. But the clips of Brazelton had been edited quite heavily, with time. Adam despised the man. There were clear, sweeping shots of the courthouse lawns, with the crowds of silent onlookers, and the heavily armed state police, and the robed Klansmen with their coneheads and sinister masks. There were brief glimpses of Sam, always in a hurry, always shielding himself from the cameras by ducking along behind a beefy deputy. After the second trial and the second hung jury, Marvin Kramer stopped his wheelchair on the side-walk in front of the Wilson County Courthouse, and with tears in his eyes bitterly condemned Sam Cayhall and the Ku Klux Klan and the hidebound justice system in Mississippi. As the cameras rolled, a pitiful incident unfolded. Marvin suddenly spotted two Klansmen in white robes not far away, and began screaming at them. One of them yelled back, but his reply was lost in the heat of the moment. Adam had tried everything to retrieve the Klansman's words from the air, but with no luck. The reply would be forever unintelligible. A couple of years earlier, while in law school at

Michigan, Adam had found one of the local reporters who was standing there at the moment, holding a microphone not far from Marvin's face. According to the reporter, the reply from across the lawn had something to do with their desire to blow off the rest of Marvin's limbs. Something this crude and cruel appeared to be true because Marvin went beserk. He screamed obscenities at the Kluckers, who were easing away, and he spun the metal wheels of his chair, lunging in their direction. He was yelling and cursing and crying. His wife and a few friends tried to restrain him, but he broke free, his hands furiously working the wheels. He rolled about twenty feet, with his wife in chase, with the cameras recording it all, until the sidewalk ended and the grass began. The wheelchair flipped, and Marvin sprawled onto the lawn. The quilt around his amputated legs flung free as he rolled hard next to a tree. His wife and friends were on him immediately, and for a moment or two he disappeared into a small huddle on the ground. But he could still be heard. As the camera backed away and shot quickly at the two Klansmen, one doubled over with laughter and one frozen in place, an odd wailing erupted from the small crowd on the ground. Marvin was moaning, but in the shrill, high-pitched howl of a wounded madman. It was a sick sound, and after a few miserable seconds of it the video cut to the next scene.

Adam had tears in his eyes the first time he watched Marvin roll on the ground, howling and groaning, and though the images and sounds still tightened his throat, he had stopped crying long ago. This video was his creation. No one had seen it but him. And he'd watched it so many times that tears were no longer possible.

Technology improved immensely from 1968 to 1981, and the footage from Sam's third and last trial was much sharper and clearer. It was February of 1981, in a pretty little town with a busy square and a quaint courthouse of red brick. The air was bitterly cold, and perhaps this kept away the crowds of onlookers and demonstrators. One report from the first day of the trial had a brief shot of three behooded

Klansmen huddled around a portable heater, rubbing their hands and looking more like Mardi Gras revelers than serious hoodlums. They were watched by a dozen or so state troopers, all in blue jackets.

Because the civil rights movement was viewed by this time as more of a historical event than a continuing struggle, the third trial of Sam Cayhall attracted more media than the first two. Here was an admitted Klansman, a real live terrorist from the distant era of Freedom Riders and church bombings. Here was a relic from those infamous days who'd been tracked down and was now being hauled to justice. The analogy to Nazi war criminals was made more than once.

Sam was not in custody during his last trial. He was a free man, and his freedom made it even more difficult to catch him on camera. There were quick shots of him darting into various doors of the courthouse. Sam had aged gracefully in the thirteen years since trial number two. The hair was still short and neat, but half gray now. He appeared a bit heavier, but fit. He moved deftly along sidewalks and in and out of automobiles as the media gave chase. One camera caught him as he stepped from a side door of the courthouse, and Adam stopped the tape just as Sam stared directly into the camera.

Much of the footage of the third and final trial centered around a cocky young prosecutor named David McAllister, a handsome man who wore dark suits and a quick smile with perfect teeth. There was little doubt that David McAllister held grand political ambitions. He had the looks, the hair, the chin, the rich voice, the smooth words, the ability to attract cameras.

In 1989, eight short years after the trial, David McAllister was elected governor of the State of Mississippi. To no one's surprise, the widest planks in his platform had been more jails, longer sentences, and an unwavering affinity for the death penalty. Adam despised him too, but he knew that in a matter of weeks, maybe days, he would be sitting in the governor's office in Jackson, Mississippi, begging for a pardon.

The video ended with Sam, in handcuffs once again, being led from the courthouse after the jury condemned him to death. His face was expressionless. His lawyer appeared to be in shock and uttered a few unremarkable comments. The reporter signed off with the news that Sam would be transported to death row in a matter of days.

Adam pushed the rewind button and stared at the blank screen. Behind the armless sofa were three cardboard boxes which contained the rest of the story: the bulky transcripts of all three trials, which Adam had purchased while at Pepperdine; copies of the briefs and motions and other documents from the appellate warfare that had been raging since Sam's conviction; a thick and carefully indexed binder with neat copies of hundreds of newspaper and magazine stories about Sam's adventures as a Klansman; death penalty materials and research; notes from law school. He knew more about his grandfather than anyone alive.

Yet, Adam knew he had not scratched the surface. He pushed another button, and watched the video again.

SEVEN

THE FUNERAL for Eddie Cayhall occurred less than a month after Sam was sentenced to die. It was held in a small chapel in Santa Monica, and attended by few friends and even fewer family members. Adam sat on a front pew between his mother and sister. They held hands and stared at the closed casket just inches away. As always, his mother was stiff and stoic. Her eyes watered occasionally, and she was forced to dab them with a tissue. She and Eddie had separated and reconciled so many times the children had lost track of whose clothes were where. Though their marriage had never been violent, it had been lived in a continual state of divorce – threats of divorce, plans for divorce, solemn chats with the kids about divorce, negotiations for divorce, filings for divorce, retreat from divorce, vows to avoid divorce. During the third trial of Sam Cayhall, Adam's mother quietly moved her possessions back into their small house, and stayed with Eddie as much as possible. Eddie stopped going to work, and withdrew once again into his dark little world. Adam quizzed his mother, but she explained in a few short words that Dad was simply having another 'bad time'. The curtains were drawn; the shades were pulled; the lights were unplugged; the voices were lowered; the television was turned off as the family endured another of Eddie's bad times.

Three weeks after the verdict he was dead. He shot himself in Adam's bedroom, on a day when he knew Adam would be the first one home. He left a note on the floor with instructions for Adam to hurry and clean up the mess before the girls got home. Another note was found in the kitchen.

Carmen was fourteen at the time, almost three years younger than Adam. She had been conceived in Mississippi, but born in California after her parents' hasty migration westward. By the time she was born, Eddie had legally transformed his little family from Cayhalls to Halls. Alan had become Adam. They lived in East L.A., in a three-room apartment with dirty sheets on the windows. Adam remembered the sheets with the holes in them. It was the first of many temporary residences.

Next to Carmen on the front pew was a mysterious woman known as Aunt Lee. She had just been introduced to Adam and Carmen as Eddie's sister, his only sibling. As children they were taught not to ask questions about family, but occasionally Lee's name would surface. She lived in Memphis, had at one point married into a wealthy Memphis family, had a child, and had nothing to do with Eddie because of some ancient feud. The kids, Adam especially, had longed to meet a relative, and since Aunt Lee was the only one ever mentioned they fantasized about her. They wanted to meet her, but Eddie always refused because she was not a nice person, he said. But their mother whispered that Lee was indeed a good person, and that one day she would take them to Memphis to meet her.

Lee, instead, made the trip to California, and together they buried Eddie Hall. She stayed for two weeks after the funeral, and became acquainted with her niece and nephew. They loved her because she was pretty and cool, wore blue jeans and tee shirts, and walked barefoot on the beach. She took them shopping, and to the movies, and they went for long walks by the shore of the ocean. She made all sorts of excuses for not visiting sooner. She wanted to, she promised, but Eddie wouldn't allow it. He didn't want to see her because they had fought in the past.

And it was Aunt Lee who sat with Adam on the end of a pier, watching the sun sink into the Pacific, and finally talked of her father, Sam Cayhall. As the waves rocked

64

gently beneath them, Lee explained to young Adam that he had a brief prior life as a toddler in a small town in Mississippi. She held his hand and at times patted his knee while she unveiled the forlorn history of their family. She laid out the barest details of Sam's Klan activities, and of the Kramer bombing, and of the trials that eventually sent him to death row in Mississippi. There were gaps in her oral history large enough to fill libraries, but she covered the high spots with a great deal of finesse.

For an insecure sixteen-year-old who'd just lost his father, Adam took the whole thing rather well. He asked a few questions as a cool wind found the coast and they huddled together, but for the most part he just listened, not in shock or anger, but with enormous fascination. This awful tale was oddly satisfying. There was a family out there! Perhaps he wasn't so abnormal after all. Perhaps there were aunts and uncles and cousins with lives to share and stories to tell. Perhaps there were old homes built by real ancestors, and land and farms upon which they settled. He had a history after all.

But Lee was wise and quick enough to recognize this interest. She explained that the Cayhalls were a strange and secret breed who kept to themselves and shunned outsiders. They were not friendly and warm people who gathered for Christmas and reunited on the Fourth of July. She lived just an hour away from Clanton, yet never saw them.

The visits to the pier at dusk became a ritual for the next week. They would stop at the market and buy a sack of red grapes, then spit seeds into the ocean until well past dark. Lee told stories of her childhood in Mississippi with her little brother Eddie. They lived on a small farm fifteen minutes from Clanton, with ponds to fish in and ponies to ride. Sam was a decent father; not overbearing but certainly not affectionate. Her mother was a weak woman who disliked Sam but doted on her children. She lost a baby, a newborn, when Lee was six and Eddie was almost four, and she stayed in her bedroom for almost a year. Sam hired a black woman to care for Eddie and Lee. Her mother died of cancer, and it was the last time the Cayhalls gathered. Eddie sneaked into town for the funeral, but tried to avoid everyone. Three years later Sam was arrested for the last time and convicted.

Lee had little to say about her own life. She left home in a hurry at the age of eighteen, the week after high school graduation, and went straight to Nashville to get famous as a recording artist. Somehow she met Phelps Booth, a graduate student at Vanderbilt whose family owned banks. They were eventually married and settled into what appeared to be a miserable existence in Memphis. They had one son, Walt, who evidently was quite rebellious and now lived in Amsterdam. These were the only details.

Adam couldn't tell if Lee had transformed herself into something other than a Cayhall, but he suspected she had. Who could blame her?

Lee left as quietly as she had come. Without a hug or a farewell, she eased from their home before dawn, and was gone. She called two days later and talked to Adam and Carmen. She encouraged them to write, which they eagerly did, but the calls and letters from her became further apart. The promise of a new relationship slowly faded. Their mother made excuses. She said Lee was a good person, but she was nonetheless a Cayhall, and thus given to a certain amount of gloom and weirdness. Adam was crushed.

The summer after his graduation from Pepperdine, Adam and a friend drove across the country to Key West. They stopped in Memphis and spent two nights with Aunt Lee. She lived alone in a spacious, modern condo on a bluff overlooking the river, and they sat for hours on the patio, just the three of them, eating homemade pizza, drinking beer, watching barges, and talking about almost everything. Family was never mentioned. Adam was excited about law school, and Lee was full of questions about his future. She was vibrant and fun and talkative, the perfect hostess and aunt. When they hugged good-bye, her eyes watered and she begged him to come again.

66

Adam and his friend avoided Mississippi. They drove eastward instead, through Tennessee and the Smoky Mountains. At one point, according to Adam's calculations, they were within a hundred miles of Parchman and death row and Sam Cayhall. That was four years ago, in the summer of 1986, and he already had collected a large box full of materials about his grandfather. His video was almost complete.

THEIR CONVERSATION on the phone last night had been brief. Adam said he would be living in Memphis for a few months, and would like to see her. Lee invited him to her condo, the same one on the bluff, where she had four bedrooms and a part-time maid. He would live with her, she insisted. Then he said he would be working in the Memphis office, working on Sam's case as a matter of fact. There was silence on the other end, then a weak offer to come on down anyway and they would talk about it.

Adam pushed her doorbell at a few minutes after nine, and glanced at his black Saab convertible. The development was nothing but a single row of twenty units, all stacked tightly together with red-tiled roofs. A broad brick wall with heavy iron grating along the top protected those inside from the dangers of downtown Memphis. An armed guard worked the only gate. If not for the view of the river on the other side, the condos would be virtually worthless.

Lee opened the door and they pecked each other on the cheeks. 'Welcome,' she said, looking at the parking lot, then locking the door behind him. 'Are you tired?'

'Not really. It's a ten-hour drive but it took me twelve. I was not in a hurry.'

'Are you hungry?'

'No. I stopped a few hours ago.' He followed her into the den where they faced each other and tried to think of something appropriate to say. She was almost fifty, and had aged a lot in the past four years. The hair was now an equal mixture of gray and brunette, and much longer. She pulled it tightly into a ponytail. Her soft blue eyes were red and worried, and surrounded by more wrinkles. She wore an oversized cotton button-down and faded jeans. Lee was still cool.

'It's good to see you,' she said with a nice smile.

'Are you sure?'

'Of course I'm sure. Let's sit on the patio.' She took his hand and led him through the glass doors onto a wooden deck where baskets of ferns and bougainvillea hung from wooden beams. The river was below them. They sat in white wicker rockers. 'How's Carmen?' she asked as she poured ice tea from a ceramic pitcher.

'Fine. Still in grad school at Berkeley. We talk once a week. She's dating a guy pretty serious.'

'What's she studying now? I forget.'

'Psychology. Wants to get her doctorate, then maybe teach.' The tea was strong on lemon and short on sugar. Adam sipped it slowly. The air was still muggy and hot. 'It's almost ten o'clock,' he said. 'Why is it so hot?'

'Welcome to Memphis, dear. We'll roast through September.'

'I couldn't stand it.'

'You get used to it. Sort of. We drink lots of tea and stay inside. How's your mother?'

'Still in Portland. Now married to a man who made a fortune in timber. I've met him once. He's probably sixty-five, but could pass for seventy. She's forty-seven and looks forty. A beautiful couple. They jet here and there, St Barts, southern France, Milan, all the places where the rich need to be seen. She's very happy. Her kids are grown. Eddie's dead. Her past is tucked neatly away. And she has plenty of money. Her life is very much in order.'

'You're too harsh.'

'I'm too easy. She really doesn't want me around because I'm a painful link to my father and his pathetic family.'

'Your mother loves you, Adam.'

'Boy that's good to hear. How do you know so much?'

'I just know.'

'Didn't realize you and Mom were so close.'

68

'We're not. Settle down, Adam. Take it easy.'

'I'm sorry. I'm wired, that's all. I need a stronger drink.'

'Relax. Let's have some fun while you're here.'

'It's not a fun visit, Aunt Lee.'

'Just call me Lee, okay.'

'Okay. I'm going to see Sam tomorrow.'

She carefully placed her glass on the table, then stood and left the patio. She returned with a bottle of Jack Daniel's, and poured a generous shot into both glasses. She took a long drink and stared at the river in the distance. 'Why?' she finally asked.

'Why not? Because he's my grandfather. Because he's about to die. Because I'm a lawyer and he needs help.'

'He doesn't even know you.'

'He will tomorrow.'

'So you'll tell him?'

'Yes, of course I'm going to tell him. Can you believe it? I'm actually going to tell a deep, dark, nasty Cayhall secret. What about that?'

Lee held her glass with both hands and slowly shook her head. 'He'll die,' she mumbled without looking at Adam.

'Not yet. But it's nice to know you're concerned.'

'I am concerned.'

'Oh really. When did you last see him?'

'Don't start this, Adam. You don't understand.'

'Fine. Fair enough. Explain it to me then. I'm listening. I want to understand.'

'Can't we talk about something else, dear? I'm not ready for this.'

'No.'

'We can talk about this later, I promise. I'm just not ready for it right now. I thought we'd just gossip and laugh for a while.'

'I'm sorry, Lee. I'm sick of gossip and secrets. I have no past because my father conveniently erased it. I want to know about it, Lee. I want to know how bad it really is.'

'It's awful,' she whispered, almost to herself.

'Okay. I'm a big boy now. I can handle it. My father

69

checked out on me before he had to face it, so I'm afraid there's no one but you.'

'Give me some time.'

'There is no time. I'll be face-to-face with him tomorrow.' Adam took a long drink and wiped his lips with his sleeve. 'Twenty-three years ago, *Newsweek* said Sam's father was also a Klansman. Was he?'

'Yes. My grandfather.'

'And several uncles and cousins as well.'

'The whole damned bunch.'

'*Newsweek* also said that it was common knowledge in Ford County that Sam Cayhall shot and killed a black man in the early fifties, and was never arrested for it. Never served a day in jail. Is this true?'

'Why does it matter now, Adam? That was years before you were born.'

'So it really happened?'

'Yes, it happened.'

'And you knew about it?'

'I saw it.'

'You saw it!' Adam closed his eyes in disbelief. He breathed heavily and sunk lower into the rocker. The horn from a tugboat caught his attention, and he followed it downriver until it passed under a bridge. The bourbon was beginning to soothe.

'Let's talk about something else,' Lee said softly.

'Even when I was a little kid,' he said, still watching the river, 'I loved history. I was fascinated by the way people lived years ago – the pioneers, the wagon trains, the gold rush, cowboys and Indians, the settling of the West. There was a kid in the fourth grade who claimed his great-great-grandfather had robbed trains and buried the money in Mexico. He wanted to form a gang and run away to find the money. We knew he was lying, but it was great fun playing along. I often wondered about my ancestors, and I remember being puzzled because I didn't seem to have any.'

'What would Eddie say?'

'He told me they were all dead; said more time is wasted

70

on family history than anything else. Every time I asked questions about my family, Mother would pull me aside and tell me to stop because it might upset him and he might go off into one of his dark moods and stay in his bedroom for a month. I spent most of my childhood walking on egg-shells around my father. As I grew older, I began to realize he was a very strange man, very unhappy, but I never dreamed he would kill himself.'

She rattled her ice and took the last sip. 'There's a lot to it, Adam.'

'So when will you tell me?'

Lee gently took the pitcher and refilled their glasses. Adam poured bourbon into both. Several minutes passed as they sipped and watched the traffic on Riverside Drive.

'Have you been to death row?' he finally asked, still staring at the lights along the river.

'No,' she said, barely audible.

'He's been there for almost ten years, and you've never gone to see him?'

'I wrote him a letter once, shortly after his last trial. Six months later he wrote me back and told me not to come. Said he didn't want me to see him on death row. I wrote him two more letters, neither of which he answered.'

'I'm sorry.'

'Don't be sorry. I'm carrying a lot of guilt, Adam, and it's not easy to talk about. Just give me some time.'

'I may be in Memphis for a while.'

'I want you to stay here. We'll need each other.' She hesitated and stirred the drink with an index finger. 'I mean, he is going to die, isn't he?'

'It's likely.'

'When?'

'Two or three months. His appeals are virtually exhausted. There's not much left.'

'Then why are you getting involved?'

'I don't know. Maybe it's because we have a fighting chance. I'll work my tail off for the next few months and pray for a miracle.'

71

'I'll be praying too,' she said as she took another sip.

'Can we talk about something?' he asked, suddenly looking at her.

'Sure.'

'Do you live here alone? I mean, it's a fair question if I'm going to be staying here.'

'I live alone. My husband lives in our house in the country.'

'Does he live alone? Just curious.'

'Sometimes. He likes young girls, early twenties, usually employees at his banks. I'm expected to call before I go to the house. And he's expected to call before he comes here.'

'That's nice and convenient. Who negotiated that agreement?'

'We just sort of worked it out over time. We haven't lived together in fifteen years.'

'Some marriage.'

'It works quite well, actually. I take his money, and I ask no questions about his private life. We do the required little social numbers together, and he's happy.'

'Are you happy?'

'Most of the time.'

'If he cheats, why don't you sue for divorce and clean him out? I'll represent you.'

'A divorce wouldn't work. Phelps comes from a very proper, stiff old family of miserably rich people. Old Memphis society. Some of these families have intermarried for decades. In fact, Phelps was expected to marry a fifth cousin, but instead he fell under my charms. His family was viciously opposed to it, and a divorce now would be a painful admission that his family was right. Plus, these people are proud bluebloods, and a nasty divorce would humiliate them. I love the independence of taking his money and living as I choose.'

'Did you ever love him?'

'Of course. We were madly in love when we married. We eloped, by the way. It was 1963, and the idea of a large wedding with his family of aristocrats and my family of

72

rednecks was not appealing. His mother would not speak to me, and my father was burning crosses. At that time, Phelps did not know my father was a Klansman, and of course I desperately wanted to keep it quiet.'

'Did he find out?'

'As soon as Daddy was arrested for the bombing, I told him. He in turn told his father, and the word was spread slowly and carefully through the Booth family. These people are quite proficient at keeping secrets. It's the only thing they have in common with us Cayhalls.'

'So only a few know you're Sam's daughter?'

'Very few. I'd like to keep it that way.'

'You're ashamed of –'

'Hell yes I'm ashamed of my father! Who wouldn't be?' Her words were suddenly sharp and bitter. 'I hope you don't have some romanticized image of this poor old man suffering on death row, about to be unjustly crucified for his sins.'

'I don't think he should die.'

'Neither do I. But he's damned sure killed enough people – the Kramer twins, their father, your father, and God knows who else. He should stay in prison for the rest of his life.'

'You have no sympathy for him?'

'Occasionally. If I'm having a good day and the sun is shining, then I might think of him and remember a small pleasant event from my childhood. But those moments are very rare, Adam. He has caused much misery in my life and in the lives of those around him. He taught us to hate everybody. He was mean to our mother. His whole damned family is mean.'

'So let's just kill him then.'

'I didn't say that, Adam, and you're being unfair. I think about him all the time. I pray for him every day. I've asked these walls a million times why and how my father became such a horrible person. Why can't he be some nice old man right now sitting on the front porch with a pipe and a cane, maybe a little bourbon in a glass, for his stomach, of course?

73

Why did my father have to be a Klansman who killed innocent children and ruined his own family?'

'Maybe he didn't intend to kill them.'

'They're dead, aren't they? The jury said he did it. They were blown to bits and buried side by side in the same neat little grave. Who cares if he intended to kill them? He was there, Adam.'

'It could be very important.'

Lee jumped to her feet and grabbed his hand. 'Come here,' she insisted. They stepped a few feet to the edge of the patio. She pointed to the Memphis skyline several blocks away. 'You see that flat building facing the river there. The nearest to us. Just over there, three or four blocks away.'

'Yes,' he answered slowly.

'The top floor is the fifteenth, okay. Now, from the right, count down six levels. Do you follow?'

'Yes,' Adam nodded and counted obediently. The building was a showy high-rise.

'Now, count four windows to the left. There's a light on. Do you see it?'

'Yes.'

'Guess who lives there.'

'How would I know?'

'Ruth Kramer.'

'Ruth Kramer! The mother?'

'That's her.'

'Do you know her?'

'We met once, by accident. She knew I was Lee Booth, wife of the infamous Phelps Booth, but that was all. It was a glitzy fundraiser for the ballet or something. I've always avoided her if possible.'

'This must be a small town.'

'It can be tiny. If you could ask her about Sam, what would she say?'

Adam stared at the lights in the distance. 'I don't know. I've read that she's still bitter.'

'Bitter? She lost her entire family. She's never remarried.

74

Do you think she cares if my father intended to kill her children? Of course not. She just knows they're dead, Adam, dead for twenty-three years now. She knows they were killed by a bomb planted by my father, and if he'd been home with his family instead of riding around at night with his idiot buddies, little Josh and John would not be dead. They instead would be twenty-eight years old, probably very well educated and married with perhaps a baby or two for Ruth and Marvin to play with. She doesn't care who the bomb was intended for, Adam, only that it was placed there and it exploded. Her babies are dead. That's all that matters.'

Lee stepped backward and sat in her rocker. She rattled her ice again and took a drink. 'Don't get me wrong, Adam. I'm opposed to the death penalty. I'm probably the only fifty-year-old white woman in the country whose father is on death row. It's barbaric, immoral, discriminatory, cruel, uncivilized – I subscribe to all the above. But don't forget the victims, okay. They have the right to want retribution. They've earned it.'

'Does Ruth Kramer want retribution?'

'By all accounts, yes. She doesn't say much to the press anymore, but she's active with victims groups. Years ago she was quoted as saying she would be in the witness room when Sam Cayhall was executed.'

'Not exactly a forgiving spirit.'

'I don't recall my father asking for forgiveness.'

Adam turned and sat on the ledge with his back to the river. He glanced at the buildings downtown, then studied his feet. Lee took another long drink.

'Well, Aunt Lee, what are we going to do?'

'Please drop the Aunt.'

'Okay, Lee. I'm here. I'm not leaving. I'll visit Sam tomorrow, and when I leave I intend to be his lawyer.'

'Do you intend to keep it quiet?'

'The fact that I'm really a Cayhall? I don't plan to tell anyone, but I'll be surprised if it's a secret much longer. When it comes to death row inmates, Sam's a famous one. The press will start some serious digging pretty soon.'

Lee folded her feet under her and stared at the river. 'Will it harm you?' she asked softly.

'Of course not. I'm a lawyer. Lawyers defend child molesters and assassins and drug dealers and rapists and terrorists. We are not popular people. How can I be harmed by the fact that he's my grandfather?'

'Your firm knows?'

'I told them yesterday. They were not exactly delighted, but they came around. I hid it from them, actually, when they hired me, and I was wrong to do so. But I think things are okay.'

'What if he says no?'

'Then we'll be safe, won't we? No one will ever know, and you'll be protected. I'll go back to Chicago and wait for CNN to cover the carnival of the execution. And I'm sure I'll drive down one cool day in the fall and put some flowers on his grave, probably look at the tombstone and ask myself again why he did it and how he became such a lowlife and why was I born into such a wretched family, you know, the questions we've been asking for many years. I'll invite you to come with me. It'll be sort of a little family reunion, you know, just us Cayhalls slithering through the cemetery with a cheap bouquet of flowers and thick sunglasses so no one will discover us.'

'Stop it,' she said, and Adam saw the tears. They were flowing and were almost to her chin when she wiped them with her fingers.

'I'm sorry,' he said, then turned to watch another barge inch north through the shadows of the river. 'I'm sorry, Lee.'

EIGHT

SO AFTER TWENTY-THREE YEARS, he was finally
returning to the state of his birth. He didn't particularly feel
welcome, and though he wasn't particularly afraid of
anything he drove a cautious fifty-five and refused to pass
anyone. The road narrowed and sunk onto the flat plain of
the Mississippi Delta, and for a mile Adam watched as a
levee snaked its way to the right and finally disappeared. He
eased through the hamlet of Walls, the first town of any size
along 61, and followed the traffic south.

Through his considerable research, he knew that this
highway had for decades served as the principal conduit for
hundreds of thousands of poor Delta blacks journeying
north to Memphis and St Louis and Chicago and Detroit,
places where they sought jobs and decent housing. It was in
these towns and farms, these ramshackle shotgun houses
and dusty country stores and colorful juke joints along
Highway 61 where the blues were born and spread
northward. The music found a home in Memphis where it
was blended with gospel and country, and together they
spawned rock and roll. He listened to an old Muddy Waters
cassette as he entered the infamous county of Tunica, said
to be the poorest in the nation.

The music did little to calm him. He had refused
breakfast at Lee's, said he wasn't hungry but in fact had a
knot in his stomach. The knot grew with each mile.

Just north of the town of Tunica, the fields grew vast and
ran to the horizon in all directions. The soybeans and cotton

77

were knee high. A small army of green and red tractors with plows behind them crisscrossed the endless neat rows of leafy foliage. Though it was not yet nine o'clock, the weather was already hot and sticky. The ground was dry, and clouds of dust smoldered behind each plow. An occasional crop duster dropped from nowhere and acrobatically skimmed the tops of the fields, then soared upward. Traffic was heavy and slow, and sometimes forced almost to a standstill as a monstrous John Deere of some variety inched along as if the highway were deserted.

Adam was patient. He was not expected until ten, and it wouldn't matter if he arrived late.

At Clarksdale, he left Highway 61 and headed southeast on 49, through the tiny settlements of Mattson and Dublin and Tutwiler, through more soybean fields. He passed cotton gins, now idle but waiting for the harvest. He passed clusters of impoverished row houses and dirty mobile homes, all for some reason situated close to the highway. He passed an occasional fine home, always at a distance, always sitting majestically under heavy oaks and elms, and usually with a fenced swimming pool to one side. There was no doubt who owned these fields.

A road sign declared the state penitentiary to be five miles ahead, and Adam instinctively slowed his car. A moment later, he ran up on a large tractor puttering casually down the road, and instead of passing he chose to follow. The operator, an old white man with a dirty cap, motioned for him to come around. Adam waved, and stayed behind the plow at twenty miles per hour. There was no other traffic in sight. A random dirt clod flung from a rear tractor tire, and landed just inches in front of the Saab. He slowed a bit more. The operator twisted in his seat, and again waved for Adam to come around. His mouth moved and his face was angry, as if this were his highway and he didn't appreciate idiots following his tractor. Adam smiled and waved again, but stayed behind him.

Minutes later, he saw the prison. There were no tall chain-link fences along the road. There were no lines of glistening razor wire to prevent escape. There were no watchtowers with armed guards. There were no gangs of inmates howling at the passerby. Instead, Adam saw an entrance to the right and the words MISSISSIPPI STATE PENITENTIARY spanning from an arch above it. Next to the entrance were several buildings, all facing the highway and apparently unguarded.

Adam waved once again at the tractor operator, then eased from the highway. He took a deep breath, and studied the entrance. A female in uniform stepped from a guard-house under the arch, and stared at him. Adam drove slowly to her, and lowered his window.

'Mornin',' she said. She had a gun on her hip and a clipboard in her hand. Another guard watched from inside. 'What can we do for you?'

'I'm a lawyer, here to see a client on death row,' Adam said weakly, very much aware of his shrill and nervous voice. Just calm down, he told himself.

'We ain't got nobody on death row, sir.'

'I'm sorry?'

'Ain't no such place as death row. We got a bunch of 'em in the Maximum Security Unit, that's MSU for short, but you can look all over this place and you won't find no death row.'

'Okay.'

'Name?' she said, studying the clipboard.

'Adam Hall.'

'And your client?'

'Sam Cayhall.' He half-expected some sort of response to this, but the guard didn't care. She flipped a sheet, and said, 'Stay right here.'

The entrance became a driveway with shade trees and small buildings on each side. This wasn't a prison – this was a pleasant little street in a small town where any minute now a group of kids would appear on bicycles and roller skates. To the right was a quaint structure with a front porch and flower beds. A sign said this was the Visitors Center, as if souvenirs and lemonade were on sale for eager tourists. A white pickup with three young blacks in it and Mississippi Department of Corrections stenciled on the door passed by without slowing a bit.

Adam caught a glimpse of the guard standing behind his car. She was writing something on the clipboard as she approached his window. 'Where'bouts in Illinois?' she asked.

'Chicago.'

'Got any cameras, guns, or tape recorders?'

'No.'

She reached inside and placed a card on his dash. Then she returned to her clipboard, and said, 'Got a note here that you're supposed to see Lucas Mann.'

'Who's that?'

'He's the prison attorney.'

'I didn't know I was supposed to see him.'

She held a piece of paper three feet from his face. 'Says so right here. Take the third left, just up there, then wind around to the back of that red brick building.' She was pointing.

'What does he want?'

She snorted and shrugged at the same time, and walked to the guardhouse shaking her head. Dumbass lawyers.

Adam gently pressed the accelerator and eased by the Visitors Center and down the shaded drive. On both sides were neat white frame houses where, he learned later, prison guards and other employees lived with their families. He followed her instructions and parked in front of an aging brick building. Two trustees in blue prison pants with white stripes down the legs swept the front steps. Adam avoided eye contact and went inside.

He found the unmarked office of Lucas Mann with little trouble. A secretary smiled at him, and opened another door to a large office where Mr Mann was standing behind his desk and talking on the phone.

'Just have a seat,' the secretary whispered as she closed the door behind him. Mann smiled and waved awkwardly as he listened to the phone. Adam sat his briefcase in a chair

80

and stood behind it. The office was large and clean. Two long windows faced the highway and provided plenty of light. On the wall to the left was a large framed photo of a familiar face, a handsome young man with an earnest smile and strong chin. It was David McAllister, governor of the State of Mississippi. Adam suspected identical photos were hung in every state government office, and also plastered in every hallway, closet, and toilet under the state's domain.

Lucas Mann stretched the phone cord and walked to a window, his back to the desk and Adam. He certainly didn't appear to be a lawyer. He was in his mid-fifties with flowing dark gray hair which he somehow pulled and kept situated on the back of his neck. His dress was the hippest of fraternity chic – severely starched khaki workshirt with two pockets and a mixed salad tie, still tied but hanging loose; top button unbuttoned to reveal a gray cotton tee shirt; brown chinos, likewise starched to the crunch with a perfect one-inch cuff falling just enough to allow a peek at white socks; loafers shined immaculately. It was obvious Lucas knew how to dress, and also obvious he was engaged in a different practice of law. If he'd had a small earring in his left lobe, he would have been the perfect aging hippie who in his later years was yielding to conformity.

The office was neatly furnished with government hand-me-downs: a worn wooden desk that seemed impeccably organized; three metal chairs with vinyl cushions; a row of mismatched file cabinets along one wall. Adam stood behind a chair and tried to calm himself. Could this meeting be required of all visiting attorneys? Surely not. There were five thousand inmates of Parchman. Garner Goodman had not mentioned a visit with Lucas Mann.

The name was vaguely familiar. Somewhere deep in one of his boxes of court files and newspaper clippings he had seen the name of Lucas Mann, and he desperately tried to remember if he was a good guy or a bad one. What exactly was his role in death penalty litigation? Adam knew for certain that the enemy was the state's Attorney General, but he couldn't fit Lucas into the scenario.

81

Mann suddenly hung up the phone and shoved a hand at Adam. 'Nice to meet you, Mr Hall. Please have a seat,' he said softly in a pleasant drawl as he waved at a chair. 'Thanks for stopping by.'

Adam took a seat. 'Sure. A pleasure to meet you,' he replied nervously. 'What's up?'

'A couple of things. First, I just wanted to meet you and say hello. I've been the attorney here for twelve years. I do most of the civil litigation that this place spews forth, you know, all kinds of crazy litigation filed by our guests – prisoners' rights, damage suits, that kind of stuff. We get sued every day, it seems. By statute, I also play a small role in the death cases, and I understand you're here to visit Sam.'

'That's correct.'

'Has he hired you?'

'Not exactly.'

'I didn't think so. This presents a small problem. You see, you're not supposed to visit an inmate unless you actually represent him, and I know that Sam has success-fully terminated Kravitz & Bane.'

'So I can't see him?' Adam asked, almost with a trace of relief.

'You're not supposed to. I had a long talk yesterday with Garner Goodman. He and I go back a few years to the Maynard Tole execution. Are you familiar with that one?'

'Vaguely.'

'Nineteen eighty–six. It was my second execution,' he said as if he'd personally pulled the switch. He sat on the edge of his desk and looked down at Adam. The starch crackled gently in his chinos. His right leg swung from the desk. 'I've had four, you know. Sam could be the fifth. Anyway, Garner represented Maynard Tole, and we got to know each other. He's a fine gentleman and fierce advocate.'

'Thanks,' Adam said because he could think of nothing else.

'I hate them, personally.'

'You're opposed to the death penalty?'

'Most of the time. I go through stages, actually. Every time we kill someone here I think the whole world's gone crazy. Then, invariably, I'll review one of these cases and remember how brutal and horrible some of these crimes were. My first execution was Teddy Doyle Meeks, a drifter who raped, mutilated, and killed a little boy. There was not much sadness here when he was gassed. But, hey, listen, I could tell war stories forever. Maybe we'll have time for it later, okay?'

'Sure,' Adam said without commitment. He could not envision a moment when he wanted to hear stories about violent murderers and their executions.

'I told Garner that I didn't think you should be permitted to visit Sam. He listened for a while, then he explained, rather vaguely I must say, that perhaps yours was a special situation, and that you should be allowed at least one visit. He wouldn't say what was so special about it, know what I mean?' Lucas rubbed his chin when he said this as if he had almost solved the puzzle. 'Our policy is rather strict, especially for MSU. But the warden will do whatever I ask.' He said this very slowly, and the words hung in the air.

'I, uh, really need to see him,' Adam said, his voice almost cracking.

'Well, he needs a lawyer. Frankly, I'm glad you're here. We've never executed one unless his lawyer was present. There's all sorts of legal maneuvering up to the very last minute, and I'll just feel better if Sam has a lawyer.' He walked around the desk and took a seat on the other side. He opened a file and studied a piece of paper. Adam waited and tried to breathe normally.

'We do a fair amount of background on our death inmates,' Lucas said, still looking at the file. The statement had the tone of a solemn warning. 'Especially when the appeals have run and the execution is looming. Do you know anything about Sam's family?'

The knot suddenly felt like a basketball in Adam's

stomach. He managed to shrug and shake his head at the same time, as if to say he knew nothing.

'Do you plan to talk to Sam's family?'

Again, no response, just the same inept shrug of the shoulders, very heavy shoulders at this moment.

'I mean, normally, in these cases, there's quite a lot of contact with the condemned man's family as the execution gets closer. You'll probably want to contact these folks. Sam has a daughter in Memphis, a Mrs Lee Booth. I have an address, if you want it.' Lucas watched him suspiciously. Adam could not move. 'Don't suppose you know her, do you?'

Adam shook his head, but said nothing.

'Sam had one son, Eddie Cayhall, but the poor guy committed suicide in 1981. Lived in California. Eddie left two children, a son born in Clanton, Mississippi, on May 12, 1964, which, oddly enough, is your birthday, according to my *Martindale-Hubbell Law Directory*. Says you were born in Memphis on the same day. Eddie also left a daughter who was born in California. These are Sam's grandchildren. I'll try and contact them, if you –'

'Eddie Cayhall was my father,' Adam blurted out, and he took a deep breath. He sank lower in the chair and stared at the top of the desk. His heart pounded furiously, but at least he was breathing again. His shoulders were suddenly lighter. He even managed a very small smile.

Mann's face was expressionless. He thought for a long minute, then said with a hint of satisfaction, 'I sort of figured that.' He immediately started flipping papers as if the file possessed many other surprises. 'Sam's been a very lonely man on death row, and I've often wondered about his family. He gets some mail, but almost none from his family. Virtually no visitors, not that he wants any. But it's a bit unusual for such a noted inmate to be ignored by his family. Especially a white one. I don't pry, you understand.'

'Of course not.'

Lucas ignored this. 'We have to make preparations for the execution, Mr Hall. For example, we have to know what to do with the body. Funeral arrangements and all. That's where the family comes in. After I talked to Garner yesterday, I asked some of our people in Jackson to track down the family. It was really quite easy. They also checked your paperwork, and immediately discovered that the State of Tennessee has no record of the birth of Adam Hall on May 12, 1964. One thing sort of led to another. It wasn't difficult.'

'I'm not hiding anymore.'

'When did you learn about Sam?'

'Nine years ago. My aunt, Lee Booth, told me after we buried my father.'

'Have you had any contact with Sam?'

'No.'

Lucas closed the file and reclined in his squeaky chair. 'So Sam has no idea who you are or why you're here?'

'That's right.'

'Wow,' he whistled at the ceiling.

Adam relaxed a bit and sat up in his chair. The cat was now out of the bag, and had it not been for Lee and her fears of being discovered he would have felt completely at ease. 'How long can I see him today?' he asked.

'Well, Mr Hall –'

'Just call me Adam, okay.'

'Sure, Adam, we really have two sets of rules for the Row.'

'Excuse me, but I was told by a guard at the gate that there was no death row.'

'Not officially. You'll never hear the guards or other personnel refer to it as anything but Maximum Security or MSU or Unit 17. Anyway, when a man's time is about up on the Row we relax the rules quite a bit. Normally, a visit with the lawyer is limited to an hour a day, but in Sam's case you can have all the time you need. I suspect you'll have a lot to talk about.'

'So there's no time limit?'

'No. You can stay all day if you like. We try to make things easy in the last days. You can come and go as you please as long as there's no security risk. I've been to death row in five other states, and, believe me, we treat them the best. Hell, in Louisiana they take the poor guy out of his unit and place him in what's called the Death House for three days before they kill him. Talk about cruel. We don't do that. Sam will be treated special until the big day.'

'The big day?'

'Yeah. It's four weeks from today, you know? August 8.' Lucas reached for some papers on the corner of his desk, then handed them to Adam. 'This came down this morning. The Fifth Circuit lifted the stay late yesterday afternoon. The Mississippi Supreme Court just set a new execution date for August 8.'

Adam held the papers without looking at them. 'Four weeks,' he said, stunned.

'Afraid so. I took a copy of it to Sam about an hour ago, so he's in a foul mood.'

'Four weeks,' Adam repeated, almost to himself. He glanced at the court's opinion. The case was styled *State of Mississippi v. Sam Cayhall*. 'I guess I'd better go see him, don't you think?' he said without thinking.

'Yeah. Look, Adam, I'm not one of the bad guys, okay?' Lucas slowly eased to his feet and walked to the edge of his desk where he gently placed his rear. He folded his arms and looked down at Adam. 'I'm just doing my job, okay. I'll be involved because I have to watch this place and make sure things are done legally, by the book. I won't enjoy it, but it'll get crazy and quite stressful, and everybody will be ringing my phone – the warden, his assistants, the Attorney General's office, the governor, you, and a hundred others. So I'll be in the middle of it, though I don't want to. It's the most unpleasant thing about this job. I just want you to realize that I'm here if you need me, okay? I'll always be fair and truthful with you.'

'You're assuming Sam will allow me to represent him.'

'Yes. I'm assuming this.'

'What are the chances of the execution taking place in four weeks?'

'Fifty-fifty. You never know what the courts will do at the last minute. We'll start preparing in a week or so. We have a rather long checklist of things to do to get ready for it.'

'Sort of a blueprint for death.'

'Something like that. Don't think we enjoy it.'

'I guess everybody here is just doing their job, right?'

'It's the law of this state. If our society wants to kill criminals, then someone has to do it.'

Adam placed the court opinion in his briefcase and stood in front of Lucas. 'Thanks, I guess, for the hospitality.'

'Don't mention it. After you visit with Sam, I'll need to know what happened.'

'I'll send you a copy of our representation agreement, if he signs it.'

'That's all I need.'

They shook hands and Adam headed for the door.

'One other thing,' Lucas said. 'When they bring Sam into the visiting room, ask the guards to remove the handcuffs. I'll make sure they do. It'll mean a lot to Sam.'

'Thanks.'

'Good luck.'

NINE

THE TEMPERATURE had risen at least ten degrees when Adam left the building and walked past the same two trustees sweeping the same dirt in the same languid motions. He stopped on the front steps, and for a moment watched a gang of inmates gather litter along the highway less than a hundred yards away. An armed guard on a horse in a ditch watched them. Traffic zipped along without slowing. Adam wondered what manner of criminals were these who were allowed to work outside the fences and so close to a highway. No one seemed to care about it but him.

He walked the short distance to his car, and was sweating by the time he opened the door and started the engine. He followed the drive through the parking lot behind Mann's office, then turned left onto the main prison road. Again, he was passing neat little white homes with flowers and trees in the front yard. What a civilized little community. An arrow on a road sign pointed left to Unit 17. He turned, very slowly, and within seconds was on a dirt road that led quickly to some serious fencing and razor wire.

The Row at Parchman had been built in 1954, and officially labeled the Maximum Security Unit, or simply MSU. An obligatory plaque on a wall inside listed the date, the name of the governor then, the names of various important and long-forgotten officials who were instrumental in its construction, and, of course, the names of the architect and contractor. It was state of the art for that period – a single-story flat roof building of red brick stretching in two long rectangles from the center.

Adam parked in the dirt lot between two other cars and stared at it. No bars were visible from the outside. No guards patrolled around it. If not for the fences and barbed wire, it could almost pass for an elementary school in the suburbs. Inside a caged yard at the end of one wing, a solitary inmate dribbled a basketball on a grassless court and flipped it against a crooked backboard.

The fence in front of Adam was at least twelve feet high, and crowned at the top with thick strands of barbed wire and a menacing roll of shiny razor wire. It ran straight and true to the corner where it joined a watchtower where guards looked down. The fence encompassed the Row on all four sides with remarkable symmetry, and in each corner an identical tower stood high above with a glass-enclosed guard station at the top. Just beyond the fence the crops started and seemed to run forever. The Row was literally in the middle of a cotton field.

Adam stepped from his car, felt suddenly claustrophobic, and squeezed the handle of his thin briefcase as he glared through the chain link at the hot, flat little building where they killed people. He slowly removed his jacket, and noticed his shirt was already spotted and sticking to his chest. The knot in his stomach had returned with a vengeance. His first few steps toward the guard station were slow and awkward, primarily because his legs were unsteady and his knees were shivering. His fancy tasseled loafers were dusty by the time he stopped under the watchtower and looked up. A red bucket, the type one might use to wash a car, was being lowered on a rope by an earnest woman in a uniform. 'Put your keys in the bucket,' she explained efficiently, leaning over the railing. The barbed wire on the top of the fence was five feet below her.

Adam quickly did as she instructed. He carefully laid his keys in the bucket where they joined a dozen other key rings. She jerked it back and he watched it rise for a few seconds, then stop. She tied the rope somehow, and the little red bucket hung innocently in the air. A nice breeze would have moved it gently, but at the moment, in this stifling vacuum, there was scarcely enough air to breathe. The winds had died years ago.

The guard was finished with him. Someone somewhere pushed a button or pulled a lever, Adam had no idea who did it, but a humming noise kicked in, and the first of two bulky, chain-link gates began to slide a few feet so he could enter. He walked fifteen feet along the dirt drive, then stopped as the first gate closed behind him. He was in the process of learning the first basic rule of prison security – every protected entrance has either two locked doors or gates.

When the first gate stopped behind him and locked itself into place, the second one dutifully snatched itself free and rolled along the fence. As this was happening, a very stocky guard with arms as big as Adam's legs appeared at the main door of the unit and began to amble along the brick path to the entrance. He had a hard belly and a thick neck, and he sort of waited for Adam as Adam waited for the gates to secure everything.

He eased forward an enormous black hand, and said, 'Sergeant Packer.' Adam shook it and immediately noticed the shiny black cowboy boots on Sergeant Packer's feet.

'Adam Hall,' he said, trying to manage the hand.

'Here to see Sam,' Packer stated as a fact.

'Yes sir,' Adam said, wondering if everyone here referred to him simply as Sam.

'Your first visit here?' They began a slow walk toward the front of the building.

'Yeah,' Adam said, looking at the open windows along the nearest tier. 'Are all death row inmates here?' he asked.

'Yep. Got forty-seven as of today. Lost one last week.'

They were almost to the main door. 'Lost one?'

'Yeah. The Big Court reversed. Had to move him in with the general population. I have to frisk you.' They were at the door, and Adam glanced nervously to see just exactly where it was that Packer wished to conduct the frisk.

'Just spread your legs a little,' Packer said, already taking the briefcase and placing it on the concrete. The fancy tasseled loafers were now stuck in place. Though he was dizzy and momentarily without the use of all his faculties, Adam could not at this horrible moment remember anyone ever asking him to spread his legs, even just a little.

But Packer was a pro. He patted expertly around the socks, moved up quite delicately to the knees, which were more than a little wobbly, then around the waist in no time flat. Adam's first frisk was mercifully finished just seconds after it started when Sergeant Packer made a rather cursory pass under both arms as if Adam might be wearing a shoulder harness with a small pistol inside it. Packer deftly stuck his massive right hand into the briefcase, then handed it back to Adam. 'Not a good day to see Sam,' he said.

'So I've heard,' Adam replied, slinging his jacket once again over his shoulder. He faced the iron door as if it was now time to enter the Row.

'This way,' Packer mumbled as he stepped down onto the grass and headed around the corner. Adam obediently followed along yet another little red-brick trail until they came to a plain, nondescript door with weeds growing beside it. The door was not marked or labeled.

'What's this?' Adam asked. He vaguely recalled Goodman's description of this place, but at the moment all details were fuzzy.

'Conference room.' Packer produced a key and unlocked the door. Adam glanced around before he entered and tried to gather his bearings. The door was next to the central section of the unit, and it occurred to Adam that perhaps the guards and their administrators didn't want the lawyers underfoot and poking around. Thus, the outside entrance.

He took a deep breath and stepped inside. There were no other lawyers visiting their clients, and this was particularly comforting to Adam. This meeting could become tumultuous and perhaps emotional, and he preferred to do it in private. At least for the moment the room was empty. It was large enough for several lawyers to visit and counsel, probably thirty feet long and twelve feet wide with a concrete floor and bright fluorescent lighting. The wall on the far end was red brick with three windows high at the top, just like the exterior of the unit's tiers. It was immediately obvious that the conference room had been added as an afterthought.

The air conditioner, a small window unit, was snarling angrily and producing much less than it should. The room was divided neatly by a solid wall of brick and metal; the lawyers had their side and the clients had theirs. The partition was made of brick for the first three feet, then a small counter provided the lawyers a place to sit their mandatory legal pads and take their pages of mandatory notes. A bright green screen of thick metal grating sat solidly on the counter and ran up to the ceiling.

Adam walked slowly to the end of the room, sidestepping a varied assortment of chairs – green and gray government throwaways, folding types, narrow cafeteria seats.

'I'm gonna lock this door,' Packer said as he stepped outside. 'We'll get Sam.' The door slammed, and Adam was alone. He quickly picked out a place at the end of the room just in case another lawyer arrived, at which time the other lawyer would undoubtedly take a position far to the other end and they could plot strategy with some measure of privacy. He pulled a chair to the wooden counter, placed his jacket on another chair, removed his legal pad, unscrewed his pen, and began chewing his fingernails. He tried to stop the chewing, but he couldn't. His stomach flipped violently, and his heels twitched out of control. He looked through the screen and studied the inmates' portion of the room – the same wooden counter, the same array of old chairs. In the center of the screen before him was a slit, four inches by ten, and it would be through this little hole that he would come face-to-face with Sam Cayhall.

He waited nervously, telling himself to be calm, take it easy, relax, he could handle this. He scribbled something on the legal pad, but honestly couldn't read it. He rolled up his sleeves. He looked around the room for hidden

92

microphones and cameras, but the place was so simple and modest he couldn't imagine anyone trying to eavesdrop. If Sergeant Packer was any indication, the staff was laid-back, almost indifferent.

He studied the empty chairs on both sides of the screen, and wondered how many desperate people, in the last hours of their lives, had met here with their attorneys and listened for words of hope. How many urgent pleas had passed through this screen as the clock ticked steadily away? How many lawyers had sat where he was now sitting and told their clients that there was nothing left to do, that the execution would proceed? It was a somber thought, and it calmed Adam quite a bit. He was not the first to be here, and he would not be the last. He was a lawyer, well trained, blessed with a quick mind, and arriving here with the formidable resources of Kravitz & Bane behind him. He could do his job. His legs slowly became still, and he quit chewing his fingernails.

A door bolt clicked, and he jumped through his skin. It opened slowly, and a young white guard stepped into the inmates' side. Behind him, in a bright red jumpsuit, hands cuffed behind, was Sam Cayhall. He glowered around the room, squinting through the screen, until his eyes focused on Adam. A guard pulled at his elbow and led him to a spot directly across from the lawyer. He was thin, pale, and six inches shorter than both guards, but they seemed to give him plenty of room.

'Who are you?' he hissed at Adam, who at the moment had a fingernail between his teeth.

One guard pulled a chair behind Sam, and the other guard sat him in it. He stared at Adam. The guards backed away, and were about to leave when Adam said, 'Could you remove the handcuffs, please?'

'No sir. We can't.'

Adam swallowed hard. 'Just take them off, okay. We're gonna be here for a while,' he said, mustering a degree of forcefulness. The guards looked at each other as if this request had never been heard. A key was quickly produced, and the handcuffs were removed.

Sam was not impressed. He glared at Adam through the opening in the screen as the guards made their noisy departure. The door slammed, and the deadbolt clicked.

They were alone, the Cayhall version of a family reunion. The air conditioner rattled and spewed, and for a long minute it made the only sounds. Though he tried valiantly, Adam was unable to look Sam in the eyes for more than two seconds. He busied himself with important note taking on the legal pad, and as he numbered each line he could feel the heat of Sam's stare.

Finally, Adam stuck a business card through the opening. 'My name is Adam Hall. I'm a lawyer with Kravitz & Bane. Chicago and Memphis.'

Sam patiently took the card and examined it front and back. Adam watched every move. His fingers were wrinkled and stained brown with cigarette smoke. His face was pallid, the only color coming from the salt and pepper stubble of five days' growth. His hair was long, gray, and oily, and slicked back severely. Adam decided quickly that he looked nothing like the frozen images from the video. Nor did he resemble the last known photos of himself, those from the 1981 trial. He was quite an old man now, with pasty delicate skin and layers of tiny wrinkles around his eyes. Deep burrows of age and misery cut through his forehead. The only attractive feature was the set of piercing, indigo eyes that lifted themselves from the card. 'You Jew boys never quit, do you?' he said in a pleasant, even tone. There was no hint of anger.

'I'm not Jewish,' Adam said, successfully returning the stare.

'Then how can you work for Kravitz & Bane?' he asked as he set the card aside. His words were soft, slow, and delivered with the patience of a man who'd spent nine and a half years alone in a six-by-nine cell.

'We're an equal opportunity employer.'

'That's nice. All proper and legal, I presume. In full compliance with all civil rights decisions and federal do-gooder laws.'

'Of course.'

'How many partners are in Kravitz & Bane now?'

Adam shrugged. The number varied from year to year. 'Around a hundred and fifty.'

'A hundred and fifty partners. And how many are women?'

Adam hesitated as he tried to count. 'I really don't know. Probably a dozen.'

'A dozen,' Sam repeated, barely moving his lips. His hands were folded and still, and his eyes did not blink. 'So, less than ten percent of your partners are women. How many nigger partners do you have?'

'Could we refer to them as blacks?'

'Oh sure, but of course that too is an antiquated term. They now want to be called African-Americans. Surely you're politically correct enough to know this.'

Adam nodded but said nothing.

'How many African-American partners do you have?'

'Four, I believe.'

'Less than three percent. My, my. Kravitz & Bane, that great bastion of civil justice and liberal political action, does, in fact, discriminate against African-Americans and Female-Americans. I just don't know what to say.'

Adam scratched something illegible on his pad. He could argue, of course, that almost a third of the associates were female and that the firm made diligent efforts to sign the top black law students. He could explain how they had been sued for reverse discrimination by two white males whose job offers disappeared at the last moment.

'How many Jewish-American partners do you have? Eighty percent?'

'I don't know. It really doesn't matter to me.'

'Well, it certainly matters to me. I was always embarrassed to be represented by such blatant bigots.'

'A lot of people would find it appropriate.'

Sam carefully reached into the only visible pocket of his jumpsuit, and removed a blue pack of Montclairs and a disposable lighter. The jumpsuit was unbuttoned halfway

95

down the chest, and a thick matting of gray hair showed through the gap. The fabric was a very light cotton. Adam could not imagine life in this place with no air conditioning.

He lit the cigarette and exhaled toward the ceiling. 'I thought I was through with you people.'

'They didn't send me down here. I volunteered.'

'Why?'

'I don't know. You need a lawyer, and –'

'Why are you so nervous?'

Adam jerked his fingernails from his teeth and stopped tapping his feet. 'I'm not nervous.'

'Sure you are. I've seen lots of lawyers around this place, and I've never seen one as nervous as you. What's the matter, kid? You afraid I'm coming through the screen after you?'

Adam grunted and tried to smile. 'Don't be silly. I'm not nervous.'

'How old are you?'

'Twenty-six.'

'You look twenty-two. When did you finish law school?'

'Last year.'

'Just great. The Jewish bastards have sent a greenhorn to save me. I've known for a long time that they secretly wanted me dead, now this proves it. I killed some Jews, now they want to kill me. I was right all along.'

'You admit you killed the Kramer kids?'

'What the hell kind of question is that? The jury said I did. For nine years, the appeals courts have said the jury was right. That's all that matters. Who the hell are you asking me questions like that?'

'You need a lawyer, Mr Cayhall. I'm here to help.'

'I need a lot of things, boy, but I damned sure don't need an eager little tenderfoot like you to give me advice. You're dangerous, son, and you're too ignorant to know it.' Again, the words came deliberately and without emotion. He held the cigarette between the index and middle finger of his right hand, and casually flipped ashes in an organized pile in a plastic bowl. His eyes blinked occasionally. His face showed neither feeling nor sentiment.

Adam took meaningless notes, then tried again to stare through the slit into Sam's eyes. 'Look, Mr Cayhall, I'm a lawyer, and I have a strong moral conviction against the death penalty. I am well educated, well trained, well read on Eighth Amendment issues, and I can be of assistance to you. That's why I'm here. Free of charge.'

'Free of charge,' Sam repeated. 'How generous. Do you realize, son, that I get at least three offers a week now from lawyers who want to represent me for free? Big lawyers. Famous lawyers. Rich lawyers. Some real slimy snakes. They're all perfectly willing to sit where you're now sitting, file all the last minute notions and appeals, do the interviews, chase the cameras, hold my hand in the last hours, watch them gas me, then do yet another press conference, then sign a book deal, a movie deal, maybe a television mini-series deal about the life and times of Sam Cayhall, a real Klan murderer. You see, son, I'm famous, and what I did is now legendary. And since they're about to kill me, then I'm about to become even more famous. Thus, the lawyers want me. I'm worth a lot of money. A sick country, right.'

Adam was shaking his head. 'I don't want any of that, I promise. I'll put it in writing. I'll sign a complete confidentiality agreement.'

Sam chuckled. 'Right, and who's going to enforce it after I'm gone?'

'Your family,' Adam said.

'Forget my family,' Sam said firmly.

'My motives are pure,' Mr Cayhall. My firm has represented you for seven years, so I know almost everything about your file. I've also done quite a lot of research into your background.'

'Join the club. I've had my underwear examined by a hundred half-ass reporters. There are many people who know much about me, it seems, and all this combined knowledge is of absolutely no benefit to me right now. I have four weeks. Do you know this?'

'I have a copy of the opinion.'

'Four weeks, and they gas me.'

'So let's get to work. You have my word that I will never talk to the press unless you authorize it, that I'll never repeat anything you tell me, and that I will not sign any book or movie deal. I swear it.'

Sam lit another cigarette and stared at something on the counter. He gently rubbed his right temple with his right thumb, the cigarette just inches from his hair. For a long time the only sound was the gurgling of the overworked window unit. Sam smoked and contemplated. Adam doodled on his pad and was quite proud that his feet were motionless and his stomach was not aching. The silence was awkward, and he figured, correctly, that Sam could sit and smoke and think in utter silence for days.

'Are you familiar with *Barroni*?' Sam asked quietly.

'*Barroni*?'

'Yes, *Barroni*. Came down last week from the Ninth Circuit. California case.'

Adam racked his brain for a trace of *Barroni*. 'I might have seen it.'

'You might have seen it? You're well trained, well read, etc., and you might have seen *Barroni*? What kind of half-ass lawyer are you?'

'I'm not a half-ass lawyer.'

'Right, right. What about *Texas v. Eekes*? Surely you've read that one?'

'When did it come down?'

'Within six weeks.'

'What court?'

'Fifth Circuit.'

'Eighth Amendment?'

'Don't be stupid,' Sam grunted in genuine disgust. 'Do you think I'd spend my time reading freedom of speech cases? This is my ass sitting over here, boy, these are my wrists and ankles that will be strapped down. This is my nose the poison will hit.'

'No. I don't remember *Eekes*.'

'What do you read?'

'All the important cases.'

'Have you read *Barefoot*?'

'Of course.'

'Tell me about *Barefoot*.'

'What is this, a pop quiz?'

'This is whatever I want it to be. Where was *Barefoot* from?' Sam asked.

'I don't remember. But the full name was *Barefoot v. Estelle*, a landmark case in 1983 in which the Supreme Court held that death row inmates cannot hold back valid claims on appeal so they can save them for later. More or less.'

'My, my, you have read it. Does it ever strike you as odd how the same court can change its mind whenever it wants to? Think about it. For two centuries the U.S. Supreme Court allowed legal executions. Said they were consitutional, covered nicely by the Eighth Amendment. Then, in 1972 the U.S. Supreme Court read the same, unchanged Constitution and outlawed the death penalty. Then, in 1976 the U.S. Supreme Court said executions were in fact constitutional after all. Same bunch of turkeys wearing the same black robes in the same building in Washington. Now, the U.S. Supreme Court is changing the rules again with the same Constitution. The Reagan boys are tired of reading too many appeals, so they declare certain avenues to be closed. Seems odd to me.'

'Seems odd to a lot of people.'

'What about *Dulaney*?' Sam asked, taking a long drag. There was little or no ventilation in the room and a cloud was forming above them.

'Where's it from?'

'Louisiana. Surely you've read it.'

'I'm sure I have. In fact, I've probably read more cases than you, but I don't always bother to memorize them unless I plan to use them.'

'Use them where?'

'Motions and appeals.'

'So you've handled death cases before. How many?'

'This is the first.'

'Why am I not comforted by this? Those Jewish-American lawyers at Kravitz & Bane sent you down here to experiment on me, right? Get yourself a little hands-on training so you can stick it on your résumé.'

'I told you – they didn't send me down here.'

'How about Garner Goodman? Is he still alive?'

'Yes. He's about your age.'

'Then he doesn't have long, does he? And Tyner?'

'Mr Tyner's doing well. I'll tell him you asked.'

'Oh please do. Tell him I really miss him, both of them, actually. Hell, it took me almost two years to fire them.'

'They worked their butts off for you.'

'Tell them to send me a bill.' Sam chuckled to himself, his first smile of the meeting. He methodically stubbed out the cigarette in the bowl, and lit another. 'Fact is, Mr Hall, I hate lawyers.'

'That's the American way.'

'Lawyers chased me, indicted me, prosecuted me, persecuted me, screwed me, then sent me to this place. Since I've been here, they've hounded me, screwed me some more, lied to me, and now they're back in the form of you, a rookie zealot without a clue of how to find the damned courthouse.'

'You might be surprised.'

'It'll be a helluva surprise, son, if you know your ass from a hole in the ground. You'll be the first clown from Kravitz & Bane to possess such information.'

'They've kept you out of the gas chamber for the past seven years.'

'And I'm supposed to be thankful? There are fifteen residents of the Row with more seniority than me. Why should I be next? I've been here for nine and a half years. Treemont's been here for fourteen years. Of course, he's an African-American and that always helps. They have more rights, you know. It's much harder to execute one of them because whatever they did was someone else's fault.'

'That's not true.'

'How the hell do you know what's true? A year ago you were still in school, still wearing faded blue jeans all day long, still drinking beer at happy hours with your idealistic little buddies. You haven't lived, son. Don't tell me what's true.'

'So you're in favor of swift executions for African-Americans?'

'Not a bad idea, really. In fact, most of these punks deserve the gas.'

'I'm sure that's a minority opinion on death row.'

'You could say that.'

'And you, of course, are different and don't belong here.'

'No, I don't belong here. I'm a political prisoner, sent here by an egomaniac who used me for his own political purposes.'

'Can we discuss your guilt or innocence?'

'No. But I didn't do what the jury said I did.'

'So you had an accomplice? Someone else planted the bomb?'

Sam rubbed the deep burrows in his forehead with his middle finger, as if he was flipping the bird. But he wasn't. He was suddenly in a deep and prolonged trance. The conference room was much cooler than his cell. The conversation was aimless, but at least it was conversation with someone other than a guard or the invisible inmate next door. He would take his time, make it last as long as possible.

Adam studied his notes and pondered what to say next. They had been chatting for twenty minutes, sparring really, with no clear direction. He was determined to confront their family's history before he left. He just didn't know how to do it.

Minutes passed. Neither looked at the other. Sam lit another Montclair.

'Why do you smoke so much?' Adam finally said.

'I'd rather die of lung cancer. It's a common desire on death row.'

'How many packs a day?'

'Three or four.'

Another minute passed. Sam slowly finished the cigarette, and kindly asked, 'Where'd you go to school?'

'Law school at Michigan. Undergrad at Pepperdine.'

'Where's that?'

'California.'

'Is that where you grew up?'

'Yeah.'

'How many states have the death penalty?'

'Thirty-eight. Most of them don't use it, though. It seems to be popular only in the Deep South, Texas, Florida, and California.'

'You know our esteemed legislature has changed the law here. Now we can die by lethal injection. It's more humane. Ain't that nice? Doesn't apply to me, though, since my conviction was years ago. I'll get to sniff the gas.'

'Maybe not.'

'You're twenty-six?'

'Yeah.'

'Born in 1964.'

'That's right.'

Sam removed another cigarette from the pack and tapped the filter on the counter. 'Where?'

'Memphis,' Adam replied without looking at him.

'You don't understand, son. This state needs an execution, and I happen to be the nearest victim. Louisiana, Texas, and Florida are killing them like flies, and the law-abiding people of this state can't understand why our little chamber is not being used. The more violent crime we have, the more people beg for executions. Makes 'em feel better, like the system is working hard to eliminate murderers. The politicians openly campaign with promises of more prisons and tougher sentences and more executions. That's why those clowns in Jackson voted for lethal injection. It's supposed to be more humane, less objectionable, thus easier to implement. You follow?'

Adam nodded his head slightly.

'It's time for an execution, and my number is up. That's why they're pushing like hell. You can't stop it.'

'We can certainly try. I want the opportunity.'

Sam finally lit the cigarette. He inhaled deeply, then whistled the smoke through a small opening in his lips. He leaned forward slightly on his elbows and peered through the hole in the screen. 'What part of California are you from?'

'Southern. L.A.' Adam glanced at the piercing eyes, then looked away.

'Your family still there?'

A wicked pain shot through Adam's chest, and for a second his heart froze. Sam puffed his cigarette and never blinked.

'My father's dead,' he said with a shaky voice, and sank a few inches in his chair.

A long minute passed as Sam sat poised on the edge of his seat. Finally, he said, 'And your mother?'

'She lives in Portland. Remarried.'

'Where's your sister?' he asked.

Adam closed his eyes and dropped his head. 'She's in college,' he mumbled.

'I believe her name is Carmen, right?' Sam asked softly.

Adam nodded. 'How'd you know?' he asked through gritted teeth.

Sam backed away from the screen and sank into the folding metal chair. He dropped his current cigarette on the floor without looking at it. 'Why did you come here?' he asked, his voice much firmer and tougher.

'How'd you know it was me?'

'The voice. You sound like your father. Why'd you come here?'

'Eddie sent me.'

Their eyes met briefly, then Sam looked away. He slowly leaned forward and planted both elbows on both knees. His gaze was fixed on something on the floor. He grew perfectly still.

Then he placed his right hand over his eyes.

TEN

PHILLIP NAIFEH was sixty-three years old, and nineteen months away from retirement. Nineteen months and four days. He had served as superintendent of the State Department of Corrections for twenty-seven years, and in doing so had survived six governors, an army of state legislators, a thousand prisoners' lawsuits, countless intrusions by the federal courts, and more executions than he cared to remember.

The warden, as he preferred to be called (although the title was officially nonexistent under the terminology of the Mississippi Code), was a full-blooded Lebanese whose parents had immigrated in the twenties and settled in the Delta. They had prospered with a small grocery store in Clarksdale where his mother had become somewhat famous for her homemade Lebanese desserts. He was educated in the public schools, went off to college, returned to the state, and, for reasons long forgotten, had become involved in criminal justice.

He hated the death penalty. He understood society's yearning for it, and long ago he had memorized all the sterile reasons for its necessity. It was a deterrent. It removed killers. It was the ultimate punishment. It was biblical. It satisfied the public's need for retribution. It relieved the anguish of the victim's family. If pressed, he could make these arguments as persuasively as any prosecutor. He actually believed one or two of them.

But the burden of the actual killing was his, and he

104

despised this horrible aspect of his job. It was Phillip Naifeh who walked with the condemned man from his cell to the Isolation Room, as it was called, to suffer the last hour before death. It was Phillip Naifeh who led him next door to the Chamber Room, and supervised the strapping of the legs, arms, and head. 'Any last words?' he had uttered twenty-two times in twenty-seven years. It was left to him to tell the guards to lock the chamber door, and it was left to him to nod to the executioner to pull the levers to mix the deadly gas. He had actually watched the faces of the first two as they died, then decided it was best to watch the faces of the witnesses in the small room behind the chamber. He had to select the witnesses. He had to do a hundred things listed in a manual of how to legally kill death row inmates, including the pronouncing of death, the removal of the body from the chamber, the spraying of it to remove the gas from the clothing, and on and on.

He had once testified before a legislative committee in Jackson, and given his opinions about the death penalty. He had a better idea, he had explained to deaf ears, and his plan would keep condemned killers in the Maximum Security Unit in solitary confinement where they couldn't kill, couldn't escape, and would never be eligible for parole. They would eventually die on death row, but not at the hands of the state.

This testimony made headlines and almost got him fired.

Nineteen months and four days, he thought to himself, as he gently ran his fingers through his thick gray hair and slowly read the latest opinion from the Fifth Circuit. Lucas Mann sat across the desk and waited.

'Four weeks,' Naifeh said, putting the opinion aside. 'How many appeals are left?' he asked in a gentle drawl.

'The usual assortment of last ditch efforts,' Mann replied.

'When did this come down?'

'Early this morning. Sam will appeal it to the Supreme Court, where it will probably be ignored. This should take a week or so.'

'What's your opinion, counselor?'

'The meritorious issues have all been presented at this point. I'd give it a fifty percent chance of happening in four weeks.'

'That's a lot.'

'Something tells me this one might go off.'

In the interminable workings of death penalty roulette, a 50 percent chance was close to a certainty. The process would have to be started. The manual would have to be consulted. After years of endless appeals and delays, the last four weeks would be over in the blink of an eye.

'Have you talked to Sam?' the warden asked.

'Briefly. I took him a copy of the opinion this morning.'

'Garner Goodman called me yesterday, said they were sending down one of their young associates to talk to Sam. Did you take care of it?'

'I talked to Garner, and I talked to the associate. His name is Adam Hall, and he's meeting with Sam as we speak. Should be interesting. Sam's his grandfather.'

'His what!'

'You heard me. Sam Cayhall is Adam Hall's paternal grandfather. We were doing a routine background on Adam Hall yesterday, and noticed a few gray spots. I called the FBI in Jackson, and within two hours they had plenty of circumstantial evidence. I confronted him this morning and he confessed. I don't think he's trying to hide it.'

'But he has a different name.'

'It's a long story. They haven't seen each other since Adam was a toddler. His father fled the state after Sam was arrested for the bombing. Moved out West, changed names, drifted around, in and out of work, sounds like a real loser. Killed himself in 1981. Anyway, Adam here goes to college and makes perfect grades. Goes to law school at Michigan, a Top Ten school, and is the editor of the law review. Takes a job with our pals at Kravitz & Bane, and he shows up this morning for the reunion with his grandfather.'

Naifeh now raked both hands through his hair and shook

his head. 'How wonderful. As if we needed more publicity, more idiotic reporters asking more asinine questions.'

'They're meeting now. I am assuming Sam will agree to allow the kid to represent him. I certainly hope so. We've never executed an inmate without a lawyer.'

'We should do some lawyers without the inmates,' Naifeh said with a forced smile. His hatred for lawyers was legendary, and Lucas didn't mind. He understood. He had once estimated that Phillip Naifeh had been named as a defendant in more lawsuits than anyone else in the history of the state. He had earned the right to hate lawyers.

'I retire in nineteen months,' he said, as if Lucas had never heard this. 'Who's next after Sam?'

Lucas thought a minute and tried to catalog the voluminous appeals of forty-seven inmates. 'No one, really. The Pizza Man came close four months ago, but he got his stay. It'll probably expire in a year or so, but there are other problems with his case. I can't see another execution for a couple of years.'

'The Pizza Man? Forgive me.'

'Malcolm Friar. Killed three pizza delivery boys in a week. At trial he claimed robbery was not the motive, said he was just hungry.'

Naifeh raised both hands and nodded. 'Okay, okay, I remember. He's the nearest after Sam?'

'Probably. It's hard to say.'

'I know.' Naifeh gently pushed away from his desk and walked to a window. His shoes were somewhere under the desk. He thrust his hands in his pockets, pressed his toes into the carpet, and thought deeply for a while. He had been hospitalized after the last execution, a mild heart flutter as his doctor preferred to call it. He'd spent a week in a hospital bed watching his little flutter on a monitor, and promised his wife he would never suffer through another execution. If he could somehow survive Sam, then he could retire at full pension.

He turned and stared at his friend Lucas Mann. 'I'm not doing this one, Lucas. I'm passing the buck to another man, one of my subordinates, a younger man, a good man, a man who can be trusted, a man who's never seen one of these shows, a man who's just itching to get blood on his hands.'

'Not Nugent.'

'That's the man. Retired Colonel George Nugent, my trusted assistant.'

'He's a nut.'

'Yes, but he's our nut, Lucas. He's a fanatic for details, discipline, organization, hell, he's the perfect choice. I'll give him the manual, tell him what I want, and he'll do a marvellous job of killing Sam Cayhall. He'll be perfect.'

George Nugent was an assistant superintendent at Parchman. He had made a name for himself by implementing a most successful boot camp for first offenders. It was a brutal, six-week ordeal in which Nugent strutted and swaggered around in black boots, cursing like a drill instructor and threatening gang rape for the slightest infraction. The first offenders rarely came back to Parchman.

'Nugent's crazy, Phillip. It's a matter of time before he hurts someone.'

'Right! Now you understand. We're going to let him hurt Sam, just the way it should be done. By the book. Heaven knows how much Nugent loves a book to go by. He's the perfect choice, Lucas. It'll be a flawless execution.'

It really mattered little to Lucas Mann. He shrugged, and said, 'You're the boss.'

'Thanks,' Naifeh said. 'Just watch Nugent, okay. I'll watch him on this end, and you watch the legal stuff. We'll get through it.'

'This will be the biggest one yet,' Lucas said.

'I know. I'll have to pace myself. I'm an old man.'

Lucas gathered his file from the desk and headed for the door. 'I'll call you after the kid leaves. He's supposed to check in with me before he goes.'

'I'd like to meet him,' Naifeh said.

'He's a nice kid.'

'Some family, huh.'

THE NICE KID and his condemned grandfather had spent fifteen minutes in silence, the only sound in the room the uneasy rattling of the overworked AC unit. At one point, Adam had walked to the wall and waved his hand before the dusty vents. There was a trace of cool air. He leaned on the counter with his arms folded and stared at the door, as far away from Sam as possible. He was leaning and staring when the door opened and the head of Sergeant Packer appeared. Just checking to see if things were okay, he said, glancing first at Adam then down the room and through the screen at Sam, who was leaning forward in his chair with a hand over his face.

'We're fine,' Adam said without conviction.

'Good, good,' Packer said and hurriedly closed the door. It locked, and Adam slowly made his way back to his chair. He pulled it close to the screen and rested on his elbows. Sam ignored him for a minute or two, then wiped his eyes with a sleeve and sat up. They looked at each other.

'We need to talk,' Adam said quietly.

Sam nodded but said nothing. He wiped his eyes again, this time with the other sleeve. He removed a cigarette and put it between his lips. His hand shook as he flicked the lighter. He puffed quickly.

'So you're really Alan,' he said in a low, husky voice.

'At one time, I guess. I didn't know it until my father died.'

'You were born in 1964.'

'Correct.'

'My first grandson.'

Adam nodded and glanced away.

'You disappeared in 1967.'

'Something like that. I don't remember it, you know. My earliest memories are from California.'

'I heard Eddie went to California, and that there was another child. Someone told me later her name was Carmen. I would hear bits and pieces over the years, knew

109

y'all were somewhere in Southern California, but he did a good job of disappearing.'

'We moved around a lot when I was a kid. I think he had trouble keeping a job.'

'You didn't know about me?'

'No. The family was never mentioned. I found out about it after his funeral.'

'Who told you?'

'Lee.'

Sam closed his eyes tightly for a moment, then puffed again. 'How is she?'

'Okay, I guess.'

'Why'd you go to work for Kravitz & Bane?'

'It's a good firm.'

'Did you know they represented me?'

'Yes.'

'So you've been planning this?'

'For about five years.'

'But why?'

'I don't know.'

'You must have a reason.'

'The reason is obvious. You're my grandfather, okay. Like it or not, you're who you are and I'm who I am. And I'm here now, so what are we going to do about it?'

'I think you should leave.'

'I'm not leaving, Sam. I've been preparing for this a long time.'

'Preparing for what?'

'You need legal representation. You need help. That's why I'm here.'

'I'm beyond help. They're determined to gas me, okay, for lots of reasons. You don't need to get involved in it.'

'Why not?'

'Well, for one, it's hopeless. You're gonna get hurt if you bust your ass and you're unsuccessful. Second, your true identity will be revealed. It'll be very embarrassing. Life for you will be much better if you remain Adam Hall.'

'I am Adam Hall, and I don't plan to change it. I'm also

110

your grandson, and we can't change that, can we? So what's the big deal?'

'It'll be embarrassing for your family. Eddie did a great job of protecting you. Don't blow it.'

'My cover's already blown. My firm knows it. I told Lucas Mann, and –'

'That jerk'll tell everybody. Don't trust him for a minute.'

'Look, Sam, you don't understand. I don't care if he tells. I don't care if the world knows that I'm your grandson. I'm tired of these dirty little family secrets. I'm a big boy now, I can think for myself. Plus, I'm a lawyer, and my skin is getting thick. I can handle it.'

Sam relaxed a bit in his chair and looked at the floor with a pleasant little smirk, the kind grown men often give to little boys who are acting bigger than their years. He grunted at something and very slowly nodded his head. 'You just don't understand, kid,' he said again, now in the measured, patient tone.

'So explain it to me,' Adam said.

'It would take forever.'

'We have four weeks. You can do a lot of talking in four weeks.'

'Just exactly what is it that you want to hear?'

Adam leaned even closer on his elbows, pen and pad ready. His eyes were inches from the slit in the screen. 'First, I want to talk about the case – appeals, strategies, the trials, the bombing, who was with you that night –'

'No one was with me that night.'

'We can talk about it later.'

'We're talking about it now. I was alone, do you hear me?'

'Okay. Second, I want to know about my family.'

'Why?'

'Why not? Why keep it buried? I want to know about your father and his father, and your brothers and cousins. I may dislike these people when it's all over, but I have the right to know about them. I've been deprived of this information all of my life, and I want to know.'

111

'It's nothing remarkable.'

'Oh really. Well, Sam, I think it's pretty remarkable that you've made it here to death row. This is a pretty exclusive society. Throw in the fact that you're white, middle class, almost seventy years old, and it becomes even more remarkable. I want to know how and why you got here. What made you do those things? How many Klansmen were in my family? And why? How many other people were killed along the way?'

'And you think I'll just spill my guts with all this?'

'Yeah, I think so. You'll come around. I'm your grandson, Sam, the only living, breathing relative who gives a damn about you anymore. You'll talk, Sam. You'll talk to me.'

'Well, since I'll be so talkative what else will we discuss?'

'Eddie.'

Sam took a deep breath and closed his eyes. 'You don't want much, do you?' he said softly. Adam scribbled something meaningless on his pad.

It was now time for the ritual of another cigarette, and Sam performed it with even more patience and care. Another blast of blue smoke joined the fog well above their heads. His hands were steady again. 'When we get finished with Eddie, who do you want to talk about?'

'I don't know. That should keep us busy for four weeks.'

'When do we talk about you?'

'Anytime.' Adam reached into his briefcase and removed a thin file. He slid a sheet of paper and a pen through the opening. 'This is an agreement for legal representation. Sign at the bottom.'

Without touching it, Sam read it from a distance. 'So I sign up again with Kravitz & Bane.'

'Sort of.'

'What do you mean, sort of? Says right here I agree to let those Jews represent me again. It took me forever to fire them, and, hell, I wasn't even paying them.'

'The agreement is with me, Sam, okay. You'll never see those guys unless you want to.'

'I don't want to.'

'Fine. I happen to work for the firm, and so the agreement must be with the firm. It's easy.'

'Ah, the optimism of youth. Everything's easy. Here I sit less than a hundred feet from the gas chamber, clock ticking away on the wall over there, getting louder and louder, and everything's easy.'

'Just sign the damned paper, Sam.'

'And then what?'

'And then we go to work. Legally, I can't do anything for you until we have that agreement. You sign it, we go to work.'

'And what's the first bit of work you'd like to do?'

'Walk through the Kramer bombing, very slowly, step by step.'

'It's been done a thousand times.'

'We'll do it again. I have a thick notebook full of questions.'

'They've all been asked.'

'Yeah, Sam, but they haven't been answered, have they?'

Sam stuck the filter between his lips.

'And they haven't been asked by me, have they?'

'You think I'm lying.'

'Are you?'

'No.'

'But you haven't told the whole story, have you?'

'What difference does it make, counselor? You've read *Bateman*.'

'Yeah, I've memorized *Bateman*, and there are a number of soft spots in it.'

'Typical lawyer.'

'If there's new evidence, then there are ways to present it. All we're doing, Sam, is trying to create enough confusion to make some judge somewhere give it a second thought. Then a third thought. Then he grants a stay so he can learn more.'

'I know how the game is played, son.'

'Adam, okay, it's Adam.'

'Yeah, and just call me Gramps. I suppose you plan to appeal to the governor.'

'Yes.'

Sam inched forward in his chair and moved close to the screen. With the index finger of his right hand, he began pointing at a spot somewhere in the center of Adam's nose. His face was suddenly harsh, his eyes narrow. 'You listen to me, Adam,' he growled, finger pointing back and forth. 'If I sign this piece of paper, you are never to talk to that bastard. Never. Do you understand?'

Adam watched the finger but said nothing.

Sam decided to continue. 'He is a bogus son of a bitch. He is vile, sleazy, thoroughly corrupt, and completely able to mask it all with a pretty smile and a clean haircut. He is the only reason I'm sitting here on death row. If you contact him in any way, then you're finished as my lawyer.'

'So I'm your lawyer.'

The finger dropped and Sam relaxed a bit. 'Oh, I may give you a shot, let you practice on me. You know, Adam, the legal profession is really screwed up. If I was a free man, just trying to make a living, minding my own business, paying my taxes, obeying the laws and such, then I couldn't find a lawyer who'd take the time to spit on me unless I had money. But here I am, a convicted killer, condemned to die, not a penny to my name, and I've got lawyers all over the country begging to represent me. Big, rich lawyers with long names preceded with initials and followed by numerals, famous lawyers with their own jets and television shows. Can you explain this?'

'Of course not. Nor do I care about it.'

'It's a sick profession you've gotten yourself in.'

'Most lawyers are honest and hardworking.'

'Sure. And most of my pals here on death row would be ministers and missionaries if they hadn't been wrongly convicted.'

'The governor might be our last chance.'

'Then they might as well gas me now. That pompous ass'll probably want to witness my execution, then he'll hold a press conference and replay every detail for the world. He's a spineless little worm who's made it this far because of me. And if he can milk me for a few more sound bites, then he'll do it. Stay away from him.'

'We can discuss it later.'

'We're discussing it now, I believe. You'll give me your word before I sign this paper.'

'Any more conditions?'

'Yeah. I want something added here so that if I decide to fire you again, then you and your firm won't fight me. That should be easy.'

'Let me see it.'

The agreement was passed through the slit again, and Adam printed a neat paragraph at the bottom. He handed it back to Sam, who read it slowly and laid it on the counter.

'You didn't sign it,' Adam said.

'I'm still thinking.'

'Can I ask some questions while you're thinking?'

'You can ask them.'

'Where did you learn to handle explosives?'

'Here and there.'

'There were at least five bombings before Kramer, all with the same type, all very basic – dynamite, caps, fuses. Kramer, of course, was different because a timing device was used. Who taught you how to make bombs?'

'Have you ever lit a firecracker?'

'Sure.'

'Same principle. A match to the fuse, run like crazy, and boom.'

'The timing device is a bit more complicated. Who taught you how to wire one?'

'My mother. When do you plan to return here?'

'Tomorrow.'

'Good. Here's what we'll do. I need some time to think about this. I don't want to talk right now, and I damned sure don't want to answer a bunch of questions. Let me look over this document, make some changes, and we'll meet again tomorrow.'

'That's wasting time.'

'I've wasted almost ten years here. What's another day?'

'They may not allow me to return if I don't officially represent you. This visit is a favor.'

'A great bunch of guys, aren't they? Tell them you're my lawyer for the next twenty-four hours. They'll let you in.'

'We have a lot of ground to cover, Sam. I'd like to get started.'

'I need to think, okay. When you spend over nine years alone in a cell, you become real good at thinking and analyzing. But you can't do it fast, understand? It takes longer to sort things out and place them in order. I'm sort of spinnin' right now, you know. You've hit me kinda hard.'

'Okay.'

'I'll be better tomorrow. We can talk then. I promise.'

'Sure.' Adam placed the cap on his pen and stuck it in his pocket. He slid the file into the briefcase, and relaxed in his seat. 'I'll be staying in Memphis for the next couple of months.'

'Memphis? I thought you lived in Chicago.'

'We have a small office in Memphis. I'll be working out of there. The number's on the card. Feel free to call anytime.'

'What happens when this thing is over?'

'I don't know. I may go back to Chicago.'

'Are you married?'

'No.'

'Is Carmen?'

'No.'

'What's she like?'

Adam folded his hands behind his head and examined the thin fog above them. 'She's very smart. Very pretty. Looks a lot like her mother.'

'Evelyn was a beautiful girl.'

'She's still beautiful.'

'I always thought Eddie was lucky to get her. I didn't like her family, though.'

And she certainly didn't like Eddie's, Adam thought to himself. Sam's chin almost dropped to his chest. He rubbed

116

his eyes and pinched the bridge of his nose. 'This family business will take some work, won't it?' he said without looking.

'Yep.'

'I may not be able to talk about some things.'

'Yes you will. You owe it to me, Sam. And you owe it to yourself.'

'You don't know what you're talking about, and you wouldn't want to know all of it.'

'Try me. I'm sick of secrets.'

'Why do you want to know so much?'

'So I can try and make some sense of it.'

'That'll be a waste of time.'

'I'll have to decide that, won't I?'

Sam placed his hands on his knees, and slowly stood. He took a deep breath and looked down at Adam through the screen. 'I'd like to go now.'

Their eyes met through the narrow diamonds in the partition. 'Sure,' Adam said. 'Can I bring you anything?'

'No. Just come back.'

'I promise.'

ELEVEN

PACKER CLOSED THE DOOR and locked it, and together they stepped from the narrow shadow outside the conference room into the blinding midday sun. Adam closed his eyes and stopped for a second, then fished through his pockets in a desperate search for sunglasses. Packer waited patiently, his eyes sensibly covered with a pair of thick imitation Ray-Bans, his face shielded by the wide' brim of an official Parchman cap. The air was suffocating and almost visible. Sweat immediately covered Adam's arms and face as he finally found the sunglasses in his briefcase and put them on. He squinted and grimaced, and once able to actually see, he followed Packer along the brick trail and baked grass in front of the unit.

'Sam okay?' Packer asked. His hands were in his pockets and he was in no hurry.

'I guess.'

'You hungry?'

'No,' Adam replied as he glanced at his watch. It was almost one o'clock. He wasn't sure if Packer was offering prison food or something else, but he was taking no chances.

'Too bad. Today's Wednesday, and that means turnip greens and corn bread. Mighty good.'

'Thanks.' Adam was certain that somewhere deep in his genes he was supposed to crave turnip greens and corn bread. Today's menu should make his mouth drool and his stomach yearn. But he considered himself a Californian, and to his knowledge had never seen turnip greens. 'Maybe next week,' he said, hardly believing he was being offered lunch on the Row.

They were at the first of the double gates. As it opened, Packer, without removing his hands from his pockets, said, 'When you coming back?'

'Tomorrow.'

'That soon?'

'Yeah. I'm going to be around for a while.'

'Well, nice to meet you.' He grinned broadly and walked away.

As Adam walked through the second gate, the red bucket began its descent. It stopped three feet from the ground, and he rattled through the selection at the bottom until he found his keys. He never looked up at the guard.

A white mini-van with official markings on the door and along the sides was waiting by Adam's car. The driver's window came down, and Lucas Mann leaned out. 'Are you in a hurry?'

Adam glanced at his watch again. 'Not really.'

'Good. Hop in. I need to talk to you. We'll take a quick tour of the place.'

Adam didn't want a quick tour of the place, but he was planning to stop by Mann's office anyway. He opened the passenger's door and threw his coat and briefcase on a rear seat. Thankfully, the air was at full throttle. Lucas, cool and still impeccably starched, looked odd sitting behind the wheel of a mini-van. He eased away from MSU and headed for the main drive.

'How'd it go?' he asked. Adam tried to recall Sam's exact description of Lucas Mann. Something to the effect that he could not be trusted.

'Okay, I guess,' he replied, carefully vague.

'Are you going to represent him?'

'I think so. He wants to dwell on it tonight. And he wants to see me tomorrow.'

'No problem, but you need to sign him up tomorrow. We need some type of written authorization from him.'

'I'll get it tomorrow. Where are we going?' They turned left and headed away from the front of the prison. They passed the last of the neat white houses with shade trees and flower beds, and now they were driving through fields of cotton and beans that stretched forever.

'Nowhere in particular. Just thought you might want to see some of our farm. We need to cover a few things.'

'I'm listening.'

'The decision of the Fifth Circuit hit the wire at mid-morning, and we've already had at least three phone calls from reporters. They smell blood, of course, and they want to know if this might be the end for Sam. I know some of these people, dealt with them before on other executions. A few are nice guys, most are obnoxious jerks. But anyway, they're all asking about Sam and whether or not he has a lawyer. Will he represent himself to the very end? You know, that kind of crap.'

In a field to the right was a large group of inmates in white pants and without shirts. They were working the rows and sweating profusely, their backs and chests drenched and glistening under the scorching sun. A guard on a horse watched them with a rifle. 'What are these guys doing?' Adam asked.

'Chopping cotton.'

'Are they required to?'

'No. All volunteers. It's either that or sit in a cell all day.'

'They wear white. Sam wears red. I saw a gang by the highway in blue.'

'It's part of the classification system. White means these guys are low risk.'

'What were their crimes?'

'Everything. Drugs, murder, repeat offenders, you name it. But they've behaved since they've been here, so they wear white and they're allowed to work.'

The mini-van turned at an intersection, and the fences and razor wire returned. To the left was a series of modern barracks built on two levels and branching in all directions from a central hub. If not for the barbed wire and guard

120

towers, the unit could pass for a badly designed college dormitory. 'What's that?' Adam asked, pointing.

'Unit 30.'

'How many units are there?'

'I'm not sure. We keep building and tearing down. Around thirty.'

'It looks new.'

'Oh yes. We've been in trouble with the federal courts for almost twenty years, so we've been doing lots of building. It's no secret that the real superintendent of this place has been a federal judge.'

'Can the reporters wait until tomorrow? I need to see what Sam has on his mind. I'd hate to talk to them now, and then things go badly tomorrow.'

'I think I can put them off a day. But they won't wait long.'

They passed the last guard tower and Unit 30 disappeared. They drove at least two miles before the gleaming razor wire of another compound peeked above the fields.

'I talked to the warden this morning, after you got here,' Lucas said. 'He said he'd like to meet you. You'll like him. He hates executions, you know. He was hoping to retire in a couple of years without going through another, but now it looks doubtful.'

'Let me guess. He's just doing his job, right?'

'We're all doing our jobs here.'

'That's my point. I get the impression that everybody here wants to pat me on the back and speak to me in sad voices about what's about to happen to poor old Sam. Nobody wants to kill him, but you're all just doing your jobs.'

'There are plenty of people who want Sam dead.'

'Who?'

'The governor and the Attorney General. I'm sure you're familiar with the governor, but the AG is the one you'd better watch. He, of course, wants to be governor one day. For some reason we've elected in this state a whole crop of these young, terribly ambitious politicians who just can't seem to sit still.'

121

'His name's Roxburgh, right?'

'That's him. He loves cameras, and I expect a press conference from him this afternoon. If he holds true to form, he'll take full credit for the victory in the Fifth Circuit, and promise a diligent effort to execute Sam in four weeks. His office handles these things, you know. And then it wouldn't surprise me if the governor himself doesn't appear on the evening news with a comment or two. My point is this, Adam – there will be enormous pressure from above to make sure there are no more stays. They want Sam dead for their own political gain. They'll milk it for all they can get.'

Adam watched the next camp as they drove by. On a concrete slab between two buildings, a game of basketball was in full force with at least a dozen players on each side. All were black. Next to the court, a row of barbells was being pumped and jerked around by some heavy lifters. Adam noticed a few whites.

Lucas turned onto another road. 'There's another reason,' he continued. 'Louisiana is killing them right and left. Texas has executed six already this year. Florida, five. We haven't had an execution in over two years. We're dragging our feet, some people say. It's time to show these other states that we're just as serious about good government as they are. Just last week in Jackson a legislative committee held hearings on the issue. There were all sorts of angry statements by our leaders about the endless delays in these matters. Not surprisingly, it was decided that the federal courts are to blame. There's lots of pressure to kill somebody. And Sam happens to be next.'

'Who's after Sam?'

'Nobody, really. It could be two years before we get this close again. The buzzards are circling.'

'Why are you telling me this?'

'I'm not the enemy, okay? I'm the attorney for the prison, not the State of Mississippi. And you've never been here before. I thought you'd want to know these things.'

'Thanks,' Adam said. Though the information was unsolicited, it was certainly useful.

'I'll help in any way I can.'

The roofs of buildings could be seen on the horizon. 'Is that the front of the prison?' Adam asked.

'Yes.'

'I'd like to leave now.'

THE MEMPHIS OFFICE of Kravitz & Bane occupied two floors of a building called Brinkley Plaza, a 1920s edifice on the corner of Main and Monroe in downtown. Main Street was also known as the Mid-America Mall. Cars and trucks had been banished when the city attempted to revitalize its downtown and converted asphalt into tiles, fountains, and decorative trees. Only pedestrian traffic was permitted on the Mall.

The building itself had been revitalized and renewed tastefully. Its main lobby was marble and bronze. The K&B offices were large and richly decorated with antiques and oak-paneled walls and Persian rugs.

Adam was escorted by an attractive young secretary to the corner office of Baker Cooley, the managing partner. They introduced themselves, shook hands, and admired the secretary as she left the room and closed the door. Cooley leered a bit too long and seemed to hold his breath until the door was completely closed and the glimpse was over.

'Welcome south,' Cooley said, finally exhaling and sitting in his posh burgundy leather swivel chair.

'Thanks. I guess you've talked to Garner Goodman.'

'Yesterday. Twice. He gave me the score. We've got a nice little conference room at the end of this hall with a phone, computer, plenty of room. It's yours for the, uh, duration.'

Adam nodded and glanced around the office. Cooley was in his early fifties, a man with an organized desk and a clean room. His words and hands were quick, and he bore the gray hair and dark circles of a frazzled accountant. 'What kind of work goes on here?' Adam asked.

'Not much litigation, and certainly no criminal work,' he

answered quickly as if criminals were not allowed to set their dirty feet on the thick carpeting and fancy rugs of this establishment. Adam remembered Goodman's description of the Memphis branch – a boutique firm of twelve good lawyers whose acquisition years earlier by Kravitz & Bane was now a mystery. But the additional address looked nice on the letterhead.

'Mostly corporate stuff,' Cooley continued. 'We represent some old banks, and we do a lot of bond work for local governmental units.'

Exhilarating work, Adam thought.

'The firm itself dates back a hundred and forty years, the oldest in Memphis, by the way. Been around since the Civil War. It split up and spun off a few times, then merged with the big boys in Chicago.'

Cooley delivered this brief chronicle with pride, as if the pedigree had a damned thing to do with practicing law in 1990.

'How many lawyers?' Adam asked, trying to fill in the gaps of a conversation that had started slow and was going nowhere.

'A dozen. Eleven paralegals. Nine clerks. Seventeen secretaries. Miscellaneous support staff of ten. Not a bad operation for this part of the country. Nothing like Chicago, though.'

You're right about that, Adam thought. 'I'm looking forward to visiting here. I hope I won't be in the way.'

'Not at all. I'm afraid we won't be much help, though. We're the corporate types, you know, office practitioners, lots of paperwork and all. I haven't seen a courtroom in twenty years.'

'I'll be fine. Mr Goodman and those guys up there will help me.'

Cooley jumped to his feet and rubbed his hands as if he wasn't sure what else to do with them. 'Well, uh, Darlene will be your secretary. She's actually in a pool, but I've sort of assigned her to you. She'll give you a key, give you the scoop on parking, security, phones, copiers, the works. All state of the art. Really good stuff. If you need a paralegal, just let me know. We'll steal one from one of the other guys, and –'

'No, that won't be necessary. Thanks.'

'Well, then, let's go look at your office.'

Adam followed Cooley down the quiet and empty hallway, and smiled to himself as he thought of the offices in Chicago. There the halls were always filled with harried lawyers and busy secretaries. Phones rang incessantly, and copiers and faxes and intercoms beeped and buzzed and gave the place the atmosphere of an arcade. It was a madhouse for ten hours a day. Solitude was found only in the alcoves of the libraries, or maybe in the corners of the building where the partners worked.

This place was as quiet as a funeral parlour. Cooley pushed open a door and flipped on a switch. 'How's this?' he asked, waving his arm in a broad circle. The room was more than adequate, a long narrow office with a beautiful polished table in the center and five chairs on each side. At one end, a makeshift workplace with a phone, computer, and executive's chair had been arranged. Adam walked along the table, glancing at the bookshelves filled with neat but unused law books. He peeked through the curtains of the window. 'Nice view,' he said, looking three floors below at the pigeons and people on the Mall.

'Hope it's adequate,' Cooley said.

'It's very nice. It'll work just fine. I'll keep to myself and stay out of your way.'

'Nonsense. If you need anything, just give me a call.' Cooley was walking slowly toward Adam. 'There is one thing, though,' he said with his eyebrows suddenly serious.

Adam faced him. 'What is it?'

'Got a call a couple of hours ago from a reporter here in Memphis. Don't know the guy, but he said he's been following the Cayhall case for years. Wanted to know if our firm was still handling the case, you know. I suggested he contact the boys in Chicago. We, of course, have nothing to do with it.' He pulled a scrap of paper from his shirt pocket and handed it to Adam. It had a name and a phone number.

'I'll take care of it,' Adam said.

Cooley took a step closer and crossed his arms on his chest. 'Look, Adam, we're not trial lawyers, you know. We do the corporate work. Money's great. We're very low key, and we avoid publicity, you know.'

Adam nodded slowly but said nothing.

'We've never touched a criminal case, certainly nothing as huge as this.'

'You don't want any of the dirt to rub off on you, right?'

'I didn't say that. Not at all. No. It's just that things are different down here. This is not Chicago. Our biggest clients happen to be some rather staid and proper old bankers, been with us for years, and, well, we're just concerned about our image. You know what I mean?'

'No.'

'Sure you do. We don't deal with criminals, and, well, we're very sensitive about the image we project here in Memphis.'

'You don't deal with criminals?'

'Never.'

'But you represent big banks?'

'Come on, Adam. You know where I'm coming from. This area of our practice is changing rapidly. Deregulation, mergers, failures, a real dynamic sector of the law. Competition is fierce among the big law firms, and we don't want to lose clients. Hell, everybody wants banks.'

'And you don't want your clients tainted by mine?'

'Look, Adam, you're from Chicago. Let's keep this matter where it belongs, okay? It's a Chicago case, handled by you guys up there. Memphis has nothing to do with it, okay?'

'This office is part of Kravitz & Bane.'

'Yeah, and this office has nothing to gain by being connected to scum like Sam Cayhall.'

'Sam Cayhall is my grandfather.'

'Shit!' Cooley's knees buckled and his arms dropped from his chest. 'You're lying!'

126

Adam took a step toward him. 'I'm not lying, and if you object to my presence here, then you need to call Chicago.'

'This is awful,' Cooley said as he retreated and headed for the door.

'Call Chicago.'

'I might do that,' he said, almost to himself, as he opened the door and disappeared, mumbling something else.

Welcome to Memphis, Adam said as he sat in his new chair and stared at the blank computer screen. He placed the scrap of paper on the table and looked at the name and phone number. A sharp hunger pain hit, and he realized he hadn't eaten in hours. It was almost four. He was suddenly weak and tired and hungry.

He gently placed both feet on the table next to the phone, and closed his eyes. The day was a blur, from the anxiety of driving to Parchman and seeing the front gate of the prison, from the unexpected meeting with Lucas Mann, to the horror of stepping onto the Row, to the fear of confronting Sam. And now the warden wanted to meet him, the press wanted to inquire, the Memphis branch of his firm wanted it all hushed up. All this, in less than eight hours.

What could he expect tomorrow?

THEY SAT next to each other on the deep cushioned sofa with a bowl of microwave popcorn between them. Their bare feet were on the coffee table amid a half dozen empty cartons of Chinese food and two bottles of wine. They peered over their toes and watched the television. Adam held the remote control. The room was dark. He slowly ate popcorn.

Lee hadn't moved in a long time. Her eyes were wet, but she said nothing. The video started for the second time.

Adam pushed the Pause button as Sam first appeared, in handcuffs, being rushed from the jail to a hearing. 'Where were you when you heard he was arrested?' he asked without looking at her.

'Here in Memphis,' she said quietly but with a strong voice. 'We had been married for a few years. I was at home.

Phelps called and said there had been a bombing in Greenville, at least two people were dead. Might be the Klan. He told me to watch the news at noon, but I was afraid to. A few hours later, my mother called and told me they had arrested Daddy for the bombing. She said he was in jail in Greenville.'

'How'd you react?'

'I don't know. Stunned. Scared. Eddie got on the phone and told me that he and Mother had been instructed by Sam to sneak over to Cleveland and retrieve his car. I remember Eddie kept saying that he'd finally done it, he'd finally done it. He'd killed someone else. Eddie was crying and I started crying, and I remember it was horrible.'

'They got the car.'

'Yeah. No one ever knew it. It never came out during any of the trials. We were scared the cops would find out about it, and make Eddie and my mother testify. But it never happened.'

'Where was I?'

'Let me see. You guys lived in a little white house in Clanton, and I'm sure you were there with Evelyn. I don't think she was working at the time. But I'm not sure.'

'What kind of work was my father doing?'

'I don't remember. At one time he worked as a manager in an auto parts store in Clanton, but he was always changing jobs.'

The video continued with clips of Sam being escorted to and from the jail and the courthouse, then there was the report that he had been formally indicted for the murders. He paused it. 'Did any one of you visit Sam in jail?'

'No. Not while he was in Greenville. His bond was very high, a half a million dollars, I think.'

'It was a half a million.'

'And at first the family tried to raise the money to bail him out. Mother, of course, wanted me to convince Phelps to write a check. Phelps, of course, said no. He wanted no part of it. We fought bitterly, but I couldn't really blame him. Daddy stayed in jail. I remember one of his brothers trying to borrow against some land, but it didn't work. Eddie didn't want to go to jail to see him, and Mother wasn't able. I'm not sure Sam wanted us there.'

'When did we leave Clanton?'

Lee leaned forward and took her wineglass from the table. She sipped and thought for a moment. 'He'd been in jail about a month, I believe. I drove down one day to see Mother, and she told me Eddie was talking about leaving. I didn't believe it. She said he was embarrassed and humiliated and couldn't face people around town. He'd just lost his job and he wouldn't leave the house. I called him and talked to Evelyn. Eddie wouldn't get on the phone. She said he was depressed and disgraced and all that, and I remember telling her that we all felt that way. I asked her if they were leaving, and she distinctly said no. About a week later, Mother called again and said you guys had packed and left in the middle of the night. The landlord was calling and wanting rent, and no one had seen Eddie. The house was empty.'

'I wish I remembered some of this.'

'You were only three, Adam. The last time I saw you you were playing by the garage of the little white house. You were so cute and sweet.'

'Gee thanks.'

'Several weeks passed, then one day Eddie called me and told me to tell Mother that you guys were in Texas and doing okay.'

'Texas?'

'Yeah. Evelyn told me much later that y'all sort of drifted westward. She was pregnant and anxious to settle down some place. He called again and said y'all were in California. That was the last call for many years.'

'Years?'

'Yeah. I tried to convince him to come home, but he was adamant. Swore he'd never return, and I guess he meant it.'

'Where were my mother's parents?'

'I don't know. They were not from Ford County. Seems like they lived in Georgia, maybe Florida.'

129

'I've never met them.'

He pushed the button again and the video continued. The first trial started in Nettles County. The camera panned the courthouse lawn with the group of Klansmen and rows of policemen and swarms of onlookers.

'This is incredible,' Lee said.

He stopped it again. 'Did you go to the trial?'

'Once. I sneaked in the courthouse and listened to the closing arguments. He forbade us to watch any of his three trials. Mother was not able. Her blood pressure was out of control, and she was taking lots of medication. She was practically bedridden.'

'Did Sam know you were there?'

'No. I sat in the back of the courtroom with a scarf over my head. He never saw me.'

'What was Phelps doing?'

'Hiding in his office, tending to his business, praying no one would find out Sam Cayhall was his father-in-law. Our first separation occurred not long after this trial.'

'What do you remember from the trial, from the courtroom?'

'I remember thinking that Sam got himself a good jury, his kind of people. I don't know how his lawyer did it, but they picked twelve of the biggest rednecks they could find. I watched the jurors react to the prosecutor, and I watched them listen carefully to Sam's lawyer.'

'Clovis Brazelton.'

'He was quite an orator, and they hung on every word. I was shocked when the jury couldn't agree on a verdict and a mistrial was declared. I was convinced he would be acquitted. I think he was shocked too.'

The video continued with reactions to the mistrial, with generous comments from Clovis Brazelton, with another shot of Sam leaving the courthouse. Then the second trial began with its similarities to the first. 'How long have you worked on this?' she asked.

'Seven years. I was a freshman at Pepperdine when the idea hit. It's been a challenge.' He fast-forwarded through the pathetic scene of Marvin Kramer spilling from his wheelchair after the second trial, and stopped with the smiling face of a local anchorwoman as she chattered on about the opening of the third trial of the legendary Sam Cayhall. It was 1981 now.

'Sam was a free man for thirteen years,' Adam said. 'What did he do?'

'He kept to himself, farmed a little, tried to make ends meet. He never talked to me about the bombing or any of his Klan activities, but he enjoyed the attention in Clanton. He was somewhat of a local legend down there, and he was sort of smug about it. Mother's health declined, and he stayed at home and took care of her.'

'He never thought about leaving?'

'Not seriously. He was convinced his legal problems were over. He'd had two trials, and walked away from both of them. No jury in Mississippi was going to convict a Klansman in the late sixties. He thought he was invincible. He stayed close to Clanton, avoided the Klan, and lived a peaceful life. I thought he'd spend his golden years growing tomatoes and fishing for bream.'

'Did he ever ask about my father?'

She finished her wine and placed the glass on the table. It had never occurred to Lee that she would one day be asked to recall in detail so much of this sad little history. She had worked so hard to forget it. 'I remember during the first year he was back home, he would occasionally ask me if I'd heard from my brother. Of course, I hadn't. We knew you guys were somewhere in California, and we hoped you were okay. Sam's a very proud and stubborn person, Adam. He would never consider chasing you guys down and begging Eddie to come home. If Eddie was ashamed of his family, then Sam felt like he should stay in California.' She paused and sunk lower into the sofa. 'Mother was diagnosed with cancer in 1973, and I hired a private investigator to find Eddie. He worked for six months, charged me a bunch of money, and found nothing.'

'I was nine years old, fourth grade, that was in Salem, Oregon.'

131

'Yeah. Evelyn told me later that you guys spent time in Oregon.'

'We moved all the time. Every year was a different school until I was in the eighth grade. Then we settled in Santa Monica.'

'You were elusive. Eddie must've hired a good lawyer, because any trace of Cayhall was eliminated. The investigator even used some people out there, but nothing.'

'When did she die?'

'Nineteen seventy-seven. We were actually sitting in the front of the church, about to start the funeral, when Eddie slid in a side door and sat behind me. Don't ask how he knew about Mother's death. He simply appeared in Clanton then disappeared again. Never said a word to Sam. Drove a rental car so no one could check his plates. I drove to Memphis the next day, and there he was, waiting in my driveway. We drank coffee for two hours and talked about everything. He had school pictures of you and Carmen, everything was just wonderful in sunny Southern California. Good job, nice house in the suburbs, Evelyn was selling real estate. The American dream. Said he would never return to Mississippi, not even for Sam's funeral. After swearing me to secrecy, he told me about the new names, and he gave me his phone number. Not his address, just his phone number. Any breach of secrecy, he threatened, and he would simply disappear again. He told me not to call him, though, unless it was an emergency. I told him I wanted to see you and Carmen, and he said that it might happen, one day. At times he was the same old Eddie, and at times he was another person. We hugged and waved good-bye, and I never saw him again.'

Adam flipped the remote and the video moved. The clear, modern images of the third and final trial moved by quickly, and there was Sam, suddenly thirteen years older, with a new lawyer as they darted through a side door of the Lakehead County Courthouse. 'Did you go to the third trial?'

'No. He told me to stay away.'

132

Adam paused the video. 'At what point did Sam realize they were coming after him again?'

'It's hard to say. There was a small story in the Memphis paper one day about this new district attorney in Greenville who wanted to reopen the Kramer case. It was not a big story, just a couple of paragraphs in the middle of the paper. I remember reading it with horror. I read it ten times and stared at it for an hour. After all these years, the name Sam Cayhall was once again in the paper. I couldn't believe it. I called him, and, of course, he had read it too. He said not to worry. About two weeks later there was another story, a little larger this time, with David McAllister's face in the middle of it. I called Daddy, he said everything was okay. That's how it got started. Rather quietly, then it just steamrolled. The Kramer family supported the idea, then the NAACP got involved. One day it became obvious that McAllister was determined to push for a new trial, and that it was not going to go away. Sam was sickened by it, and he was scared, but he tried to act brave. He'd won twice he said, he could do it again.'

'Did you call Eddie?'

'Yeah. Once it was obvious there would be a new indictment, I called him and broke the news. He didn't say much, didn't say much at all. It was a brief conversation, and I promised to keep him posted. I don't think he took it very well. It wasn't long before it became a national story, and I'm sure Eddie followed it in the media.'

They watched the remaining segments of the third trial in silence. McAllister's toothsome face was everywhere, and more than once Adam wished he'd done a bit more editing. Sam was led away for the last time in handcuffs, and the screen went blank.

'Has anyone else seen this?' Lee asked.

'No. You're the first.'

'How did you collect it all?'

'It took time, a little money, a lot of effort.'

'It's incredible.'

'When I was a junior in high school, we had this goofy

133

teacher of political science. He allowed us to haul in newspapers and magazines and debate the issues of the day. Someone brought a front page story from the *L.A. Times* about the upcoming trial of Sam Cayhall in Mississippi. We kicked it around pretty good, then we watched it closely as it took place. Everyone, including myself, was quite pleased when he was found guilty. But there was a huge debate over the death penalty. A few weeks later, my father was dead and you finally told me the truth. I was horrified that my friends would find out.'

'Did they?'

'Of course not. I'm a Cayhall, a master at keeping secrets.'

'It won't be a secret much longer.'

'No, it won't.'

There was a long pause as they stared at the blank screen. Adam finally pushed the power button and the television went off. He tossed the remote control on the table. 'I'm sorry, Lee, if this will embarrass you. I mean it. I wish there was some way to avoid it.'

'You don't understand.'

'I know. And you can't explain it, right? Are you afraid of Phelps and his family?'

'I despise Phelps and his family.'

'But you enjoy their money.'

'I've earned their money, okay? I've put up with him for twenty-seven years.'

'Are you afraid your little clubs will ostracize you? That they'll kick you out of the country clubs?'

'Stop it, Adam.'

'I'm sorry,' he said. 'It's been a weird day. I'm coming out of the closet, Lee. I'm confronting my past, and I guess I expect everyone to be as bold. I'm sorry.'

'What does he look like?'

'A very old man. Lots of wrinkles and pale skin. He's too old to be locked up in a cage.'

'I remember talking to him a few days before his last trial. I asked him why he didn't just run away, vanish into the night and hide in some place like South America. And you know what?'

'What?'

'He said he thought about it. Mother had been dead for several years. Eddie was gone. He had read books about Mengele and Eichmann and other Nazi war criminals who disappeared into South America. He even mentioned São Paulo, said it was a city of twenty million and filled with refugees of all sorts. He had a friend, another Klansman I think, who could fix the paperwork and help him hide. He gave it a lot of thought.'

'I wish he had. Maybe my father would still be with us.'

'Two days before he went to Parchman, I saw him in the jail in Greenville. It was our last visit. I asked him why he hadn't run. He said he never dreamed he would get the death penalty. I couldn't believe that for years he'd been a free man and could've easily run away. It was a big mistake, he said, not running. A mistake that would cost him his life.'

Adam placed the popcorn bowl on the table, and slowly leaned toward her. His head rested on her shoulder. She took his hand. 'I'm sorry you're in the middle of all this,' she whispered.

'He looked so pitiful sitting there in a red death row jumpsuit.'

135

TWELVE

CLYDE PACKER poured a generous serving of a strong brew into a cup with his name on it, and began filling out the morning's paperwork. He had worked the Row for twenty-one years, the last seven as the Shift Commander. For eight hours each morning, he would be one of four Tier Sergeants, in charge of fourteen condemned men, two guards, and two trustees. He completed his forms and checked a clipboard. There was a note to call the Warden. Another note said that F. M. Dempsey was low on heart pills and wanted to see the doctor. They all wanted to see the doctor. He sipped the steaming coffee as he left the office for his morning inspection. He checked the uniforms of two guards at the front door and told the young white one to get a haircut.

MSU was not a bad place to work. As a general rule, death row inmates were quiet and well behaved. They spent twenty-three hours a day alone in their cells, separated from each other and thus unable to instigate trouble. They spent sixteen hours a day sleeping. They were fed in their cells. They were allowed an hour of outdoor recreation per day, their 'hour out' as they called it, and they could have this time alone if they chose. Everyone had either a television or a radio, or both, and after breakfast the four tiers came to life with music and news and soap operas and quiet conversations through the bars. The inmates could not see their neighbors next door, but they conversed with little trouble. Arguments erupted occasionally over the volume of someone's music, but these little spats were quickly settled by the guards. The inmates had certain rights, and then they had certain privileges. The removal of a television or a radio was devastating.

The Row bred an odd camaraderie among those sentenced there. Half were white, half were black, and all had been convicted of brutal killings. But there was little concern about past deeds and criminal records, and generally no real interest in skin color. Out in the general prison population, gangs of all varieties did an effective job of classifying inmates, usually on the basis of race. On the Row, however, a man was judged by the way he handled his confinement. Whether they liked each other or not, they were all locked together in this tiny corner of the world, all waiting to die. It was a ragtag little fraternity of misfits, drifters, outright thugs, and cold-blooded killers.

And the death of one could mean the death of all. The news of Sam's new death sentence was whispered along the tiers and through the bars. When it made the noon news yesterday, the Row became noticeably quieter. Every inmate suddenly wanted to talk to his lawyer. There was a renewed interest in all matters legal, and Packer had noticed several of them plowing through their court files with televisions off and radios down.

He eased through a heavy door, took a long drink, and walked slowly and quietly along Tier A. Fourteen identical cells, six feet wide and nine feet deep, faced the hallway. The front of each cell was a wall of iron bars, so that at no time did an inmate have complete privacy. Anything he happened to be doing – sleeping, using the toilet – was subject to observation by the guards.

They were all in bed as Packer slowed in front of each little room and looked for a head under the sheets. The cell lights were off and the tier was dark. The hall man, an inmate with special privileges, would wake them, or rack-'em-up, at five. Breakfast would be served at six – eggs, toast, jam, sometimes bacon, coffee, and fruit juice. In a few minutes the Row would slowly come to life as forty-seven men shook off their sleep and resumed the interminable process of dying. It happened slowly, one day at a time, as another miserable sunrise brought another blanket of heat into their private little pockets of hell. And it happened quickly, as it had the day before, when a court somewhere rejected a plea or a motion or an appeal and said that an execution must happen soon.

Packer sipped coffee and counted heads and shuffled quietly along through his morning ritual. Generally, MSU ran smoothly when routines were unbroken and schedules were followed. There were lots of rules in the manual, but they were fair and easy to follow. Everyone knew them. But an execution had its own handbook with a different policy and fluctuating guidelines that generally upset the tranquility of the Row. Packer had great respect for Phillip Naifeh, but damned if he didn't rewrite the book before and after each execution. There was great pressure to do it all properly and constitutionally and compassionately. No two killings had been the same.

Packer hated executions. He believed in the death penalty because he was a religious man, and when God said an eye for an eye, then God meant it. He preferred, however, that they be carried out somewhere else by other people. Fortunately, they had been so rare in Mississippi that his job proceeded smoothly with little interference. He'd been through fifteen in twenty-one years, but only four since 1982.

He spoke quietly to a guard at the end of the tier. The sun was beginning to peek through the open windows above the tier walkway. The day would be hot and suffocating. It would also be much quieter. There would be fewer complaints about the food, fewer demands to see the doctor, a scattering of gripes about this and that, but on the whole they would be a docile and preoccupied group. It had been at least a year and maybe longer since a stay had been withdrawn this close to an execution. Packer smiled to himself as he searched for a head under the sheets. This day would indeed be a quiet one.

138

During the first few months of Sam's career on the Row, Packer had ignored him. The official handbook prohibited anything other than necessary contact with inmates, and Packer had found Sam an easy person to leave alone. He was a Klansman. He hated blacks. He said little. He was bitter and surly, at least in the early days. But the routine of doing nothing for eight hours a day gradually softens the edges, and with time they reached a level of communication that consisted of a handful of short words and grunts. After nine and a half years of seeing each other every day, Sam could on occasion actually grin at Packer.

There were two types of killers on the Row, Packer had decided after years of study. There were the cold-blooded killers who would do it again if given the chance, and there were those who simply made mistakes and would never dream of shedding more blood. Those in the first group should be gassed quickly. Those in the second group caused great discomfort for Packer because their executions served no purpose. Society would not suffer or even notice if these men were released from prison. Sam was a solid member of the second group. He could be returned to his home where he would soon die a lonesome death. No, Packer did not want Sam Cayhall executed.

He shuffled back along Tier A, sipping his coffee and looking at the dark cells. His tier was the nearest to the Isolation Room, which was next door to the Chamber Room. Sam was in number six on Tier A, literally less than ninety feet from the gas chamber. He had requested a move a few years back because of some silly squabble with Cecil Duff, then his next-door neighbor.

Sam was now sitting in the dark on the edge of his bed. Packer stopped, walked to the bars. 'Mornin', Sam,' he said softly.

'Mornin',' Sam replied, squinting at Packer. Sam then stood in the center of his room and faced the door. He was wearing a dingy white tee shirt and baggy boxer shorts, the usual attire for inmates on the Row because it was so hot. The rules required the bright red coveralls to be worn outside the cell, but inside they wore as little as possible.

'It's gonna be a hot one,' Packer said, the usual early morning greeting.

'Wait till August,' Sam said, the standard reply to the usual early morning greeting.

'You okay?' Packer asked.

'Never felt better.'

'Your lawyer said he was coming back today.'

'Yeah. That's what he said. I guess I need lots of lawyers, huh, Packer?'

'Sure looks that way.' Packer took a sip of coffee and glanced down the tier. The windows behind him were to the south, and a trickle of sunlight was making its way through. 'See you later, Sam,' he said and eased away. He checked the remaining cells and found all his boys. The doors clicked behind him as he left Tier A and returned to the front.

THE ONE LIGHT in the cell was above the stainless steel sink – made of stainless steel so it couldn't be chipped and then used as a weapon or suicide device. Under the sink was a stainless steel toilet. Sam turned on his light and brushed his teeth. It was almost five-thirty. Sleep had been difficult.

He lit a cigarette and sat on the edge of his bed, studying his feet and staring at the painted concrete floor that somehow retained heat in the summer and cold in the winter. His only shoes, a pair of rubber shower shoes which he loathed, were under the bed. He owned one pair of wool socks, which he slept in during the winter. His remaining assets consisted of a black and white television, a radio, a typewriter, six tee shirts with holes, five pairs of plain white boxer shorts, a toothbrush, comb, nail clippers, an oscillating fan, and a twelve-month wall calendar. His most valuable asset was a collection of law books he had gathered and memorized over the years. They were also placed neatly on the cheap wooden shelves across from his bunk. In a cardboard box on the floor between the shelves and the door

140

was an accumulation of bulky files, the chronological legal history of *State of Mississippi v. Sam Cayhall*. It, too, had been committed to memory.

His balance sheet was lean and short, and other than the death warrant there were no liabilities. The poverty had bothered him at first, but those concerns were dispelled years ago. Family legend held that his great-grandfather had been a wealthy man with acreage and slaves, but no modern Cayhall was worth much. He had known condemned men who had agonized over their wills as if their heirs would brawl over their old televisions and dirty magazines. He was considering preparing his own Last Will and Testament and leaving his wool socks and dirty underwear to the State of Mississippi, or perhaps the NAACP.

To his right was J. B. Gullitt, an illiterate white kid who'd raped and killed a homecoming queen. Three years earlier, Gullitt had come within days of execution before Sam intervened with a crafty motion. Sam pointed out several unresolved issues, and explained to the Fifth Circuit that Gullitt had no lawyer. A stay was immediately granted, and Gullitt became a friend for life.

To his left was Hank Henshaw, the reputed leader of a long-forgotten band of thugs known as the Redneck Mafia. Hank and his motley gang had hijacked an eighteen-wheeler one night, planning only to steal its cargo. The driver produced a gun, and was killed in the ensuing shootout. Hank's family was paying good lawyers, and thus he was not expected to die for many years.

The three neighbors referred to their little section of MSU as Rhodesia.

Sam flipped the cigarette into the toilet and reclined on his bed. The day before the Kramer bombing he had stopped at Eddie's house in Clanton, he couldn't remember why except that he did deliver some fresh spinach from his garden, and he had played with little Alan, now Adam, for a few minutes in the front yard. It was April, and warm, he remembered, and his grandson was barefoot. He remembered the chubby little feet with a Band-Aid around one toe. He had cut it on a rock, Alan had explained with great pride. The kid loved Band-Aids, always had one on a finger or a knee. Evelyn held the spinach and shook her head as he proudly showed his grandfather a whole box of assorted adhesives.

That was the last time he had seen Alan. The bombing took place the next day, and Sam spent the next ten months in jail. By the time the second trial was over and he was released, Eddie and his family were gone. He had too much pride to give chase. There had been rumors and gossip of their whereabouts. Lee said they were in California, but she couldn't find them. Years later, she talked to Eddie and learned of the second child, a girl named Carmen.

There were voices at the end of the tier. Then the flush of a toilet, then a radio. Death row was creaking to life. Sam combed his oily hair, lit another Montclair, and studied the calendar on the wall. Today was July 12. He had twenty-seven days.

He sat on the edge of his bed and studied his feet some more. J. B. Gullitt turned on his television to catch the news, and as Sam puffed and scratched his ankles he listened to the NBC affiliate in Jackson. After the rundown of local shootings, robberies, and killings, the anchorman delivered the hot news that an execution was materializing up at Parchman. The Fifth Circuit, he reported eagerly, had lifted the stay for Sam Cayhall, Parchman's most famous inmate, and the date was now set for August 8. Authorities believe that Cayhall's appeals have been exhausted, the voice said, and the execution could take place.

Sam turned on his television. As usual, the audio preceded the picture by a good ten seconds, and he listened as the Attorney General himself predicted justice for Mr Cayhall, after all these many years. A grainy face formed on the screen, with words spewing forth, and then there was Roxburgh smiling and frowning at the same time, deep in thought as he relished for the cameras the scenario of finally hauling Mr Cayhall into the gas chamber. Back to the anchorperson, a local kid with a peach fuzz mustache, who wrapped up the story by blitzing through Sam's horrible crime while over his shoulder in the background was a crude illustration of a Klansman in a mask and pointed hood. A gun, a burning cross, and the letters KKK finished the depiction. The kid repeated the date, August 8, as if his viewers should circle their calendars and plan to take the day off. Then they were on to the weather.

He turned off the television, and walked to the bars.

'Did you hear it, Sam?' Gullitt called out from next door.

'Yep.'

'It's gonna get crazy, man.'

'Yep.'

'Look on the bright side, man.'

'What's that?'

'You've only got four weeks of it.' Gullitt chuckled as he hit this punch line, but he didn't laugh long. Sam pulled some papers from the file and sat on the edge of his bed. There were no chairs in the cell. He read through Adam's agreement of representation, a two-page document with a page and a half of language. On all margins, Sam had made neat, precise notes with a pencil. And he had added paragraphs on the back of the sheets. Another idea hit him, and he found room to add it. With a cigarette in his right fingers, he held the document with his left and read it again. And again.

Finally, Sam reached to his shelves and carefully took down his ancient Royal portable typewriter. He balanced it perfectly on his knees. He inserted a sheet of paper, and began typing.

AT TEN MINUTES after six, the doors on the north end of Tier A clicked and opened, and two guards entered the hallway. One pushed a cart with fourteen trays stacked neatly in slots. They stopped at cell number one, and slid the metal tray through a narrow opening in the door. The occupant of number one was a skinny Cuban who was waiting at the bars, shirtless in his drooping briefs. He grabbed the tray like a starving refugee, and without a word took it to the edge of his bed.

This morning's menu was two scrambled eggs, four pieces of toasted white bread, a fat slice of bacon, two scrawny containers of grape jelly, a small bottle of pre-packed orange juice, and a large Styrofoam cup of coffee. The food was warm and filling, and had the distinction of being approved by the federal courts.

They moved to the next cell where the inmate was waiting. They were always waiting, always standing by the door like hungry dogs.

'You're eleven minutes late,' the inmate said quietly as he took his tray. The guards did not look at him.

'Sue us,' one said.

'I've got my rights.'

'Your rights are a pain in the ass.'

'Don't talk to me that way. I'll sue you for it. You're abusive.'

The guards rolled away to the next door with no further response. Just part of the daily ritual.

Sam was not waiting at the door. He was busy at work in his little law office when breakfast arrived.

'I figured you'd be typing,' a guard said as they stopped in front of number six. Sam slowly placed the typewriter on the bed.

'Love letters,' he said as he stood.

'Well, whatever you're typing, Sam, you'd better hurry. The cook's already talking about your last meal.'

'Tell him I want microwave pizza. He'll probably screw that up. Maybe I'll just go for hot dogs and beans.' Sam took his tray through the opening.

'It's your call, Sam. Last guy wanted steak and shrimp. Can you imagine? Steak and shrimp around this place.'

'Did he get it?'

'No. He lost his appetite and they filled him full of Valium instead.'

'Not a bad way to go.'

'Quiet!' J. B. Gullitt yelled from the next cell. The guards eased the cart a few feet down the tier and stopped in front of J. B., who was gripping the bars with both hands. They kept their distance.

'Well, well, aren't we frisky this morning?' one said.

'Why can't you assholes just serve the food in silence? I mean, do you think we want to wake up each morning and start the day by listening to your cute little comments? Just give me the food, man.'

'Gee, J. B. We're awful sorry. We just figured you guys were lonely.'

'You figured wrong.' J. B. took his tray and turned away.

'Touchy, touchy,' a guard said as they moved away in the direction of someone else to torment.

Sam sat his food on the bed and mixed a packet of sugar in his coffee. His daily routine did not include scrambled eggs and bacon. He would save the toast and jelly and eat it throughout the morning. He would carefully sip the coffee, rationing it until ten o'clock, his hour of exercise and sunshine.

He balanced the typewriter on his knees, and began pecking away.

THIRTEEN

SAM'S VERSION of the law was finished by nine-thirty. He was proud of it, one of his better efforts in recent months. He munched on a piece of toast as he proofed the document for the last time. The typing was neat but outdated, the result of an ancient machine. The language was effusive and repetitive, flowery and filled with words never uttered by humble laymen. Sam was almost fluent in legalese and could hold his own with any lawyer.

A door at the end of the hallway banged open, then shut. Heavy footsteps clicked along properly, and Packer appeared. 'Your lawyer's here, Sam,' he said, removing a set of handcuffs from his belt.

Sam stood and pulled up his boxer shorts. 'What time is it?'

'A little after nine-thirty. What difference does it make?'

'I'm supposed to get my hour out at ten.'

'You wanna go outside, or you wanna see your lawyer?'

Sam thought about this as he slipped into his red jumpsuit and slid his feet into his rubber sandals. Dressing was a swift procedure on death row. 'Can I make it up later?'

'We'll see.'

'I want my hour out, you know.'

'I know, Sam. Let's go.'

'It's real important to me.'

'I know, Sam. It's real important to everyone. We'll try and make it up later, okay?'

146

Sam combed his hair with great deliberation, then rinsed his hands with cold water. Packer waited patiently. He wanted to say something to J. B. Gullitt, something about the mood he was in this morning, but Gullitt was already asleep again. Most of them were asleep. The average inmate on death row made it through breakfast and an hour or so of televison before stretching out for the morning nap. Though his study was by no means scientific, Packer estimated they slept fifteen to sixteen hours a day. And they could sleep in the heat, the sweat, the cold, and amid the noise of loud televisions and radios.

The noise was much lower this morning. The fans hummed and whined, but there was no yelling back and forth.

Sam approached the bars, turned his back to Packer, and extended both hands through the narrow slot in the door. Packer applied the handcuffs, and Sam walked to his bed and picked up the document. Packer nodded to a guard at the end of the hall, and Sam's door opened electronically. Then it closed.

Leg chains were optional in these situations, and with a younger prisoner, perhaps one with an attitude and a bit more stamina, Packer probably would have used them. But this was just Sam. He was an old man. How far could he run? How much damage could he do with his feet?

Packer gently placed his hand around Sam's skinny bicep and led him along the hall. They stopped at the tier door, a row of more bars, waited for it to open and close, and left Tier A. Another guard followed behind as they came to an iron door which Packer unlocked with a key from his belt. They walked through it, and there was Adam sitting alone on the other side of the green grating.

Packer removed the handcuffs and left the room.

ADAM READ IT SLOWLY the first time. During the second reading he took a few notes and was amused at some of the language. He'd seen worse work from trained lawyers. And he'd seen much better work. Sam was suffering the same

147

affliction that hit most first-year law students. He used six words when one would suffice. His Latin was dreadful. Entire paragraphs were useless. But, on the whole, not bad for a non-lawyer.

The two-page agreement was now four, typed neatly with perfect margins and only two typos and one misspelled word.

'You do pretty good work,' Adam said as he placed the document on the counter. Sam puffed a cigarette and stared at him through the opening. 'It's basically the same agreement I handed you yesterday.'

'It's basically a helluva lot different,' Sam said, correcting him.

Adam glanced at his notes, then said, 'You seem to be concerned about five areas. The governor, books, movies, termination, and who gets to witness the execution.'

'I'm concerned about a lot of things. Those happen to be non-negotiable.'

'I promised yesterday I would have nothing to do with books and movies.'

'Good. Moving right along.'

'The termination language is fine. You want the right to terminate my representation, and that of Kravitz & Bane, at any time and for any reason, without a fight.'

'It took me a long time to fire those Jewish bastards last time. I don't want to go through it again.'

'That's reasonable.'

'I don't care whether you think it's reasonable, okay? It's in the agreement, and it's non-negotiable.'

'Fair enough. And you want to deal with no one but me.'

'That's correct. No one at Kravitz & Bane touches my file. That place is crawling with Jews, and they don't get involved, okay? Same for niggers and women.'

'Look, Sam, can we lay off the slurs? How about we refer to them as blacks?'

'Ooops. Sorry. How about we do the right thing and call them African-Americans and Jewish-Americans and Female-Americans? You and I'll be Irish-Americans, and

148

also White-Male-Americans. If you need help from your firm, try to stick with German-Americans or Italian-Americans. Since you're in Chicago, maybe use a few Polish-Americans. Gee, that'll be nice, won't it? We'll be real proper and multicultural and politically correct, won't we?'

'Whatever.'

'I feel better already.'

Adam made a check mark by his notes. 'I'll agree to it.'

'Damned right you will, if you want an agreement. Just keep the minorities out of my life.'

'You're assuming they're anxious to jump in.'

'I'm not assuming anything. I have four weeks to live, and I'd rather spend my time with people I trust.'

Adam read again a paragraph on page three of Sam's draft. The language gave Sam the sole authority to select two witnesses at his execution. 'I don't understand this clause about the witnesses,' Adam said.

'It's very simple. If we get to that point, there will be about fifteen witnesses. Since I'm the guest of honor, I get to select two. The statute, once you've had a chance to review it, lists a few who must be present. The warden, a Lebanese-American by the way, has some discretion in picking the rest. They usually conduct a lottery with the press to choose which of the vultures are allowed to gawk at it.'

'Then why do you want this clause?'

'Because the lawyer is always one of the two chosen by the gassee. That's me.'

'And you don't want me to witness the execution?'

'That's correct.'

'You're assuming I'll want to witness it.'

'I'm not assuming anything. It's just a fact that the lawyers can't wait to see their poor clients gassed once it becomes inevitable. Then they can't wait to get in front of the cameras and cry and carry on and rail against injustice.'

'And you think I'll do that?'

'No. I don't think you'll do that.'

149

'Then, why this clause?'

Sam leaned forward with his elbows on the counter. His nose was an inch from the screen. 'Because you will not witness the execution, okay?'

'It's a deal,' he said casually, and flipped to another page. 'We're not going to get that far, Sam.'

'Atta boy. That's what I want to hear.'

'Of course, we may need the governor.'

Sam snorted in disgust and relaxed in his chair. He crossed his right leg on his left knee, and glared at Adam. 'The agreement is very plain.'

Indeed it was. Almost an entire page was dedicated to a venomous attack on David McAllister. Sam forgot about the law and used words like scurrilous and egotistical and narcissistic and mentioned more than once the insatiable appetite for publicity.

'So you have a problem with the governor,' Adam said.

Sam snorted.

'I don't think this is a good idea, Sam.'

'I really don't care what you think.'

'The governor could save your life.'

'Oh really. He's the only reason I'm here, on death row, waiting to die, in the gas chamber. Why in hell would he want to save my life?'

'I didn't say he wanted to. I said that he could. Let's keep our options open.'

Sam smirked for a long minute as he lit a cigarette. He blinked and rolled his eyes as if this kid was the dumbest human he'd encountered in decades. Then he leaned forward on his left elbow and pointed at Adam with a crooked right finger. 'If you think David McAllister will grant me a last minute pardon, then you're a fool. But let me tell you what he will do. He'll use you, and me, to suck out all the publicity imaginable. He'll invite you to his office at the state capitol, and before you get there he'll tip off the media. He'll listen with remarkable sincerity. He'll profess grave reservations about whether I should die. He'll schedule another meeting, closer to the execution. And after you leave, he'll hold a couple of interviews and divulge everything you've just told him. He'll rehash the Kramer bombing. He'll talk about civil rights and all that radical nigger crap. He'll probably even cry. The closer I get to the gas chamber, the bigger the media circus will become. He'll try every way in the world to get in the middle of it. He'll meet with you every day, if we allow it. He'll take us to the wire.'

'He can do this without us.'

'And he will. Mark my word, Adam. An hour before I die, he'll hold a press conference somewhere – probably here, maybe at the governor's mansion – and he'll stand there in the glare of a hundred cameras and deny me clemency. And the bastard will have tears in his eyes.'

'It won't hurt to talk to him.'

'Fine. Go talk to him. And after you do, I'll invoke paragraph two and your ass'll go back to Chicago.'

'He might like me. We could be friends.'

'Oh, he'll love you. You're Sam's grandson. What a great story! More reporters, more cameras, more journalists, more interviews. He'd love to make your acquaintance so he can string you along. Hell, you might get him reelected.'

Adam flipped another page, made some more notes, and stalled for a while in an effort to move away from the governor. 'Where'd you learn to write like this?' he asked.

'Same place you did. I was taught by the same learned souls who provided your instruction. Dead judges. Honorable justices. Windy lawyers. Tedious professors. I've read the same garbage you've read.'

'Not bad,' Adam said, scanning another paragraph.

'I'm delighted you think so.'

'I understand you have quite a little practice here.'

'Practice. What's a practice? Why do lawyers practice? Why can't they just work like everyone else? Do plumbers practice? Do truck drivers practice? No, they simply work. But not lawyers. Hell no. They're special, and they practice. With all their damned practicing you'd think they'd know what the hell they were doing. You'd think they'd eventually become good at something.'

151

'Do you like anyone?'

'That's an idiotic question.'

'Why is it idiotic?'

'Because you're sitting on that side of the wall. And you can walk out that door and drive away. And tonight you can have dinner in a nice restaurant and sleep in a soft bed. Life's a bit different on this side. I'm treated like an animal. I have a cage. I have a death sentence which allows the State of Mississippi to kill me in four weeks, and so yes, son, it's hard to be loving and compassionate. It's hard to like people these days. That's why your question is foolish.'

'Are you saying you were loving and compassionate before you arrived here?'

Sam stared through the opening and puffed on the cigarette. 'Another stupid question.'

'Why?'

'It's irrelevant, counselor. You're a lawyer, not a shrink.'

'I'm your grandson. Therefore, I'm allowed to ask questions about your past.'

'Ask them. They might not be answered.'

'Why not?'

'The past is gone, son. It's history. We can't undo what's been done. Nor can we explain it all.'

'But I don't have a past.'

'Then you are indeed a lucky person.'

'I'm not so sure.'

'Look, if you expect me to fill in the gaps, then I'm afraid you've got the wrong person.'

'Okay. Who else should I talk to?'

'I don't know. It's not important.'

'Maybe it's important to me.'

'Well, to be honest, I'm not too concerned about you right now. Believe it or not, I'm much more worried about me. Me and my future. Me and my neck. There's a big clock ticking somewhere, ticking rather loudly, wouldn't you say? For some strange reason, don't ask me why, but I can hear the damned thing and it makes me real anxious. I find it very difficult to worry about the problems of others.'

152

'Why did you become a Klansman?'

'Because my father was in the Klan.'

'Why did he become a Klansman?'

'Because his father was in the Klan.'

'Great. Three generations.'

'Four, I think. Colonel Jacob Cayhall fought with Nathan Bedford Forrest in the war, and family legend has it that he was one of the early members of the Klan. He was my great-grandfather.'

'You're proud of this?'

'Is that a question?'

'Yes.'

'It's not a matter of pride.' Sam nodded at the counter. 'Are you going to sign that agreement?'

'Yes.'

'Then do it.'

Adam signed at the bottom of the back page and handed it to Sam. 'You're asking questions that are very confidential. As my lawyer, you cannot breathe a word.'

'I understand the relationship.'

Sam signed his name next to Adam's, then studied the signatures. 'When did you become a Hall?'

'A month before my fourth birthday. It was a family affair. We were all converted at the same time. Of course, I don't remember.'

'Why did he stick with Hall? Why not make a clean break and go with Miller or Green or something?'

'Is that a question?'

'No.'

'He was running, Sam. And he was burning bridges as he went. I guess four generations was enough for him.'

Sam placed the contract in a chair beside him, and methodically lit another cigarette. He exhaled at the ceiling and stared at Adam. 'Look, Adam,' he said slowly, his voice suddenly much softer. 'Let's lay off the family stuff for a while, okay. Maybe we'll get around to it later. Right now I need to know what's about to happen to me. What are my chances, you know? Stuff like that. How do you stop the clock? What do you file next?'

'Depends on several things, Sam. Depends on how much you tell me about the bombing.'

'I don't follow.'

'If there are new facts, then we present them. There are ways, believe me. We'll find a judge who'll listen.'

'What kind of new facts?'

Adam flipped to a clean page on his pad, and scribbled the date in the margin. 'Who delivered the green Pontiac to Cleveland on the night before the bombing?'

'I don't know. One of Dogan's men.'

'You don't know his name?'

'No.'

'Come on, Sam.'

'I swear. I don't know who did it. I never saw the man. The car was delivered to a parking lot. I found it. I was supposed to leave it where I found it. I never saw the man who delivered it.'

'Why wasn't he discovered during the trials?'

'How am I supposed to know? He was just a minor accomplice, I guess. They were after me. Why bother with a gopher? I don't know.'

'Kramer was bombing number six, right?'

'I think so.' Sam leaned forward again with his face almost touching the screen. His voice was low, his words carefully chosen as if someone might be listening somewhere.

'You think so?'

'It was a long time ago, okay.' He closed his eyes and thought for a moment. 'Yeah, number six.'

'The FBI said it was number six.'

'Then that settles it. They're always right.'

'Was the same green Pontiac used in one or all of the prior bombings?'

'Yes. In a couple, as I remember. We used more than one car.'

'All supplied by Dogan?'

'Yes. He was a car dealer.'

'I know. Did the same man deliver the Pontiac for the prior bombings?'

'I never saw or met anyone delivering the cars for the bombings. Dogan didn't work that way. He was extremely careful, and his plans were detailed. I don't know this for a fact, but I'm certain that the man delivering the cars didn't have a clue as to who I was.'

'Did the cars come with the dynamite?'

'Yes. Always. Dogan had enough guns and explosives for a small war. Feds never found his arsenal either.'

'Where'd you learn about explosives?'

'KKK boot camp and the basic training manual.'

'Probably hereditary, wasn't it?'

'No, it wasn't.'

'I'm serious. How'd you learn to detonate explosives?'

'It's very basic and simple. Any fool could pick it up in thirty minutes.'

'Then with a bit of practice you're an expert.'

'Practice helps. It's not much more difficult than lighting a fire-cracker. You strike a match, any match will do, and you place it at the end of a long fuse until the fuse lights. Then you run like hell. If you're lucky, it won't blow up for about fifteen minutes.'

'And this is something that is just sort of absorbed by all Klansmen?'

'Most of the ones I knew could handle it.'

'Do you still know any Klansmen?'

'No. They've abandoned me.'

Adam watched his face carefully. The fierce blue eyes were steady. The wrinkles didn't move. There was no emotion, no feeling or sorrow or anger. Sam returned the stare without blinking.

Adam returned to his notepad. 'On March 2, 1967, the Hirsch Temple in Jackson was bombed. Did you do it?'

'Get right to the point, don't you?'

'It's an easy question.'

Sam twisted the filter between his lips and thought for a second. 'Why is it important?'

'Just answer the damned question,' Adam snapped. 'It's too late to play games.'

'I've never been asked that question before.'

'Well I guess today's your big day. A simple yes or no will do.'

'Yes.'

'Did you use the green Pontiac?'

'I think so.'

'Who was with you?'

'What makes you think someone was with me?'

'Because a witness said he saw a green Pontiac speed by a few minutes before the explosion. And he said two people were in the car. He even made a tentative identification of you as the driver.'

'Ah, yes. Our little friend Bascar. I read about him in the newspapers.'

'He was near the corner of Fortification and State streets when you and your pal rushed by.'

'Of course he was. And he'd just left a bar at three in the morning, drunk as a goat, and stupid as hell to begin with. Bascar, as I'm sure you know, never made it near a courtroom, never placed his hand on a Bible and swore to tell the truth, never faced a cross-examination, never came forward until after I was under arrest in Greenville and half the world had seen pictures of the green Pontiac. His tentative identification occurred only after my face had been plastered all over the papers.'

'So he's lying?'

'No, he's probably just ignorant. Keep in mind, Adam, that I was never charged with that bombing. Bascar was never put under pressure. He never gave sworn testimony. His story was revealed, I believe, when a reporter with a Memphis newspaper dug through the honky-tonks and whorehouses long enough to find someone like Bascar.'

'Let's try it this way. Did you or did you not have someone with you when you bombed the Hirsch Temple synagogue on March 2, 1967?'

Sam's gaze fell a few inches below the opening, then to

156

the counter, then to the floor. He pushed away slightly from the partition and relaxed in his chair. Predictably, the blue package of Montclairs was produced from the front pocket, and he took forever selecting one, then thumping it on the filter, then inserting it just so between his moist lips. The striking of the match was another brief ceremony, but one that was finally accomplished and a fresh fog of smoke lifted toward the ceiling.

Adam watched and waited until it was obvious no quick answer was forthcoming. The delay in itself was an admission. He tapped his pen nervously on the legal pad. He took quick breaths and noticed an increase in his heartbeat. His empty stomach was suddenly jittery. Could this be the break? If there had been an accomplice, then perhaps they had worked as a team and perhaps Sam had not actually planted the dynamite that killed the Kramers. Perhaps this fact could be presented to a sympathetic judge somewhere who would listen and grant a stay. Perhaps. Maybe. Could it be?

'No,' Sam said ever so softly but firmly as he looked at Adam through the opening.

'I don't believe you.'

'There was no accomplice.'

'I don't believe you, Sam.'

Sam shrugged casually as if he couldn't care less. He crossed his legs and wrapped his fingers around a knee.

Adam took a deep breath, scribbled something routinely as if he'd been expecting this, and flipped to a clean page. 'What time did you arrive in Cleveland on the night of April 20, 1967?'

'Which time?'

'The first time.'

'I left Clanton around six. Drove two hours to Cleveland. So I got there around eight.'

'Where'd you go?'

'To a shopping center.'

'Why'd you go there?'

'To get the car.'

'The green Pontiac?'

157

'Yes. But it wasn't there. So I drove to Greenville to look around a bit.'

'Had you been there before?'

'Yes. A couple of weeks earlier, I had scouted the place. I even went in the Jew's office to get a good look.'

'That was pretty stupid, wasn't it? I mean, his secretary identified you at trial as the man who came in asking for directions and wanting to use the rest room.'

'Very stupid. But then, I wasn't supposed to get caught. She was never supposed to see my face again.' He bit the filter and sucked hard. 'A very bad move. Of course, it's awfully easy to sit here now and second-guess everything.'

'How long did you stay in Greenville?'

'An hour or so. Then I drove back to Cleveland to get the car. Dogan always had detailed plans with several alternates. The car was parked in spot B, near a truck stop.'

'Where were the keys?'

'Under the mat.'

'What did you do?'

'Took it for a drive. Drove out of town, out through some cotton fields. I found a lonely spot and parked the car. I popped the trunk to check the dynamite.'

'How many sticks?'

'Fifteen, I believe. I was using between twelve and twenty, depending on the building. Twenty for the synagogue because it was new and modern and built with concrete and stone. But the Jew's office was an old wooden structure, and I knew fifteen would level it.'

'What else was in the trunk?'

'The usual. A cardboard box of dynamite. Two blasting caps. A fifteen-minute fuse.'

'Is that all?'

'Yes.'

'Are you sure?'

'Of course I'm sure.'

'What about the timing device? The detonator?'

'Oh yeah. I forgot about that. It was in another, smaller box.'

'Describe it for me.'

'Why? You've read the trial transcripts. The FBI expert did a wonderful job of reconstructing my little bomb. You've read this, haven't you?'

'Many times.'

'And you've seen the photos they used at trial. The ones of the fragments and pieces of the timer. You've seen all this, haven't you?'

'I've seen it. Where did Dogan get the clock?'

'I never asked. You could buy one in any drugstore. It was just a cheap, windup alarm clock. Nothing fancy.'

'Was this your first job with a timing device?'

'You know it was. The other bombs were detonated by fuses. Why are you asking me these questions?'

'Because I want to hear your answers. I've read everything, but I want to hear it from you. Why did you want to delay the Kramer bomb?'

'Because I was tired of lighting fuses and running like hell. I wanted a longer break between planting the bomb and feeling it go off.'

'What time did you plant it?'

'Around 4 A.M.'

'What time was it supposed to go off?'

'Around five.'

'What went wrong?'

'It didn't go off at five. It went off a few minutes before eight, and there were people in the building by then, and some of these people got killed. And that's why I'm sitting here in a red monkey suit wondering what the gas'll smell like.'

'Dogan testified that the selection of Marvin Kramer as a target was a joint effort between the both of you; that Kramer had been on a Klan hit list for two years; that the use of a timing device was something you suggested as a way to kill Kramer because his routine was predictable; that you acted alone.'

Sam listened patiently and puffed on his cigarette. His eyes narrowed to tiny slits and he nodded at the floor. Then

159

he almost smiled. 'Well, I'm afraid Dogan went crazy, didn't he? Feds hounded him for years, and he finally caved in. He was not a strong man, you know.' He took a deep breath and looked at Adam. 'But some of it's true. Not much, but some.'

'Did you intend to kill him?'

'No. We weren't killing people. Just blowing up buildings.'

'What about the Pinder home in Vicksburg? Was that one of yours?'

Sam nodded slowly.

'The bomb went off at four in the morning while the entire Pinder family was sound asleep. Six people. Miraculously, only one minor injury.'

'It wasn't a miracle. The bomb was placed in the garage. If I'd wanted to kill anyone, I'd have put it by a bedroom window.'

'Half the house collapsed.'

'Yeah, and I could've used a clock and wiped out a bunch of Jews as they ate their bagels or whatever.'

'Why didn't you?'

'As I said, we weren't trying to kill people.'

'What were you trying to do?'

'Intimidate. Retaliate. Keep the damned Jews from financing the civil rights movement. We were trying to keep the Africans where they belonged – in their own schools and churches and neighborhoods and rest rooms, away from our women and children. Jews like Marvin Kramer were promoting an interracial society and stirring up the Africans. Son of a bitch needed to be kept in line.'

'You guys really showed him, didn't you?'

'He got what he deserved. I'm sorry about the little boys.'

'Your compassion is overwhelming.'

'Listen, Adam, and listen good. I did not intend to hurt anyone. The bomb was set to go off at 5 A.M., three hours before he usually arrived for work. The only reason his kids were there was because his wife had the flu.'

'But you feel no remorse because Marvin lost both legs?'

'Not really.'

160

'No remorse because he killed himself?'

'He pulled the trigger, not me.'

'You're a sick man, Sam.'

'Yeah, and I'm about to get a lot sicker when I sniff the gas.'

Adam shook his head in disgust, but held his tongue. They could argue later about race and hatred; not that he, at this moment, expected to make any progress with Sam on these topics. But he was determined to try. Now, however, they needed to discuss facts.

'After you inspected the dynamite, what did you do?'

'Drove back to the truck stop. Drank coffee.'

'Why?'

'Maybe I was thirsty.'

'Very funny, Sam. Just try and answer the questions.'

'I was waiting.'

'For what?'

'I needed to kill a couple of hours. By then it was around midnight, and I wanted to spend as little time in Greenville as possible. So, I killed time in Cleveland.'

'Did you talk to anyone in the café?'

'No.'

'Was it crowded?'

'I really don't remember.'

'Did you sit alone?'

'Yes.'

'At a table?'

'Yes.' Sam managed a slight grin because he knew what was coming.

'A truck driver by the name of Tommy Farris said he saw a man who greatly resembled you in the truck stop that night, and that this man drank coffee for a long time with a younger man.'

'I never met Mr Farris, but I believe he had a lapse of memory for three years. Not a word to anyone, as I recall, until another reporter flushed him out and he got his name in the paper. It's amazing how these mystery witnesses pop up years after the trials.'

'Why didn't Farris testify in your last trial?'

161

'Don't ask me. I suppose it was because he had nothing to say. The fact that I drank coffee alone or with someone seven hours before the bombing was hardly relevant. Plus, the coffee drinking took place in Cleveland, and had nothing to do with whether or not I committed the crime.'

'So Farris was lying?'

'I don't know what Farris was doing. Don't really care. I was alone. That's all that matters.'

'What time did you leave Cleveland?'

'Around three, I think.'

'And you drove straight to Greenville?'

'Yes. And I drove by the Kramers' house, saw the guard sitting on the porch, drove by his office, killed some more time, and around four or so I parked behind his office, slipped through the rear door, planted the bomb in a closet in the hallway, walked back to my car, and drove away.'

'What time did you leave Greenville?'

'I had planned to leave after the bomb went off. But, as you know, it was several months before I actually made it out of town.'

'Where did you go when you left Kramer's office?'

'I found a little coffee shop on the highway, a half mile or so from Kramer's office.'

'Why'd you go there?'

'To drink coffee.'

'What time was it?'

'I don't know. Around four-thirty or so.'

'Was it crowded?'

'A handful of people. Just your run-of-the-mill all-night diner with a fat cook in a dirty tee shirt and a waitress who smacked her chewing gum.'

'Did you talk to anybody?'

'I spoke to the waitress when I ordered my coffee. Maybe I had a doughnut.'

'And you were having a nice cup of coffee, just minding your own business, waiting for the bomb to go off.'

'Yeah. I always liked to hear the bombs go off and watch the people react.'

'So you'd done this before?'

'A couple of times. In February of that year I bombed the real estate office in Jackson – Jews had sold a house to some niggers in a white section – and I had just sat down in a diner not three blocks away when the bomb went off. I was using a fuse then, so I had to hustle away and park real fast and find a table. The girl had just sat my coffee down when the ground shook and everybody froze. I really liked that. It was four in the morning and the place was packed with truckers and deliverymen, even had a few cops over in a corner, and of course they ran to their cars and sped away with lights blazing. My table shook so hard that coffee spilled from my cup.'

'And that gave you a real thrill?'

'Yes, it did. But the other jobs were too risky. I didn't have the time to find a café or diner, so I just sort of rode around for a few minutes waiting for the fun. I'd check my watch closely, so I always knew about when it would hit. If I was in the car, I liked to be on the edge of town, you know.' Sam paused and took a long puff from his cigarette. His words were slow and careful. His eyes danced a bit as he talked about his adventures, but his words were measured. 'I did watch the Pinder bombing,' he added.

'And how'd you do that?'

'They lived in a big house in the suburbs, lots of trees, sort of in a valley. I parked on the side of a hill about a mile away, and I was sitting under a tree when it went off.'

'How peaceful.'

'It really was. Full moon, cool night. I had a great view of the street, and I could see almost all the roof. It was so calm and peaceful, everyone was asleep, then, boom, blew that roof to hell and back.'

'What was Mr Pinder's sin?'

'Just overall general Jewishness. Loved niggers. Always embraced the radical Africans when they came down from the North and agitated everybody. He loved to march and boycott with the Africans. We suspected he was financing a lot of their activities.'

163

Adam made notes and tried to absorb all of this. It was hard to digest because it was almost impossible to believe. Perhaps the death penalty was not such a bad idea after all. 'Back to Greenville. Where was this coffee shop located?'

'Don't remember.'

'What was it called?'

'It was twenty-three years ago. And it was not the kind of place you'd want to remember.'

'Was it on Highway 82?'

'I think so. What are you gonna do? Spend your time digging for the fat cook and the tacky waitress? Are you doubting my story?'

'Yes. I'm doubting your story.'

'Why?'

'Because you can't tell me where you learned to make a bomb with a timing detonator.'

'In the garage behind my house.'

'In Clanton?'

'Out from Clanton. It's not that difficult.'

'Who taught you?'

'I taught myself. I had a drawing, a little booklet with diagrams and such. Steps one, two, three. It was no big deal.'

'How many times did you practice with such a device before Kramer?'

'Once.'

'Where? When?'

'In the woods not far from my house. I took two sticks of dynamite and the necessary paraphernalia, and I went to a little creek bed deep in the woods. It worked perfectly.'

'Of course. And you did all this study and research in your garage?'

'That's what I said.'

'Your own little laboratory.'

'Call it whatever you want.'

'Well, the FBI conducted a thorough search of your house, garage, and premises while you were in custody. They didn't find a trace of evidence of explosives.'

164

'Maybe they're stupid. Maybe I was real careful and didn't leave a trail.'

'Or maybe the bomb was planted by someone with experience in explosives.'

'Nope. Sorry.'

'How long did you stay in the coffee shop in Greenville?'

'A helluva long time. Five o'clock came and went. Then it was almost six. I left a few minutes before six and drove by Kramer's office. The place looked fine. Some of the early risers were out and about, and I didn't want to be seen. I crossed the river and drove to Lake Village, Arkansas, then returned to Greenville. It was seven by then, sun was up and people were moving around. No explosion. I parked the car on a side street, and walked around for a while. The damned thing wouldn't go off. I couldn't go in after it, you know. I walked and walked, listening hard, hoping the ground would shake. Nothing happened.'

'Did you see Marvin Kramer and his sons go into the building?'

'No. I turned a corner and saw his car parked, and I thought dammit! I went blank. I couldn't think. But then I thought, what the hell, he's just a Jew and he's done many evil things. Then, I thought about secretaries and other people who might work in there, so I walked around the block again. I remember looking at my watch then when it was twenty minutes before eight, and I had this thought that maybe I should make an anonymous phone call to the office and tell Kramer that there was a bomb in the closet. And if he didn't believe me, then he could go look at it, then he could haul ass.'

'Why didn't you?'

'I didn't have a dime. I'd left all my change as a tip for the waitress, and I didn't want to walk into a store and ask for change. I have to tell you I was real nervous. My hands were shaking, and I didn't want to act suspicious in front of anybody. I was a stranger, right? That was my bomb in there, right? I was in a small town where everybody knows everyone, and they damned sure remember strangers when

165

there's a crime. I remember walking down the sidewalk, just across the street from Kramer's, and in front of a barbershop there was a newspaper rack, and this man was fumbling in his pocket for change. I almost asked him for a dime so I could make a quick call, but I was too nervous.'

'Why were you nervous, Sam? You just said you didn't care if Kramer got hurt. This was your sixth bombing, right?'

'Yeah, but the others were easy. Light the fuse, hit the door, and wait a few minutes. I kept thinking about that cute little secretary in Kramer's office, the one who'd shown me to the rest room. The same one who later testified at trial. And I kept thinking about the other people who worked in his office because when I went in that day I saw people everywhere. It was almost eight o'clock, and I knew the place opened in a few minutes. I knew a lot of people were about to get killed. My mind stopped working. I remember standing beside a phone booth a block away, staring at my watch, then staring at the phone, telling myself that I had to make the call. I finally stepped inside and looked up the number, but by the time I closed the book I'd forgotten it. So I looked it up again, and I started to dial when I remembered I didn't have a dime. So I made up my mind to go into the barbershop to get some change. My legs were heavy and I was sweatin' like hell. I walked to the barbershop, and I stopped at the plate glass window and looked in. It was packed. They were lined up against the wall, talking and reading papers, and there was a row of chairs, all filled with men talking at the same time. I remember a couple of them looked at me, then one or two more began to stare, so I walked away.'

'Where did you go?'

'I'm not sure. There was an office next door to Kramer's, and I remember seeing a car park in front of it. I thought maybe it was a secretary or someone about to go into Kramer's, and I think I was walking toward the car when the bomb went off.'

'So you were across the street?'

166

'I think so. I remember rocking on my hands and knees in the street as glass and debris fell all around me. But I don't remember much after that.'

There was a slight knock on the door from the outside, then Sergeant Packer appeared with a large Styrofoam cup, a paper napkin, a stir stick, and creamer. 'Thought you might need a little coffee. Sorry to butt in.' He placed the cup and accessories on the counter.

'Thanks,' Adam said.

Packer quickly turned and headed for the door.

'I'll take two sugars, one cream,' Sam said from the other side.

'Yes sir,' Packed snapped without slowing. He was gone.

'Good service around here,' Adam said.

'Wonderful, just wonderful.'

167

FOURTEEN

SAM, OF COURSE, was not served coffee. He knew this immediately, but Adam did not. And so after waiting for a few minutes, Sam said, 'Drink it.' He himself lit another cigarette, and paced around a bit behind his chair while Adam stirred the sugar with the plastic stick. It was almost eleven, and Sam had missed his hour out, and he had no confidence that Packer would find the time to make it up. He paced and squatted a few times, performed a half dozen deep bends, knees cracking and joints popping as he rose and sank unsteadily. During the first few months of his first year on the Row, he had grown quite disciplined with his exercise. At one point, he was doing a hundred push-ups and a hundred sit-ups in his cell each day, every day. His weight fell to a perfect one hundred and sixty pounds as the low-fat diet took its course. His stomach was flat and hard. He had never been so healthy.

Not long afterward, however, came the realization that the Row would be his final home, and that the state would one day kill him here. What's the benefit of good health and tight biceps when one is locked up twenty-three hours a day waiting to die? The exercise slowly stopped. The smoking intensified. Among his comrades, Sam was considered a lucky man, primarily because he had outside money. A younger brother, Donnie, lived in North Carolina and once a month shipped to Sam a cardboard box packed neatly with ten cartons of Montclair cigarettes. Sam averaged between three and four packs a day. He wanted to kill himself before the state got around to it. And he preferred to go by way of some protracted illness or affliction, some disease that would require expensive treatment which the State of Mississippi would be constitutionally bound to provide.

It looked as though he would lose the race.

The federal judge who had assumed control of Parchman through a prisoners' rights suit had issued sweeping orders overhauling fundamental correction procedures. He had carefully defined the rights of prisoners. And he had set forth minor details, such as the square footage of each cell on the Row and the amount of money each inmate could possess. Twenty dollars was the maximum. It was referred to as 'dust,' and it always came from the outside. Death row inmates were not allowed to work and earn money. The lucky ones received a few dollars a month from relatives and friends. They could spend it in a canteen located in the middle of MSU. Soft drinks were known as 'bottle-ups.' Candy and snacks were 'zu-zus' and 'wham-whams.' Real cigarettes in packages were 'tight-legs' and 'ready-rolls.'

The majority of the inmates received nothing from the outside. They traded, swapped, and bartered, and gathered enough coins to purchase loose leaf tobacco which they rolled into thin papers and smoked slowly. Sam was indeed a lucky man.

He took his seat and lit another one.

'Why didn't you testify at trial?' his lawyer asked through the screen.

'Which trial?'

'Good point. The first two trials.'

'Didn't need to. Brazelton picked good juries, all white, good sympathetic people who understood things. I knew I wouldn't be convicted by those people. There was no need to testify.'

'And the last trial?'

'That's a little more complicated. Keyes and I discussed it many times. He at first thought it might help, because I could explain to the jury what my intentions were. Nobody was supposed to get hurt, etc. The bomb was supposed to go off at 5 A.M. But we knew the cross-examination would be brutal. The judge had already ruled that the other bombings could be discussed to show certain things. I would be forced to admit that I did in fact plant the bomb, all fifteen sticks, which of course was more than enough to kill people.'

'So why didn't you testify?'

'Dogan. That lying bastard told the jury that our plan was to kill the Jew. He was a very effective witness. I mean, think about it, here was the former Imperial Wizard of the Mississippi Klan testifying for the prosecution against one of his own men. It was stout stuff. The jury ate it up.'

'Why did Dogan lie?'

'Jerry Dogan went crazy, Adam. I mean, really crazy. The Feds pursued him for fifteen years – bugged his phones, followed his wife around town, harassed his kinfolks, threatened his children, knocked on his door at all hours of the night. His life was miserable. Someone was always watching and listening. Then, he got sloppy, and the IRS stepped in. They, along with the FBI, told him he was looking at thirty years. Dogan cracked under the pressure. After my trial, I heard he was sent away for a while. You know, to an institution. He got some treatment, returned home, and died not long after.'

'Dogan's dead?'

Sam froze in mid-puff. Smoke leaked from his mouth and curled upward past his nose and in front of his eyes, which at the moment were staring in disbelief through the opening and into those of his grandson. 'You don't know about Dogan?' he said.

Adam's memory blitzed through the countless articles and stories which he'd collected and indexed. He shook his head. 'No. What happened to Dogan?'

'I thought you knew everything,' Sam said. 'Thought you'd memorized everything about me.'

'I know a lot about you, Sam. I really don't care about Jeremiah Dogan.'

170

'He burned in a house fire. He and his wife. They were asleep one night when a gas line somehow began leaking propane. Neighbors said it was like a bomb going off.'

'When did this happen?'

'Exactly one year to the day after he testified against me.'

Adam tried to write this down, but his pen wouldn't move. He studied Sam's face for a clue. 'Exactly a year?'

'Yep.'

'That's a nice coincidence.'

'I was in here, of course, but I heard bits and pieces of it. Cops ruled it accidental. In fact, I think there was a lawsuit against the propane company.'

'So, you don't think he was murdered?'

'Sure I think he was murdered.'

'Okay. Who did it?'

'In fact, the FBI came here and asked me some questions. Can you believe it? The Feds poking their noses around here. A couple of kids from up North. Just couldn't wait to visit death row and flash their badges and meet a real live Klan terrorist. They were so damned scared they were afraid of their shadows. They asked me stupid questions for an hour, then left. Never heard from anybody again.'

'Who would murder Dogan?'

Sam bit the filter and extracted the last mouthful of smoke from the cigarette. He stubbed it in the ashtray while exhaling through the screen. Adam waved at the smoke with exaggerated motions, but Sam ignored him. 'Lots of people,' he mumbled.

Adam made a note in the margin to talk about Dogan later. He would do the research first, then spring it again in some future conversation.

'Just for the sake of argument,' he said, still writing, 'it seems as though you should've testified to counter Dogan.'

'I almost did,' Sam said with a trace of regret. 'The last night of the trial, me and Keyes and his associate, I forget her name, stayed up until midnight discussing whether or not I should take the stand. But think about it, Adam. I would've been forced to admit that I planted the bomb, that

171

it had a timing device set to go off later, that I had been involved in other bombings, and that I was across the street from the building when it blew. Plus, the prosecution had clearly proven that Marvin Kramer was a target. I mean, hell, they played those FBI phone tapes to the jury. You should've heard it. They rigged up these huge speakers in the courtroom, and they set the tape player on a table in front of the jury like it was some kind of a live bomb. And there was Dogan on the phone to Wayne Graves, his voice was scratchy but very audible, talking about bombing Marvin Kramer for this and for that, and bragging about how he would send his Group, as he called me, to Greenville to take care of matters. The voices on that tape sounded like ghosts from hell, and the jury hung on every word. Very effective. And, then, of course, there was Dogan's own testimony. I would've looked ridiculous at that moment trying to testify and convince the jury that I really wasn't a bad guy. McAllister would've eaten me alive. So we decided I shouldn't take the stand. Looking back, it was a bad move. I should've talked.'

'But on the advice of your attorney you didn't?'

'Look, Adam, if you're thinking about attacking Keyes on the grounds of ineffective assistance of counsel, then forget it. I paid Keyes good money, mortgaged everything I had, and he did a good job. A long time ago Goodman and Tyner considered going after Keyes, but they found nothing wrong with his representation. Forget it.'

The Cayhall file at Kravitz & Bane had at least two inches of research and memos on the issue of Benjamin Keyes' representation. Ineffective assistance of trial counsel was a standard argument in death penalty appeals, but it had not been used in Sam's case. Goodman and Tyner had discussed it at length, bouncing long memos back and forth between their offices on the sixty-first and sixty-sixth floors in Chicago. The final memo declared that Keyes had done such a good job at trial that there was nothing to attack.

The file also included a three-page letter from Sam

172

expressly forbidding any attack on Keyes. He would not sign any petition doing so, he promised.

The last memo, however, had been written seven years earlier at a time when death was a distant possibility. Things were different now. Issues had to be resurrected or even fabricated. It was time to grasp at straws.

'Where is Keyes now?' Adam asked.

'Last I heard he took a job in Washington. He wrote me about five years ago, said he wasn't practising anymore. He took it pretty hard when we lost. I don't think either one of us expected it.'

'You didn't expect to be convicted?'

'Not really. I had already beaten it twice, you know. And my jury the third time had eight whites, or Anglo-Americans I should say. As bad as the trial went, I don't think I ever really believed they'd convict me.'

'What about Keyes?'

'Oh, he was worried. We damned sure didn't take it lightly. We spent months preparing for the trial. He neglected his other clients, even his family, for weeks while we were getting ready. McAllister was popping off in the papers every day, it seemed, and the more he talked the more we worked. They released the list of potential jurors, four hundred of them, and we spent days investigating those people. His pretrial preparation was impeccable. We were not naive.'

'Lee told me you considered disappearing.'

'Oh, she did.'

'Yeah, she told me last night.'

He tapped the next cigarette on the counter, and admired it for a moment as if it might be his last. 'Yeah, I thought about it. Almost thirteen years passed before McAllister came after me. I was a free man, hell I was forty-seven years old when the second trial ended and I returned home. Forty-seven years old, and I had been cleared by two juries, and all this was behind me. I was happy. Life was normal. I farmed and ran a sawmill, drank coffee in town and voted in every election. The Feds watched me for a few months, but

I guess they became convinced I'd given up bombing. From time to time, a pesky reporter or journalist would show up in Clanton and ask questions, but nobody spoke to them. They were always from up North, dumb as hell, rude and ignorant, and they never stayed long. One came to the house one day, and wouldn't leave. Instead of getting the shotgun, I just turned the dogs loose on him and they chewed his ass up. Never came back.' He chuckled to himself and lit the cigarette. 'Not in my wildest dreams did I envision this. If I'd had the slightest inkling, the faintest clue that this might happen to me, then I would have been gone years ago. I was completely free, you understand, no restrictions. I would've gone to South America, changed my name, disappeared two or three times, then settled in some place like São Paulo or Rio.'

'Like Mengele.'

'Something like that. They never caught him, you know. They never caught a bunch of those guys. I'd be living right now in a nice little house, speaking Portuguese and laughing at fools like David McAllister.' Sam shook his head and closed his eyes, and dreamed of what might have been.

'Why didn't you leave when McAllister started making noises?'

'Because I was foolish. It happened slowly. It was like a bad dream coming to life in small segments. First, McAllister got elected with all his promises. Then, a few months later Dogan got nailed by the IRS. I started hearing rumors and reading little things in the newspapers. But I simply refused to believe it could happen. Before I knew it, the FBI was following me and I couldn't run.'

Adam looked at his watch and was suddenly tired. They had been talking for more than two hours, and he needed fresh air and sunshine. His head ached from the cigarette smoke, and the room was growing warmer by the moment. He screwed the cap on his pen and slid the legal pad into his briefcase. 'I'd better go,' he said in the direction of the screen. 'I'll probably come back tomorrow for another round.'

'I'll be here.'

'Lucas Mann has given me the green light to visit anytime I want.'

'A helluva guy, isn't he?'

'He's okay. Just doing his job.'

'So's Naifeh and Nugent and all those other white folks.'

'White folks?'

'Yeah, it's slang for the authorities. Nobody really wants to kill me, but they're just doing their jobs. There's this little moron with nine fingers who's the official executioner – the guy who mixes the gas and inserts the canister. Ask him what he's doing as they strap me in, and he'll say, "Just doing my job." The prison chaplain and the prison doctor and the prison psychiatrist, along with the guards who'll escort me in and the medics who'll carry me out, well, they're nice folks, nothing really against me, but they're just doing their jobs.'

'It won't get that far, Sam.'

'Is that a promise?'

'No. But think positive.'

'Yeah, positive thinking's real popular around here. Me and the boys are big on motivational shows, along with travel programs and home shopping. The Africans prefer "Soul Train".'

'Lee's worried about you, Sam. She wanted me to tell you she's thinking about you and praying for you.'

Sam bit his bottom lip and looked at the floor. He nodded slowly but said nothing.

'I'll be staying with her for the next month or so.'

'She's still married to that guy?'

'Sort of. She wants to see you.'

'No.'

'Why not?'

Sam carefully eased from his chair and knocked on the door behind him. He turned and looked at Adam through the screen. They watched each other until a guard opened the door and took Sam away.

FIFTEEN

'THE KID left an hour ago, with authorization, though I haven't seen it in writing,' Lucas Mann explained to Phillip Naifeh, who was standing in his window watching a litter gang along the highway. Naifeh had a headache, a backache, and was in the middle of a generally awful day which had included three early phone calls from the governor and two from Roxburgh, the Attorney General. Sam, of course, had been the reason for the calls.

'So he's got himself a lawyer,' Naifeh said while gently pressing a fist in the center of his lower back.

'Yeah, and I really like this kid. He stopped by when he left and looked like he'd been run over by a truck. I think he and his grandfather are having a rough time of it.'

'It'll get worse for the grandfather.'

'It'll get worse for all of us.'

'Do you know what the governor asked me? Wanted to know if he could have a copy of our manual on how to carry out executions. I told him no, that in fact he could not have a copy. He said he was the governor of this state and he felt as though he should have a copy. I tried to explain that it wasn't really a manual as such, just a loose-leaf little book in a black binder that gets heavily revised each time we gas someone. What's it called, he wanted to know. I said it's called nothing, actually, no official name because thankfully it's not used that much, but that on further thought I myself have referred to it as the little black book. He pushed a little harder, I got a little madder, we hung up, and fifteen

176

minute later his lawyer, that little hunchback fart with eyeglasses pinching his nose—'

'Larramore.'

'Larramore called me and said that according to this code section and that code section he, the governor, has a right to a copy of the manual. I put him on hold, pulled the code sections, made him wait ten minutes, then we read the law together, and, of course, as usual, he's lying and bluffing and figuring I'm an imbecile. No such language in my copy of the code. I hung up on him. Ten minutes later the governor called back, all sugar and spice, told me to forget the little black book, that he's very concerned about Sam's constitutional rights and all, and just wants me to keep him posted as this thing unfolds. A real charmer.' Naifeh shifted weight on his feet and changed fists in his back while staring at the window.

'Then, half an hour later Roxburgh calls, and guess what he wants to know? Wants to know if I've talked to the governor. You see, Roxburgh thinks he and I are real tight, old political pals, you know, and therefore we can trust each other. And so he tells me, confidentially of course, buddy to buddy, that he thinks the governor might try to exploit this execution for his own political gain.'

'Nonsense!' Lucas hooted.

'Yeah, I told Roxburgh that I just couldn't believe he would think such a thing about our governor. I was real serious, and he got real serious, and we promised each other that we'd watch the governor real close and if we saw any sign that he was trying to manipulate this situation, then we'd call each other real quick. Roxburgh said there were some things he could do to neutralize the governor if he got out of line. I didn't dare ask what or how, but he seemed sure of himself.'

'So who's the bigger fool?'

'Probably Roxburgh. But it's a tough call.' Naifeh stretched carefully and walked to his desk. His shoes were off and his shirttail was out. He was in obvious pain. 'Both have insatiable appetites for publicity. They're like two little boys scared to death that one will get a bigger piece of candy. I hate 'em both.'

'Everybody hates them except the voters.'

There was a sharp knock on the door, three solid raps delivered at precise intervals. 'Must be Nugent,' Naifeh said and his pain suddenly intensified. 'Come in.'

The door opened quickly and Retired Colonel George Nugent marched into the room, pausing only slightly to close the door, and moved officially toward Lucas Mann, who did not stand but shook hands anyway. 'Mr Mann.' Nugent greeted him crisply, then stepped forward and shook hands across the desk with Naifeh.

'Have a seat, George,' Naifeh said, waving at an empty chair next to Mann. Naifeh wanted to order him to cut the military crap, but he knew it would do no good.

'Yes sir,' Nugent answered as he lowered himself into the seat without bending his back. Though the only uniforms at Parchman were worn by guards and inmates, Nugent had managed to fashion one for himself. His shirt and pants were dark olive, perfectly matched and perfectly ironed with precise folds and creases, and they miraculously survived each day without the slightest wrinkling. The pants stopped a few inches above the ankles where they disappeared into a pair of black leather combat boots, shined and buffed at least twice a day to a state of perpetual sparkle. There had once been a weak rumor that a secretary or maybe a trustee had seen a spot of mud on one of the soles, but the rumor had not been confirmed.

The top button was left open to form an exact triangle which revealed a gray tee shirt. The pockets and sleeves were bare and unadorned, free of his medals and ribbons, and Naifeh had long suspected that this caused the colonel no small amount of humiliation. The haircut was strict military with bare skin above the ears and a thin layer of gray sprouts on top. Nugent was fifty-two, had served his country for thirty-four years, first as a buck private in Korea and later as a captain of some variety in Vietnam, where he fought the war from behind a desk. He'd been

178

wounded in a jeep wreck and sent home with another ribbon.

For two years now Nugent had served admirably as an assistant superintendent, a trusted, loyal, and dependable underling of Naifeh's. He loved details and regulations and rules. He devoured manuals, and was constantly writing new procedures and directives and modifications for the warden to ponder. He was a significant pain in the warden's ass, but he was needed nonetheless. It was no secret that the colonel wanted Naifeh's job in a couple of years.

'George, me and Lucas have been talking about the Cayhall matter. Don't know how much you know about the appeals, but the Fifth Circuit lifted the stay and we're looking at an execution in four weeks.'

'Yes sir,' Nugent snapped, absorbing and itemizing every word. 'I read about it in today's paper.'

'Good. Lucas here is of the opinion that this one might come down, you know. Right, Lucas?'

'There's a good chance. Better than fifty-fifty.' Lucas said this without looking at Nugent.

'How long have you been here, George?'

'Two years, one month.'

The warden calculated something while rubbing his temples. 'Did you miss the Parris execution?'

'Yes sir. By a few weeks,' he answered with a trace of disappointment.

'So you haven't been through one?'

'No sir.'

'Well, they're awful, George. Just awful. Worst part of this job, by far. Frankly, I'm just not up to it. I was hoping I'd retire before we used the chamber again, but now that looks doubtful. I need some help.'

Nugent's back, though painfully stiff already, seemed to straighten even more. He nodded quickly, eyes dancing in all directions.

Naifeh delicately sat in his seat, grimacing as he eased onto the soft leather. 'Since I'm just not up to it, George,

179

Lucas and I were thinking that maybe you'd do a good job with this one.'

The colonel couldn't suppress a smile. Then it quickly disappeared and was replaced with a most serious scowl. 'I'm sure I can handle it, sir.'

'I'm sure you can too.' Naifeh pointed to a black binder on the corner of his desk. 'We have a manual of sorts. There it is, the collected wisdom of two dozen visits to the gas chamber over the past thirty years.'

Nugent's eyes narrowed and focused on the black book. He noticed that the pages were not all even and uniform, that an assortment of papers were actually folded and stuffed slovenly throughout the text, that the binder itself was worn and shabby. Within hours, he quickly decided, the manual would be transformed into a primer worthy of publication. That would be his first task. The paperwork would be immaculate.

'Why don't you read it tonight, and let's meet again tomorrow?'

'Yes sir,' he said smugly.

'Not a word to anyone about this until we talk again, understood?'

'No sir.'

Nugent nodded smartly at Lucas Mann, and left the office cradling the black book like a kid with a new toy. The door closed behind him.

'He's a nut,' Lucas said.

'I know. We'll watch him.'

'We'd better watch him. He's so damned gung-ho he might try to gas Sam this weekend.'

Naifeh opened a desk drawer and retrieved a bottle of pills. He swallowed two without the assistance of water. 'I'm going home, Lucas. I need to lie down. I'll probably die before Sam does.'

'You'd better hurry.'

THE PHONE CONVERSATION with E. Garner Goodman was brief. Adam explained with some measure of

180

pride that he and Sam had a written agreement on representation, and that they had already spent four hours together though little had been accomplished. Goodman wanted a copy of the agreement, and Adam explained that there were no copies as of now, that the original was safely tucked away in a cell on death row, and, furthermore, there would be copies only if the client decided so.

Goodman promised to review the file and get to work. Adam gave him Lee's phone number and promised to check in every day. He hung up the phone and stared at two terrifying phone messages beside his computer. Both were from reporters, one from a Memphis newspaper and one from a television station in Jackson, Mississippi.

Baker Cooley had talked to both reporters. In fact, a TV crew from Jackson had presented itself to the firm's receptionist and left only after Cooley made threats. All this attention had upset the tedious routine of the Memphis branch of Kravitz & Bane. Cooley was not happy about it. The other partners had little to say to Adam. The secretaries were professionally polite, but anxious to stay away from his office.

The reporters knew, Cooley had warned him gravely. They knew about Sam and Adam, the grandson-grandfather angle, and while he wasn't sure how they knew, it certainly hadn't come from him. He hadn't told a soul, until, of course, word was already out and he'd been forced to gather the partners and associates together just before lunch and break the news.

It was almost five o'clock. Adam sat at his desk with the door shut, listening to the voices in the hall as clerks and paralegals and other salaried staff made last minute preparations to leave for the day. He decided he would have nothing to say to the TV reporter. He dialed the number for Todd Marks at the *Memphis Press*. A recorded message guided him through the wonders of voice mail, and after a couple of minutes, Mr Marks picked up his five-digit extension and said hurriedly, 'Todd Marks.' He sounded like a teenager.

181

'This is Adam Hall, with Kravitz & Bane. I had a note to call you.'

'Yes, Mr Hall,' Marks gushed, instantly friendly and no longer in a hurry. 'Thanks for calling. I, uh, well, we, uh, picked up a rumor about your handling of the Cayhall case, and, uh, I was just trying to track it down.'

'I represent Mr Cayhall,' Adam said with measured words.

'Yes, well, that's what we heard. And, uh, you're from Chicago?'

'I am from Chicago.'

'I see. How, uh, did you get the case?'

'My firm has represented Sam Cayhall for seven years.'

'Yes, right. But didn't he terminate your services recently?'

'He did. And now he's rehired the firm.' Adam could hear keys pecking away as Marks gathered his words into a computer.

'I see. We heard a rumor, just a rumor, I guess, that Sam Cayhall is your grandfather.'

'Where'd you hear this?'

'Well, you know, we have sources, and we have to protect them. Can't really tell you where it came from, you know.'

'Yeah, I know.' Adam took a deep breath and let Marks hang for a minute. 'Where are you now?'

'At the paper.'

'And where's that? I don't know the city.'

'Where are you?' Marks asked.

'Downtown. In our office.'

'I'm not far away. I can be there in ten minutes.'

'No, not here. Let's meet somewhere else. A quiet little bar some place.'

'Fine. The Peabody Hotel is on Union, three blocks from you. There's a nice bar off the lobby called Mallards.'

'I'll be there in fifteen minutes. Just me and you, okay?'

'Sure.'

Adam hung up the phone. Sam's agreement contained some loose and ambiguous language that attempted to

182

prevent his lawyer from talking to the press. The particular clause had major loopholes that any lawyer could walk through, but Adam did not wish to push the issue. After two visits, his grandfather was still nothing but a mystery. He didn't like lawyers and would readily fire another, even his own grandson.

MALLARDS was filling up quickly with young weary professionals who needed a couple of stiff ones for the drive to the suburbs. Few people actually lived in downtown Memphis, so the bankers and brokers met here and in countless other bars and gulped beer in green bottles and sipped Swedish vodka. They lined the bar and gathered around the small tables to discuss the direction of the market and debate the future of the prime. It was a tiny place, with authentic brick walls and real hardwood floors. A table by the door held trays of chicken wings and livers wrapped with bacon.

Adam spotted a young man in jeans holding a notepad. He introduced himself, and they went to a table in the corner. Todd Marks was no more than twenty-five. He wore wire-rimmed glasses and hair to his shoulders. He was cordial and seemed a bit nervous. They ordered Heinekens.

The notepad was on the table, ready for action, and Adam decided to take control. 'A few ground rules,' he said. 'First, everything I say is off the record. You can't quote me on anything. Agreed?'

Marks shrugged as if this was okay but not exactly what he had in mind. 'Okay,' he said.

'I think you call it deep background, or something like that.'

'That's it.'

'I'll answer some questions for you, but not many. I'm here because I want you to get it right, okay?'

'Fair enough. Is Sam Cayhall your grandfather?'

'Sam Cayhall is my client, and he has instructed me not to talk to the press. That's why you can't quote me. I'm here to confirm or deny. That's all.'

183

'Okay. But is he your grandfather?'

'Yes.'

Marks took a deep breath and savored this incredible fact which no doubt led to an extraordinary story. He could see the headlines.

Then he realized he should ask some more questions. He carefully took a pen from his pocket. 'Who's your father?'

'My father is deceased.'

A long pause. 'Okay. So Sam is your mother's father?'

'No. Sam is my father's father.'

'All right. Why do you have different last names?'

'Because my father changed his name.'

'Why?'

'I don't want to answer that. I don't want to go into a lot of family background.'

'Did you grow up in Clanton?'

'No. I was born there, but left when I was three years old. My parents moved to California. That's where I grew up.'

'So you were not around Sam Cayhall?'

'No.'

'Did you know him?'

'I met him yesterday.'

Marks considered the next question, and thankfully the beer arrived. They sipped in unison and said nothing.

He stared at his notepad, scribbled something, then asked, 'How long have you been with Kravitz & Bane?'

'Almost a year.'

'How long have you worked on the Cayhall case?'

'A day and a half.'

He took a long drink, and watched Adam as if he expected an explanation. 'Look, uh, Mr Hall—'

'It's Adam.'

'Okay, Adam. There seem to be a lot of gaps here. Could you help me a bit?'

'No.'

'All right. I read somewhere that Cayhall fired Kravitz & Bane recently. Were you working on the case when this happened?'

184

'I just told you I've been working on the case for a day and a half.'

'When did you first go to death row?'

'Yesterday.'

'Did he know you were coming?'

'I don't want to get into that.'

'Why not?'

'This is a very confidential matter. I'm not going to discuss my visits to death row. I will confirm or deny only those things which you can verify elsewhere.'

'Does Sam have other children?'

'I'm not going to discuss family. I'm sure your paper has covered this before.'

'But it was a long time ago.'

'Then look it up.'

Another long drink, and another long look at the notepad. 'What are the odds of the execution taking place on August 8?'

'It's very hard to say. I wouldn't want to speculate.'

'But all the appeals have run, haven't they?'

'Maybe. Let's say I've got my work cut out for me.'

'Can the governor grant a pardon?'

'Yes.'

'Is that a possibility?'

'Rather unlikely. You'll have to ask him.'

'Will your client do any interviews before the execution?'

'I doubt it.'

Adam glanced at his watch as if he suddenly had to catch a plane. 'Anything else?' he asked, then finished off the beer.

Marks stuck his pen in a shirt pocket. 'Can we talk again?'

'Depends.'

'On what?'

'On how you handle this. If you drag up the family stuff, then forget it.'

'Must be some serious skeletons in the closet.'

'No comment.' Adam stood and offered a handshake. 'Nice meeting you,' he said as they shook hands.

'Thanks. I'll give you a call.'

Adam walked quickly by the crowd at the bar, and disappeared through the hotel lobby.

SIXTEEN

OF ALL THE SILLY, nitpicking rules imposed upon inmates at the Row, the one that irritated Sam the most was the five-inch rule. This little nugget of regulatory brilliance placed a limit on the volume of legal papers a death row inmate could possess in his cell. The documents could be no thicker than five inches when placed on end and squeezed together. Sam's file was not much different from the other inmates', and after nine years of appellate warfare the file filled a large cardboard box. How in hell was he supposed to research and study and prepare with such limitations as the five-inch rule?

Packer had entered his cell on several occasions with a yardstick which he waved around like a bandleader then carefully placed against the papers. Each time Sam had been over the limit; once being caught, according to Packer's assessment, with twenty-one inches. And each time Packer wrote an RVR, a rules violation report, and some more paperwork went into Sam's institutional file. Sam often wonderered if his file in the main administration building was thicker than five inches. He hoped so. And who cared? They'd kept him in a cage for nine and a half years for the sole purpose of sustaining his life so they could one day take it. What else could they do to him?

Each time Packer had given him twenty-four hours to thin his file. Sam usually mailed a few inches to his brother in North Carolina. A few times he had reluctantly mailed an inch or two to E. Garner Goodman.

At the present time, he was about twelve inches over. And he had a thin file of recent Supreme Court cases under his mattress. And he had two inches next door where Hank Henshaw watched it on the bookshelf. And he had about three inches next door in J. B. Gullitt's stack of papers. Sam reviewed all documents and letters for Henshaw and Gullitt. Henshaw had a fine lawyer, one purchased with family money. Gullitt had a fool from a big-shot firm in D. C. who'd never seen a courtroom.

The three-book rule was another baffling limitation on what inmates could keep in their cells. This rule simply said that a death row inmate could possess no more than three books. Sam owned fifteen; six in his cell, and nine scattered among his clients on the Row. He had no time for fiction. His collection was solely law books about the death penalty and the Eighth Amendment.

He had finished a dinner of boiled pork, pinto beans, and corn bread, and he was reading a case from the Ninth Circuit in California about an inmate who faced his death so calmly his lawyers decided he must be crazy. So they filed a series of motions claiming their client was indeed too crazy to execute. The Ninth Circuit was filled with California liberals opposed to the death penalty, and they jumped at this novel argument. The execution was stayed. Sam liked this case. He had wished many times that he had the Ninth Circuit looking down upon him instead of the Fifth.

Gullitt next door said, 'Gotta kite, Sam,' and Sam walked to his bars. Flying a kite was the only method of correspondence for inmates several cells away. Gullitt handed him the note. It was from Preacher Boy, a pathetic white kid seven doors down. He had become a country preacher at the age of fourteen, a regular hellfire-and-brimstoner, but that career was cut short and perhaps delayed forever when he was convicted of the rape and murder of a deacon's wife. He was twenty-four now, a resident of the Row for three years, and had recently made a glorious return to the gospel. The note said:

Dear Sam, I am down here praying for you right now. I really believe God will step into this matter and stop this thing. But if he don't, I'm asking him to take you quickly, no pain or nothing, and take you home. Love, Randy.

How wonderful, thought Sam, they're already praying that I go quickly, no pain or nothing. He sat on the edge of his bed and wrote a brief message on a scrap of paper.

Dear Randy:
Thanks for the prayers. I need them. I also need one of my books. It's called Bronstein's Death Penalty Review. It's a green book. Send it down. Sam.

He handed it to J.B., and waited with his arms through the bars as the kite made its way along the tier. It was almost eight o'clock, still hot and muggy but mercifully growing dark outside. The night would lower the temperature to the high seventies, and with the fans buzzing away the cells became tolerable.

Sam had received several kites during the day. All had expressed sympathy and hope. All offered whatever help was available. The music had been quieter and the yelling that erupted occasionally when someone's rights were being tampered with had not occurred. For the second day, the Row had been a more peaceful place. The televisions rattled along all day and into the night, but the volume was lower. Tier A was noticeably calmer.

'Got myself a new lawyer,' Sam said quietly as he leaned on his elbows with his hands hanging into the hallway. He wore nothing but his boxer shorts. He could see Gullitt's hands and wrists, but he could never see his face when they talked in their cells. Each day as Sam was led outside for his hour of exercise, he walked slowly along the tier and stared into the eyes of his comrades. And they stared at him. He had their faces memorized, and he knew their voices. But it was cruel to live next door to a man for years and have long conversations about life and death while looking only at his hands.

'That's good, Sam. I'm glad to hear it.'

'Yeah. Pretty sharp kid, I think.'

'Who is it?' Gullitt's hands were clasped together. They didn't move.

'My grandson.' Sam said this just loud enough for Gullitt to hear. He could be trusted with secrets.

Gullitt's fingers moved slightly as he pondered this. 'Your grandson?'

'Yep. From Chicago. Big firm. Thinks we might have a chance.'

'You never told me you had a grandson.'

'I hadn't seen him in twenty years. Showed up yesterday and told me he was a lawyer and wanted to take my case.'

'Where's he been for the past ten years?'

'Growing up, I guess. He's just a kid. Twenty-six, I think.'

'You're gonna let a twenty-six-year-old kid take your case?'

This irritated Sam a bit. 'I don't exactly have a lot of choices at this moment in my life.'

'Hell, Sam, you know more law than he does.'

'I know, but it'll be nice to have a real lawyer out there typing up motions and appeals on real computers and filing them in the proper courts, you know. It'll be nice to have somebody who can run to court and argue with judges, somebody who can fight with the state on equal footing.'

This seemed to satisfy Gullitt because he didn't speak for several minutes. His hands were still, but then he began rubbing his fingertips together and this of course meant something was bothering him. Sam waited.

'I've been thinking about something, Sam. All day long this has been eatin' at me.'

'What is it?'

'Well, for three years now you've been right there and I've been right here, you know, and you're my best friend in the world. You're the only person I can trust, you know, and I don't know what I'm gonna do if they walk you down the hall and into the chamber. I mean, I've always had you

190

right there to look over my legal stuff, stuff that I'll never understand, and you've always given me good advice and told me what to do. I can't trust my lawyer in D.C. He never calls me or writes me, and I don't know what the hell's going on with my case. I mean, I don't know if I'm a year away or five years away, and it's enough to drive me crazy. If it hadn't been for you, I'd be a nut case by now. And what if you don't make it?' By now his hands were jumping and thrusting with all sorts of intensity. His words stopped and his hands died down.

Sam lit a cigarette and offered one to Gullitt, the only person on death row with whom he'd share. Hank Henshaw, to his left, did not smoke. They puffed for a moment, each blowing clouds of smoke at the row of windows along the top of the hallway.

Sam finally said, 'I'm not going anywhere, J.B. My lawyer says we've got a good chance.'

'Do you believe him?'

'I think so. He's a smart kid.'

'That must be weird, man, having a grandson as your lawyer. I can't imagine.' Gullitt was thirty-one, childless, married, and often complained about his wife's jody, or free world boyfriend. She was a cruel woman who never visited and had once written a short letter with the good news that she was pregnant. Gullitt pouted for two days before admitting to Sam that he had beaten her for years and chased lots of women himself. She wrote again a month later and said she was sorry. A friend loaned her the money for an abortion, she explained, and she didn't want a divorce after all. Gullitt couldn't have been happier.

'It's somewhat strange, I guess,' Sam said. 'He looks nothing like me, but he favors his mother.'

'So the dude just came right out and told you he was your long-lost grandson?'

'No. Not at first. We talked for a while and his voice sounded familiar. Sounded like his father's.'

'His·father is your son, right?'

'Yeah. He's dead.'

191

'Your son is dead?'

'Yeah.'

The green book finally arrived from Preacher Boy with another note about a magnificent dream he had just two nights ago. He had recently acquired the rare spiritual gift of dream interpretation, and couldn't wait to share it with Sam. The dream was still revealing itself to him, and once he had it all pieced together he would decode it and untangle it and illustrate it for Sam. It was good news, he already knew that much.

At least he's stopped singing, Sam said to himself as he finished the note and sat on his bed. Preacher Boy had also been a gospel singer of sorts and a songwriter on top of that, and periodically found himself seized with the spirit to the point of serenading the tier at full volume and at all hours of the day and night. He was an untrained tenor with little pitch but incredible volume, and the complaints came fast and furious when he belted his new tunes into the hallway. Packer himself usually intervened to stop the racket. Sam had even threatened to step in legally and speed up the kid's execution if the caterwauling didn't stop, a sadistic move that he later apologized for. The poor kid was just crazy, and if Sam lived long enough he planned to use an insanity strategy that he'd read about from the California case.

He reclined on his bed and began to read. The fan ruffled the pages and circulated the sticky air, but within minutes the sheets under him were wet. He slept in dampness until the early hours before dawn when the Row was almost cool and the sheets were almost dry.

192

SEVENTEEN

THE AUBURN HOUSE had never been a house or a home, but for decades had been a quaint little church of yellow brick and stained glass. It sat surrounded by an ugly chain-link fence on a shaded lot a few blocks from downtown Memphis. Graffiti littered the yellow brick and the stained glass windows had been replaced with plywood. The congregation had fled east years ago, away from the inner city, to the safety of the suburbs. They took their pews and songbooks, and even their steeple. A security guard paced along the fence ready to open the gate. Next door was a crumbling apartment building, and a block behind was a deteriorating federal housing project from which the patients of Auburn House came.

They were all young mothers, teenagers without exception whose mothers had also been teenagers and whose fathers were generally unknown. The average age was fifteen. The youngest had been eleven. They drifted in from the project with a baby on a hip and sometimes another one trailing behind. They came in packs of three and four and made their visits a social event. They came alone and scared. They gathered in the old sanctuary which was now a waiting room where paperwork was required. They waited with their infants while their toddlers played under the seats. They chatted with their friends, other girls from the project who'd walked to Auburn House because cars were scarce and they were too young to drive.

Adam parked in a small lot to the side and asked the

193

security guard for directions. He examined Adam closely then pointed to the front door where two young girls were holding babies and smoking. He entered between them, nodding and trying to be polite, but they only stared. Inside he found a half dozen of the same mothers sitting in plastic chairs with children swarming at their feet. A young lady behind a desk pointed at a door and told him to take the hallway on the left.

The door to Lee's tiny office was open and she was talking seriously to a patient. She smiled at Adam. 'I'll be five minutes,' she said, holding something that appeared to be a diaper. The patient did not have a child with her, but one was due very shortly.

Adam eased along the hallway and found the men's room. Lee was waiting for him in the hall when he came out. They pecked each other on the cheeks. 'What do you think of our little operation?' she asked.

'What exactly do you do here?' They walked through the narrow corridor with worn carpet and peeling walls.

'Auburn House is a nonprofit organization staffed with volunteers. We work with young mothers.'

'It must be depressing.'

'Depends on how you look at it. Welcome to my office.' Lee waved at her door and they stepped inside. The walls were covered with colorful charts, one showing a series of babies and the foods they eat; another listed in large simple words the most common ailments of newborns; another cartoonish illustration hailed the benefits of condoms. Adam took a seat and assessed the walls.

'All of our kids come from the projects, so you can imagine the postnatal instruction they receive at home. None of them are married. They live with their mothers or aunts or grandmothers. Auburn House was founded by some nuns twenty years ago to teach these kids how to raise healthy babies.'

Adam nodded at the condom poster. 'And to prevent babies?'

'Yes. We're not family planners, don't want to be, but it doesn't hurt to mention birth control.'

194

'Maybe you should do more than mention it.'

'Maybe. Sixty percent of the babies born in this county last year were out of wedlock, and the numbers go up each year. And each year there are more cases of battered and abandoned children. It'll break your heart. Some of these little fellas don't have a chance.'

'Who funds it?'

'It's all private. We spend half our time trying to raise money. We operate on a very lean budget.'

'How many counselors like you?'

'A dozen or so. Some work a few afternoons a week, a few Saturdays. I'm lucky. I can afford to work here full-time.'

'How many hours a week?'

'I don't know. Who keeps up with them? I get here around ten and leave after dark.'

'And you do this for free?'

'Yeah. You guys call it pro bono, I think.'

'It's different with lawyers. We do volunteer work to justify ourselves and the money we make, our little contribution to society. We still make plenty of money, you understand. This is a little different.'

'It's rewarding.'

'How'd you find this place?'

'I don't know. It was a long time ago. I was a member of a social club, a hot-tea-drinkers club, and we'd meet once a month for a lovely lunch and discuss ways to raise a few pennies for the less fortunate. One day a nun spoke to us about Auburn House, and we adopted it as our beneficiary. One thing led to another.'

'And you're not paid a dime?'

'Phelps has plenty of money, Adam. In fact, I donate a lot of it to Auburn House. We have an annual fundraiser now at the Peabody, black tie and champagne, and I make Phelps lean on his banker buddies to show up with their wives and fork over the money. Raised over two hundred thousand last year.'

'Where does it go?'

'Some goes to overhead. We have two full-time staffers.

The building is cheap but it still costs. The rest goes for baby supplies, medicine, and literature. There's never enough.'

'So you sort of run the place?'

'No. We pay an administrator. I'm just a counselor.'

Adam studied the poster behind her, the one with a bulky yellow condom snaking its way harmlessly across the wall. He gathered from the latest surveys and studies that these little devices were not being used by teenagers, in spite of television campaigns and school slogans and MTV spots by responsible rock stars. He could think of nothing worse than sitting in this cramped little room all day discussing diaper rashes with fifteen-year-old mothers.

'I admire you for this,' he said, looking at the wall with the baby food poster.

Lee nodded but said nothing. Her eyes were tired and she was ready to go. 'Let's go eat,' she said.

'Where?'

'I don't know. Anywhere.'

'I saw Sam today. Spent two hours with him.'

Lee sunk in her seat, and slowly placed her feet on the desk. As usual, she was wearing faded jeans and a button-down.

'I'm his lawyer.'

'He signed the agreement?'

'Yes. He prepared one himself, four pages. We both signed it, and so now it's up to me.'

'Are you scared?'

'Terrified. But I can handle it. I talked to a reporter with the *Memphis Press* this afternoon. They've heard the rumor that Sam Cayhall is my grandfather.'

'What did you tell him?'

'Couldn't really deny it, could I? He wanted to ask all kinds of questions about the family, but I told him little. I'm sure he'll dig around and find some more.'

'What about me?'

'I certainly didn't tell him about you, but he'll start digging. I'm sorry.'

'Sorry about what?'

'Sorry that maybe they'll expose your true identity. You'll be branded as the daughter of Sam Cayhall, murderer, racist, anti-Semite, terrorist, Klansman, the oldest man ever led to the gas chamber and gassed like an animal. They'll run you out of town.'

'I've been through worse.'

'What?'

'Being the wife of Phelps Booth.'

Adam laughed at this, and Lee managed a smile. A middle-aged lady walked to the open door and told Lee she was leaving for the day. Lee jumped to her feet and quickly introduced her handsome young nephew, Adam Hall, a lawyer from Chicago, who was visiting for a spell. The lady was sufficiently impressed as she backed out of the office and disappeared down the hall.

'You shouldn't have done that,' Adam said.

'Why not?'

'Because my name will be in the paper tomorrow – Adam Hall, lawyer from Chicago, and grandson.'

Lee's mouth dropped an inch before she caught it. She then gave a shrug as if she didn't care, but Adam saw the fear in her eyes. What a stupid mistake, she was telling herself. 'Who cares?' she said as she picked up her purse and briefcase. 'Let's go find a restaurant.'

THEY WENT to a neighborhood bistro, an Italian family place with small tables and few lights in a converted bungalow. They sat in a dark corner and ordered drinks, iced tea for her and mineral water for him. When the waiter left, Lee leaned over the table and said, 'Adam, there's something I need to tell you.'

He nodded but said nothing.

'I'm an alcoholic.'

His eyes narrowed then froze. They'd had drinks together the last two nights.

'It's been about ten years, now,' she explained, still low over the table. The nearest person was fifteen feet away.

197

'There were a lot of reasons, okay, some of which you could probably guess. I went through recovery, came out clean, and lasted about a year. Then, rehab again. I've been through treatment three times, the last was five years ago. It's not easy.'

'But you had a drink last night. Several drinks.'

'I know. And the night before. And today I emptied all the bottles and threw away the beer. There's not a drop in the apartment.'

'That's fine with me. I hope I'm not the reason.'

'No. But I need your help, okay. You'll be living with me for a couple of months, and we'll have some bad times. Just help me.'

'Sure, Lee. I wish you'd told me when I arrived. I don't drink much. I can take it or leave it.'

'Alcoholism is a strange animal. Sometimes I can watch people drink and it doesn't bother me. Then I'll see a beer commercial and break into a sweat. I'll see an ad in a magazine for a wine I used to enjoy, and the craving is so intense I'll become nauseated. It's an awful struggle.'

The drinks arrived and Adam was afraid to touch his mineral water. He poured it over the ice and stirred it with a spoon. 'Does it run in the family?' he asked, almost certain that it did.

'I don't think so. Sam would sneak around and drink a little when we were kids, but he kept it from us. My mother's mother was an alcoholic, so my mother never touched the stuff. I never saw it in the house.'

'How'd it happen to you?'

'Gradually. When I left home I couldn't wait to give it a try because it was taboo when Eddie and I were growing up. Then I met Phelps, and he comes from a family of heavy social drinkers. It became an escape, and then it became a crutch.'

'I'll do whatever I can. I'm sorry.'

'Don't be sorry. I've enjoyed having a drink with you, but it's time to quit, okay. I've fallen off the wagon three times, and it all starts with the idea that I can have a drink or two and keep it under control. I went a month one time sipping wine and limiting myself to a glass a day. Then it was a glass and a half, then two, then three. Then rehab. I'm an alcoholic, and I'll never get over it.'

Adam lifted his glass and touched it to hers. 'Here's to the wagon. We'll ride it together.' They gulped their soft drinks.

The waiter was a student with a quick idea of what they should eat. He suggested the chef's baked ravioli because it was simply the best in town and would be on the table in ten minutes. They agreed.

'I often wondered what you did with your time but I was afraid to ask,' Adam said.

'I had a job once. After Walt was born and started school I got bored, so Phelps found me a job with one of his friend's companies. Big salary, nice office. I had my own secretary who knew much more about my job than I did. I quit after a year. I married money, Adam, so I'm not supposed to work. Phelps' mother was appalled that I would draw a salary.'

'What do rich women do all day long?'

'Carry the burdens of the world. They must first make sure hubby is off to work, then they must plan the day. The servants have to be directed and supervised. The shopping is divided into at least two parts – morning and afternoon – with the morning usually consisting of several rigorous phone calls to Fifth Avenue for the necessities. The afternoon shopping is sometimes actually done in person, with the driver waiting in the parking lot, of course. Lunch takes up most of the day because it requires hours to plan and at least two hours to execute. It's normally a small banquet attended by more of the same harried souls. Then there's the social responsibility part of being a rich woman. At least three times a week she attends tea parties in the homes of her friends where they nibble on imported biscuits and whimper about the plight of abandoned babies or mothers on crack. Then, it's back home in a hurry to freshen up for hubby's return from the office wars. She'll sip her first martini with him by the pool while four people prepare their dinner.'

'What about sex?'

'He's too tired. Plus, he probably has a mistress.'

'This is what happened to Phelps?'

'I guess, although he couldn't complain about the sex. I had a baby, I got older, and he's always had a steady supply of young blondes from his banks. You wouldn't believe his office. It's filled with gorgeous women with impeccable teeth and nails, all with short skirts and long legs. They sit behind nice desks and talk on the phone, and wait for his beck and call. He has a small bedroom next to a conference room. The man's an animal.'

'So you gave up the hard life of a rich woman and moved out?'

'Yeah. I was not a very good rich woman, Adam. I hated it. It was fun for a very short while, but I didn't fit in. Not the right blood type. Believe it or not, my family was not known in the social circles of Memphis.'

'You must be kidding.'

'I swear. And to be a proper rich woman with a future in this city you have to come from a family of rich fossils, preferably with a great-grandfather who made money in cotton. I just didn't fit in.'

'But you still play the social game.'

'No. I still make appearances, but only for Phelps. It's important for him to have a wife who's his age but with a touch of gray, a mature wife who looks nice in an evening dress and diamonds and can hold her own while gabbing with his boring friends. We go out three times a year. I'm sort of an aging trophy wife.'

'Seems to me like he'd want a real trophy wife, one of the slinky blondes.'

'No. His family would be crushed, and there's a lot of money in trust. Phelps walks on eggshells around his family. When his parents are gone, then he'll be ready to come out of the closet.'

'I thought his parents hated you.'

'Of course they do. It's ironic that they're the reason we're still married. A divorce would be scandalous.'

Adam laughed and shook his head in bewilderment. 'This is crazy.'

'Yes, but it works. I'm happy. He's happy. He has his little girls. I fool around with whomever I want. No questions are asked.'

'What about Walt?'

She slowly sat her glass of tea on the table and looked away. 'What about him?' she said, without looking.

'You never talk about him.'

'I know,' she said softly, still watching something across the room.

'Let me guess. More skeletons in the closet. More secrets.'

She looked at him sadly, then gave a slight shrug as if to say, what the hell.

'He is, after all, my first cousin,' Adam said. 'And to my knowledge, and barring any further revelations, he's the only first cousin I have.'

'You wouldn't like him.'

'Of course not. He's part Cayhall.'

'No. He's all Booth. Phelps wanted a son, why I don't know. And so we had a son. Phelps, of course, had little time for him. Always too busy with the bank. He took him to the country club and tried to teach him golf, but it didn't work. Walt never liked sports. They went to Canada once to hunt pheasants, and didn't speak to each other for a week when they came home. He wasn't a sissy, but he wasn't athletic either. Phelps was a big prep school jock – football, rugby, boxing, all that. Walt tried to play, but the talent just wasn't there. Phelps drove him even harder, and Walt rebelled. So, Phelps, with the typical heavy hand, sent him away to boarding school. My son left home at the age of fifteen.'

'Where did he go to college?'

'He spent one year at Cornell, then dropped out.'

'He dropped out?'

201

'Yes. He went to Europe after his freshman year, and he's been there ever since.'

Adam studied her face and waited for more. He sipped his water, and was about to speak when the waiter appeared and rapidly placed a large bowl of green salad between them.

'Why did he stay in Europe?'

'He went to Amsterdam and fell in love.'

'A nice Dutch girl?'

'A nice Dutch boy.'

'I see.'

She was suddenly interested in the salad, which she served on her plate and began cutting into small pieces. Adam did likewise, and they ate in silence for a while as the bistro filled up and became noisier. An attractive couple of tired yuppies sat at the small table next to them and ordered strong drinks.

Adam smeared butter on a roll, took a bite, then asked, 'How did Phelps react?'

She wiped the corners of her mouth. 'The last trip Phelps and I took together was to Amsterdam to find our son. He'd been gone for almost two years. He'd written a few times and called me occasionally, but then all correspondence stopped. We were worried, of course, so we flew over and camped out in a hotel until we found him.'

'What was he doing?'

'Working as a waiter in a café. Had an earring in each ear. His hair was chopped off. Weird clothes. He was wearing those damned clogs with wool socks. Spoke perfect Dutch. We didn't want to make a scene, so we asked him to come to our hotel. He did. It was horrible. Just horrible. Phelps handled it like the idiot he is, and the damage was irreparable. We left and came home. Phelps made a big production of redoing his will and revoking Walt's trust.'

'He's never come home?'

'Never. I meet him in Paris once a year. We both arrive alone, that's the only rule. We stay in a nice hotel and spend a week together, roaming the city, eating the food, visiting the museums. It's the highlight of my year. But he hates Memphis.'

'I'd like to meet him.'

Lee watched him carefully, then her eyes watered. 'Bless you. If you're serious, I'd love for you to go with me.'

'I'm serious. I don't care if he's gay. I'd enjoy meeting my first cousin.'

She took a deep breath and smiled. The ravioli arrived on two heaping plates with steam rising in all directions. A long loaf of garlic bread was placed along the edge of the table, and the waiter was gone.

'Does Walt know about Sam?' Adam asked.

'No. I've never had the guts to tell him.'

'Does he know about me and Carmen? About Eddie? About any of our family's glorious history?'

'Yes, a little. When he was a little boy, I told him he had cousins in California, but that they never came to Memphis. Phelps, of course, told him that his California cousins were of a much lower social class and therefore not worthy of his attention. Walt was groomed by his father to be a snob, Adam, you must understand this. He attended the most prestigious prep schools, hung out at the nicest country clubs, and his family consisted of a bunch of Booth cousins who were all the same. They're all miserable people.'

'What do the Booths think of having a homosexual in the family?'

'They hate him, of course. And he hates them.'

'I like him already.'

'He's not a bad kid. He wants to study art and paint. I send him money all the time.'

'Does Sam know he has a gay grandson?'

'I don't think so. I don't know who would tell him.'

'I probably won't tell him.'

'Please don't. He has enough on his mind.'

The ravioli cooled enough to eat, and they enjoyed it in silence. The waiter brought more water and tea. The couple next to them ordered a bottle of red wine, and Lee glanced at it more than once.

Adam wiped his mouth and rested for a moment. He leaned over the table. 'Can I ask you something personal?' he said quietly.

'All your questions seem to be personal.'

'Right. So can I ask you one more?'

'Please do.'

'Well, I was just thinking. Tonight you've told me you're an alcoholic, your husband's an animal, and your son is gay. That's a lot for one meal. But is there anything else I should know?'

'Lemme see. Yes, Phelps is an alcoholic too, but he won't admit it.'

'Anything else?'

'He's been sued twice for sexual harassment.'

'Okay. Forget about the Booths. Any more surprises from our side of the family?'

'We haven't scratched the surface, Adam.'

'I was afraid of that.'

EIGHTEEN

A LOUD THUNDERSTORM rolled across the Delta before dawn, and Sam was awakened by the crack of lightning. He heard raindrops dropping hard against the open windows above the hallway. Then he heard them drip and puddle against the wall under the windows not far from his cell. The dampness of his bed was suddenly cool. Maybe today would not be so hot. Maybe the rain would linger and shade the sun, and maybe the wind would blow away the humidity for a day or two. He always had these hopes when it rained, but in the summer a thunderstorm usually meant soggy ground which under a glaring sun meant nothing but more suffocating heat.

He raised his head and watched the rain fall from the windows and gather on the floor. The water flickered in the reflected light of a distant yellow bulb. Except for this faint light, the Row was dark. And it was silent.

Sam loved the rain, especially at night and especially in the summer. The State of Mississippi, in its boundless wisdom, had built its prison in the hottest place it could find. And it designed its Maximum Security Unit along the same lines as an oven. The windows to the outside were small and useless, built that way for security reasons, of course. The planners of this little branch of hell also decided that there would be no ventilation of any sort, no chance for a breeze getting in or the dank air getting out. And after they built what they considered to be a model penal facility, they decided they would not air condition it.

It would sit proudly beside the soybeans and cotton, and absorb the same heat and moisture from the ground. And when the land was dry, the Row would simply bake along with the crops.

But the State of Mississippi could not control the weather, and when the rains came and cooled the air, Sam smiled to himself and offered a small prayer of thanks. A higher being was in control after all. The state was helpless when it rained. It was a small victory.

He eased to his feet and stretched his back. His bed consisted of a piece of foam, six feet by two and a half, four inches thick, otherwise known as a mattress. It rested on a metal frame fastened securely to the floor and wall. It was covered with two sheets. Sometimes they passed out blankets in the winter. Back pain was common throughout the Row, but with time the body adjusted and there were few complaints. The prison doctor was not considered to be a friend of death row inmates.

He took two steps and leaned on his elbows through the bars. He listened to the wind and thunder, and watched the drops bounce along the windowsill and splatter on the floor. How nice it would be to step through that wall and walk through the wet grass on the other side, to stroll around the prison grounds in the driving rain, naked and crazy, soaking wet with water dripping from his hair and beard.

The horror of death row is that you die a little each day. The waiting kills you. You live in a cage and when you wake up you mark off another day and you tell yourself that you are now one day closer to death.

Sam lit a cigarette and watched the smoke float upward toward the raindrops. Weird things happen with our absurd judicial system. Courts rule this way one day and the other way the next. The same judges reach different conclusions on familiar issues. A court will ignore a wild motion or appeal for years, then one day embrace it and grant relief. Judges die and they're replaced by judges who think differently. Presidents come and go and they appoint their pals to the bench. The Supreme Court drifts one way, then another.

At times, death would be welcome. And if given the choice of death on one hand, or life on death row on the other, Sam would quickly take the gas. But there was always hope, always the slight glimmering promise that something somewhere in the vast maze of the judicial jungle would strike a chord with someone; and his case would be reversed. Every resident of the Row dreamed of the miracle reversal from heaven. And their dreams sustained them from one miserable day to the next.

Sam had recently read that there were almost twenty-five hundred inmates sentenced to die in America, and last year, 1989, only sixteen were executed. Mississippi had executed only four since 1977, the year Gary Gilmore insisted on a firing squad in Utah. There was safety in those numbers. They fortified his resolve to file even more appeals.

He smoked through the bars as the storm passed and the rain stopped. He took his breakfast as the sun rose, and at seven o'clock he turned on the television for the morning news. He had just bitten into a piece of cold toast when suddenly his face appeared on the screen behind a Memphis morning anchorperson. She eagerly reported the thrilling top story of the day, the bizarre case of Sam Cayhall and his new lawyer. Seems his new lawyer was his long-lost grandson, one Adam Hall, a young lawyer from the mammoth Chicago firm of Kravitz & Bane, the outfit who'd represented Sam for the past seven years or so. The photo of Sam was at least ten years old, the same one they used every time his name was mentioned on TV or in print. The photo of Adam was a bit stranger. He obviously had not posed for it. Someone had snapped it outdoors while he wasn't looking. She explained with wild eyes that the *Memphis Press* was reporting this morning that Adam Hall had confirmed that he was in fact the grandson of Sam Cayhall. She gave a fleeting sketch of Sam's crime, and twice gave the date of his pending execution. More on the story later, she promised, perhaps maybe as soon as the 'Noon Report'. Then she was off on the morning summary of last night's murders.

Sam threw the toast on the floor next to the bookshelves

and stared at it. An insect found it almost immediately and crawled over and around it a half dozen times before deciding it wasn't worth eating. His lawyer had already talked to the press. What do they teach these people in law school? Do they give instruction on media control?

'Sam, you there?' It was Gullitt.

'Yeah. I'm here.'

'Just saw you on channel four.'

'Yeah. I saw it.'

'You pissed?'

'I'm okay.'

'Take a deep breath, Sam. It's okay.'

Among men sentenced to die in the gas chamber, the expression 'Take a deep breath' was used often and considered nothing more than an effort at humor. They said it to each other all the time, usually when one was angry. But when used by the guards it was far from funny. It was a constitutional violation. It had been mentioned in more than one lawsuit as an example of the cruel treatment dispensed on death row.

Sam agreed with the insect and ignored the rest of his breakfast. He sipped coffee and stared at the floor.

AT NINE-THIRTY, Sergeant Packer was on the tier looking for Sam. It was time for his hour of fresh air. The rains were far away and the sun was blistering the Delta. Packer had two guards with him and a pair of leg irons. Sam pointed at the chains, and asked, 'What are they for?'

'They're for security, Sam.'

'I'm just going out to play, aren't I?'

'No, Sam. We're taking you to the law library. Your lawyer wants to meet you there so y'all can talk amongst the law books. Now turn around.'

Sam stuck both hands through the opening of his door. Packer cuffed them loosely, then the door opened and Sam stepped into the hall. The guards dropped to their knees and were securing the leg irons when Sam asked Packer, 'What about my hour out?'

'What about it?'

'When do I get it?'

'Later.'

'You said that yesterday and I didn't get my rec time. You lied to me yesterday. Now you're lying to me again. I'll sue you for this.'

'Lawsuits take a long time, Sam. They take years.'

'I want to talk to the warden.'

'And I'm sure he wants to talk to you too, Sam. Now, do you want to see your lawyer or not?'

'I have a right to my lawyer and I have a right to my rec time.'

'Get off his ass, Packer!' Hank Henshaw shouted from less than six feet away.

'You lie, Packer! You lie!' J. B. Gullitt added from the other side.

'Down, boys,' Packer said coolly. 'We'll take care of old Sam, here.'

'Yeah, you'd gas him today if you could,' Henshaw yelled.

The leg irons were in place, and Sam shuffled into his cell to get a file. He clutched it to his chest and waddled down the tier with Packer at his side and the guards following.

'Give 'em hell, Sam,' Henshaw yelled as they walked away.

There were other shouts of support for Sam and catcalls at Packer as they left the tier. They were cleared through a set of doors and Tier A was behind them.

'The warden says you get two hours out this afternoon, and two hours a day till it's over,' Packer said as they moved slowly through a short hallway.

'Till what's over?'

'This thang.'

'What thang?'

Packer and most of the guards referred to an execution as a thang.

'You know what I mean,' Packer said.

'Tell the warden he's a real sweetheart. Ask him if I get

209

two hours if this thang doesn't go off, okay? And while you're at it, tell him I think he's a lying son of a bitch.'

'He already knows.'

They stopped at a wall of bars and waited for the door to open. They passed through it and stopped again by two guards at the front door. Packer made quick notes on a clipboard, and they walked outside where a white van was waiting. The guards took Sam by the arm and lifted him and his chains into the side door. Packer sat in the front with the driver.

'Does this thing have air conditioning?' Sam snapped at the driver, whose window was down.

'Yep,' the driver said as they backed away from the front of MSU.

'Then turn the damned thing on, okay.'

'Knock it off, Sam,' Packer said without conviction.

'It's bad enough to sweat all day in a cage with no air conditioning, but it's pretty stupid to sit here and suffocate. Turn the damned thing on. I've got my rights.'

'Take a deep breath, Sam,' Packer drawled and winked at the driver.

'That'll cost you, Packer. You'll wish you hadn't said that.'

The driver hit a switch and the air started blowing. The van was cleared through the double gates and slowly made its way down the dirt road away from the Row.

Though he was handcuffed and shackled, this brief journey on the outside was refreshing. Sam stopped the bitching and immediately ignored the others in the van. The rains had left puddles in the grassy ditches beside the road, and they had washed the cotton plants, now more than knee-high. The stalks and leaves were dark green. Sam remembered picking cotton as a boy, then quickly dismissed the thought. He had trained his mind to forget the past, and on those rare occasions when a childhood memory flashed before him, he quickly snuffed it out.

The van crept along, and he was thankful for this. He stared at two inmates sitting under a tree watching a buddy lift weights in the sun. There was a fence around them, but how nice, he thought, to be outside walking and talking, exercising and lounging, never giving a thought to the gas chamber, never worrying about the last appeal.

THE LAW LIBRARY was known as the Twig because it was too small to be considered a full branch. The main prison law library was deeper into the farm, at another camp. The Twig was used exclusively by death row inmates. It was stuck to the rear of an administration building, with only one door and no windows. Sam had been there many times during the past nine years. It was a small room with a decent collection of current law books and up-to-date reporting services. A battered conference table sat in the center with shelves of books lining the four walls. Every now and then a trustee would volunteer to serve as the librarian, but good help was hard to find and the books were seldom where they were supposed to be. This irritated Sam immensely because he admired neatness and he despised the Africans, and he was certain that most if not all of the librarians were black, though he did not know this for a fact.

The two guards unshackled Sam at the door.

'You got two hours,' Packer said.

'I got as long as I want,' Sam said, rubbing his wrists as if the handcuffs had broken them.

'Sure, Sam. But when I come after you in two hours, I'll bet we load your gimpy little ass into the van.'

Packer opened the door as the guards took their positions beside it. Sam entered the library and slammed the door behind him. He laid his file on the table and stared at his lawyer.

Adam stood at the far end of the conference table, holding a book and waiting for his client. He'd heard voices outside, and he watched Sam enter the room without guards or handcuffs. He stood there in his red jumpsuit, much smaller now without the thick metal screen between them.

They studied each other for a moment across the table,

211

grandson and grandfather, lawyer and client, stranger and stranger. It was an awkward interval in which they sized each other up and neither knew what to do with the other.

'Hello, Sam,' Adam said, walking toward him.

'Mornin'. Saw us on TV a few hours ago.'

'Yeah. Have you seen the paper?'

'Not yet. It comes later.'

Adam slid the morning paper across the table and Sam stopped it. He held it with both hands, eased into a chair, and raised the paper to within six inches of his nose. He read it carefully and studied the pictures of himself and Adam.

Todd Marks had evidently spent most of the evening digging and making frantic phone calls. He had verified that one Alan Cayhall had been born in Clanton, in Ford County, in 1964, and the father's name listed on the birth certificate was one Edward S. Cayhall. He checked the birth certificate for Edward S. Cayhall and found that his father was Samuel Lucas Cayhall, the same man now on death row. He reported that Adam Hall had confirmed that his father's name had been changed in California, and that his grandfather was Sam Cayhall. He was careful not to attribute direct quotes to Adam, but he nonetheless violated their agreement. There was little doubt the two had talked.

Quoting unnamed sources, the story explained how Eddie and his family left Clanton in 1967 after Sam's arrest, and fled to California where Eddie later killed himself. The trail ended there because Marks obviously ran out of time late in the day and could confirm nothing from California. The unnamed source or sources didn't mention Sam's daughter living in Memphis, so Lee was spared. The story ran out of steam with a series of no-comments from Baker Cooley, Garner Goodman, Phillip Naifeh, Lucas Mann, and a lawyer with the Attorney General's office in Jackson. Marks finished strong, though, with a sensational recap of the Kramer bombing.

The story was on the front page of the *Press*, above the main headline. The ancient picture of Sam was to the right,

212

and next to it was a strange photo of Adam from the waist up. Lee had brought the paper to him hours earlier as he sat on the terrace and watched the early morning river traffic. They drank coffee and juice, and read and reread the story. After much analysis, Adam had decided that Todd Marks had placed a photographer across the street from the Peabody Hotel, and when Adam left their little meeting yesterday and stepped onto the sidewalk, he got his picture taken. The suit and tie were definitely worn yesterday.

'Did you talk to this clown?' Sam growled as he placed the paper on the table. Adam sat across from him.

'We met.'

'Why?'

'Because he called our office in Memphis, said he'd heard some rumors, and I wanted him to get it straight. It's no big deal.'

'Our pictures on the front page is no big deal?'

'You've been there before.'

'And you?'

'I didn't exactly pose. It was an ambush, you see. But I think I look rather dashing.'

'Did you confirm these facts for him?'

'I did. We agreed it would be background, and he could not quote me on anything. Nor was he supposed to use me as a source. He violated our agreement, and ripped his ass with me. He also planted a photographer, so I've spoken for the first and last time to the *Memphis Press*.'

Sam looked at the paper for a moment. He was relaxed, and his words were as slow as ever. He managed a trace of a smile. 'And you confirmed that you are my grandson?'

'Yes. Can't really deny it, can I?'

'Do you want to deny it?'

'Read the paper, Sam. If I wanted to deny it, would it be on the front page?'

This satisfied Sam, and the smile grew a bit. He bit his lip and stared at Adam. Then he methodically removed a fresh pack of cigarettes, and Adam glanced around for a window.

After the first one was properly lit, Sam said, 'Stay away

from the press. They're ruthless and they're stupid. They lie and they make careless mistakes.'

'But I'm a lawyer, Sam. It's inbred.'

'I know. It's hard, but try to control yourself. I don't want it to happen again.'

Adam reached into his briefcase, smiled, and pulled out some papers. 'I have a wonderful idea how to save your life.' He rubbed his hands together then removed a pen from his pocket. It was time for work.

'I'm listening.'

'Well, as you might guess, I've been doing a lot of research.'

'That's what you're paid to do.'

'Yes. And I've come up with a marvelous little theory, a new claim which I intend to file on Monday. The theory is simple. Mississippi is one of only five states still using the gas chamber, right?'

'That's right.'

'And the Mississippi Legislature in 1984 passed a law giving a condemned man the choice of dying by lethal injection or in the gas chamber. But the new law applies only to those convicted after July 1, 1984. Doesn't apply to you.'

'That's correct. I think about half the guys on the Row will get their choice. It's years away, though.'

'One of the reasons the legislature approved lethal injection was to make the killings more humane. I've studied the legislative history behind the law and there was a lot of discussion of problems the state's had with gas chamber executions. The theory is simple: make the executions quick and painless, and there will be fewer constitutional claims that they are cruel. Lethal injections raise fewer legal problems, thus the killings are easier to carry out. Our theory, then, is that since the state has adopted lethal injection, it has in effect said that the gas chamber is obsolete. And why is it obsolete? Because it's a cruel way to kill people.'

Sam puffed on this for a minute and nodded slowly. 'Keep going,' he said.

'We attack the gas chamber as a method of execution.'

'Do you limit it to Mississippi?'

'Probably. I know there were problems with Teddy Doyle Meeks and Maynard Tole.'

Sam snorted and blew smoke across the table. 'Problems? You could say that.'

'How much do you know?'

'Come on. They died within fifty yards of me. We sit in our cells all day long and think about death. Everyone on the Row knows what happened to those boys.'

'Tell me about them.'

Sam leaned forward on his elbows and stared absently at the newspaper in front of him. 'Meeks was the first execution in Mississippi in ten years, and they didn't know what they were doing. It was 1982. I'd been here for almost two years, and until then we were living in a dream world. We never thought about the gas chamber and cyanide pellets and last meals. We were sentenced to die, but, hell, they weren't killing anyone, so why worry? But Meeks woke us up. They killed him, so they could certainly kill the rest of us.'

'What happened to him?' Adam had read a dozen stories about the botched execution of Teddy Doyle Meeks, but he wanted to hear it from Sam.

'Everything went wrong. Have you seen the chamber?'

'Not yet.'

'There's a little room off to the side where the executioner mixes his solution. The sulfuric acid is in a canister which he takes from his little laboratory to a tube running into the bottom of the chamber. With Meeks, the executioner was drunk.'

'Come on, Sam.'

'I didn't see him, okay. But everyone knows he was drunk. State law designates an official state executioner, and the warden and his gang didn't think about it until just a few hours before the execution. Keep in mind, no one thought Meeks would die. We were all waiting on a last minute stay, because he'd been through it twice already.

215

But there was no stay, and they scrambled around at the last minute trying to locate the official state executioner. They found him, drunk. He was a plumber, I think. Anyway, his first batch of brew didn't work. He placed the canister into the tube, pulled a lever, and everyone waited for Meeks to take a deep breath and die. Meeks held his breath as long as he could, then inhaled. Nothing happened. They waited. Meeks waited. The witnesses waited. Everybody slowly turned to the executioner, who was also waiting and cussing. He went back to his little room, and fixed up another mix of sulfuric acid. Then he had to retrieve the old canister from the chute, and that took ten minutes. The warden and Lucas Mann and the rest of the goons were standing around waiting and fidgeting and cussing this drunk plumber, who finally plugged in the new canister and pulled the lever. This time the sulfuric acid landed where it was supposed to – in a bowl under the chair where Meeks was strapped. The executioner pulled the second lever dropping the cyanide pellets, which were also under the chair, hovering above the sulfuric acid. The pellets dropped, and sure enough, the gas drifted upward to where old Meeks was holding his breath again. You can see the vapors, you know. When he finally sucked in a nose full of it, he started shaking and jerking, and this went on quite a while. For some reason, there's a metal pole that runs from the top of the chamber to the bottom, and it's directly behind the chair. Just about the time Meeks got still and everybody thought he was dead, his head started banging back and forth, striking this pole, just beating it like hell. His eyes were rolled back, his lips were wide open, he was foaming at the mouth, and there he was beating the back of his head in on this pole. It was sick.'

'How long did it take to kill him?'

'Who knows. According to the prison doctor, death was instant and painless. According to some of the eye-witnesses, Meeks convulsed and heaved and pounded his head for five minutes.'

The Meeks execution had provided death penalty

abolitionists with much ammunition. There was little doubt he had suffered greatly, and many accounts were written of his death. Sam's version was remarkably consistent with those of the eyewitnesses.

'Who told you about it?' Adam asked.

'A couple of the guards talked about it. Not to me, of course, but word spread quickly. There was a public outcry, which would've been even worse if Meeks hadn't been such a despicable person. Everyone hated him. And his little victim had suffered greatly, so it was hard to feel sympathetic.'

'Where were you when he was executed?'

'In my first cell, Tier D, on the far side away from the chamber. They locked everybody down that night, every inmate at Parchman. It happened just after midnight, which is sort of amusing because the state has a full day to carry out the execution. The death warrant does not specify a certain time, just a certain day. So these gung-ho bastards are just itching to do it as soon as possible. They plan every execution for one minute after midnight. That way, if there's a stay, then they have the entire day for their lawyers to get it lifted. Buster Moac went down that way. They strapped him in at midnight, then the phone rang and they took him back to the holding room where he waited and sweated for six hours while the lawyers ran from one court to the next. Finally, as the sun was rising, they strapped him in for the last time. I guess you know what his last words were.'

Adam shook his head. 'I have no idea.'

'Buster was a friend of mine, a class guy. Naifeh asked him if he had any last words, and he said yes, as a matter of fact, he did have something to say. He said the steak they'd cooked for his last meal was a bit too rare. Naifeh mumbled something to the effect that he'd speak to the cook about it. Then Buster asked if the governor had granted a last minute pardon. Naifeh said no. Buster then said, "Well, tell that son of a bitch he's lost my vote." They slammed the door and gassed him.'

217

Sam was obviously amused by this, and Adam was obliged to offer an awkward laugh. He looked at his legal pad while Sam lit another cigarette.

Four years after the execution of Teddy Doyle Meeks, the appeals of Maynard Tole reached a dead end and it was time for the chamber to be used again. Tole was a Kravitz & Bane pro bono project. A young lawyer named Peter Wiesenberg represented Tole, under the supervision of E. Garner Goodman. Both Wiesenberg and Goodman witnessed the execution, which in many ways was dreadfully similar to Meeks'. Adam had not discussed the Tole execution with Goodman, but he'd studied the file and read the eyewitness accounts written by Wiesenberg and Goodman.

'What about Maynard Tole?' Adam asked.

'He was an African, a militant who killed a bunch of people in a robbery and, of course, blamed everything on the system. Always referred to himself as an African warrior. He threatened me several times, but for the most part he was just selling wolf.'

'Selling wolf?'

'Yeah, that means a guy is talking bad, talking trash. It's common with the Africans. They're all innocent, you know. Every damned one of them. They're here because they're black and the system is white, and even though they've raped and murdered it's someone else's fault. Always, always someone else's fault.'

'So you were happy when he went?'

'I didn't say that. Killing is wrong. It's wrong for the Africans to kill. It's wrong for the Anglos to kill. And it's wrong for the people of the State of Mississippi to kill death row inmates. What I did was wrong, so how do you make it right by killing me?'

'Did Tole suffer?'

'Same as Meeks. They found them a new executioner and he got it right the first time. The gas hit Tole and he went into convulsions, started banging his head on the pole just like Meeks, except Tole evidently had a harder head

218

because he kept beating the pole with it. It went on and on, and finally Naifeh and the goon squad got real anxious because the boy wouldn't die and things were getting sloppy, so they actually made the witnesses leave the witness room. It was pretty nasty.'

'I read somewhere that it took ten minutes for him to die.'

'He fought it hard, that's all I know. Of course, the warden and his doctor said death was instant and painless. Typical. They did, however, make one slight change in their procedure after Tole. By the time they got to my buddy Moac, they had designed this cute little head brace made of leather straps and buckles and attached to that damned pole. With Moac, and later with Jumbo Parris, they belted their heads down so tight there was no way they could flop around and whip the pole. A nice touch, don't you think? That makes it easier on Naifeh and the witnesses because now they don't have to watch as much suffering.'

'You see my point, Sam? It's a horrible way to die. We attack the method. We find witnesses who'll testify about these executions and we try to convince a judge to rule the gas chamber unconstitutional.'

'So what? Do we then ask for lethal injection? What's the point? Seems kind of silly for me to say I prefer not to die in the chamber, but, what the hell, lethal injection will do just fine. Put me on the gurney and fill me up with drugs. I'll be dead, right? I don't get it.'

'True. But we buy ourselves some time. We'll attack the gas chamber, get a temporary stay, then pursue it through the higher courts. We could jam this thing for years.'

'It's already been done.'

'What do you mean it's already been done?'

'Texas, 1983. Case called *Larson*. The same arguments were made with no result. The court said gas chambers have been around for fifty years, and they've proven themselves quite efficient at killing humanely.'

'Yeah, but there's one big difference.'

'What?'

'This ain't Texas. Meeks and Tole and Moac and Parris

weren't gassed in Texas. And, by the way, Texas has already gone to lethal injection. They threw away their gas chamber because they found a better way to kill. Most gas chamber states have traded them in for better technology.'

Sam stood and walked to the other end of the table. 'Well, when it's my time, I damned sure want to go with the latest technology.' He paced along the table, back and forth three or four times, then stopped. 'It's eighteen feet from one end of this room to the other. I can walk eighteen feet without hitting bars. Do you realize what it's like spending twenty-three hours a day in a cell that's six feet by nine? This is freedom, man.' He paced some more, puffing as he came and went.

Adam watched the frail figure bounce along the edge of the table with a trail of smoke behind him. He had no socks and wore navy-colored rubber shower shoes that squeaked when he paced. He suddenly stopped, yanked a book from a shelf, threw it hard on the table, and began flipping pages with a flourish. After a few minutes of intense searching, he found exactly what he was looking for and spent five minutes reading it.

'Here it is,' he mumbled to himself. 'I knew I'd read this before.'

'What is it?'

'A 1984 case from North Carolina. The man's name was Jimmy Old, and evidently Jimmy did not want to die. They had to drag him into the chamber, kicking and crying and screaming, and it took a while to strap him in. They slammed the door and dropped the gas, and his chin crashed onto his chest. Then his head rolled back and began twitching. He turned to the witness who could see nothing but the whites of his eyeballs, and he began salivating. His head rocked and swung around forever while his body shook and his mouth foamed. It went on and on, and one of the witnesses, a journalist, vomited. The warden got fed up with it and closed the black curtains so the witness couldn't see anymore. They estimate it took fourteen minutes for Jimmy Old to die.'

220

'Sounds cruel to me.'

Sam closed the book and placed it carefully onto the shelf. He lit a cigarette and studied the ceiling. 'Virtually every gas chamber was built long ago by Eaton Metal Products in Salt Lake City. I read somewhere that Missouri's was built by inmates. But our little chamber was built by Eaton, and they're all basically the same – made of steel, octagonal in shape with a series of windows placed here and there so folks can watch the death. There's not much room inside the actual chamber, just a wooden seat with straps all over it. There's a metal bowl directly under the chair, and just inches above the bowl is a little bag of cyanide tablets which the executioner controls with a lever. He also controls the sulfuric acid which is introduced into the affair by means of the canister. The canister makes its way through a tube to the bowl, and when the bowl fills with acid, he pulls the lever and drops the cyanide pellets. This causes the gas, which of course causes death, which of course is designed to be painless and quick.'

'Wasn't it designed to replace the electric chair?'

'Yes. Back in the twenties and thirties, everyone had an electric chair, and it was just the most marvelous device ever invented. I remember as a boy they had a portable electric chair which they simply loaded into a trailer and took around to the various counties. They'd pull up at the local jail, bring 'em out in shackles, line 'em up outside the trailer, then run 'em through. It was an efficient way to alleviate overcrowded jails.' He shook his head in disbelief. 'Anyway, they, of course, had no idea what they were doing, and there were some horrible stories of people suffering. This is capital punishment, right? Not capital torture. And it wasn't just Mississippi. Many states were using these old, half-ass rigged electric chairs with a bunch of jakelegs pulling the switches, and there were all sorts of problems. They'd strap in some poor guy, pull the switch, give him a good jolt but not good enough, guy was roasting on the inside but wouldn't die, so they'd wait a few minutes, and hit him again. This might go on for fifteen minutes.

221

They wouldn't fasten the electrodes properly, and it was not uncommon for flames and sparks to shoot from the eyes and ears. I read an account of a guy who received an improper voltage. The steam built up in his head and his eyeballs popped out. Blood ran down his face. During an electrocution, the skin gets so hot that they can't touch the guy for a while, so in the old days they had to let him cool off before they could tell if he was dead. There are lots of stories about men who would sit still after the initial jolt, then start breathing again. So they would of course hit 'em with another current. This might happen four or five times. It was awful, so this Army doctor invented the gas chamber as a more humane way to kill people. It is now, as you say, obsolete because of lethal injection.'

Sam had an audience, and Adam was captivated. 'How many men have died in Mississippi's chamber?' he asked.

'It was first used here in 1954, or thereabouts. Between then and 1970, they killed thirty-five men. No women. After *Furman* in 1972, it sat idle until Teddy Doyle Meeks in 1982. They've used it three times since then, so that's a total of thirty-nine. I'll be number forty.'

He began pacing again, now much slower. 'It's a terribly inefficient way to kill people,' he said, much like a professor in front of a classroom. 'And it's dangerous. Dangerous of course to the poor guy strapped in the chair, but also to those outside the chamber. These damned things are old and they all leak to some degree. The seals and gaskets rot and crumble, and the cost of building a chamber that will not leak is prohibitive. A small leak could be deadly to the executioner or anyone standing nearby. There are always a handful of people – Naifeh, Lucas Mann, maybe a minister, the doctor, a guard or two – standing in the little room just outside the chamber. There are two doors to this little room, and they are always closed during an execution. If any of the gas leaked from the chamber into the room, it would probably hit Naifeh or Lucas Mann and they'd croak right there on the floor. Not a bad idea, come to think of it.

'The witnesses are also in a great deal of danger, and they

222

don't have a clue. There's nothing between them and the chamber except for a row of windows, which are old and equally subject to leakage. They're also in a small room with the door closed, and if there's a gas leak of any size these gawking fools get gassed too.

'But the real danger comes afterward. There's a wire they stick to your ribs and it runs through a hole in the chamber to outside where a doctor monitors the heartbeat. Once the doctor says the guy is dead, they open a valve on top of the chamber and the gas is supposed to evaporate. Most of it does. They'll wait fifteen minutes or so, then open the door. The cooler air from the outside that's used to evacuate the chamber causes a problem because it mixes with the remaining gas and condenses on everything inside. It creates a death trap for anyone going in. It's extremely dangerous, and most of these clowns don't realize how serious it is. There's a residue of prussic acid on everything – walls, windows, floor, ceiling, door, and, of course, the dead guy.

'They spray the chamber and the corpse with ammonia to neutralize the remaining gas, then the removal team or whatever it's called goes in with oxygen masks. They'll wash the inmate a second time with ammonia or chlorine bleach because the poison oozes through the pores in the skin. While he's still strapped in the chair, they cut his clothes off, put them in a bag, and burn them. In the old days they allowed the guy to wear only a pair of shorts so their job would be easier. But now they're such sweethearts they allow us to wear whatever we want. So if I get that far, I'll have a hell of a time selecting my wardrobe.'

He actually spat on the floor as he thought about this. He cursed under his breath and stomped around the far end of the table.

'What happens to the body?' Adam asked, somewhat ashamed to tread on such sensitive matters but nonetheless anxious to complete the story.

Sam grunted a time or two, then stuck the cigarette in his mouth. 'Do you know the extent of my wardrobe?'

'No.'

'Consists of two of these red monkey suits, four or five sets of clean underwear, and one pair of these cute little rubber shower shoes that look like leftovers from a nigger fire sale. I refuse to die in one of these red suits. I've thought about exercising my constitutional rights and parading into the chamber buck naked. Wouldn't that be a sight? Can you see those goons trying to shove me around and strap me in and trying like hell not to touch my privates. And when they get me strapped down, I'll reach over and take the little heart monitor gizmo and attach it to my testicles. Wouldn't the doctor love that? And I'd make sure the witnesses saw my bare ass. I think that's what I'll do.'

'What happens to the body?' Adam asked again.

'Well, once it's sufficiently washed and disinfected, they dress it in prison garb, pull it out of the chair, then put it in a body bag. They place it on a stretcher which goes into the ambulance which takes it to a funeral home somewhere. The family takes over at that point. Most families.'

Sam was now standing with his back to Adam, talking to a wall and leaning on a bookshelf. He was silent for a long time, silent and still as he gazed into the corner and thought about the four men he'd known who had already gone to the chamber. There was an unwritten rule on the Row that when your time came you did not go to the chamber in a red prison suit. You did not give them the satisfaction of killing you in the clothes they'd forced you to wear.

Maybe his brother, the one who sent the monthly supply of cigarettes, would help with a shirt and a pair of pants. New socks would be nice. And anything but the rubber shower shoes. He'd rather go barefoot than wear those damned things.

He turned and walked slowly to Adam's end of the table and took a seat. 'I like this idea,' he said, very quiet and composed. 'It's worth a try.'

'Good. Let's get to work. I want you to find more cases like Jimmy Old from North Carolina. Let's dig up every wretched and botched gas chamber execution known to man. We'll throw 'em all in the lawsuit. I want you to make a list of people who might testify about the Meeks and Tole executions. Maybe even Moac and Parris.'

Sam was already on his feet again, pulling books from shelves and mumbling to himself. He piled them on the table, dozens of them, then buried himself among the stacks.

NINETEEN

THE ROLLING WHEAT FIELDS stretched for miles then grew steeper as the foothills began. The majestic mountains lined the farmland in the distance. In a sweeping valley above the fields, with a view for miles in front and with the mountains as a barrier to the rear, the Nazi compound lay sprawled over a hundred acres. Its barbed-wire fences were camouflaged with hedgerows and underbrush. Its firing ranges and combat grounds were likewise screened to prevent detection from the air. Only two innocuous log cabins sat above the ground, and if seen from the outside would appear only to be fishing lodges. But below them, deep in the hills, were two shafts with elevators which dropped into a maze of natural caverns and man-made caves. Large tunnels, wide enough for golf carts, ran in all directions and connected a dozen different rooms. One room had a printing press. Two stored weapons, and ammunition. Three large ones were living quarters. One was a small library. The largest room, a cavern forty feet from top to bottom, was the central hall where the members gathered for speeches and films and rallies.

It was a state-of-the-art compound, with satellite dishes feeding televisions with news from around the world, and computers linked to other compounds for the quick flow of information, and fax machines, cellular phones, and every current electronic device in vogue.

No less than ten newspapers were received into the compound each day, and they were taken to a table in a room next to the library where they were first read by a man named Roland. He lived in the compound most of the time, along with several other members who maintained the place. When the newspapers arrived from the city, usually around nine in the morning, Roland poured himself a large cup of coffee and started reading. It was not a chore. He had traveled the world many times, spoke four languages, and had a voracious appetite for knowledge. If a story caught his attention, he would mark it, and later he would make a copy of it and give it to the computer desk.

His interests were varied. He barely scanned the sports, and never looked at the want ads. Fashion, style, living, fanfare, and related sections were browsed with little curiosity. He collected stories about groups similar to his – Aryans, Nazis, the KKK. Lately, he'd been flagging many stories from Germany and Eastern Europe, and was quite thrilled with the rise of fascism there. He spoke fluent German and spent at least one month a year in that great country. He watched the politicians, with their deep concern about hate crimes and their desire to restrict the rights of groups such as his. He watched the Supreme Court. He followed the trials of skinheads in the United States. He followed the tribulations of the KKK.

He normally spent two hours each morning absorbing the latest news and deciding which stories should be kept for future reference. It was routine, but he enjoyed it immensely.

This particular morning would be different. The first glimpse of trouble was a picture of Sam Cayhall buried deep in the front section of a San Francisco daily. The story had but three paragraphs, but sufficiently covered the hot news that the oldest man on death row in America would now be represented by his grandson. Roland read it three times before he believed it, then marked the story to be saved. After an hour, he'd read the same story five or six times. Two papers had the snapshot of young Adam Hall that appeared on the front page of the Memphis paper the day before.

Roland had followed the case of Sam Cayhall for many years, and for several reasons. First, it was normally the type of case that would interest their computers – an aging Klan terrorist from the sixties biding his time on death row. The Cayhall printout was already a foot thick. Though he was certainly no lawyer, Roland shared the prevailing opinion that Sam's appeals had run their course and he was about to die. This suited Roland just fine, but he kept his opinion to himself. Sam Cayhall was a hero to white supremacists, and Roland's own little band of Nazis had already been asked to participate in demonstrations before the execution. They had no direct contact with Cayhall because he had never answered their letters, but he was a symbol and they wanted to make the most of his death.

Roland's last name, Forchin, was of Cajun extraction from down around Thibodaux. He had no Social Security number; never filed tax returns; did not exist, as far as the government was concerned. He had three beautifully forged passports, one of which was German, and one allegedly issued by the Republic of Ireland. Roland crossed borders and cleared immigration with no worries.

One of Roland's other names, known only to himself and never divulged to a breathing soul, was Rollie Wedge. He had fled the United States in 1967 after the Kramer bombing, and had lived in Northern Ireland. He had also lived in Libya, Munich, Belfast, and Lebanon. He had returned to the United States briefly in 1967 and 1968 to observe the two trials of Sam Cayhall and Jeremiah Dogan. By then, he was traveling effortlessly with perfect papers.

There had been a few other quick trips back to the United States, all required because of the Cayhall mess. But as time passed, he worried about it less. He had moved to this bunker three years earlier to spread the message of Nazism. He no longer considered himself a Klansman. Now, he was a proud fascist.

When he finished his morning reading, he had found the Cayhall story in seven of the ten papers. He placed them in a metal basket, and decided to see the sun. He poured more coffee in his Styrofoam cup, and rode an elevator eighty feet to a foyer in a log cabin. It was a beautiful day, cool and sunny, not a cloud to be seen. He walked upward along a narrow trail toward the mountains, and within ten minutes was looking at the valley below him. The wheat fields were in the distance.

Roland had been dreaming of Cayhall's death for twenty-three years. They shared a secret, a heavy burden which would be lifted only when Sam was executed. He admired the man greatly. Unlike Jeremiah Dogan, Sam had honored his oath and never talked. Through three trials, several lawyers, countless appeals, and millions of inquiries, Sam Cayhall had never yielded. He was an honorable man, and Roland wanted him dead. Oh sure, he'd been forced to deliver a few threats to Cayhall and Dogan during the first two trials, but that was so long ago. Dogan cracked under pressure, and he talked and testified against Sam. And Dogan died.

This kid worried him. Like everyone else, Roland had lost track of Sam's son and his family. He knew about the daughter in Memphis, but the son had disappeared. And now this – this nice-looking, well-educated young lawyer from a big, rich Jewish law firm had popped up from nowhere and was primed to save his grandfather. Roland knew enough about executions to understand that in the waning hours the lawyers try everything. If Sam was going to crack, he would do it now, and he would do it in the presence of his grandson.

He tossed a rock down the hillside and watched it bounce out of sight. He'd have to go to Memphis.

SATURDAY was typically just another day of hard labor at Kravitz & Bane in Chicago, but things were a bit more laid-back at the Memphis branch. Adam arrived at the office at nine and found only two other attorneys and one paralegal at work. He locked himself in his room and closed the blinds.

He and Sam had worked for two hours yesterday, and by

the time Packer returned to the law library with the handcuffs and the shackles they had managed to cover the table with dozens of law books and legal pads. Packer had waited impatiently as Sam slowly reshelved the books.

Adam reviewed their notes. He entered his own research into the computer, and revised the petition for the third time. He had already faxed a copy of it to Garner Goodman, who in turn had revised it and sent it back.

Goodman was not optimistic about a fair hearing on the suit, but at this stage of the proceedings there was nothing to lose. If by chance an expedited hearing was held in federal court, Goodman was ready to testify about the Maynard Tole execution. He and Peter Wiesenberg had witnessed it. In fact, Wiesenberg had been so sickened by the sight of a living person being gassed that he resigned from the firm and took a job teaching. His grandfather had survived the Holocaust; his grandmother had not. Goodman promised to contact Wiesenberg, and felt confident he too would testify.

By noon, Adam was tired of the office. He unlocked his door and heard no sounds on the floor. The other lawyers were gone. He left the building.

He drove west, over the river into Arkansas, past the truck stops and dog track in West Memphis, and finally through the congestion and into the farm country. He passed the hamlets of Earle and Parkin and Wynne, where the hills began. He stopped for a Coke at a country grocery where three old men in faded overalls sat on a porch swatting flies and suffering in the heat. He lowered the convertible top and sped away.

Two hours later he stopped again, this time in the town of Mountain View to get a sandwich and ask directions. Calico Rock was not far up the road, he was told, just follow the White River. It was a lovely road, winding through the foothills of the Ozarks, through heavy woods and across mountain streams. The White River snaked its way along to the left, and it was dotted with trout fishermen in jon boats.

Calico Rock was a small town on a bluff above the river.

Three trout docks lined the east bank near the bridge. Adam parked by the river and walked to the first one, an outfitter called Calico Marina. The building floated on pontoons, and was held close to the bank by thick cables. A row of empty rental boats was strung together next to the pier. The pungent smell of gasoline and oil emanated from a solitary gas pump. A sign listed the rates for boats, guides, gear, and fishing licenses.

Adam walked onto the covered dock and admired the river a few feet away. A young man with dirty hands emerged from a back room and asked if he could be of assistance. He examined Adam from top to bottom, and apparently decided that he was no fisherman.

'I'm looking for Wyn Lettner.'

The name Ron was stitched above the shirt pocket and slightly covered with a smudge of grease. Ron walked back to his room and yelled, 'Mr. Lettner!' in the direction of a screen door that led to a small shop. Ron disappeared.

Wyn Lettner was a huge man, well over six feet tall with a large frame that was quite overloaded. Garner had described him as a beer drinker, and Adam remembered this as he glanced at the large stomach. He was in his late sixties, with thinning gray hair tucked neatly under an EVINRUDE cap. There were at least three newspaper photographs of Special Agent Lettner indexed away somewhere in Adam's files, and in each he was the standard G-Man – dark suit, white shirt, narrow tie, military haircut. And he was much trimmer in those days.

'Yes, sir,' he said loudly as he walked through the screen door, wiping crumbs from his lips. 'I'm Wyn Lettner.' He had a deep voice and a pleasant smile.

Adam pushed forward a hand, and said, 'I'm Adam Hall. Nice to meet you.'

Lettner took his hand and shook it furiously. His forearms were massive and his biceps bulged. 'Yes sir,' he boomed. 'What can I do for you?'

Thankfully the dock was deserted, with the exception of Ron, who was out of sight but making noises with a tool in

231

his room. Adam fidgeted a bit, and said, 'Well, I'm a lawyer, and I represent Sam Cayhall.'

The smile grew and revealed two rows of strong yellow teeth. 'Got your work cut out for you, don't you?' he said with a laugh and slapped Adam on the back.

'I guess so,' Adam said awkwardly as he waited for another assault. 'I'd like to talk about Sam.'

Lettner was suddenly serious. He stroked his chin with a beefy hand and studied Adam with narrow eyes. 'I saw it in the papers, son. I know Sam's your grandfather. Must be tough on you. Gonna get tougher, too.' Then he smiled again. 'Tougher on Sam as well.' His eyes twinkled as if he'd just delivered a side-splitting punch line and he wanted Adam to double over with laughter.

Adam missed the humor. 'Sam has less than a month, you know,' he said, certain that Lettner had also read about the execution date.

A heavy hand was suddenly on Adam's shoulder and was shoving him in the direction of the shop. 'Step in here, son. We'll talk about Sam. You wanna beer?'

'No. Thanks.' They entered a narrow room with fishing gear hanging from the walls and ceilings, with rickety wooden shelves covered with food – crackers, sardines, canned sausages, bread, pork and beans, cupcakes – all the necessities for a day on the river. A soft drink cooler sat in one corner.

'Take a seat,' Lettner said, waving to a corner near the cash register. Adam sat in a shaky wooden chair as Lettner fished through an ice chest and found a bottle of beer. 'Sure you don't want one?'

'Maybe later.' It was almost five o'clock.

He twisted the top, drained at least a third of the bottle with the first gulp, smacked his lips, then sat in a beaten leather captain's chair which had no doubt been removed from a customized van. 'Are they finally gonna get old Sam?' he asked.

'They're trying awfully hard.'

'What're the odds?'

'Not good. We have the usual assortment of last minute appeals, but the clock's ticking.'

'Sam's not a bad guy,' Lettner said with a trace of remorse, then washed it away with another long drink. The floor creaked quietly as the dock shifted with the river.

'How long were you in Mississippi?' Adam asked.

'Five years. Hoover called me after the three civil rights workers disappeared. Nineteen sixty-four. We set up a special unit and went to work. After Kramer, the Klan sort of ran out of gas.'

'And you were in charge of what?'

'Mr Hoover was very specific. He told me to infiltrate the Klan at all costs. He wanted it busted up. To be truthful, we were slow getting started in Mississippi. Bunch of reasons for it. Hoover hated the Kennedys and they were pushing him hard, so he dragged his feet. But when those three boys disappeared, we got off our asses. Nineteen sixty-four was a helluva year in Mississippi.'

'I was born that year.'

'Yeah, paper said you were born in Clanton.'

Adam nodded. 'I didn't know it for a long time. My parents told me I was born in Memphis.'

The door jingled and Ron entered the shop. He looked at them, then studied the crackers and sardines. They watched him and waited. He glanced at Adam as if to say, 'Keep talking. I'm not listening.'

'What do you want?' Lettner snapped at him.

He grabbed a can of Vienna sausage with his dirty hand and showed it to them. Lettner nodded and waved at the door. Ron ambled toward it, checking the cupcakes and potato chips as he went.

'He's nosy as hell,' Lettner said after he was gone. 'I talked to Garner Goodman a few times. It was years ago. Now, that's a weird bird.'

'He's my boss. He gave me your name, said you'd talk to me.'

'Talk about what?' Lettner asked, then took another drink.

'The Kramer case.'

233

'The Kramer case is closed. The only thing left is Sam and his date with the gas chamber.'

'Do you want him executed?'

Voices followed footsteps, then the door opened again. A man and a boy entered and Lettner got to his feet. They needed food and supplies, and for ten minutes they shopped and talked and decided where the fish were biting. Lettner was careful to place his beer under the counter while his customers were present.

Adam removed a soft drink from the cooler and left the shop. He walked along the edge of the wooden dock next to the river, and stopped by the gas pump. Two teenagers in a boat were casting near the bridge, and it struck Adam that he'd never been fishing in his life. His father had not been a man of hobbies and leisure. Nor had he been able to keep a job. At the moment, Adam could not remember exactly what his father had done with his time.

The customers left and the door slammed. Lattner lumbered to the gas pump. 'You like to trout fish?' he asked, admiring the river.

'No. Never been.'

'Let's go for a ride. I need to check out a spot two miles downriver. The fish are supposed to be thick.'

Lettner was carrying his ice chest which he dropped carefully into a boat. He stepped down from the dock, and the boat rocked violently from side to side as he grabbed the motor. 'Come on,' he yelled at Adam, who was studying the thirty-inch gap between himself and the boat. 'And grab that rope,' Lettner yelled again, pointing to a thin cord hooked to a grapple.

Adam unhitched the rope and stepped nervously into the boat, which rocked just as his foot touched it. He slipped and landed on his head and came within inches of taking a swim. Lettner howled with laughter as he pulled the starter rope. Ron, of course, had watched this and was grinning stupidly on the dock. Adam was embarrassed but laughed as if it was all very funny. Lettner gunned the engine, the front of the boat jerked upward, and they were off.

234

Adam clutched the handles on both sides as they sped through the water and under the bridge. Calico Rock was soon behind them. The river turned and twisted its way through scenic hills and around rocky bluffs. Lettner navigated with one hand and sipped a fresh beer with the other. After a few minutes, Adam relaxed somewhat and managed to pull a beer from the cooler without losing his balance. The bottle was ice cold. He held it with his right hand and clutched the boat with his left. Lettner was humming or singing something behind him. The high-pitched roar of the motor prevented conversation.

They passed a small trout dock where a group of clean-cut city slickers were counting fish and drinking beer, and they passed a flotilla of rubber rafts filled with mangy teenagers smoking something and absorbing the sun. They waved at other fishermen who were hard at work.

The boat slowed finally and Lettner maneuvered it carefully through a bend as if he could see the fish below and had to position himself perfectly. He turned off the engine. 'You gonna fish or drink beer?' he asked, staring at the water.

'Drink beer.'

'Figures.' His bottle was suddenly of secondary importance as he took the rod and cast to a spot toward the bank. Adam watched for a second, and when there was no immediate result he reclined and hung his feet over the water. The boat was not comfortable.

'How often do you fish?' he asked.

'Every day. It's part of my job, you know, part of my service to my customers. I have to know where the fish are biting.'

'Tough job.'

'Somebody has to do it.'

'What brought you to Calico Rock?'

'Had a heart attack in '75, so I had to retire from the Bureau. Had a nice pension and all, but, hell, you get bored just sitting around. The wife and I found this place and found the marina for sale. One mistake led to another, and here I am. Hand me a beer.'

He cast again as Adam dispensed the beer. He quickly counted fourteen bottles remaining in the ice. The boat drifted with the river, and Lettner grabbed a paddle. He fished with one hand, sculled the boat with the other, and somehow balanced a fresh beer between his knees. The life of a fishing guide.

They slowed under some trees, and the sun was mercifully shielded for a while. He made the casting look easy. He whipped the rod with a smooth wrist action, and sent the lure anywhere he wanted. But the fish weren't biting. He cast toward the middle of the river.

'Sam's not a bad guy.' He'd already said this once.

'Do you think he should be executed?'

'That's not up to me, son. The people of the state want the death penalty, so it's on the books. The people said Sam was guilty and then said he should be executed, so who am I?'

'But you have an opinion.'

'What good is it? My thoughts are completely worthless.'

'Why do you say Sam's not a bad guy?'

'It's a long story.'

'We have fourteen beers left.'

Lettner laughed and the vast smile returned. He gulped from the bottle and looked down the river, away from his line. 'Sam was of no concern to us, you understand. He was not active in the really nasty stuff, at least not at first. When those civil rights workers disappeared, we went in with a fury. We spread money all over the place, and before long we had all sorts of Klan informants. These people were basically just ignorant rednecks who'd never had a dime, and we preyed on their craving for money. We'd have never found those three boys had we not dropped some cash. About thirty thousand, as I remember it, though I didn't deal directly with the informant. Hell, son, they were buried in a levee. We found them, and it made us look good, you understand. Finally, we'd accomplished something. Made a bunch of arrests, but the convictions were difficult. The violence continued. They bombed black churches and

236

black homes so damned often we couldn't keep up. It was like a war down there. It got worse, and Mr Hoover got madder, and we spread around more money.

'Listen, son, I'm not going to tell you anything useful, you understand?'

'Why not?'

'Some things I can talk about, some I can't.'

'Sam wasn't alone when he bombed the Kramer office, was he?'

Lettner smiled again and studied his line. The rod was sitting in his lap. 'Anyway, by late '65 and early '66, we had a helluva network of informants. It really wasn't that difficult. We'd learn that some guy was in the Klan, and so we'd trail him. We'd follow him home at night, flashing our lights behind him, parking in front of his house. It'd usually scare him to death. Then we'd follow him to work, sometimes we'd go talk to his boss, flash our badges around, act like we were about to shoot somebody. We'd go talk to his parents, show them our badges, let them see us in our dark suits, let them hear our Yankee accents, and these poor country people would literally crack up right in front of us. If the guy went to church, we'd follow him one Sunday, then the next day we'd go talk to his preacher. We'd tell him that we had heard a terrible rumor that Mr Such and Such was an active member of the Klan, and did he know anything about it. We acted like it was a crime to be a member of the Klan. If the guy had teenage children, we'd follow them on dates, sit behind them at the movies, catch them parking in the woods. It was nothing but pure harassment, but it worked. Finally, we'd call the poor guy or catch him alone somewhere, and offer him some money. We'd promise to leave him alone, and it always worked. Usually, they were nervous wrecks by this time, they couldn't wait to cooperate. I saw them cry, son, if you can believe it. Actually cry when they finally came to the altar and confessed their sins.' Lettner laughed in the direction of his line, which was quite inactive.

Adam sipped his beer. Perhaps if they drank it all it would eventually loosen his tongue.

'Had this guy one time, I'll never forget him. We caught him in bed with his black mistress, which was not unusual. I mean, these guys would go out burning crosses and shooting into black homes, then sneak around like crazy to meet their black girlfriends. Never could understand why the black women put up with it. Anyway, he had a little hunting lodge deep in the woods, and he used it for a love nest. He met her there one afternoon for a quickie, and when he was finished and ready to go, he opened the front door and we took his picture. Got her picture too, and then we talked to him. He was a deacon or an elder in some country church, a real pillar, you know, and we talked to him like he was a dog. We ran her off and sat him down inside the little lodge there, and before long he was crying. As it turned out, he was one of our best witnesses. But he later went to jail.'

'Why?'

'Well, it seems that while he was sneaking around with his girlfriend, his wife was doing the same thing with a black kid who worked on their farm. Lady got pregnant, baby was half and half, so our informant goes to the hospital and kills mother and child. He spent fifteen years at Parchman.'

'Good.'

'We didn't get a lot of convictions back in those days, but harassed them to a point where they were afraid to do much. The violence had slowed considerably until Dogan decided to go after the Jews. That caught us off guard, I have to admit. We had no clue.'

'Why not?'

'Because he got smart. He learned the hard way that his own people would talk to us, so he decided to operate with a small, quiet unit.'

'Unit? As in more than one person?'

'Something like that.'

'As in Sam and who else?'

Lettner snorted and chuckled at once, and decided the fish had moved elsewhere. He placed his rod and reel in the boat, and yanked on the starter cord. They were off, racing once again downstream. Adam left his feet over the side, and his leather moccasins and bare ankles were soon wet. He sipped the beer. The sun was finally beginning to disappear behind the hills, and he enjoyed the beauty of the river.

The next stop was a stretch of still water below a bluff with a rope hanging from it. Lettner cast and reeled, all to no effect, and assumed the role of interrogator. He asked a hundred questions about Adam and his family – the flight westward, the new identities, the suicide. He explained that while Sam was in jail they checked out his family and knew he had a son who had just left town, but since Eddie appeared to be harmless they did not pursue the investigation. Instead, they spent their time watching Sam's brothers and cousins. He was intrigued by Adam's youth, and how he was raised with virtually no knowledge of kinfolks.

Adam asked a few questions, but the answers were vague and immediately twisted into more questions about his past. Adam was sparring with a man who'd spent twenty-five years asking questions.

The third and final hot spot was not far from Calico Rock, and they fished until it was dark. After five beers, Adam mustered the courage to wet a hook. Lettner was a patient instructor, and within minutes Adam had caught an impressive trout. For a brief interlude, they forgot about Sam and the Klan and other nightmares from the past, and they simply fished. They drank and fished.

MRS LETTNER'S FIRST NAME was Irene, and she welcomed her husband and his unexpected guest with grace and nonchalance. Wyn had explained, as Ron drove them home, that Irene was accustomed to drop-ins. She certainly seemed to be unruffled as they staggered through the front door and handed her a string of trout.

The Lettner home was a cottage on the river a mile north of town. The rear porch was screened to protect it from

239

insects, and not far below it was a splendid view of the river. They sat in wicker rockers on the porch, and opened another round of brew as Irene fried the fish.

Putting food on the table was a new experience for Adam, and he ate the fish he'd caught with great gusto. It always tastes better, Wyn assured him as he chomped and drank, when you catch it yourself. About half-way through the meal, Wyn switched to Scotch. Adam declined. He wanted a simple glass of water, but machismo drove him to continue with the beer. He couldn't wimp out at this point. Lettner would certainly chastise him.

Irene sipped wine and told stories about Mississippi. She had been threatened on several occasions, and their children refused to visit them. They were both from Ohio, and their families worried constantly about their safety. Those were the days, she said more than once with a certain longing for excitement. She was extremely proud of her husband and his performance during the war for civil rights.

She left them after dinner and disappeared somewhere in the cottage. It was almost ten o'clock, and Adam was ready for sleep. Wyn rose to his feet while holding onto a wooden beam, and excused himself for a visit to the bathroom. He returned in due course with two fresh Scotches in tall glasses. He handed one to Adam, and returned to his rocker.

They rocked and sipped in silence for a moment, then Lettner said, 'So you're convinced Sam had some help.'

'Of course he had some help.' Adam was very much aware that his tongue was thick and his words were slow. Lettner's speech was remarkably articulate.

'And what makes you so certain?'

Adam lowered the heavy glass and vowed not to take another drink. 'The FBI searched Sam's house after the bombing, right?'

'Right.'

'Sam was in jail in Greenville, and you guys got a warrant.'

'I was there, son. We went in with a dozen agents and spent three days.'

240

'And found nothing.'

'You could say that.'

'No trace of dynamite. No trace of blasting caps, fuses, detonators. No trace of any device or substance used in any of the bombings. Correct?'

'That's correct. So what's your point?'

'Sam had no knowledge of explosives, nor did he have a history of using them.'

'No, I'd say he had quite a history of using them. Kramer was the sixth bombing, as I recall. Those crazy bastards were bombing like hell, son, and we couldn't stop them. You weren't there. I was in the middle of it. We had harassed the Klan and infiltrated to a point where they were afraid to move, then all of a sudden another war erupted and bombs were falling everywhere. We listened where we were supposed to listen. We twisted familiar arms until they broke. And we were clueless. Our informants were clueless. It was like another branch of the Klan had suddenly invaded Mississippi without telling the old one.'

'Did you know about Sam?'

'His name was in our records. As I recall, his father had been a Klucker, and maybe a brother or two. So we had their names. But they seemed harmless. They lived in the northern part of the state, in an area not known for serious Klan violence. They probably burned some crosses, maybe shot up a few houses, but nothing compared to Dogan and his gang. We had our hands full with murderers. We didn't have time to investigate every possible Klucker in the state.'

'Then how do you explain Sam's sudden shift to violence?'

'Can't explain it. He was no choirboy, okay? He had killed before.'

'Are you sure?'

'You heard me. He shot and killed one of his black employees in the early fifties. Never spent a day in jail for it. In fact, I'm not sure, but I don't think he was ever arrested for it. There may have been another killing, too. Another black victim.'

241

'I'd rather not hear it.'

'Ask him. See if the old bastard has guts enough to admit it to his grandson.' He took another sip. 'He was a violent man, son, and he certainly had the capability to plant bombs and kill people. Don't be naive.'

'I'm not naive. I'm just trying to save his life.'

'Why? He killed two very innocent little boys. Two children. Do you realize this?'

'He was convicted of the murders. But if the killings were wrong, then it's wrong for the state to kill him.'

'I don't buy that crap. The death penalty is too good for these people. It's too clean and sterile. They know they're about to die, so they have time to say their prayers and say good-bye. What about the victims? How much time did they have to prepare?'

'So you want Sam executed?'

'Yeah. I want 'em all executed?'

'I thought you said he wasn't a bad guy.'

'I lied. Sam Cayhall is a cold-blooded killer. And he's guilty as hell. How else can you explain the fact that the bombings stopped as soon as he was in custody?'

'Maybe they were scared after Kramer?'

'They? Who the hell is they?'

'Sam and his partner. And Dogan.'

'Okay. I'll play along. Let's assume Sam had an accomplice.'

'No. Let's assume Sam was the accomplice. Let's assume the other guy was the explosives expert.'

'Expert? These were very crude bombs, son. The first five were nothing more than a few sticks wrapped together with a fuse. You light the match, run like hell, and fifteen minutes later, Boom! The Kramer bomb was nothing but a half-ass rig with an alarm clock wired to it. They were lucky it didn't go off while they were playing with it.'

'Do you think it was deliberately set to go off when it did?'

'The jury thought so. Dogan said they planned to kill Marvin Kramer.'

'Then why was Sam hanging around? Why was he close enough to the bomb to get hit with debris?'

'You'll have to ask Sam, which I'm sure you've already done. Does he claim he had an accomplice?'

'No.'

'Then that settles it. If your own client says no, what the hell are you digging for?'

'Because I think my client is lying.'

'Too bad for your client, then. If he wants to lie and protect the identity of someone, then why should you care?'

'Why would he lie to me?'

Lettner shook his head in frustration, then mumbled something and took a drink. 'How the hell am I supposed to know? I don't want to know, okay? I honestly don't care if Sam's lying or if Sam's telling the truth. But if he won't level with you, his lawyer and his own grandson, then I say gas him.'

Adam took a long drink and stared into the darkness. He actually felt silly at times digging around trying to prove his own client was lying to him. He'd give this another shot, then talk about something else. 'You don't believe the witnesses who saw Sam with another person?'

'No. They were pretty shaky, as I recall. The guy at the truck stop didn't come forward for a long time. The other guy had just left a honky-tonk. They weren't credible.'

'Do you believe Dogan?'

'The jury did.'

'I didn't ask about the jury.'

Lettner's breathing was finally getting heavy, and he appeared to be fading. 'Dogan was crazy, and Dogan was a genius. He said the bomb was intended to kill, and I believe him. Keep in mind, Adam, they almost wiped out an entire family in Vicksburg. I can't remember the name –'

'Pinder. And you keep saying *they* did this and that.'

'I'm just playing along, okay. We're assuming Sam had a buddy with him. They planted a bomb at the Pinder house in the middle of the night. An entire family could've been killed.'

'Sam said he placed the bomb in the garage so no one would get hurt.'

'Sam told you this? Sam admitted he did it? Then why in the hell are you asking me about an accomplice? Sounds like you need to listen to your client. Son of a bitch is guilty, Adam. Listen to him.'

Adam took another drink and his eyelids grew heavier. He looked at his watch, but couldn't see it. 'Tell me about the tapes,' he said, yawning.

'What tapes?' Lettner asked, yawning.

'The FBI tapes they played at Sam's trial. The ones with Dogan talking to Wayne Graves about bombing Kramer.'

'We had lots of tapes. And they had lots of targets. Kramer was just one of many. Hell, we had a tape with two Kluckers talking about bombing a synagogue while a wedding was in progress. They wanted to bolt the doors and shoot some gas through the heating ducts so the entire congregation would be wiped out. Sick bastards, man. It wasn't Dogan, just a couple of his idiots talking trash, and so we dismissed it. Wayne Graves was a Klucker who was also on our payroll, and he allowed us to tap his phones. He called Dogan one night, said he was on a pay phone, and they got to talking about hitting Kramer. They also talked about other targets. It was very effective at Sam's trial. But the tapes did not help us stop a single bombing. Nor did they help us identify Sam.'

'You had no idea Sam Cayhall was involved?'

'None whatsoever. If the fool had left Greenville when he should have, he'd probably still be a free man.'

'Did Kramer know he was a target?'

'We told him. But by then he was accustomed to threats. He kept a guard at his house.' His words were starting to slur a bit, and his chin had dropped an inch or two.

Adam excused himself and cautiously made his way to the bathroom. As he returned to the porch, he heard heavy snoring. Lettner had slumped in his chair and collapsed with the drink in his hand. Adam removed it, then left in search of a sofa.

TWENTY

THE LATE MORNING was warm but seemed downright feverish in the front of the Army surplus jeep, which lacked air conditioning and other essentials. Adam sweated and kept his hand on the handle of the door which he hoped would open promptly in the event Irene's breakfast came roaring up.

He had awakened on the floor beside a narrow sofa in a room which he had mistaken for the den, but was in fact the washroom beside the kitchen. And the sofa was a bench, Lettner had explained with much laughter, that he used to sit on to take off his boots. Irene had eventually found his body after searching the house, and Adam apologized profusely until they both asked him to stop. She had insisted on a heavy breakfast. It was their one day of the week to eat pork, a regular tradition around the Lettner cottage, and Adam had sat at the kitchen table guzzling ice water while the bacon fried and Irene hummed and Wyn read the paper. She also scrambled eggs and mixed bloody marys.

The vodka deadened some of the pain in his head, but it also did nothing to calm his stomach. As they bounced toward Calico Rock on the bumpy road, Adam was terrified that he would be sick.

Though Lettner had passed out first, he was remarkably healthy this morning. No sign of a hangover. He'd eaten a plate full of grease and biscuits, and he'd sipped only one bloody mary. He'd diligently read the paper and

245

commented about this and that, and Adam figured he was one of those functional alcoholics who got plastered every night but shook it off easily.

The village was in view. The road was suddenly smoother and Adam's stomach stopped bouncing. 'Sorry about last night,' Lettner said.

'What?' Adam asked.

'About Sam. I was harsh. I know he's your grandfather and you're very concerned. I lied about something. I really don't want Sam to be executed. He's not a bad guy.'

'I'll tell him.'

'Yeah. I'm sure he'll be thrilled.'

They entered the town and turned toward the bridge. 'There's something else,' Lettner said. 'We always suspected Sam had a partner.'

Adam smiled and looked through his window. They passed a small church with elderly people standing under a shade tree in their pretty dresses and neat suits.

'Why?' Adam asked.

'For the same reasons. Sam had no history with bombs. He had not been involved in Klan violence. The two witnesses, especially the truck driver in Cleveland, always bothered us. The trucker had no reason to lie, and he seemed awfully certain of himself. Sam just didn't seem like the type to start his own bombing campaign.'

'So who's the man?'

'I honestly don't know.' They rolled to a stop by the river, and Adam opened his door just in case. Lettner leaned on the steering wheel, and cocked his head toward Adam. 'After the third or fourth bombing, I think maybe it was the synagogue in Jackson, some big Jews in New York and Washington met with LBJ, who in turn called in Mr Hoover, who in turn called me. I went to D.C., where I met with Mr Hoover and the President, and they pretty much crawled my ass. I returned to Mississippi with renewed determination. We came down hard on our informants. I mean, we hurt some people. We tried everything, but to no avail. Our sources simply did not know who was doing the

246

bombing. Only Dogan knew, and it was obvious he wasn't telling anybody. But after the fifth bomb, which I think was the newspaper office, we got a break.'

Lettner opened his door and walked to the front of the jeep. Adam joined him there, and they watched the river ease along through Calico Rock. 'You wanna beer? I keep it cold in the bait shop.'

'No, please. I'm half-sick now.'

'Just kidding. Anyway, Dogan ran this huge used car lot, and one of his employees was an illiterate old black man who washed the cars and swept the floors. We had carefully approached the old man earlier, but he was hostile. But out of the blue he tells one of our agents that he saw Dogan and another man putting something in the trunk of a green Pontiac a couple of days earlier. He said he waited, then opened the trunk and saw it was dynamite. The next day he heard that there was another bombing. He knew the FBI was swarming all around Dogan, so he figured it was worth mentioning to us. Dogan's helper was a Klucker named Virgil, also an employee. So I went to see Virgil. I knocked on his door at three o'clock one morning, just beat it like hell, you know, like we always did in those days, and before long he turned on the light and stepped on the porch. I had about eight agents with me, and we all stuck our badges in Virgil's face. He was scared to death. I told him we knew he had delivered the dynamite to Jackson the night before, and that he was looking at thirty years. You could hear his wife crying through the screen door. Virgil was shaking and ready to cry himself. I left him my card with instructions to call me before noon that very day, and I threatened him if he told Dogan or anybody else. I told him we'd be watching him around the clock.

'I doubt if Virgil went back to sleep. His eyes were red and puffy when he found me a few hours later. We got to be friends. He said the bombings were not the work of Dogan's usual gang. He didn't know much, but he'd heard enough from Dogan to believe that the bomber was a very young man from another state. This guy had dropped in

247

from nowhere, and was supposed to be very good with explosives. Dogan picked the targets, planned the jobs, then called this guy, who sneaked into town, carried out the bombings, then disappeared.'

'Did you believe him?'

'For the most part, yes. It just made sense. It had to be someone new, because by then we had riddled the Klan with informants. We knew virtually every move they made.'

'What happened to Virgil?'

'I spent some time with him, gave him some money, you know, the usual routine. They always wanted money. I became convinced he had no idea who was planting the bombs. He would never admit that he'd been involved, that he'd delivered the cars and dynamite, and we didn't press him. We weren't after him.'

'Was he involved with Kramer?'

'No. Dogan used someone else for that one. At times, Dogan seemed to have a sixth sense about when to mix things up, to change routines.'

'Virgil's suspect certainly doesn't sound like Sam Cayhall, does he?' Adam asked.

'No.'

'And you had no suspects?'

'No.'

'Come on, Wyn. Surely you guys had some idea.'

'I swear. We did not. Shortly after we met Virgil, Kramer got bombed and it was all over. If Sam had a buddy, then the buddy left him.'

'And the FBI heard nothing afterward?'

'Not a peep. We had Sam, who looked and smelled extremely guilty.'

'And, of course, you guys were anxious to close the case.'

'Certainly. And the bombings stopped, remember. There were no bombings after Sam got caught, don't forget that. We had our man. Mr Hoover was happy. The Jews were happy. The President was happy. Then they couldn't convict him for fourteen years, but that was a different story. Everyone was relieved when the bombings stopped.'

'So why didn't Dogan squeal on the real bomber when he squealed on Sam?'

They had eased down the bank to a point just inches above the water. Adam's car sat nearby. Lettner cleared his throat and spat into the river. 'Would you testify against a terrorist who was not in custody?'

Adam thought for a second. Lettner smiled, flashed his big yellow teeth, then chuckled as he started for the dock. 'Let's have a beer.'

'No. Please. I need to go.'

Lettner stopped, and they shook hands and promised to meet again. Adam invited him to Memphis, and Lettner invited him back to Calico Rock for more fishing and drinking. At the moment, his invitation was not well received. Adam sent his regards to Irene, apologized again for passing out in the washroom, and thanked him again for the chat.

He left the small town behind, driving gingerly around the curves and hills, still careful not to upset his stomach.

LEE WAS STRUGGLING with a pasta dish when he entered her apartment. The table was set with china and silver and fresh flowers. The recipe was baked manicotti, and things were not going well in the kitchen. On more than one occasion in the past week she'd confessed to being a lousy cook, and now she was proving it. Pots and pans were scattered along the countertops. Her seldom used apron was covered with tomato sauce. She laughed as they kissed each other on the cheeks and said there was a frozen pizza if matters got worse.

'You look awful,' she said, suddenly staring at his eyes.

'It was a rough night.'

'You smell like alcohol.'

'I had two bloody marys for breakfast. And I need another one now.'

'The bar's closed.' She picked up a knife and stepped to a pile of vegetables. A zucchini was the next victim. 'What did you do up there?'

'Got drunk with the FBI man. Slept on the floor next to his washer and dryer.'

'How nice.' She came within a centimeter of drawing blood. She jerked her hand away from the chopping block and examined a finger. 'Have you seen the Memphis paper?'

'No. Should I?'

'Yes. It's over there.' She nodded to a corner of the snack bar.

'Something bad?'

'Just read it.'

Adam took the Sunday edition of the *Memphis Press* and sat in a chair at the table. On the front page of the second section, he suddenly encountered his smiling face. It was a familiar photo, one taken not long ago when he was a second-year law student at Michigan. The story covered half the page, and his photo was joined by many others – Sam, of course, Marvin Kramer, Josh and John Kramer, Ruth Kramer, David McAllister, the Attorney General, Steve Roxburgh, Naifeh, Jeremiah Dogan, and Mr Elliot Kramer, father of Marvin.

Todd Marks had been busy. His narrative began with a succinct history of the case which took an entire column, then he moved quickly to the present and recapped the same story he'd written two days earlier. He found a bit more biographical data on Adam – college at Pepperdine, law school at Michigan, law review editor, brief employment history with Kravitz & Bane. Naifeh had very little to say, only that the execution would be carried out according to the law. McAllister, on the other hand, was full of wisdom. He had lived with the Kramer nightmare for twenty-three years, he said gravely, thinking about it every day of his life since it happened. It had been his honor and privilege to prosecute Sam Cayhall and bring the killer to justice, and only the execution could close this awful chapter of Mississippi's history. No, he said after much thought, the idea of clemency was out of the question. Just wouldn't be fair to the little Kramer boys. And on and on.

Steve Roxburgh had evidently enjoyed his interview too. He stood ready to fight the final efforts by Cayhall and his lawyer to thwart the execution. He and his staff were prepared to work eighteen hours a day to carry out the wishes of the people. This matter had dragged on long enough, he was quoted as saying more than once, and it was time for justice. No, he was not worried about the last ditch legal challenges of Mr Cayhall. He had confidence in his skills as a lawyer, the people's lawyer.

Sam Cayhall refused to comment, Marks explained, and Adam Hall couldn't be reached, as if Adam was eager to talk but simply couldn't be found.

The comments from the family were both interesting and disheartening. Elliot Kramer, now seventy-seven and still working, was described as spry and healthy in spite of heart trouble. He was also very bitter. He blamed the Klan and Sam Cayhall not only for killing his two grandsons, but also for Marvin's death. He'd been waiting twenty-three years for Sam to be executed, and it couldn't come a minute too soon. He lashed out at a judicial system that allows a convict to live for almost ten years after the jury gives him a death penalty. He was not certain if he would witness the execution, it would be up to his doctors, he said, but he wanted to be there and look Cayhall in the eyes when they strapped him in.

Ruth Kramer was a bit more moderate. Time had healed many of the wounds, she said, and she was unsure how she would feel after the execution. Nothing would bring back her sons. She had little to say to Todd Marks.

Adam folded the paper and placed it beside the chair. He suddenly had a knot in his fragile stomach, and it came from Steve Roxburgh and David McAllister. As the lawyer expected to save Sam's life, it was frightening to see his enemies so eager for the final battle. He was a rookie. They were veterans. Roxburgh in particular had been through it before, and he had an experienced staff which included a renowned specialist known as Dr Death, a skilled advocate with a passion for executions. Adam had nothing but an exhausted file full of unsuccessful appeals, and a prayer that a miracle would happen. At this moment he felt completely vulnerable and hopeless.

Lee sat next to him with a cup of espresso. 'You look worried,' she said, stroking his arm.

'My buddy at the trout dock was of no help.'

'Sounds like old man Kramer is hell-bent.'

Adam rubbed his temples and tried to ease the pain. 'I need a painkiller.'

'How about a Valium?'

'Wonderful.'

'Are you real hungry?'

'No. My stomach is not doing well.'

'Good. Dinner has been terminated. A slight problem with the recipe. It's frozen pizza or nothing.'

'Nothing sounds good to me. Nothing but a Valium.'

TWENTY-ONE

ADAM DROPPED HIS KEYS in the red bucket and watched it ascend to a point twenty feet off the ground where it stopped and spun slowly on the end of a rope. He walked to the first gate, which jerked before sliding open. He walked to the second gate, and waited. Packer emerged from the front door a hundred feet away, stretching and yawning as if he'd been napping on the Row.

The second gate closed behind him, and Packer waited nearby. 'Good day,' he said. It was almost two, the hottest time of the day. A morning radio forecaster had merrily predicted the first one-hundred-degree day of the year.

'Hello, Sergeant,' Adam said as if they were old friends now. They walked along the brick path to the small door with the weeds in front of it. Packer unlocked it, and Adam stepped inside.

'I'll get Sam,' Packer said, in no hurry, and disappeared.

The chairs on his side of the metal screen were scattered about. Two were flipped over, as if the lawyers and visitors had been brawling. Adam pulled one close to the counter at the far end, as far as possible from the air conditioner.

He removed a copy of the petition he'd filed at nine that morning. By law, no claim or issue could be raised in federal court unless it had first been presented and denied in state court. The petition attacking the gas chamber had been filed in the Mississippi Supreme Court under the state's postconviction relief statutes. It was a formality, in Adam's opinion, and in the opinion of Garner Goodman. Goodman had worked on the claim throughout the weekend. In fact, he'd worked all day Saturday while Adam was drinking beer and trout fishing with Wyn Lettner.

Sam arrived as usual, hands cuffed behind his back, no expression on his face, red jumpsuit unbuttoned almost to the waist. The gray hair on his pale chest was slick with perspiration. Like a well-trained animal, he turned his back to Packer, who quickly removed the cuffs, then left through the door. Sam immediately went for the cigarettes, and made certain one was lit before he sat down and said, 'Welcome back.'

'I filed this at nine this morning,' Adam said, sliding the petition through the narrow slit in the screen. 'I talked to the clerk with the Supreme Court in Jackson. She seemed to think the court will rule on it with due speed.'

Sam took the papers, and looked at Adam. 'You can bet on that. They'll deny it with great pleasure.'

'The state will be required to respond immediately, so we've got the Attorney General scrambling right now.'

'Great. We can watch the latest on the evening news. He's probably invited the cameras into his office while they prepare their response.'

Adam removed his jacket and loosened his tie. The room was humid and he was already sweating. 'Does the name Wyn Lettner ring a bell?'

Sam tossed the petition onto an empty chair and sucked hard on the filter. He released a steady stream of exhaust at the ceiling. 'Yes. Why?'

'Did you ever meet him?'

Sam thought about this for a moment, before speaking, and, as usual, spoke with measured words. 'Maybe. I'm not sure. I knew who he was at the time. Why?'

'I found him over the weekend. He's retired now, and runs a trout dock on the White River. We had a long talk.'

'That's nice. And what exactly did you accomplish?'

'He says he still thinks you had someone working with you.'

'Did he give you any names?'

254

'No. They never had a suspect, or so he says. But they had an informant, one of Dogan's people, who told Lettner that the other guy was someone new, not one of the usual gang. They thought he was from another state, and that he was very young. That's all Lettner knew.'

'And you believe this?'

'I don't know what I believe.'

'What difference does it make now?'

'I don't know. It could give me something to use as I try to save your life. Nothing more than that. I'm desperate, I guess.'

'And I'm not?'

'I'm grasping for straws, Sam. Grasping and filling in holes.'

'So my story has holes?'

'I think so. Lettner said he was always doubtful because they found no trace of explosives when they searched your house. And you had no history of using them. He said you didn't seem to be the type to initiate your own bombing campaign.'

'And you believe everything Lettner says?'

'Yeah. Because it makes sense.'

'Let me ask you this. What if I told you there was someone else? What if I gave you his name, address, phone number, blood type, and urine analysis? What would you do with it?'

'Start screaming like hell. I'd file motions and appeals by the truckload. I'd get the media stirred up, and make a scapegoat out of you. I'd try to sensationalize your innocence and hope someone noticed, someone like an appellate judge.'

Sam nodded slowly as if this was quite ridiculous and exactly what he'd expected. 'It wouldn't work, Adam,' he said carefully, as if lecturing to a child. 'I have three and a half weeks. You know the law. There's no way to start screaming John Doe did it, when John Doe has never been mentioned.'

'I know. But I'd do it anyway.'

255

'It won't work. Stop trying to find John Doe.'

'Who is he?'

'He doesn't exist.'

'Yes he does.'

'Why are you so sure?'

'Because I want to believe you're innocent, Sam. It's very important to me.'

'I told you I'm innocent. I planted the bomb, but I had no intentions of killing anyone.'

'But why'd you plant the bomb? Why'd you bomb the Pinder house, and the synagogue, and the real estate office? Why were you bombing innocent people?'

Sam just puffed and looked at the floor.

'Why do you hate, Sam? Why does it come so easy? Why were you taught to hate blacks and Jews and Catholics and anyone slightly different from you? Have you ever asked yourself why?'

'No. Don't plan to.'

'So, it's just you, right. It's your character, your composition, same as your height and blue eyes. It's something you were born with and can't change. It was passed down in the genes from your father and grandfather, faithful Kluckers all, and it's something you'll proudly take to your grave, right?'

'It was a way of life. It was all I knew.'

'Then what happened to my father? Why couldn't you contaminate Eddie?'

Sam thumped the cigarette onto the floor and leaned forward on his elbows. The wrinkles tightened in the corners of his eyes and across his forehead. Adam's face was directly through the slit, but he did not look at him. Instead, he stared down at the base of the screen. 'So this is it. Time for our Eddie talk.' His voice was much softer and his words even slower.

'Where did you go wrong with him?'

'This, of course, has not a damned thing to do with the little gas party they're planning for me. Does it? Nothing to do with issues and appeals, lawyers and judges, motions and stays. This is a waste of time.'

'Don't be a coward, Sam. Tell me where you went wrong with Eddie. Did you teach him the word nigger? Did you teach him to hate little black kids? Did you try to teach him how to burn crosses or build bombs? Did you take him to his first lynching? What did you do with him, Sam? Where did you go wrong?'

'Eddie didn't know I was in the Klan until he was in high school.'

'Why not? Surely you weren't ashamed of it. It was a great source of family pride, wasn't it?'

'It was not something we talked about.'

'Why not? You were the fourth generation of Cayhall Klansmen, with roots all the way back to the Civil War, or something like that. Isn't that what you told me?'

'Yes.'

'Then why didn't you sit little Eddie down and show him pictures from the family album? Why didn't you tell him bedtime stories of the heroic Cayhalls and how they rode around at night with masks on their brave faces and burned Negro shacks? You know, war stories. Father to son.'

'I repeat, it was not something we talked about.'

'Well, when he got older, did you try to recruit him?'

'No. He was different.'

'You mean, he didn't hate?'

Sam jerked forward and coughed, the deep, scratchy hacking action of a chain-smoker. His face reddened as he struggled for breath. The coughing grew worse and he spat on the floor. He stood and leaned at the waist with both hands on his hips, coughing and hacking while shuffling around and trying to stop it.

Finally, a break. He stood straight and breathed rapidly. He swallowed and spat again, then relaxed and inhaled slowly. The seizure was over, and his red face was suddenly pale again. He took his seat across from Adam, and puffed mightily on the cigarette as if some other device or habit was to blame for the coughing. He took his time, breathing deeply and clearing his throat.

'Eddie was a tender child,' he began hoarsely. 'He got it

257

from his mother. He wasn't a sissy. In fact, he was just as tough as other little boys.' A long pause, another drag of nicotine. 'Not far from our house was a nigger family –'

'Could we just call them blacks, Sam? I've asked you this already.'

'Forgive me. There was an African family on our place. The Lincolns. Joe Lincoln was his name, and he'd worked for us for many years. Had a common-law wife and a dozen common-law children. One of the boys was the same age as Eddie, and they were inseparable, best of friends. It was not that unusual in those days. You played with whoever lived nearby. I even had little African buddies, believe it or not. When Eddie started school, he got real upset because he rode one bus and his African pal rode another. Kid's name was Quince. Quince Lincoln. They couldn't wait to get home from school and go play on the farm. I remember Eddie was always disturbed because they couldn't go to school together. And Quince couldn't spend the night in our house, and Eddie couldn't spend the night with the Lincolns. He was always asking me questions about why the Africans in Ford County were so poor, and lived in run-down houses, and didn't have nice clothes, and had so many children in each family. He really suffered over it, and that made him different. As he got older, he grew even more sympathetic toward the Africans. I tried to talk to him.'

'Of course you did. You tried to straighten him out, didn't you?'

'I tried to explain things to him.'

'Such as?'

'Such as the need to keep the races separate. There's nothing wrong with separate but equal schools. Nothing wrong with laws prohibiting miscegenation. Nothing wrong with keeping the Africans in their place.'

'Where's their place?'

'Under control. Let 'em run wild, and look at what's happened. Crime, drugs, AIDS, illegitimate births, general breakdown in the moral fabric of society.'

'What about nuclear proliferation and killer bees?'

'You get my point.'

'What about basic rights, radical concepts like the right to vote, the right to use public rest rooms, the right to eat in restaurants and stay in hotels, the right not to be discriminated against in housing, employment, and education?'

'You sound like Eddie.'

'Good.'

'By the time he was finishing high school he was spouting off like that, talking about how badly the Africans were being mistreated. He left home when he was eighteen.'

'Did you miss him?'

'Not at first, I guess. We were fighting a lot. He knew I was in the Klan, and he hated the sight of me. At least, he said he did.'

'So you thought more of the Klan than you did your own son?'

Sam stared at the floor. Adam scribbled on a legal pad. The air conditioner rattled and faded, and for a moment seemed determined to finally quit. 'He was a sweet kid,' Sam said quietly. 'We used to fish a lot, that was our big thing together. I had an old boat, and we'd spend hours on the lake fishing for crappie and bream, sometimes bass. Then he grew up and didn't like me. He was ashamed of me, and of course it hurt. He expected me to change, and I expected him to see the light like all the other white kids his age. It never happened. We drifted apart when he was in high school, then it seems like the civil rights crap started, and there was no hope after that.'

'Did he participate in the movement?'

'No. He wasn't stupid. He might have been sympathetic, but he kept his mouth shut. You just didn't go around talking that trash if you were local. There were enough Northern Jews and radicals to keep things stirred up. They didn't need any help.'

'What did he do after he left home?'

'Joined the Army. It was an easy way out of town, away from Mississippi. He was gone for three years, and when he came back he brought a wife. They lived in Clanton and we barely saw them. He talked to his mother occasionally, but didn't have much to say to me. It was the early sixties by then, and the African movement was getting cranked up. There were a lot of Klan meetings, a lot of activity, most to the south of us. Eddie kept his distance. He was very quiet, never had much to say anyway.'

'Then I was born.'

'You were born around the time those three civil rights workers disappeared. Eddie had the nerve to ask me if I was involved in it.'

'Were you?'

'Hell no. I didn't know who did it for almost a year.'

'They were Kluckers, weren't they?'

'They were Klansmen.'

'Were you happy when those boys were murdered?'

'How the hell is that relevant to me and the gas chamber in 1990?'

'Did Eddie know it when you got involved with the bombing?'

'No one knew it in Ford County. We had not been too active. As I said, most of it was to the south of us, around Meridian.'

'And you couldn't wait to jump in the middle of it?'

'They needed help. The Fibbies had infiltrated so deep hardly anyone could be trusted. The civil rights movement was snowballing fast. Something had to be done. I'm not ashamed of it.'

Adam smiled and shook his head. 'Eddie was ashamed, wasn't he?'

'Eddie didn't know anything about it until the Kramer bombing.'

'Why did you involve him?'

'I didn't.'

'Yes you did. You told your wife to get Eddie and drive to Cleveland and pick up your car. He was an accessory after the fact.'

'I was in jail, okay. I was scared. And no one ever knew. It was harmless.'

'Perhaps Eddie didn't think so.'

'I don't know what Eddie thought, okay. By the time I got out of jail, he had disappeared. Y'all were gone. I never saw him again until his mother's funeral, and then he slipped in and out without a word to anyone.' He rubbed the wrinkles on his forehead with his left hand, then ran it through his oily hair. His face was sad, and as he glanced through the slit Adam saw a trace of moisture in the eyes. 'The last time I saw Eddie, he was getting in his car outside the church after the funeral service. He was in a hurry. Something told me I'd never see him again. He was there because his mother had died, and I knew that would be his last visit home. There was no other reason for him to come back. I was on the front steps of the church, Lee was with me, and we both watched him drive away. There I was burying my wife, and at the same time watching my son disappear for the last time.'

'Did you try to find him?'

'No. Not really. Lee said she had a phone number, but I didn't feel like begging. It was obvious he didn't want anything to do with me, so I left him alone. I often wondered about you, and I remember telling your grandmother how nice it would be to see you. But I wasn't about to spend a lot of time trying to track y'all down.'

'It would've been hard to find us.'

'That's what I heard. Lee talked to Eddie occasionally, and she would report to me. It sounded like you guys were moving all over California.'

'I went to six schools in twelve years.'

'But why? What was he doing?'

'A number of things. He'd lose his job, and we'd move because we couldn't pay the rent. Then Mother would find a job, and we'd move somewhere else. Then Dad would get mad at my school for some vague reason, and he'd yank me out.'

'What kind of work did he do?'

'Once he worked for the post office, until he got fired. He threatened to sue them, and for a long time he maintained this massive little war against the postal system. He couldn't find a lawyer to take his case, so he abused them with paperwork. He always had a small desk with an old typewriter and boxes filled with his papers, and they were his most valuable possessions. Every time we moved, he took great care with his office, as he called it. He didn't care about anything else, there wasn't much, but he protected his office with his life. I can remember many nights lying in bed trying to sleep and listening to that damned typewriter pecking away at all hours. He hated the federal government.'

'That's my boy.'

'But for different reasons, I think. The IRS came after him one year, which I always found odd because he didn't earn enough to pay three dollars in taxes. So he declared war on the Infernal Revenue, as he called it, and that raged for years. The State of California revoked his driver's license one year when he didn't renew, and this violated all sorts of civil and human rights. Mother had to drive him for two years until he surrendered to the bureaucracy. He was always writing letters to the governor, the President, U.S. senators, congressmen, anyone with an office and staff. He would just raise hell about this and that, and when they wrote him back he'd declare a small victory. He saved every letter. He got in a fight one time with a next-door neighbor, something to do with a strange dog peeing on our porch, and they were yelling at each other across the hedgerow. The madder they got, the more powerful their friends became, and both were just minutes away from making phone calls to all sorts of hotshots who would instantly inflict punishment on the other. Dad ran in the house, and within seconds returned to the argument with thirteen letters from the governor of the State of California. He counted them loudly and waved them under the neighbor's nose, and the poor guy was crushed. End of argument. End of dog pissing on our porch. Of course, every one of the letters had asked him, in a nice way, to get lost.'

Though they didn't realize it, they were both smiling by the end of this brief story.

'If he couldn't keep a job, how did y'all survive?' Sam asked, staring through the opening.

'I don't know. Mother always worked. She was very resourceful, and she sometimes kept two jobs. Cashier in a grocery store. Clerk in a pharmacy. She could do anything, and I remember a couple of pretty good jobs as a secretary. At some point, Dad got a license to sell life insurance, and that became a permanent part-time job. I guess he was good at it, because things improved as I got older. He could work his own hours and reported to no one. This suited him, although he said he hated insurance companies. He sued one for canceling a policy or something, I really didn't understand it, and he lost the case. Of course, he blamed it all on his lawyer, who made the mistake of sending Eddie a long letter full of strong statements. Dad typed for three days, and when his masterpiece was finished he proudly showed it to Mother. Twenty-one pages of mistakes and lies by the lawyer. She just shook her head. He fought with that poor lawyer for years.'

'What kind of father was he?'

'I don't know. That's a hard question, Sam.'

'Why?'

'Because of the way he died. I was mad at him for a long time after his death, and I didn't understand how he could decide that he should leave us, that we didn't need him anymore, that it was time for him to check out. And after I learned the truth, I was mad at him for lying to me all those years, for changing my name and running away. It was terribly confusing for a young kid. Still is.'

'Are you still angry?'

'Not really. I tend to remember the good things about Eddie. He was the only father I've had, so I don't know how to rate him. He didn't smoke, drink, gamble, do drugs, chase women, beat his kids, or any of that. He had trouble keeping a job, but we never went without food or shelter. He and Mother were constantly talking about divorce, but it didn't work out. She moved out several times, and then he would move out. It was disruptive, but Carmen and I became accustomed to it. He had his dark days, or bad times, as they were known, when he would withdraw to his room and lock the door and pull the shades. Mother would gather us around her and explain that he was not feeling well, and that we should be very quiet. No television or radios. She was very supportive when he withdrew. He would stay in his room for days, then suddenly emerge as if nothing happened. We learned to live with Eddie's bad times. He looked and dressed normal. He was almost always there if we needed him. We played baseball in the backyard and rode rides at the carnival. He took us to Disneyland a couple of times. I guess he was a good man, a good father who just had this dark, strange side that flared up occasionally.'

'But you weren't close.'

'No, we weren't close. He helped me with my homework and science projects, and he insisted on perfect report cards. We talked about the solar system and the environment, but never about girls and sex and cars. Never about family and ancestors. There was no intimacy. He was not a warm person. There were times when I needed him and he was locked up in his room.'

Sam rubbed the corners of his eyes, then he leaned forward again on his elbows with his face close to the screen and looked directly at Adam. 'What about his death?' he asked.

'What about it?'

'How'd it happen?'

Adam waited for a long time before answering. He could tell this story several ways. He could be cruel and hateful and brutally honest, and in doing so destroy the old man. There was a mighty temptation to do this. It needed to be done, he'd told himself many times before. Sam needed to suffer; he needed to be slapped in the face with the guilt of

264

Eddie's suicide. Adam wanted to really hurt the old bastard and make him cry.

But at the same time he wanted to tell the story quickly, glossing over the painful parts and then moving on to something else. The poor old man sitting captive on the other side of the screen was suffering enough. The government was planning to kill him in less than four weeks. Adam suspected he knew more about Eddie's death than he let on.

'He was going through a bad time,' Adam said, gazing at the screen but avoiding Sam. 'He'd been in his room for three weeks, which was longer than usual. Mother kept telling us that he was getting better, just a few more days and he'd come out. We believed her, because he always seemed to bounce out of it. He picked a day when she was at work and Carmen was at a friend's house, a day when he knew I'd be the first one home. I found him lying on the floor of my bedroom, still holding the gun, a thirty-eight. One shot to the right temple. There was a neat circle of blood around his head. I sat on the edge of my bed.'

'How old were you?'

'Almost seventeen. A junior in high school. Straight A's. I realized he'd carefully arranged half a dozen towels on the floor then placed himself in the middle of them. I checked the pulse in his wrist, and he was already stiff. Coroner said he'd been dead three hours. There was a note beside him, typed neatly on white paper. The note was addressed Dear Adam. Said he loved me, that he was sorry, that he wanted me to take care of the girls, and that maybe one day I would understand. Then he directed my attention to a plastic garbage bag, also on the floor, and said I should place the dirty towels in the garbage bag, wipe up the mess, then call the police. Don't touch the gun, he said. And hurry, before the girls get home.' Adam cleared his throat and looked at the floor.

'And so I did exactly what he said, and I waited for the police. We were alone for fifteen minutes, just the two of us. He was lying on the floor, and I was lying on my bed looking down at him. I started crying and crying, asking him why and how and what happened and a hundred other questions. There was my dad, the only dad I would ever have, lying there in his faded jeans and dirty socks and favorite UCLA sweatshirt. From the neck down he could've been napping, but he had a hole in his head and the blood had dried in his hair. I hated him for dying, and I felt so sorry for him because he was dead. I remember asking him why he hadn't talked to me before this. I asked a lot of questions. I heard voices, and suddenly the room was filled with cops. They took me to the den and put a blanket around me. And that was the end of my father.'

Sam was still on his elbows, but one hand was now over his eyes. There were just a couple more things Adam wanted to say.

'After the funeral, Lee stayed with us for a while. She told me about you and about the Cayhalls. She filled in a lot of gaps about my father. I became fascinated with you and the Kramer bombing, and I began reading old magazine articles and newspaper stories. It took about a year for me to figure out why Eddie killed himself when he did. He'd been hiding in his room during your trial, and he killed himself when it was over.'

Sam removed his hand and glared at Adam with wet eyes. 'So you blame me for his death, right, Adam? That's what you really want to say, isn't it?'

'No. I don't blame you entirely.'

'Then how much? Eighty percent? Ninety percent? You've had time to do the numbers. How much of it's my fault?'

'I don't know, Sam. Why don't you tell me?'

Sam wiped his eyes and raised his voice. 'Oh what the hell! I'll claim a hundred percent. I'll take full responsibility for his death, okay? Is that what you want?'

'Take whatever you want.'

'Don't patronize me! Just add my son's name to my list, is that what you want? The Kramer twins, their father, then Eddie. That's four I've killed, right? Anyone else you want

266

to tack on here at the end? Do it quick, old boy, because the clock is ticking.'

'How many more are out there?'

'Dead bodies?'

'Yes. Dead bodies. I've heard the rumors.'

'And of course your believe them, don't you? You seem eager to believe everything bad about me.'

'I didn't say I believed them.'

Sam jumped to his feet and walked to the end of the room. 'I'm tired of this conversation!' he yelled from thirty feet away. 'And I'm tired of you! I almost wish I had those damned Jew lawyers harassing me again.'

'We can accommodate you,' Adam shot back.

Sam walked slowly back to his chair. 'Here I am worried about my ass, twenty-three days away from the chamber, and all you want to do is talk about dead people. Just keep chirping away, old boy, and real soon you can start talking about me. I want some action.'

'I filed a petition this morning.'

'Fine! Then leave, dammit. Just get the hell out and stop tormenting me!'

TWENTY-TWO

THE DOOR on Adam's side opened, and Packer entered with two gentlemen behind him. They were obviously lawyers – dark suits, frowns, thick bulging briefcases. Packer pointed to some chairs under the air conditioner, and they sat down. He looked at Adam, and paid particular attention to Sam, who was still standing on the other side. 'Everything okay?' he asked Adam.

Adam nodded and Sam eased into his chair. Packer left and the two new lawyers efficiently went about their business of pulling heavy documents from fat files. Within a minute, both jackets were off.

Five minutes passed without a word from Sam. Adam caught a few glimpses from the lawyers on the other end. They were in the same room with the most famous inmate on the Row, the next one to be gassed, and they couldn't help but steal curious peeks at Sam Cayhall and his lawyer.

Then the door opened behind Sam, and two guards entered with a wiry little black man who was shackled and manacled and cuffed as if he might erupt any moment and kill dozens with his bare hands. They led him to a seat across from his lawyers, and went about the business of liberating most of his limbs. The hands remained cuffed behind his back. One of the guards left the room, but the other took a position halfway between Sam and the black inmate.

Sam glanced down the counter at his comrade, a nervous type who evidently was not happy with his lawyers. His lawyers did not appear to be thrilled either. Adam watched them from his side of the screen, and within minutes their heads were closer together and they were talking in unison through the slit while their client sat militantly on his hands. Their low voices were audible, but their words were indecipherable.

Sam eased forward again, on his elbows, and motioned for Adam to do likewise. Their faces met ten inches apart with the opening between them.

'That's Stockholm Turner,' Sam said, almost in a whisper.

'Stockholm?'

'Yeah, but he goes by Stock. These rural Africans love unusual names. He says he has a brother named Denmark and one named Germany. Probably does.'

'What'd he do?' Adam asked, suddenly curious.

'Robbed a whiskey store, I think. Shot the owner. About two years ago he got a death warrant, and it went down to the wire. He came within two hours of the chamber.'

'What happened?'

'His lawyers got a stay, and they've been fighting ever since. You can never tell, but he'll probably be the next after me.'

They both looked toward the end of the room where the conference was raging in full force. Stock was off his hands and sitting on the edge of his chair and raising hell with his lawyers.

Sam grinned, then chuckled, then leaned even closer to the screen. 'Stock's family is dirt poor, and they have little to do with him. It's not unusual, really, especially with the Africans. He seldom gets mail or visitors. He was born fifty miles from here, but the free world has forgotten about him. As his appeals were losing steam, Stock started worrying about life and death and things in general. Around here, if no one claims your body, then the state buries you like a pauper in some cheap grave. Stock got concerned about what would happen to his body, and he started asking all kinds of questions. Packer and some of the guards picked up on it, and they convinced Stock that his body would be sent to a crematorium where it would be burned. The ashes would be dropped from the air and spread over Parchman. They told him that since he'd be full of gas anyway, when they stuck a match to him he'd go off like a bomb. Stock was devastated. He had trouble sleeping and lost weight. He started writing letters to his family and friends begging them for a few dollars so he could have a Christian burial, as he called it. The money trickled in, and he wrote more letters. He wrote to ministers and civil rights groups. Even his lawyers sent money.

'When his stay was lifted, Stock had close to four hundred dollars, and he was ready to die. Or so he thought.'

Sam's eyes were dancing and his voice was light. He told the story slowly, in a low voice, and savored the details. Adam was amused more by the telling than by the narrative.

'They have a loose rule here that allows almost unlimited visitation for seventy-two hours prior to the execution. As long as there's no security risk, they'll allow the condemned man to do damned near anything. There's a little office up front with a desk and phone, and that becomes the visiting room. It's usually filled with all sorts of people – grandmothers, nieces, nephews, cousins, aunties – especially with these Africans. Hell, they run 'em in here by the busload. Kinfolks who haven't spent five minutes thinking about the inmate suddenly show up to share his last moments. It almost becomes a social event.

'They also have this rule, it's unwritten I'm sure, that allows one final conjugal visit with the wife. If there's no wife, then the warden in his boundless mercy allows a brief appointment with a girlfriend. One last little quickie before lover boy checks out.' Sam glanced along the counter at Stock, then leaned even closer.

'Well, ole Stock here is one of the more popular residents of the Row, and he somehow convinced the warden that he had both a wife and a girlfriend, and that these ladies would agree to spend a few moments with him before he died. At

270

the same time! All three of them, together! The warden allegedly knew something fishy was going on, but everyone likes Stock, and, well, they were about to kill him anyway, so what's the harm. So Stock here was sitting in the little room with his mother and sisters and cousins and nieces, a whole passel of Africans, most of whom hadn't uttered his name in ten years, and he was eating his last meal of steak and potatoes while everybody else was crying and grieving and praying. With about four hours to go, they emptied the room and sent the family to the chapel. Stock waited for a few minutes while another van brought his wife and his girlfriend here to the Row. They arrived with guards, and were taken to the little office up front where Stock was waiting, all wild-eyed and ready. Poor guy'd been on the Row for twelve years.

'Well, they brought in a little cot for this liaison, and Stock and his gals got it on. The guards said later that Stock had some fine-looking women, and the guards also said they commented at the time on how young they looked. Stock was just about to have a go with either his wife or his girlfriend, it didn't really matter, when the phone rang. It was his lawyer. And his lawyer was crying and out of breath as he yelled out the great news that the Fifth Circuit had issued a stay.

'Stock hung up on him. He had more important matters at hand. A few minutes passed, then the phone rang again. Stock grabbed it. It was his lawyer again, and this time he was much more composed as he explained to Stock the legal maneuvering that had saved his life, for the moment. Stock offered his appreciation, then asked his lawyer to keep it quiet for another hour.'

Adam glanced to his right, and wondered which of the two lawyers had called Stock while he was exercising his constitutional right of the last conjugal visit.

'Well, by this time, the Attorney General's office had talked to the warden, and the execution had been called off, or aborted as they like to say. Made no difference to Stock. He was proceeding as if he would never see another woman.

271

The door to the room cannot be locked from the inside, for obvious reasons, so Naifeh, after waiting patiently, gently knocked on the door and asked Stock to come on out. Time to go back to your cell, Stock, he said. Stock said he needed just another five minutes. No, said Naifeh. Please, Stock begged, and suddenly there were noises again. So the warden grinned at the guards who grinned at the warden, and for five minutes they studied the floor while the cot rattled and bounced around the little room.

'Stock finally opened the door and strutted out like the heavyweight champ of the world. The guards said he was happier about his performance than he was about his stay. They quickly got rid of the women, who as it turned out, were not really his wife and girlfriend after all.'

'Who were they?'

'A couple of prostitutes.'

'Prostitutes!' Adam said a bit too loud, and one of the lawyers stared at him.

Sam leaned so close his nose was almost in the slit. 'Yeah, local whores. His brother somehow arranged it for him. Remember the funeral money he worked so hard to raise.'

'You're kidding.'

'That's it. Four hundred bucks spent on whores which at first seems a bit stiff, especially for local African whores, but it seems they were scared to death about coming to death row, which I guess makes sense. They took all Stock's money. He told me later he didn't give a damn how they buried him. Said it was worth every dime. Naifeh got embarrassed, and he threatened to prohibit the conjugal visits. But Stock's lawyer, that little dark-haired one over there, filed a lawsuit and got a ruling that ensures one last quickie. I think Stock's almost looking forward to his next one.'

Sam leaned back in his chair and the smile slowly left his face. 'Personally, I haven't given much thought to my conjugal visit. It's intended for husband and wife relations only, you know, that's what the term means. But the warden'll probably bend the rules for me. What do you think?'

'I really haven't thought about it.'

'I'm just kidding, you know. I'm an old man. I'd settle for a back rub and a stiff drink.'

'What about your last meal?' Adam asked, still very quietly.

'That's not funny.'

'I thought we were kidding.'

'Probably something gross like boiled pork and rubber peas. Same crap they've been feeding me for almost ten years. Maybe an extra piece of toast. I'd hate to give the cook the opportunity to prepare a meal fit for free world humans.'

'Sounds delicious.'

'Oh, I'll share it with you. I've often wondered why they feed you before they kill you. They also bring the doctor in and give you a preexecution physical. Can you believe it? Gotta make sure you're fit to die. And they have a shrink on staff here who examines you before the execution, and he must report to the warden in writing that you're mentally sound enough to gas. And they have a minister on the payroll who'll pray and meditate with you and make sure your soul is headed in the right direction. All paid for by the taxpayers of the State of Mississippi and administered by these loving people around here. Don't forget the conjugal visit. You can die with your lust satisfied. They think of everything. They're very considerate. Really concerned about your appetite and health and spiritual well-being. Right at the very last, they put a catheter in your penis and a plug up your ass so you won't make a mess. This is for their benefit, not yours. They don't wanna have to clean you afterward. So, they feed you real good, anything you want, then they plug you up. Sick, isn't it? Sick, sick, sick, sick.'

'Let's talk about something else.'

Sam finished the last cigarette and thumped it on the floor in front of the guard. 'No. Let's stop talking. I've had enough for one day.'

'Fine.'

'And no more about Eddie, okay? It's really not fair to come in here and hit me with stuff like that.'

'I'm sorry. No more about Eddie.'

'Let's try to focus on me the next three weeks, okay? That's more than enough to keep us busy.'

'It's a deal, Sam.'

ALONG HIGHWAY 82 from the east, Greenville was growing in an unsightly sprawl, with its strip shopping centers filled with video rental and dinky liquor stores, and its endless fast-food franchises and drive-up motels with free cable and breakfast. The river blocked such progress to the west, and since 82 was the main corridor it had evidently become the developers' favorite territory.

In the past twenty-five years, Greenville had grown from a sleepy river town of thirty-five thousand to a busy river city of sixty thousand. It was prosperous and progressive. In 1990, Greenville was the fifth-largest city in the state.

The streets leading into the central district were shaded and lined with stately old homes. The center of the town was pretty and quaint, well preserved and apparently unchanged, Adam thought, in stark contrast to the thoughtless chaos along Highway 82. He parked on Washington Street, a few minutes after five, as downtown merchants and their customers were busy preparing for the end of the day. He removed his tie and left it with his jacket in the car because the temperature was still in the nineties and showed no sign of relenting.

He walked three blocks, and found the park with the life-sized bronze statue of two little boys in the center. They were the same size with the same smile and the same eyes. One was running while the other one skipped, and the sculptor had captured them perfectly. Josh and John Kramer, forever five years old, frozen in time with copper and tin. A brass plate below them said simply:

JOSH AND JOHN KRAMER
DIED HERE ON APRIL 21, 1967
(MARCH 2, 1962–APRIL 21, 1967)

The park was a perfect square, half a city block which had once held Marvin's law office and an old building next to it. The land had been in the Kramer family for years, and Marvin's father gave it to the city to be used as a memorial. Sam had done a fine job of leveling the law office, and the city had razed the building next to it. Some money had been spent on Kramer Park, and a lot of thought had gone into it. It was completely fenced with ornamental wrought iron and an entrance on each side from the sidewalks. Perfect rows of oaks and maples followed the fencing. Lines of manicured shrubs met at precise angles, then encirled flower beds of begonias and geraniums. A small amphitheater sat in one corner under the trees, and across the way a group of black children sailed through the air on wooden swings.

It was small and colorful, a pleasant little garden amid the streets and buildings. A teenaged couple argued on a bench as Adam walked by. A bicycle gang of eight-year-olds roared around a fountain. An ancient policeman ambled by and actually tipped his hat to Adam as he said hello.

He sat on a bench and stared at Josh and John, less than thirty feet away. 'Never forget the victims,' Lee had admonished. 'They have the right to want retribution. They've earned it.'

He remembered all the gruesome details from the trials – the FBI expert who testified about the bomb and the speed at which it ripped through the building; the medical examiner who delicately described the little bodies and what exactly killed them; the firemen who tried to rescue but were much too late and were left only to retrieve. There had been photographs of the building and the boys, and the trial judges had used great restraint in allowing just a few of these to go to the jury. McAllister, typically, had wanted to show huge enlarged color pictures of the mangled bodies, but they were excluded.

Adam was now sitting on ground which had once been the office of Marvin Kramer, and he closed his eyes and tried to feel the ground shake. He saw the footage from his video of smoldering debris and the cloud of dust suspended over the scene. He heard the frantic voice of the news reporter, the sirens shrieking in the background.

Those bronze boys were not much older than he was when his grandfather killed them. They were five and he was almost three, and for some reason he kept up with their ages. Today, he was twenty-six and they would be twenty-eight.

The guilt hit hard and low in the stomach. It made him shudder and sweat. The sun hid behind two large oaks to the west, and as it flickered through the branches the boys' faces gleamed.

How could Sam have done this? Why was Sam Cayhall his grandfather and not someone else's? When did he decide to participate in the Klan's holy war against Jews? What made him change from a harmless cross-burner to a full-fledged terrorist?

Adam sat on the bench, stared at the statue, and hated his grandfather. He felt guilty for being in Mississippi trying to help the old bastard.

He found a Holiday Inn and paid for a room. He called Lee and reported in, then watched the evening news on the Jackson channels. Evidently, it had been just another languid summer day in Mississippi with little happening. Sam Cayhall and his latest efforts to stay alive were the hot topics. Each station carried somber comments by the governor and the Attorney General about the newest petition for relief filed by the defense this morning, and each man was just sick and tired of the endless appeals. Each would fight valiantly to pursue this matter until justice was realized. One station began its own countdown – twenty-three days until execution, the anchorperson rattled off, as if reciting the number of shopping days left until Christmas. The number 23 was plastered under the same overworked photo of Sam Cayhall.

Adam ate dinner in a small downtown café. He sat alone in a booth, picking at roast beef and peas, listening to harmless chatter around him. No one mentioned Sam.

At dusk, he walked the sidewalks in front of the shops

and stores, and thought of Sam pacing along these same streets, on the same concrete, waiting for the bomb to go off and wondering what in the world had gone wrong. He stopped by a phone booth, maybe the same one Sam had tried to use to call and warn Kramer.

The park was deserted and dark. Two gaslight street lamps stood by the front entrance, providing the only light. Adam sat at the base of the statue, under the boys, under the brass plate with their names and dates of birth and death. On this very spot, it said, they died.

He sat there for a long time, oblivious to the darkness, pondering imponderables, wasting time with fruitless considerations of what might have been. The bomb had defined his life, he knew that much. It had taken him away from Mississippi and deposited him in another world with a new name. It had transformed his parents into refugees, fleeing their past and hiding from their present. It had killed his father, in all likelihood, though no one could predict what might have happened to Eddie Cayhall. The bomb had played a principal role in Adam's decision to become a lawyer, a calling he'd never felt until he learned of Sam. He'd dreamed of flying airplanes.

And now the bomb had led him back to Mississippi for an undertaking laden with agony and little hope. The odds were heavy that the bomb would claim its final victim in twenty-three days, and Adam wondered what would happen to him after that.

What else could the bomb have in store for him?

TWENTY-THREE

FOR THE MOST PART, death penalty appeals drag along for years at a snail's pace. A very old snail. No one is in a hurry. The issues are complicated. The briefs, motions, petitions, etc., are thick and burdensome. The court dockets are crowded with more pressing matters.

Occasionally, though, a ruling can come down with stunning speed. Justice can become terribly efficient. Especially in the waning days, when a date for an execution has been set and the courts are tired of more motions, more appeals. Adam received his first dose of quick justice while he was wandering the streets of Greenville Monday afternoon.

The Mississippi Supreme Court took one look at his petition for postconviction relief, and denied it around 5 P.M. Monday. Adam was just arriving in Greenville and knew nothing about it. The denial was certainly no surprise, but its speed certainly was. The court kept the petition less than eight hours. In all fairness, the court had dealt with Sam Cayhall off and on for over ten years.

In the final days of death cases, the courts watch each other closely. Copies of filings and rulings are faxed along so that the higher courts know what's coming. The denial by the Mississippi Supreme Court was routinely faxed to the federal district court in Jackson, Adam's next forum. It was sent to the Honorable F. Flynn Slattery, a young federal judge who was new to the bench. He had not been involved with the Cayhall appeals.

278

Judge Slattery's office attempted to locate Adam Hall between 5 and 6 P.M. Monday, but he was sitting in Kramer Park. Slattery called the Attorney General, Steve Roxburgh, and at eight-thirty a brief meeting took place in the judge's office. The judge happened to be a workaholic, and this was his first death case. He and his clerk studied the petition until midnight.

If Adam had watched the late news Monday, he would have learned that his petition had already been denied by the supreme court. He was, however, sound asleep.

At six Tuesday morning, he casually picked up the Jackson paper and learned that the supreme court had turned him down, that the matter was now in federal court, assigned to Judge Slattery, and that both the Attorney General and the governor were claiming another victory. Odd, he thought, since he hadn't yet officially filed anything in federal court. He jumped in his car and raced to Jackson, two hours away. At nine, he entered the federal courthouse on Capitol Street in downtown, and met briefly with Breck Jefferson, an unsmiling young man, fresh from law school and holding the important position of Slattery's law clerk. Adam was told to return at eleven for a meeting with the judge.

ALTHOUGH HE ARRIVED at Slattery's office at exactly eleven, it was obvious a meeting of sorts had been in progress for some time. In the center of Slattery's huge office was a mahogany conference table, long and wide with eight black leather chairs on each side. Slattery's throne was at one end, near his desk, and before him on the table were stacks of papers, legal pads, and other effects. The side to his right was crowded with young white men in navy suits, all bunched together along the table, with another row of eager warriors seated close behind. This side belonged to the state, with His Honor, the governor, Mr David McAllister, sitting closest to Slattery. His Honor, the Attorney General, Steve Roxburgh, had been banished to the middle of the table in an obvious losing battle over turf.

Each distinguished public servant had brought to the table his most trusted litigators and thinkers, and this squadron of strategists had obviously been meeting with the judge and plotting long before Adam arrived.

Breck, the clerk, swung the door open and greeted Adam pleasantly enough, then asked him to step inside. The room was instantly silent as Adam slowly approached the table. Slattery reluctantly rose from his chair and introduced himself to Adam. The handshake was cold and fleeting. 'Have a seat,' he said ominously, fluttering his left hand at the eight leather chairs on the defense side of the table. Adam hesitated, then picked one directly across from a face he recognized as belonging to Roxburgh. He placed his briefcase on the table, and sat down. Four empty chairs were to his right, in the direction of Slattery, and three to his left. He felt like a lonesome trespasser.

'I assume you know the governor and the Attorney General,' Slattery said, as if everyone had personally met these two.

'Neither,' Adam said, shaking his head slightly.

'I'm David McAllister, Mr Hall, nice to meet you,' the governor said quickly, ever the anxious glad-handing politician, with an incredibly rapid flash of flawless teeth.

'A pleasure,' Adam said, barely moving his lips.

'And I'm Steve Roxburgh,' said the Attorney General.

Adam only nodded at him. He'd seen his face in the newspapers.

Roxburgh took the initiative. He began talking and pointing at people. 'These are attorneys from my criminal appeals division. Kevin Laird, Bart Moody, Morris Henry, Hugh Simms, and Joseph Ely. These guys handle all death penalty cases.' They all nodded obediently while maintaining their suspicious frowns. Adam counted eleven people on the other side of the table.

McAllister chose not to introduce his band of clones, all of whom were suffering from either migraines or hemorrhoids. Their faces were contorted from pain, or perhaps from quite serious deliberation about legal matters at hand.

280

'Hope we haven't jumped the gun, Mr Hall,' Slattery said as he slipped a pair of reading glasses on his nose. He was in his early forties, one of the young Reagan appointees. 'When do you expect to officially file your petition here in federal court?'

'Today,' Adam said nervously, still astounded by the speed of it all. This was a positive development though, he'd decided while driving to Jackson. If Sam got any relief, it would be in federal court, not state.

'When can the state respond?' the judge asked Roxburgh.

'Tomorrow morning. Assuming the petition here raises the same issues as those raised in the supreme court.'

'They're the same,' Adam said to Roxburgh, then he turned to Slattery. 'I was told to be here at eleven o'clock. What time did the meeting start?'

'The meeting started when I decided it would start, Mr Hall,' Slattery said icily. 'Do you have a problem with that?'

'Yes. It's obvious this conference started some time ago, without me.'

'What's wrong with that? This is my office, and I'll start meetings whenever I want.'

'Yeah, but it's my petition, and I was invited here to discuss it. Seems as though I should've been here for the entire meeting.'

'You don't trust me, Mr Hall?' Slattery was easing forward on his elbows, thoroughly enjoying this.

'I don't trust anybody,' Adam said, staring at His Honor.

'We're trying to accommodate you, Mr Hall. Your client doesn't have much time, and I'm only trying to move things along. I thought you'd be pleased that we were able to arrange this meeting with such speed.'

'Thank you,' Adam said, and looked at his legal pad. There was a brief silence as the tension eased a bit.

Slattery held a sheet of paper. 'Get the petition filed today. The state will file its response tomorrow. I'll consider it over the weekend and issue a ruling on Monday. In the event I decide to conduct a hearing, I need to know

281

from both sides how long it will take to prepare. How about you, Mr Hall? How long to get ready for a hearing?'

Sam had twenty-two days to live. Any hearing would have to be a hurried, concise affair with quick witnesses and, he hoped, a swift ruling by the court. Adding to the stress of the moment was the crucial fact that Adam had no idea how long it would take to prepare for a hearing because he'd never tried such a matter. He'd participated in a few minor skirmishes in Chicago, but always with Emmit Wycoff close by. He was just a rookie, dammit! He wasn't even certain where the courtroom was located.

And something told him that the eleven vultures examining him at this precise second knew full well he didn't know what the hell he was doing. 'I can be ready in a week,' he said with a steady poker face and as much faith as he could muster.

'Very well,' Slattery said, as if this was fine, a good answer, Adam, good boy. A week was reasonable. Then Roxburgh whispered something to one of his warlocks, and the whole bunch thought it was funny. Adam ignored them.

Slattery scribbled something with an ink pen, then studied it. He gave it to Breck the clerk who treasured it and raced off to do something else with it. His Honor looked along the wall of legal infantry to his right, then he dropped his gaze upon young Adam. 'Now, Mr Hall, there's something else I'd like to discuss. As you know, this execution is scheduled to take place in twenty-two days, and I would like to know if this court can expect any additional filings on behalf of Mr Cayhall. I know this is an unusual request, but we're operating here in an unusual situation. Frankly, this is my first involvement with a death penalty case as advanced as this one, and I think it's best if we all work together here.'

In other words, Your Honor, you want to make damned sure there are no stays. Adam thought for a second. It was an unusual request, and one that was quite unfair. But Sam had a constitutional right to file anything at anytime, and

Adam could not be bound by any promises made here. He decided to be polite. 'I really can't say, Your Honor. Not now. Maybe next week.'

'Surely you'll file the usual gangplank appeals,' Roxburgh said, and the smirking bastards around him all looked at Adam with wondrous amazement.

'Frankly, Mr Roxburgh, I'm not required to discuss my plans with you. Or with the court, for that matter.'

'Of course not,' McAllister chimed in for some reason, probably just his inability to stay quiet for more than five minutes.

Adam had noticed the lawyer sitting to Roxburgh's right, a methodical sort with steely eyes that seldom left Adam. He was young but gray, clean-shaven, and very neat. McAllister favored him, and had leaned to his right several times as if receiving advice. The others from the AG's office seemed to accede to his thoughts and movements. There was a reference in one of the hundred articles Adam had clipped and filed away about an infamous litigator in the AG's office known as Dr Death, a clever bird with a penchant for pushing death penalty cases to their conclusion. Either his first or last name was Morris, and Adam vaguely recalled a Morris something or other mentioned moments earlier during Roxburgh's garbled introduction of his staff.

Adam assumed him to be the nefarious Dr Death. Morris Henry was his name.

'Well, hurry up and file them then,' Slattery said with a good dose of frustration. 'I don't want to work around the clock as this thing goes down to the wire.'

'No sir,' Adam said in mock sympathy.

Slattery glared at him for a moment, then returned to the paperwork in front of him. 'Very well, gentlemen, I suggest you stick by your telephones Sunday night and Monday morning. I'll be calling as soon as I've made a decision. This meeting is adjourned.'

The conspiracy on the other side broke up in a flurry of papers and files snatched from the table and sudden mumbled conversations. Adam was nearest the door. He nodded at Slattery, offered a feeble 'Good day, Your Honor,' and left the office. He gave a polite grin to the secretary and was into the hallway when someone called his name. It was the governor, with two flunkies in tow.

'Can we talk a minute?' McAllister asked, thrusting a hand at Adam's waist. They shook for a second.

'What about?'

'Just five minutes, okay.'

Adam looked at the governor's boys waiting a few feet away. 'Alone. Private. And off the record,' he said.

'Sure,' McAllister said, then pointed to a set of double doors. They stepped inside a small empty courtroom with the lights off. The governor's hands were free. Someone else carried his briefcase and bags. He stuck them deep in his pockets and leaned against a railing. He was lean and well dressed, nice suit, fashionable silk tie, obligatory white cotton shirt. He was under forty and aging remarkably well. Only a touch of gray tinted his sideburns. 'How's Sam?' he asked, feigning deep concern.

Adam snorted, looked away, then sat his briefcase on the floor. 'Oh, he's wonderful. I'll tell him you asked. He'll be thrilled.'

'I'd heard he was in bad health.'

'Health? You're trying to kill him. How can you be worried about his health?'

'Just heard a rumor.'

'He hates your guts, okay? His health is bad, but he can hang on for another three weeks.'

'Hate is nothing new for Sam, you know.'

'What exactly do you want to talk about?'

'Just wanted to say hello. I'm sure we'll get together shortly.'

'Look, Governor, I have a signed contract with my client that expressly forbids me from talking to you. I repeat, he hates you. You're the reason he's on death row. He blames you for everything, and if he knew we were talking now, he'd fire me.'

284

'Your own grandfather would fire you?'

'Yes. I truly believe it. So if I read in tomorrow's paper that you met with me today and we discussed Sam Cayhall, then I'll be on my way back to Chicago, which will probably screw up your execution because Sam won't have a lawyer. Can't kill a man if he doesn't have a lawyer.'

'Says who?'

'Just keep it quiet, okay?'

'You have my word. But if we can't talk, then how do we discuss the issue of clemency?'

'I don't know. I haven't reached that point yet.'

McAllister's face was always pleasant. The comely smile was always in place or just beneath the surface. 'You have thought about clemency, haven't you?'

'Yes. With three weeks to go, I've thought about clemency. Every death row inmate dreams of a pardon, Governor, and that's why you can't grant one. You pardon one convict, and you'll have the other fifty pestering you for the same favor. Fifty families writing letters and calling night and day. Fifty lawyers pulling strings and trying to get in your office. You and I both know it can't be done.'

'I'm not sure he should die.'

He said this while looking away, as if a change of heart was under way, as if the years had matured him and softened his zeal to punish Sam. Adam started to say something, then realized the magnitude of these last words. He watched the floor for a minute, paying particular attention to the governor's tasseled loafers. The governor was deep in thought.

'I'm not sure he should die, either,' Adam said.

'How much has he told you?'

'About what?'

'About the Kramer bombing.'

'He says he's told me everything.'

'But you have doubts?'

'Yes.'

'So do I. I always had doubts.'

'Why?'

285

'Lots of reasons. Jeremiah Dogan was a notorious liar, and he was scared to death of going to prison. The IRS had him cold, you know, and he was convinced that if he went to prison he'd be raped and tortured and killed by gangs of blacks. He was the Imperial Wizard, you know. Dogan was also ignorant about a lot of things. He was sly and hard to catch when it came to terrorism, but he didn't understand the criminal justice system. I always thought someone, probably the FBI, told Dogan that Sam had to be convicted or they'd ship him off to prison. No conviction, no deal. He was a very eager witness on the stand. He desperately wanted the jury to convict Sam.'

'So he lied?'

'I don't know. Maybe.'

'About what?'

'Have you asked Sam if he had an accomplice?'

Adam paused for a second and analyzed the question. 'I really can't discuss what Sam and I have talked about. It's confidential.'

'Of course it is. There are a lot of people in this state who secretly do not wish to see Sam executed.' McAllister was now watching Adam closely.

'Are you one of them?'

'I don't know. But what if Sam didn't plan to kill either Marvin Kramer or his sons? Sure Sam was there, right in the thick of it. But what if someone else possessed the intent to murder?'

'Then Sam isn't as guilty as we think.'

'Right. He's certainly not innocent, but not guilty enough to be executed either. This bothers me, Mr Hall. Can I call you Adam?'

'Of course.'

'I don't suppose Sam has mentioned anything about an accomplice?'

'I really can't discuss that. Not now.'

The governor slipped a hand from a pocket and gave Adam a business card. 'Two phone numbers on the back. One is my private office number. The other is my home number. All phone calls are confidential, I swear. I play for the cameras sometimes, Adam, it goes with the job, but I can also be trusted.'

Adam took the card and looked at the handwritten numbers.

'I couldn't live with myself if I failed to pardon a man who didn't deserve to die,' McAllister said as he walked to the door. 'Give me a call, but don't wait too late. This thing's already heating up. I'm getting twenty phone calls a day.'

He winked at Adam, showed him the sparkling teeth once again, and left the room.

Adam sat in a metal chair against the wall, and looked at the front of the card. It was gold-embossed with an official seal. Twenty calls a day. What did that mean? Did the calls want Sam dead or did they want him pardoned?

A lot of people in this state do not wish to see Sam executed, he'd said, as if he was already weighing the votes he'd lose against those he might gain.

TWENTY-FOUR

THE SMILE from the receptionist in the foyer was not as quick as usual, and as Adam walked to his office he detected a more somber atmosphere among the staff and the handful of lawyers. The chatter was an octave lower. Things were a bit more urgent.

Chicago had arrived. It happened occasionally, not necessarily for purposes of inspection, but more often than not to service a local client or to conduct bureaucratic little firm meetings. No one had ever been fired when Chicago arrived. No one had ever been cursed or abused. But it always provided for a few anxious moments until Chicago left and headed back North.

Adam opened his office door and nearly smacked into the worried face of E. Garner Goodman, complete with green paisley bow tie, white starched shirt, bushy gray hair. He'd been pacing around the room and happened to be near the door when it opened. Adam stared at him, then took his hand and shook it quickly.

'Come in, come in,' Goodman said, closing the door as he invited Adam into his own office. He hadn't smiled yet.

'What are you doing here?' Adam asked, throwing his briefcase on the floor and walking to his desk. They faced each other.

Goodman stroked his neat gray beard, then adjusted his bow tie. 'There's a bit of an emergency, I'm afraid. Could be bad news.'

'What?'

'Sit down, sit down. This might take a minute.'

'No. I'm fine. What is it?' It had to be horrible if he needed to take it sitting down.

Goodman tinkered with his bow tie, rubbed his beard, then said, 'Well, it happened at nine this morning. You see, the Personnel Committee is made up of fifteen partners, almost all are younger guys. The full committee has several subcommittees, of course, one for recruiting, hiring, one for discipline, one for disputes, and on and on. And, as you might guess, there's one for terminations. The Termination Subcommittee met this morning, and guess who was there to orchestrate everything.'

'Daniel Rosen.'

'Daniel Rosen. Evidently, he's been working the Termination Subcommittee for ten days trying to line up enough votes for your dismissal.'

Adam sat in a chair at the table, and Goodman sat across from him.

'There are seven members of the subcommittee, and they met this morning at Rosen's request. There were five members present, so they had a quorum. Rosen, of course, did not notify me or anyone else. Termination meetings are strictly confidential, for obvious reasons, so there was no requirement that he notify anyone.'

'Not even me?'

'No, not even you. You were the only item on the agenda, and the meeting lasted less than an hour. Rosen had the deck stacked before he went in, but he presented his case very forcefully. Remember, he was a courtroom brawler for thirty years. They record all termination meetings, just in case there's litigation afterward, so Rosen made a complete record. He, of course, claims that you were deceitful when you applied for employment with Kravitz & Bane; that it presents the firm with a conflict of interest, and on and on. And he had copies of a dozen or so newspaper articles about you and Sam and the grandfather-grandson angle. His argument was that you had embarrassed the firm. He was very prepared. I think we underestimated him last Monday.'

'And so they voted.'

'Four to one to terminate you.'

'Bastards!'

'I know. I've seen Rosen in tough spots before, and the guy can be brutally persuasive. He usually gets his way. He can't go to courtrooms anymore, so he's picking fights around the office. He'll be gone in six months.'

'That's a small comfort at the moment.'

'There's hope. Word finally filtered to my office around eleven, and luckily Emmitt Wycoff was in. We went to Rosen's office and had a terrible fight, then we got on the phone. Bottom line is this – the full Personnel Committee meets at eight o'clock in the morning to review your dismissal. You need to be there.'

'Eight o'clock in the morning!'

'Yeah. These guys are busy. Many have court dates at nine. Some have depositions all day. Out of fifteen, we'll be lucky to have a quorum.'

'How much is a quorum?'

'Two-thirds. Ten. And if there's no quorum, then we might be in trouble.'

'Trouble! What do you call this?'

'It could get worse. If there's no quorum in the morning, then you have the right to request another review in thirty days.'

'Sam will be dead in thirty days.'

'Maybe not. At any rate, I think we'll have the meeting in the morning. Emmitt and I have commitments from nine of the members to be there.'

'What about the four who voted against me this morning?'

Goodman grinned and glanced away. 'Guess. Rosen made sure his votes can be there tomorrow.'

Adam suddenly slapped the table with both hands. 'I quit dammit!'

'You can't quit. You've just been terminated.'

'Then I won't fight it. Sonofabitches!'

'Listen, Adam –'

290

'Sonofabitches!'

Goodman retreated for a moment to allow Adam to cool. He straightened his bow tie and checked the growth of his beard. He tapped his fingers on the table. Then he said, 'Look, Adam, we're in good shape in the morning, okay. Emmitt thinks so. I think so. The firm's behind you on this. We believe in what you're doing, and, frankly, we've enjoyed the publicity. There've been nice stories in the Chicago papers.'

'The firm certainly appears to be supportive.'

'Just listen to me. We can pull this off tomorrow. I'll do most of the talking. Wycoff's twisting arms right now. We've got other people twisting arms.'

'Rosen's not stupid, Mr Goodman. He wants to win, that's all. He doesn't care about me, doesn't care about Sam, or you, or anyone else involved. He simply wants to win. It's a contest, and I'll bet he's on the phone right now trying to line up votes.'

'Then let's go fight his cranky ass, okay. Let's walk into that meeting tomorrow with a chip on our shoulders. Let's make Rosen the bad guy. Honestly, Adam, the man does not have a lot of friends.'

Adam walked to the window and peeked through the shades. Foot traffic was heavy on the Mall below. It was almost five. He had close to five thousand dollars in mutual funds, and if he was frugal and if he made certain lifestyle changes the money might last for six months. His salary was sixty-two thousand, and replacing it in the very near future would be difficult. But he had never been one to worry about money, and he wouldn't start now. He was much more concerned about the next three weeks. After a ten-day career as a death penalty lawyer, he knew he needed help.

'What will it be like at the end?' he asked after a heavy silence.

Goodman slowly rose from his chair and walked to another window. 'Pretty crazy. You won't sleep much the last four days. You'll be running in all directions. The courts are unpredictable. The system is unpredictable. You keep filing petitions and appeals knowing full well they won't work. The press will be dogging you. And, most importantly, you'll need to spend as much time as possible with your client. It's crazy work and it's all free.'

'So I'll need some help.'

'Oh yes. You can't do it alone. When Maynard Tole was executed, we had a lawyer from Jackson staked out at the governor's office, one at the supreme court clerk's office in Jackson, one in Washington, and two on death row. That's why you have to go fight tomorrow, Adam. You'll need the firm and its resources. You can't do it by yourself. It takes a team.'

'This is a real kick in the crotch.'

'I know. A year ago you were in law school, now you've been terminated. I know it hurts. But believe me, Adam, it's just a fluke. It won't stand. Ten years from now you'll be a partner in this firm, and you'll be terrorizing young associates.'

'Don't bet on it.'

'Let's go to Chicago. I've got two tickets for a seven-fifteen flight. We'll be in Chicago by eight-thirty, and we'll find a nice restaurant.'

'I need to get some clothes.'

'Fine. Meet me at the airport at six-thirty.'

THE MATTER was effectively settled before the meeting began. Eleven members of the Personnel Committee were present, a sufficient number for a quorum. They gathered in a locked library on the sixtieth floor, around a long table with gallons of coffee in the center of it, and they brought with them thick files and portable Dictaphones and fatigued pocket schedules. One brought his secretary, and she sat in the hallway and worked furiously. These were busy people, all of them less than an hour away from another frantic day of endless conferences, meetings, briefings, depositions, trials, telephones, and significant lunches. Ten men, one woman, all in their late thirties or early forties, all partners of K&B, all in a hurry to return to their cluttered desks.

The matter of Adam Hall was a nuisance to them. The Personnel Committee, in fact, was a nuisance to them. It was not one of the more pleasant panels upon which to serve, but they'd been duly elected and no one dared decline. All for the firm. Go team Go!

Adam had arrived at the office at seven-thirty. He'd been gone for ten days, his longest absence yet. Emmitt Wycoff had shifted Adam's work to another young associate. There was never a shortage of rookies at Kravitz & Bane.

By eight o'clock he was hiding in a small, useless conference room near the library on the sixtieth floor. He was nervous, but worked hard at not showing it. He sipped coffee and read the morning papers. Parchman was a world away. And he studied the list of fifteen names on the Personnel Committee, none of whom he knew. Eleven strangers who would kick his future around for the next hour, then vote quickly and get on with more important matters. Wycoff checked in and said hello a few minutes before eight. Adam thanked him for everything, apologized for being so much trouble, and listened as Emmitt promised a speedy and satisfactory outcome.

Garner Goodman opened the door at five minutes after eight. 'Looks pretty good,' he said, almost in a whisper. 'Right now there are eleven present. We have commitments from at least five. Three of Rosen's votes from the subcommittee are here, but it looks like he might be a vote or two shy.'

'Is Rosen here?' Adam asked, knowing the answer but hoping that maybe the old bastard had died in his sleep.

'Yes, of course. And I think he's worried. Emmitt was still making phone calls at ten last night. We've got the votes, and Rosen knows it.' Goodman eased through the door and was gone.

At eight-fifteen, the chairman called the meeting to order and declared a quorum. The termination of Adam Hall was the sole issue on the agenda, indeed the only reason for this special meeting. Emmitt Wycoff went first, and in ten minutes did a fine job of telling how wonderful Adam was.

293

He stood at one end of the table in front of a row of bookshelves, and chatted comfortably as if trying to persuade a jury. At least half of the eleven did not hear a word. They scanned documents and juggled their calendars.

Garner Goodman spoke next. He quickly summarized the case of Sam Cayhall, and provided the honest assessment that, in all likelihood, Sam would be executed in three weeks. Then he bragged on Adam, said he might have been wrong in not disclosing his relationship with Sam, but what the hell. That was then, and this is now, and the present is a helluva lot more important when your client has only three weeks to live.

Not a single question was asked of either Wycoff or Goodman. The questions, evidently, were being saved for Rosen.

Lawyers have long memories. You cut one's throat today, and he'll wait patiently in the weeds for years until he can return the favor. Daniel Rosen had lots of favors lying around the hallways of Kravitz & Bane, and as managing partner he was in the process of collecting them. He'd stepped on people, his own people, for years. He was a bully, a liar, a thug. In his glory days, he'd been the heart and soul of the firm, and he knew it. No one would challenge him. He had abused young associates and tormented his fellow partners. He had run roughshod over committees, ignored firm policies, stolen clients from other lawyers at Kravitz & Bane, and now in the decline of his career he was collecting favors.

Two minutes into his presentation, he was interrupted for the first time by a young partner who rode motorcycles with Emmitt Wycoff. Rosen was pacing, as if playing to a packed courtroom in his glory days, when the question stopped him. Before he could think of a sarcastic answer, another question hit him. By the time he could think of an answer to either of the first two, a third came from nowhere. The brawl was on.

The three interrogators worked like an efficient tag team,

and it was apparent that they had been practicing. They took turns needling Rosen with relentless questions, and within a minute he was cursing and throwing insults. They kept their collective cool. Each had a legal pad with what appeared to be long lists of questions.

'Where's the conflict of interest, Mr Rosen?'

'Certainly a lawyer can represent a family member, right, Mr Rosen?'

'Did the application for employment specifically ask Mr Hall if this firm represented a member of his family?'

'Do you have something against publicity, Mr Rosen?'

'Why do you consider the publicity to be negative?'

'Would you try to help a family member on death row?'

'What are your feelings about the death penalty, Mr Rosen?'

'Do you secretly want to see Sam Cayhall executed because he killed Jews?'

'Don't you think you've ambushed Mr Hall?'

It was not a pleasant sight. Some of the greatest courtroom victories in recent Chicago history belonged to Daniel Rosen, and here he was getting his teeth kicked in in a meaningless fight before a committee. Not a jury. Not a judge. A committee.

The idea of retreat had never entered his mind. He pressed on, growing louder and more caustic. His retorts and acid replies grew personal, and he said some nasty things about Adam.

This was a mistake. Others joined the fray, and soon Rosen was flailing like wounded prey, just a few steps in front of the wolf pack. When it was apparent that he could never reach a majority of the committee, he lowered his voice and regained his composure.

He rallied nicely with a quiet summation about ethical considerations and avoiding the appearance of impropriety, scriptures that lawyers learn in law school and spit at each other when fighting but otherwise ignore when convenient.

When Rosen finished, he stormed out of the room, mentally taking notes of those who'd had the nerve to grill him. He'd write their names in a file the minute he got to his desk, and one day, well, one day he'd just do something about it.

Papers and pads and electronic equipment vanished from the table which was suddenly clean except for the coffee and empty cups. The chairman called for a vote. Rosen got five. Adam got six, and the Personnel Committee adjourned itself immediately and disappeared in a rush.

'Six to five?' Adam repeated as he looked at the relieved but unsmiling faces of Goodman and Wycoff.

'A regular landslide,' Wycoff quipped.

'Could be worse,' Goodman said. 'You could be out of a job.'

'Why am I not ecstatic? I mean, one lousy vote and I'd be history.'

'Not really,' Wycoff explained. 'The votes were counted before the meeting. Rosen had maybe two solid votes, and the others stuck with him because they knew you would win. You have no idea of the amount of arm twisting that took place last night. This does it for Rosen. He'll be gone in three months.'

'Maybe quicker,' added Goodman. 'He's a loose cannon. Everybody's sick of him.'

'Including me,' Adam said.

Wycoff glanced at his watch. It was eight forty-five, and he had to be in court at nine. 'Look, Adam, I've gotta run,' he said, buttoning his jacket. 'When are you going back to Memphis?'

'Today, I guess.'

'Can we have lunch? I'd like to talk to you.'

'Sure.'

He opened the door, and said, 'Great. My secretary will give you a call. Gotta run. See you.' And he was gone.

Goodman suddenly glanced at his watch too. His watch ran much slower than the real lawyers in the firm, but he did have appointments to keep. 'I need to see someone in my office. I'll join you guys for lunch.'

'One lousy vote,' Adam repeated, staring at the wall.

'Come on, Adam. It wasn't that close.'

'It certainly feels close.'

'Look, we need to spend a few hours together before you leave. I wanna hear about Sam, okay? Let's start with lunch.' He opened the door and was gone.

Adam sat on the table, shaking his head.

TWENTY-FIVE

IF BAKER COOLEY and the other lawyers in the Memphis office knew anything about Adam's sudden termination and its quick reversal, it was not apparent. They treated him the same, which was to say they kept to themselves and stayed away from his office. They were not rude to him, because, after all, he was from Chicago. They smiled when forced to, and they could muster a moment of small talk in the hallways if Adam was in the mood. But they were corporate lawyers, with starched shirts and soft hands which were unaccustomed to the dirt and grime of criminal defense. They did not go to jails or prisons or holding tanks to visit with clients, nor did they wrangle with cops and prosecutors and cranky judges. They worked primarily behind their desks and around mahogany conference tables. Their time was spent talking to clients who could afford to pay them several hundred dollars an hour for advice, and when they weren't talking to clients they were on the phone or doing lunch with other lawyers and bankers and insurance executives.

There'd been enough in the newspapers already to arouse resentment around the office. Most of the lawyers were embarrassed to see the name of their firm associated with a character such as Sam Cayhall. Most of them had no idea that he'd been represented by Chicago for seven years. Now friends were asking questions. Other lawyers were making wisecracks. Wives were humiliated over garden club teas. In-laws were suddenly interested in their legal careers.

Sam Cayhall and his grandson had quickly become a pain in the ass for the Memphis office, but nothing could be done about it.

Adam could sense it but didn't care. It was a temporary office, suitable for three more weeks and hopefully not a day longer. He stepped from the elevator Friday morning, and ignored the receptionist who was suddenly busy arranging magazines. He spoke to his secretary, a young woman named Darlene, and she handed him a phone message from Todd Marks at the *Memphis Press.*

He took the pink phone message to his office and threw it in the wastebasket. He hung his coat on a hanger, and began covering the table with paper. There were pages of notes he'd taken on the flights to and from Chicago, and similar pleadings he'd borrowed from Goodman's files, and dozens of copies of recent federal decisions.

He was soon lost in a world of legal theories and strategies. Chicago was a fading memory.

ROLLIE WEDGE entered the Brinkley Plaza building through the front doors to the Mall. He had waited patiently at a table of a sidewalk café until the black Saab appeared then turned into a nearby parking garage. He was dressed in a white shirt with a tie, seersucker slacks, casual loafers. He sipped an iced tea while watching Adam walk along the sidewalk and enter the building.

The lobby was empty as Wedge scanned the directory. Kravitz & Bane had the third and fourth floors. There were four identical elevators, and he rode one to the eighth floor. He stepped into a narrow foyer. To the right was a door with the name of a trust company emblazoned in brass and to the left was an adjoining hallway lined with doors to all kinds of enterprises. Next to the water fountain was a door to the stairway. He casually walked down eight flights, checking doors as he went. No one passed him in the stairwell. He reentered the lobby, then rode the other elevator, alone, to the third floor. He smiled at the receptionist, who was still busy with the magazines, and was about to ask directions to the trust company when the phone rang and she became occupied with it. A set of double glass doors separated the reception area from the entryway to the elevators. He rode to the fourth floor, and found an identical set of doors, but no receptionist. The doors were locked. On a wall to the right was a coded entry panel with nine numbered buttons.

He heard voices, and stepped into the stairwell. There was no lock on the door from either side. He waited for a moment, then eased through the door and took a long drink of water. An elevator opened, and a young man in khakis and blue blazer bounced out with a cardboard box under one arm and a thick book in his right hand. He headed for the Kravitz & Bane doors. He hummed a loud tune and did not notice as Wedge fell in behind him. He stopped and carefully balanced the law book on top of the box, freeing his right hand to punch the code. Seven, seven, three, and the panel beeped with each number. Wedge was inches away, peering over his shoulder and gathering the code.

The young man quickly grabbed the book, and was about to turn around when Wedge bumped into him slightly, and said, 'Damn! Sorry! I wasn't –' Wedge took a step backwards and looked at the lettering above the door. 'This isn't Riverbend Trust,' he said, dazed and bewildered.

'Nope. This is Kravitz & Bane.'

'What floor is this? Wedge asked. Something clicked and the door was free.

'Fourth. Riverbend Trust is on the eighth.'

'Sorry,' Wedge said again, now embarrassed and almost pitiful. 'Must've got off on the wrong floor.'

The young man frowned and shook his head, then opened the door.

'Sorry,' Wedge said for the third time as he backed away. The door closed and the kid was gone. Wedge rode the elevator to the main lobby and left the building.

He left downtown, and drove east and north for ten minutes until he came to a section of the city filled with government housing. He pulled into the driveway beside the Auburn House, and was stopped by a uniformed guard. He was just turning around, he explained, lost again, and he was very sorry. As he backed into the street, he saw the burgundy Jaguar owned by Lee Booth parked between two subcompacts.

He headed toward the river, toward downtown again, and twenty minutes later parked at an abandoned red-brick warehouse on the bluffs. While sitting in his car, he quickly changed into a tan shirt with blue trim around the short sleeves and the name Rusty stitched above the pocket. Then he was moving swiftly but inconspicuously on foot around the corner of the building and down a slope through weeds until he stopped in the brush. A small tree provided shade as he caught his breath and hid from the scorching sun. In front of him was a small field of Bermuda grass, thick and green and obviously well tended, and beyond the grass was a row of luxury condominiums hanging over the edge of the bluff. A fence of brick and iron presented a vexing problem, and he studied it patiently from the privacy of the brush.

One side of the condos was the parking lot with a closed gate leading to the only entrance and exit. A uniformed guard manned the small, boxlike, air-conditioned gatehouse. Few cars were in sight. It was almost 10 A.M. The outline of the guard could be seen through tinted glass.

Wedge ignored the fence and chose instead to penetrate from the bluff. He crawled along a row of boxwoods, clutching handfuls of grass to keep from sliding eighty feet into Riverside Drive. He slid under wooden patios, some of which hung ten feet into the air as the bluff dropped fast below them. He stopped at the seventh condo, and swung himself onto the patio.

He rested for a moment in a wicker chair and toyed with an outside cable as if on a routine service call. No one was watching. Privacy was important to these wealthy people, they paid for it dearly, and each little terrace was shielded from the next by decorative wooden planks and all sorts of hanging vegetation. His shirt by now was sticky and clinging to his back.

301

The sliding glass door from the patio to the kitchen was locked, of course, a rather simple lock that slowed him for almost one minute. He picked it, leaving neither damage nor evidence, then glanced around for another look before he went in. This was the tricky part. He assumed there was a security system, probably one with contacts on every window and door. Since no one was home it was highly probable the system would be activated. The delicate question was exactly how much noise would be made when he opened the door. Would there be a silent alert, or would he be startled with a screaming siren?

He took a breath, then carefully slid the door open. No siren greeted him. He took a quick look at the monitor above the door, then stepped inside.

The relay immediately alerted Willis, the guard at the gate, who heard a frantic though not very loud beeping sound from his monitoring screen. He looked at the red light blinking at Number 7, home of Lee Booth, and he waited for it to stop. Mrs Booth tripped her alarm at least twice a month, which was about the average for the flock he guarded. He checked his clipboard and noticed that Mrs Booth had left at nine-fifteen. But she occasionally had sleepovers, usually men, and now she had her nephew staying with her, and so Willis watched the red light for forty-five seconds until it stopped blinking and fixed itself in a permanent ON position.

This was unusual, but no need to panic. These people lived behind walls and paid for around-the-clock armed guards, so they were not serious about their alarm systems. He quickly dialed Mrs Booth's number, and there was no answer. He punched a button and set in motion a recorded 911 call requesting police assistance. He opened the key drawer and selected one for Number 7, then left the gatehouse and walked quickly across the parking lot to see about Mrs Booth's unit. He unfastened his holster so he could grab his revolver, just in case.

Rollie Wedge stepped into the gatehouse and saw the open key drawer. He took a set marked for Unit 7, along with a card with the alarm code and instructions, and for good measure he also grabbed keys and cards for Numbers 8 and 13, just to baffle old Willis and the cops.

TWENTY-SIX

THEY WENT to the cemetery first, to pay their respects to the dead. It covered two small hills on the edge of Clanton, one lined with elaborate tombstones and monuments where prominent families had buried themselves together, over time, and had their names carved in heavy granite. The second hill was for the newer graves, and as time had passed in Mississippi the tombstones had grown smaller. Stately oaks and elms shaded most of the cemetery. The grass was trimmed low and the shrubs were neat. Azaleas were in every corner. Clanton placed a priority on its memories.

It was a lovely Saturday, with no clouds and a slight breeze that had started during the night and chased away the humidity. The rains were gone for a while, and the hillsides were lush with greenery and wild flowers. Lee knelt by her mother's headstone and placed a small bouquet of flowers under her name. She closed her eyes as Adam stood behind her and stared at the grave. Anna Gates Cayhall, September 3, 1922 – September 18, 1977. She was fifty-five when she died, Adam calculated, so he was thirteen, still living in blissful ignorance somewhere in Southern California.

She was buried alone, under a single headstone, and this in itself had presented some problems. Mates for life are usually buried side by side, at least in the South, with the first one occupying the first slot under a double headstone. Upon each visit to the deceased, the survivor gets to see his or her name already carved and just waiting.

'Daddy was fifty-six when Mother died,' Lee explained as she took Adam's hand and inched away from the grave. 'I wanted him to bury her in a plot where he could one day join her, but he refused. I guess he figured he still had a few years left, and he might remarry.'

'You told me once that she didn't like Sam.'

'I'm sure she loved him in a way, they were together for almost forty years. But they were never close. As I grew older I realized she didn't like to be around him. She confided in me at times. She was a simple country girl who married young, had babies, stayed home with them, and was expected to obey her husband. And this was not unusual for those times. I think she was a very frustrated woman.'

'Maybe she didn't want Sam next to her for eternity.'

'I thought about that. In fact, Eddie wanted them separated and buried at opposite ends of the cemetery.'

'Good for Eddie.'

'He wasn't joking either.'

'How much did she know about Sam and the Klan?'

'I have no idea. It was not something we discussed. I remember she was humiliated after his arrest. She even stayed with Eddie and you guys for a while because the reporters were bothering her.'

'And she didn't attend any of his trials.'

'No. He didn't want her to watch. She had a problem with high blood pressure, and Sam used that as an excuse to keep her away from it.'

They turned and walked along a narrow lane through the old section of the cemetery. They held hands and looked at the passing tombstones. Lee pointed to a row of trees across the street on another hill. 'That's where the blacks are buried,' she said. 'Under those trees. It's a small cemetery.'

'You're kidding? Even today?'

'Sure, you know, keep 'em in their place. These people couldn't stand the idea of a Negro lying amongst their ancestors.'

Adam shook his head in disbelief. They climbed the hill

and rested under an oak. The rows of graves spread peacefully beneath them. The dome of the Ford County Courthouse glittered in the sun a few blocks away.

'I played here as a little girl,' she said quietly. She pointed to her right, to the north. 'Every Fourth of July the city celebrates with a firework display, and the best seats in the house are here in the cemetery. There's a park down there, and that's where they shoot from. We'd load up our bikes and come to town to watch the parade and swim in the city pool and play with our friends. And right after dark, we'd all gather around here, in the midst of the dead, and sit on these tombstones to watch the fireworks. The men would stay by their trucks where the beer and whiskey were hidden, and the women would lie on quilts and tend to the babies. We would run and romp and ride bikes all over the place.'

'Eddie?'

'Of course. Eddie was just a normal little brother, pesky as hell sometimes, but very much a boy. I miss him, you know. I miss him very much. We weren't close for many years, but when I come back to this town I think of my little brother.'

'I miss him too.'

'He and I came here, to this very spot, the night he graduated from high school. I had been in Nashville for two years, and I came back because he wanted me to watch him graduate. We had a bottle of cheap wine, and I think it was his first drink. I'll never forget it. We sat here on Emil Jacob's tombstone and sipped wine until the bottle was empty.'

'What year was it?'

'Nineteen sixty-one, I think. He wanted to join the Army so he could leave Clanton and get away from Sam. I didn't want my little brother in the Army, and we discussed it until the sun came up.'

'He was pretty confused?'

'He was eighteen, probably as confused as most kids who've just finished high school. Eddie was terrified that if he stayed in Clanton something would happen to him, some

306

mysterious genetic flaw would surface and he'd become another Sam. Another Cayhall with a hood. He was desperate to run from this place.'

'But you ran as soon as you could.'

'I know, but I was tougher than Eddie, at least at the age of eighteen. I couldn't see him leaving home so young. So we sipped wine and tried to get a handle on life.'

'Did my father ever have a handle on life?'

'I doubt it, Adam. We were both tormented by our father and his family's hatred. There are things I hope you never learn, stories that I pray remain untold. I guess I pushed them away, while Eddie couldn't.'

She took his hand again and they strolled into the sunlight and down a dirt path toward the newer section of the cemetery. She stopped and pointed to a row of small headstones. 'Here are your great-grandparents, along with aunts, uncles, and other assorted Cayhalls.'

Adam counted eight in all. He read the names and dates, and spoke aloud the poetry and the Scriptures and farewells inscribed in granite.

'There are lots more out in the country,' Lee said. 'Most of the Cayhalls originated around Karaway, fifteen miles from here. They were country people, and they're buried behind rural churches.'

'Did you come here for these burials?'

'A few. It's not a close family, Adam. Some of these people had been dead for years before I knew about it.'

'Why wasn't your mother buried here?'

'Because she didn't want to be. She knew she was about to die, and she picked the spot. She never considered herself a Cayhall. She was a Gates.'

'Smart woman.'

Lee pulled a handful of weeds from her grandmother's grave, and rubbed her fingers over the name of Lydia Newsome Cayhall, who died in 1961 at the age of seventy-two. 'I remember her well,' Lee said, kneeling on the grass. 'A fine, Christian woman. She'd roll over in her grave if she knew her third son was on death row.'

'What about him?' Adam asked pointing to Lydia's husband, Nathaniel Lucas Cayhall, who died in 1952 at the age of sixty-four. The fondness left Lee's face. 'A mean old man,' she said. 'I'm sure he'd be proud of Sam. Nat, as he was known, was killed at a funeral.'

'A funeral?'

'Yes. Traditionally, funerals were social occasions around here. They were preceded by long wakes with lots of visiting and eating. And drinking. Life was hard in the rural South, and often the funerals turned into drunken brawls. Nat was very violent, and he picked a fight with the wrong men just after a funeral service. They beat him to death with a stick of wood.'

'Where was Sam?'

'Right in the middle of it. He was beaten too, but survived. I was a little girl, and I remember Nat's funeral. Sam was in hospital and couldn't attend.'

'Did he get retribution?'

'Of course.'

'How?'

'Nothing was ever proven, but several years later the two men who'd beaten Nat were released from prison. They surfaced briefly around here, then disappeared. One body was found months later next door in Milburn County. Beaten, of course. The other man was never found. The police questioned Sam and his brothers, but there was no proof.'

'Do you think he did it?'

'Sure he did. Nobody messed with the Cayhalls back then. They were known to be half-crazy and mean as hell.'

They left the family gravesites and continued along the path. 'So Adam, the question for us is, where do we bury Sam?'

'I think we should bury him over there, with the blacks. That would serve him right.'

'What makes you think they'd want him?'

'Good point.'

'Seriously.'

'Sam and I have not reached that point yet.'

'Do you think he'll want to be buried here? In Ford County?'

'I don't know. We haven't discussed it, for obvious reasons. There's still hope.'

'How much hope?'

'A trace. Enough to keep fighting.'

They left the cemetery on foot, and walked along a tranquil street with worn sidewalks and ancient oaks. The homes were old and well painted, with long porches and cats resting on the front steps. Children raced by on bikes and skateboards, and old people rocked in their porch swings and waved slowly. 'These are my old stomping grounds, Adam,' Lee said as they walked aimlessly along. Her hands were stuck deep in denim pockets, her eyes moistened with memories that were at once sad and pleasant. She looked at each house as if she'd stayed there as a child and could remember the little girls who'd been her friends. She could hear the giggles and laughs, and silly games and the serious fights of ten-year-olds.

'Were those happy times?' Adam asked.

'I don't know. We never lived in town, so we were known as country kids. I always longed for one of these houses, with friends all around and stores a few blocks away. The town kids considered themselves to be a bit better than us, but it wasn't much of a problem. My best friends lived here, and I spent many hours playing in these streets, climbing these trees. Those were good times, I guess. The memories from the house in the country are not pleasant.'

'Because of Sam?'

An elderly lady in a flowered dress and large straw hat was sweeping around her front steps as they approached. She glanced at them, then she froze and stared. Lee slowed then stopped near the walkway to the house. She looked at the old woman, and the old woman looked at Lee. 'Mornin', Mrs Langston,' Lee said in a friendly drawl.

Mrs Langston gripped the broom handle and stiffened her back, and seemed content to stare.

309

'I'm Lee Cayhall. You remember me,' Lee drawled again.

As the name Cayhall drifted across the tiny lawn, Adam caught himself glancing around to see if anyone else heard it. He was prepared to be embarrassed if the name fell on other ears. If Mrs Langston remembered Lee, it was not apparent. She managed a polite nod of the head, just a quick up and down motion, rather awkward as if to say, 'Good morning to you. Now move along.'

'Nice to see you again,' Lee said and began walking away. Mrs Langston scurried up the steps and disappeared inside. 'I dated her son in high school,' Lee said, shaking her head in disbelief.

'She was thrilled to see you.'

'She was always sort of wacky,' Lee said without conviction. 'Or maybe she's afraid to talk to a Cayhall. Afraid of what the neighbors might say.'

'I think it might be best if we go incognito for the rest of the day. What about it?'

'It's a deal.'

They passed other folks puttering in their flower beds and waiting for the mailman, but they said nothing. Lee covered her eyes with sun shades. They zigzagged through the neighborhood in the general direction of the central square, chatting about Lee's old friends and where they were now. She kept in touch with two of them, one in Clanton and one in Texas. They avoided family history until they were on a street with smaller, wood-framed houses stacked tightly together. They stopped at the corner, and Lee nodded at something down the street.

'You see the third house on the right, the little brown one there?'

'Yes.'

'That's where you lived. We could walk down there but I see people moving about.'

Two small children played with toy guns in the front yard and someone was swinging on the narrow front porch. It

310

was a square house, small, neat, perfect for a young couple having babies.

Adam had been almost three when Eddie and Evelyn disappeared, and as he stood on the corner he tried desperately to remember something about the house. He couldn't.

'It was painted white back then, and of course the trees were smaller. Eddie rented it from a local real estate agent.'

'Was it nice?'

'Nice enough. They hadn't been married long. They were just kids with a new child. Eddie worked in an auto parts store, then he worked for the state highway department. Then he took another job.'

'Sounds familiar.'

'Evelyn worked part-time in a jewelry store on the square. I think they were happy. She was not from here, you know, and so she didn't know a lot of people. They kept to themselves.'

They walked by the house and one of the children aimed an orange machine gun at Adam. There were no memories of the place to be evoked at that moment. He smiled at the child and looked away. They were soon on another street with the square in sight.

Lee was suddenly a tour guide and historian. The Yankees had burned Clanton in 1863, the bastards, and after the war, General Clanton, a Confederate hero whose family owned the county, returned, with only one leg, the other one lost somewhere on the battlefield at Shiloh, and designed the new courthouse and the streets around it. His original drawings were on the wall upstairs in the courthouse. He wanted lots of shade so he planted oaks in perfect rows around the new courthouse. He was a man of vision who could see the small town rising from the ashes and prospering, so he designed the streets in an exact square around the courthouse common. They had walked by the great man's grave, she said, just a moment ago, and she would show it to him later.

There was a struggling mall north of town and a row of

discount supermarkets to the east, but the people of Ford County still enjoyed shopping around the square on Saturday morning, she explained as they strolled along the sidewalk next to Washington Street. Traffic was slow and the pedestrians were even slower. The buildings were old and adjoining, filled with lawyers and insurance agents, banks and cafés, hardware stores and dress shops. The sidewalk was covered with canopies, awnings, and verandas from the offices and stores. Creaky fans hung low and spun sluggishly. They stopped in front of an ancient pharmacy, and Lee removed her sunglasses. 'This was a hangout,' she explained. 'There was a soda fountain in the back with a jukebox and racks of comic books. You could buy an enormous cherry sundae for a nickel, and it took hours to eat it. It took even longer if the boys were here.'

Like something from a movie, Adam thought. They stopped in front of a hardware store, and for some reason examined the shovels and hoes and rakes leaning against the window. Lee looked at the battered double doors, opened and held in place by bricks, and thought of something from her childhood. But she kept it to herself.

They crossed the street, hand in hand, and passed a group of old men whittling wood and chewing tobacco around the war memorial. She nodded at a statue and informed him quietly that it was General Clanton, with both legs. The courthouse was not open for business on Saturdays. They bought colas from a machine outside and sipped them in a gazebo on the front lawn. She told the story of the most famous trial in the history of Ford County, the murder trial of Carl Lee Hailey in 1984. He was a black man who shot and killed two rednecks who'd raped his little daughter. There were marches and protests by blacks on one side and Klansmen on the other, and the National Guard actually camped out here, around the courthouse, to keep the peace. Lee had driven down from Memphis one day to watch the spectacle. He was acquitted by an all-white jury.

Adam remembered the trial. He'd been a junior at

312

Pepperdine, and had followed it in the papers because it was happening in the town of his birth.

When she was a child, entertainment was scarce, and trials were always well attended. Sam had brought her and Eddie here once to watch the trial of a man accused of killing a hunting dog. He was found guilty and spent a year in prison. The county was split – the city folks were against the conviction for such a lowly crime, while the country folks placed a higher value on good beagles. Sam had been particularly happy to see the man sent away.

Lee wanted to show him something. They walked around the courthouse to the rear door where two water fountains stood ten feet apart. Neither had been used in years. One had been for whites, the other for blacks. She remembered the story of Rosia Alfie Gateswood, Miss Allie as she was known, the first black person to drink from the white fountain and escape without injury. Not long after that, the water lines were disconnected.

They found a table in a crowded café known simply as The Tea Shoppe, on the west side of the square. She told stories, all of them pleasant and most of them funny, as they ate BLT's and french fries. She kept her sunglasses on, and Adam caught her watching the people.

THEY LEFT CLANTON after lunch, and after a leisurely walk back to the cemetery. Adam drove, and Lee pointed this way and that until they were on a county highway running through small, neat farms with cows grazing the hillsides. They passed occasional pockets of white trash – dilapidated double-wide trailers with junk cars strewn about – and they passed run-down shotgun houses still inhabited by poor blacks. But the hilly countryside was pretty, for the most part, and the day was beautiful.

She pointed again, and they turned onto a smaller, paved road that snaked its way deeper into the sticks. They finally stopped in front of an abandoned white frame house with weeds shooting from the porch and ivy swarming into the windows. It was fifty yards from the road, and the gravel

313

drive leading to it was gullied and impassable. The front lawn was overgrown with Johnson grass and cocklebur. The mailbox was barely visible in the ditch beside the road.

'The Cayhall estate,' she mumbled, and they sat for a long time in the car and looked at the sad little house.

'What happened to it?' Adam finally asked.

'Oh, it was a good house. Didn't have much of a chance, though. The people were a disappointment.' She slowly removed her sunglasses and wiped her eyes. 'I lived here for eighteen years, and I couldn't wait to leave it.'

'Why is it abandoned?'

She took a deep breath, and tried to arrange the story. 'I think it was paid for many years ago, but Daddy mortgaged it to pay the lawyers for his last trial. He, of course, never came home again, and at some point the bank foreclosed. There are eighty acres around it, and everything was lost. I haven't been back here since the foreclosure. I asked Phelps to buy it, and he said no. I couldn't blame him. I really didn't want to own it for myself. I heard later from some friends here that it was rented several times, and I guess eventually abandoned. I didn't know if the house was still standing.'

'What happened to the personal belongings?'

'The day before the foreclosure, the bank allowed me to go in and box up anything I wanted. I saved some things – photo albums, keepsakes, yearbooks, bibles, some of Mother's valuables. They're in storage in Memphis.'

'I'd like to see them.'

'The furniture was not worth saving, not a decent piece of anything. My mother was dead, my brother had just committed suicide, and my father had just been sent to death row, and I was not in the mood to keep a lot of memorabilia. It was a horrible experience, going through that dirty little house and trying to salvage objects that might one day bring a smile. Hell, I wanted to burn everything. Almost did.'

'You're not serious.'

'Of course I am. After I'd been here for a couple of hours,

314

I decided to just burn the damn house and everything in it. Happens all the time, right? I found an old lantern with some kerosene in it, and I sat it on the kitchen table and talked to it as I boxed stuff up. It would've been easy.'

'Why didn't you?'

'I don't know. I wish I'd had the guts to do it, but I remember worrying about the bank and the foreclosure and, well, arson is a crime, isn't it? I remember laughing at the idea of going off to prison where I'd be with Sam. That's why I didn't strike a match. I was afraid I'd get in trouble and go to prison.'

The car was hot now, and Adam opened his door. 'I want to look around,' he said, getting out. They picked their way down the gravel drive, stepping over gullies two feet wide. They stopped at the front porch and looked at the rotting boards.

'I'm not going in there,' she said firmly and pulled her hand away from his. Adam studied the decaying porch and decided against stepping on it. He walked along the front of the house, looking at the broken windows with vines disappearing inside. He followed the drive around the house, and Lee tagged along.

The backyard was shaded by old oaks and maples, and the ground was bare in places where the sun was kept out. It stretched for an eighth of a mile down a slight incline until it stopped at a thicket. The plot was surrounded by woods in the distance.

She took his hand again, and they walked to a tree beside the wooden shed that, for some reason, was in much better condition than the house. 'This was my tree,' she said, looking up at the branches. 'My own pecan tree.' Her voice had a slight quiver.

'It's a great tree.'

'Wonderful for climbing. I'd spend hours here, sitting in those branches, swinging my feet and resting my chin on a limb. In the spring and summer, I'd climb about halfway up, and no one could see me. I had my own little world up there.'

She suddenly closed her eyes and covered her mouth with a hand. Her shoulders trembled. Adam placed his arm around her and tried to think of something to say.

'This is where it happened,' she said after a moment. She bit her lip and fought back tears. Adam said nothing.

'You asked me once about a story,' she said with clenched teeth as she wiped her cheeks with the backs of her hands. 'The story of Daddy killing a black man.' She nodded toward the house. Her hands shook so she stuck them in her pockets.

A minute passed as they stared at the house, neither wanting to speak. The only rear door opened onto a small square porch with a railing around it. A delicate breeze ruffled the leaves above them and made the only sound.

She took a deep breath, then said, 'His name was Joe Lincoln, and he lived down the road there with his family.' She nodded at the remnants of a dirt trail that ran along the edge of a field then disappeared into the woods. 'He had about a dozen kids.'

'Quince Lincoln?' Adam asked.

'Yeah. How'd you know about him?'

'Sam mentioned his name the other day when we were talking about Eddie. He said Quince and Eddie were good friends when they were kids.'

'He didn't talk about Quince's father, did he?'

'No.'

'I didn't think so. Joe worked here on the farm for us, and his family lived in a shotgun house that we also owned. He was a good man with a big family, and like most poor blacks back then they just barely survived. I knew a couple of his kids, but we weren't friends like Quince and Eddie. One day the boys were playing here in the backyard, it was summertime and we weren't in school. They got into an argument over a small toy, a Confederate Army soldier, and Eddie accused Quince of stealing it. Typical boy stuff, you know. I think they were eight or nine years old. Daddy happened to walk by, over there, and Eddie ran to him and told how Quince had stolen the toy. Quince emphatically

316

denied it. Both boys were really mad and on the verge of tears. Sam, typically, flew into a rage and cursed Quince, calling him all sorts of names like "thieving little nigger" and "sorry little nigger bastard". Sam demanded the soldier, and Quince started crying. He kept saying he didn't have it, and Eddie kept saying he did. Sam grabbed the boy, shook him real hard, and started slapping him on the butt. Sam was yelling and screaming and cursing, and Quince was crying and pleading. They went around the yard a few times with Sam shaking him and hitting him. Quince finally pulled free, and ran home. Eddie ran into our house, and Daddy followed him inside. A moment later, Sam stepped through the door there, with a walking cane, which he carefully laid on the porch. He then sat on the steps and waited patiently. He smoked a cigarette and watched the dirt road. The Lincoln house was not far away, and, sure enough, within a few minutes Joe came running out of the trees there with Quince right behind him. As he got close to the house, he saw Daddy waiting on him, and he slowed to a walk. Daddy yelled over his shoulder, "Eddie! Come here! Watch me whip this nigger!" '

She began walking very slowly to the house, then stopped a few feet from the porch. 'When Joe was right about here, he stopped and looked at Sam. He said something like, "Quince says you hit him, Mr Sam." To which my father replied something like, "Quince is a thieving little nigger, Joe. You should teach your kids not to steal." They began to argue, and it was obvious there was going to be a fight. Sam suddenly jumped from the porch, and threw the first punch. They fell to the ground, right about here, and fought like cats. Joe was a few years younger and stronger, but Daddy was so mean and angry that the fight was pretty even. They struck each other in the face and cursed and kicked like a couple of animals.' She stopped the narrative and looked around the yard, then she pointed to the back door. 'At some point, Eddie stepped onto the porch to watch it. Quince was standing a few feet away, yelling at his father. Sam made a dash for the porch and grabbed the

317

walking cane, and the matter got out of hand. He beat Joe in the face and head until he fell to his knees, and he poked him in the stomach and groin until he could barely move. Joe looked at Quince and yelled for him to run get the shotgun. Quince took off. Sam stopped beating, and turned to Eddie. "Go get my shotgun," he said. Eddie froze, and Daddy yelled at him again. Joe was on the ground, on all fours, trying to collect himself, and just as he was about to stand, Sam beat him again and knocked him down. Eddie went inside and Sam walked to the porch. Eddie returned in a matter of seconds with a shotgun, and Daddy made him go inside. The door closed.'

Lee walked to the porch and sat on the edge of it. She buried her face in her hands, and cried for a long time. Adam stood a few feet away, staring at the ground, listening to the sobs. When she finally looked at him, her eyes were glazed, her mascara was running, her nose dripped. She wiped her face with her hands, then rubbed them on her jeans. 'I'm sorry,' she whispered.

'Finish it, please,' he said quickly.

She breathed deeply for a moment, then wiped her eyes some more. 'Joe was just over there,' she said, pointing to a spot in the grass not far from Adam. 'He'd made it to his feet, and he turned and saw Daddy with the gun. He glanced around in the direction of his house, but there was no sign of Quince and his gun. He turned back to Daddy, who was standing right there, on the edge of the porch. Then my dear sweet father slowly raised the gun, hesitated for a second, looked around to see if anyone was watching, and pulled the trigger. Just like that. Joe fell hard and never moved.'

'You saw this happen, didn't you?'

'Yes, I did.'

'Where were you?'

'Over there,' she nodded, but didn't point. 'In my pecan tree. Hidden from the world.'

'Sam couldn't see you?'

'No one could see me. I watched the whole thing.' She

covered her eyes again and fought back the tears. Adam eased onto the porch and sat beside her.

She cleared her throat and looked away. 'He watched Joe for a minute, ready to shoot again if necessary. But Joe never moved. He was quite dead. There was some blood around his head on the grass, and I could see it from the tree. I remember digging my fingernails into the bark to keep from falling, and I remember wanting to cry but being too scared. I didn't want him to hear me. Quince appeared after a few minutes. He'd heard the shot, and he was crying by the time I saw him. Just running like crazy and crying, and when he saw his father on the ground he started screaming like any child would've done. My father raised the gun again, and for a second I knew he was about to shoot the boy. But Quince threw Joe's shotgun to the ground and ran to his father. He was bawling and wailing. He wore a light-colored shirt, and soon it was covered with blood. Sam eased to the side and picked up Joe's shotgun, then he went inside with both guns.'

She stood slowly and took several measured steps. 'Quince and Joe were right about here,' she said, marking the spot with her heel. 'Quince held his father's head next to his stomach, blood was everywhere, and he made strange moaning sounds, like the whimper of a dying animal.' She turned and looked at the tree. 'And there I was sitting up there like a little bird, crying too. I hated my father so badly at that moment.'

'Where was Eddie?'

'Inside the house, in his room with the door locked.' She pointed to a window with broken panes and a shutter missing. 'That was his room. He told me later he looked outside when he heard the shot, and he saw Quince clutching his father. Within minutes, Ruby Lincoln came running up with a string of children behind her. They all collapsed around Quince and Joe, and, God, it was horrible. They were screaming and weeping and yelling at Joe to get up, to please not die on them.

'Sam went inside and called an ambulance. He also called

319

one of his brothers, Albert, and a couple of neighbors. Pretty soon there was a crowd in the backyard. Sam and his gang stood on the porch with their guns and watched the mourners, who dragged the body under that tree over there.' She pointed to a large oak. 'The ambulance arrived after an eternity, and took the body away. Ruby and her children walked back to their house, and my father and his buddies had a good laugh on the porch.'

'How long did you stay in the tree?'

'I don't know. As soon as everybody was gone, I climbed down and ran into the woods. Eddie and I had a favorite place down by a creek, and I knew he would come looking for me. He did. He was scared and out of breath; told me all about the shooting, and I told him that I'd seen it. He didn't believe me at first, but I gave him the details. We were both scared to death. He reached in his pocket and pulled out something. It was the little Confederate soldier he and Quince had fought over. He'd found it under his bed, and so he decided on the spot that everything was his fault. We swore each other to secrecy. He promised he would never tell anyone that I had witnessed the killing, and I promised I would never tell anyone that he'd found the soldier. He threw it in the creek.'

'Did either of you ever tell?'

She shook her head for a long time.

'Sam never knew you were in the tree?' Adam asked.

'Nope. I never told my mother. Eddie and I talked about it occasionally over the years, and as time passed we just sort of buried it away. When we returned to the house, our parents were in the middle of a huge fight. She was hysterical and he was wild-eyed and crazy. I think he'd hit her a few times. She grabbed us and told us to get in the car. As we were backing out of the driveway, the sheriff pulled up. We drove around for a while, Mother in the front seat, and Eddie and I in the back, both of us too scared to talk. She didn't know what to say. We assumed he would be taken to jail, but when we parked in the driveway he was sitting on the front porch as if nothing had happened.'

'What did the sheriff do?'

'Nothing, really. He and Sam talked for a bit. Sam showed him Joe's shotgun and explained how it was a simple matter of self-defense. Just another dead nigger.'

'He wasn't arrested?'

'No, Adam. This was Mississippi in the early fifties. I'm sure the sheriff had a good laugh about it, patted Sam on the back, and told him to be a good boy, and then left. He even allowed Sam to keep Joe's shotgun.'

'That's incredible.'

'We were hoping he'd go to jail for a few years.'

'What did the Lincolns do?'

'What could they do? Who would listen to them? Sam forbade Eddie from seeing Quince, and to make sure the boys didn't get together, he evicted them from their house.'

'Good God!'

'He gave them one week to get out, and the sheriff arrived to fulfill his sworn duties by forcing them out of the house. The eviction was legal and proper, Sam assured Mother. It was the only time I thought she might leave him. I wish she had.'

'Did Eddie ever see Quince?'

'Years later. When Eddie started driving, he started looking for the Lincolns. They had moved to a small community on the other side of Clanton, and Eddie found them there. He apologized and said he was sorry a hundred times. But they were never friends again. Ruby asked him to leave. He told me they lived in a run-down shack with no electricity.'

She walked to her pecan tree and sat against its trunk. Adam followed and leaned against it. He looked down at her and thought of all the years she'd been carrying this burden. And he thought of his father, of his anguish and torment, of the indelible scars he'd borne to his death. Adam now had the first clue to his father's destruction, and he wondered if the pieces might someday fit together. He thought of Sam, and as he glanced at the porch he could see a younger man with a gun and hatred in his face. Lee was sobbing quietly.

'What did Sam do afterwards?'

She struggled to control herself. 'The house was so quiet for a week, maybe a month, I don't know. But it seemed like years before anyone spoke over dinner. Eddie stayed in his room with the door locked. I would hear him crying at night, and he told me again and again how much he hated his father. He wanted him dead. He wanted to run away from home. He blamed himself for everything. Mother became concerned, and she spent a lot of time with him. As for me, they thought I was off playing in the woods when it happened. Shortly after Phelps and I married, I secretly began seeing a psychiatrist. I tried to work it out in therapy, and I wanted Eddie to do the same. But he wouldn't listen. The last time I talked to Eddie before he died, he mentioned the killing. He never got over it.'

'And you got over it?'

'I didn't say that. Therapy helped, but I still wonder what would've happened if I had screamed at Daddy before he pulled the trigger. Would he have killed Joe with his daughter watching? I don't think so.'

'Come on Lee. That was forty years ago. You can't blame yourself.'

'Eddie blamed me. And he blamed himself, and we blamed each other until we were grown. We were children when it happened, and we couldn't run to our parents. We were helpless.'

Adam could think of a hundred questions about the killing of Joe Lincoln. The subject was not likely to be raised again with Lee, and he wanted to know everything that happened, every small detail. Where was Joe buried? What happened to his shotgun? Was the shooting reported in the local paper? Was the case presented to a grand jury? Did Sam ever mention it to his children? Where was her mother during the fight? Did she hear the argument and the gunshot? What happened to Joe's family? Did they still live in Ford County?

'Let's burn it, Adam,' she said strongly, wiping her face and glaring at him.

322

'You're not serious.'

'Yes I am! Let's burn the whole damned place, the house, the shed, the tree, the grass and weeds. It won't take much. Just a couple of matches here and there. Come on.'

'No, Lee.'

'Come on.'

Adam bent over gently and took her by the arm. 'Let's go, Lee. I've heard enough for one day.'

She didn't resist. She too had had enough for one day. He helped her through the weeds, around the house, over the ruins of the driveway, and back to the car.

They left the Cayhall estate without a word. The road turned to gravel, then stopped at the intersection of a highway. Lee pointed to the left, then closed her eyes as if trying to nap. They bypassed Clanton and stopped at a country store near Holly Springs. Lee said she needed a cola, and insisted on getting it herself. She returned to the car with a six-pack of beer and offered a bottle to Adam. 'What's this?' he asked.

'Just a couple,' she said. 'My nerves are shot. Don't let me drink more than two, okay. Only two.'

'I don't think you should, Lee.'

'I'm okay,' she insisted with a frown, and took a drink.

Adam declined and sped away from the store. She drained two bottles in fifteen minutes, then went to sleep. Adam placed the sack in the backseat, and concentrated on the road.

He had a sudden desire to leave Mississippi, and longed for the lights of Memphis.

TWENTY-SEVEN

EXACTLY ONE WEEK earlier, he had awakened with a fierce headache and a fragile stomach, and had been forced to face the greasy bacon and oily eggs of Irene Lettner. And in the past seven days, he'd been to the courtroom of Judge Slattery, and to Chicago, Greenvile, Ford County, and Parchman. He'd met the governor, and the Attorney General. He hadn't talked to his client in six days.

To hell with his client. Adam had sat on the patio watching the river traffic and sipping decaffeinated coffee until 2 A.M. He swatted mosquitoes and struggled with the vivid images of Quince Lincoln grasping at his father's body while Sam Cayhall stood on the porch and admired his handiwork. He could hear the muted laughter of Sam and his buddies on the narrow porch as Ruby Lincoln and her children fell around the corpse and eventually dragged it across the yard to the shade of a tree. He could see Sam on the front lawn with both shotguns explaining to the sheriff exactly how the crazy nigger was about to kill him, and how he acted reasonably and in self-defense. The sheriff was quick to see Sam's point, of course. He could hear the whispers of the tormented children, Eddie and Lee, as they blamed themselves and struggled with the horror of Sam's deed. And he cursed a society so willing to ignore violence against a despised class.

He'd slept fitfully, and at one point had sat on the edge of his bed and declared to himself that Sam could find another lawyer, that the death penalty might in fact be appropriate

324

for some people, notably his grandfather, and that he would return to Chicago immediately and change his name again. But that dream passed, and when he awoke for the last time the sunlight filtered through the blinds and cast neat lines across his bed. He contemplated the ceiling and crown molding along the walls for half an hour as he remembered the trip to Clanton. Today, he hoped, would be a late Sunday with a thick newspaper and strong coffee. He would go to the office later in the afternoon. His client had seventeen days.

Lee had finished a third beer after they arrived at the condo, then she'd gone to bed. Adam had watched her carefully, half-expecting a wild binge or sudden slide into an alcoholic stupor. But she'd been very quiet and composed, and he heard nothing from her during the night.

He finished his shower, didn't shave, and walked into the kitchen where the syrupy remains of the first pot of coffee awaited him. Lee had been up for some time. He called her name, then walked to her bedroom. He quickly checked the patio, then roamed through the condo. She was not there. The Sunday paper was stacked neatly on the coffee table in the den.

He fixed fresh coffee and toast, and took his breakfast on the patio. It was almost nine-thirty, and thankfully the sky was cloudy and the temperature was not suffocating. It would be a good Sunday for office work. He read the paper, starting with the front section.

Perhaps she'd run to the store or something. Maybe she'd gone to church. They hadn't yet reached the point of leaving notes for each other. But there'd been no talk of Lee going anywhere this morning.

He'd eaten one piece of toast with strawberry jam when his appetite suddenly vanished. The front page of the Metro section carried another story on Sam Cayhall, with the same picture from ten years ago. It was a chatty little summary of the past week's developments, complete with a chronological chart giving the important dates in the history of the case. A cute question mark was left dangling by the date of

August 8, 1990. Would there be an execution then? Evidently, Todd Marks had been given unlimited column inches by the editors because the story contained almost nothing new. The disturbing part was a few quotes from a law professor at Ole Miss, an expert in constitutional matters who'd worked on many death penalty cases. The learned professor was generous with his opinions, and his bottom line was that Sam's goose was pretty much cooked. He'd studied the file at length, and followed it for many years in fact, and was of the opinion that there was basically nothing left for Sam to do. He explained that in many death penalty cases, miracles can sometimes be performed at the last moment because usually the inmate has suffered from mediocre legal representation, even during his appeals. In those cases, experts such as himself can often pull rabbits out of hats because they're just so damned brilliant, and thus able to create issues ignored by lesser legal minds. But, regrettably, Sam's case was different because he had been competently represented by some very fine lawyers from Chicago.

Sam's appeals had been handled skillfully, and now the appeals had run their course. The professor, evidently a gambling man, gave five to one odds the execution would take place on August 8. And for all of this, the opinion and the odds, he got his picture in the paper.

Adam was suddenly nervous. He'd read dozens of death cases in which lawyers at the last minute grabbed ropes they'd never grabbed before, and convinced judges to listen to new arguments. The lore of capital litigation was full of stories about latent legal issues undiscovered and untapped until a different lawyer with a fresh eye entered the arena and captured a stay. But the law professor was right. Sam had been lucky. Though Sam despised the lawyers at Kravitz & Bane, they had provided superb representation. Now there was nothing left but a bunch of desperate motions, the gangplank appeals, as they were known.

He flung the paper on the wooden deck and went inside for more coffee. The sliding door beeped, a new sound from

326

the new security system installed last Friday after the old one malfunctioned and some keys mysteriously disappeared. There was no evidence of a break-in. Security was tight at the complex. And Willis didn't really know how many sets of keys he kept for each unit. The Memphis police decided the sliding door had been left unlocked and slipped open somehow. Adam and Lee had not worried about it.

He inadvertently struck a glass tumbler next to the sink, and it shattered as it hit the floor. Bits of glass bounced around his bare feet, and he tiptoed gingerly to the pantry to get a broom and dustpan. He carefully swept the debris, without bloodshed, into a neat pile and dumped it into a wastebasket under the sink. Something caught his attention. He slowly reached into the black plastic garbage bag, and felt his way through warm coffee grounds and broken glass until he found a bottle and pulled it out. It was an empty pint of vodka.

He raked the coffee grounds from it and studied the label. The trash basket was small and normally emptied every other day, sometimes once a day. It was now half-filled. The bottle had not been there long. He opened the refrigerator and looked for the remaining three bottles of beer from yesterday's six-pack. She'd had two en route back to Memphis, then one at the condo. He did not remember where they had been stored, but they were not in the refrigerator. Nor in the trash in the kitchen, den, bathrooms or bedrooms. The more he searched the more determined he became to find the bottles. He inspected the pantry, the broom closet, the linen closet, the kitchen cabinets. He went through her closets and drawers, and felt like a thief and a cheat but pressed on because he was scared.

They were under her bed, empty of course, and carefully hidden in an old Nike shoe box. Three empty bottles of Heineken stacked neatly together, as if they were to be shipped somewhere as a gift. He sat on the floor and examined them. They were fresh, with a few drops still rolling around the bottoms.

He guessed her weight to be around a hundred and thirty pounds, and her height at five feet six or seven. She was slender but not too thin. Her body couldn't handle much booze. She'd gone to bed early, around nine, then at some point sneaked around the condo fetching beer and vodka. Adam leaned against the wall, his mind racing wildly. She'd given much thought to the hiding of the green bottles, but she knew she'd get caught. She had to know Adam would look for them later. Why hadn't she been more careful with the empty pint bottle? Why was it hidden in the trash, and the beer bottles tucked away under her bed?

Then he realized he was attempting to track a rational mind, instead of a drunk one. He closed his eyes and tapped the back of his head against the wall. He'd taken her to Ford County, where they looked at graves and relived a nightmare, and where she'd worn sunglasses to hide her face. For two weeks now, he'd been demanding family secrets and yesterday he'd been kicked in the face with a few. He needed to know, he'd told himself. He wasn't certain why, but he just felt as if he had to know the reasons his family was strange and violent and hateful.

And now, it occurred to him for the first time, perhaps this was much more complicated than the casual telling of family stories. Perhaps this was painful for everyone involved. Maybe his selfish interest in closeted skeletons wasn't as important as Lee's stability.

He slid the shoe box back to its original position, then threw the vodka bottle in the wastebasket for the second time. He dressed quickly and left the building. He asked the gate man about Lee. According to a sheet of paper on his clipboard, she'd left almost two hours ago, at eight-ten.

IT WAS CUSTOMARY for lawyers at Kravitz & Bane in Chicago to spend Sunday at the office, but evidently the practice was frowned upon in Memphis. Adam had the place entirely to himself. He locked his door anyway, and was soon lost in the murky legal world of federal habeas corpus practice.

His concentration, though, was difficult and only lasted for short intervals. He worried about Lee, and he hated Sam. It would be difficult to look at him again, probably tomorrow, through the metal screen at the Row. He was frail and bleached and wrinkled, and by all rights entitled to a little sympathy from someone. Their last discussion had been about Eddie, and when it ended Sam had asked him to leave the family stuff outside the Row. He had enough on his mind at the moment. It wasn't fair to confront a condemned man with his ancient sins.

Adam was not a biographer, nor a genealogist. He hadn't been trained in sociology or psychiatry, and, frankly, he was, at the moment, quite weary of further expeditions into the cryptic history of the Cayhall family. He was simply a lawyer, a rather green one, but an advocate nonetheless whose client needed him.

It was time to practice law and forget the folklore.

At eleven-thirty, he dialed Lee's number and listened to the phone ring. He left a message on the recorder, telling her where he was and would she please call. He called again at one, and at two. No answer. He was preparing an appeal when the phone rang.

Instead of Lee's pleasant voice, he heard the clipped words of the Honorable F. Flynn Slattery. 'Yes, Mr Hall, Judge Slattery here. I've carefully considered this matter, and I'm denying all relief, including your request for a stay of execution,' he said, almost with a trace of cheer. 'Lots of reasons, but we won't go into them. My clerk will fax you my opinion right away, so you'll have it in a moment.'

'Yes sir,' Adam said.

'You'll need to appeal as soon as possible, you know. I suggest you do so in the morning.'

'I'm working on the appeal now, Your Honor. In fact, it's almost finished.'

'Good. So you were expecting this.'

'Yes sir. I started working on the appeal right after I left your office on Tuesday.' It was tempting to take a shot or two at Slattery. He was after all, two hundred miles away.

329

But he was also, after all, a federal judge. Adam was very aware that one day very soon he might need His Honor again.

'Good day, Mr Hall.' And with that, Slattery hung up.

Adam walked around the table a dozen times, then watched the light rain on the Mall below. He swore quietly about federal judges in general and Slattery in particular, then returned to his computer where he stared at the screen and waited for inspiration.

He typed and read, researched and printed, looked from his windows and dreamed of miracles until it was dark. He had killed several hours with footless piddling, and one reason he worked until eight o'clock was to give Lee plenty of time to return to the condo.

There was no sign of her. The security guard said she had not returned. There was no message on the recorder, other than his. He dined on microwave popcorn, and watched two movies on video. The idea of calling Phelps Booth was so repugnant he nearly shuddered at the thought.

He thought of sleeping on the sofa in the den so he would hear her if she came home, but after the last movie he retired to his room upstairs and closed the door.

TWENTY-EIGHT

THE EXPLANATION for yesterday's disappearance was slow in coming, but sounded plausible by the time she finished with it. She'd been at the hospital all day, she said as she moved slowly around the kitchen, with one of her kids from the Auburn House. Poor little girl was only thirteen, baby number one but of course there would be others, and she had gone into labor a month early. Her mother was in jail and her aunt was off selling drugs, and she had no one else to turn to. Lee'd held her hand throughout the complicated delivery. The girl was fine and the baby was okay, and now there was another unwanted little child in the Memphis ghettos.

Lee's voice was scratchy and her eyes were puffy and red. She said she'd returned a few minutes after one, and she would've called earlier but they were in the labor room for six hours and the delivery room for two. St Peter's Charity Hospital is a zoo, especially the maternity wing, and, well, she just couldn't get to a phone.

Adam sat in his pajamas at the table, sipping coffee and studying the paper as she talked. He hadn't asked for the explanation. He tried his best to act unconcerned about her. She insisted on cooking breakfast: scrambled eggs and canned biscuits. And she was doing a good job of busying herself in the kitchen as she talked and avoided eye contact.

'What's the kid's name?' he asked seriously as if he was deeply concerned with Lee's story.

'Uh, Natasha. Natasha Perkins.'

331

'And she's only thirteen?'

'Yes. Her mother is twenty-nine. Can you believe it? A twenty-nine-year-old grandmother.'

Adam shook his head in disbelief. He happened to be looking at the small section of the *Memphis Press* where it registered the county's vital records. Marriage licenses. Divorce petitions. Births. Arrests. Deaths. He scanned the list of yesterday's births as if he were checking scores, and found no record of a new mother named Natasha Perkins.

Lee finished her struggle with the canned biscuits. She placed them on a small platter along with the eggs and served them, then sat at the other end of the table, as far away from Adam as possible. *'Bon appétit,'* she said with a forced smile. Her cooking was already a rich source of humor.

Adam smiled as if everything was fine. They needed humor at this moment, but wit failed them. 'Cubs lost again,' he said, taking a bite of eggs and glancing at the folded newspaper.

'The Cubs always lose, don't they?'

'Not always. You follow baseball?'

'I hate baseball. Phelps turned me against every sport known to man.'

Adam grinned and read the paper. They ate without talking for a few minutes, and the silence grew heavy. Lee punched the remote and the television on the counter came on and created noise. They were both suddenly interested in the weather, which was again hot and dry. She played with her food, nibbling on a half-baked biscuit and pushing the eggs around her plate. Adam suspected her stomach was feeble at the moment.

He finished quickly and took his plate to the kitchen sink. He sat again at the table to finish the paper. She was staring at the television, anything to keep her eyes away from her nephew.

'I'll probably go see Sam today,' he said. 'I haven't been in a week.'

Her gaze fell to a spot somewhere in the middle of the table. 'I wish we hadn't gone to Clanton Saturday,' she said.

332

'I know.'

'It was not a good idea.'

'I'm sorry, Lee. I insisted on going, and it was not a good idea. I've insisted on a lot of things, and maybe I've been wrong.'

'It's not fair –'

'I know it's not fair. I realize now that it's not a simple matter of learning family history.'

'It's not fair to him, Adam. It's almost cruel to confront him with these things when he has only two weeks to live.'

'You're right. And it's wrong to make you relive them.'

'I'll be fine.' She said this as if she certainly wasn't fine now, but there might be a bit of hope for the future.

'I'm sorry, Lee. I'm truly sorry.'

'It's okay. What will you and Sam do today?'

'Talk, primarily. The local federal court ruled against us yesterday, and so we'll appeal this morning. Sam likes to talk legal strategies.'

'Tell him I'm thinking about him.'

'I will.'

She pushed her plate away and cuddled her cup with both hands. 'And ask him if he wants me to come see him.'

'Do you really want to?' Adam asked, unable to conceal his surprise.

'Something tells me I should. I haven't seen him in many years.'

'I'll ask him.'

'And don't mention Joe Lincoln, okay Adam? I never told Daddy what I saw.'

'You and Sam never mentioned the killing?'

'Never. It became well known in the community. Eddie and I grew up with it and carried it as a burden, but, to be honest, Adam, it was not a big deal to the neighbors. My father killed a black man. It was 1950, and it was Mississippi. It was never discussed in our house.'

'So Sam makes it to his grave without being confronted with the killing?'

333

'What do you accomplish by confronting him? It was forty years ago.'

'I don't know. Maybe he'll say he was sorry.'

'To you? He apologizes to you, and that makes everything okay? Come on, Adam, you're young and you don't understand. Leave it alone. Don't hurt the old man anymore. Right now, you're the only bright spot in his pathetic life.'

'Okay, okay.'

'You have no right to ambush him with the story of Joe Lincoln.'

'You're right. I won't. I promise.'

She stared at him with bloodshot eyes until he looked at the television, and she quickly excused herself and disappeared through the den. Adam heard the bathroom door close and lock. He eased across the carpet and stood in the hallway, listening as she heaved and vomited. The toilet flushed, and he ran upstairs to his room to shower and change.

BY 10 A.M., Adam had perfected the appeal to the Fifth Circuit Court of Appeals in New Orleans. Judge Slattery had already faxed a copy of his order to the clerk of the Fifth Circuit, and Adam faxed his appeal shortly after arriving at the office. He Fed-Exed the original by overnight.

He also had his first conversation with the Death Clerk, a full-time employee of the United States Supreme Court who does nothing but monitor the final appeals of all death row inmates. The Death Clerk often works around the clock as executions go down to the wire. E. Garner Goodman had briefed Adam on the machinations of the Death Clerk and his office, and it was with some reluctance that Adam placed the first call.

The clerk's name was Richard Olander, a rather efficient sort who sounded quite tired early Monday morning. 'We've been expecting this,' he said to Adam, as if the damned thing should've been filed some time ago. He asked Adam if this was his first execution.

'Afraid so,' Adam said. 'And I hope it's my last.'

'Well, you've certainly picked a loser,' Mr Olander said, then explained in tedious detail exactly how the Court expected the final appeals to be handled. Every filing from this point forward, until the *end*, regardless of where it's filed or what it's about, must also simultaneously be filed with his office, he stated flatly as if reading from a textbook. In fact, he would immediately fax to Adam a copy of the Court's rules, all of which had to be meticulously followed up until the very *end*. His office was on call, around the clock, he repeated more than once, and it was essential that they receive copies of everything. That was, of course, if Adam wanted his client to have a fair hearing with the Court. If Adam didn't care, then, well, just follow the rules haphazardly and his client would pay for it.

Adam promised to follow the rules. The Supreme Court had become increasingly weary of the endless claims in death cases, and wanted to have all motions and appeals in hand to expedite matters. Adam's appeal to the Fifth Circuit would be scrutinized by the justices and their clerks long before the Court actually received the case from New Orleans. The same would be true for all his eleventh-hour filings. The Court would then be able to grant immediate relief, or deny it quickly.

So efficient and speedy was the Death Clerk that the Court had recently been embarrassed by denying an appeal before it was actually filed.

Then Mr Olander explained that his office had a checklist of every conceivable last minute appeal and motion, and he and his quite able staff monitored each case to see if all possible filings took place. And if a lawyer somewhere missed a potential issue, then they would actually notify the lawyer that he should pursue the forgotten claim. Did Adam desire a copy of their checklist?

No, Adam explained that he already had a copy. E. Garner Goodman had written the book on gangplank appeals.

Very well, said Mr Olander. Mr Cayhall had sixteen days,

335

and, of course, a lot can happen in sixteen days. But Mr Cayhall had been ably represented, in his humble opinion, and the matter had been thoroughly litigated. He would be surprised, he ventured, if there were additional delays.

Thanks for nothing, Adam thought.

Mr Olander and his staff were watching a case in Texas very closely, he explained. The execution was set for a day before Sam's, but, in his opinion, there was a likely chance for a stay. Florida had one scheduled for two days after Mr Cayhall's. Georgia had two set for a week later, but, well, who knows. He or someone on his staff would be available at all hours, and he himself would personally be by the phone for the twelve-hour period leading up to the execution.

Just call anytime, he said, and ended the conversation with a terse promise to make things as easy as possible for Adam and his client.

Adam slammed the phone down and stalked around his office. His door was locked, as usual, and the hallway was busy with eager Monday morning gossip. His face had been in the paper again yesterday, and he did not want to be seen. He called the Auburn House and asked for Lee Booth, but she was not in. He called her condo, and there was no answer. He called Parchman, and told the officer at the front gate to expect him around one.

He went to his computer and found one of his current projects, a condensed, chronological history of Sam's case.

THE LAKEHEAD COUNTY JURY convicted Sam on February 12, 1981, and two days later handed him a verdict of death. He appealed directly to the Mississippi Supreme Court, claiming all sorts of grievances with the trial and the prosecution but taking particular exception to the fact that the trial occurred almost fourteen years after the bombing. His lawyer, Benjamin Keyes, argued vehemently that Sam was denied a speedy trial, and that he was subjected to double jeopardy, being tried three times for the same crime. Keyes presented a very strong argument. The Mississippi

Supreme Court was bitterly divided over these issues, and on July 23, 1982, handed down a split decision affirming Sam's conviction. Five justices voted to affirm, three to reverse, and one abstained.

Keyes then filed a petition for writ of certiorari with the U.S. Supreme Court, which, in effect, asked that Court to review Sam's case. Since the Supreme Court 'grants cert' on such a small number of cases, it was somewhat of a surprise when, on March 4, 1983, the Court agreed to review Sam's conviction.

The U.S. Supreme Court split almost as badly as Mississippi's on the issue of double jeopardy, but nonetheless reached the same conclusion. Sam's first two juries had been hopelessly deadlocked, hung up by the shenanigans of Clovis Brazelton, and thus Sam was not protected by the double jeopardy clause of the Fifth Amendment. He was not acquitted by either of the first two juries. Each had been unable to reach a verdict, so reprosecution was quite constitutional. On September 21, 1983, the U.S. Supreme Court ruled six to three that Sam's conviction should stand. Keyes immediately filed some motions requesting a rehearing, but to no avail.

Sam had hired Keyes to represent him during the trial and on appeal to the Mississippi Supreme Court, if necessary. By the time the U.S. Supreme Court affirmed the conviction, Keyes was working without getting paid. His contract for legal representation had expired, and he wrote Sam a long letter and explained that it was now time for Sam to make other arrangements. Sam understood this.

Keyes also wrote a letter to an ACLU lawyer-friend of his in Washington, who in turn wrote a letter to his pal E. Garner Goodman at Kravitz & Bane in Chicago. The letter landed on Goodman's desk at precisely the right moment. Sam was running out of time and was desperate. Goodman was looking for a pro bono project. They swapped letters, and on December 18, 1983, Wallace Tyner, a partner in the white-collar criminal defense section of Kravitz & Bane, filed a petition seeking postconviction relief with the Mississippi Supreme Court.

Tyner alleged many errors in Sam's trial, including the admission into evidence of the gory pictures of the bodies of Josh and John Kramer. He attacked the selection of the jury, and claimed that McAllister systematically picked blacks over whites. He claimed a fair trial was not possible because the social environment was far different in 1981 than in 1967. He maintained the venue selected by the trial judge was unfair. He raised yet again the issues of double jeopardy and speedy trial. In all, Wallace Tyner and Garner Goodman raised eight separate issues in the petition. They did not, however, maintain that Sam had suffered because of ineffective trial counsel, the primary claim of all death row inmates. They had wanted to, but Sam wouldn't allow it. He initially refused to sign the petition because it attacked Benjamin Keyes, a lawyer Sam was fond of.

On June 1, 1985, the Mississippi Supreme Court denied all of the postconviction relief requested. Tyner again appealed to the U.S. Supreme Court, but cert was denied. He then filed Sam's first petition for writ of habeas corpus and request for a stay of execution in federal court in Mississippi. Typically, the petition was quite thick, and contained every issue already raised in state court.

Two years later, on May 3, 1987, the district court denied all relief, and Tyner appealed to the Fifth Circuit in New Orleans, which in due course affirmed the lower court's denial. On March 20, 1988, Tyner filed a petition for a rehearing with the Fifth Circuit, which was also denied. On September 3, 1988, Tyner and Goodman again trekked to the Supreme Court and asked for cert. A week later, Sam wrote the first of many letters to Goodman and Tyner threatening to fire them.

The U.S. Supreme Court granted Sam his last stay on May 14, 1989, pursuant to a grant of certiorari being granted in a Florida case the Court had decided to hear. Tyner argued successfully that the Florida case raised similar issues, and the Supreme Court granted stays in several dozen death cases around the country.

Nothing was filed in Sam's case while the Supreme Court delayed and debated the Florida case. Sam, however, had begun his own efforts to rid himself of Kravitz & Bane. He filed a few clumsy motions himself, all of which were quickly denied. He did succeed, however, in obtaining an order from the Fifth Circuit which effectively terminated the pro bono services of his lawyers. On June 29, 1990, the Fifth Circuit allowed him to represent himself, and Garner Goodman closed the file on Sam Cayhall. It wasn't closed for long.

On July 9, 1990, the Supreme Court vacated Sam's stay. On July 10, the Fifth Circuit vacated Sam's stay, and on the same day the Mississippi Supreme Court set his execution date for August 8, four weeks away.

After nine years of appellate warfare, Sam now had sixteen days to live.

TWENTY-NINE

THE ROW was quiet and still as another day dragged itself toward noon. The diverse collection of fans buzzed and rattled in the tiny cells, trying valiantly to push around air that grew stickier by the moment.

The early television news had been filled with excited reports that Sam Cayhall had lost his latest legal battle. Slattery's decision was trumpeted around the state as if it were indeed the final nail in the coffin. A Jackson station continued its countdown, only sixteen days to go. Day Sixteen! it said in bold letters under the same old photo of Sam. Bright-eyed reporters with heavy makeup and no knowledge of the law spouted at the cameras with fearless predictions: 'According to our sources, Sam Cayhall's legal options are virtually gone. Many people believe that his execution will take place, as scheduled, on August 8.' Then on to sports and weather.

There was much less talk on the Row, less yelling back and forth, fewer kites being floated along the cells. There was about to be an execution.

Sergeant Packer smiled to himself as he shuffled along Tier A. The bitching and griping that was so much a part of his daily work had almost disappeared. Now, the inmates were concerned with appeals and their lawyers. The most common request in the past two weeks had been to use the phone to call a lawyer.

Packer did not look forward to another execution, but he did enjoy the quiet. And he knew it was only temporary. If

340

Sam got a stay tomorrow, the noise would increase immediately.

He stopped in front of Sam's cell. 'Hour out, Sam.'

Sam was sitting on his bed, typing and smoking as usual. 'What time is it?' he asked, placing the typewriter to his side and standing.

'Eleven.'

Sam turned his back to Packer and stuck his wrists through the opening in the door. Packer carefully cuffed them together. 'You out by yourself?' he asked.

Sam turned with his hands behind him. 'No. Henshaw wants to come out too.'

'I'll get him,' Packer said, nodding at Sam then nodding at the end of the tier. The door opened, and Sam slowly followed him past the other cells. Each inmate was leaning on the bars with hands and arms dangling through, each watching Sam closely as he walked by.

They made their way through more bars and more hallways, and Packer unlocked an unpainted metal door. It opened to the outside, and the sunlight burst through. Sam hated this part of his hour out. He stepped onto the grass and closed his eyes tightly as Packer uncuffed him, then opened them slowly as they focused and adjusted to the painful glow of the sun.

Packer disappeared inside without a word, and Sam stood in the same spot for a full minute as lights flashed and his head pounded. The heat didn't bother him because he lived with it, but the sunlight hit like lasers and caused a severe headache each time he was allowed to venture from the dungeon. He could easily afford a pair of cheap sunglasses, similar to Packer's, but of course that would be too sensible. Sunglasses were not on the approved list of items an inmate could own.

He walked unsteadily through the clipped grass, looking through the fence to the cotton fields beyond. The recreation yard was nothing more than a fenced-in plot of dirt and grass with two wooden benches and a basketball hoop for the Africans. It was known to guards and prisoners alike as the bullpen. Sam had stepped it off carefully a thousand times, and had compared his measurements with those of other inmates. The yard was fifty-one feet long and thirty-six feet wide. The fence was ten feet tall and crowned with another eighteen inches of razor wire. Beyond the fence was a stretch of grass which ran a hundred feet or so to the main fence, which was watched by the guards in the towers.

Sam walked in a straight line next to the fence, and when it stopped he turned ninety degrees and continued his little routine, counting every step along the way. Fifty-one feet by thirty-six. His cell was six by nine. The law library, the Twig, was eighteen by fifteen. His side of the visitors' room was six by thirty. He'd been told the Chamber Room was fifteen by twelve, and the chamber itself was a mere cube barely four feet wide.

During the first year of his confinement, he had jogged around the edges of the yard, trying to sweat and give his heart a workout. He'd also tossed shots at the basketball hoop, but quit when he went days without making one. He had eventually quit exercising, and for years had used this hour to do nothing but enjoy the freedom from his cell. At one time, he'd fallen into the habit of standing at the fence and staring past the fields to the trees where he imagined all sorts of things. Freedom. Highways. Fishing. Food. Sex occasionally. He could almost picture his little farm in Ford County not far over there between two small patches of woods. He would dream of Brazil or Argentina or some other laid-back hiding place where he should be living with a new name.

And then he'd stopped the dreaming. He'd stopped gazing through the fence as if a miracle would take him away. He walked and smoked, almost always by himself. His most rigorous activity was a game of checkers.

The door opened again, and Hank Henshaw walked through it. Packer uncuffed him as he squinted furiously and looked at the ground. He rubbed his wrists as soon as they were free, then stretched his back and legs. Packer walked to one of the benches and placed a worn cardboard box on it.

The two inmates watched Packer until he left the yard, then they walked to the bench and assumed their positions astraddle the wooden plank with the box between them. Sam carefully placed the checkerboard on the bench as Henshaw counted the checkers.

'My turn to be red,' Sam said.

'You were red last time,' Henshaw said, staring at him.

'I was black last time.'

'No, I was black last time. It's my turn to be red.'

'Look, Hank. I've got sixteen days, and if I want to be red, then I get to be red.'

Henshaw shrugged and conceded. They arranged their checkers meticulously.

'I guess you get the first move,' Henshaw said.

'Of course.' Sam slid a checker to a vacant square, and the match was on. The midday sun baked the ground around them and within minutes their red jumpsuits stuck to their backs. They both wore rubber shower shoes with no socks.

Hank Henshaw was forty-one, now a resident of the Row for seven years but not expected to ever see the gas chamber. Two crucial errors had been made at trial, and Henshaw had a decent chance of getting reversed and freed from the Row.

'Bad news yesterday,' he said as Sam pondered the next move.

'Yes, things are lookin' pretty grim, wouldn't you say?'

'Yeah. What does your lawyer say?' Neither of them looked up from the checkerboard.

'He says we have a fightin' chance.'

'What the hell does that mean?' Henshaw asked as he made a move.

'I think it means they're gonna gas me, but I'll go down swinging.'

'Does the kid know what he's doing?'

'Oh yeah. He's sharp. Runs in the blood, you know.'

'But he's awfully young.'

'He's a smart kid. Great education. Number two in his law class at Michigan, you know. Editor of the law review.'

'What does that mean?'

'Means he's brilliant. He'll think of something.'

'Are you serious, Sam? Do you think it's gonna happen?'

Sam suddenly jumped two black checkers, and Henshaw cursed. 'You're pitiful,' Sam said with a grin. 'When was the last time you beat me?'

'Two weeks ago.'

'You liar. You haven't beat me in three years.'

Henshaw made a tentative move, and Sam jumped him again. Five minutes later, the game was over with Sam victorious again. They cleared the board, and started over.

AT NOON, Packer and another guard appeared with handcuffs, and the fun was over. They were led to their cells where lunch was in progress. Beans, peas, mashed potatoes, and several slices of dry toast. Sam ate less than a third of the bland food on his plate, and waited patiently for a guard to come after him. He held a pair of clean boxer shorts and a bar of soap. It was time to bathe.

The guard arrived and led Sam to a small shower at the end of the tier. By court order, death row inmates were allowed five quick showers a week, whether they needed them or not, as the guards liked to say.

Sam showered quickly, washing his hair twice with the soap and rinsing himself in the warm water. The shower itself was clean enough, but used by all fourteen inmates on the tier. Thus, the rubber shower shoes remained on the feet. After five minutes, the water stopped, and Sam dripped for a few more minutes as he stared at the moldy tiled walls. There were some things about the Row that he would not miss.

Twenty minutes later, he was loaded into a prison van and driven a half a mile to the law library.

Adam was waiting inside. He removed his coat and rolled up his sleeves as the guards uncuffed Sam and left the room. They greeted each other and shook hands. Sam quickly took a seat and lit a cigarette. 'Where've you been?' he asked.

'Busy,' Adam said, sitting across the table. 'I had an unexpected trip to Chicago last Wednesday and Thursday.'

'Anything to do with me?'

'You could say that. Goodman wanted to review the case, and there were a couple of other matters.'

'So Goodman's still involved?'

'Goodman is my boss right now, Sam. I have to report to him if I want to keep my job. I know you hate him, but he's very concerned about you and your case. Believe it or not, he does not want to see you gassed.'

'I don't hate him anymore.'

'Why the change of heart?'

'I don't know. When you get this close to death, you do a lot of thinking.'

Adam was anxious to hear more, but Sam let it pass. Adam watched him smoke and tried not to think about Joe Lincoln. He tried not to think of Sam's father being beaten in a drunken brawl at a funeral, and he tried to ignore all the other miserable stories Lee had told him in Ford County. He tried to block these things from his mind, but he couldn't.

He had promised her he would not mention any more nightmares from the past. 'I guess you've heard about our latest defeat,' he said as he pulled papers from his briefcase.

'It didn't take long, did it?'

'No. A rather quick loss, but I've already appealed to the Fifth Circuit.'

'I've never won in the Fifth Circuit.'

'I know. But we can't select our review court at this point.'

'What can we do at this point?'

'Several things. I bumped into the governor last Tuesday after a meeting with the federal judge. He wanted to talk in private. He gave me his private phone numbers and invited me to call and talk about the case. Said he had doubts about the extent of your guilt.'

Sam glared at him. 'Doubts? He's the only reason I'm here. He can't wait to see me executed.'

'You're probably right, but —'

'You promised not to talk to him. You signed an agreement with me expressly prohibiting any contact with that fool.'

'Relax, Sam. He grabbed me outside the judge's office.'

'I'm surprised he didn't call a press conference to talk about it.'

'I threatened him, okay. I made him promise not to talk.'

'Then you're the first person in history to silence that bastard.'

'He's open to the idea of clemency.'

'He told you this?'

'Yes.'

'Why? I don't believe it.'

'I don't know why, Sam. And I don't really care. But how can it hurt? What's the danger in requesting a clemency hearing? So he gets his picture in the paper. So the TV cameras chase him around some more. If there's a chance he'll listen, then why should you care if he gets some mileage from it?'

'No. The answer is no. I will not authorize you to request a clemency hearing. Hell no. A thousand times no. I know him, Adam. He's trying to suck you into his game plan. It's all a sham, a show for the public. He'll grieve over this until the very end, milking it for all he can. He'll get more attention than I will, and it's my execution.'

'So what's the harm?'

Sam slapped the table with the palm of his hand. 'Because it won't do any good, Adam! He will not change his mind.'

Adam scribbled something on a legal pad and let a moment pass. Sam eased back in his seat, and lit another cigarette. His hair was still wet and he combed it back with his fingernails.

Adam placed his pen on the table and looked at his client. 'What do you want to do, Sam? Quit? Throw in the towel? You think you know so damned much law, tell me what you want to do.'

346

'Well, I've been thinking about it.'

'I'm sure you have.'

'The lawsuit on its way to the Fifth Circuit has merit, but it doesn't look promising. There's not much left, as I see things.'

'Except Benjamin Keyes.'

'Right. Except Keyes. He did a fine job for me at trial and on appeal, and he was almost a friend. I hate to go after him.'

'It's standard in death cases, Sam. You always go after the trial lawyer and claim ineffective assistance of counsel. Goodman told me he wanted to do it, but you refused. It should've been done years ago.'

'He's right about that. He begged me to do it, but I said no. I guess it was a mistake.'

Adam was on the edge of his seat taking notes. 'I've studied the record, and I think Keyes made a mistake when he didn't put you on the stand to testify.'

'I wanted to talk to the jury, you know. I think I've already told you that. After Dogan testified, I thought it was essential for me to explain to the jury that I did in fact plant the bomb, but there was no intent to kill anyone. That's the truth, Adam. I didn't intend to kill anyone.'

'You wanted to testify, but your lawyer said no.'

Sam smiled and looked at the floor. 'Is that what you want me to say?'

'Yes.'

'I don't have much of a choice, do I?'

'No.'

'Okay. That's the way it happened. I wanted to testify, but my lawyer wouldn't allow it.'

'I'll file first thing in the morning.'

'It's too late, isn't it?'

'Well, it's certainly late, and this issue should've been raised a long time ago. But what's there to lose?'

'Will you call Keyes and tell him?'

'If I have time. I'm really not concerned with his feelings at the moment.'

347

'Then neither am I. To hell with him. Who else can we attack?'

'The list is rather short.'

Sam jumped to his feet and began pacing along the table in measured steps. The room was eighteen feet long. He walked round the table, behind Adam, and along each of the four walls, counting as he went. He stopped and leaned against a shelf of books.

Adam finished some notes and watched him carefully. 'Lee wants to know if she can come visit,' he said.

Sam stared at him, then slowly returned to his seat across the table. 'She wants to?'

'I think so.'

'I'll have to think about it.'

'Well hurry.'

'How's she doing?'

'Pretty fair, I guess. She sends her love and prayers, and she thinks about you a lot these days.'

'Do people in Memphis know she's my daughter?'

'I don't think so. It hasn't been in the papers yet.'

'I hope they keep it quiet.'

'She and I went to Clanton last Saturday.'

Sam looked at him sadly, then gazed at the ceiling. 'What did you see?' he asked.

'Lots of things. She showed me my grandmother's grave, and the plot with the other Cayhalls.'

'She didn't want to be buried with the Cayhalls, did Lee tell you that?'

'Yes. Lee asked me where you wanted to be buried.'

'I haven't decided yet.'

'Sure. Just let me know when you make the decision. We walked through the town, and she showed me the house we lived in. We went to the square and sat in the gazebo on the courthouse lawn. The town was very busy. People were packed around the square.'

'We used to watch fireworks in the cemetery.'

'Lee told me all about it. We ate lunch at The Tea

Shoppe, and took a drive in the country. She took me to her childhood home.'

'It's still there?'

'Yeah, it's abandoned. The house is run-down and the weeds have taken over. We walked around the place. She told me lots of stories of her childhood. Talked a lot about Eddie.'

'Does she have fond memories?'

'Not really.'

Sam crossed his arms and looked at the table. A minute passed without a word. Finally, Sam asked, 'Did she tell you about Eddie's little African friend, Quince Lincoln?'

Adam nodded slowly, and their eyes locked together. 'Yes, she did.'

'And about his father, Joe?'

'She told me the story.'

'Do you believe her?'

'I do. Should I?'

'It's true. It's all true.'

'I thought so.'

'How did you feel when she told you the story? I mean, how did you react to it?'

'I hated your guts.'

'And how do you feel now?'

'Different.'

Sam slowly rose from his seat and walked to the end of the table where he stopped and stood with his back to Adam. 'That was forty years ago,' he mumbled, barely audible.

'I didn't come here to talk about it,' Adam said, already feeling guilty.

Sam turned and leaned on the same bookshelf. He crossed his arms and stared at the wall. 'I've wished a thousand times it hadn't happened.'

'I promised Lee I wouldn't bring it up, Sam. I'm sorry.'

'Joe Lincoln was a good man. I've often wondered what happened to Ruby and Quince and the rest of the kids.'

'Forget it, Sam. Let's talk about something else.'

'I hope they're happy when I'm dead.'

THIRTY

AS ADAM drove past the security station at the main gate the guard waved, as if by now he was a regular customer. He waved back as he slowed and pushed a button to release his trunk. No paperwork was required for visitors to leave, only a quick look in the trunk to make sure no prisoners had caught a ride. He turned onto the highway, heading south, away from Memphis, and calculated that this was his fifth visit to Parchman. Five visits in two weeks. He had a suspicion that the place would be his second home for the next sixteen days. What a rotten thought.

He was not in the mood to deal with Lee tonight. He felt some responsibility for her relapse into alcohol, but by her own admission this had been a way of life for many years. She was an alcoholic, and if she chose to drink there was nothing he could do to stop her. He would be there tomorrow night, to make coffee and conversation. Tonight, he needed a break.

It was mid-afternoon, the heat emanated from the asphalt highway, the fields were dusty and dry, the farm implements languid and slow, the traffic light and sluggish. Adam pulled to the shoulder and raised the convertible top. He stopped at a Chinese grocery in Ruleville and bought a can of iced tea, then sped along a lonely highway in the general direction of Greenville. He had an errand to run, probably an unpleasant one, but something he felt obligated to do. He hoped he had the courage to go through with it.

He stayed on the back roads, the small paved county routes, and zipped almost aimlessly across the Delta. He got lost twice, but worked himself out of it. He arrived in Greenville a few minutes before five, and cruised the downtown area in search of his target. He passed Kramer Park twice. He found the synagogue, across the street from the First Baptist Church. He parked at the end of Main Street, at the river where a levee guarded the city. He straightened his tie and walked three blocks along Washington Street to an old brick building with the sign Kramer Wholesale hanging from a veranda above the sidewalk in front of it. The heavy glass door opened to the inside, and the ancient wooden floors squeaked as he walked on them. The front part of the building had been preserved to resemble an old-fashioned retail store, with glass counters in front of wide shelves that ran to the ceiling. The shelves and counters were filled with boxes and wrappings of food products sold years ago, but now extinct. An antique cash register was on display. The little museum quickly yielded to modern commerce. The rest of the huge building was renovated and gave the appearance of being quite efficient. A wall of paned glass cut off the front foyer, and a wide carpeted hallway ran down the center of the building and led, no doubt, to offices and secretaries, and somewhere in the rear there had to be a warehouse.

Adam admired the displays in the front counters. A young man in jeans appeared from the back and asked, 'Can I help you?'

Adam smiled, and was suddenly nervous. 'Yes, I'd like to see Mr Elliot Kramer.'

'Are you a salesman?'

'No.'

'Are you a buyer?'

'No.'

The young man was holding a pencil and had things on his mind. 'Then, may I ask what you need?'

'I need to see Mr Elliot Kramer. Is he here?'

'He spends most of his time at the main warehouse south of town.'

Adam took three steps toward the guy and handed him a business card. 'My name is Adam Hall. I'm an attorney from Chicago. I really need to see Mr Kramer.'

He took the card and studied it for a few seconds, then he looked at Adam with a great deal of suspicion. 'Just a minute,' he said, and walked away.

Adam leaned on a counter and admired the cash register. He had read somewhere in his voluminous research that Marvin Kramer's family had been prosperous merchants in the Delta for several generations. An ancestor had made a hasty exit from a steamboat at the port in Greenville, and decided to call it home. He opened a small dry goods store, and one thing led to another. Throughout the ordeal of Sam's trials, the Kramer family was repeatedly described as wealthy.

After twenty minutes of waiting, Adam was ready to leave, and quite relieved. He'd made the effort. If Mr Kramer didn't want to meet with him, there was nothing he could do about it.

He heard footsteps on the wooden floor, and turned around. An elderly gentleman stood with a business card in his hand. He was tall and thin, with wavy gray hair, dark brown eyes with heavy shadows under them, a lean, strong face which at the moment was not smiling. He stood erect, no cane to aid him, no eyeglasses to help him see. He scowled at Adam, but said nothing.

For an instant, Adam wished he'd left five minutes ago. Then he asked himself why he was there to begin with. Then he decided to go for it anyway. 'Good afternoon,' he said, when it was obvious the gentleman would not speak. 'Mr Elliot Kramer?'

Mr Kramer nodded in the affirmative, but nodded ever so slowly as if challenged by the question.

'My name is Adam Hall. I'm an attorney from Chicago. Sam Cayhall is my grandfather, and I represent him.' It was obvious Mr Kramer had already figured this out, because Adam's words didn't faze him. 'I would like to talk to you.'

'Talk about what?' Mr Kramer said in a slow drawl.

'About Sam.'

'I hope he rots in hell,' he said, as if he was already certain of Sam's eternal destination. His eyes were so brown they were almost black.

Adam glanced at the floor, away from the eyes, and tried to think of something noninflammatory. 'Yes sir,' he said, very much aware that he was in the Deep South where politeness went a long way. 'I understand how you feel. I don't blame you, but I just wanted to talk to you for a few minutes.'

'Does Sam send his apologies?' Mr Kramer asked. The fact that he referred to him simply as Sam struck Adam as odd. Not Mr Cayhall, not Cayhall, just Sam, as if the two were old friends who'd been feuding and now it was time to reconcile. Just say you're sorry, Sam, and everything's fine.

The thought of a quick lie raced through Adam's mind. He could lay it on thick, say how terrible Sam felt in these, his last days, and how he desperately wanted forgiveness. But Adam couldn't bring himself to do it. 'Would it make any difference?' he asked.

Mr Kramer carefully placed the card in his shirt pocket, and began what would become a long stare past Adam and through the front window. 'No,' he said, 'it wouldn't make any difference. It's something that should've been done long ago.' His words were accented with the heavy drip of the Delta, and even though their meanings were not welcome, their sounds were very soothing. They were slow and thoughtful, uttered as if time meant nothing. They also conveyed the years of suffering, and the hint that life had ceased long ago.

'No, Mr Kramer. Sam does not know I'm here, so he does not send his apologies. But I do.'

The gaze through the window and into the past did not flinch or waver. But he was listening.

Adam continued, 'I feel the obligation to at least say, for

myself and Sam's daughter, that we're terribly sorry for all that's happened.'

'Why didn't Sam say it years ago?'

'I can't answer that.'

'I know. You're new.'

Ah, the power of the press. Of course Mr Kramer had been reading the papers like everyone else.

'Yes sir. I'm trying to save his life.'

'Why?'

'Many reasons. Killing him will not bring back your grandsons, nor your son. He was wrong, but it's also wrong for the government to kill him.'

'I see. And you think I've never heard this before?'

'No sir. I'm sure you've heard it all. You've seen it all. You've felt it all. I can't imagine what you've been through. I'm just trying to avoid it myself.'

'What else do you want?'

'Could you spare five minutes?'

'We've been talking for three minutes. You have two more.' He glanced at his watch as if to set a timer, then eased his long fingers into the pockets of his pants. His eyes returned to the window and the street beyond it.

'The Memphis paper quoted you as saying you wanted to be there when they strapped Sam Cayhall in the gas chamber; that you wanted to look him in the eyes.'

'That's an accurate quote. But I don't believe it'll ever happen.'

'Why not?'

'Because we have a rotten criminal justice system. He's been coddled and protected in prison for almost ten years now. His appeals go on and on. You're filing appeals and pulling strings at this very moment to keep him alive. The system is sick. We don't expect justice.'

'I assure you he's not being coddled. Death row is a horrible place. I just left it.'

'Yeah, but he's alive. He's living and breathing and watching television and reading books. He's talking to you. He's filing lawsuits. And when and if death gets near, he'll

354

have plenty of time to make plans for it. He can say his good-byes. Say his prayers. My grandsons didn't have time to say good-bye, Mr Hall. They didn't get to hug their parents and give them farewell kisses. They were simply blown to bits while they were playing.'

'I understand that, Mr Kramer. But killing Sam will not bring them back.'

'No, it won't. But it'll make us feel a helluva lot better. It'll ease a lot of pain. I've prayed a million times that I'll live long enough to see him dead. I had a heart attack five years ago. They had me strapped to machines for two weeks, and the one thing that kept me alive was my desire to outlive Sam Cayhall. I'll be there, Mr Hall, if my doctors allow it. I'll be there to watch him die, then I'll come home and count my days.'

'I'm sorry you feel this way.'

'I'm sorry I do too. I'm sorry I ever heard the name Sam Cayhall.'

Adam took a step backward and leaned on the counter near the cash register. He stared at the floor, and Mr Kramer stared through the window. The sun was falling to the west, behind the building, and the quaint little museum was growing dimmer.

'I lost my father because of this,' Adam said softly.

'I'm sorry. I read where he had committed suicide shortly after the last trial.'

'Sam has suffered too, Mr Kramer. He wrecked his family, and he wrecked yours. And he carries more guilt than you or I could ever imagine.'

'Perhaps he won't be as burdened when he's dead.'

'Perhaps. But why don't we stop the killing?'

'How do you expect me to stop it?'

'I read somewhere that you and the governor are old friends.'

'Why is it any of your business?'

'It's true, isn't it?'

'He's a local boy. I've known him for many years.'

355

'I met him last week for the first time. He has the power to grant clemency, you know.'

'I wouldn't count on that.'

'I'm not. I'm desperate, Mr Kramer. I have nothing to lose at this point, except my grandfather. If you and your family are hell-bent on pushing for the execution, then the governor will certainly listen to you.'

'You're right.'

'And if you decided you didn't want an execution, I think the governor might listen to that as well.'

'So it's all up to me,' he said, finally moving. He walked in front of Adam and stopped near the window. 'You're not only desperate, Mr Hall, you're also naive.'

'I won't argue that.'

'It's nice to know I have so much power. If I had known this before now, your grandfather would've been dead years ago.'

'He doesn't deserve to die, Mr Kramer,' Adam said as he walked to the door. He hadn't expected to find sympathy. It was important only for Mr Kramer to see him and know that other lives were being affected.

'Neither did my grandsons. Neither did my son.'

Adam opened the door, and said, 'I'm sorry for the intrusion, and I thank you for your time. I have a sister, a cousin, and an aunt, Sam's daughter. I just wanted you to know that Sam has a family, such as it is. We will suffer if he dies. If he's not executed, he'll never leave prison. He'll simply wilt away and die some day very soon of natural causes.'

'You will suffer?'

'Yes sir. It's a pathetic family, Mr Kramer, filled with tragedy. I'm trying to avoid another one.'

Mr Kramer turned and looked at him. His face bore no expression. 'Then I feel sorry for you.'

'Thanks again,' Adam said.

'Good day, sir,' Mr Kramer said without a smile.

Adam left the building and walked along a shaded street until he was in the center of town. He found the memorial park, and sat on the same bench not far from the bronze statue of the little boys. After a few minutes, though, he was tired of the guilt and memories, and he walked away.

He went to the same café a block away, drank coffee, and toyed with a grilled cheese. He heard a Sam Cayhall conversation several tables away, but couldn't discern what exactly was being said.

He checked into a motel and called Lee. She sounded sober, and maybe a bit relieved that he would not be there tonight. He promised to return tomorrow evening. By the time it was dark, Adam had been asleep for half an hour.

THIRTY-ONE

ADAM DROVE through downtown Memphis in the predawn hours, and was locked in his office by 7 A.M. By eight, he'd talked to E. Garner Goodman three times. Goodman, it seemed, was wired and also having trouble sleeping. They discussed at length the issue of Keyes' representation at trial. The Cayhall file was filled with memos and research about what went wrong at trial, but little of it placed blame on Benjamin Keyes.

But that had been many years ago, when the gas chamber seemed too distant to worry about. Goodman was pleased to hear that Sam now felt he should've testified at trial, and that Keyes had stopped him. Goodman was skeptical of the truth at this point, but he would take Sam's word for it.

Both Goodman and Adam knew the issue should've been raised years ago, and that to do so now was a long shot at best. Law books were getting thicker by the week with Supreme Court decisions barring legitimate claims because they weren't timely filed. But it was a real issue, one always examined by the courts, and Adam got excited as he drafted and redrafted the claim and swapped faxes with Goodman.

Again, the claim would first be filed under the post-conviction relief statutes in state court. He hoped for a quick denial there so he could immediately run to federal court.

At ten, he faxed his final draft to the clerk of the Mississippi Supreme Court, and also faxed a copy of it to the attention of Breck Jefferson in Slattery's office. Faxes

358

also went to the clerk of the Fifth Circuit in New Orleans. Then he called the Death Clerk at the Supreme Court, and told Mr Olander what he was doing. Mr Olander instructed him to immediately fax a copy to Washington.

Darlene knocked on the door, and Adam unlocked it. He had a visitor waiting in the reception area, a Mr Wyn Lettner. Adam thanked her, and a few minutes later walked down the hall and greeted Lettner, who was alone and dressed like a man who owned a trout dock. Deck shoes, fishing cap. They exchanged pleasantries: fish were biting, Irene was fine, when was he coming back to Calico Rock?

'I'm in town on business, and I just wanted to see you for a few minutes,' he said in a low whisper with his back to the receptionist.

'Sure,' Adam whispered. 'My office is down the hall.'

'No. Let's take a walk.'

They rode the elevator to the lobby, and stepped from the building onto the pedestrian mall. Lettner bought a bag of roasted peanuts from a pushcart vendor, and offered Adam a handful. He declined. They walked slowly north toward city hall and the federal building. Lettner alternately ate the peanuts and tossed them to the pigeons.

'How's Sam?' he finally asked.

'He has two weeks. How would you feel if you had two weeks?'

'Guess I'd be praying a lot.'

'He's not at that point yet, but it won't be long.'

'Is it gonna happen?'

'It's certainly being planned. There's nothing in writing to stop it.'

Lettner threw a handful of peanuts into his mouth. 'Well, good luck to you. Since you came to see me, I've found myself pulling for you and ol' Sam.'

'Thanks. And you came to Memphis to wish me luck?'

'Not exactly. After you left, I thought a lot about Sam and the Kramer bombing. I looked at my personal files and records – stuff I haven't thought about in years. It brought back a lot of memories. I called a few of my old buddies and we told war stories about the Klan. Those were the days.'

'I'm sorry that I missed them.'

'Anyway, I thought of a few things that maybe I should've told you.'

'Such as.'

'There's more to the Dogan story. You know he died a year after he testified.'

'Sam told me.'

'He and his wife were killed when their house blew up. Some kind of propane leak in the heater. House filled up with gas, and something ignited it. Went off like a bomb, a huge fireball. Buried them in sandwich bags.'

'Sad, but so what?'

'We never believed it was an accident. The crime lab boys down there tried to reconstruct the heater. A lot of it was destroyed, but they were of the opinion it had been rigged to leak.'

'How does this affect Sam?'

'It doesn't affect Sam.'

'Then why are we talking about it?'

'It might affect you.'

'I really don't follow.'

'Dogan had a son, a kid who joined the Army in 1979 and was sent to Germany. At some point in the summer of 1980, Dogan and Sam were indicted again by the circuit court in Greenville, and shortly thereafter it became widely known that Dogan had agreed to testify against Sam. It was a big story. In October of 1980, Dogan's son went AWOL in Germany. Vanished.' He crunched on some peanuts and tossed the hulls to a covey of pigeons. 'Never found him either. Army searched high and low. Months went by. Then a year. Dogan died not knowing what happened to the kid.'

'What happened to him?'

'Don't know. To this day, he's never turned up.'

'He died?'

360

'Probably. There was no sign of him.'

'Who killed him?'

'Maybe the same person who killed his parents.'

'And who might that be?'

'We had a theory, but no suspect. We thought at the time that the son was grabbed before the trial as a warning to Dogan. Perhaps Dogan knew secrets.'

'Then why kill Dogan after the trial?'

They stopped under a shade tree and sat on a bench in Court Square. Adam finally took some peanuts.

'Who knew the details of the bombing?' Lettner asked. 'All the details.'

'Sam. Jeremiah Dogan.'

'Right. And who was their lawyer in the first two trials?'

'Clovis Brazelton.'

'Would it be safe to assume Brazelton knew the details?'

'I suppose. He was active in the Klan, wasn't he?'

'Yep, he was a Klucker. That makes three – Sam, Dogan, and Brazelton. Anybody else?'

Adam thought for a second. 'Perhaps the mysterious accomplice.'

'Perhaps. Dogan's dead. Sam wouldn't talk. And Brazelton died many years ago.'

'How'd he die?'

'Plane crash. The Kramer case made him a hero down there, and he was able to parlay his fame into a very successful law practice. He liked to fly, so he bought himself a plane and buzzed around everywhere trying lawsuits. A real big shot. He was flying back from the Coast one night when the plane disappeared from radar. They found his body in a tree. The weather was clear. The FAA said there'd been some type of engine failure.'

'Another mysterious death.'

'Yep. So everybody's dead but Sam, and he's getting close.'

'Any link between Dogan's death and Brazelton's?'

'No. They were years apart. But the theory includes the scenario that the deaths were the work of the same person.'

'So who's at work here?'

'Someone who's very concerned about secrets. Could be Sam's mysterious accomplice, John Doe.'

'That's a pretty wild theory.'

'Yes, it is. And it's one with absolutely no proof to support it. But I told you in Calico Rock that we always suspected Sam had help. Or perhaps Sam was merely a helper for John Doe. At any rate, when Sam screwed up and got caught, John Doe vanished. Perhaps he's been at work eliminating witnesses.'

'Why would he kill Dogan's wife?'

'Because she happened to be in bed with him when the house blew up.'

'Why would he kill Dogan's son?'

'To keep Dogan quiet. Remember, when Dogan testified his son had been missing for four months.'

'I've never read anything about the son.'

'It was not well known. It happened in Germany. We advised Dogan to keep it quiet.'

'I'm confused. Dogan didn't finger anybody else at trial. Only Sam. Why would John Doe kill him afterward?'

'Because he still knew secrets. And because he testified against another Klansman.'

Adam cracked two shells and dropped the peanuts in front of a single, fat pigeon. Lettner finished the bag and threw another handful of hulls on the sidewalk near a water fountain. It was almost noon, and dozens of office workers hurried through the park in pursuit of the perfect thirty-minute lunch.

'You hungry?' Lettner asked, glancing at his watch.

'No.'

'Thirsty? I need a beer.'

'No. How does John Doe affect me?'

'Sam's the only witness left, and he's scheduled to be silenced in two weeks. If he dies without talking, then John Doe can live in peace. If Sam doesn't die in two weeks, then John Doe is still anxious. But if Sam starts talking, then somebody might get hurt.'

'Me?'

'You're the one trying to find the truth.'

'You think he's out there?'

'Could be. Or he might be driving a cab in Montreal. Or maybe he never existed.'

Adam glanced over both shoulders with exaggerated looks of fear.

'I know it sounds crazy,' Lettner said.

'John Doe is safe. Sam ain't talking.'

'There's a potential danger, Adam. I just wanted you to know.'

'I'm not scared. If Sam gave me John Doe's name right now, I'd scream it in the streets and file motions by the truckload. And it wouldn't do any good. It's too late for new theories of guilt or innocence.'

'What about the governor?'

'I doubt it.'

'Well, I want you to be careful.'

'Thanks, I guess.'

'Let's get a beer.'

I've got to keep this guy away from Lee, Adam thought. 'It's five minutes before noon. Surely you don't start this early.'

'Oh, sometimes I start with breakfast.'

JOHN DOE sat on a park bench with a newspaper in front of his face and pigeons around his feet. He was eighty feet away, so he couldn't hear what they were saying. He thought he recognized the old man with Adam as an FBI agent whose face had appeared in the newspapers years ago. He would follow the guy and find out who he was and where he lived.

Wedge was getting bored with Memphis, and this suited him fine. The kid worked at the office and drove to Parchman and slept at the condo, and seemed to be spinning his wheels. Wedge followed the news carefully. His name had not been mentioned. No one knew about him.

THE NOTE on the counter was dated properly. She had given the time as 7:15 P.M. It was Lee's handwriting, which was not neat to begin with but was even sloppier now. She said she was in bed with what appeared to be the flu. Please don't disturb. She'd been to the doctor who told her to sleep it off. For added effect, a prescription bottle from a local pharmacy was sitting nearby next to a half-empty glass of water. It had today's date on it.

Adam quickly checked the wastebasket under the sink – no sign of booze.

He quietly put a frozen pizza in the microwave and went to the patio to watch the barges on the river.

THIRTY-TWO

THE FIRST KITE of the morning arrived shortly after breakfast, as Sam stood in his baggy boxer shorts and leaned through the bars with a cigarette. It was from Preacher Boy, and it brought bad news. It read:

Dear Sam:
The dream is finished. The Lord worked on me last night and finally showed me the rest of it. I wish he hadn't done it. There's a lot to it, and I'll explain it all if you want. Bottom line is that you'll be with him shortly. He told me to tell you to get things right with him. He's waiting. The journey will be rough, but the rewards will be worth it. I love you.
                                                    Brother Randy

Bon voyage, Sam mumbled to himself as he crumpled the paper and threw it on the floor. The kid was slowly deteriorating, and there was no way to help him. Sam had already prepared a series of motions to be filed at some uncertain point in the future when Brother Randy was thoroughly insane.

He saw Gullitt's hands come through the bars next door.

'How you doin', Sam?' Gullitt finally asked.

'God's upset with me,' Sam said.

'Really?'

'Yeah. Preacher Boy finished his dream last night.'

'Thank God for that.'

'It was more like a nightmare.'

'I wouldn't worry too much about it. Crazy bastard has

dreams when he's wide awake. They said yesterday he's been crying for a week.'

'Can you hear him?'

'No. Thank God.'

'Poor kid. I've done some motions for him, just in case I leave this place. I want to leave them with you.'

'I don't know what to do with them.'

'I'll leave instructions. They're to be sent to his lawyer.'

Gullitt whistled softly. 'Man oh man, Sam. What am I gonna do if you leave? I ain't talked to my lawyer in a year.'

'Your lawyer is a moron.'

'Then help me fire him, Sam. Please. You just fired yours. Help me fire mine. I don't know how to do it.'

'Then who'll represent you?'

'Your grandson. Tell him he can have my case.'

Sam smiled, then he chuckled. And then he laughed at the idea of rounding up his buddies on the Row and delivering their hopeless cases to Adam.

'What's so damned funny?' Gullitt demanded.

'You. What makes you think he'll want your case?'

'Come on, Sam. Talk to the kid for me. He must be smart if he's your grandson.'

'What if they gas me? Do you want a lawyer who's just lost his first death row client?'

'Hell, I can't be particular right now.'

'Relax, J.B. You have years to go.'

'How many years?'

'At least five, maybe more.'

'You swear?'

'You have my word. I'll put it in writing. If I'm wrong, you can sue me.'

'Real funny, Sam. Real funny.'

A door clicked open at the end of the hall, and heavy footsteps came their way. It was Packer, and he stopped in front of number six. 'Mornin', Sam,' he said.

'Mornin', Packer.'

'Put your reds on. You have a visitor.'

'Who is it?'

'Somebody who wants to talk to you.'

'Who is it?' Sam repeated as he quickly slipped into his red jumpsuit. He grabbed his cigarettes. He didn't care who the visitor was or what he wanted. A visit by anyone was a welcome relief from his cell.

'Hurry up, Sam,' Packer said.

'Is it my lawyer?' Sam asked as he slid his feet into the rubber shower shoes.

'No.' Packer handcuffed him through the bars, and the door to his cell opened. They left Tier A and headed for the same little room where the lawyers always waited.

Packer removed the handcuffs and slammed the door behind Sam, who focused on the heavy-set woman seated on the other side of the screen. He rubbed his wrists for her benefit and took a few steps to the seat opposite her. He did not recognize the woman. He sat down, lit a cigarette, and glared at her.

She scooted forward in her chair, and nervously said, 'Mr Cayhall, my name is Dr Stegall.' She slipped a business card through the opening. 'I'm the psychiatrist for the State Department of Corrections.'

Sam studied the card on the counter in front of him. He picked it up and examined it suspiciously. 'Says here your name is N. Stegall. Dr N. Stegall.'

'That's correct.'

'That's a strange name, N. I've never met a woman named N. before.'

The small, anxious grin disappeared from her face, and her spine stiffened. 'It's just an initial, okay. There are reasons for it.'

'What's it stand for?'

'That's really none of your business.'

'Nancy? Nelda? Nona?'

'If I wanted you to know, I would've put it on the card, now wouldn't I?'

'I don't know. Must be something horrible, whatever it is. Nick? Ned? I can't imagine hiding behind an initial.'

'I'm not hiding, Mr Cayhall.'

'Just call me S., okay?'

367

Her jaws clenched and she scowled through the screen.
'I'm here to help you.'

'You're too late, N.'

'Please call me Dr Stegall.'

'Oh, well, in that case you can call me Lawyer Cayhall.'

'Lawyer Cayhall?'

'Yes. I know more law than most of the clowns who sit over there where you are.'

She managed a slight, patronizing smile, then said, 'I'm supposed to consult you at this stage of the proceedings to see if I can be of any assistance. You don't have to cooperate if you don't want.'

'Thank you so much.'

'If you need to talk to me, or if you need any medication now or later, just let me know.'

'How about some whiskey?'

'I can't prescribe that.'

'Why not?'

'Prison regulations, I guess.'

'What can you prescribe?'

'Tranquilizers, Valium, sleeping pills, things like that.'

'For what?'

'For your nerves.'

'My nerves are fine.'

'Are you able to sleep?'

Sam thought for a moment. 'Well, to be honest, I am having a little trouble. Yesterday I slept off and on for no more than twelve hours. Usually I'm good for fifteen or sixteen.'

'Twelve hours?'

'Yeah. How often do you get over here to death row?'

'Not very often.'

'That's what I thought. If you knew what you were doing, you'd know that we average about sixteen hours a day.'

'I see. And what else might I learn?'

'Oh, lots of things. You'd know that Randy Dupree is slowly going insane, and no one around here cares about him. Why haven't you been to see him?'

368

'There are five thousand inmates here, Mr Cayhall. I—'

'Then leave. Go away. Go tend to the rest of them. I've been here for nine and a half years and never met you. Now that y'all are about to gas me, you come running over with a bag full of drugs to calm my nerves so I'll be sweet and gentle when you kill me. Why should you care about my nerves and my sleeping habits? You're working for the state and the state is working like hell to execute me.'

'I'm doing my job, Mr Cayhall.'

'Your job stinks, Ned. Get a real job where you can help people. You're here right now because I've got thirteen days and you want me to go in peace. You're just another flunkie for the state.'

'I didn't come here to be abused.'

'Then get your big ass out of here. Leave. Go and sin no more.'

She jumped to her feet and grabbed her briefcase. 'You have my card. If you need anything, let me know.'

'Sure, Ned. Don't sit by the phone.' Sam stood and walked to the door on his side. He banged it twice with the palm of his hand, and waited with his back to her until Packer opened it.

ADAM WAS PACKING his briefcase in preparation for a quick trip to Parchman when the phone rang. Darlene said it was urgent. She was right.

The caller identified himself as the clerk of the Fifth Circuit Court of Appeals in New Orleans, and was remarkably friendly. He said the Cayhall petition attacking the constitutionality of the gas chamber had been received on Monday, had been assigned to a three-judge panel, and that the panel wanted to hear oral argument from both sides. Could he be in New Orleans at 1 P.M. tomorrow, Friday, for the oral argument?

Adam almost dropped the phone. Tomorrow? Of course, he said after a slight hesitation. One o'clock sharp, the clerk said, then explained that the court did not normally hear oral argument in the afternoon. But because of the urgency of this matter the court had scheduled a special hearing. He asked Adam if he'd ever argued before the Fifth Circuit before.

Are you kidding, Adam thought. A year ago I was studying for the bar exam. He said no, in fact he had not, and the clerk said he would immediately fax to Adam a copy of the court's rules governing oral argument. Adam thanked him profusely, and hung up.

He sat on the edge of the table and tried to collect his thoughts. Darlene brought the fax to him, and he asked her to check the flights to New Orleans.

Had he caught the attention of the court with his issues? Was this good news, or just a formality? In his brief career as a lawyer, he had stood alone before the bench to argue a client's position on only one occasion. But Emmitt Wycoff had been seated nearby, just in case. And the judge had been a familiar one. And it had happened in downtown Chicago, not far from his office. Tomorrow he would walk into a strange courtroom in a strange city and try to defend an eleventh-hour plea before a panel of judges he'd never heard of.

He called E. Garner Goodman with the news. Goodman had been to the Fifth Circuit many times, and as he talked Adam relaxed. It was neither good news nor bad, in Goodman's opinion. The court was obviously interested in the lawsuit, but they'd heard it all before. Both Texas and Louisiana had sent similar constitutional claims to the Fifth Circuit in recent years.

Goodman assured him that he could handle the arguments. Just be prepared, he said. And try to relax. It might be possible for him to fly to New Orleans and be there, but Adam said no. He said he could do it alone. Keep in touch, Goodman said.

Adam checked with Darlene, then locked himself in his office. He memorized the rules for oral argument. He studied the lawsuit attacking the gas chamber. He read briefs and cases. He called Parchman and left word for Sam that he would not be there today.

HE WORKED UNTIL DARK, then made the dreaded trip to Lee's condo. The same note was sitting on the counter, untouched and still declaring that she was in bed with the flu. He eased around the apartment and saw no signs of movement or life during the day.

Her bedroom door was slightly opened. He tapped on it while pushing. 'Lee,' he called out gently into the darkness. 'Lee, are you all right?'

There was movement in the bed, though he couldn't see what it was. 'Yes dear,' she said. 'Come in.'

Adam slowly sat on the edge of the bed and tried to focus on her. The only light was a faint beam from the hallway. She pushed herself up and rested on the pillows. 'I'm better,' she said with a scratchy voice. 'How are you, dear?'

'I'm fine, Lee. I'm worried about you.'

'I'll be okay. It's a wicked little virus.'

The first pungent vapor wafted from the bedsheets and covers, and Adam wanted to cry. It was the reeking odor of stale vodka or gin or sour mash, or maybe a combination of everything. He couldn't see her eyes in the murky shadows, only the vague outline of her face. She was wearing a dark shirt of some sort.

'What type of medication?' he asked.

'I don't know. Just some pills. The doctor said it'll last for a few days, then quickly disappear. I feel better already.'

Adam started to say something about the oddity of a flu-like virus in late July, but let it pass. 'Are you able to eat?'

'No appetite, really.'

'Is there anything I can do?'

'No dear. How have you been? What day is it?'

'It's Thursday.'

'I feel like I've been in a cave for a week.'

Adam had two choices. He could play along with the wicked little virus act and hope she stopped the drinking before it got worse. Or he could confront her now and make her realize she was not fooling him. Maybe they would fight, and maybe this was what you were supposed to do

371

with drunks who'd fallen off the wagon. How was he supposed to know what to do?

'Does your doctor know you're drinking?' he asked, holding his breath.

There was a long pause. 'I haven't been drinking,' she said, almost inaudible.

'Come on, Lee. I found the vodka bottle in the wastebasket. I know the other three bottles of beer disappeared last Saturday. You smell like a brewery right now. You're not fooling anyone, Lee. You're drinking heavily, and I want to help.'

She sat straighter, and pulled her legs up to her chest. Then she was still for a long time. Adam glanced at her silhouette. Minutes passed. The apartment was deathly quiet.

'How's my dear father?' she muttered. Her words were sluggish, but still bitter.

'I didn't see him today.'

'Don't you think we'll be better off when he's dead?'

Adam looked at her silhouette. 'No, Lee, I don't. Do you?'

She was silent and still for at least a minute. 'You feel sorry for him, don't you?' she finally asked.

'Yes, I do.'

'Is he pitiful?'

'Yes, he is.'

'What does he look like?'

'A very old man, with plenty of gray hair that's always oily and pulled back. He has a short gray beard. Lots of wrinkles. His skin is very pale.'

'What does he wear?'

'A red jumpsuit. All death row inmates wear the same thing.'

Another long pause as she thought about this. Then she said, 'I guess it's easy to feel sorry for him.'

'It is for me.'

'But you see, Adam, I've never seen him the way you see him. I saw a different person.'

'And what did you see?'

She adjusted the blanket around her legs, then grew still again. 'My father was a person I despised.'

'Do you still despise him?'

'Yes. Very much so. I think he should go ahead and die. God knows he deserves it.'

'Why does he deserve it?'

This prompted another spell of silence. She moved slightly to her left and took a cup or glass from the nightstand. She sipped slowly, as Adam watched her shadows. He didn't ask what she was drinking.

'Does he talk to you about the past?'

'Only when I ask questions. We've talked about Eddie, but I promised we wouldn't do it again.'

'He's the reason Eddie's dead. Does he realize this?'

'Maybe.'

'Did you tell him? Did you blame him for Eddie?'

'No.'

'You should have. You're too easy on him. He needs to know what he's done.'

'I think he does. But you said yourself it's not fair to torment him at this point of his life.'

'How about Joe Lincoln? Did you talk to him about Joe Lincoln?'

'I told Sam that you and I went to the old family place. He asked me if I knew about Joe Lincoln. I said that I did.'

'Did he deny it?'

'No. He showed a lot of remorse.'

'He's a liar.'

'No. I think he was sincere.'

Another long pause as she sat motionless. Then, 'Has he told you about the lynching?'

Adam closed his eyes and rested his elbows on his knees. 'No,' he mumbled.

'I didn't think so.'

'I don't want to hear it, Lee.'

'Yes you do. You came down here full of questions about the family and about your past. Two weeks ago you just couldn't get enough of the Cayhall family misery. You wanted all the blood and gore.'

'I've heard enough,' he said.

'What day is it?' she asked.

'It's Thursday, Lee. You've already asked once.'

'One of my girls was due today. Her second child. I didn't call the office. I guess it's the medication.'

'And the alcohol.'

'All right, dammit. So I'm an alcoholic. Who can blame me? Sometimes I wish I had the guts to do what Eddie did.'

'Come on, Lee. Let me help you.'

'Oh, you've already helped a great deal, Adam. I was fine, nice and sober until you arrived.'

'Okay. I was wrong. I'm sorry. I just didn't realize—' His words trailed off, then quit.

She moved slightly and Adam watched as she took another sip. A heavy silence engulfed them as minutes passed. The rancid smell emanated from her end of the bed.

'Mother told me the story,' she said quietly, almost whispering. 'She said she'd heard rumours about it for years. Long before they married she knew he'd helped lynch a young black man.'

'Please, Lee.'

'I never asked him about it, but Eddie did. We had whispered about it for many years, and finally one day Eddie just up and confronted him with the story. They had a nasty fight, but Sam admitted it was true. It really didn't bother him, he said. The black kid had allegedly raped a white girl, but she was white trash and many people doubted if it was really a rape. This is according to Mother's version. Sam was fifteen or so at the time, and a bunch of men went down to the jail, got the black kid, and took him out in the woods. Sam's father, of course, was the ringleader, and his brothers were involved.'

'That's enough, Lee.'

'They beat him with a bullwhip, then hung him from a tree. My dear father was right in the middle of it. He

374

couldn't really deny it, you know, because somebody took a picture of it.'

'A photograph?'

'Yeah. A few years later the photo found its way into a book about the plight of Negroes in the Deep South. It was published in 1947. My mother had a copy of it for years. Eddie found it in the attic.'

'And Sam's in the photograph.'

'Sure. Smiling from ear to ear. They're standing under the tree and the black guy's feet are dangling just above their heads. Everybody's having a ball. Just another nigger lynching. There are no credits with the photo, no names. The picture speaks for itself. It's described as a lynching in rural Mississippi, 1936.'

'Where's the book?'

'Over there in the drawer. I've kept it in storage with other family treasures since the foreclosure. I got it out the other day. I thought you might want to see it.'

'No. I don't want to see it.'

'Go ahead. You wanted to know about your family. Well, there they are. Grandfather, great-grandfather, and all sorts of Cayhalls at their very best. Caught in the act, and quite proud of it.'

'Stop it, Lee.'

'There were other lynchings, you know.'

'Shut up, Lee. Okay? I don't want to hear any more.'

She leaned to her side and reached for the nightstand.

'What are you drinking, Lee?'

'Cough syrup.'

'Bullshit!' Adam jumped to his feet and walked through the darkness to the nightstand. Lee quickly gulped the last of the liquid. He grabbed the glass from her hand and sniffed the top of it. 'This is bourbon.'

'There's more in the pantry. Would you get it for me?'

'No! You've had more than enough.'

'If I want it, I'll get it.'

'No you won't, Lee. You're not drinking any more

tonight. Tomorrow I'll take you to the doctor, and we'll get some help.'

'I don't need help. I need a gun.'

Adam placed the glass on the dresser and switched on a lamp. She shielded her eyes for a few seconds, then looked at him. They were red and puffy. Her hair was wild, dirty, and unkempt.

'Not a pretty sight, huh,' she said, slurring her words, and looking away.

'No. But we'll get help, Lee. We'll do it tomorrow.'

'Get me a drink, Adam. Please.'

'No.'

'Then leave me alone. This is all your fault, you know. Now, leave, please. Go on to bed.'

Adam grabbed a pillow from the center of the bed and threw it against the door. 'I'm sleeping here tonight,' he said, pointing at the pillow. 'I'm locking the door, and you're not leaving this room.'

She glared at him, but said nothing. He switched off the lamp, and the room was completely dark. He pressed the lock on the knob and stretched out on the carpet against the door. 'Now sleep it off, Lee.'

'Go to bed, Adam. I promise I won't leave the room.'

'No. You're drunk, and I'm not moving. If you try to open this door, I'll physically put you back in the bed.'

'That sounds sort of romantic.'

'Knock it off, Lee. Go to sleep.'

'I can't sleep.'

'Try it.'

'Let's tell Cayhall stories, okay, Adam? I know a few more lynching stories.'

'Shut up, Lee!' Adam screamed, and she was suddenly quiet. The bed squeaked as she wiggled and flipped and got herself situated. After fifteen minutes, she was subdued. After thirty minutes, the floor became uncomfortable and Adam rolled from side to side.

Sleep came in brief naps, interrupted by long periods of staring at the ceiling and worrying about her, and about the

376

Fifth Circuit. At one point during the night he sat with his back to the door and stared through the darkness in the direction of the drawer. Was the book really there? He was tempted to sneak over and get it, then ease into the bathroom to look for the picture. But he couldn't risk waking her. And he didn't want to see it.

Erith cargo, he got out of his chair and crept the length of the corridor.

cave of the door and turned the knob. She shut herself in the bathroom of the driver. She stood back until she heard. He was prepared to sneak over and get in. She crept into the bathroom to knock on the bedroom, the room talk at long last, and he quickly went to sleep.

THIRTY-THREE

HE FOUND a pint of bourbon hidden behind a box of saltines in the pantry, and emptied it in the sink. It was dark outside. Sunlight was an hour away. He made the coffee strong, and sipped it on the sofa while he rehearsed the arguments he would present in a few hours in New Orleans.

He reviewed his notes on the patio at dawn, and by seven he was in the kitchen making toast. No sign of Lee. He didn't want a confrontation, but one was necessary. He had things to say, and she had apologies to make, and he rattled plates and forks on the counter. The volume was increased for the morning news.

But there was no movement from her part of the condo. After he showered and dressed, he gently turned the knob to her door. It was locked. She had sealed herself in her cave, and prevented the painful talk of the morning after. He wrote a note and explained that he would be in New Orleans today and tonight, and he would see her tomorrow. He said he was sorry for now, and they would talk about it later. He pleaded with her not to drink.

The note was placed on the counter where she couldn't miss it. Adam left the condo and drove to the airport.

The direct flight to New Orleans took fifty-five minutes. Adam drank fruit juice and tried to sit comfortably to soothe his stiff back. He'd slept less than three hours on the floor by the door, and vowed not to do it again. By her own admission, she'd been through recovery three times over the years, and if she couldn't stay off the booze by herself

378

there was certainly nothing he could do to help. He would stay in Memphis until this miserable case was over, and if his aunt couldn't stay sober, then he could manage things from a hotel room.

He fought himself to forget about her for the next few hours. He needed to concentrate on legal matters, not lynchings and photographs and horror stories from the past; not his beloved aunt and her problems.

The plane touched down in New Orleans, and suddenly his concentration became sharper. He mentally clicked off the names of dozens of recent death penalty cases from the Fifth Circuit and the U.S. Supreme Court.

The hired car was a Cadillac sedan, one arranged by Darlene and charged to Kravitz & Bane. It came with a driver, and as Adam relaxed in the rear seat he conceded that life in a big firm did indeed have certain advantages. Adam had never been to New Orleans before, and the drive from the airport could've taken place in any city. Just traffic and expressways. The driver turned onto Poydras Street by the Superdome, and suddenly they were downtown. He explained to his passenger that the French Quarter was a few blocks away, not far from Adam's hotel. The car stopped on Camp Street, and Adam stepped onto the sidewalk in front of a building simply called the Fifth Circuit Court of Appeals. It was an impressive structure, with Greek columns and lots of steps leading to the front entrance.

He found the clerk's office on the main floor, and asked for the gentleman he'd spoken to, a Mr Feriday. Mr Feriday was as sincere and courteous in person as he'd been on the phone. He properly registered Adam, and explained some of the rules of the court. He asked Adam if he wanted a quick tour of the place. It was almost noon, the place was not busy, and it was the perfect time for a look around. They headed for the courtrooms, passing along the way various offices of the judges and staff.

'The Fifth Circuit has fifteen judges,' Mr Feriday explained as they walked casually over marble floors, 'and their offices are along these hallways. Right now the court has three vacancies, and the nominations are tied up in Washington.' The corridors were dark and quiet, as if great minds were at work behind the broad wooden doors.

Mr Feriday went first to the En Banc courtroom, a large, intimidating stage with fifteen chairs sitting snugly together in a half-circle in the front of the room. 'Most of the work here is assigned to three-judge panels. But occasionally the entire body sits en banc,' he explained quietly, as if still in awe of the spectacular room. The bench was elevated well above the rest of the room, so that the lawyers at the podium below looked upward as they pleaded. The room was marble and dark wood, heavy drapes and a huge chandelier. It was ornate but understated, old but meticulously maintained, and as Adam inspected it he felt quite frightened. Only rarely does the entire court sit en banc, Mr Feriday explained again as if he were instructing a first-year student of the law. The great civil rights decisions of the sixties and seventies took place right here, he said with no small amount of pride. Portraits of deceased justices hung behind the bench.

As beautiful and stately as it was, Adam hoped he never saw it again, at least not as a lawyer representing a client. They walked down the hall to the West Courtroom, which was smaller than the first but just as intimidating. This is where the three-judge panels operate, Mr Feriday explained as they walked past the seats in the spectators' section, through the bar and to the podium. The bench again was elevated, though not as lofty or as long as En Banc.

'Virtually all oral arguments take place in the morning, beginning at nine,' Mr Feriday said. 'Your case is a bit different because it's a death case that's going down to the wire.' He pointed a crooked finger at the seats in the back. 'You'll need to be seated out there a few minutes before one, and the clerk will call the case. Then you come through the bar and sit right here at counsel table. You'll go first, and you have twenty minutes.'

Adam knew this, but it was certainly nice to be walked through it.

Mr Feriday pointed to a device on the podium which resembled a traffic light. 'This is the timer,' he said gravely. 'And it is very important. Twenty minutes, okay. There are horrific stories of long-winded lawyers who ignored this. Not a pretty sight. The green is on when you're talking. The yellow comes on when you want your warning – two minutes, five minutes, thirty seconds, whatever. When the red comes on, you simply stop in mid-sentence and go sit down. It's that simple. Any questions?'

'Who are the judges?'

'NcNeely, Robichaux, and Judy.' He said this as if Adam personally knew all three. 'There's a waiting room over there, and there's a library on the third floor. Just be here about ten minutes before one. Any more questions?'

'No sir. Thanks.'

'I'm in my office if you need me. Good luck.' They shook hands. Mr Feriday left Adam standing at the podium.

AT TEN MINUTES BEFORE ONE, Adam walked through the massive oak doors of the West Courtroom for the second time, and found other lawyers preparing for battle. On the first row behind the bar, Attorney General Steve Roxburgh and his cluster of assistants were huddled together plotting tactics. They hushed when Adam walked in, and a few nodded and tried to smile. Adam sat by himself along the aisle and ignored them.

Lucas Mann was seated on their side of the courtroom, though several rows behind Roxburgh and his boys. He casually read a newspaper, and waved to Adam when their eyes met. It was good to see him. He was starched from head to toe in wrinkle-free khaki, and his tie was wild enough to glow in the dark. It was obvious Mann was not intimidated by the Fifth Circuit and its trappings, and equally as obvious that he was keeping his distance from Roxburgh. He was only the attorney for Parchman, only doing his job. If the Fifth Circuit granted a stay and Sam didn't die, Lucas Mann would be pleased. Adam nodded and smiled at him.

Roxburgh and his gang rehuddled. Morris Henry, Dr Death, was in the middle of it, explaining things to lesser minds.

Adam breathed deeply and tried to relax. It was quite difficult. His stomach was churning and his feet twitched, and he kept telling himself that it would only last for twenty minutes. The three judges couldn't kill him, they could only embarrass him, and even that could last for only twenty minutes. He could endure anything for twenty minutes. He glanced at his notes, and to calm himself he tried to think of Sam – not Sam the racist, the murderer, the lynch mob thug, but Sam the client, the old man wasting away on death row who was entitled to die in peace and dignity. Sam was about to get twenty minutes of this court's valuable time, so his lawyer had to make the most of it.

A heavy door thudded shut somewhere, and Adam jumped in his seat. The court crier appeared from behind the bench and announced that the honorable court was now in session. He was followed by three figures in flowing black robes – McNeely, Robichaux, and Judy, each of whom carried files and seemed to be totally without humour or goodwill. They sat in their massive leather chairs high up on the shiny, dark, oak-paneled bench, and looked down upon the courtroom. The case of *State of Mississippi v. Sam Cayhall* was called, and the attorneys were summoned from the back of the room. Adam nervously walked through the swinging gate in the bar, and was followed by Steve Roxburgh. The Assistant Attorney Generals kept their seats, as did Lucas Mann and a handful of spectators. Most of these, Adam would later learn, were reporters.

The presiding judge was Judy, the Honorable T. Eileen Judy, a young woman from Texas. Robichaux was from Louisiana, and in his late fifties. McNeely looked to be a hundred and twenty, and was also from Texas. Judy made a brief statement about the case, then asked Mr Adam Hall from Chicago if he was ready to proceed. He stood nervously, his knees rubber-like, his bowels jumping, his voice high and nervous, and he said that, yes, in fact he was ready to go. He made it to the podium in the center of the room and looked up, way up, it seemed, at the panel behind the bench.

The green light beside him came on, and he assumed correctly this meant to get things started. The room was silent. The judges glared down at him. He cleared his throat, glanced at the portraits of dead honorables hanging on the wall, and plunged into a vicious attack on the gas chamber as a means of execution.

He avoided eye contact with the three of them, and for five minutes or so was allowed to repeat what he'd already submitted in his brief. It was post-lunch, in the heat of the summer, and it took a few minutes for the judges to shrug off the cobwebs.

'Mr Hall, I think you're just repeating what you've already said in your brief,' Judy said testily. 'We're quite capable of reading, Mr Hall.'

Mr Hall took it well, and thought to himself that this was his twenty minutes, and if he wanted to pick his nose and recite the alphabet then he should be allowed to do so. For twenty minutes. As green as he was, Adam had heard this comment before from an appellate judge. It happened while he was in law school and watching a case being argued. It was standard fare in oral argument.

'Yes, Your Honor,' Adam said, carefully avoiding any reference to gender. He then moved on to discuss the effect of cyanide gas on laboratory rats, a study not included in his brief. The experiments had been conducted a year ago by some chemists in Sweden for the purpose of proving that humans do not die instantly when they inhale the poison. It had been funded by a European organization working to abolish the death penalty in America.

The rats went into seizures and convulsed. Their lungs and hearts stopped and started erratically for several minutes. The gas burst blood vessels throughout their bodies, including their brains. Their muscles quivered uncontrollably. They salivated and squeaked.

The obvious point of the study was that the rats did not die quickly, but in fact suffered a great deal. The tests were conducted with scientific integrity. Appropriate doses were given to the small animals. On the average, it took almost ten minutes for death to occur. Adam labored over the details, and as he warmed to his presentation his nerves settled a bit. The judges were not only listening, but seemed to be enjoying this discussion of dying rats.

Adam had found the study in a footnote to a recent North Carolina case. It was in the fine print, and had not been widely reported.

'Now, let me get this straight,' Robichaux interrupted in a high-pitched voice. 'You don't want your client to die in the gas chamber because it's a cruel way to go, but are you telling us you don't mind if he's executed by lethal injection?'

'No, Your Honour. That's not what I'm saying. I do not want my client executed by any method.'

'But lethal injection is the least offensive?'

'All methods are offensive, but lethal injection seems to be the least cruel. There's no doubt the gas chamber is a horrible way to die.'

'Worse than being bombed? Blown up by dynamite?'

A heavy silence fell over the courtroom as Robichaux's words settled in. He had emphasized the word 'dynamite,' and Adam struggled for something appropriate. McNeely shot a nasty look at his colleague on the other side of the bench.

It was a cheap shot, and Adam was furious. He controlled his temper, and said firmly, 'We're talking about methods of execution, Your Honor, not the crimes that send men to death row.'

'Why don't you want to talk about the crime?'

'Because the crime is not an issue here. Because I have only twenty minutes, and my client has only twelve days.'

'Perhaps your client shouldn't have been planting bombs?'

'Of course not. But he was convicted of his crime, and

now he faces death in the gas chamber. Our point is that the chamber is a cruel way to execute people.'

'What about the electric chair?'

'The same argument applies. There have been some hideous cases of people suffering terribly in the chair before they died.'

'What about a firing squad?'

'Sounds cruel to me.'

'And hanging?'

'I don't know much about hanging, but it too sounds awfully cruel.'

'But you like the idea of lethal injection?'

'I didn't say I like it. I believe I said it was not as cruel as the other methods.'

Justice McNeely interrupted and asked, 'Mr Hall, why did Mississippi switch from the gas chamber to lethal injection?'

This was covered thoroughly in the lawsuit and the brief, and Adam sensed immediately that McNeely was a friend. 'I've condensed the legislative history of the law in my brief, Your Honor, but it was done principally to facilitate executions. The legislature admitted it was an easier way to die, and so to sidestep constitutional challenges such as this one it changed the method.'

'So the State has effectively admitted that there is a better way to execute people?'

'Yes sir. But the law took effect in 1984, and applies only to those inmates convicted afterward. It does not apply to Sam Cayhall.'

'I understand that. You're asking us to strike down the gas chamber as a method. What happens if we do? What happens to your client and those like him who were convicted prior to 1984? Do they fall through the cracks? There is no provision in the law to execute them by lethal injection.'

Adam was anticipating the obvious question. Sam had already asked it. 'I can't answer that, Your Honor, except to say that I have great confidence in the Mississippi

Legislature's ability and willingness to pass a new law covering my client and those in his position.'

Judge Judy inserted herself at this point. 'Assuming they do, Mr Hall, what will you argue when you return here in three years?'

Thankfully, the yellow light came on, and Adam had only one minute remaining. 'I'll think of something,' he said with a grin. 'Just give me time.'

'We've already seen a case like this, Mr Hall,' Robichaux said. 'In fact, it's cited in your brief. A Texas case.'

'Yes, Your Honor. I'm asking the court to reconsider its decision on this issue. Virtually every state with a gas chamber or an electric chair has switched to lethal injection. The reason is obvious.'

He had a few seconds left, but decided it was a good place to stop. He didn't want another question. 'Thank you,' he said, and walked confidently back to his seat. It was over. He had held his breakfast, and performed quite well for a rookie. It would be easier the next time.

Roxburgh was wooden and methodical, and thoroughly prepared. He tried a few one-liners about rats and the crimes they commit, but it was a dismal effort at humor. McNeely peppered him with similar questions about why the states were rushing to lethal injection. Roxburgh stuck to his guns, and recited a long line of cases where the various federal circuits had endorsed death by gas, electricity, hanging, and firing squads. The established law was on his side, and he made the most of it. His twenty minutes raced by, and he returned to his seat as quickly as Adam had.

Judge Judy talked briefly about the urgency of this matter, and promised a ruling within days. Everyone rose in unison, and the three judges disappeared from the bench. The court crier declared matters to be in recess until Monday morning.

Adam shook hands with Roxburgh and made it through the doors before a reporter stopped him. He was with a paper in Jackson, and just had a couple of questions. Adam was polite, but declined comment. He then did the same for two more reporters. Roxburgh, typically, had things to say, and as Adam walked away, the reporters surrounded the Attorney General and shoved recorders near his face.

Adam wanted to leave the building. He stepped into the tropical heat, and quickly covered his eyes with sunglasses. 'Have you had lunch?' a voice asked from close behind. It was Lucas Mann, in aviator sunglasses. They shook hands between the columns.

'I couldn't eat,' Adam admitted.

'You did fine. It's quite nerve-racking, isn't it?'

'Yes, it is. Why are you here?'

'It's part of my job. The warden asked me to fly down and watch the argument. We'll wait until there's a ruling before we start preparations. Let's go eat.'

Adam's driver stopped the car at the curb, and they got in.

'Do you know the city?' Mann asked.

'No. This is my first visit.'

'The Bon Ton Café,' Mann told the driver. 'It's a wonderful old place just around the corner. Nice car.'

'The benefits of working for a wealthy firm.'

LUNCH BEGAN with a novelty – raw oysters on the half shell. Adam had heard of them before, but had never been tempted. Mann artfully demonstrated the proper blending of horseradish, lemon juice, Tabasco, and cocktail sauce, then dropped the first oyster into the mixture. It was then delicately placed on a cracker and eaten in one bite. Adam's first oyster slid off the cracker and onto the table, but his second slid properly down his throat.

'Don't chew it,' Mann instructed. 'Just let it slither down.' The next ten slithered down, and not soon enough for Adam. He was happy when the dozen shells on his plate were empty. They sipped Dixie beer and waited for shrimp remoulade.

'I saw where you're claiming ineffective assistance of counsel,' Mann said, nibbling on a cracker.

'I'm sure we'll be filing everything from now on.'

387

'The supreme court didn't waste any time with it.'

'No, they didn't. Seems as if they're tired of Sam Cayhall. I'll file it in district court today, but I don't expect any relief from Slattery.'

'I wouldn't either.'

'What are my odds, with twelve days to go?'

'Getting slimmer by the day, but things are wildly unpredictable. Probably still around fifty-fifty. A few years back we came very close with Stockholm Turner. With two weeks to go, it looked certain. With a week to go, there was simply nothing else for him to file. He had a decent lawyer, but the appeals had run. He was given his last meal, and—'

'And his conjugal visit, with two prostitutes.'

'How'd you know?'

'Sam told me all about it.'

'It's true. He got a last minute stay, and now he's years away from the chamber. You never know.'

'But what's your gut feeling?'

Mann took a long drink of beer and leaned backward as two large platters of shrimp remoulade were placed before them. 'I don't have gut feelings when it comes to executions. Anything can happen. Just keep filing writs and appeals. It becomes a marathon. You can't give up. The lawyer for Jumbo Parris collapsed with twelve hours to go, and was in a hospital bed when his client went down.'

Adam chewed on a boiled shrimp and washed it down with beer. 'The governor wants me to talk to him. Should I?'

'What does your client want?'

'What do you think? He hates the governor. He has forbidden me to talk to him.'

'You have to ask for a clemency hearing. That's standard practice.'

'How well do you know McAllister?'

'Not very well. He's a political animal with great ambitions, and I wouldn't trust him for a minute. He does, however, have the power to grant clemency. He can commute the death sentence. He can impose life, or he can set him free. The statute grants broad discretionary authority to the governor. He'll probably be your last hope.'

'God help us.'

'How's the remoulade?' Mann asked with a mouthful.

'Delicious.'

They busied themselves with eating for a while. Adam was thankful for the company and conversation, but decided to limit the talk to appeals and strategy. He liked Lucas Mann, but his client did not. As Sam would say, Mann worked for the state and the state was working to execute him.

A LATE AFTERNOON FLIGHT would have taken him back to Memphis by six-thirty, long before dark. And once there he could've killed an hour or so at the office before returning to Lee's. But he wasn't up to it. He had a fancy room in a modern hotel by the river, paid for without question by the boys at Kravitz & Bane. All expenses were covered. He'd never seen the French Quarter.

And so he awoke at six after a three-hour nap brought on by three Dixies for lunch and a bad night's rest. He was lying across the bed with his shoes on, and he studied the ceiling fan for half an hour before he moved. The sleep had been heavy.

Lee did not answer the phone. He left a message on her recorder, and hoped she was not drinking. And if she was, then he hoped she'd locked herself in her room where she couldn't hurt anyone. He brushed his teeth and hair, and rode an elevator to the spacious lobby where a jazz band performed for happy hour. Five-cent oysters on the half shell were being hawked from a corner bar.

He walked in the sweltering heat along Canal Street until he came to Royal, where he took a right and was soon lost in a throng of tourists. Friday night was coming to life in the Quarter. He gawked at the strip clubs, trying desperately to peek inside. He was stopped cold by an open door which revealed a row of male strippers on stage – men who looked like beautiful women. He ate an egg roll on a stick from a Chinese carryout. He stepped around a wino vomiting in the street. He spent an hour at a small table in a jazz club, listening to a delightful combo and sipping a four-dollar beer. When it was dark, he walked to Jackson Square and watched the artists pack up their easels and leave. The street musicians and dancers were out in force in front of an old cathedral, and he clapped for an amazing string quartet comprised of Tulane students. People were everywhere, drinking and eating and dancing, enjoying the festiveness of the French Quarter.

He bought a dish of ice cream, and headed for Canal. On another night and under far different circumstances, he might be tempted to take in a strip show, sitting in the rear, of course, where no one could see him, or he might hang out in a trendy bar looking for lonely, beautiful women.

But not tonight. The drunks reminded him of Lee, and he wished he'd returned to Memphis to see her. The music and laughter reminded him of Sam, who at this very moment was sitting in a humid oven, staring at the bars and counting the days, hoping and perhaps praying now that his lawyer might work a miracle. Sam would never see New Orleans, never again eat oysters or red beans and rice, never taste a cold beer or a good coffee. He would never hear jazz or watch artists paint. He would never again fly on a plane or stay in a nice hotel. He would never fish or drive or do a thousand things free people take for granted.

Even if Sam lived past August 8, he would simply continue the process of dying a little each day.

Adam left the Quarter and walked hurriedly to his hotel. He needed rest. The marathon was about to begin.

390

THIRTY-FOUR

THE GUARD NAMED TINY handcuffed Sam and led him off Tier A. Sam carried a plastic bag filled tightly with the last two weeks' worth of fan mail. For most of his career as a death row inmate, he had averaged a handful of letters a month from supporters – Klansmen and their sympathizers, racial purists, anti-Semites, all types of bigots. For a couple of years he had answered these letters, but with time had grown weary of it. What was the benefit? To some he was a hero, but the more he swapped words with his admirers the wackier they became. There were a lot of nuts out there. The idea had crossed his mind that perhaps he was safer on the Row than in the free world.

Mail had been declared to be a right by the federal court, not a privilege. Thus, it could not be taken away. It could, however, be regulated. Each letter was opened by an inspector unless the envelope clearly was from an attorney. Unless an inmate was under mail censorship, the letters were not read. They were delivered to the Row in due course and dispensed to the inmates. Boxes and packages were also opened and inspected.

The thought of losing Sam was frightening to many fanatics, and his mail had picked up dramatically since the Fifth Circuit lifted his stay. They offered their unwavering support, and their prayers. A few offered money. Their letters tended to run long as they invariably blasted Jews and blacks and liberals and other conspirators. Some bitched about taxes, gun control, the national debt. Some delivered sermons.

Sam was tired of the letters. He was averaging six per day. He placed them on the counter as the handcuffs were removed, then asked the guard to unlock a small door in the screen. The guard shoved the plastic bag through the door and Adam took it on the other side. The guard left, locking the door behind.

'What's this?' Adam asked, holding the bag.

'Fan mail.' Sam took his regular seat and lit a cigarette.

'What am I supposed to do with it?'

'Read it. Burn it. I don't care. I was cleaning my cell this morning and the stuff got in the way. I understand you were in New Orleans yesterday. Tell me about it.'

Adam placed the letters on a chair, and sat across from Sam. The temperature outside was a hundred and two, and not much cooler inside the visitors' room. It was Saturday, and Adam was dressed in jeans, loafers, and a very light cotton polo. 'The Fifth Circuit called Thursday, and said they wanted to hear from me on Friday. I went down, dazzled them with my brilliance, and flew back to Memphis this morning.'

'When do they rule?'

'Soon.'

'A three-judge panel?'

'Yes.'

'Who?'

'Judy, Robichaux, and McNeely.'

Sam contemplated the names for a moment. 'McNeely's an old warrior who'll help us. Judy's a conservative bitch, oops, sorry, I mean a conservative Female-American, a Republican appointee. I doubt if she'll help. I'm not familiar with Robichaux. Where's he from?'

'Southern Louisiana.'

'Ah, a Cajun-American.'

'I guess. He's a hard-ass. He won't help.'

'Then we'll lose by two to one. I thought you said you dazzled them with your brilliance.'

'We haven't lost yet.' Adam was surprised to hear Sam

392

speak with such familiarity about the individual judges. But then, he'd been studying the court for many years.

'Where's the ineffective counsel claim?' Sam asked.

'Still in district court here. It's a few days behind the other.'

'Let's file something else, okay.'

'I'm working on it.'

'Work fast. I've got eleven days. There's a calendar on my wall, and I spend at least three hours a day staring at it. When I wake up in the morning I make a big X over the date for the day before. I've got a circle around August 8. My X's are getting close to the circle. Do something.'

'I'm working, okay. In fact, I'm developing a new theory of attack.'

'Atta boy.'

'I think we can prove you're mentally unbalanced.'

'I've been considering that.'

'You're old. You're senile. You're too calm about this. Something must be wrong. You're unable to comprehend the reason for your execution.'

'We've been reading the same cases.'

'Goodman knows an expert who'll say anything for a fee. We're considering bringing him down here to examine you.'

'Wonderful. I'll pull out my hair and chase butterflies around the room.'

'I think we can make a hard run at a mental incompetency claim.'

'I agree. Go for it. Let's file lots of things.'

'I'll do it.'

Sam puffed and pondered for a few minutes. They were both sweating, and Adam needed fresh air. He needed to get in his car with the windows up and turn the air on high.

'When are you coming back?' Sam asked.

'Monday. Listen, Sam, this is not a pleasant subject, but we need to address it. You're gonna die one of these days. It might be on August 8, or it might be five years from now. At the rate you're smoking, you can't last for long.'

'Smoking is not my most pressing health concern.'

'I know. But your family, Lee and I, need to make some burial arrangements. It can't be done overnight.'

Sam stared at the rows of tiny triangles in the screen. Adam scribbled on a legal pad. The air conditioner spewed and hissed, accomplishing little.

'Your grandmother was a fine lady, Adam. I'm sorry you didn't know her. She deserved better than me.'

'Lee took me to her grave.'

'I caused her a lot of suffering, and she bore it well. Bury me next to her, and maybe I can tell her I'm sorry.'

'I'll take care of it.'

'Do that. How will you pay for the plot?'

'I can handle it, Sam.'

'I don't have any money, Adam. I lost it years ago, for reasons which are probably obvious. I lost the land and the house, so there are no assets to leave behind.'

'Do you have a will?'

'Yes. I prepared it myself.'

'We'll look at it next week.'

'You promise you'll be here Monday.'

'I promise, Sam. Can I bring you anything?'

Sam hesitated for a second and almost seemed embarrassed. 'You know what I'd really like?' he asked with a childish grin.

'What? Anything, Sam.'

'When I was a kid, the biggest thrill in life was an Eskimo Pie.'

'An Eskimo Pie?'

'Yeah, it's a little ice cream treat on a stick. Vanilla, with a chocolate coating. I ate them until I came to this place. I think they still make them.'

'An Eskimo Pie?' Adam repeated.

'Yeah. I can still taste it. The greatest ice cream in the world. Can you imagine how good one would taste right now in this oven?'

'Then, Sam, you shall have an Eskimo Pie.'

'Bring more than one.'

'I'll bring a dozen. We'll eat 'em right here while we sweat.'

SAM'S SECOND VISITOR on Saturday was not expected. He stopped at the guard station by the front gate, and produced a North Carolina driver's license with his picture on it. He explained to the guard that he was the brother of Sam Cayhall, and had been told he could visit Sam on death row at his convenience between now and the scheduled execution. He had talked to a Mr Holland somewhere deep in Administration yesterday, and Mr Holland had assured him the visitation rules were relaxed for Sam Cayhall. He could visit anytime between 8 A.M. and 5 P.M., any day of the week. The guard stepped inside and made a phone call.

Five minutes passed as the visitor sat patiently in his rented car. The guard made two more calls, then copied the registration number of the car onto her clipboard. She instructed the visitor to park a few feet away, lock his car, and wait by the guard station. He did so, and within a few minutes a white prison van appeared. An armed, uniformed guard was behind the wheel, and he motioned for the visitor to get in.

The van was cleared through the double gates at MSU, and driven to the front entrance where two other guards waited. They frisked him on the steps. He was carrying no packages or bags.

They led him around the corner and into the empty visitors' room. He took a seat near the middle of the screen. 'We'll get Sam,' one of the guards said. 'Take about five minutes.'

Sam was typing a letter when the guards stopped at his door. 'Let's go Sam. You have a visitor.'

He stopped typing and stared at them. His fan was blowing hard and his television was tuned to a baseball game. 'Who is it?' he snapped.

'Your brother.'

Sam gently placed the typewriter on the bookshelf and grabbed his jumpsuit. 'Which brother?'

'We didn't ask any questions, Sam. Just your brother. Now come on.'

They handcuffed him and he followed them along the tier. Sam once had three brothers, but his oldest had died of a heart attack before Sam was sent to prison. Donnie, the youngest at age sixty-one, now lived near Durham, North Carolina. Albert, age sixty-seven, was in bad health and lived deep in the woods of rural Ford County. Donnie sent the cigarettes each month, along with a few dollars and an occasional note. Albert hadn't written in seven years. A spinster aunt had written until her death in 1985. The rest of the Cayhalls had forgotten Sam.

It had to be Donnie, he said to himself. Donnie was the only one who cared enough to visit. He hadn't seen him in two years, and he stepped lighter as they neared the door to the visitors' room. What a pleasant surprise.

Sam stepped through the door and looked at the man sitting on the other side of the screen. It was a face he didn't recognize. He glanced around the room, and confirmed it was empty except for this visitor, who at the moment was staring at Sam with a cool and even gaze. The guards watched closely as they sprang the handcuffs, so Sam smiled and nodded at the man. Then he stared at the guards until they left the room and shut the door. Sam sat opposite his visitor, lit a cigarette, and said nothing.

There was something familiar about him, but he couldn't identify him. They watched each other through the opening in the screen.

'Do I know you?' Sam finally asked.

'Yes,' the man answered.

'From where?'

'From the past, Sam. From Greenville and Jackson and Vicksburg. From the synagogue and the real estate office and the Pinder home and Marvin Kramer's.'

'Wedge?'

The man nodded slowly, and Sam closed his eyes and exhaled at the ceiling. He dropped his cigarette and slumped in his chair. 'God, I was hoping you were dead.'

'Too bad.'

Sam glared wildly at him. 'You son of a bitch,' he said with clenched teeth. 'Son of a bitch. I've hoped and dreamed for twenty-three years that you were dead. I've killed you a million times myself, with my bare hands, with sticks and knives and every weapon known to man. I've watched you bleed and I've heard you scream for mercy.'

'Sorry. Here I am, Sam.'

'I hate you more than any person has ever been hated. If I had a gun right now I'd blow your sorry ass to hell and back. I'd pump your head full of lead and laugh until I cried. God, how I hate you.'

'Do you treat all your visitors like this, Sam?'

'What do you want, Wedge?'

'Can they hear us in here?'

'They don't give a damn what we're saying.'

'But this place could be wired, you know.'

'Then leave, fool, just leave.'

'I will in a minute. But first I just wanted to say that I'm here, and I'm watching things real close, and I'm very pleased that my name has not been mentioned. I certainly hope this continues. I've been very effective at keeping people quiet.'

'You're very subtle.'

'Just take it like a man, Sam. Die with dignity. You were with me. You were an accomplice and a conspirator, and under the law you're just as guilty as me. Sure I'm a free man, but who said life is fair. Just go on and take our little secret to your grave, and no one gets hurt, okay?'

'Where have you been?'

'Everywhere. My name's not really Wedge, Sam, so don't get any ideas. It was never Wedge. Not even Dogan knew my real name. I was drafted in 1966, and I didn't want to go to Vietnam. So I went to Canada and came back to the underground. Been there ever since. I don't exist, Sam.'

'You should be sitting over here.'

'No, you're wrong. I shouldn't, and neither should you. You were an idiot for going back to Greenville. The FBI

397

was clueless. They never would've caught us. I was too smart. Dogan was too smart. You, however, happened to be the weak link. It would've been the last bombing too, you know, with the dead bodies and all. It was time to quit. I fled the country and would've never returned to this miserable place. You would've gone home to your chickens and cows. Who knows what Dogan would've done. But the reason you're sitting over there, Sam, is because you were a dumbass.'

'And you're a dumbass for coming here today.'

'Not really. No one would believe you if you started screaming. Hell, they all think you're crazy anyway. But just the same, I'd rather keep things the way they are. I don't need the hassle. Just accept what's coming, Sam, and do it quietly.'

Sam carefully lit another cigarette, and thumped the ashes in the floor. 'Leave, Wedge. And don't ever come back.'

'Sure. I hate to say it, Sam, but I hope they gas you.'

Sam stood and walked to the door behind him. A guard opened it, and took him away.

THEY SAT IN THE REAR of the cinema and ate popcorn like two teenagers. The movie was Adam's idea. She'd spent three days in her room, with the virus, and by Saturday morning the binge was over. He had selected a family restaurant for dinner, one with quick food and no alcohol on the menu. She'd devoured pecan waffles with whipped cream.

The movie was a western, politically correct with the Indians as the good guys and the cowboys as scum. All pale faces were evil and eventually killed. Lee drank two large Dr Peppers. Her hair was clean and pulled back over her ears. Her eyes were clear and pretty again. Her face was made up and the wounds of the past week were hidden. She was as cool as ever in jeans and cotton button-down. And she was sober.

Little had been said about last Thursday night when Adam slept by the door. They had agreed to discuss it later, at some distant point in the future when she could handle it. That was fine with him. She was walking a shaky tightrope, teetering on the edge of another plunge into the blackness of dipsomania. He would protect her from torment and distress. He would make things pleasant and enjoyable. No more talk of Sam and his killings. No more talk of Eddie. No more Cayhall family history.

She was his aunt, and he loved her dearly. She was fragile and sick, and she needed his strong voice and broad shoulders.

THIRTY-FIVE

PHILLIP NAIFEH awoke in the early hours of Sunday morning with severe chest pains, and was rushed to the hospital in Cleveland. He lived in a modern home on the grounds at Parchman with his wife of forty-one years. The ambulance ride took twenty minutes, and he was stable by the time he entered the emergency room on a gurney.

His wife waited anxiously in the corridor as the nurses scurried about. She had waited there before, three years earlier with the first heart attack. A somber-faced young doctor explained that it was a mild one, that he was quite steady and secure and resting comfortably with the aid of medication. He would be monitored diligently for the next twenty-four hours, and if things went as expected he'd be home in less than a week.

He was absolutely forbidden from getting near Parchman, and could have nothing to do with the Cayhall execution. Not even a phone call from his bed.

SLEEP WAS BECOMING a battle. Adam habitually read for an hour or so in bed, and had learned in law school that legal publications were marvelous sleeping aids. Now, however, the more he read the more he worried. His mind was burdened with the events of the past two weeks – the people he'd met, the things he'd learned, the places he'd been. And his mind raced wildly with what was to come.

He slept fitfully Saturday night, and was awake for long stretches of time. When he finally awoke for the last time, the sun was up. It was almost eight o'clock. Lee had mentioned the possibility of another foray into the kitchen. She had once been quite good with sausage and eggs, she'd said, and anybody could handle canned biscuits, but as he pulled up his jeans and slipped on a tee shirt, he could smell nothing.

The kitchen was quiet. He called her name as he examined the coffee pot – half full. Her bedroom door was open and the lights were off. He quickly checked every room. She was not on the patio sipping coffee and reading the paper. A sick feeling came over him and grew worse with each empty room. He ran to the parking lot – no sign of her car. He stepped barefoot across the hot asphalt and asked the security guard when she'd left. He checked a clipboard, and said it had been almost two hours ago. She appeared to be fine, he said.

He found it on a sofa in the den, a three-inch stack of news and ads known as the Sunday edition of the *Memphis Press*. It had been left in a neat pile with the Metro section on top. Lee's face was on the front of this section, in a photo taken at a charity ball years earlier. It was a close-up of Mr and Mrs Phelps Booth, all smiles for the camera. Lee was smashing in a strapless black dress. Phelps was decorated fashionably in black tie. They seemed to be a wonderfully happy couple.

The story was Todd Marks' latest exploitation of the Cayhall mess, and with each report the series was becoming more tabloid-like. It started friendly enough, with a weekly summary of the events swirling around the execution. The same voices were heard – McAllister's, Roxburgh's, Lucas Mann's, and Naifeh's steady 'no comments.' Then it turned mean-spirited quickly as it gleefully exposed Lee Cayhall Booth: prominent Memphis socialite, wife of important banker Phelps Booth of the renowned and rich Booth family, community volunteer, aunt of Adam Hall, and, believe it or not, daughter of the infamous Sam Cayhall!

The story was written as if Lee herself were guilty of a

terrible crime. It quoted alleged friends, unnamed of course, as being shocked to learn her true identitiy. It talked about the Booth family and its money, and pondered how a blue blood such as Phelps could stoop to marry into a clan such as the Cayhalls. It mentioned their son Walt, and again quoted unnamed sources who speculated about his refusal to return to Memphis. Walt had never married, it reported breathlessly, and lived in Amsterdam.

And then, worst of all, it quoted another nameless source and told the story of a charity event not too many years ago at which Lee and Phelps Booth were present and sat at a table near Ruth Kramer. The source had also been at the dinner, and distinctly remembered where these people had sat. The source was a friend of Ruth's and an acquaintance of Lee's, and was just plain shocked to learn that Lee had such a father.

A smaller photo of Ruth Kramer accompanied the story. She was an attractive woman in her early fifties.

After the sensational uncovering of Lee, the story went on to summarize Friday's oral argument in New Orleans and the latest maneuverings of the Cayhall defense.

Taken as a whole, it was sleazy narrative that accomplished nothing except that it pushed the daily murder summaries onto the second page.

Adam threw the paper on the floor and sipped coffee. She had awakened on this warm Sunday, clean and sober for the first time in days, probably in much better spirits, and had settled on the sofa with a fresh cup of coffee and the paper. Within minutes she'd been slapped in the face and kicked in the stomach, and now she'd left again. Where did she go during these times? Where was her sanctuary? Certainly she stayed away from Phelps. Maybe she had a boyfriend somewhere who took her in and gave her comfort, but that was doubtful. He prayed she wasn't driving the streets aimlessly with a bottle in her hand.

No doubt, things were hopping around the Booth estates this morning. Their dirty little secret was out, plastered on the front page for the world to see. How would they cope with the humiliation? Imagine, a Booth marrying and producing offspring with such white trash, and now everyone knew. The family might never recover. Madame Booth was certainly distressed, and probably bedridden by now.

Good for them, Adam thought. He showered and changed clothes, then lowered the top of the Saab. He didn't expect to see Lee's maroon Jaguar on the deserted streets of Memphis, but he drove around anyway. He started at Front Street near the river, and with Springsteen blaring from the speakers he randomly made his way east, past the hospitals on Union, through the stately homes of midtown, and back to the projects near Auburn House. Of course he didn't find her, but the drive was refreshing. By noon, the traffic had resumed, and Adam went to the office.

SAM'S ONLY GUEST on Sunday was again an unexpected one. He rubbed his wrists when the handcuffs were removed, and sat across the screen from the gray-haired man with a jolly face and a warm smile.

'Mr Cayhall, my name is Ralph Griffin, and I'm the chaplain here at Parchman. I'm new, so we haven't met.'

Sam nodded, and said, 'Nice to meet you.'

'My pleasure. I'm sure you knew my predecessor.'

'Ah yes, the Right Reverend Rucker. Where is he now?'

'Retired.'

'Good. I never cared for him. I doubt if he makes it to heaven.'

'Yes, I've heard he wasn't too popular.'

'Popular? He was despised by everyone here. For some reason we didn't trust him. Don't know why. Could be because he was in favor of the death penalty. Can you imagine? He was called by God to minister to us, yet he believed we should die. Said it was in the Scriptures. You know, the eye for an eye routine.'

'I've heard that before.'

'I'm sure you have. What kind of preacher are you? What denomination?'

403

'I was ordained in a Baptist church, but I'm sort of nondenominational now. I think the Lord's probably frustrated with all this sectarianism.'

'He's frustrated with me too, you know.'

'How's that?'

'You're familiar with Randy Dupree, an inmate here. Just down the tier from me. Rape and murder.'

'Yes, I've read his file. He was a preacher at one time.'

'We call him Preacher Boy, and he's recently acquired the spiritual gift of interpreting dreams. He also sings and heals. He'd probably play with snakes if they allowed it. You know, take up the serpents, from the book of Mark, sixteenth chapter, eighteenth verse. Anyway, he just finished this long dream, took over a month, sort of like a mini-series, and it eventually was revealed to him that I will in fact be executed, and that God is waiting for me to clean up my act.'

'It wouldn't be a bad idea, you know. To get things in order.'

'What's the rush? I have ten days.'

'So you believe in God?'

'Yes, I do. Do you believe in the death penalty?'

'No, I don't.'

Sam studied him for a while, then said, 'Are you serious?'

'Killing is wrong, Mr Cayhall. If in fact you are guilty of your crime, then you were wrong to kill. It's also wrong for the government to kill you.'

'Hallelujah, brother.'

'I've never been convinced that Jesus wanted us to kill as a punishment. He didn't teach that. He taught love and forgiveness.'

'That's the way I read the Bible. How in hell did you get a job here?'

'I have a cousin in the state senate.'

Sam smiled and chuckled at this response. 'You won't last long. You're too honest.'

'No. My cousin is the chairman of the Committee on Corrections, and rather powerful.'

'Then you'd better pray he gets reelected.'

'I do every morning. I just wanted to stop by and introduce myself. I'd like to talk to you during the next few days. I'd like to pray with you if you want. I've never been through an execution before.'

'Neither have I.'

'Does it scare you?'

'I'm an old man, Reverend. I'll be seventy in a few months, if I make it. At times, the thought of dying is quite pleasant. Leaving this godforsaken place will be a relief.'

'But you're still fighting.'

'Sure, though sometimes I don't know why. It's like a long bout with cancer. You gradually decline and grow weak. You die a little each day, and you reach the point where death would be welcome. But no one really wants to die. Not even me.'

'I've read about your grandson. That must be heart-warming. I know you're proud of him.'

Sam smiled and looked at the floor.

'Anyway,' the reverend continued, 'I'll be around. Would you like for me to come back tomorrow?'

'That would be nice. Let me do some thinking, okay?'

'Sure. You know the procedures around here, don't you? During your last few hours you're allowed to have only two people present. Your lawyer and your spiritual adviser. I'll be honored to stay with you.'

'Thanks. And can you find the time to talk to Randy Dupree? The poor kid is cracking up, and he really needs help.'

'I'll do it tomorrow.'

'Thanks.'

ADAM WATCHED a rented movie by himself, with the phone nearby. There had been no word from Lee. At ten, he made two calls to the West Coast. The first was to his mother in Portland. She was subdued, but glad to hear from him, she said. She did not ask about Sam, and Adam did not offer. He reported that he was working hard, that he was

405

hopeful, and that he would, in all likelihood return to Chicago in a couple of weeks. She'd seen a few stories in the papers, and she was thinking about him. Lee was fine, Adam said.

The second call was to his younger sister, Carmen, in Berkeley. A male voice answered the phone in her apartment, Kevin somebody if Adam remembered correctly, a steady companion for several years now. Carmen was soon on the phone, and seemed anxious to hear about events in Mississippi. She too had followed the news closely, and Adam put an optimistic spin on things. She was worried about him down there in the midst of all those horrible Kluckers and racists. Adam insisted he was safe, things were quite peaceful, actually. The people were surprisingly gentle and laid-back. He was staying at Lee's and they were making the best of it. To Adam's surprise, she wanted to know about Sam – what was he like, his appearance, his attitude, his willingness to talk about Eddie. She asked if she should fly down and see Sam before August 8, a meeting Adam had not contemplated. Adam said he would think about it, and that he would ask Sam.

He fell asleep on the sofa, with the television on.

At three-thirty Monday morning, he was awakened by the phone. A voice he'd never heard before crisply identified himself as Phelps Booth. 'You must be Adam,' he said.

Adam sat up and rubbed his eyes. 'Yes, that's me.'

'Have you seen Lee?' Phelps asked, neither calm nor urgent.

Adam glanced at a clock on the wall above the television. 'No, what's the matter?'

'Well, she's in trouble. The police called me about an hour ago. They picked her up for drunk driving at eight-twenty last night, and took her to jail.'

'Oh no,' Adam said.

'This is not the first time. She was taken in, refused the breath test of course, and was put in the drunk tank for five hours. She listed my name on the paperwork, so the cops called me. I ran downtown to the jail, and she had already

406

posted bail and walked out. I thought maybe she'd called you.'

'No. She was not here when I woke up yesterday morning, and this is the first thing I've heard. Who would she call?'

'Who knows? I hate to start calling her friends and waking them up. Maybe we should just wait.'

Adam was uncomfortable with his sudden inclusion into the decision making. These people had been married, for better or for worse, for almost thirty years, and they had obviously been through this before. How was he supposed to know what to do? 'She didn't drive away from the jail, did she?' he asked timidly, certain of the answer.

'Of course not. Someone picked her up. Which brings up another problem. We need to get her car. It's in a lot by the jail. I've already paid the towing charges.'

'Do you have a key?'

'Yes. Can you help me get it?'

Adam suddenly remembered the newspaper story with the smiling photo of Phelps and Lee, and he also remembered his speculation about the Booth family's reaction to it. He was certain most of the blame and venom had been directed at him. If he'd stayed in Chicago, none of this would've happened.

'Sure. Just tell me what—'

'Go wait by the guardhouse. I'll be there in ten minutes.'

Adam brushed his teeth and laced up his Nikes, and spent fifteen minutes chatting about this and that with Willis, the guard, at the gate. A black Mercedes, the longest model in history, approached and stopped. Adam said good-bye to Willis, and got in the car.

They shook hands because it was the polite thing to do. Phelps was dressed in a white jogging suit and wore a Cubs cap. He drove slowly on the empty street. 'I guess Lee has told you some things about me,' he said, without a trace of concern or regret.

'A few things,' Adam said carefully.

407

'Well, there's a lot to tell, so I'm not going to ask what subjects she's covered.'

A very good idea, Adam thought. 'It's probably best if we just talk about baseball or something. I take it you're a Cubs fan.'

'Always a Cubs fan. You?'

'Sure. This is my first season in Chicago, and I've been to Wrigley a dozen times. I live pretty close to the park.'

'Really. I go up three or four times a year. I have a friend with a box. Been doing it for years. Who's your favorite player?'

'Sandberg, I guess. How about you?'

'I like the old guys. Ernie Banks and Ron Santo. Those were the good days of baseball, when the players had loyalty and you knew who'd be on your team from one year to the next. Now, you never know. I love the game, but greed's corrupted it.'

It struck Adam as odd that Phelps Booth would denounce greed. 'Maybe, but the owners wrote the book on greed for the first hundred years of baseball. What's wrong with the players asking for all the money they can get?'

'Who's worth five million a year?'

'Nobody. But if rock stars make fifty, what's wrong with baseball players making a few million? It's entertainment. The players are the game, not the owners. I go to Wrigley to see the players, not because the *Tribune* happens to be the current owner.'

'Yeah, but look at ticket prices. Fifteen bucks to watch a game.'

'Attendance is up. The fans don't seem to mind.'

They drove through downtown, deserted at four in the morning, and within minutes were near the jail. 'Listen, Adam, I don't know how much Lee has told you about her drinking problem.'

'She told me she's an alcoholic.'

'Definitely. This is the second drunk driving charge. I was able to keep the first out of the papers, but I don't know about this. She's suddenly become an item around town.

408

Thank heaven she hasn't hurt anybody.' Phelps stopped the car at a curb near a fenced lot. 'She's been in and out of recovery half a dozen times.'

'Half a dozen. She told me she'd been through treatment three times.'

'You can't believe alcoholics. I know of at least five times in the past fifteen years. Her favorite place is a swanky little abuse center called Spring Creek. It's on a river a few miles north of the city, real nice and peaceful. It's for the wealthy only. They get dried out and pampered. Good food, exercise, saunas, you know, all the bells and whistles. It's so damned nice I think people want to go there. Anyway, I have a hunch she'll turn up there later today. She has some friends who'll help her get checked in. She's well known around the place. Sort of a second home.'

'How long will she stay there?'

'It varies. The minimum is a week. She has stayed as long as a month. Costs two thousand bucks a day, and of course they send me the bills. But I don't mind. I'll pay any amount to help her.'

'What am I supposed to do?'

'First, we try to find her. I'll get my secretaries on the phones in a few hours, and we'll track her down. She's fairly predictable at this point, and I'm sure she'll turn up in a detox ward, probably at Spring Creek. I'll start pulling strings in a few hours and try to keep it out of the paper. It won't be easy, in light of everything else that's been printed recently.'

'I'm sorry.'

'Once we find her, you need to go see her. Take some flowers and candy. I know you're busy, and I know what's ahead for the next, uh—'

'Nine days.'

'Nine days. Right. Well, try to see her. And, when the thing down at Parchman is over, I suggest you go back to Chicago, and leave her alone.'

'Leave her alone?'

'Yeah. It sounds harsh, but it's necessary. There are

409

many reasons for her many problems. I'll admit I'm one of the reasons, but there's lots of stuff you don't know. Her family is another reason. She adores you, but you also bring back nightmares and a lot of suffering. Don't think bad of me for saying this. I know it hurts, but it's the truth.'

Adam stared at the chain-link fence across the sidewalk next to his door.

'She was sober once for five years,' Phelps continued. 'And we thought she'd stay that way forever. Then Sam was convicted, and then Eddie died. When she returned from his funeral, she fell into the black hole, and I thought many times that she'd never get out. It's best for her if you stay away.'

'But I love Lee.'

'And she loves you. But you need to adore her from a distance. Send her letters and cards from Chicago. Flowers for her birthday. Call once a month and talk about movies and books, but stay away from the family stuff.'

'Who'll take care of her?'

'She's almost fifty years old, Adam, and for the most part she's very independent. She's been an alcoholic for many years, and there's nothing you or I can do to help her. She knows the disease. She'll stay sober when she wants to stay sober. You're not a good influence. Nor am I. I'm sorry.'

Adam breathed deeply and grabbed the door latch. 'I'm sorry, Phelps, if I've embarrassed you and your family. It was not intentional.'

Phelps smiled and placed a hand on Adam's shoulder. 'Believe it or not, my family is in many ways more dysfunctional than yours. We've been through worse.'

'That sir, is difficult to believe.'

'It's true.' Phelps handed him a key ring and pointed to a small building inside the fence. 'Check in there, and they'll show you the car.'

Adam opened the door and got out. He watched the Mercedes ease away and disappear. As Adam walked through a gate in the fence, he couldn't shake the unmistakable feeling that Phelps Booth actually still loved his wife.

THIRTY-SIX

RETIRED COLONEL George Nugent was barely ruffled by the news of Naifeh's heart attack. The old guy was doing quite well by Monday morning, resting comfortably and out of danger, and what the hell he was only months away from retirement anyway. Naifeh was a good man, but past his usefulness and hanging on simply to bolster his pension. Nugent was considering a run for the head position if he could get his politics straight.

Now, however, he was pressed with a more critical matter. The Cayhall execution was nine days away, actually only eight because it was scheduled for one minute after midnight on Wednesday of next week, which meant that Wednesday counted as another day though only one minute of it was used. Tuesday of next week was actually the last day.

On his desk was a shiny leather-bound notebook with the words Mississippi Protocol printed professionally on the front. It was his masterpiece, the result of two weeks of tedious organizing. He'd been appalled at the haphazard guides and outlines and checklists thrown together by Naifeh for previous executions. It was a wonder they'd actually been able to gas anyone. But now there was a plan, a detailed and carefully arranged blueprint which included everything, in his opinion. It was two inches thick and a hundred and eighty pages long, and of course had his name all over it.

Lucas Mann entered his office at fifteen minutes after

411

eight, Monday morning. 'You're late,' Nugent snapped, now a man in charge of things. Mann was just a simple lawyer. Nugent was the head of an execution team. Mann was content with his work. Nugent had aspirations, which in the past twenty-four hours had been bolstered considerably.

'So what,' Mann said as he stood by a chair facing the desk. Nugent was dressed in his standard dark olive pants with no wrinkles and heavily starched dark olive shirt with gray tee shirt underneath. His boots gleamed with heavily buffed polish. He marched to a point behind his desk. Mann hated him.

'We have eight days,' Nugent said as if this were known only to him.

'I think it's nine,' Mann said. Both men were standing.

'Next Wednesday doesn't count. We have eight working days left.'

'Whatever.'

Nugent sat stiffly in his chair. 'Two things. First, here is a manual I've put together for executions. A protocol. From A to Z. Completely organized, indexed, cross-indexed. I'd like for you to review the statutes contained herein and make sure they're current.'

Mann stared at the black binder but did not touch it.

'And second, I'd like a report each day on the status of all appeals. As I understand it, there are no legal impediments as of this morning.'

'That's correct, sir,' Mann answered.

'I'd like something in writing first thing each morning with the updates.'

'Then hire yourself a lawyer, sir. You're not my boss, and I'll be damned if I'll write a little brief for your morning coffee. I'll let you know if something happens, but I won't push paper for you.'

Ah, the frustrations of civilian life. Nugent longed for the discipline of the military. Damned lawyers. 'Very well. Will you please review the protocol?'

Mann flipped it open and turned a few pages. 'You know, we've managed four executions without all this.'

'I find that very surprising, frankly.'

'Frankly, I don't. We've become quite efficient, I'm sad to say.'

'Look, Lucas, I don't relish this,' Nugent said wistfully. 'Phillip asked me to do it. I hope there's a stay. I really do. But if not, then we must be prepared. I want this to run smoothly.'

Mann acknowledged the obvious lie, and picked up the manual. Nugent had yet to witness an execution, and he was counting hours, not days. He couldn't wait to see Sam strapped in the chair, sniffing gas.

Lucas nodded and left the office. In the hallway, he passed Bill Monday, the state executioner, no doubt headed to Nugent's for a quiet pep talk.

ADAM ARRIVED at the Twig shortly before 3 P.M. The day had begun with the panic over Lee's drunk driving mess, and had not improved.

He had been sipping coffee at his desk, nursing a headache and trying to do some research, when in the span of ten minutes Darlene brought a fax from New Orleans and a fax from the district council. He'd lost twice. The Fifth Circuit upheld the decision of the federal court on Sam's claim that the gas chamber was unconstitutional because it was cruel and obsolete, and the district court denied the claim that Benjamin Keyes had performed ineffectively at trial. The headache had suddenly been forgotten. Within an hour, the Death Clerk, Mr Richard Olander, had called from Washington inquiring about Adam's plans to appeal, and he also wanted to know what other filings might be contemplated by the defense. He told Adam that there were only eight working days to go, you know, as if Adam had to be reminded. Thirty minutes after Olander's call, a clerk at the death desk of the Fifth Circuit called and asked Adam when he planned to appeal the district court's ruling.

Adam had explained to both death clerks at both courts that he was perfecting his appeals as quickly as possible,

413

and he would try to file by the end of the day. When he stopped to think about it, it was a little unnerving practicing law with such an audience. At this moment of the process, there were courts and justices watching to see what he would do next. There were clerks calling and asking what he might be contemplating. The reason was obvious and disheartening. They weren't concerned with whether or not Adam would seize the magical issue that would prevent an execution. They were concerned only about logistics. The death clerks had been instructed by their superiors to monitor the waning days so the courts could rule quickly, usually against the inmate. These justices did not enjoy reading briefs at three in the morning. They wanted copies of all last minute filings on their desks long before the appeals officially arrived.

Phelps had called him at the office just before noon with the news that Lee had not been found. He had checked every detox and recovery facility within a hundred miles, and no one had admitted a Lee Booth. He was still searching, but was very busy now with meetings and such.

Sam arrived at the prison library thirty minutes later in a somber mood. He'd heard the bad news at noon on television, on the Jackson station that was counting down the days. Only nine more. He sat at the table and stared blankly at Adam. 'Where are the Eskimo Pies?' he asked sadly, like a small child who wanted candy.

Adam reached under the table and retrieved a small Styrofoam cooler. He placed it on the table and opened it. 'They almost confiscated these at the front gate. Then the guards picked through and threatened to throw them out. So, enjoy.'

Sam grabbed one, admired it for a long second, then carefully peeled off the wrapper. He licked the chocolate coating, then took a massive bite. He chewed it slowly with his eyes closed.

Minutes later, the first Eskimo Pie was gone, and Sam started on the second. 'Not a good day,' he said, licking the edges.

Adam slid some papers to him. 'Here are both decisions. Short, to the point, and strongly against us. You don't have a lot of friends on these courts, Sam.'

'I know. At least the rest of the world adores me. I don't wanna read that crap. What do we do next?'

'We're gonna prove you're too crazy to execute, that because of your advanced age you don't fully comprehend the nature of your punishment.'

'Won't work.'

'You liked the idea Saturday. What's happened?'

'It won't work.'

'Why not?'

'Because I'm not insane. I know full well why I'm being executed. You're doing what lawyers do best – dreaming up offbeat theories, then finding wacky experts to prove them.' He took a large bite of ice cream and licked his lips.

'You want me to quit?' Adam snapped.

Sam pondered his yellow fingernails. 'Maybe,' he said, quickly running his tongue across a finger.

Adam slid into the seat next to him, as opposed to his usual lawyerly position across the table, and studied him closely. 'What's the matter, Sam?'

'I don't know. I've been thinking.'

'I'm listening.'

'When I was very young, my best friend was killed in a car wreck. He was twenty-six, had a new wife, new child, new house, his whole life in front of him. Suddenly, he was dead. I've outlived him by forty-three years. My oldest brother died when he was fifty-six. I've outlived him by thirteen years. I'm an old man, Adam. A very old man. I'm tired. I feel like giving it up.'

'Come on, Sam.'

'Look at the advantages. It takes the pressure off you. You won't be forced to spend the next week running crazy and filing useless claims. You won't feel like a failure when it's over. I won't spend my last days praying for a miracle, but instead I can get my things in order. We can spend more time together. It'll make a lot of people happy – the

415

Kramers, McAllister, Roxburgh, eighty percent of the American people who favour the death penalty. It'll be another glorious moment for law and order. I can go out with a little dignity, instead of looking like a desperate man who's afraid to die. It's really quite appealing.'

'What's happened to you, Sam? Last Saturday you were still ready to fight the bear.'

'I'm tired of fighting. I'm an old man. I've had a long life. And what if you're successful in saving my skin? Where does that leave me? I'm not going anyplace, Adam. You'll go back to Chicago and bury yourself in your career. I'm sure you'll come down whenever you can. We'll write letters and send cards. But I have to live on the Row. You don't. You have no idea.'

'We're not quitting, Sam. We still have a chance.'

'It's not your decision.' He finished the second Eskimo Pie and wiped his mouth with a sleeve.

'I don't like you like this, Sam. I like it when you're mad and nasty and fighting.'

'I'm tired, okay?'

'You can't let them kill you. You have to fight to the bitter end, Sam.'

'Why?'

'Because it's wrong. It's morally wrong for the state to kill you, and that's why we can't give up.'

'But we're gonna lose anyway.'

'Maybe. Maybe not. But you've been fighting for almost ten years. Why quit with a week to go?'

'Because it's over, Adam. This thing has finally run its course.'

'Perhaps, but we can't quit. Please don't throw in the towel. Hell, I'm making progress. I've got these clowns on the run.'

Sam offered a gentle smile and a patronizing gaze.

Adam inched closer and placed his hand on Sam's arm. 'I've thought of several new strategies,' he said in earnest. 'In fact, tomorrow we've got an expert coming to examine you.'

416

Sam looked at him. 'What kind of expert?'

'A shrink.'

'A shrink?'

'Yeah. From Chicago.'

'I've already talked to a shrink. It didn't go well.'

'This guy's different. He works for us and he'll say that you've lost your mental faculties.'

'You're assuming I had them when I got here.'

'Yes, we're assuming that. This psychiatrist will examine you tomorrow, then he'll quickly prepare a report to the effect that you're senile and insane and just a blithering idiot, and who knows what else he'll say.'

'How do you know he'll say this?'

'Because we're paying him to say it.'

'Who's paying him?'

'Kravitz & Bane, those dedicated Jewish-Americans in Chicago you hate, but who've been busting their asses to keep you alive. It's Goodman's idea, actually.'

'Must be a fine expert.'

'We can't be too particular at this point. He's been used by some of the other lawyers in the firm on various cases, and he'll say whatever we want him to say. Just act bizarre when you talk to him.'

'That shouldn't be too difficult.'

'Tell him all the horror stories about this place. Make it sound atrocious and deplorable.'

'No problem there.'

'Tell him how you've deteriorated over the years, and how it's especially hard on a man your age. You're by far the oldest one here, Sam, so tell him how it's affected you. Lay it on thick. He'll fix up a compelling little report, and I'll run to court with it.'

'It won't work.'

'It's worth a try.'

'The Supreme Court allowed Texas to execute a retarded boy.'

'This ain't Texas, Sam. Every case is different. Just work with us on this, okay.'

417

'Us? Who is us?'

'Me and Goodman. You said you didn't hate him anymore, so I figured I'd let him in on the fun. Seriously, I need help. There's too much work for only one lawyer.'

Sam scooted his chair away from the table, and stood. He stretched his arms and legs, and began pacing along the table, counting steps as he went.

'I'll file a petition for cert to the Supreme Court in the morning,' Adam said as he looked at a checklist on his legal pad. 'They probably won't agree to hear it, but I'll do it anyway. I'll also finish the appeal to the Fifth Circuit on the ineffectiveness claim. The shrink will be here tomorrow afternoon. I'll file the mental competency claim Wednesday morning.'

'I'd rather go peacefully, Adam.'

'Forget it, Sam. We're not quitting. I talked to Carmen last night, and she wants to come see you.'

Sam sat on the edge of the table and watched the floor. His eyes were narrow and sad. He puffed and blew smoke at his feet. 'Why would she want to do that?'

'I didn't ask why, nor did I suggest it. She brought it up. I told her I'd ask you.'

'I've never met her.'

'I know. She's your only granddaughter, Sam, and she wants to come.'

'I don't want her to see me like this,' he said, waving at his red jumpsuit.

'She won't mind.'

Sam reached into the cooler and took another Eskimo Pie. 'Do you want one?' he asked.

'No. What about Carmen?'

'Let me think about it. Does Lee still want to visit?'

'Uh, sure. I haven't talked to her in a couple of days, but I'm sure she wants to.'

'I thought you were staying with her.'

'I am. She's been out of town.'

'Let me think about it. Right now I'm against it. I haven't seen Lee in almost ten years, and I just don't want

418

her to remember me like this. Tell her I'm thinking about it, but right now I don't think so.'

'I'll tell her,' Adam promised, uncertain if he would see her anytime soon. If she had in fact sought treatment, she would undoubtedly be secluded for several weeks.

'I'll be glad when the end comes, Adam. I'm really sick of all this.' He took a large bite of ice cream.

'I understand. But let's put it off for a while.'

'Why?'

'Why? It's obvious. I don't want to spend my entire legal career encumbered with the knowledge that I lost my first case.'

'That's not a bad reason.'

'Great. So we're not quitting?'

'I guess not. Bring on the shrink. I'll act as loony as possible.'

'That's more like it.'

LUCAS MANN was waiting for Adam at the front gate of the prison. It was almost five, the temperature still hot and the air still sticky. 'Gotta minute?' he asked through the window of Adam's car.

'I guess. What's up?'

'Park over there. We'll sit under the shade.'

They walked to a picnic table by the Visitors Center, under a mammoth oak with the highway in view not far away. 'A couple of things,' Mann said. 'How's Sam? Is he holding up okay?'

'As well as can be expected. Why?'

'Just concerned, that's all. At last count, we had fifteen requests for interviews today. Things are heating up. The press is on its way.'

'Sam is not talking.'

'Some want to talk to you.'

'I'm not talking either.'

'Fine. We have a form that Sam needs to sign. It gives us written authorization to tell the reporters to get lost. Have you heard about Naifeh?'

'I saw it in the paper this morning.'

'He'll be okay, but he can't supervise the execution. There's a nut named George Nugent, an assistant superintendent, who'll coordinate everything. He's a commandant. Retired military and all, a real gung-ho type.'

'It really makes no difference to me. He can't carry out the death warrant unless the courts allow it.'

'Right. I just wanted you to know who he was.'

'I can't wait to meet him.'

'One more thing. I have a friend, an old buddy from law school who now works in the governor's administration. He called this morning, and it seems as if the governor is concerned about Sam's execution. According to my friend, who no doubt was told by the governor to solicit me to speak to you, they would like to conduct a clemency hearing, preferably in a couple of days.'

'Are you close to the governor?'

'No. I despise the governor.'

'So do I. So does my client.'

'That's why my friend was recruited to call and lean on me. Allegedly, the governor is having serious doubts about whether Sam should be executed.'

'Do you believe it?'

'It's doubtful. The governor's reputation was made at the expense of Sam Cayhall, and I'm certain he's fine-tuning his media plan for the next eight days. But what is there to lose?'

'Nothing.'

'It's not a bad idea.'

'I'm all for it. My client, however, has given me strict orders not to request such a hearing.'

Mann shrugged as if he really didn't care what Sam did. 'It's up to Sam then. Does he have a will?'

'Yes.'

'How about burial arrangements?'

'I'm working on them. He wants to be buried in Clanton.'

They started walking toward the front gate. 'The body

420

goes to a funeral home in Indianola, not far from here. It'll be released to the family there. All visitation ends four hours before the scheduled execution. From that point on, Sam can have only two people with him – his lawyer and his spiritual adviser. He also needs to select his two witnesses, if he so chooses.'

'I'll speak to him.'

'We need his approved list of visitors between now and then. It's usually family and close friends.'

'That'll be a very short list.'

'I know.'

THIRTY-SEVEN

EVERY OCCUPANT of the Row knew the procedure, though it had never been reduced to writing. The veterans, including Sam, had endured four executions over the past eight years, and with each the procedure had been followed with small variations. The old hands talked and whispered among themselves, and they were usually quick to dispense descriptions of the last hours to the new guys, most of whom arrived at the Row with muted questions about how it's done. And the guards liked to talk about it.

The last meal was to be taken in a small room near the front of the Row, a room referred to simply as the front office. It had a desk and some chairs, a phone and an air conditioner, and it was in this room that the condemned man received his last visitors. He sat and listened as his lawyers tried to explain why things were not developing as planned. It was a plain room with locked windows. The last conjugal visit was held here, if in fact the inmate was up to it. Guards and administrators loitered in the hallway outside.

The room was not designed for the last hours, but when Teddy Doyle Meeks became the first in many years to be executed in 1982, such a room was suddenly needed for all sorts of purposes. It once belonged to a lieutenant, then a case manager. It had no other name except for the front office. The phone on the desk was the last one used by the inmate's lawyer when he received the final word that there would be no more stays, no more appeals. He then made the

422

long walk back to Tier A, to the far end where his client waited in the Observation Cell.

The Observation Cell was nothing more than a regular cell on Tier A, just eight doors down from Sam. It was six by nine, with a bunk, a sink, and a toilet, just like Sam's, just like all the others. It was the last cell on the tier, and the nearest to the Isolation Room, which was next to the Chamber Room. The day before the execution, the inmate was to be taken for the last time from his cell and placed in Observation. His personal belongings were to be moved too, which was usually a quick task. There he waited. Usually, he watched his own private drama on television as the local television stations monitored his last ditch appeals. His lawyer waited with him, seated on the flimsy bed, in the dark cell, watching the news reports. The lawyer ran back and forth to the front office. A minister or spiritual adviser was also allowed in the cell.

The Row would be dark and deathly quiet. Some of the inmates would hover above their televisions. Others would hold hands and pray through the bars. Others would lie on their beds and wonder when their time would come. The outside windows above the hallway were all closed and bolted. The Row was locked down. But there were voices between the tiers, and there were lights from the outside. For men who sit for hours in tiny cells, seeing and hearing everything, the flurry of strange activity was nerve-racking.

At eleven, the warden and his team would enter Tier A and stop at the Observation Cell. By now, the hope of a last minute stay was virtually exhausted. The inmate would be sitting on his bed, holding hands with his lawyer and his minister. The warden would announce that it was time to go to the Isolation Room. The cell door would clang and open, and the inmate would step into the hallway. There would be shouts of support and reassurance from the other inmates, many of whom would be in tears. The Isolation Room is no more than twenty feet from the Observation Cell. The inmate would walk through the center of two rows of armed and bulky security guards, the largest the warden could find. There was never any resistance. It wouldn't do any good.

The warden would lead the inmate into a small room, ten feet by ten, with nothing in it except a foldaway bed. The inmate would sit on the bed with his lawyer by his side. At this point, the warden, for some baffling reason, would feel the need to spend a few moments with the inmate, as if he, the warden, was the last person the inmate wanted to chat with. The warden eventually would leave. The room would be quiet except for an occasional bang or knock from the room next door. Prayers were normally completed at this point. There were just minutes to go.

Next door to the Isolation Room was the Chamber Room itself. It was approximately fifteen feet by twelve, with the gas chamber in the center of it. The executioner would be hard at work while the inmate prayed in isolation. The warden, the prison attorney, the doctor, and a handful of guards would be making preparations. There would be two telephones on the wall for the last minute clearance. There was a small room to the left where the executioner mixed his solutions. Behind the chamber was a series of three windows, eighteen inches by thirty, and covered for the moment by black drapes. On the other side of the windows was the witness room.

At twenty minutes before midnight, the doctor would enter the Isolation Room and attach a stethoscope to the inmate's chest. He would leave, and the warden would enter to take the condemned man to see the chamber.

The Chamber Room was always filled with people, all anxious to help, all about to watch a man die. They would back him into the chamber, strap him in, close the door, and kill him.

It was a fairly straightforward procedure, varied a bit to accommodate the individual case. For example, Buster Moac was in the chair with half the straps in place when the phone rang in the Chamber Room. He went back to the Isolation Room and waited six miserable hours until they came for him again. Jumbo Parris was the smartest of the

424

four. A longtime drug user before he made it to the Row, he began asking the psychiatrist for Valium days before his execution. He chose to spend his last hours alone, no lawyer or minister, and when they came to fetch him from the Observation Cell, he was stoned. He had evidently stockpiled the Valium, and had to be dragged to the Isolation Room where he slept in peace. He was then dragged to the chamber and given his final dosage.

It was a humane and thoughtful procedure. The inmate remained in his cell, next to his pals, up to the very end. In Louisiana, they were removed from the Row and placed in a small building known as the Death House. They spent their final three days there, under constant supervision. In Virginia, they were moved to another city.

Sam was eight doors from the Observation Cell, about forty-eight feet. Then another twenty feet to the Isolation Room, then another twelve feet to the chamber. From a point in the center of his bed, he'd calculated many times that he was approximately eighty-five feet from the gas chamber.

And he made the calculation again Tuesday morning as he carefully made an X on his calendar. Eight days. It was dark and hot. He had slept off and on and spent most of the night sitting in front of his fan. Breakfast and coffee were an hour away now. This would be day number 3,449 on the Row, and the total did not include time spent in the county jail in Greenville during his first two trials. Only eight more days.

His sheets were soaked with sweat, and as he lay on the bed and watched the ceiling for the millionth time he thought of death. The actual act of dying would not be too terrible. For obvious reasons, no one knew the exact effects of the gas. Maybe they would give him an extra dose so he'd be dead long before his body twitched and jerked. Maybe the first breath would knock him senseless. At any rate, it wouldn't take long, he hoped. He'd watched his wife shrivel and suffer greatly from cancer. He'd watched kinfolks grow old and vegetate. Surely, this was a better way to go.

425

'Sam,' J. B. Gullitt whispered, 'you up?'

Sam walked to his door and leaned through the bars. He could see Gullitt's hands and forearms. 'Yeah. I'm up. Can't seem to sleep.' He lit the first cigarette of the day.

'Me neither. Tell me it's not gonna happen, Sam.'

'It's not gonna happen.'

'You serious?'

'Yeah, I'm serious. My lawyer's about to unload the heavy stuff. He'll probably walk me outta here in a coupla weeks.'

'Then why can't you sleep?'

'I'm so excited about gettin' out.'

'Have you talked to him about my case?'

'Not yet. He's got a lot on his mind. As soon as I get out, we'll go to work on your case. Just relax. Try and get some sleep.'

Gullitt's hands and forearms slowly withdrew, then his bed squeaked. Sam shook his head at the kid's ignorance. He finished his cigarette and thumped it down the hall, a breach of the rules which would earn him a violation report. As if he cared.

He carefully took his typewriter from the shelf. He had things to say and letters to write. There were people out there he needed to speak to.

GEORGE NUGENT entered the Maximum Security Unit like a five-star general and glared disappovingly at the hair and then at the unshined boots of a white security guard. 'Get a haircut,' he growled, 'or I'll write you up. And work on those boots.'

'Yes sir,' the kid said, and almost saluted.

Nugent jerked his head and nodded at Packer, who led the way through the center of the Row to Tier A. 'Number six,' Packer said as the door opened.

'Stay here,' Nugent instructed. His heels clicked as he marched along the tier, gazing with disdain into each cell. He stopped at Sam's, and peered inside. Sam was stripped to his boxers, his thin and wrinkled skin gleaming with

426

sweat as he pecked away. He looked at the stranger staring at him through the bars, then returned to his work.

'Sam, my name is George Nugent.'

Sam hit a few keys. The name was not familiar, but Sam assumed he worked somewhere up the ladder since he had access to the tiers. 'What do you want?' Sam asked without looking.

'Well, I wanted to meet you.'

'My pleasure, now shove off.'

Gullitt to the right and Henshaw to the left were suddenly leaning through the bars, just a few feet from Nugent. They snickered at Sam's response.

Nugent glared at them, and cleared his throat. 'I'm an assistant superintendent, and Phillip Naifeh has placed me in charge of your execution. There are a few things we need to discuss.'

Sam concentrated on his correspondence, and cursed when he hit a wrong key. Nugent waited. 'If I could have a few minutes of your valuable time, Sam.'

'Better call him Mr Cayhall,' Henshaw added helpfully. 'He's a few years older than you, and it means a lot to him.'

'Where'd you get those boots?' Gullitt asked, staring at Nugent's feet.

'You boys back away,' Nugent said sternly. 'I need to talk to Sam.'

'Mr Cayhall's busy right now,' Henshaw said. 'Perhaps you should come back later. I'll be happy to schedule an appointment for you.'

'Are you some kinda military asshole?' Gullitt asked.

Nugent stood stiffly and glanced to his right and to his left. 'I'm ordering you two to get back, okay. I need to speak to Sam.'

'We don't take orders,' Henshaw said.

'And what're you gonna do about it?' Gullitt asked. 'Throw us in solitary? Feed us roots and berries? Chain us to the walls? Why don't you just go ahead and kill us?'

Sam placed his typewriter on the bed, and walked to the bars. He took a long drag, and shot smoke through them in

427

the general direction of Nugent. 'What do you want?' he demanded.

'I need a few things from you.'

'Such as?'

'Do you have a will?'

'That's none of your damned business. A will is a private document to be seen only if it's probated, and it's probated only after a person dies. That's the law.'

'What a dumbass!' Henshaw shrieked.

'I don't believe this,' Gullitt offered. 'Where did Naifeh find this idiot?' he asked.

'Anything else?' Sam asked.

Nugent's face was changing colors. 'We need to know what to do with your things.'

'It's in my will, okay.'

'I hope you're not going to be difficult, Sam.'

'It's Mr Cayhall,' Henshaw said again.

'Difficult?' Sam asked. 'Why would I be difficult? I intend to cooperate fully with the state while it goes about its business of killing me. I'm a good patriot. I would vote and pay taxes if I could. I'm proud to be an American, an Irish-American, and at this moment I'm still very much in love with my precious state, even though it plans to gas me. I'm a model prisoner, George. No problems out of me.'

Packer was thoroughly enjoying this as he waited at the end of the tier. Nugent stood firm.

'I need a list of people you want to witness the execution,' he said. 'You're allowed two.'

'I'm not giving up yet, George. Let's wait a few days.'

'Fine. I'll also need a list of your visitors for the next few days.'

'Well, this afternoon I have this doctor coming down from Chicago, you see. He's a psychiatrist, and he's gonna talk to me and see how nutty I really am, then my lawyers will run to court and say that you, George, can't execute me because I'm crazy. He'll have time to examine you, if you want. It won't take long.'

Henshaw and Gullitt horselaughed, and within seconds

most of the other inmates on the tier were chiming in and cackling loudly. Nugent took a step backward and scowled up and down the tier. 'Quiet!' he demanded, but the laughter increased. Sam continued puffing and blowing smoke through the bars. Catcalls and insults could be heard amid the ruckus.

'I'll be back,' Nugent shouted angrily at Sam.

'He shall return!' Henshaw yelled, and the commotion grew even louder. The commandant stormed away, and as he marched swiftly to the end of the hall, shouts of 'Heil Hitler' rang through the tier.

Sam smiled at the bars for a moment as the noise died, then returned to his position on the edge of the bed. He took a bite of dry toast, a sip of cold coffee. He resumed his typing.

THE AFTERNOON DRIVE to Parchman was not a particularly pleasant one. Garner Goodman sat in the front seat as Adam drove, and they talked strategy and brainstormed about the last minute appeals and procedures. Goodman planned to return to Memphis over the weekend, and be available during the last three days. The psychiatrist was Dr Swinn, a cold, unsmiling man in a black suit. He had wild, bushy hair, dark eyes hidden behind thick glasses, and was completely incapable of small talk. His presence in the backseat was discomfiting. He did not utter a single word from Memphis to Parchman.

The examination had been arranged by Adam and Lucas Mann to take place in the prison hospital, a remarkably modern facility. Dr Swinn had very plainly informed Adam that neither he nor Goodman could be present during his evaluation of Sam. And this was perfectly fine with Adam and Goodman. A prison van met them at the front gate, and carried Dr Swinn to the hospital deep inside the farm.

Goodman had not seen Lucas Mann in several years. They shook hands like old friends, and immediately lapsed into war stories about executions. The conversation was kept away from Sam, and Adam appreciated it.

They walked from Mann's office across a parking lot to a small building behind the administration complex. The building was a restaurant, designed along the lines of a neighborhood tavern. Called The Place, it served basic food to the office workers and prison employees. No alcohol. It was on state property.

They drank iced tea and talked about the future of capital punishment. Both Goodman and Mann agreed that executions would soon become even more commonplace. The U.S. Supreme Court was continuing its swing to the right, and it was weary of the endless appeals. Ditto for the lower levels of the federal judiciary. Plus, American juries were becoming increasingly reflective of society's intolerance of violent crime. There was much less sympathy for death row inmates, a much greater desire to fry the bastards. Fewer federal dollars were being spent to fund groups opposed to the death penalty, and fewer lawyers and their firms were willing to make the enormous pro bono commitments. The death row population was growing faster than the number of lawyers willing to take capital cases.

Adam was quite bored with the conversation. He'd read and heard it a hundred times. He excused himself and found a pay phone in a corner. Phelps was not in, a young secretary said, but he'd left a message for Adam: no word from Lee. She was scheduled to be in court in two weeks; maybe she'd turn up then.

DARLENE typed Dr Swinn's report while Adam and Garner Goodman worked on the petition to accompany it. The report was twenty pages long in rough draft, and sounded like soft music. Swinn was a hired gun, a prostitute who'd sell an opinion to the highest bidder, and Adam detested him and his ilk. He roamed the country as a professional testifier, able to say this today and that tomorrow, depending on who had the deepest pockets. But for the moment, he was their whore, and he was quite good. Sam was suffering from advanced senility. His mental faculties had eroded to the point where he did not know and appreciate the nature

430

of his punishment. He lacked the requisite competence to be executed, and therefore the execution would not serve any purpose. It was not an entirely unique legal argument, nor had the courts exactly embraced it. But, as Adam found himself saying every day, what was there to lose? Goodman seemed to be more than a little optimistic, primarily because of Sam's age. He could not recall an execution of a man over the age of fifty.

They, Darlene included, worked until almost eleven.

THIRTY-EIGHT

GARNER GOODMAN did not return to Chicago Wednesday morning, but instead flew to Jackson, Mississippi. The flight took thirty minutes, hardly time for a cup of coffee and an unthawed croissant. He rented a car at the airport and drove straight to the state capitol. The legislature was not in session, and there were plenty of parking places on the grounds. Like many county courthouses rebuilt after the Civil War, the capitol defiantly faced south. He stopped to admire the war monument to Southern women, but spent more time studying the splendid Japanese magnolias at the bottom of the front steps.

Four years earlier, during the days and hours prior to the Maynard Tole execution, Goodman had made this same journey on two occasions. There was a different governor then, a different client, and a different crime. Tole had murdered several people in a two-day crime spree, and it had been quite difficult to arouse sympathy for him. He hoped Sam Cayhall was different. He was an old man who'd probably die within five years anyway. His crime was ancient history to many Mississippians. And on and on.

Goodman had been rehearsing his routine all morning. He entered the capitol building and once again marveled at its beauty. It was a smaller version of the U.S. Capitol in Washington, and no expense had been spared. It had been built in 1910 with prison labor. The state had used the proceeds from a successful lawsuit against a railroad to construct itself this monument.

He entered the governor's office on the second floor and handed his card to the lovely receptionist. The governor was not in this morning, she said, and did he have an appointment? No, Goodman explained pleasantly, but it was very important, and would it be possible for him to see Mr Andy Larramore, chief counsel for the governor?

He waited as she made several calls, and half an hour later Mr Larramore presented himself. They made their introductions and disappeared into a narrow hallway that ran through a maze of small offices. Larramore's cubbyhole was cluttered and disorganized, much like the man himself. He was a small guy with a noticeable bend at the waist and absolutely no neck. His long chin rested on his chest, and when he talked his eyes, nose, and mouth all squeezed together tightly. It was a horrible sight. Goodman couldn't tell if he was thirty or fifty. He had to be a genius.

'The governor is speaking to a convention of insurance agents this morning,' Larramore said, holding an itinerary as if it were a piece of fine jewelry. 'And then he visits a public school in the inner city.'

'I'll wait,' Goodman said. 'It's very important, and I don't mind hanging around.'

Larramore placed the sheet of paper aside, and folded his hands on the table. 'What happened to that young fellow, Sam's grandson?'

'Oh, he's still lead counsel. I'm the director of pro bono for Kravitz & Bane, so I'm here to assist him.'

'We're monitoring this thing very closely,' Larramore said, his face wrinkling fiercely in the center, then relaxing at the end of each sentence. 'Looks like it will go down to the wire.'

'They always do,' Goodman said. 'How serious is the governor about a clemency hearing?'

'I'm sure he'll entertain the idea of a hearing. The granting of clemency is an entirely different matter. The statute is very broad, as I'm sure you know. He can commute the death sentence and instantly parole the convict. He can commute it to life in prison, or something less than that.'

Goodman nodded. 'Will it be possible for me to see him?'

'He's scheduled to return here at eleven. I'll speak to him then. He'll probably eat lunch at his desk, so there may be a gap around one. Can you be here?'

'Yes. This must be kept quiet. Our client is very much opposed to this meeting.'

'Is he opposed to the idea of clemency?'

'We have seven days to go, Mr Larramore. We're not opposed to anything.'

Larramore crinkled his nose and exposed his upper teeth, and picked up the itinerary again. 'Be here at one. I'll see what I can do.'

'Thanks.' They chatted aimlessly for five minutes, then Larramore was besieged by a series of urgent telephone calls. Goodman excused himself and left the capitol. He paused again at the Japanese magnolias and removed his jacket. It was nine-thirty, and his shirt was wet under the arms and sticking to his back.

He walked south in the general direction of Capitol Street, four blocks away and considered to be the main street of Jackson. In the midst of the buildings and traffic of downtown, the governor's mansion sat majestically on manicured grounds and faced the capitol. It was a large antebellum home surrounded by gates and fences. A handful of death penalty opponents had gathered on the sidewalk the night Tole was executed and yelled at the governor. Evidently, he had not heard them. Goodman stopped on the sidewalk and remembered the mansion. He and Peter Wiesenberg had walked hurriedly through a gate to the left of the main drive with their last plea, just hours before Tole was gassed. The governor at that time was having a late dinner with important people, and had become quite irritated with their interruption. He denied their final request for clemency, then, in the finest Southern tradition, invited them to stay for dinner.

They'd politely declined. Goodman explained to His

434

Honor that they had to hurry back to Parchman to be with their client as he died. 'Be careful,' the governor had told them, then returned to his dinner party.

Goodman wondered how many protestors would be standing on this spot in a few short days, chanting and praying and burning candles, waving placards, and yelling at McAllister to spare old Sam. Probably not very many.

There has seldom been a shortage of office space in the central business district in Jackson, and Goodman had little trouble finding what he wanted. A sign directed his attention to vacant footage on the third floor of an ugly building. He inquired at the front desk of a finance company on the ground level, and an hour later the owner of the building arrived and showed him the available space. It was a dingy two-room suite with worn carpet and holes in the wallboard. Goodman walked to the lone window and looked at the front of the capitol building three blocks away. 'Perfect,' he said.

'It's three hundred a month, plus electricity. Rest room's down the hall. Six-month minimum.'

'I need it for only two months,' Goodman said, reaching into his pocket and withdrawing a neatly folded collection of cash.

The owner looked at the money, and asked, 'What kind of business are you in?'

'Marketing analysis.'

'Where are you from?'

'Detroit. We're thinking about establishing a branch in this state, and we need this space to get started. But for only two months. All cash. Nothing in writing. We'll be out before you know it. Won't make a sound.'

The owner took the cash and handed Goodman two keys, one for the office, the other for the entrance on Congress Street. They shook hands and the deal was closed.

Goodman left the dump and returned to his car at the capitol. Along the way he chuckled at the scheme he was pursuing. The idea was Adam's brainchild, another long shot in a series of desperate plots to save Sam. There was

435

nothing illegal about it. The cost would be slight, and who cared about a few dollars at this point? He was, after all, Mr Pro Bono at the firm, the source of great pride and self-righteousness among his peers. Nobody, not even Daniel Rosen, would question his expenditures for a little rent and a few phones.

AFTER THREE WEEKS as a death row lawyer, Adam was beginning to yearn for the predictability of his office in Chicago, if, in fact, he still had an office. Before ten o'clock Wednesday, he had finished a claim for postconviction relief. He had talked with various court clerks four times, then with a court administrator. He had talked with Richard Olander in Washington twice concerning the habeas claim attacking the gas chamber, and he had talked with a clerk of the death desk at the Fifth Circuit in New Orleans regarding the ineffectiveness claim.

The claim alleging Sam's lack of mental competence was now in Jackson, by fax with the original to follow by Fed-Ex, and Adam was forced to politely beg the court's administrator to speed things up. Hurry up and deny it, he said, though not in those words. If a stay of execution was forthcoming, it would in all likelihood be issued by a federal judge.

Each new claim brought with it a scant new ray of hope, and, as Adam was quickly learning, also the potential for another loss. A claim had to clear four obstacles before it was extinguished – the Mississippi Supreme Court, the federal district court, the Fifth Circuit, and the U.S. Supreme Court – so the odds were against success, especially at this stage of the appeals. Sam's bread and butter issues had been litigated thoroughly by Wallace Tyner and Garner Goodman years ago. Adam was now filing the crumbs.

The clerk at the Fifth Circuit doubted if the court would care to indulge in another oral argument, especially since it appeared that Adam would be filing new claims every day. The three-judge panel would probably consider only the

436

briefs. Conference calls would be used if the judges wished to hear his voice.

Richard Olander called again to say the Supreme Court had received Adam's petition for cert, or request to hear the case, and that it had been assigned. No, he did not think the Court would care to hear oral argument. Not this late in the game. He also informed Adam that he had received by fax a copy of the new claim of mental incompetency, and that he would monitor it through the local courts. Interesting, he said. He asked again what new claims Adam might be contemplating, but Adam wouldn't say.

Judge Slattery's law clerk, Breck Jefferson, he of the permanent scowl, called to inform Adam that His Honor had received by fax a copy of the new claim filed with the Mississippi Supreme Court, and frankly His Honor didn't think much of it but would nevertheless give it full consideration once it arrived in their court.

Adam took a little satisfaction in the knowledge that he had managed to keep four very different courts hopping at the same time.

At eleven, Morris Henry, the infamous Dr Death in the Attorney General's office, called to inform Adam that they had received the latest round of gangplank appeals, as he enjoyed calling them, and Mr Roxburgh himself had assigned a dozen lawyers to produce the responding paperwork. Henry was nice enough on the phone, but the call had made its point – we have lots of lawyers, Adam.

The paperwork was being generated by the pound now, and the small conference table was covered with neat stacks of it. Darlene was in and out of the office constantly – making copies, delivering phone messages, fetching coffee, proofreading briefs and petitions. She'd been trained in the tedious field of government bonds, so the detailed and voluminous documents did not intimidate her. She confessed more than once that this was an exciting change from her normal drudgery. 'What's more exciting than a looming execution?' Adam asked.

Even Baker Cooley managed to tear himself away from

the latest updates in federal banking regulations and popped in for a look.

Phelps called around eleven to ask if Adam wanted to meet for lunch. Adam did not, and begged off by blaming deadlines and cranky judges. Neither had heard from Lee. Phelps said she'd disappeared before, but never for more than two days. He was worried and thinking about hiring a private investigator. He'd keep in touch.

'There's a reporter here to see you,' Darlene said, handing him a business card declaring the presence of Anne L. Piazza, correspondent for *Newsweek*. She was the third reporter who'd contacted the office on Wednesday. 'Tell her I'm sorry,' Adam said with no regret.

'I did that already, but I thought that since it was *Newsweek* you might wanna know.'

'I don't care who it is. Tell her the client's not talking either.'

She left in a hurry as the phone was ringing. It was Goodman, reporting from Jackson that he was to see the governor at one. Adam brought him up to date on the flurry of activity and phone calls.

Darlene delivered a deli sandwich at twelve-thirty. Adam ate it quickly, then napped in a chair as his computer spewed forth another brief.

GOODMAN FLIPPED through a car magazine as he waited alone in the reception area next to the governor's office. The same pretty secretary worked on her nails between phone calls at her switchboard. One o'clock came and went without comment. Same for one-thirty. The receptionist, now with glorious peach nails, apologized at two. No problem, said Goodman with a warm smile. The beauty of a pro bono career was that labor was not measured by time. Success meant helping people, regardless of hours billed.

At two-fifteen, an intense young woman in a dark suit appeared from nowhere and walked to Goodman. 'Mr Goodman, I'm Mono Stark, the governor's chief of staff. The governor will see you now.' She smiled correctly, and

438

Goodman followed her through a set of double doors and into a long, formal room with a desk at one end and a conference table far away at the other.

McAllister was standing by the window with his jacket off, tie loosened, sleeves up, very much the beleaguered and overworked servant of the people. 'Hello, Mr Goodman,' he said with a hand thrust forward and teeth flashing brilliantly.

'Governor, my pleasure,' Goodman said. He had no briefcase, no standard lawyer accessories. He looked as if he'd simply passed by on the street and decided to stop and meet the governor.

'You've met Mr Larramore and Ms Stark,' McAllister said, waving a hand at each.

'Yes. We've met. Thanks for seeing me on such short notice.' Goodman tried to match his dazzling smile, but it was hopeless. At the moment, he was most humble and appreciative just to be in this great office.

'Let's sit over here,' the governor said, waving at the conference table and leading the way. The four of them sat on separate sides of the table. Larramore and Mona withdrew pens and were poised for serious note-taking. Goodman had nothing but his hands in front of him.

'I understand there've been quite a lot of filings in the past few days,' McAllister said.

'Yes sir. Just curious, have you been through one of these before?' Goodman asked.

'No. Thankfully.'

'Well, this is not unusual. I'm certain we'll be filing petitions until the last moment.'

'Can I ask you something, Mr Goodman?' the governor said sincerely.

'Certainly.'

'I know you've handled many of these cases. What's your prediction at this point? How close will it get?'

'You never know. Sam's a bit different from most inmates on death row because he's had good lawyers – good trial counsel, then superb appellate work.'

'By you, I believe.'

Goodman smiled, then McAllister smiled, then Mona managed a grin. Larramore remained hunched over his legal pad, his face contorted in furious concentration.

'That's right. So Sam's major claims have already been ruled on. What you're seeing now are the desperate moves, but they often work. I'd say fifty-fifty, today, seven days away.'

Mona quickly recorded this on paper as if it carried some enormous legal significance. Larramore had written every word so far.

McAllister thought about it for a few seconds. 'I'm a little confused, Mr Goodman. Your client does not know we're meeting. He's opposed to the idea of a clemency hearing. You want this meeting kept quiet. So why are we here?'

'Things change, Governor. Again, I've been here many times before. I've watched men count down their last days. It does strange things to the mind. People change. As the lawyer, I have to cover every base, every angle.'

'Are you asking for a hearing?'

'Yes sir. A closed hearing.'

'When?'

'What about Friday?'

'In two days,' McAllister said as he gazed through a window. Larramore cleared his throat, and asked, 'What sort of witnesses do you anticipate?'

'Good question. If I had names, I'd give them to you now, but I don't. Our presentation will be brief.'

'Who will testify for the state?' McAllister asked Larramore, whose moist teeth glistened as he pondered. Goodman looked away.

'I'm certain the victims' family will want to say something. The crime is usually discussed. Someone from the prison might be needed to discuss the type of inmate he's been. These hearings are quite flexible.'

'I know more about the crime than anyone,' McAllister said, almost to himself.

'It's a strange situation,' Goodman confessed. 'I've had

440

my share of clemency hearings, and the prosecutor is usually the first witness to testify against the defendant. In this case, you were the prosecutor.'

'Why do you want the hearing closed?'

'The governor has long been an advocate of open meetings,' Mona added.

'It's really best for everyone,' Goodman said, much like the learned professor. 'It's less pressure on you, Governor, because it's not exposed and you don't have a lot of unsolicited advice. We, of course, would like for it to be closed.'

'Why?' McAllister asked.

'Well, frankly, sir, we don't want the public to see Ruth Kramer talking about her little boys.' Goodman watched them as he delivered this. The real reason was something else altogether. Adam was convinced that the only way to talk Sam into a clemency hearing was to promise him it would not be a public spectacle. If such a hearing was closed, then Adam could maybe convince Sam that McAllister would be prevented from grandstanding.

Goodman knew dozens of people around the country who would gladly come to Jackson on a moment's notice to testify on Sam's behalf. He had heard these people make some persuasive, last minute arguments against death. Nuns, priests, ministers, psychologists, social workers, authors, professors, and a couple of former death row inmates. Dr Swinn would testify about how dreadfully Sam was doing these days, and he would do an excellent job of trying to convince the governor that the state was about to kill a vegetable.

In most states, the inmate has a right to a last minute clemency hearing, usually before the governor. In Mississippi, however, the hearing was discretionary.

'I guess that makes sense,' the governor actually said.

'There's enough interest already,' Goodman said, knowing that McAllister was giddy with dreams of the forthcoming media frenzy. 'It will benefit no one if the hearing is open.'

Mona, the stauch open meetings advocate, frowned even harder and wrote something in block letters. McAllister was deep in thought.

'Regardless of whether it's open or closed,' he said, 'there's no real reason for such a hearing unless you and your client have something new to add. I know this case, Mr Goodman. I smelled the smoke. I saw the bodies. I cannot change my mind unless there's something new.'

'Such as?'

'Such as a name. You give me the name of Sam's accomplice, and I'll agree to a hearing. No promise of clemency, you understand, just a regular clemency hearing. Otherwise, this is a waste of time.'

'Do you believe there was an accomplice?' Goodman asked.

'We were always suspicious. What do you think?'

'Why is it important?'

'It's important because I make the final decision, Mr Goodman. After the courts are finished with it, and the clock ticks down next Tuesday night, I'm the only person in the world who can stop it. If Sam deserves the death penalty, then I have no problem sitting by while it happens. But if he doesn't, then the execution should be stopped. I'm a young man. I do not want to be haunted by this for the rest of my life. I want to make the right decision.'

'But if you believe there was an accomplice, and you obviously do, then why not stop it anyway?'

'Because I want to be sure. You've been his lawyer for many years. Do you think he had an accomplice?'

'Yes. I've always thought there were two of them. I don't know who was the leader and who was the follower, but Sam had help.'

McAllister leaned closer to Goodman and looked into his eyes. 'Mr Goodman, if Sam will tell me the truth, then I will grant a closed hearing, and I will consider clemency. I'm not promising a damned thing, you understand, only that we'll have the hearing. Otherwise, there's nothing new to add to the story.'

Mona and Larramore scribbled faster than court reporters.

'Sam says he's telling the truth.'

'Then forget the hearing. I'm a busy man.'

Goodman sighed in frustration, but kept a smile in place. 'Very well, we'll talk to him again. Can we meet here again tomorrow?'

The governor looked at Mona, who consulted a pocket calendar and began shaking her head as if tomorrow was hopelessly filled with speeches and appearances and meetings. 'You're booked,' she said in a commanding tone.

'What about lunch?'

'Nope. Wouldn't work. You're speaking to the NRA convention.'

'Why don't you call me?' Larramore offered.

'Good idea,' the governor said, standing now and buttoning his sleeves.

Goodman stood and shook hands with the three. 'I'll call if something breaks. We are requesting a hearing as soon as possible, regardless.'

'The request is denied unless Sam talks,' said the governor.

'Please put the request in writing, sir, if you don't mind,' Larramore asked.

'Certainly.'

They walked Goodman to the door, and after he left the office McAllister sat in his official chair behind his desk. He unbuttoned his sleeves again. Larramore excused himself and went to his little room down the hall.

Ms Stark studied a printout while the governor watched the rows of buttons blink on the phone. 'How many of these calls are about Sam Cayhall?' he asked. She moved a finger along a column.

'Yesterday, you had twenty-one calls regarding the Cayhall execution. Fourteen in favour of gassing him. Five said to spare him. Two couldn't make up their minds.'

'That's an increase.'

'Yeah, but the paper had that article about Sam's last

443

ditch efforts. It mentioned the possibility of a clemency hearing.'

'What about the polls?'

'No change. Ninety percent of the white poeple in this state favour the death penalty, and about half the blacks do. Overall, it's around eighty-four percent.'

'Where's my approval?'

'Sixty-two. But if you pardon Sam Cayhall, I'm sure it'll drop to single digits.'

'So you're against the idea.'

'There's absolutely nothing to gain, and much to lose. Forget polls and numbers, if you pardon one of those thugs up there you'll have the other fifty sending lawyers and grandmothers and preachers down here begging for the same favor. You have enough on your mind. It's foolish.'

'Yeah, you're right. Where's the media plan?'

'I'll have it in an hour.'

'I need to see it.'

'Nagel's putting the final touches on it. I think you should grant the request for a clemency hearing anyway. But hold it Monday. Announce it tomorrow. Let it simmer over the weekend.

'It shouldn't be closed.'

'Hell no! We want Ruth Kramer crying for the cameras.'

'It's my hearing. Sam and his lawyers will not dictate its conditions. If they want it, they'll do it my way.'

'Right. But keep in mind, you want it too. Tons of coverage.'

GOODMAN SIGNED a three-month lease for four cellular phones. He used a Kravitz & Bane credit card and deftly dodged the barrage of questions by the chirpy young salesman. He went to a public library on State Street and found a reference table filled with phonebooks. Judging by their thickness, he selected those of the larger Mississippi towns, places like Laurel, Hattiesburg, Tupelo, Vicksburg, Biloxi, and Meridian. Then he picked the thinner ones – Tunica, Calhoun City, Bude, Long Beach,

West Point. At the information desk, he converted bills to quarters, and spent two hours copying pages from the phonebooks.

He went merrily about his work. No one would've believed the natty little man with bushy gray hair and bow tie was in fact a partner in a major Chicago firm with secretaries and paralegals at his beck and call. No one would've believed he earned over four hundred thousand dollars a year. And he couldn't have cared less. E. Garner Goodman was happy with his work. He was trying his best to save another soul from being legally killed.

He left the library and drove a few blocks to the Mississippi College School of Law. A professor there by the name of John Bryan Glass taught criminal procedure and law, and also had begun publishing scholarly articles against the death penalty. Goodman wanted to make his acquaintance, and to see if maybe the professor had a few bright students interested in a research project.

The professor was gone for the day, but scheduled to teach a 9 A.M. class on Thursday. Goodman checked out the law school's library, then left the building. He drove a few blocks to the Old State Capitol Building, just killing time, and took an extended tour of it. It lasted for thirty minutes, half of which was spent at the Civil Rights Exhibit on the ground floor. He asked the clerk in the gift shop about a bed and breakfast, and she suggested the Millsaps-Buie House, about a mile down the street. He found the lovely Victorian mansion just where she'd said, and took the last vacant room. The house was immaculately restored with period pieces and furnishings. The butler fixed him a Scotch and water, and he took it to his room.

THIRTY-NINE

THE AUBURN HOUSE opened for business at eight. A feeble and dispirited security guard in a bad uniform unlocked the gate across the drive, and Adam was the first person into the parking lot. He waited in his car for ten minutes until another parked nearby. He recognized the woman as the counselor he'd met in Lee's office two weeks earlier. He stopped her on the sidewalk as she was entering a side door. 'Excuse me,' he said. 'We've met before. I'm Adam Hall. Lee's nephew. I'm sorry, but I don't remember your name.'

The lady held a worn briefcase in one hand and a brown lunch bag in the other. She smiled and said, 'Joyce Cobb. I remember. Where's Lee?'

'I don't know. I was hoping you might know something. You haven't heard from her?'

'No. Not since Tuesday.'

'Tuesday? I haven't talked to her since Saturday. Did you talk to her Tuesday?'

'She called here, but I didn't talk to her. It was the day they ran that drunk driving story in the paper.'

'Where was she?'

'She never said. She asked for the administrator, said she would be out for a while, had to get some help, stuff like that. Never said where she was or when she was coming back.'

'What about her patients?'

'We're covering for her. It's always a struggle, you know. But we'll manage.'

446

'Lee wouldn't forget these girls. Do you think maybe she's talked to them this week?'

'Look, Adam, most of these girls don't have phones, okay? And Lee certainly would not go into the projects. We're seeing her girls, and I know they haven't talked to her.'

Adam took a step back and looked at the gate. 'I know. I need to find her. I'm really worried.'

'She'll be okay. She's done this once before, and everything worked out.' Joyce was suddenly in a hurry to get inside. 'If I hear something, I'll let you know.'

'Please do. I'm staying at her place.'

'I know.'

Adam thanked her, and drove away. By nine, he was at the office, buried in paper.

COLONEL NUGENT sat at the end of a long table in the front of a room filled with guards and staff people. The table was on a slight platform twelve inches above the rest of the room, and behind it on the wall was a large chalkboard. A portable podium sat in a corner. The chairs along the table to his right were empty, so that the guards and staff sitting in the folding chairs could see the faces of the more important ones on Nugent's left. Morris Henry from the Attorney General's office was there, thick briefs lying before him. Lucas Mann sat at the far end taking notes. Two assistant superintendents were next to Henry. A flunkie from the governor's office was next to Lucas.

Nugent glanced at his watch, then began his little pep talk. He referred to his notes, and aimed his comments at the guards and staff. 'As of this morning, August 2, all stays have been lifted by the various courts, and there's nothing to stop the execution. We are proceeding as if it will take place as planned, at one minute after midnight next Wednesday. We have six full days to prepare, and I am determined for this thing to take place smoothly, without a hitch.

'The inmate has at least three petitions and appeals

447

currently working their way through the various courts, and, of course, there's no way to predict what might happen. We are in constant contact with the Attorney General's office. In fact, Mr Morris Henry is here with us today. It is his opinion, and an opinion shared by Mr Lucas Mann, that this thing will go down to the wire. A stay could be granted at any moment, but that looks doubtful. We have to be ready regardless. The inmate is also expected to request a clemency hearing from the governor, but, frankly, that is not expected to be successful. From now until next Wednesday, we will be in a state of preparedness.'

Nugent's words were strong and clear. He had center stage, and was obviously enjoying every moment of it. He glanced at his notes, and continued. 'The gas chamber itself is being prepared. It's old and it hasn't been used in two years, so we're being very careful with it. A representative of the manufacturer arrives this morning, and will conduct tests today and tonight. We'll go through a complete rehearsal of the execution over the weekend, probably Sunday night, assuming there's no stay. I have collected the lists of volunteers for the execution team, and I'll make that determination this afternoon.

'Now, we're being inundated with requests from the media for all sorts of things. They want to interview Mr Cayhall, his lawyer, our lawyer, the warden, the guards, other inmates on the row, the executioner, everybody. They want to witness the execution. They want pictures of his cell and the chamber. Typical media silliness. But we must deal with it. There is to be no contact with any member of the press unless I first approve it. That goes for every employee of this institution. No exceptions. Most of these reporters are not from around here, and they get their jollies making us look like a bunch of ignorant rednecks. So don't talk to them. No exceptions. I'll issue the appropriate releases when I deem necessary. Be careful with these people. They're vultures.

'We're also expecting trouble from outside. As of about ten minutes ago, the first group of Ku Klux Klansmen

448

arrived at the front gate. They were directed to the usual spot between the highway and the administration building where the protests take place. We've also heard that other such groups will be here shortly, and it appears as if they plan to protest until this thing is over. We'll watch them closely. They have the right to do this, so long as it's peaceful. Though I wasn't here for the last four executions, I've been told that groups of death penalty supporters usually show up and raise hell. We plan to keep these two groups separated, for obvious reasons. '

Nugent couldn't sit any longer, and stood stiffly at the end of the table. All eyes were on him. He studied his notes for a second.

'This execution will be different because of Mr Cayhall's notoriety. It will attract a lot of attention, a lot of media, a lot of other loonies. We must act professionally at all times, and I will not tolerate any breach of the rules of conduct. Mr Cayhall and his family are entitled to respect during these last few days. No off-color comments about the gas chamber or the execution. I will not stand for it. Any questions?'

Nugent surveyed the room and was quite pleased with himself. He'd covered it all. No questions. 'Very well. We'll meet again in the morning at nine.' He dismissed them, and the room emptied hurriedly.

GARNER GOODMAN caught Professor John Bryan Glass as he was leaving his office and headed for a lecture. The class was forgotten as the two stood in the hallway and swapped compliments. Glass had read all of Goodman's books, and Goodman had read most of Glass' recent articles condemning the death penalty. The conversation quickly turned to the Cayhall mess, and specifically to Goodman's pressing need for a handful of trustworthy law students who could assist with a quick research project over the weekend. Glass offered his help, and the two agreed to have lunch in a few hours to pursue the matter.

Three blocks away from the Mississippi College School

of Law, Goodman found the small and cramped offices of Southern Capital Defense Group, a quasi federal agency with small, cramped offices in every state in the Death Belt. The director was a young, black, Yale-educated lawyer named Hez Kerry, who had forsaken the riches of the big firms and dedicated his life to abolishing the death penalty. Goodman had met him on two prior occasions at conferences. Though Kerry's Group, as it was referred to, did not directly represent every inmate on death row, it did have the responsibility of monitoring every case. Hez was thirty-one years old and aging quickly. The gray hair was evidence of the pressure of forty-seven men on death row.

On a wall above the secretary's desk in the foyer was a small calendar, and across the top of it someone had printed the words BIRTHDAYS ON DEATH ROW. Everybody got a card, nothing more. The budget was tight, and the cards were usually purchased with pocket change collected around the office.

The group had two lawyers working under Kerry's supervision, and only one full-time secretary. A few students from the law school worked several hours a week, for free.

Goodman talked with Hez Kerry for more than an hour. They planned their movements for next Tuesday – Kerry himself would camp out at the clerk's office at the Mississippi Supreme Court. Goodman would stay at the governor's office. John Bryan Glass would be recruited to sit in the Fifth Circuit satellite office in the federal courthouse in Jackson. One of Goodman's former associates at Kravitz & Bane now worked in Washington, and he had already agreed to wait at the Death Clerk's desk. Adam would be left to sit on the Row with the client and coordinate the last minute calls.

Kerry agreed to participate in Goodman's market analysis project over the weekend.

At eleven, Goodman returned to the governor's office in the state capitol, and handed to Lawyer Larramore a written request for a clemency hearing. The governor was out of the office, very busy these days, and he, Larramore, would see him just after lunch. Goodman left his phone number at the Millsaps-Buie House, and said he would call in periodically.

He then drove to his new office, now supplied with the finest rental furniture available on two months' lease, cash of course. The folding chairs were leftovers from a church fellowship hall, according to the markings under the seats. The rickety tables too had seen their share of potluck suppers and wedding receptions.

Goodman admired his hastily assembled little hole-in-the-wall. He took a seat, and on a new cellular phone he called his secretary in Chicago, Adam's office in Memphis, his wife at home, and the governor's hotline.

By 4 P.M. Thursday, the Mississippi Supreme Court still had not denied the claim based on Sam's alleged mental incompetence. Almost thirty hours had passed since Adam filed it. He'd made a nuisance of himself calling the court's clerk. He was tired of explaining the obvious – he needed an answer, please. There was not the slightest trace of optimism that the court was actually considering the merits of the claim. The court, in Adam's opinion, was dragging its feet and delaying his rush to federal court. At this point, relief in the state supreme court was impossible, he felt.

He wasn't exactly on a roll in the federal courts either. The U.S. Supreme Court had not ruled on his request to consider the claim that the gas chamber was unconstitutional. The Fifth Circuit was sitting on his ineffectiveness of counsel claim.

Nothing was moving on Thursday. The courts were just sitting there as if these were ordinary lawsuits to be filed and assigned and docketed, then continued and delayed for years. He needed action, preferably a stay granted at some level, or if not a stay then an oral argument, or a hearing on the merits, or even a denial so he could move on to the next court.

He paced around the table in his office and listened for

the phone. He was tired of pacing and sick of the phone. The office was littered with the debris of a dozen briefs. The table was blanketed with disheveled piles of paper. Pink and yellow phone messages were stuck along one bookshelf.

Adam suddenly hated the place. He needed fresh air. He told Darlene he was going for a walk, and left the building. It was almost five, still bright and very warm. He walked to the Peabody Hotel on Union, and had a drink in a corner of the lobby near the piano. It was his first drink since Friday in New Orleans, and although he enjoyed it he worried about Lee. He looked for her in the crowd of conventioneers flocking around the registration desk. He watched the tables in the lobby fill up with well-dressed people, hoping that for some reason she would appear. Where do you hide when you're fifty years old and running from life?

A man with a ponytail and hiking boots stopped and stared, then walked over. 'Excuse me, sir. Are you Adam Hall, the lawyer for Sam Cayhall?'

Adam nodded.

The man smiled, obviously pleased that he'd recognized Adam, and walked to his table. 'I'm Kirk Kleckner with the *New York Times*.' He laid a business card in front of Adam. 'I'm here covering the Cayhall execution. Just arrived, actually. May I sit down?'

Adam waved at the empty seat across the small round table. Kleckner sat down. 'Lucky to find you here,' he said, all smiles. He was in his early forties with a rugged, globe-trotting journalist look – scruffy beard, sleeveless cotton vest over a denim shirt, jeans. 'Recognized you from some pictures I studied on the flight down.'

'Nice to meet you,' Adam said dryly.

'Can we talk?'

'About what?'

'Oh, lots of things. I understand your client will not give interviews.'

'That's correct.'

'What about you?'

'The same. We can chat, but nothing for the record.'

452

'That makes it diffcult.'

'I honestly don't care. I'm not concerned with how difficult your job may be.'

'Fair enough.' A pliant young waitress in a short skirt stopped by long enough to take his order. Black coffee. 'When did you last see your grandfather?'

'Tuesday.'

'When will you see him again?'

'Tomorrow.'

'How is he holding up?'

'He's surviving. The pressure is building, but he's taking it well, so far.'

'What about you?'

'Just having a ball.'

'Seriously. Are you losing sleep, you know, things like that?'

'I'm tired. Yeah, I'm losing sleep. I'm working lots of hours, running back and forth to the prison. It'll go down to the wire, so the next few days will be hectic.'

'I covered the Bundy execution in Florida. Quite a circus. His lawyer went days without sleep.'

'It's difficult to relax.'

'Will you do it again? I know this is not your speciality, but will you consider another death case?'

'Only if I find another relative on death row. Why do you cover these things?'

'I've written for years on the death penalty. It's fascinating. I'd like to interview Mr Cayhall.'

Adam shook his head and finished his drink. 'No. There's no way. He's not talking to anyone.'

'Will you ask him for me?'

'No.'

The coffee arrived. Kleckner stirred it with a spoon. Adam watched the crowd. 'I interviewed Benjamin Keyes yesterday in Washington,' Kleckner said. 'He said he wasn't surprised that you're now saying he made mistakes at trial. He said he figured it was coming.'

At the moment, Adam didn't care about Benjamin Keyes

or any of his opinions. 'It's standard. I need to run. Nice to meet you.'

'But I wanted to talk about—'

'Listen, you're lucky you caught me,' Adam said, standing abruptly.

'Just a couple of things,' Kleckner said as Adam walked away.

Adam left the Peabody, and strolled to Front Street near the river, passing along the way scores of well-dressed young people very much like himself, all in a hurry to go home. He envied them; whatever their vocations or careers, whatever their pressures at the moment, they weren't carrying burdens as heavy as his.

He ate a sandwich at a delicatessen, and by seven was back in his office.

THE RABBIT had been trapped in the woods at Parchman by two of the guards, who named him Sam for the occasion. He was a brown cottontail, the largest of the four captured. The other three had already been eaten.

Late Thursday night, Sam the rabbit and his handlers, along with Colonel Nugent and the execution team, entered the Maximum Security Unit in prison vans and pickups. They drove slowly by the front and around the bullpens on the west end. They parked by a square, red-brick building attached to the southwest corner of MSU.

Two white, metal doors without windows led to the interior of the square building. One, facing south, opened to a narrow room, eight feet by fifteen, where the witnesses sat during the execution. They faced a series of black drapes which, when opened, revealed the rear of the chamber itself, just inches away.

The other door opened into the Chamber Room, a fifteen-by-twelve room with a painted concrete floor. The octagonal-shaped gas chamber sat squarely in the middle, glowing smartly from a fresh coat of silver enamel varnish and smelling like the same. Nugent had inspected it a week earlier and ordered a new paint job. The death room, as it was also known, was spotless and sanitized. The black drapes over the windows behind the chamber were pulled.

Sam the rabbit was left in the bed of a pickup while a small guard, about the same height and weight as Sam Cayhall, was led by two of his larger colleagues into the Chamber Room. Nugent strutted and inspected like General Patton – pointing and nodding and frowning. The small guard was pushed gently into the chamber first, then joined by the two guards who turned him around and eased him into the wooden chair. Without a word or a smile, neither a grin nor a joke, they strapped his wrists first with leather bands to the arms of the chair. Then his knees, then his ankles. Then one lifted his head up an inch or two and held it in place while the other manged to buckle the leather head strap.

The two guards stepped carefully from the chamber, and Nugent pointed to another member of the team who stepped forward as if to say something to the condemned.

'At this point, Lucas Mann will read the death warrant to Mr Cayhall,' Nugent explained like an amateur movie director. 'Then I will ask if he has any last words.' He pointed again, and a designated guard closed the heavy door to the chamber and sealed it.

'Open it,' Nugent barked, and the door came open. The small guard was set free.

'Get the rabbit,' Nugent ordered. One of the handlers retrieved Sam the rabbit from the pickup. He sat innocently in a wire cage which was handed to the same two guards who'd just left the chamber. They carefully placed him in the wooden chair, then went about their task of strapping in an imaginary man. Wrists, knees, ankles, head, and the rabbit was ready for the gas. The two guards left the chamber.

The door was shut and sealed, and Nugent signaled for the executioner, who placed a canister of sulfuric acid into a tube which ran into the bottom of the chamber. He pulled a lever, a clicking sound occurred, and the canister made its way to the bowl under the chair.

Nugent stepped to one of the windows and watched intently. The other members of the team did likewise. Petroleum jelly had been smeared around the edges of the windows to prevent seepage.

The poisonous gas was released slowly, and a faint mist of visible vapors rose from under the chair and drifted upwards. At first, the rabbit didn't react to the steam that permeated his little cell, but it hit him soon enough. He stiffened, then hopped a few times, banging into the sides of his cage, then he went into violent convulsions, jumping and jerking and twisting frantically. In less than a minute, he was still.

Nugent smiled as he glanced at his watch. 'Clear it,' he ordered, and a vent at the top of the chamber was opened, releasing the gas.

The door from the Chamber Room to the outside was opened, and most of the execution team walked out for fresh air or a smoke. It would be at least fifteen minutes before the chamber could be opened and the rabbit removed. Then they had to hose it down and clean up. Nugent was still inside, watching everything. So they smoked and had a few laughs.

Less than sixty feet away, the windows above the hallway of Tier A were open. Sam could hear their voices. It was after ten and the lights were off, but in every cell along the tier two arms protruded from the bars as fourteen men listened in dark silence.

A death row inmate lives in a six-by-nine cell for twenty-three hours a day. He hears everything – the strange clicking sound of a new pair of boots in the hallway; the unfamiliar pitch and accent of a different voice; the faraway hum of a lawn mower or weedeater. And he can certainly hear the opening and closing of the door to the Chamber Room. He can hear the satisfied and important chuckles of the execution team.

Sam leaned on his forearms and watched the windows above the hallway. They were practicing for him out there.

FORTY

BETWEEN THE WESTERN EDGE of Highway 49 and the front lawn of the administrative buildings of Parchman, a distance of fifty yards, there was a grassy strip of land that was smooth and noticeable because it was once a railroad track. It was where the death penalty protestors were corralled and monitored at every execution. They invariably arrived, usually small groups of committed souls who sat in folding chairs and held homemade placards. They burned candles at night and sang hymns during the final hours. They sang hymns, offered prayers, and wept when the death was announced.

A new twist had occurred during the hours preceding the execution of Teddy Doyle Meeks, a child rapist and killer. The somber, almost sacred protest had been disrupted by carloads of unruly college students who suddenly appeared without warning and had a delightful time demanding blood. They drank beer and played loud music. They chanted slogans and heckled the shaken death protestors. The situation deteriorated as the two groups exchanged words. Prison officials moved in and restored order.

Maynard Tole was next, and during the planning of his execution another section of turf on the other side of the main drive was designated for the death penalty proponents. Extra security was assigned to keep things peaceful.

When Adam arrived Friday morning, he counted seven Ku Klux Klansmen in white robes. Three were engaged in some attempt at synchronized protest, a casual walking along the edge of the grassy strip near the highway with posters strung over their shoulders. The other four were erecting a large blue and white canopy. Metal poles and ropes were scattered on the ground. Two ice chests sat next to several lawn chairs. These guys were planning to stay awhile.

Adam stared at them as he rolled to a stop at the front gate of Parchman. He lost track of time as he watched the Kluckers for minutes. So this was his heritage, his roots. These were the brethren of his grandfather and his grandfather's relatives and ancestors. Were some of these figures the same ones who'd been recorded on film and edited by Adam into the video about Sam Cayhall? Had he seen them before?

Instinctively, Adam opened the door of his car and got out. His coat and briefcase were in the rear seat. He began walking slowly in their direction, and stopped near their ice chests. Their placards demanded freedom for Sam Cayhall, a political prisoner. Gas the real criminals, but release Sam. For some reason, Adam was not comforted by their demands.

'What do you want?' demanded one with a sign draped over his chest. The other six stopped what they were doing and stared.

'I don't know,' Adam said truthfully.

'Then what are you looking at?'

'I'm not sure.'

Three others joined the first, and they stepped together near Adam. Their robes were identical – white and made of a very light fabric with red crosses and other markings. It was almost 9 A.M., and they were already sweating. 'Who the hell are you?'

'Sam's grandson.'

The other three crowded behind the others, and all seven examined Adam from a distance of no more than five feet. 'Then you're on our side,' one said, relieved.

'No. I'm not one of you.'

'That's right. He's with that bunch of Jews from

458

Chicago,' another said for the edification of the rest, and this seemed to stir them up a bit.

'Why are you people here?' Adam asked.

'We're trying to save Sam. Looks like you're not gonna do it.'

'You're the reason he's here.'

A young one with a red face and rows of sweat on his forehead took the lead and walked even closer to Adam. 'No. He's the reason we're here. I wasn't even born when Sam killed those Jews, so you can't blame it on me. We're here to protest his execution. He's being persecuted for political reasons.'

'He wouldn't be here had it not been for the Klan. Where are your masks? I thought you people always hid your faces.'

They twitched and fidgeted as a group, uncertain what to do next. He was, after all, the grandson of Sam Cayhall, their idol and champion. He was the lawyer trying to save a most precious symbol.

'Why don't you leave?' Adam asked. 'Sam doesn't want you here.'

'Why don't you go to hell?' the young one sneered.

'How eloquent. Just leave, okay. Sam's worth much more to you dead than alive. Let him die in peace, then you'll have a wonderful martyr.'

'We ain't leavin'. We'll be here till the end.'

'And what if Sam asks you to leave? Will you go then?'

'No,' he sneered again, then glanced over his shoulders at the others who all seemed to agree that they would, in fact, not leave. 'We plan to make a lot of noise.'

'Great. That'll get your pictures in the papers. That's what this is about, isn't it? Circus clowns in funny costumes always attract attention.'

Car doors slammed somewhere behind Adam, and as he looked around he saw a television crew making a speedy exit from a van parked near his Saab.

'Well, well,' he said to the group. 'Smile, fellas. This is your big moment.'

459

'Go to hell,' the young one snapped angrily. Adam turned his back to them and walked toward his car. A hurried reporter with a cameraman in tow rushed to him.

'Are you Adam Hall?' she asked breathlessly. 'Cayhall's lawyer?'

'Yes,' he said without stopping.

'Could we have a few words?'

'No. But those boys are anxious to talk,' he said, pointing over his shoulder. She walked along beside him while the cameraman fumbled with his equipment. Adam opened his car door, then slammed it as he turned the ignition.

Louise, the guard at the gate, handed him a numbered card for his dashboard, then waved him through.

PACKER WENT THROUGH the motions of the obligatory frisk inside the front door of the Row. 'What's in there?' he asked, pointing to the small cooler Adam held in his left hand.

'Eskimo Pies, Sergeant. Would you like one?'

'Lemme see.' Adam handed the cooler to Packer, who flipped open the top just long enough to count half a dozen Eskimo Pies, still frozen under a layer of ice.

He handed the cooler back to Adam, and pointed to the door of the front office, a few feet away. 'Y'all will be meetin' in here from now on,' he explained. They stepped into the room.

'Why?' Adam asked as he looked around the room. There was a metal desk with a phone, three chairs, and two locked file cabinets.

'That's just the way we do things. We lighten up some as the big day gets close. Sam gets to have his visitors here. No time limit either.'

'How sweet.' Adam placed his briefcase on the desk and picked up the phone. Packer left to fetch Sam.

The kind lady in the clerk's office in Jackson informed Adam that the Mississippi Supreme Court had denied, just minutes ago, his client's petition for postconviction relief on the grounds that he was mentally incompetent. He thanked her, said something to the effect that this was what he expected and that it could've been done a day earlier, then asked her to fax a copy of the court's decision to his office in Memphis, and also to Lucas Mann's office at Parchman. He called Darlene in Memphis and told her to fax the new petition to the federal district court, with copies faxed to the Fifth Circuit and to Mr Richard Olander's rather busy death desk at the Supreme Court in Washington. He called Mr Olander to inform him it was coming, and was told that the U.S. Supreme Court had just denied cert on Adam's claim that the gas chamber was unconstitutional.

Sam entered the front office without handcuffs while Adam was on the phone. They shook hands quickly, and Sam took a seat. Instead of a cigarette, he opened the cooler and removed an Eskimo Pie. He ate it slowly while listening as Adam talked with Olander. 'U.S. Supreme Court just denied cert,' Adam whispered to Sam with his hand over the receiver.

Sam smiled oddly and studied some envelopes he'd brought with him.

'The Mississippi Supreme Court also turned us down,' Adam explained to his client as he punched more numbers. 'But that was to be expected. We're filing it in federal court right now.' He was calling the Fifth Circuit to check the status of the ineffective counsel claim. The clerk in New Orleans informed him that no action had been taken that morning. Adam hung up and sat on the edge of the desk.

'Fifth Circuit is still sitting on the ineffectiveness claim,' he reported to his client, who knew the law and the procedure and was absorbing it like a learned attorney. 'All in all, not a very good morning.'

'The Jackson TV station this morning said I've requested a clemency hearing from the governor,' Sam said, between bites. 'Certainly this can't be true. I didn't approve it.'

'Relax, Sam. It's routine.'

'Routine my ass. I thought we had an agreement. They even had McAllister on the tube talking about how he was

461

grieving over his decision about a clemency hearing. I warned you.'

'McAllister is the least of our problems, Sam. The request was a formality. We don't have to participate.'

Sam shook his head in frustration. Adam watched him closely. He wasn't really angry, nor did he really care what Adam had done. He was resigned, almost defeated. The little bit of bitching came naturally. A week earlier he would've lashed out.

'They practiced last night, you know. They cranked up the gas chamber, killed a rat or something, everything worked perfectly and so now everyone's excited about my execution. Can you believe it? They had a dress rehearsal for me. The bastards.'

'I'm sorry, Sam.'

'Do you know what cyanide gas smells like?'

'No.'

'Cinnamon. It was in the air last night. The idiots didn't bother to close the windows on our tier, and I got a whiff of it.'

Adam didn't know if this was true or not. He knew the chamber was vented for several minutes after an execution and the gas escaped into the air. Surely it couldn't filter onto the tiers. Maybe Sam had heard stories about the gas from the guards. Maybe it was just part of the lore. He sat on the edge of the desk, casually swinging his feet, staring at the pitiful old man with the skinny arms and oily hair. It was such a horrible sin to kill an aged creature like Sam Cayhall. His crimes were committed a generation ago. He had suffered and died many times in his six-by-nine cell. How would the state benefit by killing him now?

Adam had things on his mind, not the least of which was perhaps their last, gasping effort. 'I'm sorry, Sam,' he said again, very compassionately. 'But we need to talk about some items.'

'Were there Klansmen outside this morning? The television had a shot of them here yesterday.'

'Yes. I counted seven a few minutes ago. Full uniforms except for the masks.'

'I used to wear one of those, you know,' he said, much like a war veteran bragging to little boys.

'I know, Sam. And because you wore one, you're now sitting here on death row with your lawyer counting the hours before they strap you in the gas chamber. You should hate those silly fools out there.'

'I don't hate them. But they have no right to be here. They abandoned me. Dogan sent me here, and when he testified against me he was the Imperial Wizard of Mississippi. They gave me not one dime for legal fees. They forgot about me.'

'What do you expect from a bunch of thugs? Loyalty?'

'I was loyal.'

'And look where you are, Sam. You should denounce the Klan and ask them to leave, to stay away from your execution.'

Sam fiddled with his envelopes, then placed them carefully in a chair.

'I told them to leave,' Adam said.

'When?'

'Just a few minutes ago. I exchanged words with them. They don't give a damn about you, Sam, they're just using this execution because you'll make such a marvelous martyr, someone to rally around and talk about for years to come. They'll chant your name when they burn crosses, and they'll make pilgrimages to your gravesite. They want you dead, Sam. It's great PR.'

'You confronted them?' Sam asked, with a trace of amusement and pride.

'Yeah. It was no big deal. What about Carmen? If she's coming, she needs to make travel arrangements.'

Sam took a thoughtful puff. 'I'd like to see her, but you've gotta warn her about my appearance. I don't want her to be shocked.'

'You look great, Sam.'

'Gee thanks. What about Lee?'

'What about her?'

'How's she doing? We get newspapers in here. I saw her

in the Memphis paper last Sunday, then I read about her drunk driving charge on Tuesday. She's not in jail, is she?'

'No. She's in a rehab clinic,' Adam said as if he knew exactly where she was.

'Can she come visit?'

'Do you want her to?'

'I think so. Maybe on Monday. Let's wait and see.'

'No problem,' Adam said, wondering how in the world he could find her. 'I'll talk to her over the weekend.'

Sam handed Adam one of the envelopes, unsealed. 'Give this to the people up front. It's a list of approved visitors from now until then. Go ahead, open it.'

Adam looked at the list. There were four names. Adam, Lee, Carmen, and Donnie Cayhall. 'Not a very long list.'

'I have lots of relatives, but I don't want them here. They haven't visited me in nine and a half years, so I'll be damned if they'll come draggin' in here at the last minute to say good-bye. They can save it for the funeral.'

'I'm getting all kinds of requests from reporters and journalists for interviews.'

'Forget it.'

'That's what I've told them. But there's one inquiry that might interest you. There's a man named Wendall Sherman, an author of some repute who's published four or five books and won some awards. I haven't read any of his work, but he checks out. He's legitimate. I talked to him yesterday by phone, and he wants to sit with you and record your story. He seemed to be very honest, and said that the recording could take hours. He's flying to Memphis today, just in case you say yes.'

'Why does he want to record me?'

'He wants to write a book about you.'

'A romance novel?'

'I doubt it. He's willing to pay fifty thousand dollars up front, with a percentage of the royalties later on.'

'Great. I get fifty thousand a few days before I die. What shall I do with it?'

'I'm just relaying the offer.'

464

'Tell him to go to hell. I'm not interested.'

'Fine.'

'I want you to draw up an agreement whereby I assign all rights to my life story to you, and after I'm gone you do whatever the hell you want with it.'

'It wouldn't be a bad idea to record it.'

'You mean—'

'Talk into a little machine with little tapes. I can get one for you. Sit in your cell and talk about your life.'

'How boring.' Sam finished the Eskimo Pie and tossed the stick in the wastebasket.

'Depends on how you look at it. Things seem rather exciting now.'

'Yeah, you're right. A pretty dull life, but the end was sensational.'

'Sounds like a bestseller to me.'

'I'll think about it.'

Sam suddenly jumped to his feet, leaving the rubber shower shoes under his chair. He loped across the office in long strides, measuring and smoking as he went. 'Thirteen by sixteen and a half,' he mumbled to himself, then measured some more.

Adam made notes on a legal pad and tried to ignore the red figure bouncing off the walls. Sam finally stopped and leaned on a file cabinet. 'I want you to do me a favour,' he said, staring at a wall across the room. His voice was much lower. He breathed slowly.

'I'm listening,' Adam said.

Sam took a step to the chair and picked up an envelope. He handed it to Adam and returned to his position against the file cabinet. The envelope was turned over so that Adam could see the writing on it.'

'I want you to deliver that,' Sam said.

'To whom?'

'Quince Lincoln.'

Adam placed it to his side on the desk, and watched Sam carefully. Sam, however, was lost in another world. His wrinkled eyes stared blankly at something on the wall

465

across the room. 'I've worked on it for a week,' he said, his voice almost hoarse, 'but I've thought about it for forty years.'

'What's in the letter?' Adam asked slowly.

'An apology. I've carried the guilt for many years, Adam. Joe Lincoln was a good and decent man, a good father. I lost my head and killed him for no reason. And I knew before I shot him that I could get by with it. I've always felt bad about it. Real bad. There's nothing I can do now except say that I'm sorry.'

'I'm sure it'll mean something to the Lincolns.'

'Maybe. In the letter I ask them for forgiveness, which I believe is the Christian way of doing things. When I die, I'd like to have the knowledge that I tried to say I'm sorry.'

'Any idea where I might find him?'

'That's the hard part. I've heard through family that the Lincolns are still in Ford County. Ruby, his widow, is probably still alive. I'm afraid you'll just have to go to Clanton and start asking questions. They have an African sheriff, so I'd start with him. He probably knows all the Africans in the county.'

'And if I find Quince?'

'Tell him who you are. Give him the letter. Tell him that I died with a lot of guilt. Can you do that?'

'I'll be happy to. I'm not sure when I can do it.'

'Wait until I'm dead. You'll have plenty of time once this is over.'

Sam again walked to the chair, and this time picked up two envelopes. He handed them to Adam, and began pacing slowly, back and forth across the room. The name of Ruth Kramer was typed on one, no address, and Elliot Kramer on the other. 'Those are for the Kramers. Deliver them, but wait until the execution is over.'

'Why wait?'

'Because my motives are pure. I don't want them to think I'm doing this to arouse sympathy in my dying hours.'

Adam placed the Kramers letters next to Quince Lincoln's – three letters, three dead bodies. How many more letters would Sam crank out over the weekend? How many more victims were out there?

'You're sure you're about to die, aren't you, Sam?'

He stopped by the door and pondered this for a moment. 'The odds are against us. I'm getting prepared.'

'We still have a chance.'

'Sure we do. But I'm getting ready, just in case. I've hurt a lot of people, Adam, and I haven't always stopped to think about it. But when you have a date with the grim reaper, you think about the damage you've done.'

Adam picked up the three envelopes and looked at them. 'Are there others?'

Sam grimaced and looked at the floor. 'That's all, for now.'

THE JACKSON PAPER on Friday morning carried a front-page story about Sam Cayhall's request for a clemency hearing. The story included a slick photo of Governor David McAllister, a bad one of Sam, and lots of self-serving comments by Mona Stark, the governor's chief of staff, all to the effect that the governor was struggling with the decision.

Since he was a real man of the people, a regular servant to all Mississippians, McAllister had installed an expensive telephone hotline system shortly after he was elected. The toll-free number was plastered all over the state, and his constituents were constantly barraged with public service ads to use the People's Hotline. Call the governor. He cared about your opinions. Democracy at its finest. Operators were standing by.

And because he had more ambition than fortitude, McAllister and his staff tracked the phone calls on a daily basis. He was a follower, not a leader. He spent serious money on polls, and had proven adept at quietly discovering the issues that bothered people, then jumping out front to lead the parade.

Both Goodman and Adam suspected this. McAllister seemed too obsessed with his destiny to launch new initiatives. The man was a shameless vote-counter, so they had decided to give him something to count.

Goodman read the story early, over coffee and fruit, and by seven-thirty was on the phone with Professor John Bryan Glass and Hez Kerry. By eight, three of Glass' students were sipping coffee from paper cups in the grungy, temporary office. The marketing analysis was about to begin.

Goodman explained the scheme and the need for secrecy. They were breaking no laws, he assured them, just manipulating public opinion. The cellular phones were on the tables, along with pages of phone numbers Goodman had copied on Wednesday. The students were a little apprehensive, but nonetheless anxious to begin. They would be paid well. Goodman demonstrated the technique with the first call. He dialed the number.

'People's Hotline,' a pleasant voice answered.

'Yes, I'm calling about the story in this morning's paper, the one about Sam Cayhall,' Goodman said slowly in his best imitation of a drawl. It left a lot to be desired. The students were very amused.

'And your name is?'

'Yes, I'm Ned Lancaster, from Biloxi, Mississippi,' Goodman replied, reading from the phone lists. 'And I voted for the governor, a fine man,' he threw in for good measure.

'And how do you feel about Sam Cayhall?'

'I don't think he should be executed. He's an old man who's suffered a lot, and I want the governor to give him a pardon. Let him die in peace up there at Parchman.'

'Okay. I'll make sure the governor knows about your call.'

'Thank you.'

Goodman pushed a button on the phone, and took a bow before his audience. 'Nothing to it. Let's get started.'

The white male selected a phone number. His conversation went something like this: 'Hello, this is Lester Crosby, from Bude, Mississippi. I'm calling about the execution of

Sam Cayhall. Yes ma'am. My number? It's 555-9084. Yes, that's right, Bude, Mississippi, down here in Franklin County. That's right. Well, I don't think Sam Cayhall ought to be sent to the gas chamber. I'm just opposed to it. I think the governor should step in and stop this thing. Yes ma'am, that's right. Thank you.' He smiled at Goodman, who was punching another number.

The white female was a middle-aged student. She was from a small town in a rural section of the state, and her accent was naturally twangy. 'Hello, is this the governor's office? Good. I'm calling about the Cayhall story in today's paper. Susan Barnes. Decatur, Mississippi. That's right. Well, he's an old man who'll probably die in a few years anyway. What good will it do for the state to kill him now? Give the guy a break. What? Yes, I want the governor to stop it. I voted for the governor, and I think he's a fine man. Yes. Thank you too.'

The black male was in his late twenties. He simply informed the hotline operator that he was a black Mississippian, very much opposed to the ideas Sam Cayhall and the Klan promoted, but nonetheless opposed to the execution. 'The government does not have the right to determine if someone lives or dies,' he said. He did not favor the death penalty under any circumstances.

And so it went. The calls poured in from all over the state, one after the other, each from a different person with a different logic for stopping the execution. The students became creative, trying assorted accents and novel reasonings. Occasionally, their calls would hit busy signals, and it was amusing to know that they had jammed the hotline. Because of his crisp accent, Goodman assumed the role of the outsider, sort of a traveling death penalty abolitionist who bounced in from all over the country with a dazzling array of ethnic aliases and strange locales.

Goodman had worried that McAllister might be paranoid enough to trace the calls to his hotline, but had decided that the operators would be too busy.

And busy they were. Across town, John Bryan Glass

canceled a class and locked the door to his office. He had a delightful time making repeated calls under all sorts of names. Not far from him, Hez Kerry and one of his staff attorneys were also bombarding the hotline with the same messages.

ADAM HURRIED to Memphis. Darlene was in his office, trying vainly to organize the mountain of paperwork. She pointed to a stack nearest his computer. 'The decision denying cert is on top, then the decision from the Mississippi Supreme Court. Next to it is the petition for writ of habeas corpus to be filed in federal district court. I've already faxed everything.'

Adam removed his jacket and threw it on a chair. He looked at a row of pink telephone messages tacked to a bookshelf. 'Who are these people?'

'Reporters, writers, quacks, a couple are other lawyers offering their assistance. One is from Garner Goodman in Jackson. He said the market analysis is going fine, don't call. What is the market analysis?'

'Don't ask. No word from the Fifth Circuit?'

'No.'

Adam took a deep breath and eased into his chair.

'Lunch?' she asked.

'Just a sandwich, if you don't mind. Can you work tomorrow and Sunday?'

'Of course.'

'I need for you to stay here all weekend, by the phone and the fax. I'm sorry.'

'I don't mind. I'll get a sandwich.'

She left, closing the door behind her. Adam called Lee's condo, and there was no answer. He called the Auburn House, but no one had heard from her. He called Phelps Booth, who was in a board meeting. He called Carmen in Berkeley and told her to make arrangements to fly to Memphis on Sunday.

He looked at the phone messages, and decided none were worth returning.

AT ONE O'CLOCK, Mona Stark spoke to the press loitering around the governor's office in the capitol. She said that after much deliberation, the governor had decided to grant a clemency hearing on Monday at 10 A.M., at which time the governor would listen to the issues and appeals, and make a fair decision. It was an awesome responsibility, she explained, this weighing of life or death. But David McAllister would do what was just and right.

FORTY-ONE

PACKER WENT TO THE CELL at five-thirty Saturday morning, and didn't bother with the handcuffs. Sam was waiting, and they quietly left Tier A. They walked through the kitchen where the trustees were scrambling eggs and frying bacon. Sam had never seen the kitchen, and he walked slowly, counting his steps, checking the dimensions. Packer opened a door and motioned for Sam to hurry and follow. They stepped outside, into the darkness. Sam stopped and looked at the square brick room to his right, the little building that housed the gas chamber. Packer pulled his elbow, and they walked together to the east end of the row where another guard was watching and waiting. The guard handed Sam a large cup of coffee, and led him through a gate into a recreation yard similar to the bullpens on the west end of the Row. It was fenced and wired, with a basketball goal and two benches. Packer said he would return in an hour, and left with the guard.

Sam stood in place for a long time, sipping the hot coffee and absorbing the landscape. His first cell had been on Tier D, on the east wing, and he'd been here many times before. He knew the exact dimensions – fifty-one feet by thirty-six. He saw the guard in the tower sitting under a light and watching him. Through the fences and over the tops of the rows of cotton, he could see the lights of other buildings. He slowly walked to a bench and sat down.

How thoughtful of these kind people to grant his request to see one final sunrise. He hadn't seen one in nine and a half

472

years, and at first Nugent said no. Then Packer intervened, and explained to the colonel that it was okay, no security risk at all, and what the hell, the man was supposed to die in four days. Packer would take responsibility for it.

Sam stared at the eastern sky, where a hint of orange was peeking through scattered clouds. During his early days on the Row, when his appeals were fresh and unresolved, he had spent hours remembering the glorious humdrum of everyday life, the little things like a warm shower every day, the companionship of his dog, extra honey on his biscuits. He actually believed back then that one day he would again be able to hunt squirrels and quail, to fish for bass and bream, to sit on the porch and watch the sun come up, to drink coffee in town, and drive his old pickup wherever he wanted. His goal during those early fantasies on the Row had been to fly to California and find his grandchildren. He had never flown.

But the dreams of freedom had died long ago, driven away by the tedious monotony of life in a cell, and killed by the harsh opinions of many judges.

This would be his final sunrise, he truly believed that. Too many people wanted him dead. The gas chamber was not being used often enough. It was time for an execution, dammit, and he was next in line.

The sky grew brighter and the clouds dissipated. Though he was forced to watch this magnificent act of nature through a chain-link fence, it was satisfying nonetheless. Just a few more days and the fences would be gone. The bars and razor wire and prison cells would be left for someone else.

TWO REPORTERS smoked cigarettes and drank machine coffee as they waited by the south entrance to the capitol early Saturday morning. Word had been leaked that the governor would spend a long day at the office, struggling with the Cayhall thing.

At seven-thirty, his black Lincoln rolled to a stop nearby, and he made a quick exit from it. Two well-dressed bodyguards escorted him to the entrance, with Mona Stark a few steps behind.

'Governor, do you plan to attend the execution?' the first reporter asked hurriedly. McAllister smiled and raised his hands as if he'd love to stop and chat but things were much too critical for that. Then he saw a camera hanging from the other reporter's neck.

'I haven't made a decision yet,' he answered, stopping just for a second.

'Will Ruth Kramer testify at the clemency hearing on Monday?'

The camera was raised and ready. 'I can't say right now,' he answered, smiling into the lens. 'Sorry, guys, I can't talk now.'

He entered the building and rode the elevator to his office on the second floor. The bodyguards assumed their positions in the foyer, behind morning newspapers.

Lawyer Larramore was waiting with his updates. He explained to the governor and Ms Stark that there had been no changes in the various Cayhall petitions and appeals since 5 P.M. yesterday. Nothing had happened overnight. The appeals were becoming more desperate, and the courts would deny them more quickly, in his opinion. He had already spoken with Morris Henry at the AG's office, and, in the learned judgement of Dr Death, there was now an 80 percent chance that the execution would take place.

'What about the clemency hearing on Monday? Any word from Cayhall's lawyers?' McAllister asked.

'No. I asked Garner Goodman to stop by at nine this morning. Thought we'd talk to him about it. I'll be in my office if you need me.'

Larramore excused himself. Ms Stark was performing her morning ritual of scanning the dailies from around the state and placing them on the conference table. Of the nine papers she monitored, the Cayhall story was on the front page of eight. The announcement of a clemency hearing was of special interest Saturday morning. Three of the

474

papers carried the same AP photo of the Klansmen roasting idly under the fierce August sun outside of Parchman.

McAllister removed his coat, rolled up his sleeves, and began peering over the papers. 'Get the numbers,' he said tersely.

Mona left the office, and returned in less than a minute. She carried a computer printout, which obviously bore dreadful news.

'I'm listening,' he said.

'The calls stopped around nine last night, last one was at nine-o-seven. The total for the day was four hundred and eighty-six, and at least ninety percent voiced strong opposition to the execution.'

'Ninety percent,' McAllister said in disbelief. He was no longer in shock, though. By noon yesterday, the hotline operators had reported an unusual number of calls, and by one Mona was analyzing printouts. They had spent much of yesterday afternoon staring at the numbers, contemplating the next move. He had slept little.

'Who are these people?' he said, staring through a window.

'Your constituents. The calls are coming from all over the state. The names and numbers appear to be legitimate.'

'What was the old record?'

'I don't know. Seems like we had around a hundred one day when the legislature gave itself another pay rise. But nothing like this.'

'Ninety percent,' he mumbled again.

'And there's something else. There were lots of other calls to various numbers in this office. My secretary took a dozen or so.'

'All for Sam, right?'

'Yes, all opposed to the execution. I've talked to some of our people, and everybody got nailed yesterday. And Roxburgh called me at home last night and said that his office had been besieged with calls against the execution.'

'Good. I want him to sweat too.'

'Do we close the hotline?'

475

'How many operators work on Saturday and Sunday?'

'Only one.'

'No. Leave it open today. Let's see what happens today and tomorrow.' He walked to another window and loosened his tie. 'When does the polling start?'

'Three this afternoon.'

'I'm anxious to see those numbers.'

'They could be just as bad.'

'Ninety percent,' he said, shaking his head.

'Over ninety percent,' Mona corrected him.

THE WAR ROOM was littered with pizza boxes and beer cans, evidence of a long day of market analysis. A tray of fresh doughnuts and a row of tall paper coffee cups now awaited the analysts, two of whom had just arrived with newspapers. Garner Goodman stood at the window with a new pair of binoculars, watching the capitol three blocks away, and paying particular attention to the windows of the governor's office. During a moment of boredom yesterday, he'd gone to a mall in search of a bookstore. He'd found the binoculars in the window of a leather shop, and throughout the afternoon they'd had great fun trying to catch the governor pondering through his windows, no doubt wondering where all those damned calls were coming from.

The students devoured the doughnuts and newspapers. There was a brief but serious discussion about some obvious procedural deficiencies in Mississippi's postconviction relief statutes. The third member of the shift, a first-year student from New Orleans, arrived at eight, and the calls started.

It was immediately apparent that the hotline was not as efficient as the day before. It was difficult to get through to an operator. No problem. They used alternate numbers – the switchboard at the governor's mansion, the lines to the cute little regional offices he'd established, amid great fanfare, around the state so that he, a common man, could stay close to the people.

476

The people were calling.

Goodman left the office and walked along Congress Street to the capitol. He heard the sounds of a loudspeaker being tested, and then saw the Klansmen. They were organizing themselves, at least a dozen in full parade dress, around the monument to Confederate women at the base of the front steps to the capitol. Goodman walked by them, actually said hello to one, so that when he returned to Chicago he could say he talked to some real Kluckers.

The two reporters who'd waited for the governor were now on the front steps watching the scene below. A local television crew arrived as Goodman entered the capitol.

The governor was too busy to meet with him, Mona Stark explained gravely, but Mr Larramore could spare a few minutes. She looked a bit frazzled, and this pleased Goodman greatly. He followed her to Larramore's office where they found the lawyer on the phone. Goodman hoped it was one of his calls. He obediently took a seat. Mona closed the door and left them.

'Good morning,' Larramore said as he hung up.

Goodman nodded politely, and said, 'Thanks for the hearing. We didn't expect the governor to grant one, in light of what he said on Wednesday.'

'He's under a lot of pressure. We all are. Is your client willing to talk about his accomplice?'

'No. There's been no change.'

Larramore ran his fingers through his sticky hair and shook his head in frustration. 'Then what's the purpose of a clemency hearing? The governor is not going to budge on this, Mr Goodman.'

'We're working on Sam, okay. We're talking to him. Let's plan on going through with the hearing on Monday. Maybe Sam will change his mind.'

The phone rang and Larramore snatched it angrily. 'No, this is not the governor's office. Who is this?' He scribbled down a name and phone number. 'This is the governor's legal department.' He closed his eyes and shook his head. 'Yes, yes, I'm sure you voted for the governor.' He listened

477

some more. 'Thank you, Mr Hurt. I'll tell the governor you called. Yes, thanks.'

He returned the receiver to the phone. 'So, Mr Gilbert Hurt from Dumas, Mississippi, is against the execution,' he said, staring at the phone, dazed. 'The phones have gone crazy.'

'Lots of calls, huh?' Goodman asked, sympathetically.

'You wouldn't believe.'

'For or against?'

'About fifty-fifty, I'd say,' Larramore said. He took the phone again and punched in the number for Mr Gilbert Hurt of Dumas, Mississippi. No one answered. 'This is strange,' he said, hanging up again. 'The man just called me, left a legitimate number, now there's no answer.'

'Probably just stepped out. Try again later.' Goodman hoped he wouldn't have the time to try again later. In the first hour of the market analysis yesterday, Goodman had made a slight change in technique. He had instructed his callers to first check the phone numbers to make certain there was no answer. This prevented some curious type such as Larramore or perhaps a nosy hotline operator from calling back and finding the real person. Odds were the real person would greatly support the death penalty. It slowed things a bit for the market analysts, but Goodman felt safer with it.

'I'm working on an outline for the hearing,' Larramore said, 'just in case. We'll probably have it in the House Ways and Means Committee Room, just down the hall.'

'Will it be closed?'

'No. Is this a problem?'

'We have four days left, Mr Larramore. Everything's a problem. But the hearing belongs to the governor. We're just thankful he's granted one.'

'I have your numbers. Keep in touch.'

'I'm not leaving Jackson until this is over.'

They shook hands quickly and Goodman left the office. He sat on the front steps for half an hour and watched the Klansmen get organized and attract the curious.

FORTY-TWO

THOUGH HE'D WORN a white robe and pointed hood as a much younger man, Donnie Cayhall kept his distance from the lines of Klansmen patrolling the grassy strip near the front gate of Parchman. Security was tight, with armed guards watching the protestors. Next to the canopy where the Klansmen gathered was a small group of skinheads in brown shirts. They held signs demanding freedom for Sam Cayhall.

Donnie watched the spectacle for a moment, then followed the directions of a security guard and parked along the highway. His name was checked at the guardhouse, and a few minutes later a prison van came for him. His brother had been at Parchman for nine and a half years, and Donnie had tried to visit at least once a year. But the last visit had been two years ago, he was ashamed to admit.

Donnie Cayhall was sixty-one, the youngest of the four Cayhall brothers. All had followed the teachings of their father and joined the Klan in their teens. It had been a simple decision with little thought given to it, one expected by the entire family. Later he had joined the Army, fought in Korea, and traveled the world. In the process, he had lost interest in wearing robes and burning crosses. He left Mississippi in 1961, and went to work for a furniture company in North Carolina. He now lived near Durham.

Every month for nine and a half years, he had shipped to Sam a box of cigarettes and a small amount of cash. He'd written a few letters, but neither he nor Sam were interested in correspondence. Few people in Durham knew he had a brother on death row.

He was frisked inside the front door, and shown to the front office. Sam was brought in a few minutes later, and they were left alone. Donnie hugged him for a long time, and when they released each other both had moist eyes. They were of similar height and build, though Sam looked twenty years older. He sat on the edge of the desk and Donnie took a chair nearby.

Both lit cigarettes and stared into space.

'Any good news?' Donnie finally asked, certain of the answer.

'No. None. The courts are turning everything down. They're gonna do it, Donnie. They're gonna kill me. They'll walk me to the chamber and gas me like an animal.'

Donnie's face fell to his chest. 'I'm sorry, Sam.'

'I'm sorry too, but, dammit, I'll be glad when it's over.'

'Don't say that.'

'I mean it. I'm tired of living in a cage. I'm an old man and my time has come.'

'But you don't deserve to be killed, Sam.'

'That's the hardest part, you know. It's not that I'm gonna die, hell, we're all dying. I just can't stand the thought of these jackasses getting the best of me. They're gonna win. And their reward is to strap me in and watch me choke. It's sick.'

'Can't your lawyer do something?'

'He's trying everything, but it looks hopeless. I want you to meet him.'

'I saw his picture in the paper. He doesn't resemble our people.'

'He's lucky. He looks more like his mother.'

'Sharp kid?'

Sam managed a smile. 'Yeah, he's pretty terrific. He's really grieving over this.'

'Will he be here today?'

'Probably. I haven't heard from him. He's staying with Lee in Memphis,' Sam said with a touch of pride. Because

480

of him, his daughter and his grandson had become close and were actually living together peacefully.

'I talked to Albert this morning,' Donnie said. 'He says he's too sick to come over.'

'Good. I don't want him here. And I don't want his kids and grandkids here either.'

'He wants to pay his respects, but he can't.'

'Tell him to save it for the funeral.'

'Come on, Sam.'

'Look, no one's gonna cry for me when I'm dead. I don't want a lot of false pity before then.'

'I need something from you, Donnie. And it'll cost a little money.'

'Sure. Anything.'

Sam pulled at the waist of his red jumpsuit. 'You see this damned thing. They're called reds, and I've worn them every day for almost ten years. This is what the State of Mississippi expects me to wear when it kills me. But, you see, I have the right to wear anything I want. It would mean a lot if I die in some nice clothes.'

Donnie was suddenly hit with emotion. He tried to speak, but words didn't come. His eyes were wet and his lip quivered. He nodded, and managed to say, 'Sure, Sam.'

'You know those work pants called Dickies? I wore them for years. Sort of like khakis.'

Donnie was still nodding.

'A pair of them would be nice, with a white shirt of some sort, not a pullover but one with buttons on it. Small shirt, small pants, thirty-two in the waist. A pair of white socks, and some kind of cheap shoes. Hell, I'll just wear them once, won't I? Go to Wal-Mart or some place and you can probably get the whole thing for less than thirty bucks. Do you mind?'

Donnie wiped his eyes and tried to smile. 'No, Sam.'

'I'll be a dude, won't I?'

'Where will you be buried?'

'Clanton, next to Anna. I'm sure that'll upset her peaceful rest. Adam's taking care of the arrangements.'

'What else can I do?'

'Nothing. If you'll just get me a change of clothes.'

'I'll do it today.'

'You're the only person in the world who's cared about me all these years, do you know that? Aunt Barb wrote me for years before she died, but her letters were always stiff and dry, and I figured she was doing it so she could tell her neighbors.'

'Who the hell was Aunt Barb?'

'Hubert Cain's mother. I'm not even sure she's related to us. I hardly knew her until I arrived here, then she started this awful correspondence. She was just all tore up by the fact that one of her own had been sent to Parchman.'

'May she rest in peace.'

Sam chuckled, and was reminded of an ancient childhood story. He told it with great enthusiasm, and minutes later both brothers were laughing loudly. Donnie was reminded of another tale, and so it went for an hour.

BY THE TIME Adam arrived late Saturday afternoon, Donnie had been gone for hours. He was taken to the front office, where he spread some papers on the desk. Sam was brought in, his handcuffs removed, and the door was closed behind them. He held more envelopes, which Adam noticed immediately.

'More errands for me?' he asked suspiciously.

'Yeah, but they can wait until it's over.'

'To whom?'

'One is to the Pinder family I bombed in Vicksburg. One is to the Jewish synagogue I bombed in Jackson. One is to the Jewish real estate agent, also in Jackson. There may be others. No hurry, since I know you're busy right now. But after I'm gone, I'd appreciate it if you'd take care of them.'

'What do these letters say?'

'What do you think they say?'

'I don't know. That you're sorry, I guess.'

'Smart boy. I apologize for my deeds, repent of my sins, and ask them to forgive me.'

'Why are you doing this?'

Sam stopped and leaned on a file cabinet. 'Because I sit in a little cage all day. Because I have a typewriter and plenty of paper. I'm bored as hell, okay, so maybe I want to write. Because I have a conscience, not much of one, but it's there, and the closer I get to death the guiltier I feel about the things I've done.'

'I'm sorry. They'll be delivered.' Adam circled something on his checklist. 'We have two appeals left. The Fifth Circuit is sitting on the ineffectiveness claim. I expected something by now, but there's been no movement for two days. The district court has the mental claim.'

'It's all hopeless, Adam.'

'Maybe, but I'm not quitting. I'll file a dozen more petitions if I have to.'

'I'm not signing anything else. You can't file them if I don't sign them.'

'Yes, I can. There are ways.'

'Then you're fired.'

'You can't fire me, Sam. I'm your grandson.'

'We have an agreement saying I can fire you whenever I want. We put it in writing.'

'It's a flawed document, drafted by a decent jailhouse lawyer, but fatally defective nonetheless.'

Sam huffed and puffed and began striding again on his row of tiles. He made half a dozen passes in front of Adam, his lawyer now, tomorrow, and for the remainder of his life. He knew he couldn't fire him.

'We have a clemency hearing scheduled for Monday,' Adam said, looking at his legal pad and waiting for the explosion. But Sam took it well and never missed a step.

'What's the purpose of the clemency hearing?' he asked.

'To appeal for clemency.'

'Appeal to whom?'

'The governor.'

'And you think the governor will consider granting me clemency?'

'What's there to lose?'

483

'Answer the question, smartass. Do you, with all your training, experience, and judicial brilliance, seriously expect this governor to entertain ideas of granting me clemency?'

'Maybe.'

'Maybe my ass. You're stupid.'

'Thank you, Sam.'

'Don't mention it.' He stopped directly in front of Adam and pointed a crooked finger at him. 'I've told you from the very beginning that I, as the client and as such certainly entitled to some consideration, will have nothing to do with David McAllister. I will not appeal to that fool for clemency. I will not ask him for a pardon. I will have no contact with him, whatsoever. Those are my wishes, and I made this very plain to you, young man, from day one. You, on the other hand, as the lawyer, have ignored my wishes and gone about your merry business doing whatever the hell you wanted. You are the lawyer, nothing more or less. I, on the other hand, am the client, and I don't know what they taught you in your fancy law school, but I make the decisions.'

Sam walked to an empty chair and picked up another envelope. He handed it to Adam, and said, 'This is a letter to the governor requesting him to cancel the clemency hearing on Monday. If you refuse to get it canceled, then I will make copies of this and give it to the press. I will embarrass you, Garner Goodman, and the governor. Do you understand?'

'Plain enough.'

Sam returned the envelope to the chair, and lit another cigarette.

Adam made another circle on his list. 'Carmen will be here Monday. I'm not sure about Lee.'

Sam eased to a chair and sat down. He did not look at Adam. 'Is she still in rehab?'

'Yes, and I'm not sure when she'll get out. Do you want her to visit?'

'Let me think about it.'

484

'Think fast, okay.'

'Funny, real funny. My brother Donnie stopped by earlier. He's my youngest brother, you know. He wants to meet you.'

'Was he in the Klan?'

'What kind of question is that?'

'It's a simple yes or no question.'

'Yes. He was in the Klan.'

'Then I don't want to meet him.'

'He's not a bad guy.'

'I'll take your word for it.'

'He's my brother, Adam. I want you to meet my brother.'

'I have no desire to meet new Cayhalls, Sam, especially ones who wore robes and hoods.'

'Oh, really. Three weeks ago you wanted to know everything about the family. Just couldn't get enough of it.'

'I surrender, okay? I've heard enough.'

'Oh, there's lots more.'

'Enough, enough. Spare me.'

Sam grunted and smiled smugly to himself. Adam glanced at his legal pad, and said, 'You'll be happy to know that the Kluckers outside have now been joined by some Nazis and Aryans and skinheads and other hate groups. They're all lined along the highway, waving posters at cars passing by. The posters, of course, demand the freedom of Sam Cayhall, their hero. It's a regular circus.'

'I saw it on television.'

'They're also marching in Jackson around the state capitol.'

'This is my fault?'

'No. It's your execution. You're a symbol now. About to become a martyr.'

'What am I supposed to do?'

'Nothing. Just go ahead and die, and they'll all be happy.'

'Aren't you an asshole today?'

'Sorry, Sam. The pressure's getting to me.'

'Throw in the towel. I have. I highly recommend it.'

'Forget it. I've got these clowns on the run, Sam. I have not yet begun to fight.'

'Yeah, you've filed three petitions, and a total of seven courts have turned you down. Zero for seven. I hate to see what'll happen when you really get cranked up.' Sam said this with a wicked smile, and the humor found its mark. Adam laughed at it, and both breathed a bit easier. 'I have this great idea for a lawsuit after you're gone,' he said, feigning excitement.

'After I'm gone?'

'Sure. We'll sue them for wrongful death. We'll name McAllister, Nugent, Roxburgh, the State of Mississippi. We'll bring in everybody.'

'It's never been done,' Sam said, stroking his beard, as if deep in thought.

'Yeah, I know. Thought of it all by myself. We might not win a dime, but think of the fun I'll have harassing those bastards for the next five years.'

'You have permission to file it. Sue them!'

The smiles slowly disappeared and the humor was gone. Adam found something else on his checklist. 'Just a couple more items. Lucas Mann asked me to ask you about your witnesses. You're entitled to have two people in the witness room, in case this gets that far.'

'Donnie doesn't want to do it. I will not allow you to be there. I can't imagine anybody else who'd want to see it.'

'Fine. Speaking of them, I have at least thirty requests for interviews. Virtually every major paper and news magazine wants access.'

'No.'

'Fine. Remember that writer we discussed last time, Wendall Sherman? The one who wants to record your story on tape and –'

'Yeah. For fifty thousand bucks.'

'Now it's a hundred thousand. His publisher will put up the money. He wants to get everything on tape, watch the execution, do extensive research, then write a big book about it.'

'No.'

'Fine.'

'I don't want to spend the next three days talking about my life. I don't want some stranger poking his nose around Ford County. And don't particularly need a hundred thousand dollars at this point in my life.'

'Fine with me. You once mentioned the clothing you wanted to wear –'

'Donnie's taking care of it.'

'Okay. Moving right along. Barring a stay, you're allowed to have two people with you during your final hours. Typically, the prison has a form for you to sign designating these people.'

'It's always the lawyer and the minister, right?'

'That's correct.'

'Then it's you, and Ralph Griffin, I guess.'

Adam filled the names in on the form. 'Who's Ralph Griffin?'

'The new minister here. He's opposed to the death penalty, can you believe it? His predecessor thought we should all be gassed, in the name of Jesus, of course.'

Adam handed the form to Sam. 'Sign here.'

Sam scribbled his name and handed it back.

'You're entitled to a last conjugal visit.'

Sam laughed loudly. 'Come on, son. I'm an old man.'

'It's on the checklist, okay. Lucas Mann whispered to me the other day that I should mention it to you.'

'Okay. You've mentioned it.'

'I have another form here for your personal effects. Who gets them?'

'You mean my estate?'

'Sort of.'

'This is morbid as hell, Adam. Why are we doing this now?'

'I'm a lawyer, Sam. We get paid to sweat the details. It's just paperwork.'

487

'Do you want my things?'

Adam thought about this for a moment. He didn't want to hurt Sam's feelings, but at the same time he couldn't imagine what he'd do with a few ragged old garments, worn books, portable television, and rubber shower shoes. 'Sure,' he said.

'Then they're yours. Take them and burn them.'

'Sign here,' Adam said, shoving the form under his face. Sam signed it, then jumped to his feet and started pacing again. 'I really want you to meet Donnie.'

'Sure. Whatever you want,' Adam said, stuffing his legal pad and the forms into his briefcase. The nitpicking details were now complete. The briefcase seemed much heavier.

'I'll be back in the morning,' he said to Sam.

'Bring me some good news, okay.'

COLONEL NUGENT strutted along the edge of the highway with a dozen armed prison guards behind him. He glared at the Klansmen, twenty-six at last count, and he scowled at the brown-shirted Nazis, ten in all. He stopped and stared at the group of skinheads mingling next to the Nazis. He swaggered around the edge of the grassy protest strip, pausing for a moment to speak to two Catholic nuns sitting under a large umbrella, as far away from the other demonstrators as possible. The temperature was one hundred degrees, and the nuns were broiling under the shade. They sipped ice water, their posters resting on their knees and facing the highway.

The nuns asked him who he was and what he wanted. He explained that he was the acting warden for the prison, and that he was simply making sure the demonstration was orderly.

They asked him to leave.

FORTY-THREE

PER.IAPS IT WAS BECAUSE it was Sunday, or maybe it was the rain, but Adam drank his morning coffee in unexpected serenity. It was still dark outside, and the gentle dripping of a warm, summer shower on the patio was mesmerizing. He stood in the open door and listened to the splashing of the raindrops. It was too early for traffic on Riverside Drive below. There were no noises from the tugboats on the river. All was quiet and peaceful.

And there wasn't a heckuva lot to be done this day, Day Three before the execution. He would start at the office, where another last minute petition had to be organized. The issue was so ridiculous Adam was almost embarrassed to file it. Then he would drive to Parchman and sit with Sam for a spell.

It was unlikely there would be movement by any court on Sunday. It was certainly possible since the death clerks and their staffs were on call when an execution was looming. But Friday and Saturday had passed without rulings coming down, and he expected the same inactivity today. Tomorrow would be much different, in his untrained and untested opinion.

Tomorrow would be nothing but frenzy. And Tuesday, which of course was scheduled to be Sam's last day as a breathing soul, would be a nightmare of stress.

But this Sunday morning was remarkably calm. He had slept almost seven hours, another recent record. His head was clear, his pulse normal, his breathing relaxed. His mind was uncluttered and composed.

He flipped through the Sunday paper, scanning the headlines but reading nothing. There were at least two stories about the Cayhall execution, one with more pictures of the growing circus outside the prison gate. The rain stopped when the sun came up, and he sat in a wet rocker for an hour scanning Lee's architectural magazines. After a couple of hours of peace and tranquility, Adam was bored and ready for action.

There was unfinished business in Lee's bedroom, a matter Adam had tried to forget but couldn't. For ten days now, a silent battle had raged in his soul over the book in her drawer. She'd been drunk when she told him about the lynching photo, but it was not the delirious talk of an addict. Adam knew the book existed. There was a real book with a real photo of a young black man hanging by a rope, and somewhere under his feet was a crowd of proud white people, mugging for the camera, immune from prosecution. Adam had mentally pieced the pictured together, adding faces, sketching the tree, drawing the rope, adding titles to the space under it. But there were some things he didn't know, he couldn't visualize. Was the dead man's face perceptible? Was he wearing shoes, or barefoot? Was a very young Sam easily recognizable? How many white faces were in the photo? And how old were they? Any women? Any guns? Blood? Lee said he'd been bullwhipped. Was the whip in the photo? He had imagined the picture for days now, and it was time to finally look in the book. He couldn't wait until later. Lee might make a triumphant return. She might move the book, hide it again. He planned to spend the next two or three nights here, but that could change with one phone call. He could be forced to rush to Jackson or sleep in his car at Parchman. Such routine matters as lunch and dinner and sleeping were suddenly unpredictable when your client had less than a week to live.

This was the perfect moment, and he decided that he was now ready to face the lynch mob. He walked to the front door and scanned the parking lot, just to make sure she hadn't decided to drop in. He actually locked the door to her bedroom, and pulled open the top drawer. It was filled with her lingerie, and he was embarrassed for this intrusion.

The book was in the third drawer, lying on top of a faded sweatshirt. It was thick and bound in green fabric – *Southern Negroes and the Great Depression*. Published in 1947 by Toffler Press, Pittsburgh. Adam clutched it and sat on the edge of her bed. The pages were immaculate and pristine, as if the book had never been handled or read. Who in the Deep South would read such a book anyway? And if the book had been in the Cayhall family for several decades, then Adam was positive it had never been read. He studied the binder and pondered what set of circumstances brought this particular book into the custody of the Sam Cayhall family.

The book had three sections of photos. The first was a series of pictures of shotgun houses and ramshackle sheds where blacks were forced to live on plantations. There were family portraits on front porches with dozens of children, and there were the obligatory shots of farm workers stooped low in the fields picking cotton.

The second section was in the center of the book, and ran for twenty pages. There were actually two lynching photos, the first a horribly gruesome scene with two robed and hooded Kluckers holding rifles and posing for the camera. A badly beaten black man swung from a rope behind them, his eyes half open, his face pulverized and bloody. KKK lynching, Central Mississippi, 1939, explained the caption under it, as if these rituals could be defined simply by locale and time.

Adam gaped at the horror of the picture, then turned the page to find the second lynching scene, this one almost tame compared to the first. The lifeless body at the end of the rope could be seen only from the chest down. The shirt appeared to be torn, probably by the bullwhip, if in fact one had been used. The black man was very thin, his oversized pants drawn tightly at the waist. He was barefoot. No blood was visible.

The rope that held his body could be seen tied to a lower branch in the background. The tree was large with bulky limbs and a massive trunk.

A festive group had gathered just inches under his dangling feet. Men, women, and boys clowned for the camera, some striking exaggerated poses of anger and manliness – hard frowns, fierce eyes, tight lips, as if they possessed unlimited power to protect their women from Negro aggression; others smiled and seemed to be giggling, especially the women, two of whom were quite pretty; a small boy held a pistol and aimed it menacingly at the camera; a young man held a bottle of liquor, twisted just so to reveal the label. Most of the group seemed quite joyous that this event had occurred. Adam counted seventeen people in the group, and every single one was staring at the camera without shame or worry, without the slightest hint a wrong had been committed. They were utterly immune from prosecution. They had just killed another human, and it was painfully obvious they had done so with no fear of the consequences.

This was a party. It was at night, the weather was warm, liquor was present, pretty women. Surely they'd brought food in baskets and were about to throw quilts on the ground for a nice picnic around the tree.

Lynching in rural Mississippi, 1936, read the caption.

Sam was in the front row, crouched and resting on a knee between two other young men, all three posing hard for the camera. He was fifteen or sixteen, with a slender face that was trying desperately to appear dangerous – lip curled, eyebrows pinched, chin up. The cocky braggadocio of a boy trying to emulate the more mature thugs around him.

He was easy to spot because someone had drawn, in faded blue ink, a line across the photo to the margin where the name Sam Cayhall was printed in block letters. The line crossed the bodies and faces of others and stopped at Sam's left ear. Eddie. It had to be Eddie. Lee said that Eddie had found this book in the attic, and Adam could see his father hiding in the darkness, weeping over the photograph, identifying Sam by pointing the accusatory arrow at his head.

Lee also had said that Sam's father was the leader of this ragtag little mob, but Adam couldn't distinguish him. Perhaps Eddie couldn't either because there were no markings. There were at least seven men old enough to be Sam's father. How many of these people were Cayhalls? She'd also said that his brothers were involved, and perhaps one of the younger men resembled Sam, but it was impossible to tell for certain.

He studied the clear, beautiful eyes of his grandfather, and his heart ached. He was just a boy, born and reared in a household where hatred of blacks and others was simply a way of life. How much of it could be blamed on him? Look at those around him, his father, family, friends and neighbors, all probably honest, poor, hardworking people caught for the moment at the end of a cruel ceremony that was commonplace in their society. Sam didn't have a chance. This was the only world he knew.

How would Adam ever reconcile the past with the present? How could he fairly judge these people and their horrible deed when, but for a quirk of fate, he would've been right there in the middle of them had he been born forty years earlier?

As he looked at their faces, an odd comfort engulfed him. Though Sam was obviously a willing participant, he was only one member of the mob, only partly guilty. Clearly, the older men with the stern faces had instigated the lynching, and the rest had come along for the occasion. Looking at the photo, it was inconceivable to think that Sam and his younger buddies had initiated this brutality. Sam had done nothing to stop it. But maybe he had done nothing to encourage it.

The scene produced a hundred unanswered questions. Who was the photographer, and how did he happen to be there with his camera? Who was the young black man?

493

Where was his family, his mother? How'd they catch him? Had he been in jail and released by the authorities to the mob? What did they do with his body when it was over? Was the alleged rape victim one of the young women smiling at the camera? Was her father one of the men? Her brothers?

If Sam was lynching at such an early age, what could be expected of him as an adult? How often did these folks gather and celebrate like this in rural Mississippi?

How in God's world could Sam Cayhall have become anything other than himself? He never had a chance.

SAM WAITED PATIENTLY in the front office, sipping coffee from a different pot. It was strong and rich, unlike the watered-down brew they served the inmates each morning. Packer had given it to him in a large paper cup. Sam sat on the desk with his feet on a chair.

The door opened and Colonel Nugent marched inside with Packer behind. The door was closed. Sam stiffened and snapped off a smart salute.

'Good morning, Sam,' Nugent said somberly. 'How you doing?'

'Fabulous. You?'

'Getting by.'

'Yeah, I know you gotta lot on your mind. This is tough on you, trying to arrange my execution and making sure it goes real smooth. Tough job. My hat's off to you.'

Nugent ignored the sarcasm. 'Need to talk to you about a few things. Your lawyers now say you're crazy, and I just wanted to see for myself how you're doing.'

'I feel like a million bucks.'

'Well, you certainly look fine.'

'Gee thanks. You look right spiffy yourself. Nice boots.'

The black combat boots were sparkling, as usual. Packer glanced down at them and grinned.

'Yes,' Nugent said, sitting in a chair and looking at a sheet of paper. 'The psychiatrist said you're uncooperative.'

494

'Who? N.?'

'Dr Stegall.'

'That big lard-ass gal with an incomplete first name? I've only talked to her once.'

'Were you uncooperative?'

'I certainly hope so. I've been here for almost ten years, and she finally trots her big ass over here when I've got one foot in the grave to see how I'm getting along. All she wanted to do was give me some dope so I'll be stoned when you clowns come after me. Makes your job easier, doesn't it.'

'She was only trying to help.'

'Then God bless her. Tell her I'm sorry. It'll never happen again. Write me up with an RVR. Put it in my file.'

'We need to talk about your last meal.'

'Why is Packer in here?'

Nugent glanced at Packer, then looked at Sam. 'Because it's procedure.'

'He's here to protect you, isn't he? You're afraid of me. You're scared to be left alone with me in this room, aren't you, Nugent? I'm almost seventy years old, feeble as hell, half dead from cigarettes, and you're afraid of me, a convicted murderer.'

'Not in the least.'

'I'd stomp your ass all over this room, Nugent, if I wanted to.'

'I'm terrified. Look, Sam, let's get down to business. What would you like for your last meal?'

'This is Sunday. My last meal is scheduled for Tuesday night. Why are you bothering me with it now?'

'We have to make plans. You can have anything, within reason.'

'Who's gonna cook it?'

'It'll be prepared in the kitchen here.'

'Oh, wonderful! By the same talented chefs who've been feeding me hogslop for nine and a half years. What a way to go!'

'What would you like, Sam? I'm trying to be reasonable.'

'How about toast and boiled carrots? I'd hate to burden them with something new.'

'Fine, Sam. When you decide, tell Packer here and he'll notify the kitchen.'

'There won't be a last meal, Nugent. My lawyer will unload the heavy artillery tomorrow. You clowns won't know what hit you.'

'I hope you're right.'

'You're a lying sonofabitch. You can't wait to walk me in there and strap me down. You're giddy with the thought of asking me if I have any last words, then nodding at one of your gophers to lock the door. And when it's all over, you'll face the press with a sad face and announce that "As of twelve-fifteen, this morning, August 8, Sam Cayhall was executed in the gas chamber here at Parchman, pursuant to an order of the Circuit Court of Lakehead County, Mississippi." It'll be your finest hour, Nugent. Don't lie to me.'

The colonel never looked from the sheet of paper. 'We need your list of witnesses.'

'See my lawyer.'

'And we need to know what to do with your things.'

'See my lawyer.'

'Okay. We have numerous requests for interviews from the press.'

'See my lawyer.'

Nugent jumped to his feet and stormed from the office. Packer caught the door, waited a few seconds, then calmly said, 'Sit tight, Sam, there's someone else to see you.'

Sam smiled and winked at Packer. 'Then get me some more coffee, would you Packer?'

Packer took the cup, and returned with it a few minutes later. He also handed Sam the Sunday paper from Jackson, and Sam was reading all sorts of stories about his execution when the chaplain, Ralph Griffin, knocked and entered.

Sam placed the paper on the desk and inspected the minister. Griffin wore white sneakers, faded jeans, and a black shirt with a white clerical collar. 'Mornin', Reverend,' Sam said, sipping his coffee.

'How are you, Sam?' Griffin asked as he pulled a chair very near the desk and sat in it.

'Right now my heart's filled with hate,' Sam said gravely.

'I'm sorry. Who's it directed at?'

'Colonel Nugent. But I'll get over it.'

'Have you been praying, Sam?'

'Not really.'

'Why not?'

'What's the hurry? I have today, tomorrow, and Tuesday. I figure you and I'll be doing lots of praying come Tuesday night.'

'If you want. It's up to you. I'll be here.'

'I want you to be with me up to the last moment, Reverend, if you don't mind. You and my lawyer. Y'all are allowed to sit with me during the last hours.'

'I'd be honored.'

'Thanks.'

'What exactly do you want to pray about, Sam?'

Sam took a long drink of coffee. 'Well, first of all, I'd like to know that when I leave this world, all the bad things I've done have been forgiven.'

'Your sins?'

'That's right.'

'God expects us to confess our sins to him and ask for forgiveness.'

'All of them? One at a time?'

'Yes, the ones we can remember.'

'Then we'd better start now. It'll take a while.'

'As you wish. What else would you like to pray for?'

'My family, such as it is. This will be hard on my grandson, and my brother, and maybe my daughter. There won't be a lot of tears shed for me, you understand, but I would like for them to be comforted. And I'd like to say a prayer for my friends here on the Row. They'll take it hard.'

'Anyone else?'

'Yeah. I want to say a good prayer for the Kramers, especially Ruth.'

'The family of the victims?'

'That's right. And also the Lincolns.'

'Who are the Lincolns?'

'It's a long story. More victims.'

'This is good, Sam. You need to get this off your chest, to cleanse your soul.'

'It'll take years to cleanse my soul, Reverend.'

'More victims?'

Sam sat the cup on the desk and gently rubbed his hands together. He searched the warm and trusting eyes of Ralph Griffin. 'What if there are other victims?' he asked.

'Dead people?'

Sam nodded, very slowly.

'People you've killed?'

Sam kept nodding.

Griffin took a deep breath, and contemplated matters for a moment. 'Well, Sam, to be perfectly honest, I wouldn't want to die without confessing these sins and asking God for forgiveness.'

Sam kept nodding.

'How many?' Griffin asked.

Sam slid off the desk and eased into his shower shoes. He slowly lit a cigarette, and began pacing back and forth behind Griffin's chair. The reverend changed positions so he could watch and hear Sam.

'There was Joe Lincoln, but I've already written a letter to his family and told them I was sorry.'

'You killed him?'

'Yes. He was an African. Lived on our place. I always felt bad about it. It was around 1950.'

Sam stopped and leaned on a file cabinet. He spoke to the floor, as if in a daze. 'And there were two men, white men, who killed my father at a funeral, many years ago. They served some time in jail, and when they got out, me and my brothers waited patiently. We killed both of them, but I never felt bad about it, to be honest. They were scum, and they'd killed our father.'

'Killing is always wrong, Sam. You're fighting your own legal killing right now.'

498

'I know.'

'Did you and your brothers get caught?'

'No. The old sheriff suspected us, but he couldn't prove anything. We were too careful. Besides, they were real lowlifes, and nobody cared.'

'That doesn't make it right.'

'I know. I always figured they deserved what they got, then I was sent to this place. Life has new meaning when you're on death row. You realize how valuable it is. Now I'm sorry I killed those boys. Real sorry.'

'Anybody else?'

Sam walked the length of the room, counting each step, and returned to the file cabinet. The minister waited. Time meant nothing right now.

'There were a couple of lynchings, years ago,' Sam said, unable to look Griffin in the eyes.

'Two?'

'I think. Maybe three. No, yes, there were three, but at the first one I was just a kid, a small boy, and all I did was watch, you know, from the bushes. It was Klan lynching, and my father was involved in it, and me and my brother Albert sneaked into the woods and watched it. So that doesn't count, does it?'

'No.'

Sam's shoulders sank against the wall. He closed his eyes and lowered his head. 'The second one was a regular mob. I was about fifteen, I guess, and I was right in the middle of it. A girl got raped by an African, at least she said it was a rape. Her reputation left a lot to be desired, and two years later she had a baby that was half-African. So who knows? Anyway, she pointed the finger, we got the boy, took him out, and lynched him. I was as guilty as the rest of the mob.'

'God will forgive you, Sam.'

'Are you sure?'

'I'm positive.'

'How many murders will he forgive?'

'All of them. If you sincerely ask forgiveness, then he'll wipe the slate clean. It's in the Scriptures.'

499

'That's too good to be true.'

'What about the other lynching?'

Sam began shaking his head, back and forth, eyes closed. 'Now, I can't talk about that one, preacher,' he said, exhaling heavily.

'You don't have to talk to me about it, Sam. Just talk to God.'

'I don't know if I can talk to anybody about it.'

'Sure you can. Just close your eyes one night, between now and Tuesday, while you're in your cell, and confess all those deeds to God. He'll instantly forgive you.'

'Just doesn't seem right, you know. You kill someone, then in a matter of minutes God forgives you. Just like that. It's too easy.'

'You must be truly sorry.'

'Oh, I am. I swear.'

'God forgets about it, Sam, but man does not. We answer to God, but we also answer to the laws of man. God will forgive you, but you suffer the consequences according to the dictates of the government.'

'Screw the government. I'm ready to check outta here anyway.'

'Well, let's make sure you're ready, okay?'

Sam walked to the desk and sat on the corner next to Griffin. 'You stick close, okay, Reverend? I'll need some help. There's some bad things buried in my soul. It might take some time to get them out.'

'It won't be hard, Sam, if you're really ready.'

Sam patted him on the knee. 'Just stick close, okay?'

FORTY-FOUR

THE FRONT OFFICE was filled with blue smoke when Adam entered. Sam was puffing away on the desk, reading about himself in the Sunday paper. Three empty coffee cups and several candy wrappers littered the desk. 'You've made yourself at home, haven't you?' Adam said, noticing the debris.

'Yeah, I've been here all day.'

'Lots of guests?'

'I wouldn't call them guests. The day started with Nugent, so that pretty well ruined things. The minister stopped by to see if I've been praying. I think he was depressed when he left. Then the doctor came by to make sure I'm fit enough to kill. Then my brother Donnie stopped by for a short visit. I really want you to meet him. Tell me you've brought some good news.'

Adam shook his head and sat down. 'No. Nothing's changed since yesterday. The courts have taken the week-end off.'

'Do they realize that Saturdays and Sundays count? That the clock doesn't stop ticking for me on the weekends?'

'It could be good news. They could be considering my brilliant appeals.'

'Maybe, but I suspect the honorable brethren are more likely at their lake homes drinking beer and cooking ribs. Don't you think?'

'Yeah, you're probably right. What's in the paper?'

'Same old rehash of me and my brutal crime, pictures of

501

those people out front demonstrating, comments from McAllister. Nothing new. I've never seen such excitement.'

'You're the man of the hour, Sam. Wendall Sherman and his publisher are now at a hundred and fifty thousand, but the deadline is six o'clock tonight. He's in Memphis, sitting with his tape recorders, just itching to get down here. He says he'll need at least two full days to record your story.'

'Great. What exactly am I supposed to do with the money?'

'Leave it to your precious grandchildren.'

'Are you serious? Will you spend it? I'll do it if you'll spend it.'

'No. I'm just kidding. I don't want the money, and Carmen doesn't need it. I couldn't spend it with a clear conscience.'

'Good. Because the last thing I wanna do between now and Tuesday night is to sit with a stranger and talk about the past. I don't care how much money he has. I'd rather not have a book written about my life.'

'I've already told him to forget it.'

'Atta boy.' Sam eased to his feet and began walking back and forth across the room. Adam took his place on the edge of the desk and read the sports section of the Memphis paper.

'I'll be glad when it's over, Adam,' Sam said, still walking, talking with his hands. 'I can't stand this waiting. I swear I wish it was tonight.' He was suddenly nervous and irritable, his voice louder.

Adam placed the paper to his side. 'We're gonna win, Sam. Trust me.'

'Win what!' he snapped angrily. 'Win a reprieve? Big deal! What do we gain from that? Six months? A year? You know what that means? It means we'll get to do this again someday. I'll go through the whole damned ritual again – counting days, losing sleep, plotting last minute strategies, listening to Nugent or some other fool, talking to the shrink, whispering to the chaplain, being patted on the ass

502

and led up here to this cubbyhole because I'm special.' He stopped in front of Adam and glared down at him. His face was angry, his eyes wet and bitter. 'I'm sick of this, Adam! Listen to me! This is worse than dying.'

'We can't quit, Sam.'

'We? Who the hell is we? It's my neck on the line, not yours. If I get a stay, then you'll go back to your fancy office in Chicago and get on with your life. You'll be the hero because you saved your client. You'll get your picture in *Lawyer's Quarterly*, or whatever you guys read. The bright young star who kicked ass in Mississippi. Saved his grandfather, a wretched Klucker, by the way. Your client, on the other hand, is led back to his little cage where he starts counting days again.' Sam threw his cigarette on the floor and grabbed Adam by the shoulders. 'Look at me, son. I can't go through this again. I want you to stop everything. Drop it. Call the courts and tell them we're dismissing all the petitions and appeals. I'm an old man. Please allow me to die with dignity.'

His hands were shaking. His breathing was labored. Adam searched his brilliant blue eyes, surrounded with layers of dark wrinkles, and saw a stray tear ease out of one corner and fall slowly down his cheek until it vanished in the gray beard.

For the first time, Adam could smell his grandfather. The strong nicotine aroma mixed with an odor of dried perspiration to form a scent that was not pleasant. It was not repulsive, though, the way it would have been if radiated by a person with access to plenty of soap and hot water, air conditioning, and deodorant. After the second breath, it didn't bother Adam at all.

'I don't want you to die, Sam.'

Sam squeezed his shoulders harder. 'Why not?' he demanded.

'Because I've just found you. You're my grandfather.'

Sam stared for a second longer, then relaxed. He released Adam and took a step backward. 'I'm sorry you found me like this,' he said, wiping his eyes.

'Don't apologize.'

'But I have to. I'm sorry I'm not a better grandfather. Look at me,' he said, glancing down at his legs. 'A wretched old man in a red monkey suit. A convicted murderer about to be gassed like an animal. And look at you. A fine young man with a beautiful education and a bright future. Where in the world did I go wrong? What happened to me? I've spent my life hating people, and look what I have to show for it. You, you don't hate anybody. And look where you're headed. We have the same blood. Why am I here?'

Sam slowly sat in a chair, put his elbows on his knees, and covered his eyes. Neither moved or spoke for a long time. The occasional voice of a guard could be heard in the hall, but the room was quiet.

'You know, Adam, I'd rather not die in such an awful way,' Sam said hoarsely with his fists resting on his temples, still looking blankly at the floor. 'But death itself don't worry me now. I've known for a long time that I would die here, and my biggest fear was dying without knowing anyone would care. That's an awful thought, you know. Dying and nobody cares. There's nobody to cry and grieve, to mourn properly at the funeral and burial. I've had dreams where I saw my body in a cheap wooden casket lying in the funeral home in Clanton, and not a soul was in the room with me. Not even Donnie. In the same dream, the preacher chuckled through the funeral service because it was just the two of us, all alone in the chapel, rows and rows of empty pews. But that's different now. I know somebody cares about me. I know you'll be sad when I die because you care, and I know you'll be there when I'm buried to make sure it's done properly. I'm really ready to go now, Adam. I'm ready.'

'Fine, Sam, I respect that. And I promise I'll be there to the bitter end, and I'll grieve and mourn, and after it's over I'll make sure you're buried properly. No one's gonna screw around with you, Sam, as long as I'm here. But, please, look at it through my eyes. I have to give it my best shot, because I'm young and I've got the rest of my life.

504

Don't make me leave here knowing I could've done more. It's not fair to me.'

Sam folded his arms across his chest and looked at Adam. His pale face was calm, his eyes still wet. 'Let's do it this way,' he said, his voice still low and pained. 'I'm ready to go. I'll spend tomorrow and Tuesday night making final preparations. I'll assume it's gonna happen at midnight Tuesday, and I'll be ready for it. You, on the other hand, play it like a game. If you can win it, good for you. If you lose it, I'll be ready to face the music.'

'So you'll cooperate?'

'No. No clemency hearing. No more petitions or appeals. You have enough junk floating around out there to keep you busy. Two issues are still alive. I'm not signing any more petitions.'

Sam stood, his decrepit knees popping and wobbling. He walked to the door and leaned on it. 'What about Lee?' he asked softly, reaching for his cigarettes.

'She's still in rehab,' Adam lied. He was tempted to blurt out the truth. It seemed childish to be lying to Sam in these declining hours of his life, but Adam still held a strong hope that she would be found before Tuesday. 'Do you want to see her?'

'I think so. Can she get out?'

'It may be difficult, but I'll try. She's sicker than I first thought.'

'She's an alcoholic?'

'Yes.'

'Is that all? No drugs?'

'Just alcohol. She told me she's had a problem for many years. Rehab is nothing new.'

'Bless her heart. My children didn't have a chance.'

'She's a fine person. She's had a rough time with her marriage. Her son left home at an early age and never returned.'

'Walt, right?'

'Right,' Adam answered. What a heartbroken bunch of people. Sam was not even certain of the name of his grandson.

505

'How old is he?'

'I'm not sure. Probably close to my age.'

'Does he even know about me?'

'I don't know. He's been gone for many years. Lives in Amsterdam.'

Sam picked up a cup from the desk and took a drink of cold coffee. 'What about Carmen?' he asked.

Adam instinctively glanced at his watch. 'I pick her up at the Memphis airport in three hours. She'll be here in the morning.'

'That just scares the hell outta me.'

'Relax, Sam. She's a great person. She's smart, ambitious, pretty, and I've told her all about you.'

'Why'd you do that?'

'Because she wants to know.'

'Poor child. Did you tell her what I look like?'

'Don't worry about it, Sam. She doesn't care what you look like.'

'Did you tell her I'm not some savage monster?'

'I told her you were a sweetheart, a real dear, sort of a delicate little fella with an earring, a ponytail, limp wrist, and these cute little rubber shower shoes that you sort of glide in.'

'You kiss my ass!'

'And that you seemed a real favorite of the boys here in prison.'

'You're lying! You didn't tell her all that!' Sam was grinning, but half serious, and his concern was amusing. Adam laughed, a bit too long and a bit too loud, but the humor was welcome. They both chuckled and tried their best to seem thoroughly amused by their own wit. They tried to stretch it out, but soon the levity passed and gravity sank in. Soon they were sitting on the edge of the desk, side by side, feet on separate chairs, staring at the floor while heavy clouds of tobacco smoke boiled above them in the motionless air.

There was so much to talk about, yet there was so little to say. The legal theories and maneuverings had been beaten to death. Family was a subject they'd covered as much as they'd dared. The weather was good for no more than five minutes of conjecture. And both men knew they would spend much of the next two and a half days together. Serious matters could wait. Unpleasant subjects could be shoved back just a bit longer. Twice Adam glanced at his watch and said he'd best be going, and both times Sam insisted he stay. Because when Adam left, they would come for him and take him back to his cell, his little cage where the temperature was over a hundred. Please stay, he begged.

LATE THAT NIGHT, well after midnight, long after Adam had told Carmen about Lee and her problems, and about Phelps and Walt, about McAllister and Wyn Lettner, and the theory of the accomplice, hours after they'd finished a pizza and discussed their mother and father and grandfather and the whole pathetic bunch, Adam said the one moment he'd never forget was the two of them sitting there on the desk, passing time in silence as an invisible clock ticked away, with Sam patting him on the knee. It was like he had to touch me in some affectionate way, he explained to her, like a good grandfather would touch a small loved one.

Carmen had heard enough for one night. She'd been on the patio for four hours, suffering through the humidity and absorbing the desolate oral history of her father's family.

But Adam had been very careful. He'd hit the peaks and skipped the woeful valleys – no mention of Joe Lincoln or lynchings or sketchy hints of other crimes. He portrayed Sam as a violent man who made terrible mistakes and was now burdened with remorse. He had toyed with the idea of showing her his video of Sam's trials, but decided against it. He would do it later. She could handle only so much in one night. At times, he couldn't believe the things he'd heard in the past four weeks. It would be cruel to hit her with all of it in one sitting. He loved his sister dearly. They had years to discuss the rest of the story.

FORTY-FIVE

MONDAY, AUGUST 6, 6 A.M. Forty-two hours to go. Adam entered his office and locked the door.

He waited until seven, then called Slattery's office in Jackson. There was no answer, of course, but he was hoping for a recorded message that might direct him to another number that might lead to someone down there who could tell him something. Slattery was sitting on the mental claim; just ignoring it as if it was simply another little lawsuit.

He called information and received the home number for F. Flynne Slattery, but decided not to bother him. He could wait until nine.

Adam had slept less than three hours. His pulse was pounding, his adrenaline was pumping. His client was now down to the last forty-two hours, and dammit, Slattery should quickly rule one way or the other. It wasn't fair to sit on the damned petition when he could be racing off to other courts with it.

The phone rang and he lunged for it. The Death Clerk from the Fifth Circuit informed him that the court was denying the appeal of Sam's claim of ineffective assistance of counsel. It was the opinion of the court that the claim was procedurally barred. It should've been filed years ago. The court did not get to the merits of the issue.

'Then why'd the court sit on it for a week?' Adam demanded. 'They could've reached this nitpicking decision ten days ago.'

'I'll fax you a copy right now,' the clerk said.

'Thanks. I'm sorry, okay.'

'Keep in touch, Mr Hall. We'll be right here waiting on you.'

Adam hung up, and went to find coffee. Darlene arrived, tired, haggard, and early, at seven-thirty. She brought the fax from the Fifth Circuit, along with a raisin bagel. Adam asked her to fax to the U.S. Supreme Court the petition for cert on the ineffectiveness claim. It had been prepared for three days, and Mr Olander in Washington had told Darlene that the Court was already reviewing it.

Darlene then brought two aspirin and a glass of water. His head was splitting as he packed most of the Cayhall file into a large briefcase and a cardboard box. He gave Darlene a list of instructions.

Then he left the office, the Memphis branch of Kravitz & Bane, never to return.

COLONEL NUGENT waited impatiently for the tier door to open, then rushed into the hallway with eight members of his select execution team behind him. They swarmed into the quietness of Tier A with all the finesse of a Gestapo squad – eight large men, half in uniform, half plainclothed, following a strutting little rooster. He stopped at cell six, where Sam was lying on his bed, minding his own business. The other inmates were instantly watching and listening, their arms hanging through the bars.

'Sam, it's time to go to the Observation Cell,' Nugent said as if he was truly bothered by this. His men lined the wall behind him, under the row of windows.

Sam slowly eased himself from the bed, and walked to the bars. He glared at Nugent, and asked, 'Why?'

'Because I said so.'

'But why move me eight doors down the tier? What purpose does it serve?'

'It's procedure, Sam. It's in the book.'

'So you don't have a good reason, do you?'

'I don't need one. Turn around.'

509

Sam walked to his sink and brushed his teeth for a long time. Then he stood over his toilet and urinated with his hands on his hips. Then he washed his hands, as Nugent and his boys watched and fumed. Then he lit a cigarette, stuck it between his teeth, and eased his hands behind his back and through the narrow opening in the door. Nugent slapped the cuffs on his wrists, and nodded at the end of the tier for the door to be opened. Sam stepped onto the tier. He nodded at J. B. Gullitt, who was watching in horror and ready to cry. He winked at Hank Henshaw.

Nugent took his arm and walked him to the end of the hall, past Gullitt and Loyd Eaton and Stock Turner and Harry Ross Scott and Buddy Lee Harris, and, finally, past Preacher Boy, who at the moment was lying on his bed, face down, crying. The tier ran to a wall of iron bars, identical to those on the front of the cells, and the wall had a heavy door in the center of it. On the other side was another group of Nugent's goons, all watching quietly and loving every moment of it. Behind them was a short, narrow hallway which led to the Isolation Room. And then to the chamber.

Sam was being moved forty-eight feet closer to death. He leaned against the wall, puffing, watching in stoic silence. This was nothing personal, just part of the routine.

Nugent walked back to cell six and barked orders. Four of the guards entered Sam's cell and began grabbing his possessions. Books, typewriter, fan, television, toiletries, clothing. They held the items as if they were contaminated and carried them to the Observation Cell. The mattress and bedding were rolled up and moved by a burly plainclothed guard who accidentally stepped on a dragging sheet and ripped it.

The inmates watched this sudden flurry of activity with a saddened curiosity. Their cramped little cells were like additional layers of skin, and to see one so unmercifully violated was painful. It could happen to them. The reality of an execution was crashing in; they could hear it in the heavy boots shuffling along the tier, and in the stern muted voices of the death team. The distant slamming of a door

510

would've barely been noticed a week ago. Now, it was a jolting shock that rattled the nerves.

The officers trooped back and forth with Sam's assets until cell six was bare. It was quick work. They arranged things in his new home without the slightest care.

None of the eight worked on the Row. Nugent had read somewhere in Naifeh's haphazard notes that the members of the execution team should be total strangers to the inmate. They should be pulled from the other camps. Thirty-one officers and guards had volunteered for this duty. Nugent had chosen only the best.

'Is everything in?' he snapped at one of his men.

'Yes sir.'

'Very well. It's all yours, Sam.'

'Oh thank you, sir,' Sam sneered as he entered the cell. Nugent nodded to the far end of the hall, and the door closed. He walked forward and grabbed the bars with both hands. 'Now, listen, Sam,' he said gravely. Sam was leaning with his back to the wall, looking away from Nugent. 'We'll be right here if you need anything, okay. We moved you down here to the end so we can watch you better. All right? Is there anything I can do for you?'

Sam continued to look away, thoroughly ignoring him.

'Very well.' He backed away, and looked at his men. 'Let's go,' he said to them. The tier door opened less than ten feet from Sam, and the death team filed out. Sam waited. Nugent glanced up and down the hall, then stepped from the tier.

'Hey, Nugent!' Sam suddenly yelled. 'How 'bout taking these handcuffs off?'

Nugent froze and the death team stopped.

'You dumbass!' Sam yelled again, as Nugent scurried backward, fumbling for keys, barking orders. Laughter erupted along the tier, loud horselaughs and guffaws and boisterous catcalls. 'You can't leave me handcuffed!' Sam screamed into the hallway.

Nugent was at Sam's door, gritting his teeth, cursing, finally getting the right key. 'Turn around,' he demanded.

511

'You ignorant sonofabitch!' Sam yelled through the bars directly into the colonel's red face, which was less than two feet away. The laughter roared even louder.

'And you're in charge of my execution!' Sam said angrily, and rather loudly for the benefit of others. 'You'll probably gas yourself!'

'Don't bet on it,' Nugent said tersely. 'Now turn around.'

Someone, either Hank Henshaw or Harry Ross Scott, yelled out, 'Barney Fife!' and instantly the chant reverberated along the tier:

'Barney Fife! Barney Fife! Barney Fife!'

'Shut up!' Nugent yelled back.

'Barney Fife! Barney Fife!'

'Shut up!'

Sam finally turned around and stuck out his hands so Nugent could reach them. The cuffs came off, and the colonel quick-stepped it through the tier door.

'Barney Fife! Barney Fife! Barney Fife!' they chanted in perfect unison until the door clanged shut and the hallway was empty again. Their voices died suddenly, the laughter was gone. Slowly, their arms disappeared from the bars.

Sam stood facing the hall and glared at the two guards who were watching him from the other side of the tier door. He spent a few minutes organizing the place – plugging in the fan and television, stacking his books neatly as if they would be used, checking to see if the toilet flushed and the water ran. He sat on the bed and inspected the torn sheet.

This was his fourth cell on the Row, and undoubtedly the the one he would occupy for the briefest period of time. He reminisced about the first two, especially the second, on Tier B, where his close friend Buster Moac had lived next door. One day they came for Buster and brought him here, to the Observation Cell, where they watched him around the clock so he wouldn't commit suicide. Sam had cried when they took Buster away.

Virtually every inmate who made it this far also made it to the next stop. And then to the last.

GARNER GOODMAN was the first guest of the day in the splendid foyer of the governor's office. He actually signed the guestbook, chatted amiably with the pretty receptionist, and just wanted the governor to know that he was available. She was about to say something else when the phone buzzed on her switchboard. She punched a button, grimaced, listened, frowned at Goodman who looked away, then thanked the caller. 'These people,' she sighed.

'Beg your pardon,' Goodman offered, ever the innocent.

'We've been swamped with calls about your client's execution.'

'Yes, it's a very emotional case. Seems as if most people down here are in favor of the death penalty.'

'Not this one,' she said, recording the call on a pink form. 'Almost all of these calls are opposed to his execution.'

'You don't say. What a surprise.'

'I'll inform Ms Stark you're here.'

'Thank you.' Goodman took his familiar seat in the foyer. He glanced through the morning papers again. On Saturday, the daily paper in Tupelo made the mistake of beginning a telephone survey to gauge public opinion on the Cayhall execution. A toll-free number was given on the front page with instructions, and, of course, Goodman and his team of market analysts had bombarded the number over the weekend. The Monday edition ran the results for the first time, and they were astounding. Of three hundred and twenty calls, three hundred and two were opposed to the execution. Goodman smiled to himself as he scanned the paper.

Not too far away, the governor was sitting at the long table in his office and scanning the same papers. His face was troubled. His eyes were sad and worried.

Mona Stark walked across the marbled floor with a cup of coffee. 'Garner Goodman's here. Waiting in the foyer.'

'Let him wait.'

'The hotline's already flooded.'

McAllister calmly looked at his watch. Eleven minutes

513

before nine. He scratched his chin with his knuckles. From 3 P.M. Saturday until 8 P.M. Sunday, his pollster had called over two hundred Mississippians. Seventy-eight percent favored the death penalty, which was not surprising. However, of the same sample polled, fifty-one percent believed Sam Cayhall should not be executed. Their reasons varied. Many felt he was simply too old to face it. His crime had been committed twenty-three years ago, in a generation different from today's. He would die in Parchman soon enough anyway, so leave him alone. He was being persecuted for political reasons. Plus, he was white, and McAllister and his pollsters knew that factor was very important, if unspoken.

That was the good news. The bad news was contained in a printout next to the newspapers. Working with only one operator, the hotline received two hundred and thirty-one calls on Saturday, and one hundred and eighty on Sunday. A total of four hundred and eleven. Over ninety-five percent opposed the execution. Since Friday morning, the hotline had officially recorded eight hundred and ninety-seven calls about old Sam, with a strong ninety percent plus opposed to his execution. And now the hotline was hopping again.

There was more. The regional offices were reporting an avalanche of calls, almost all opposed to Sam dying. Staff members were coming to work with stories of long weekends with the phones. Roxburgh had called to say his lines had been flooded.

The governor was already tired. 'There's something at ten this morning,' he said to Mona without looking at her.

'Yes, a meeting with a group of Boy Scouts.'

'Cancel it. Give my apologies. Reschedule it. I'm not in the mood for any photographs this morning. It's best if I stay here. Lunch?'

'With Senator Pressgrove. You're supposed to discuss the lawsuit against the universities.'

'I can't stand Pressgrove. Cancel it, and order some chicken. And, on second thought, bring in Goodman.'

She walked to the door, disappeared for a minute, and returned with Garner Goodman. McAllister was standing by the window, staring at the buildings downtown. He turned and flashed a weary smile. 'Good morning, Mr Goodman.'

They shook hands and took seats. Late Sunday afternoon, Goodman had delivered to Larramore a written request to cancel the clemency hearing, pursuant to their client's rather strident demands.

'Still don't want a hearing, huh?' the governor said with another tired smile.

'Our client says no. He has nothing else to add. We've tried everything.' Mona handed Goodman a cup of black coffee.

'He has a very hard head. Always has, I guess. Where are the appeals right now?' McAllister was so sincere.

'Proceeding as expected.'

'You've been through this before, Mr Goodman. I haven't. What's your prediction, as of right now?'

Goodman stirred his coffee and pondered the question. There was no harm in being honest with the governor, not at this point. 'I'm one of his lawyers, so I lean toward optimism. I'd say seventy percent chance of it happening.'

The governor thought about this for a while. He could almost hear the phones ringing off the walls. Even his own people were getting skittish. 'Do you know what I want, Mr Goodman?' he asked sincerely.

Yeah, you want those damned phones to stop ringing, Goodman thought to himself. 'What?'

'I'd really like to talk to Adam Hall. Where is he?'

'Probably at Parchman. I talked to him an hour ago.'

'Can he come here today?'

'Yes, in fact he was planning on arriving in Jackson this afternoon?'

'Good. I'll wait for him.'

Goodman suppressed a smile. Perhaps a small hole had ruptured in the dam.

Oddly, though, it was on a different, far more unlikely front where the first hint of relief surfaced.

SIX BLOCKS AWAY in the federal courthouse, Breck Jefferson entered the office of his boss, the Honorable F. Flynn Slattery, who was on the phone and rather perturbed at a lawyer. Breck held a thick petition for writ of habeas corpus, and a legal pad filled with notes.

'Yes?' Slattery barked, slamming down the phone.

'We need to talk about Cayhall,' Breck said somberly. 'You know we've got his petition alleging mental incompetence.'

'Let's deny it and get it outta here. I'm too busy to worry with it. Let Cayhall take it to the Fifth Circuit. I don't want that damned thing lying around here.'

Breck looked troubled, and his words came slower. 'But there's something you need to take a look at.'

'Aw, come on, Breck. What is it?'

'He may have a valid claim.'

Slattery's face fell and his shoulders slumped. 'Come on. Are you kidding? What is it? We have a trial starting in thirty minutes. There's a jury waiting out there.'

Breck Jefferson had been the number-two student in his law class at Emory. Slattery trusted him implicitly. 'They're claiming Sam lacks the mental competence to face an execution, pursuant to a rather broad Mississippi statute.'

'Everybody knows he's crazy.'

'They have an expert who's willing to testify. It's not something we can ignore.'

'I don't believe this.'

'You'd better look at it.'

His Honor massaged his forehead with his fingertips. 'Sit down. Let me see it.'

'JUST A FEW MORE MILES,' Adam said as they sped toward the prison. 'How you doing?'

Carmen had said little since they left Memphis. Her first journey into Mississippi had been spent looking at the vastness of the Delta, admiring the lushness of its miles of

516

cotton and beans, watching in amazement as crop dusters bounced along the tops of the fields, shaking her head at the clusters of impoverished shacks. 'I'm nervous,' she admitted, not for the first time. They had talked briefly about Berkeley and Chicago and what the next years might bring. They had said nothing about their mother or father. Sam and his family were likewise neglected.

'He's nervous too.'

'This is bizarre, Adam. Rushing along this highway in this wildnerness, hurrying to meet a grandfather who's about to be executed.'

He patted her firmly on the knee. 'You're doing the right thing.' She wore oversized chinos, hiking boots, a faded red denim shirt. Very much the grad student in psychology.

'There it is.' He suddenly pointed ahead. On both sides of the highway, cars had parked bumper to bumper. Traffic was slow as people walked toward the prison.

'What's all this?' she asked.

'This is a circus.'

They passed three Klansmen walking on the edge of the pavement. Carmen stared at them, then shook her head in disbelief. They inched forward, going slightly faster than the people hurrying to the demonstrations. In the middle of the highway in front of the entrance, two state troopers directed traffic. They motioned for Adam to turn right, which he did. A Parchman guard pointed to an area along a shallow road ditch.

They held hands and walked to the front gate, pausing for a moment to stare at the dozens of robed Klansmen milling about in front of the prison. A fiery speech was being delivered into a megaphone that malfunctioned every few seconds. A group of brownshirts stood shoulder to shoulder, holding signs and facing the traffic. No less than five television vans were parked on the other side of the highway. Cameras were everywhere. A news helicopter circled above.

At the front gate, Adam introduced Carmen to his new pal Louise, the guard who took care of the paperwork. She was nervous and frazzled. There'd been an altercation or

517

two between the Kluckers and the press and the guards. Things were dicey at the moment, and not likely to improve, in her opinion.

A uniformed guard escorted them to a prison van, and they hurriedly left the front entrance.

'Unbelievable,' Carmen said.

'It gets worse each day. Wait till tomorrow.'

The van slowed as they eased along the main drive, under the large shade trees and in front of the neat, white houses. Carmen watched everything.

'This doesn't look like a prison,' she said.

'It's a farm. Seventeen thousand acres. Prison employees live in those houses.'

'With children,' she said, looking at bicycles and scooters lying in the front yards. 'It's so peaceful. Where are the prisoners?'

'Just wait.'

The van turned to the left. The pavement stopped and the dirt road began. Just ahead was the Row.

'See the towers there?' Adam pointed. 'The fences and the razor wire?' She nodded.

'That's the Maximum Security Unit. Sam's home for the past nine and a half years.'

'Where's the gas chamber?'

'In there.'

Two guards looked inside the van, then waved it through the double gates. It stopped near the front door where Packer was waiting. Adam introduced him to Carmen, who by now was barely able to speak. They stepped inside, where Packer frisked them gently. Three other guards watched. 'Sam's already in there,' Packer said nodding to the front office. 'Go on in.'

Adam took her hand and clenched it tightly. She nodded and they walked to the door. He opened it.

Sam was sitting on the edge of the desk, as usual. His feet were swinging under him and he was not smoking. The air in the room was clear and cool. He glanced at Adam, then looked at Carmen. Packer closed the door behind them.

She released Adam's hand and walked to the desk, looking Sam squarely in the eyes. 'I'm Carmen,' she said softly. Sam eased from the desk. 'I'm Sam, Carmen. Your wayward grandfather.' He drew her to him and they embraced.

It took a second or two for Adam to realize Sam had shaved his beard. His hair was shorter and looked much neater. His jumpsuit was zipped to the neck.

Sam squeezed her shoulders and examined her face. 'You're as pretty as your mother,' he said hoarsely. His eyes were moist and Carmen was fighting back tears.

She bit her lip and tried to smile.

'Thanks for coming,' he said, trying to grin. 'I'm sorry you had to find me like this.'

'You look great,' she said.

'Don't start lying, Carmen,' Adam said, breaking the ice. 'And let's stop the crying before it gets outta hand.'

'Sit down,' Sam said to her, pointing to a chair. He sat next to her, holding her hand.

'Business first, Sam,' Adam said as he leaned on the desk. 'Fifth Circuit turned us down early this morning. So we're off to greener pastures.'

'Your brother here is quite a lawyer,' Sam said to Carmen. 'He gives me this same news every day.'

'Of course, I don't have much to work with,' Adam said.

'How's your mother?' Sam asked her.

'She's fine.'

'Tell her I asked about her. I remember her as a fine person.'

'I will.'

'Any word on Lee?' Sam asked him.

'No. Do you want to see her?'

'I think so. But if she can't make it, I'll understand.'

'I'll see what I can do,' Adam said confidently. His last two phone calls to Phelps had not been returned. Frankly, he didn't have time at the moment to look for Lee.

Sam leaned closer to her. 'Adam tells me you're studying psychology.'

'That's right. I'm in grad school at Cal Berkeley. I'll –'

A sharp knock on the door interrupted the conversation. Adam opened it slightly, and saw the anxious face of Lucas Mann. 'Excuse me for a minute,' he said to Sam and Carmen, and stepped into the hall.

'What's up?' he asked.

'Garner Goodman's looking for you,' Mann said, almost in a whisper. 'He wants you in Jackson immediately.'

'Why? What's going on?'

'Looks like one of your claims has found its mark.'

Adam's heart stopped. 'Which one?'

'Judge Slattery wants to talk about the mental incompetence. He's scheduled a hearing for five this afternoon. Don't say anything to me, because I might be a witness for the state.'

Adam closed his eyes and gently tapped his head against the wall. A thousand thoughts swirled wildly through his brain. 'Five this afternoon. Slattery?'

'Hard to believe. Look, you need to move fast.'

'I need a phone.'

'There's one in there,' Mann said, nodding to the door behind Adam. 'Look, Adam, it's none of my business, but I wouldn't tell Sam. This is still a long shot, and there's no sense getting his hopes up. If it was my decision, I'd wait until the hearing is over.'

'You're right. Thanks, Lucas.'

'Sure. I'll see you in Jackson.'

Adam returned to the room, where the discussion had drifted to life in the Bay Area. 'It's nothing,' Adam said with a frown and went casually to the phone. He ignored their quiet talk as he punched the numbers.

'Garner, it's Adam. I'm here with Sam. What's up?'

'Get your ass down here, old boy,' Goodman said calmly. 'Things are moving.'

'I'm listening.' Sam was describing his first and only trip to San Francisco, decades ago.

'First, the governor wants to talk privately with you. He seems to be suffering. We're wearing his ass out with the phones, and he's feeling the heat. More importantly, Slattery, of all people, is hung up on the mental claim. I talked with him thirty minutes ago, and he's just thoroughly confused. I didn't help matters. He wants a hearing at five this afternoon. I've already talked to Dr Swinn, and he's on standby. He'll land in Jackson at three-thirty and be ready to testify.'

'I'm on my way,' Adam said with his back to Sam and Carmen.

'Meet me at the governor's office.'

Adam hung up. 'Just getting the appeals filed,' he explained to Sam, who at the moment was totally indifferent. 'I need to get to Jackson.'

'What's the hurry?' Sam asked, like a man with years to live and nothing to do.

'Hurry? Did you say hurry? It's ten o'clock, Sam, on Monday. We have exactly thirty-eight hours to find a miracle.'

'There won't be any miracles, Adam.' He turned to Carmen, still holding her hand. 'Don't get your hopes up, dear.'

'Maybe –'

'No. It's my time, okay. And I'm very ready. I don't want you to be sad when it's over.'

'We need to go, Sam,' Adam said, touching his shoulder. 'I'll be back either late tonight or early in the morning.'

Carmen leaned over and kissed Sam on the cheek. 'My heart is with you, Sam,' she whispered.

He hugged her for a second, then stood by the desk. 'You take care, kid. Study hard and all that. And don't think badly of me, okay? I'm here for a reason. It's nobody's fault but mine. There's a better life waiting on me outside this place.'

Carmen stood and hugged him again. She was crying as they left the room.

FORTY-SIX

BY NOON, Judge Slattery had fully embraced the gravity of the moment, and though he tried hard to conceal it, he was enjoying immensely this brief interval in the center of the storm. First, he had dismissed the jury and lawyers in the civil trial pending before him. He had twice talked to the clerk of the Fifth Circuit in New Orleans, then to Justice McNeely himself. The big moment had come a few minutes after eleven when Supreme Court Justice Edward F. Allbright called from Washington to get an update. Allbright was monitoring the case by the hour. They talked law and theory. Neither man was opposed to the death penalty, and both had particular problems with the Mississippi statute in question. They were concerned that it could be abused by any death row inmate who could pretend to be insane and find a wacky doctor to play along.

The reporters quickly learned that a hearing of some type was scheduled, and they not only flooded Slattery's office with calls, but parked themselves in his receptionist's office. The U.S. marshall was called to disperse the reporters.

The secretary brought messages by the minute. Breck Jefferson dug through countless law books and scattered research over the long conference table. Slattery talked to the governor, the Attorney General, Garner Goodman, dozens of others. His shoes were under his massive desk. He walked around it, holding the receiver with a long cord, thoroughly enjoying the madness.

IF SLATTERY'S OFFICE was hectic, then the Attorney General's was pure chaos. Roxburgh had gone ballistic with the news that one of Cayhall's shots in the dark had hit a target. You fight these bears for ten years, up and down the appellate ladders, out of one courtroom and into another, battling the creative legal minds of the ACLU and similar outfits, producing along the way enough paperwork to destroy a rain forest, and right when you've got him in your sights, he files a ton of gangplank appeals and one of them gets noticed by a judge somewhere who just happens to be in a tender mood.

He had stormed down the hall to the office of Morris Henry, Dr Death himself, and together they hastily had assembled a team of their best criminal boys. They met in a large library with rows and stacks of the latest books. They reviewed the Cayhall petition and the applicable law, and they plotted strategy. Witnesses were needed. Who had seen Cayhall in the last month? Who could testify about the things he said and did? There was no time for one of their doctors to examine him. He had a doctor, but they didn't. This was a significant problem. To get their hands on him with a reputable doctor, the state would be forced to ask for time. And time meant a stay of execution. A stay was out of the question.

The guards saw him every day. Who else? Roxburgh called Lucas Mann, who suggested that he talk to Colonel Nugent. Nugent said he'd seen Sam just hours earlier, and, yes, of course, he would be happy to testify. Son of a bitch wasn't crazy. He was just mean. And Sergeant Packer saw him every day. And the prison psychiatrist, Dr N. Stegall, had met with Sam, and she could testify. Nugent was anxious to help. He also suggested the prison chaplain. And he would think about others.

Morris Henry organized a hit squad of four lawyers to do nothing but dig for dirt on Dr Anson Swinn. Find other cases he'd been involved in. Talk to other lawyers around the country. Locate transcripts of his testimony. The guy was nothing but a hired mouthpiece, a professional testifier. Get the goods to discredit him.

Once Roxburgh had the attack planned and others doing the work, he rode the elevator to the lobby of the building to chat with the press.

ADAM PARKED in a vacant spot on the grounds of the state capitol. Goodman was waiting under a shade tree with his jacket off and sleeves rolled up, his paisley bow tie perfect. Adam quickly introduced Carmen to Mr Goodman.

'The governor wants to see you at two. I just left his office, for the third time this morning. Let's walk to our place,' he said, waving toward downtown. 'It's just a coupla blocks.'

'Did you meet Sam?' Goodman asked Carmen.

'Yes. This morning.'

'I'm glad you did.'

'What's on the governor's mind?' Adam asked. They were walking much too slow to suit him. Relax, he told himself. Just relax.

'Who knows? He wants to meet with you privately. Maybe the market analysis is getting to him. Maybe he's planning a media stunt. Maybe he's sincere. I can't read him. He does look tired, though.'

'The phone calls are getting through?'

'Splendidly.'

'No one's suspicious?'

'Not yet. Frankly, we're hitting them so fast and so hard I doubt they have time to trace calls.'

Carmen shot a blank look at her brother, who was too preoccupied to see it.

'What's the latest from Slattery?' Adam asked as they crossed a street, pausing for a minute in silence to watch the demonstration under way on the front steps of the capitol.

'Nothing since ten this morning. His clerk called you in Memphis, and your secretary gave him my number here. That's how they found me. He told me about the hearing, and said Slattery wants the lawyers in his chamber at three to plan things.'

524

'What does this mean?' Adam asked, desperate for his mentor to say that they were on the brink of a major victory.

Goodman sensed Adam's anxiety. 'I honestly don't know. It's good news, but no one knows how permanent it is. Hearings at this stage are not unusual.'

They crossed another street and entered the building. Upstairs, the temporary office was buzzing as four law students rattled away on cordless phones. Two were sitting with their feet on the table. One stood in the window and talked earnestly. One was pacing along the far wall, phone stuck to her head. Adam stood by the door and tried to absorb the scene. Carmen was hopelessly confused.

Goodman explained things, in a loud whisper. 'We're averaging about sixty calls an hour. We dial more than that, but the lines stay jammed, obviously. We're responsible for the jamming, and this keeps other people from getting through. It was much slower over the weekend. The hotline used only one operator.' He delivered this summary like a proud plant manager showing off the latest in automated machinery.

'Who are they calling?' Carmen asked.

A law student stepped forward and introduced himself to Adam, and then to Carmen. He was having a ball, he said.

'Would you like something to eat?' Goodman asked. 'We have some sandwiches.' Adam declined.

'Who are they calling?' Carmen asked again.

'The governor's hotline,' Adam replied, without explanation. They listened to the nearest caller as he changed his voice and read a name from a phone list. He was now Benny Chase from Hickory Flat, Mississippi, and he had voted for the governor and didn't think Sam Cayhall should be executed. It was time for the governor to step forward and take care of this situation.

Carmen cut her eyes at her brother, but he ignored her.

'These four are law students in Mississippi College,' Goodman explained further. 'We've used about a dozen students since Friday, different ages, whites and blacks, male and female. Professor Glass has been most helpful in finding these people. He's made calls too. So have Hez Kerry and his boys at the Defense Group. We've had at least twenty people calling.'

They pulled three chairs to the end of a table and sat down. Goodman found soft drinks in a plastic cooler, and sat them on the table. He continued talking in a low voice. 'John Bryan Glass is doing some research as we speak. He'll have a brief prepared by four. Hez Kerry is also at work. He's checking with his counterparts in other death states to see if similar statutes have been used recently.'

'Kerry is the black guy?' Adam said.

'Yeah, he's the director of the Southern Capital Defense Group. Very sharp.'

'A black lawyer busting his butt to save Sam.'

'It makes no difference to Hez. It's just another death case.'

'I'd like to meet him.'

'You will. All these guys will be at the hearing.'

'And they're working for free?' Carmen asked.

'Sort of. Kerry is on salary. Part of his job is to monitor every death case in this state, but since Sam has private lawyers Kerry is off the hook. He's donating his time, but it's something he wants to do. Professor Glass is on salary at the law school, but this is definitely outside the scope of his employment there. We're paying these students five bucks an hour.'

'Who's paying them?' she asked.

'Dear old Kravitz & Bane.'

Adam grabbed the nearby phonebook. 'Carmen needs to get a flight out of here this afternoon,' he said, flipping to the yellow pages.

'I'll take care of it,' Goodman said, taking the phonebook. 'Where to?'

'San Francisco.'

'I'll see what's available. Look, there's a little deli around the corner. Why don't you two get something to eat? We'll walk to the governor's office at two.'

'I need to get to a library,' Adam said, looking at his watch. It was almost one o'clock.

'Go eat, Adam. And try to relax. We'll have time later to sit down with the brain trust and talk strategy. Right now, you need to relax and eat.'

'I'm hungry,' Carmen said, anxious to be alone with her brother for a few minutes. They eased from the room, and closed the door behind them.

She stopped him in the shabby hallway before they reached the stairs. 'Please explain that to me,' she insisted, grabbing his arm.

'What?'

'That little room in there.'

'It's pretty obvious, isn't it?'

'Is it legal?'

'It's not illegal.'

'Is it ethical?'

Adam took a deep breath and stared at the wall. 'What are they planning to do with Sam?'

'Execute him.'

'Execute, gas, exterminate, kill, call it what you want. But it's murder, Carmen. Legal murder. It's wrong, and I'm trying to stop it. It's a dirty business, and if I have to bend a few ethics, I don't care.'

'It stinks.'

'So does the gas chamber.'

She shook her head and held her words. Twenty-four hours earlier she'd been eating lunch with her boyfriend at a sidewalk café in San Francisco. Now, she wasn't sure where she was.

'Don't condemn me for this, Carmen. These are desperate hours.'

'Okay,' she said, and headed down the stairs.

THE GOVERNOR and the young lawyer were alone in the vast office, in the comfortable leather chairs, their legs crossed and feet almost touching. Goodman was rushing Carmen to the airport to catch a flight. Mona Stark was nowhere in sight.

'It's strange, you know, you're the grandson, and you've known him for less than a month.' McAllister's words were calm, almost tired. 'But I've known him for many years. In fact, he's been a part of my life for a long time. And I've always thought that I'd look forward to this day. I've wanted him to die, you know, to be punished for killing those boys.' He flipped his bangs and gently rubbed his eyes. His words were so genuine, as if two old friends were catching up on the gossip. 'But now I'm not so sure. I have to tell you, Adam, the pressure's getting to me.'

He was either being brutally honest, or he was a talented actor. Adam couldn't tell. 'What will the state prove if Sam dies?' Adam asked. 'Will this be a better place to live when the sun comes up Wednesday morning and he's dead?'

'No. But then you don't believe in the death penalty. I do.'

'Why?'

'Because there has to be an ultimate punishment for murder. Put yourself in Ruth Kramer's position, and you'd feel differently. The problem you have, Adam, and people like you, is that your forget about the victims.'

'We could argue for hours about the death penalty.'

'You're right. Let's skip it. Has Sam told you anything new about the bombing?'

'I can't divulge what Sam's told me. But the answer is no.'

'Maybe he acted alone, I don't know.'

'What difference would it make today, the day before the execution?'

'I'm not sure, to be honest. But if I knew that Sam was only an accomplice, that someone else was responsible for the killings, then it would be impossible for me to allow him to be executed. I could stop it, you know. I could do that. I'd catch hell for it. It would hurt me politically. The damage would be irreparable, but I wouldn't mind. I'm getting tired of politics. And I don't enjoy being placed in this position, the giver or taker of life. But I could pardon Sam, if I knew the truth.'

'You believe he had help. You've told me that already. The FBI agent in charge of the investigation believes it too. Why don't you act on your beliefs and grant clemency?'

'Because we're not certain.'

'So, one word from Sam, just one name thrown out here in the final hours, and, bingo, you take your pen and save his life?'

'No, but I might grant a reprieve so the name could be investigated.'

'It won't happen, Governor. I've tried. I've asked so often, and he's denied so much, that it's not even discussed any more.'

'Who's he protecting?'

'Hell if I know.'

'Perhaps we're wrong. Has he ever given you the details of the bombing?'

'Again, I can't talk about our conversations. But he takes full responsibility for it.'

'Then why should I consider clemency? If the criminal himself claims he did the crime, and acted alone, how am I supposed to help him?'

'Help him because he's an old man who'll die soon enough anyway. Help him because it's the right thing to do, and deep down in your heart you want to do it. It'll take guts.'

'He hates me, doesn't he?'

'Yes. But he could come around. Give him a pardon and he'll be your biggest fan.'

McAllister smiled and unwrapped a peppermint. 'Is he really insane?'

'Our expert says he is. We'll do our best to convince Judge Slattery.'

'I know, but really? You've spent hours with him. Does he know what's happening?'

At this point, Adam decided against honesty. McAllister was not a friend, and not at all trustworthy. 'He's pretty sad,' Adam admitted. 'Frankly, I'm surprised any person can keep his mind after a few months on death row. Sam was an old man when he got there, and he's slowly wasted away. That's one reason he's declined all interviews. He's quite pitiful.'

Adam couldn't tell if the governor believed this, but he certainly absorbed it.

'What's your schedule tomorrow?' McAllister asked.

'I have no idea. It depends on what happens in Slattery's court. I had planned to spend most of the day with Sam, but I might be running around filing last minute appeals.'

'I gave you my private number. Let's keep in touch tomorrow.'

SAM TOOK THREE BITES of pinto beans and some of the corn bread, then placed the tray at the end of his bed. The same idiot guard with the blank face watched him through the bars of the tier door. Life was bad enough in these cramped cubicles, but living like an animal and being watched was unbearable.

It was six o'clock, time for the evening news. He was anxious to hear what the world was saying about him. The Jackson station began with the breaking story of a last minute hearing before federal Judge F. Flynn Slattery. The report cut to the outside of the federal courthouse in Jackson where an anxious young man with a microphone explained that the hearing had been delayed a bit as the lawyers wrangled in Slattery's office. He tried his best to briefly explain the issue. The defense was now claiming that Mr Cayhall lacked sufficient mental capacity to understand why he was being executed. He was senile and insane, claimed the defense, which would call a noted psychiatrist in this last ditch effort to stop the execution. The hearing was expected to get under way at any moment, and no one knew when a decision might be reached by Judge Slattery. Back to the anchorwoman, who said that, meanwhile, up at the state penitentiary at Parchman, all systems were go for the execution. Another young man with a microphone was suddenly on the screen, standing somewhere near the front gate of the prison, describing the increased security. He pointed to his right, and the camera panned the area near the highway where a regular carnival was happening. The highway patrol was out in force, directing traffic and keeping a wary eye on an assemblage of several dozen Ku Klux Klansmen. Other protestors included various groups of white supremacists and the usual death penalty abolitionists, he said.

The camera swung back to the reporter, who now had with him Colonel George Nugent, acting superintendent for Parchman, and the man in charge of the execution. Nugent grimly answered a few questions, said things were very much under control, and if the courts gave the green light then the execution would be carried out according to the law.

Sam turned off the television. Adam had called two hours earlier and explained the hearing, so he was prepared to hear that he was senile and insane and God knows what else. Still, he didn't like it. It was bad enough waiting to be executed, but to have his sanity slandered so nonchalantly seemed like a cruel invasion of privacy.

The tier was hot and quiet. The televisions and radios were turned down. Next door, Preacher Boy softly sang 'The Old Rugged Cross,' and it was not unpleasant.

In a neat pile on the floor against the wall was his new outfit – a plain white cotton shirt, Dickies, white socks, and a pair of brown loafers. Donnie had spent an hour with him during the afternoon.

He turned off the light and relaxed on his bed. Thirty hours to live.

THE MAIN COURTROOM in the federal building was packed when Slattery finally released the lawyers from his chamber for the third time. It was the last of a series of heated conferences that had dragged on for most of the afternoon. It was now almost seven.

They filed into the courtroom and took their places behind the appropriate tables. Adam sat with Garner Goodman. In a row of chairs behind them were Hez Kerry,

John Bryan Glass, and three of his law students. Roxburgh, Morris Henry, and a half dozen assistants crowded around the state's table. Two rows behind them, behind the bar, sat the governor with Mona Stark on one side and Larramore on the other.

The rest of the crowd was primarily reporters – no cameras were allowed. There were curious spectators, law students, other lawyers. It was open to the public. In the back row, dressed comfortably in a sports coat and tie, was Rollie Wedge.

Slattery made his entrance and everyone stood for a moment. 'Be seated,' he said into his microphone. 'Let's go on the record,' he said to the court reporter. He gave a succinct review of the petition and the applicable law, and outlined the parameters of the hearing. He was not in the mood for lengthy arguments and pointless questions, so move it along, he told the lawyers.

'Is the petitioner ready?' he asked in Adam's direction. Adam stood nervously, and said, 'Yes sir. The petitioner calls Dr Anson Swinn.'

Swinn stood from the first row and walked to the witness stand where he was sworn in. Adam walked to the podium in the center of the courtroom, holding his notes and pushing himself to be strong. His notes were typed and meticulous, the result of some superb research and preparation by Hez Kerry and John Bryan Glass. The two, along with Kerry's staff, had devoted the entire day to Sam Cayhall and this hearing. And they were ready to work all night and throughout tomorrow.

Adam began by asking Swinn some basic questions about his education and training. Swinn's answers were accented with the crispness of the upper Midwest, and this was fine. Experts should talk differently and travel great distances in order to be highly regarded. With his black hair, black beard, black glasses, and black suit, he indeed gave the appearance of an ominously brilliant master of his field. The preliminary questions were short and to the point, but only because Slattery had already reviewed Swinn's

532

qualifications and ruled that he could in fact testify as an expert. The state could attack his credentials on cross-examination, but his testimony would go into the record.

With Adam leading the way, Swinn talked about his two hours with Sam Cayhall on the previous Tuesday. He described his physical condition, and did so with such relish that Sam sounded like a corpse. He was quite probably insane, though insanity was a legal term, not medical. He had difficulty answering even basic questions like What did you eat for breakfast? Who is in the cell next to you? When did your wife die? Who was your lawyer during the first trial? And on and on.

Swinn very carefully covered his tracks by repeatedly telling the court that two hours simply was not enough time to thoroughly diagnose Mr Cayhall. More time was needed.

In his opinion, Sam Cayhall did not appreciate the fact that he was about to die, did not understand why he was being executed, and certainly didn't realize he was being punished for a crime. Adam gritted his teeth to keep from wincing at times, but Swinn was certainly convincing. Mr Cayhall was completely calm and at ease, clueless about his fate, wasting away his days in a six-by-nine cell. It was quite sad. One of the worst cases he'd encountered.

Under different circumstances, Adam would've been horrified to place on the stand a witness so obviously full of bull. But at this moment, he was mighty proud of this bizarre little man. Human life was at stake.

Slattery was not about to cut short the testimony of Dr Swinn. This case would be reviewed instantly by the Fifth Circuit and perhaps the U.S. Supreme Court, and he wanted no one from above second-guessing him. Goodman suspected this, and Swinn had been prepped to ramble. So with the court's indulgence, Swinn launched into the likely causes of Sam's problems. He described the horrors of living in a cell twenty-three hours a day; of knowing the gas chamber is a stone's throw away; of being denied companionship, decent food, sex, movement, plenty of exercise, fresh air. He'd worked with many death row inmates around the country and knew their problems well. Sam, of course, was much different because of his age. The average death row inmate is thirty-one years old, and has spent four years waiting to die. Sam was sixty when he first arrived at Parchman. Physically and mentally, he was not suited for it. It was inevitable he would deteriorate.

Swinn was under Adam's direct examination for forty-five minutes. When Adam had exhausted his questions, he sat down. Steve Roxburgh strutted to the podium, and stared at Swinn.

Swinn knew what was coming, and he was not the least bit concerned. Roxburgh began by asking who was paying for his services, and how much he was charging. Swinn said Kravitz & Bane was paying him two hundred dollars an hour. Big deal. There was no jury in the box. Slattery knew that all experts get paid, or they couldn't testify. Roxburgh tried to chip away at Swinn's professional qualifications, but got nowhere. The man was a well-educated, well-trained, experienced psychiatrist. So what if he decided years ago he could make more money as an expert witness. His qualifications weren't diminished. And Roxburgh was not about to argue medicine with a doctor.

The questions grew even stranger as Roxburgh began asking about other lawsuits in which Swinn had testified. There was a kid who was burned in a car wreck in Ohio, and Swinn had given his opinion that the child was completely, mentally disabled. Hardly an extreme opinion.

'Where are you going with this?' Slattery interrupted loudly.

Roxburgh glanced at his notes, then said, 'Your Honor, we're attempting to discredit this witness.'

'I know that. But it's not working, Mr Roxburgh. This court knows that the witness has testified in many trials around the country. What's the point?'

'We are attempting to show that he is willing to state some pretty wild opinions if the money is right.'

'Lawyers do that every day, Mr Roxburgh.'

There was some very light laughter in the audience, but very reserved.

'I don't want to hear it,' Slattery snapped. 'Now move on.'

Roxburgh should've sat down, but the moment was too rich for that. He moved to the next minefield, and began asking questions about Swinn's examination of Sam. He went nowhere. Swinn fielded each question with a fluid answer that only added to his testimony on direct examination. He repeated much of the sad description of Sam Cayhall. Roxburgh scored no points, and once thoroughly trounced, finally went to his seat. Swinn was dismissed from the stand.

The next and last witness for the petitioner was a surprise, though Slattery had already approved him. Adam called Mr E. Garner Goodman to the stand.

Goodman was sworn, and took his seat. Adam asked about his firm's representation of Sam Cayhall, and Goodman briefly outlined the history of it for the record. Slattery already knew most of it. Goodman smiled when he recalled Sam's efforts to fire Kravitz & Bane.

'Does Kravitz & Bane represent Mr Cayhall at this moment?' Adam asked.

'Indeed we do.'

'And you're here in Jackson at this moment working on the case?'

'That's correct.'

'In your opinion, Mr Goodman, do you believe Sam Cayhall has told his lawyers everything about the Kramer bombing?'

'No I do not.'

Rollie Wedge sat up a bit and listened intensely.

'Would you please explain?'

'Certainly. There has always been strong circumstantial evidence that another person was with Sam Cayhall during the Kramer bombing, and the bombings which preceded it. Mr Cayhall always refused to discuss this with me, his lawyer, and even now will not cooperate with his attorneys.

535

Obviously, at this point in the case, it is crucial that he fully divulge everything to his lawyers. And he is unable to do so. There are facts we should know, but he won't tell us.'

Wedge was at once nervous and relieved. Sam was holding fast, but his lawyers were trying everything.

Adam asked a few more questions, and sat down. Roxburgh asked only one. 'When was the last time you spoke with Mr Cayhall?'

Goodman hesitated and thought about the answer. He honestly couldn't remember exactly when. 'I'm not sure. It's been two or three years.'

'Two or three years? And you're his lawyer?'

'I'm one of his lawyers. Mr Hall is now the principal lawyer on this case, and he's spent innumerable hours with the client during the last month.'

Roxburgh sat down, and Goodman returned to his seat at the table.

'We have no more witnesses, Your Honor,' Adam said for the record.

'Call your first witness, Mr Roxburgh,' Slattery said.

'The state calls Colonel George Nugent,' Roxburgh announced. Nugent was found in the hallway, and escorted to the witness stand. His olive shirt and pants were wrinkle-free. The boots were gleaming. He stated for the record who he was and what he was doing. 'I was at Parchman an hour ago,' he said, looking at his watch. 'Just flew down on the state helicopter.'

'When did you last see Sam Cayhall?' Roxburgh asked.

'He was moved to the Observation Cell at nine this morning. I spoke with him then.'

'Was he mentally alert, or just drooling over in the corner like an idiot?'

Adam started to jump and object, but Goodman grabbed his arm.

'He was extremely alert,' Nugent said eagerly. 'Very sharp. He asked me why he was being moved from his cell to another one. He understood what was happening. He didn't like it, but then Sam doesn't like anything these days.'

536

'Did you see him yesterday?'

'Yes.'

'And was he able to speak, or just lying around like a vegetable?'

'Oh, he was quite talkative.'

'What did you talk about?'

'I had a checklist of things I needed to cover with Sam. He was very hostile, even threatened me with bodily harm. He's a very abrasive person with a sharp tongue. He settled down a bit, and we talked about his last meal, his witnesses, what to do with his personal effects. Things such as that. We talked about the execution.'

'Is he aware he is about to be executed?'

Nugent burst into laughter. 'What kind of question is that?'

'Just answer it,' Slattery said without a smile.

'Of course he knows. He knows damned well what's going on. He's not crazy. He told me the execution would not take place because his lawyers were about to unload the heavy artillery, as he put it. They've planned all this.' Nugent waved both hands at the entire courtroom.

Roxburgh asked about prior meetings with Sam, and Nugent spared no details. He seemed to remember every word Sam had uttered in the past two weeks, especially the biting sarcasm and caustic remarks.

Adam knew it was all true. He huddled quickly with Garner Goodman, and they decided to forgo any cross-examination. Little could be gained from it.

Nugent marched down the aisle and out of the courtroom. The man had a mission. He was needed at Parchman.

The state's second witness was Dr N. Stegall, psychiatrist for the Department of Corrections. She made her way to the witness stand as Roxburgh conferred with Morris Henry.

'State your name for the record,' Slattery said.

'Dr N. Stegall.'

'Ann?' His Honor asked.

'No. N. It's an initial.'

537

Slattery looked down at her, then looked at Roxburgh who shrugged as if he didn't know what to say.

The judge eased even closer to the edge of his bench, and peered down at the witness stand. 'Look, Doctor, I didn't ask for your initial, I asked for your name. Now, you state it for the record, and be quick about it.'

She jerked her eyes away from his, cleared her throat, and reluctantly said, 'Neldeen.'

No wonder, thought Adam. Why hadn't she changed it to something else?

Roxburgh seized the moment and asked her a rapid series of questions about her qualifications and training. Slattery had already deemed her fit to testify.

'Now, Dr Stegall,' Roxburgh began, careful to avoid any reference to Neldeen, 'when did you meet with Sam Cayhall?'

She held a sheet of paper which she looked at. 'Thursday, July 26.'

'And the purpose of this visit?'

'As part of my job, I routinely visit death row inmates, especially those with executions approaching. I provide counseling and medication, if they request it.'

'Describe Mr Cayhall's mental condition?'

'Extremely alert, very bright, very sharp-tongued, almost to the point of being rude. In fact, he was quite rude to me, and he asked me not to come back.'

'Did he discuss his execution?'

'Yes. In fact, he knew that he had thirteen days to go, and he accused me of trying to give him medication so he wouldn't be any trouble when his time came. He also expressed concern for another death row inmate, Randy Dupree, who Sam thinks is deteriorating mentally. He was most concerned about Mr Dupree, and chastised me for not examining him.'

'In your opinion, is he suffering from any form of decreased mental capacity?'

'Not at all. His mind is very sharp.'

'No further questions,' Roxburgh said, and sat down.

Adam walked purposefully to the podium. 'Tell us, Dr Stegall, how is Randy Dupree doing?' he asked at full volume.

'I, uh, I haven't had a chance to see him yet.'

'Sam told you about him eleven days ago, and you haven't bothered to meet with him.'

'I've been busy.'

'How long have you held your present job?'

'Four years.'

'And in four years how many times have you talked to Sam Cayhall?'

'Once.'

'You don't care much for the death row inmates, do you, Dr Stegall?'

'I certainly do.'

'How many men are on death row right now?'

'Well, uh, I'm not sure. Around forty, I think.'

'How many have you actually talked to? Give us a few names.'

Whether it was fear or anger or ignorance, no one could tell. But Neldeen froze. She grimaced and cocked her head to one side, obviously trying to pull a name from the air, and obviously unable to do so. Adam allowed her to hang for a moment, then said, 'Thank you, Dr Stegall.' He turned and walked slowly back to his chair.

'Call your next witness,' Slattery demanded.

'The state calls Sergeant Clyde Packer.'

Packer was fetched from the hallway and led to the front of the courtroom. He was still in uniform, but the gun had been removed. He swore to tell the truth, and took his seat on the witness stand.

Adam was not surprised at the effect of Packer's testimony. He was an honest man who simply told what he'd seen. He'd known Sam for nine and a half years, and he was the same today as he was when he first arrived. He typed letters and law papers all day long, read many books, especially legal ones. He typed writs for his buddies on the Row, and he typed letters to wives and girlfriends for some

539

of the guys who couldn't spell. He chain-smoked because he wanted to kill himself before the state got around to it. He loaned money to friends. In Packer's humble opinion, Sam was as mentally alert now as he'd been nine and a half years earlier. And his mind was very quick.

Slattery leaned a bit closer to the edge of the bench when Packer described Sam's checkers game with Henshaw and Gullitt.

'Does he win?' His Honor asked, interrupting.

'Almost always.'

Perhaps the turning point of the hearing came when Packer told the story of Sam wanting to see a sunrise before he died. It happened late last week when Packer was making his rounds one morning. Sam had quietly made the request. He knew he was about to die, said he was ready to go, and that he'd like to sneak out early one morning to the bullpen on the east end and see the sun come up. So Packer took care of it, and last Saturday Sam spent an hour sipping coffee and waiting for the sun. Afterward, he was very grateful.

Adam had no questions for Packer. He was excused, and left the courtroom.

Roxburgh announced that the next witness was Ralph Griffin, the prison chaplain. Griffin was led to the stand, and looked uncomfortably around the courtroom. He gave his name and occupation, then glanced warily at Roxburgh.

'Do you know Sam Cayhall?' Roxburgh asked.

'I do.'

'Have you counseled him recently?'

'Yes.'

'When did you last see him?'

'Yesterday. Sunday.'

'And how would you describe his mental state?'

'I can't.'

'I beg your pardon.'

'I said I can't describe his mental condition.'

'Why not?'

'Because right now I'm his minister, and anything he says

540

or does in my presence is strictly confidential. I can't testify against Mr Cayhall.'

Roxburgh stalled for a moment, trying to decide what to do next. It was obvious neither he nor his learned underlings had given any thought to this situation. Perhaps they'd just assumed that since the chaplain was working for the state, then he'd cooperate with them. Griffin waited expectantly for an assault from Roxburgh.

Slattery settled the matter quickly. 'A very good point, Mr Roxburgh. This witness should not be here. Who's next'''

'No further witnesses,' the Attorney General said, anxious to leave the podium and get to his seat.

His Honor scribbled some notes at length, then looked at the crowded courtroom. 'I will take this matter under advisement and render an opinion, probably early in the morning. As soon as my decision is ready, we will notify the attorneys. You don't need to hang around here. We'll call you. Court's adjourned.'

Everyone stood and hurried for the rear doors. Adam caught the Reverend Ralph Griffin and thanked him, then he returned to the table where Goodman, Hez Kerry, Professor Glass, and the students were waiting. They huddled and whispered until the crowd was gone, then left the courtroom. Someone mentioned drinks and dinner. It was almost nine.

Reporters were waiting outside the door to the courtroom. Adam threw out a few polite no-comments and kept walking. Rollie Wedge eased behind Adam and Goodman as they inched through the crowded hallway. He vanished as they left the building.

Two groups of cameras were ready outside. On the front steps, Roxburgh was addressing one batch of reporters, and not far away on the sidewalk, the governor was holding forth. As Adam walked by, he heard McAllister say that clemency was being considered, and that it would be a long night. Tomorrow would be even tougher. Would he attend the execution? someone asked. Adam couldn't hear the reply.

THEY MET at Hal and Mal's, a popular downtown restaurant and watering hole. Hez found a large table in a corner near the front and ordered a round of beer. A blues band was cranked up in the back. The dining room and bar were crowded.

Adam sat in a corner, next to Hez, and relaxed for the first time in hours. The beer went down fast and calmed him. They ordered red beans and rice, and chatted about the hearing. Hez said he'd performed wonderfully, and the law students were full of compliments. The mood was optimistic. Adam thanked them for their help. Goodman and Glass were at the far end of the table, lost in a conversation about another death row case. Time passed slowly, and Adam attacked his dinner when it arrived.

'This is probably not a good time to bring this up,' Hez said out of the corner of his mouth. He wanted no one to hear but Adam. The band was even louder now.

'I guess you'll go back to Chicago when this is over,' he said, looking at Goodman to make sure he was still engaged with Glass.

'I guess so,' Adam said, without conviction. He'd had little time to think past tomorrow.

'Well, just so you'll know, there's an opening in our office. One of my guys is going into private practice, and we're looking for a new lawyer. It's nothing but death work, you know.'

'You're right,' Adam said quietly. 'This is a lousy time to bring it up.'

'It's tough work, but it's satisfying. It's also heartbreaking. And necessary.' Hez chewed on a bite of sausage, and washed it down with beer. 'The money is lousy, compared with what you're making with the firm. Tight budget, long hours, lots of clients.'

'How much?'

'I can start you at thirty thousand.'

'I'm making sixty-two right now. With more on the way.'

'I've been there. I was making seventy with a big firm in

542

D.C. when I gave it up to come here. I was on the fast track to a partnership, but it was easy to quit. Money's not everything.'

'You enjoy this?'

'It grows on you. It takes strong moral convictions to fight the system like this. Just think about it.'

Goodman was now looking their way. 'Are you driving to Parchman tonight?' he asked loudly.

Adam was finishing his second beer. He wanted a third, but no more. Exhaustion was rapidly setting in. 'No. I'll wait until we hear something in the morning.'

They ate and drank and listened to Goodman and Glass and Kerry tell war stories of other executions. The beer flowed, and the atmosphere went from optismism to outright confidence.

SAM LAY in the darkness and waited for midnight. He'd watched the late news and learned that the hearing was over, and that the clock was still ticking. There was no stay. His life was in the hands of a federal judge.

At one minute after midnight, he closed his eyes and said a prayer. He asked God to help Lee with her troubles, to be with Carmen, and to give Adam the strength to survive the inevitable.

He had twenty-four hours to live. He folded his hands over his chest and fell asleep.

FORTY-SEVEN

NUGENT WAITED until exactly seven-thirty to close the door and start the meeting. He walked to the front of the room, and surveyed his troops. 'I just left MSU,' he said somberly. 'The inmate is awake and alert, not at all the blithering zombie we read about in the paper this morning.' He paused and smiled and expected everyone to admire his humor. It went undetected.

'In fact, he's already had his breakfast, and is already bitching about wanting his recreation time. So at least something is normal around here. There's no word from the federal court in Jackson, so this thing is on schedule unless we hear otherwise. Correct, Mr Mann?'

Lucas was sitting at the table across the front of the room, reading the paper and trying to ignore the colonel. 'Right.'

'Now, there are two areas of concern. First is the press. I've assigned Sergeant Moreland here to handle these bastards. We're gonna move them to the Visitors Center just inside the front gate, and try to keep them pinned down there. We're gonna surround them with guards, and just dare them to venture about. At four this afternoon, I'll conduct the lottery to see which reporters get to watch the execution. As of yesterday, there were over a hundred names on the request list. They get five seats.

'The second problem is what's happening outside the gate. The governor has agreed to assign three dozen troopers for today and tomorrow, and they'll be here shortly. We have to keep our distance from these nuts,

544

especially the skinheads, sumbitches are crazy, but at the same time we have to maintain order. There were two fights yesterday, and things could've deteriorated rapidly if we hadn't been watching. If the execution takes place, there could be some tense moments. Any questions?'

There were none.

'Very well. I'll expect everyone to act professionally today, and carry this out in a responsible manner. Dismissed.' He snapped off a smart salute, and proudly watched them leave the room.

SAM STRADDLED THE BENCH with the checkerboard in front of him, and waited patiently for J. B. Gullitt to enter the bullpen. He sipped the stale remains of a cup of coffee.

Gullitt stepped through the door, and paused as the handcuffs were removed. He rubbed his wrists, shielded his eyes from the sun, and looked at his friend sitting alone. He walked to the bench and took his position across the board.

Sam never looked up.

'Any good news, Sam?' Gullitt asked nervously. 'Tell me it won't happen.'

'Just move,' Sam said, staring at the checkers.

'It can't happen, Sam,' he pleaded.

'It's your turn to go first. Move.'

Gullitt slowly lowered his eyes to the board.

THE PREVAILING THEORY of the morning was that the longer Slattery sat on the petition, the greater the likelihood of a stay. But this was the conventional wisdom of those who were praying for a reprieve. No word had come by 9 A.M., nothing by 9:30.

Adam waited in Hez Kerry's office, which had become the operations center during the past twenty-four hours. Goodman was across town supervising the relentless hounding of the governor's hotline, a task he seemed to savor. John Bryan Glass had parked himself outside Slattery's office.

In the event Slattery denied a stay, they would immediately appeal to the Fifth Circuit. The appeal was completed by nine, just in case. Kerry had also prepared a petition for cert to the U.S. Supreme Court if the Fifth Circuit turned them down. The paperwork was waiting. Everything was waiting.

To occupy his mind, Adam called everyone he could think of. He called Carmen in Berkeley. She was asleep and fine. He called Lee's condo, and, of course, there was no answer. He called Phelps' office and talked to a secretary. He called Darlene to tell her he had no idea when he might return. He called McAllister's private number, but got a busy signal. Perhaps Goodman had it jammed too.

He called Sam and talked about the hearing last night, with special emphasis on the Reverend Ralph Griffin. Packer had testified too, he explained, and told only the truth. Nugent, typically, was an ass. He told Sam he would be there around noon. Sam asked him to hurry.

By eleven, Slattery's name was being cursed and defamed with righteous fervor. Adam had had enough. He called Goodman and said he was driving to Parchman. He said farewell to Hez Kerry, and thanked him again.

Then he raced away, out of the city of Jackson, north on Highway 49. Parchman was two hours away if he drove within the speed limit. He found a talk radio station that promised the latest news twice an hour, and listened to an interminable discussion about casino gambling in Mississippi. There was nothing new on the Cayhall execution at the eleven-thirty newsbreak.

He drove eighty and ninety, passing on yellow lines and on curves and over bridges. He sped through speed zones in tiny towns and hamlets. He was uncertain what drew him to Parchman with such speed. There wasn't much he could do once he got there. The legal maneuverings had been left behind in Jackson. He would sit with Sam and count the hours. Or maybe they would celebrate a wonderful gift from federal court.

He stopped at a roadside grocery near the small town of

Flora for gas and fruit juice, and he was driving away from the pumps when he heard the news. The bored and listless talk show host was now filled with excitement as he relayed the breaking story in the Cayhall case. United States District Court Judge F. Flynn Slattery had just denied Cayhall's last petition, his claim to be mentally incompetent. The matter would be appealed to the Fifth Circuit within the hour. Sam Cayhall had just taken a giant step toward the Mississippi gas chamber, the host said dramatically.

Instead of punching the accelerator, Adam slowed to a reasonable speed and sipped his drink. He turned off the radio. He cracked his window to allow the warm air to circulate. He cursed Slattery for many miles, talking vainly at the windshield and dragging up all sorts of vile names. It was now a little past noon. Slattery, in all fairness, could've ruled five hours ago. Hell, if he had guts he could've ruled last night. They could be in front of the Fifth Circuit already. He cursed Breck Jefferson also, for good measure.

Sam had told him from the beginning that Mississippi wanted an execution. It was lagging behind Louisiana and Texas and Florida, even Alabama and Georgia and Virginia were killing at a more enviable rate. Something had to be done. The appeals were endless. The criminals were coddled. Crime was rampant. It was time to execute somebody and show the rest of the country that this state was serious about law and order.

Adam finally believed him.

He stopped the swearing after a while. He finished the drink and threw the bottle over the car and into a ditch, in direct violation of Mississippi laws against littering. It was difficult to express his present opinions of Mississippi and its laws.

He could see Sam sitting in his cell, watching the television, hearing the news.

Adam's heart ached for the old man. He had failed as a lawyer. His client was about to die at the hands of the government, and there wasn't a damned thing he could do about it.

THE NEWS electrified the army of reporters and cameramen now sprawled about the small Visitors Center just inside the front gate. They gathered around portable televisions and watched their stations in Jackson and Memphis. At least four shot live segments from Parchman while countless others milled around the area. Their little section of ground had been cordoned off by ropes and barricades, and was being watched closely by Nugent's troops.

The racket increased noticeably along the highway when the news spread. The Klansmen, now a hundred strong, began chanting loudly in the direction of the administration buildings. The skinheads and Nazis and Aryans hurled obscenities at anyone who would listen to them. The nuns and other silent protestors sat under umbrellas and tried to ignore their rowdy neighbors.

Sam heard the news as he was holding a bowl of turnip greens, his final meal before his last meal. He stared at the television, watched the scenes switch from Jackson to Parchman and back again. A young black lawyer he'd never heard of was talking to a reporter and explaining what he and the rest of the Cayhall defense team would do next.

His friend Buster Moac had complained that there were so damned many lawyers involved with his case in the last days that he couldn't keep up with who was on his side and who was trying to kill him. But Sam was certain Adam was in control.

He finished the turnip greens, and placed the bowl on the tray at the foot of his bed. He walked to the bars and sneered at the blank-faced guard watching him from behind the tier door. The hall was silent. The televisions were on in every cell, all turned low and being watched with morbid interest. Not a single voice could be heard, and that in itself was extremely rare.

He pulled off his red jumpsuit for the last time, wadded it up and threw it in a corner. He kicked the rubber shower shoes under his bed, never to see them again. He carefully placed his new outfit on the bed, arranged it just so, then slowly unbuttoned the short-sleeved shirt and put it on. It fit nicely. He slid his legs into the stiff work khakis, pulled the zipper up and buttoned the waist. The pants were two inches too long, so he sat on the bed and turned them up into neat, precise cuffs. The cotton socks were thick and soothing. The shoes were a bit large but not a bad fit.

The sensation of being fully dressed in real clothes brought sudden, painful memories of the free world. These were the pants he'd worn for forty years, until he'd been incarcerated. He'd bought them at the old dry goods store on the square in Clanton, always keeping four or five pairs in the bottom drawer of his large dresser. His wife pressed them with no starch, and after a half dozen washings they felt like old pajamas. He wore them to work and he wore them to town. He wore them on fishing trips with Eddie, and he wore them on the porch swinging little Lee. He wore them to the coffee shop and to Klan meetings. Yes, he'd even worn them on that fateful trip to Greenville to bomb the office of the radical Jew.

He sat on his bed and pinched the sharp creases under his knees. It had been nine years and six months since he had worn these pants. Only fitting, he guessed, that he should now wear them to the gas chamber.

They'd be cut from his body, placed in a bag, and burned.

ADAM STOPPED FIRST at Lucas Mann's office. Louise at the front gate had given him a note saying it was important. Mann closed the door behind him and offered a seat. Adam declined. He was anxious to see Sam.

'The Fifth Circuit received the appeal thirty minutes ago,' Mann said. 'I thought you might want to use my phone to call Jackson.'

'Thanks. But I'll use the one at the Row.'

'Fine. I'm talking to the AG's office every half hour, so if I hear something I'll give you a call.'

'Thanks.' Adam was fidgeting.

'Does Sam want a last meal?'

'I'll ask him in a minute.'

'Fine. Give me a call, or just tell Packer. What about witnesses?'

'Sam will have no witnesses.'

'What about you?'

'No. He won't allow it. We agreed on it a long time ago.'

'Fine. I can't think of anything else. I have a fax and a phone, and things may be a bit quieter in here. Feel free to use my office.'

'Thanks,' Adam said, stepping from the office. He drove slowly to the Row and parked for the last time in the dirt lot next to the fence. He walked slowly to the guard tower and placed his keys in the bucket.

Four short weeks ago he had stood there and watched the red bucket descend for the first time, and he'd thought how crude but effective this little system was. Only four weeks! It seemed like years.

He waited for the double gates, and met Tiny on the steps.

Sam was already in the front office, sitting on the edge of the desk, admiring his shoes. 'Check out the new threads,' he said proudly when Adam entered.

Adam stepped close and inspected the clothing from shoes to shirt. Sam was beaming. His face was clean-shaven. 'Spiffy. Real spiffy.'

'A regular dude, aren't I?'

'You look nice, Sam, real nice. Did Donnie bring these?'

'Yeah. He got them at the dollar store. I started to order some designer threads from New York, but what the hell. It's only an execution. I told you I wouldn't allow them to kill me in one of those red prison suits. I took it off a while ago, never to wear one again. I have to admit, Adam, it was a good feeling.'

'You've heard the latest?'

'Sure. It's all over the news. Sorry about the hearing.'

'It's in the Fifth Circuit now, and I feel good about it. I like our chances there.'

Sam smiled and looked away, as if the little boy was

telling his grandfather a harmless lie. 'They had a black lawyer on television at noon, said he was working for me. What the hell's going on?'

'That was probably Hez Kerry.' Adam placed his briefcase on the desk and sat down.

'Am I paying him too?'

'Yeah, Sam, you're paying him at the same rate you're paying me.'

'Just curious. That screwball doctor, what's his name, Swinn? He must've done a number on me.'

'It was pretty sad, Sam. When he finished testifying, the entire courtroom could see you floating around your cell, scratching your teeth and peeing on the floor.'

'Well, I'm about to be put out of my misery.' Sam's words were strong and loud, almost defiant. There was not a trace of fear. 'Look, I have a small favor to ask of you,' he said, reaching for yet another envelope.

'Who is it this time?'

Sam handed it to him. 'I want you to take this to the highway by the front gate, and I want you to find the leader of that bunch of Kluckers out there, and I want you to read it to him. Try and get the cameras to film it, because I want people to know what it says.'

Adam held it suspiciously. 'What does it say?'

'It's quick and to the point. I ask them all to go home. To leave me alone, so that I can die in peace. I've never heard of some of those groups, and they're getting a lot of mileage out of my death.'

'You can't make them leave, you know.'

'I know. And I don't expect them to. But the television makes it appear as if these are my friends and cronies. I don't know a single person out there.'

'I'm not so sure it's a good idea right now,' Adam said, thinking out loud.

'Why not?'

'Because as we speak, we're telling the Fifth Circuit that you're basically a vegetable, incapable of putting together thoughts like this.'

551

Sam was suddenly angry. 'You lawyers,' he sneered. 'Don't you ever give up? It's over, Adam, stop playing games.'

'It's not over.'

'As far as I'm concerned it is. Now, take the damned letter and do as I say.'

'Right now?' Adam asked, looking at his watch. It was one-thirty.

'Yes! Right now. I'll be waiting here.'

ADAM PARKED by the guardhouse at the front gate, and explained to Louise what he was about to do. He was nervous. She gave a leery look at the white envelope in his hand, and yelled for two uniformed guards to walk over. They escorted Adam through the front gate and toward the demonstration area. Some reporters covering the protestors recognized Adam, and immediately flocked to him. He and the guards walked quickly along the front fence, ignoring their questions. Adam was scared but determined, and more than a little comforted by his newly found bodyguards.

He walked directly to the blue and white canopy which marked the headquarters for the Klan, and by the time he stopped, a group of white-robes was waiting for him. The press encircled Adam, his guards, the Klansmen. 'Who's in charge here?' Adam demanded, holding his breath.

'Who wants to know?' asked a burly young man with a black beard and sunburned cheeks. Sweat dripped from his eyebrows as he stepped forward.

'I have a statement here from Sam Cayhall,' Adam said loudly, and the circle compressed. Cameras clicked. Reporters shoved microphones and recorders into the air around Adam.

'Quiet,' someone yelled.

'Get back!' one of the guards snapped.

A tense group of Klansmen, all in matching robes but most without the hoods, packed tighter together in front of Adam. He recognized none of them from his last

552

confrontation on Friday. These guys did not look too friendly.

The racket stopped along the grassy strip as the crowd pushed closer to hear Sam's lawyer.

Adam pulled the note from the envelope and held it with both hands. 'My name is Adam Hall, and I'm Sam Cayhall's lawyer. This is a statement from Sam,' he repeated. 'It's dated today, and addressed to all members of the Ku Klux Klan, and to the other groups demonstrating on his behalf here today. I quote: "Please leave. Your presence here is of no comfort to me. You're using my execution as a means to further your own interests. I do not know a single one of you, nor do I care to meet you. Please go away immediately. I prefer to die without the benefit of your theatrics." '

Adam glanced at the stern faces of the Klansmen, all hot and dripping with perspiration. 'The last paragraph reads as follows, and I quote: "I am no longer a member of the Ku Klux Klan. I repudiate that organization and all that it stands for. I would be a free man today had I never heard of the Ku Klux Klan." It's signed by Sam Cayhall.' Adam flipped it over and thrust it toward the Kluckers, all of whom were speechless and stunned.

The one with the black beard and sunburned cheeks lunged at Adam in an attempt to grab the letter. 'Gimme that!' he yelled, but Adam yanked it away. The guard to Adam's right stepped forward quickly and blocked the man, who pushed the guard. The guard shoved him back, and for a few terrifying seconds Adam's bodyguards scuffled with a few of the Kluckers. Other guards had been watching nearby, and within seconds they were in the middle of the shoving match. Order was restored quickly. The crowd backed away.

Adam smirked at the Kluckers. 'Leave!' Adam shouted. 'You heard what he said! He's ashamed of you!'

'Go to hell!' the leader yelled back.

The two guards grabbed Adam and led him away before he stirred them up again. They moved rapidly toward the front gate, knocking reporters and cameramen out of the way. They practically ran through the entrance, past another line of guards, past another swarm of reporters, and finally to Adam's car.

'Don't come back up here, okay?' one of the guards pleaded with him.

MCALLISTER'S OFFICE was known to have more leaks than an old toilet. By early afternoon, Tuesday, the hottest gossip in Jackson was that the governor was seriously considering clemency for Sam Cayhall. The gossip spread rapidly from the capitol to the reporters outside where it was picked up by other reporters and onlookers and repeated, not as gossip, but as solid rumor. Within an hour of the leak, the rumor had risen to the level of near-fact.

Mona Stark met in the rotunda with the press and promised a statement by the governor at a later hour. The courts were not finished with the case, she explained. Yes, the governor was under tremendous pressure.

FORTY-EIGHT

IT TOOK THE FIFTH CIRCUIT less than three hours to bump the last of the gangplank appeals along to the U.S. Supreme Court. A brief telephone conference was held at three. Hez Kerry and Garner Goodman raced to Roxburgh's office across from the state capitol building. The Attorney General had a phone system fancy enough to hook up himself, Goodman, Kerry, Adam and Lucas Mann at Parchman, Justice Robichaux in Lake Charles, Justice Judy in New Orleans, and Justice McNeely in Amarillo, Texas. The three-judge panel allowed Adam and Roxburgh to make their arguments, then the conference was disbanded. At four o'clock, the clerk of the court called all parties with the denial, and faxes soon followed. Kerry and Goodman quickly faxed the appeal to the U.S. Supreme Court.

Sam was in the process of receiving his last physical exam when Adam finished his short chat with the clerk. He slowly hung up the phone. Sam was scowling at the young, frightened doctor, who was taking his blood pressure. Packer and Tiny stood nearby, at the request of the doctor. With five people present, the front office was crowded.

'Fifth Circuit just denied,' Adam said solemnly. 'We're on our way to the Supreme Court.'

'Not exactly the promised land,' Sam said, still staring at the doctor.

'I'm optimistic,' Adam said halfheartedly for the benefit of Packer.

The doctor quickly placed his instruments in his bag. 'That's it,' he said heading for the door.

'So I'm healthy enough to die?' Sam asked.

The doctor opened the door and left, followed by Packer and Tiny. Sam stood and stretched his back, then began pacing slowly across the room. The shoes slipped on his heels and affected his stride. 'Are you nervous?' he asked with a nasty smile.

'Of course. And I guess you're not.'

'The dying cannot be worse than the waiting. Hell, I'm ready. I'd like to get it over with.'

Adam almost said something trite about their reasonable chances in the Supreme Court, but he was not in the mood to be rebuked. Sam paced and smoked and was not in a talkative mood. Adam, typically, got busy with the telephone. He called Goodman and Kerry, but their conversations were brief. There was little to say, and no optimism whatsoever.

COLONEL NUGENT stood on the porch of the Visitors Center and asked for quiet. Assembled before him on the lawn was the small army of reporters and journalists, all anxiously awaiting the lottery. Next to him on a table was a tin bucket. Each member of the press wore an orange, numbered button dispensed by the prison administration as credentials. The mob was unusually quiet.

'According to prison regulations, there are eight seats allotted to members of the press,' Nugent explained slowly, his words carrying almost to the front gate. He was basking in the spotlight. 'One seat is allotted to the AP, one to the UPI, and one to the Mississippi Network. That leaves five to be selected at random. I'll pull five numbers from this bucket, and if one of them corresponds to your credentials, then it's your lucky day. Any questions?'

Several dozen reporters suddenly had no questions. Many of them pulled at their orange badges to check their numbers. A ripple of excitement went through the group. Nugent dramatically reached into the bucket and pulled out a slip of paper. 'Number four-eight-four-three,' he announced, with all the skill of a seasoned bingo caller.

'Here you go,' an excited young man called back, tugging at his lucky badge.

'Your name?' Nugent yelled.

'Edwin King, with the *Arkansas Gazette*.'

A deputy warden next to Nugent wrote down the name and paper. Edwin King was admired by his colleagues.

Nugent quickly called the other four numbers and completed the pool. A noticeable ebb of despair rolled through the group as the last number was called out. The losers were crushed. 'At exactly eleven, two vans will pull up over there.' Nugent pointed to the main drive. 'The eight witnesses must be present and ready. You will be driven to the Maximum Security Unit to witness the execution. No cameras or recorders of any type. You will be searched once you arrive there. Sometime around twelve-thirty, you will reboard the vans and return to this point. A press conference will then be held in the main hall of the new administration building, which will be opened at 9 P.M. for your convenience. Any questions?'

'How many people will witness the execution?' someone asked.

'There will be approximately thirteen or fourteen people in the witness room. And in the Chamber Room, there will be myself, one minister, one doctor, the state executioner, the attorney for the prison, and two guards.'

'Will the victims' family witness the execution?'

'Yes. Mr Elliot Kramer, the grandfather, is scheduled to be a witness.'

'How about the governor?'

'By statute, the governor has two seats in the witness room at his discretion. One of those seats will go to Mr Kramer. I have not been told whether the governor will be here.'

'What about Mr Cayhall's family?'

'No. None of his relatives will witness the execution.'

Nugent had opened a can of worms. The questions were

popping up everywhere, and he had things to do. 'No more questions. Thank you,' he said, and walked off the porch.

DONNIE CAYHALL arrived for his last visit a few minutes before six. He was led straight to the front office, where he found his well-dressed brother laughing with Adam Hall. Sam introduced the two.

Adam had carefully avoided Sam's brother until now. Donnie, as it turned out, was clean and neat, well groomed and dressed sensibly. He also resembled Sam, now that Sam had shaved, cut his hair, and shed the red jumpsuit. They were the same height, and though Donnie was not overweight, Sam was much thinner.

Donnie was clearly not the hick Adam had feared. He was genuinely happy to met Adam and proud of the fact that he was a lawyer. He was a pleasant man with an easy smile, good teeth, but very sad eyes at the moment. 'What's it look like?' he asked after a few minutes of small talk. He was referring to the appeals.

'It's all in the Supreme Court.'

'So there's still hope?'

Sam snorted at this suggestion.

'A little,' Adam said, very much resigned to fate.

There was a long pause as Adam and Donnie searched for less sensitive matters to discuss. Sam really didn't care. He sat calmly in a chair, legs crossed, puffing away. His mind was occupied with things they couldn't imagine.

'I stopped by Albert's today,' Donnie said.

Sam's gaze never left the floor. 'How's his prostrate?'

'I don't know. He thought you were already dead.'

'That's my brother.'

'I also saw Aunt Finnie.'

'I thought she was already dead,' Sam said with a smile.

'Almost. She's ninety-one. Just all tore up over what's happened to you. Said you were always her favorite nephew.'

'She couldn't stand me, and I couldn't stand her. Hell, I didn't see her for five years before I came here.'

558

'Well, she's just plain crushed over this.'

'She'll get over it.'

Sam's face suddenly broke into a wide smile, and he started laughing. 'Remember the time we watched her go to the outhouse behind Grandmother's, then peppered it with rocks? She came out screaming and crying.'

Donnie suddenly remembered, and began to shake with laughter. 'Yeah, it had a tin roof,' he said between breaths, 'and every rock sounded like a bomb going off.'

'Yeah, it was me and you and Albert. You couldn't have been four years old.'

'I remember though.'

The story grew and the laughter was contagious. Adam caught himself chuckling at the sight of these two old men laughing like boys. The one about Aunt Finnie and the outhouse led to one about her husband, Uncle Garland, who was mean and crippled, and the laughs continued.

SAM'S LAST MEAL was a deliberate snub at the fingerless cooks in the kitchen and the uninspired rations they'd tormented him with for nine and a half years. He requested something that was light, came from a carton, and could be found with ease. He had often marveled at his predecessors who'd ordered seven-course dinners – steaks and lobster and cheesecake. Buster Moac had consumed two dozen raw oysters, then a Greek salad, then a large rib eye and a few other courses. He'd never understood how they summoned such appetites only hours before death.

He wasn't the least bit hungry when Nugent knocked on the door at seven-thirty. Behind him was Packer, and behind Packer was a trustee holding a tray. In the center of the tray was a large bowl with three Eskimo Pies in it, and to the side was a small thermos of French Market coffee, Sam's favorite. The tray was placed on the desk.

'Not much of a dinner, Sam,' Nugent said.

'Can I enjoy it in peace, or will you stand there and pester me with your idiot talk?'

Nugent stiffened and glared at Adam. 'We'll come back

559

in an hour. At that time, your guest must leave, and we'll return you to the Observation Cell. Okay?'

'Just leave,' Sam said, sitting at the desk.

As soon as they were gone, Donnie said, 'Damn, Sam, why didn't you order something we could enjoy? What kind of a last meal is this?'

'It's my last meal. When your time comes, order what you want.' He picked up a fork and carefully scraped the vanilla ice cream and chocolate covering off the stick. He took a large bite, then slowly poured the coffee into the cup. It was dark and strong with a rich aroma.

Donnie and Adam sat in the chairs along a wall, watching Sam's back as he slowly ate his last meal.

THEY'D BEEN ARRIVING since five o'clock. They came from all over the state, all driving alone, all riding in big four-door cars of varied colors with elaborate seals and emblems and markings on the doors and fenders. Some had racks of emergency lights across the roof. Some had shotguns mounted on the screens above the front seats. All had tall antennas swinging in the wind.

They were the sheriffs, each elected in his own county to protect the citizenry from lawlessness. Most had served for many years, and most had already taken part in the unrecorded ritual of the execution dinner.

A cook named Miss Mazola prepared the feast, and the menu never varied. She fried large chickens in animal fat. She cooked black-eyed peas in ham hocks. And she made real buttermilk biscuits the size of small saucers. Her kitchen was in the rear of a small cafeteria near the main administration building. The food was always served at seven, regardless of how many sheriffs were present.

Tonight's crowd would be the largest since Teddy Doyle Meeks was put to rest in 1982. Miss Mazola anticipated this because she read the papers and everybody knew about Sam Cayhall. She expected at least fifty sheriffs.

They were waved through the front gates like dignitaries, and they parked haphazardly around the cafeteria. For the most part they were big men, with earnest stomachs and voracious appetites. They were famished after the long drive.

Their banter was light over dinner. They ate like hogs, then retired outside to the front of the building where they sat on the hoods of their cars and watched it grow dark. They picked chicken from their teeth and bragged on Miss Mazola's cooking. They listened to their radios squawk, as if the news of Cayhall's death would be transmitted at any moment. They talked about other executions and heinous crimes back home, and about local boys on the Row. Damned gas chamber wasn't used enough.

They stared in amazement at the hundreds of demonstrators near the highway in front of them. They picked their teeth some more, then went back inside for chocolate cake.

It was a wonderful night for law enforcement.

FORTY-NINE

DARKNESS BROUGHT an eerie quiet to the highway in front of Parchman. The Klansmen, not a single one of whom had considered leaving after Sam asked them to, sat in folding chairs and on the trampled grass, and waited. The skinheads and like-minded brethren who'd roasted in the August sun sat in small groups and drank ice water. The nuns and other activists had been joined by a contingent from Amnesty International. They lit candles, said prayers, hummed songs. They tried to keep their distance from the hate groups. Pick any other day, another execution, another inmate, and those same hateful people would be screaming for blood.

The calm was broken momentarily when a pickup load of teenagers slowed near the front entrance. They suddenly began shouting loudly and in unison, 'Gas his ass! Gas his ass! Gas his ass!' The truck squealed tires and sped away. Some of the Klansmen jumped to their feet, ready for battle, but the kids were gone, never to return.

The imposing presence of the highway patrol kept matters under control. The troopers stood about in groups, watching the traffic, keeping close watch on the Klansmen and the skinheads. A helicopter made its rounds above.

GOODMAN FINALLY CALLED a halt to the market analysis. In five long days, they had logged over two thousand calls. He paid the students, confiscated the cellular phones, and thanked them profusely. None of them

562

seemed willing to throw in the towel, so they walked with him to the capitol where another candlelight vigil was under way on the front steps. The governor was still in his office on the second floor.

One of the students volunteered to take a phone to John Bryan Glass, who was across the street at the Mississippi Supreme Court. Goodman called him, then called Kerry, then called Joshua Caldwell, an old friend who'd agreed to wait at the Death Clerk's desk in Washington. Goodman had everyone in place. All the phones were working. He called Adam. Sam was finishing his last meal, Adam said, and didn't wish to talk to Goodman. But he did want to say thanks for everything.

WHEN THE COFFEE and ice cream were gone, Sam stood and stretched his legs. Donnie had been quiet for a long time. He was suffering and ready to go. Nugent would come soon, and he wanted to say good-bye now.

There was a spot where Sam had spilled ice cream on his new shirt, and Donnie tried to remove it with a cloth napkin. 'It's not that important,' Sam said, watching his brother.

Donnie kept wiping. 'Yeah, you're right. I'd better go now, Sam. They'll be here in minute.'

The two men embraced for a long time, patted each other gently on the backs. 'I'm so sorry, Sam,' Donnie said, his voice shaking. 'I'm so sorry.'

They pulled apart, still clutching each other's shoulders, both men with moist eyes but no tears. They would not dare cry before each other. 'You take care,' Sam said.

'You too. Say a prayer, Sam, okay?'

'I will. Thanks for everything. You're the only one who cared.'

Donnie bit his lip and hid his eyes from Sam. He shook hands with Adam, but could not utter a word. He walked behind Sam to the door, then left them.

'No word from the Supreme Court?' Sam asked out of nowhere, as if he suddenly believed there was a chance.

'No,' Adam said sadly.

He sat on the desk, his feet swinging beneath him. 'I really want this to be over, Adam,' he said, each word carefully measured. 'This is cruel.'

Adam could think of nothing to say.

'In China, they sneak up behind you and put a bullet through your head. No last bowl of rice. No farewells. No waiting. Not a bad idea.'

Adam looked at his watch for the millionth time in the past hour. Since noon, there had been gaps when hours seemed to vanish, then suddenly time would stop. It would fly, then it would crawl. Someone knocked on the door. 'Come in,' Sam said faintly.

The Reverend Ralph Griffin entered and closed the door. He'd met with Sam twice during the day, and was obviously taking this hard. It was his first execution, and he'd already decided it would be his last. His cousin in the state senate would have to find him another job. He nodded at Adam and sat by Sam on the desk. It was almost nine o'clock.

'Colonel Nugent's out there, Sam. He said he's waiting on you.'

'Well, then, let's not go out. Let's just sit here.'

'Suits me.'

'You know, preacher, my heart has been touched these past few days in ways I never dreamed possible. But, for the life of me, I hate that jerk out there. And I can't overcome it.'

'Hate's an awful thing, Sam.'

'I know. But I can't help it.'

'I don't particularly like him either, to be honest.'

Sam grinned at the minister and put his arm around him. The voices outside grew louder, and Nugent barged into the room. 'Sam, it's time to go back to the Observation Cell,' he said.

Adam stood, his knees weak with fear, his stomach in knots, his heart racing wildly. Sam, however, was unruffled. He jumped from the desk. 'Let's go,' he said.

They followed Nugent from the front office into the narrow hallway where some of the largest guards at

Parchman were waiting along the wall. Sam took Adam by the hand, and they walked slowly together with the reverend trailing behind.

Adam squeezed his grandfather's hand, and ignored the faces as they walked by. They went through the center of the Row, through two sets of doors, then through the bars at the end of Tier A. The tier door closed behind them, and they followed Nugent past the cells.

Sam glanced at the faces of the men he'd known so well. He winked at Hank Henshaw, nodded bravely at J. B. Gullitt who had tears in his eyes, smiled at Stock Turner. They were all leaning through the bars, heads hung low, fear stamped all over their faces. Sam gave them his bravest look.

Nugent stopped at the last cell and waited for the door to be opened from the end of the tier. It clicked loudly, then rolled open. Sam, Adam, and Ralph entered, and Nugent gave the signal to close the door.

The cell was dark, the solitary light and television both off. Sam sat on the bed between Adam and the reverend. He leaned on his elbows with his head hanging low.

Nugent watched them for a moment, but could think of nothing to say. He'd be back in a couple of hours, at eleven, to take Sam to the Isolation Room. They all knew he was coming back. It seemed too cruel at this moment to tell Sam he was leaving, but that he would return. So he stepped away and left through the tier door where his guards were waiting and watching in the semidarkness. Nugent walked to the Isolation Room where a foldaway cot had been installed for the prisoner's last hour. He walked through the small room, and stepped into the Chamber Room where final preparations were being made.

The state executioner was busy and very much in control. He was a short, wiry man named Bill Monday. He had nine fingers and would earn five hundred dollars for his services if the execution took place. By statute, he was appointed by the governor. He was in a tiny closet known simply as the chemical room, less than five feet from the gas chamber. He

565

was studying a checklist on a clipboard. Before him on the counter was a one-pound can of sodium cyanide pellets, a nine-pound bottle of sulfuric acid, a one-pound container of caustic acid, a fifty-pound steel bottle of anhydrous ammonia, and a five-gallon container of distilled water. To his side on another, smaller counter were three gas masks, three pair of rubber gloves, a funnel, hand soap, hand towels, and a mop. Between the two counters was an acid mixing pot mounted on a two-inch pipe that ran into the floor, under the wall, and resurfaced next to the chamber near the levers.

Monday had three checklists, actually. One contained instructions for mixing the chemicals: the sulfuric acid and distilled water would be mixed to obtain approximately a 41 percent concentration; the caustic soda solution was made by dissolving one pound of caustic acid in two and a half gallons of water; and there were a couple of other brews that had to be mixed to clean the chamber after the execution. One list included all the necessary chemicals and supplies. The third list was the procedure to follow during an actual execution.

Nugent spoke to Monday; all was proceeding as planned. One of Monday's assistants was smearing petroleum jelly around the edges of the chamber's windows. A plainclothed member of the execution team was checking the belts and straps on the wooden chair. The doctor was fiddling with his EKG monitor. The door was open to the outside, where an ambulance was already parked.

Nugent glanced at the checklists once more, though he'd memorized them long ago. In fact, he'd even rewritten one other checklist, a suggested chart to record the execution. The chart would be used by Nugent, Monday, and Monday's assistant. It was a numbered, chronological list of the events of the execution: water and acid mixed, prisoner enters chamber, chamber door locked, sodium cyanide enters acid, gas strikes prisoner's face, prisoner apparently unconscious, prisoner certainly unconscious, movements of prisoner's body, last visible movement, heart stopped, respiration stopped, exhaust valve opened, drain valves opened, air valve opened, chamber door opened, prisoner removed from chamber, prisoner pronounced dead. Beside each was a blank line to record the time elapsed from the prior event.

And there was an execution list, a chart of the twenty-nine steps to be taken to begin and complete the task. Of course, the execution list had an appendix, a list of the fifteen things to do in the step-down, the last of which was to place the prisoner in the ambulance.

Nugent knew every step on every list. He knew how to mix the chemicals, how to open the valves, how long to leave them open, and how to close them. He knew it all.

He stepped outside to speak to the ambulance driver and get some air, then he walked back through the Isolation Room to Tier A. Like everyone else, he was waiting for the damned Supreme Court to rule one way or the other.

He sent the two tallest guards onto the tier to close the windows along the top of the outside wall. Like the building, the windows had been there for thirty-six years and they did not shut quietly. The guards pushed them up until they slammed, each one echoing along the tier. Thirty-five windows in all, every inmate knew the exact number, and with each closing the tier became darker and quieter.

The guards finally finished and left. The Row was now locked down – every inmate in his cell, all doors secured, all windows closed.

Sam had begun shaking with the closing of the windows. His head dropped even lower. Adam placed an arm around his frail shoulders.

'I always liked those windows,' Sam said, his voice low and hoarse. A squad of guards stood less than fifteen feet away, peering through the tier door like kids at the zoo, and Sam didn't want his words to be heard. It was hard to imagine Sam liking anything about this place. 'Used to, when it came a big rain the water would splash on the windows, and some of it would make it inside and trickle down to the floor. I always liked the rain. And the moon. Sometimes, if the clouds were gone, I could stand just right in my cell and catch a glimpse of the moon through those windows. I always wondered why they didn't have more windows around here. I mean, hell, sorry preacher, but if they're determined to keep you in a cell all day, why shouldn't you be able to see outdoors? I never understood that. I guess I never understood a lot of things. Oh well.' His voice trailed off, and he didn't speak again for a while.

From the darkness came the mellow tenor of Preacher Boy singing 'Just a Closer Walk with Thee.' It was quite pretty.

> 'Just a closer walk with Thee,
> Grant it, Jesus, is my plea,
> Daily walking close to Thee . . .'

'Quiet!' a guard yelled.

'Leave him alone!' Sam yelled back, startling both Adam and Ralph. 'Sing it, Randy,' Sam said just loud enough to be heard next door. Preacher Boy took his time, his feelings obviously wounded, then began again.

A door slammed somewhere, and Sam jumped. Adam squeezed his shoulder, and he settled down. His eyes were lost somewhere in the darkness of the floor.

'I take it Lee wouldn't come,' he said, his words haunted.

Adam thought for a second, and decided to tell the truth. 'I don't know where she is. I haven't talked to her in ten days.'

'Thought she was in a rehab clinic.'

'I think she is too, but I just don't know where. I'm sorry. I tried everything to find her.'

'I've thought about her a lot these past days. Please tell her.'

'I will.' If Adam saw her again, he would struggle to keep from choking her.

'And I've thought a lot about Eddie.'

'Look, Sam, we don't have long. Let's talk about pleasant things, okay?'

568

'I want you to forgive me for what I did to Eddie.'

'I've already forgiven you, Sam. It's taken care of. Carmen and I both forgive you.'

Ralph lowered his head next to Sam's, and said, 'Perhaps there are some others we should think about too, Sam.'

'Maybe later,' Sam said.

The tier door opened at the far end of the hallway, and footsteps hurried toward them. Lucas Mann, with a guard behind him, stopped at the last cell and looked at the three shadowy figures huddled together on the bed. 'Adam, you have a phone call,' he said nervously. 'In the front office.'

The three shadowy figures stiffened together. Adam jumped to his feet, and without a word stepped from the cell as the door opened. His belly churned violently as he half-ran down the tier. 'Give 'em hell, Adam,' J. B. Gullitt said as he raced by.

'Who is it?' Adam asked Lucas Mann, who was beside him, step for step.

'Garner Goodman.'

They weaved through the center of MSU and hurried to the front office. The receiver was lying on the desk. Adam grabbed it and sat on the desk. 'Garner, this is Adam.'

'I'm at the capitol, Adam, in the rotunda outside the governor's office. The Supreme Court just denied all of our cert petitions. There's nothing left up there.'

Adam closed his eyes and paused. 'Well, I guess that's the end of that,' he said, and looked at Lucas Mann. Lucas frowned and dropped his head.

'Sit tight. The governor's about to make an announcement. I'll call you in five minutes.' Goodman was gone.

Adam hung up the phone and stared at it. 'The Supreme Court turned down everything,' he reported to Mann. 'The governor's making a statement. He'll call back in a minute.'

Mann sat down. 'I'm sorry, Adam. Very sorry. How's Sam holding up?'

'Sam is taking this much better than I am, I think.'

'It's strange, isn't it? This is my fifth one, and I'm always amazed at how calmly they go. They give up when it gets dark. They have their last meal, say good-bye to their families, and become oddly placid about the whole thing. Me, I'd be kicking and screaming and crying. It would take twenty men to drag me out of the Observation Cell.'

Adam managed a quick smile, then noticed an open shoe box on the desk. It was lined with aluminum foil with a few broken cookies in the bottom. It had not been there when they left an hour earlier. 'What's that?' he asked, not really curious.

'Those are the execution cookies?'

'The execution cookies?'

'Yeah, this sweet little lady who lives down the road bakes them every time there's an execution.'

'Why?'

'I don't know. In fact, I have no idea why she does it.'

'Who eats them?' Adam asked, looking at the remaining cookies and crumbs as if they were poison.

'The guards and trustees.'

Adam shook his head. He had too much on his mind to analyze the purpose of a batch of execution cookies.

FOR THE OCCASION, David McAllister changed into a dark navy suit, freshly starched white shirt, and dark burgundy tie. He combed and sprayed his hair, brushed his teeth, then walked into his office from a side door. Mona Stark was crunching numbers.

'The calls finally stopped,' she said, somewhat relieved.

'I don't want to hear it,' McAllister said, checking his tie and teeth in a mirror. 'Let's go.'

He opened the door and stepped into the foyer where two bodyguards met him. They flanked him as he walked into the rotunda where bright lights were waiting. A throng of reporters and cameras pressed forward to hear the announcement. He stepped to a makeshift stand with a dozen microphones wedged together. He grimaced at the lights, waited for quiet, then spoke.

'The Supreme Court of the United States has just denied the last appeals from Sam Cayhall,' he said dramatically, as

570

if the reporters hadn't already heard this. Another pause as the cameras clicked and the microphones waited. 'And so, after three jury trials, after nine years of appeals through every court available under our Constitution, after having the case reviewed by no less than forty-seven judges, justice has finally arrived for Sam Cayhall. His crime was committed twenty-three years ago. Justice may be slow, but it still works. I have been called upon by many people to pardon Mr Cayhall, but I cannot do so. I cannot overrule the wisdom of the jury that sentenced him, nor can I impose my judgment upon that of our distinguished courts. Neither am I willing to go against the wishes of my friends the Kramers.' Another pause. He spoke without notes, and it was immediately obvious he'd worked on these remarks for a long time. 'It is my fervent hope that the execution of Sam Cayhall will help erase a painful chapter in our state's tortured history. I call upon all Mississippians to come together from this sad night forward, and work for equality. May God have mercy on his soul.'

He backed away as the questions flew. The bodyguards opened a side door, and he was gone. They darted down the stairs and out the north entrance where a car was waiting. A mile away, a helicopter was also waiting.

Goodman walked outside and stood by an old cannon, aimed for some reason at the tall buildings downtown. Below him, at the foot of the front steps, a large group of protestors held candles. He called Adam with the news, then he walked through the people and the candles and left the capitol grounds. A hymn started as he crossed the street, and for two blocks it slowly faded away. He drifted for a while, then walked toward Hez Kerry's office.

FIFTY

THE WALK BACK to the Observation Cell was much longer than before. Adam made it alone, by now on familiar terrain. Lucas Mann disappeared somewhere in the labyrinth of the Row.

As Adam waited before a heavy barred door in the center of the building, he was immediately aware of two things. First, there were many more people hanging around now – more guards, more strangers with plastic badges and guns on their hips, more stern-faced men with short-sleeved shirts and polyester ties. This was a happening, a singular phenomenon too thrilling to be missed. Adam speculated that any prison employee with enough pull and enough clout just had to be on the Row when Sam's death sentence was carried out.

The second thing he realized was that his shirt was soaked and the collar was sticking to his neck. He loosened his tie as the door clicked loudly then slid open under the hum of a hidden electric motor. A guard somewhere in the maze of concrete walls and windows and bars was watching and punching the right buttons. He stepped through, still pulling on the knot of his tie and the button under it, and walked to the next barrier, a wall of bars leading to Tier A. He patted his forehead, but there was no sweat. He filled his lungs with muggy, dank air.

With the windows shut, the tier was now suffocating. Another loud click, another hum, and he stepped into the thin hallway, which Sam had told him was seven and a half feet wide. Three dingy sets of fluorescent bulbs cast dim shadows on the ceiling and floor. He pushed his heavy feet past the dark cells, all filled with brutal murderers, each one now praying or meditating, a couple even crying.

'Good news, Adam?' J. B. Gullitt pleaded from the darkness.

Adam didn't answer. Still walking, he glanced up at the windows with their various shades of paint splattered around the ancient panes, and was struck by the question of how many lawyers before him had made this final walk from the front office to the Observation Cell to inform a dying man that the last thin shred of hope was now gone. This place had a rich history of executions, and so he concluded that many others had suffered along this trail. Garner Goodman himself had carried the final news to Maynard Tole, and this gave Adam a much needed shot of strength.

He ignored the curious stares of the small mob standing and gawking at him at the end of the tier. He stopped at the last cell, waited, and the door obediently opened.

Sam and the reverend were still sitting low on the bed, heads nearly touching in the darkness, whispering. They looked up at Adam, who sat next to Sam and placed his arm around his shoulders, shoulders that now seemed even frailer. 'The Supreme Court just denied everything,' he said very softly, his voice on the verge of cracking. The reverend exhaled a painful moan. Sam nodded as if this was certainly expected. 'And the governor just denied clemency.'

Sam tried to raise his shoulders bravely, but power failed him. He slumped even lower.

'Lord have mercy,' Ralph Griffin said.

'Then it's all over,' Sam said.

'There's nothing left,' Adam whispered.

Excited murmurings could be heard from the death squad squeezed together at the end of the tier. This thing would happen after all. A door slammed somewhere behind them, in the direction of the chamber, and Sam's knees jerked together.

He was silent for a moment – one minute or fifteen, Adam couldn't tell. The clock was still lurching and stopping.

'I guess we oughta pray now, preacher,' Sam said.

'I reckon so. We've waited long enough.'

'How do you wanna do it?'

'Well, Sam, just exactly what do you want to pray about?'

Sam pondered this for a moment, then said, 'I'd like to make sure God's not angry with me when I die.'

'Good idea. And why do you think God might be angry with you?'

'Pretty obvious, isn't it?'

Ralph rubbed his hands together. 'I guess the best way to do this is to confess your sins, and ask God to forgive you.'

'All of them?'

'You don't have to list them all, just ask God to forgive everything.'

'Sort of a blanket repentance.'

'Yeah, that's it. And it'll work, if you're serious.'

'I'm serious as hell.'

'Do you believe in hell, Sam?'

'I do.'

'Do you believe in heaven?'

'I do.'

'Do you believe that all Christians go to heaven?'

Sam thought about this for a long time, then nodded slightly before asking, 'Do you?'

'Yes, Sam. I do.'

'Then I'll take your word for it.'

'Good. Trust me on this one, okay?'

'It seems too easy, you know. I just say a quick prayer, and everything's forgiven.'

'Why does that bother you?'

'Because I've done some bad things, preacher.'

'We've all done bad things. Our God is a God of infinite love.'

'You haven't done what I've done.'

'Will you feel better if you talk about it?'

'Yeah, I won't ever feel right unless I talk about it.'

574

'I'm here, Sam.'

'Should I leave for a minute?' Adam asked. Sam clutched his knee. 'No.'

'We don't have a lot of time, Sam,' Ralph said, glancing through the bars.

Sam took a deep breath, and spoke in a low monotone, careful that only Adam and Ralph could hear. 'I killed Joe Lincoln in cold blood. I've already said I was sorry.'

Ralph was mumbling something to himself as he listened. He was already in prayer.

'And I helped my brothers kill those two men who murdered our father. Frankly, I've never felt bad about it until now. Human life seems a whole lot more valuable these days. I was wrong. And I took part in a lynching when I was fifteen or sixteen. I was just part of a mob, and I probably couldn't have stopped it if I'd tried. But I didn't try, and I feel guilty about it.'

Sam stopped. Adam held his breath and hoped the confessional was over. Ralph waited and waited, and finally asked, 'Is that it, Sam?'

'No. There's one more.'

Adam closed his eyes and braced for it. He was dizzy and wanted to vomit.

'There was another lynching. A boy named Cletus. I can't remember his last name. A Klan lynching. I was eighteen. That's all I can say.'

This nightmare will never end, Adam thought.

Sam breathed deeply and was silent for several minutes. Ralph was praying hard. Adam just waited.

'And I didn't kill those Kramer boys,' Sam said, his voice shaking. 'I had no business being there, and I was wrong to be involved in that mess. I've regretted it for many years, all of it. It was wrong to be in the Klan, hating everybody and planting bombs. But I didn't kill those boys. There was no intent to harm anyone. That bomb was supposed to go off in the middle of the night when no one would be anywhere near it. That's what I truly believed. But it was wired by someone else, not me. I was just a lookout, a driver, a

575

flunky. This other person rigged the bomb to go off much later than I thought. I've never known for sure if he intended to kill anyone, but I suspect he did.'

Adam heard the words, received them, absorbed them, but was too stunned to move.

'But I could've stopped it. And that makes me guilty. Those little boys would be alive today if I had acted differently after the bomb was planted. Their blood is on my hands, and I've grieved over this for many years.'

Ralph gently placed a hand on the back of Sam's head. 'Pray with me, Sam.' Sam covered his eyes with both hands and rested his elbows on his knees.

'Do you believe Jesus Christ was the son of God; that he came to this earth, born of a virgin, lived a sinless life, was persecuted, and died on the cross so that we might have eternal salvation? Do you believe this, Sam?'

'Yes,' he whispered.

'And that he arose from the grave and ascended into heaven?'

'Yes.'

'And that through him all of your sins are forgiven? All the terrible things that burden your heart are now forgiven. Do you believe this, Sam?'

'Yes, yes.'

Ralph released Sam's head, and wiped tears from his eyes. Sam didn't move, but his shoulders were shaking. Adam squeezed him even tighter.

Randy Dupree started whistling another stanza of 'Just a Closer walk with Thee.' His notes were clear and precise, and they echoed nicely along the tier.

'Preacher,' Sam said as his back stiffened, 'will those little Kramer boys be in heaven?'

'Yes.'

'But they were Jews.'

'All children go to heaven, Sam.'

'Will I see them up there?'

'I don't know. There's a lot about heaven we don't know.

576

But the Bible promises that there will be no sorrow when we get there.'

'Good. Then I hope I see them.'

The unmistakable voice of Colonel Nugent broke the calm. The tier door clanged, rattled, and opened. He marched five feet to the door of the Observation Cell. Six guards were behind him. 'Sam, it's time to go to the Isolation Room,' he said. 'It's eleven o'clock.'

The three men stood, side by side. The cell door opened, and Sam stepped out. He smiled at Nugent, then he turned and hugged the reverend. 'Thanks,' he said.

'I love you, brother!' Randy Dupree yelled from his cell, not ten feet away.

Sam looked at Nugent, and asked, 'Could I say good-bye to my friends?'

A deviation. The manual plainly said that the prisoner was to be taken directly from the Observation Cell to the Isolation Room, with nothing being mentioned about a final promenade down the tier. Nugent was dumbstruck, but after a few seconds rallied nicely. 'Sure, but make it quick.'

Sam took a few steps and clasped Randy's hands through the bars. Then he stepped to the next cell and shook hands with Harry Ross Scott.

Ralph Griffin eased past the guards and left the tier. He found a dark corner and wept like a child. He would not see Sam again. Adam stood in the door of the cell, near Nugent, and together they watched Sam work his way down the hallway, stopping at each cell, whispering something to each inmate. He spent the most time with J. B. Gullitt, whose sobs could be heard.

Then he turned and walked bravely back to them, counting steps as he went, smiling at his pals along the way. He took Adam by the hand. 'Let's go,' he said to Nugent.

There were so damned many guards packed together at the end of the tier that it was a tight squeeze just to get by them. Nugent went first, then Sam and Adam. The mass of human congestion added several degrees to the temperature and several layers to the stuffy air. The show of force was necessary, of course, to subdue a reluctant prisoner, or perhaps to scare one into submission. It seemed awfully silly with a little old man like Sam Cayhall.

The walk from one room to another took only seconds, a distance of twenty feet, but Adam winced with every painful step. Through the human tunnel of armed guards, through the heavy steel door, into the small room. The door on the opposite wall was shut. It led to the chamber.

A flimsy cot had been hauled in for the occasion. Adam and Sam sat on it. Nugent closed the door, and knelt before them. The three of them were alone. Adam again placed his arm around Sam's shoulders.

Nugent was wearing a terribly pained expression. He placed a hand on Sam's knee, and said, 'Sam, we're gonna get through this together. Now—'

'You goofy fool,' Adam blurted, amazed at this remarkable utterance.

'He can't help it,' Sam said helpfully to Adam. 'He's just stupid. He didn't even realize it.'

Nugent felt the sharp rebuke, and tried to think of something proper to say. 'I'm just trying to get through this, okay?' he said to Adam.

'Why don't you just leave?' Adam said.

'You know something, Nugent?' Sam asked. 'I've read tons of law books. And I've read pages and pages of prison regulations. And nowhere have I read anything that requires me to spend my last hour with you. No law, statute, regulation, nothing.'

'Just get the hell out of here,' Adam said, ready to strike if necessary.

Nugent jumped to his feet. 'The doctor will enter through that door at eleven-forty. He'll stick a stethoscope to your chest, then leave. At eleven fifty-five, I will enter, also through that door. At that time, we'll go into the Chamber Room. Any questions?'

'No. Leave,' Adam said, waving at the door. Nugent made a quick exit.

Suddenly, they were alone. With an hour to go.

TWO IDENTICAL PRISON VANS rolled to a stop in front of the Visitors Center, and were boarded by the eight lucky reporters and one lone sheriff. The law allowed, but did not require, the sheriff of the county where the crime was committed to witness the execution.

The man who was the sheriff of Washington County in 1967 had been dead for fifteen years, but the current sheriff was not about to miss this event. He had informed Lucas Mann earlier in the day that he fully intended to invoke the power of the law. Said he felt like he owed it to the people of Greenville and Washington County.

Mr Elliot Kramer was not present at Parchman. He had planned the trip for years, but his doctor intervened at the last moment. His heart was weak and it was just too risky. Ruth Kramer had never thought seriously of witnessing the execution. She was at home in Memphis, sitting with friends, waiting for it to end.

There would be no members of the victims' family present to witness the killing of Sam Cayhall.

The vans were heavily photographed and filmed as they left and disappeared on the main drive. Five minutes later, they stopped at the gates of MSU. Everyone was asked to step outside, where they were checked for cameras and recorders. They reboarded the vans and were cleared through the gates. The vans drove through the grass along the front of MSU, then around the bullpens on the west end, then stopped very near the ambulance.

Nugent himself was waiting. The reporters stepped from the vans and instinctively began looking wildly around, trying to grasp it all to record later. They were just outside a square red-brick building that was somehow attached to the low, flat structure that was MSU. The little building had two doors. One was closed, the other was waiting for them.

Nugent was not in the mood for nosy reporters. He hurriedly guided them through the open door. They stepped into a small room where two rows of folding chairs were waiting, facing an ominous panel of black drapes.

'Take a seat please,' he said rudely. He counted eight reporters, one sheriff. Three seats were empty. 'It is now eleven-ten,' he said dramatically. 'The prisoner is in the Isolation Room. Before you here, on the other side of these curtains, is the Chamber Room. He will be brought in at five minutes before twelve, strapped in, the door locked. The curtains will be opened at exactly midnight, and when you see the chamber the prisoner will already be inside it, less than two feet from the windows. You will see only the back of his head. I didn't design this, okay? It should take about ten minutes before he is pronounced dead, at which time the curtains will be closed and you'll return to the vans. You'll have a long wait, and I'm sorry this room has no air conditioning. When the curtains open, things will happen quickly. Any questions?'

'Have you talked to the prisoner?'

'Yes.'

'How's he holding up?'

'I'm not getting into all that. A press conference is planned at one, and I'll answer those questions then. Right now I'm busy.' Nugent left the witness room and slammed the door behind him. He walked quickly around the corner, and entered the Chamber Room.

'WE HAVE LESS than an hour. What would you like to talk about?' Sam asked.

'Oh, lots of things. Most of it unpleasant, though.'

'It's kinda hard to have an enjoyable conversation at this point, you know.'

'What are you thinking right now, Sam? What's going through your mind?'

'Everything.'

'What are you afraid of?'

'The smell of the gas. Whether or not it's painful. I don't want to suffer, Adam. I hope it's quick. I want a big whiff of it, and maybe I'll just float away. I'm not afraid of death, Adam, but right now I'm afraid of dying. I just wish it was over. This waiting is cruel.'

580

'Are you ready?'

'My hard little heart is at peace. I've done some bad things, son, but I feel like God might give me a break. I certainly don't deserve one.'

'Why didn't you tell me about the man who was with you?'

'It's a long story. We don't have much time.'

'It could've saved your life.'

'No, nobody would've believed it. Think about it. Twenty-three years later I suddenly change my story and blame it all on a mystery man. It would've been ridiculous.'

'Why'd you lie to me?'

'I have reasons.'

'To protect me?'

'That's one of them.'

'He's still out there, isn't he?'

'Yes. He's close by. In fact he's probably out front with all the other loonies right now. Just watching. You'd never see him, though.'

'He killed Dogan and his wife?'

'Yes.'

'And Dogan's son?'

'Yes.'

'And Clovis Brazelton?'

'Probably. He's a very talented killer, Adam. He's deadly. He threatened me and Dogan during the first trial.'

'Does he have a name?'

'Not really. I wouldn't tell you anyway. You can never breathe a word of this.'

'You're dying for someone else's crime.'

'No. I could've saved those little boys. And God knows I've killed my share of people. I deserve this, Adam.'

'No one deserves this.'

'It's far better than living. If they took me back to my cell right now and told me I'd stay there until I died, you know what I'd do?'

'What?'

'I'd kill myself.'

581

After spending the last hour in a cell, Adam couldn't argue with this. He could not begin to comprehend the horror of living twenty-three hours a day in a tiny cage.

'I forgot my cigarettes,' Sam said, patting his shirt pocket. 'I guess this is a good time to quit.'

'Are you trying to be funny?'

'Yeah.'

'It's not working.'

'Did Lee ever show you the book with my lynching picture in it?'

'She didn't show it to me. She told me where it was, and I found it.'

'You saw the picture.'

'Yes.'

'A regular party, wasn't it?'

'Pretty sad.'

'Did you see the other picture of the lynching, one page over?'

'Yes. Two Kluckers.'

'With robes and hoods and masks.'

'Yes, I saw it.'

'That was me and Albert. I was hiding behind one of the masks.'

Adam's senses were beyond the point of shock. The gruesome photograph flashed through his mind, and he tried to purge it. 'Why are you telling me this, Sam?'

'Because it feels good. I've never admitted it before, and there's a certain relief in facing the truth. I feel better already.'

'I don't want to hear any more.'

'Eddie never knew it. He found that book in the attic, and somehow figured out I was in the other party photo. But he didn't know I was one of the Kluckers.'

'Let's not talk about Eddie, okay?'

'Good idea. What about Lee?'

'I'm mad at Lee. She skipped out on us.'

'It would've been nice to see her, you know. That hurts. But I'm so glad Carmen came.'

582

Finally, a pleasant subject. 'She's a fine person,' Adam said.

'A great kid. I'm very proud of you, Adam, and of Carmen. Y'all got the good genes from your mother. I'm so lucky to have two wonderful grandchildren.'

Adam listened and didn't try to respond. Something banged next door, and they both jumped.

'Nugent must be playing with his gadgets in there,' Sam said, his shoulders vibrating again. 'You know what hurts?'

'What?'

'I've been thinking a lot about this, really flogging myself the last couple of days. I look at you, and I look at Carmen, and I see two bright young people with open minds and hearts. You don't hate anybody. You're tolerant and broad-minded, well educated, ambitious, going places without the baggage I was born with. And I look at you, my grandson, my flesh and blood, and I ask myself, Why didn't I become something else? Something like you and Carmen? It's hard to believe we're actually related.'

'Come on, Sam. Don't do this.'

'I can't help it.'

'Please, Sam.'

'Okay, okay. Something pleasant.' His voice trailed off and he leaned over. His head was low and hanging almost between his legs.

Adam wanted an in-depth conversation about the mysterious accomplice. He wanted to know it all – the real details of the bombing, the disappearance, how and why Sam got caught. He also wanted to know what might become of this guy, especially since he was out there, watching and waiting. But these questions would not be answered, so he let them pass. Sam would take many secrets to his grave.

THE ARRIVAL of the governor's helicopter created a stir along the front entrance of Parchman. It landed on the other side of the highway where another prison van waited. With a bodyguard on each elbow and Mona Stark racing behind,

McAllister scampered into the van. 'It's the governor!' someone yelled. The hymns and prayers stopped momentarily. Cameras raced to film the van, which raced through the front gate and disappeared.

Minutes later, it stopped near the ambulance behind MSU. The bodyguards and Ms Stark remained in the van. Nugent met the governor and escorted him into the witness room where he took a seat in the front row. He nodded at the other witnesses, all sweating profusely by now. The room was an oven. Black mosquitoes bounced along the walls. Nugent asked if there was anything he could fetch for the governor.

'Popcorn,' McAllister cracked, but no one laughed. Nugent frowned and left the room.

'Why are you here?' a reporter asked immediately.

'No comment,' McAllister said smugly.

The ten of them sat in silence, staring at the black drapes and anxiously checking their watches. The nervous chatter had ended. They avoided eye contact, as if they were ashamed to be participants in such a macabre event.

Nugent stopped at the door of the gas chamber and consulted a checklist. It was eleven-forty. He told the doctor to enter the Isolation Room, then he stepped outside and gave the signal for the guards to be removed from the four towers around MSU. The odds of escaping gas injuring a tower guard after the execution were miniscule, but Nugent loved the details.

THE KNOCK on the door was faint indeed, but at the moment it sounded as if a sledgehammer were being used. It cracked through the silence, startling both Adam and Sam. The door opened. The young doctor stepped in, tried to smile, dropped to one knee, and asked Sam to unbutton his shirt. A round stethoscope was stuck to his pale skin, with a short wire left hanging to his belt.

The doctor's hands shook. He said nothing.

584

FIFTY-ONE

AT ELEVEN-THIRTY, Hez Kerry, Garner Goodman, John Bryan Glass, and two of his students stopped their idle talk and held hands around the cluttered table in Kerry's office. Each offered a silent prayer for Sam Cayhall, then Hez voiced one for the group. They sat in their seats, deep in thought, deep in silence, and said another short one for Adam.

THE END CAME QUICKLY. The clock, sputtering and braking for the last twenty-four hours, suddenly roared ahead.

For a few minutes after the doctor left, they shared a light, nervous chatter as Sam walked twice across the small room, measuring it, then leaned on the wall opposite the bed. They talked about Chicago, and Kravitz & Bane, and Sam couldn't imagine how three hundred lawyers existed in the same building. There was a jittery laugh or two, and a few tense smiles as they waited for the next dreaded knock.

It came at precisely eleven fifty-five. Three sharp raps, then a long pause. Nugent waited before barging in.

Adam immediately jumped to his feet. Sam took a deep breath, and clenched his jaws. He pointed a finger at Adam. 'Listen to me,' he said firmly. 'You can walk in there with me, but you cannot stay.'

'I know. I don't want to stay, Sam.'

'Good.' The crooked finger dropped, the jaws slackened, the face sank. Sam reached forward and took Adam by the shoulders. Adam pulled him close and hugged him gently.

'Tell Lee I love her,' Sam said, his voice breaking. He pulled away slightly and looked Adam in the eyes. 'Tell her I thought about her to the very end. And I'm not mad at her for not coming. I wouldn't want to come here either if I didn't have to.'

Adam's head nodded quickly, and he struggled not to cry. Anything, Sam, anything.

'Say hello to your mom. I always liked her. Give my love to Carmen, she's a great kid. I'm sorry about all this, Adam. It's a terrible legacy for you guys to carry.'

'We'll do fine, Sam.'

'I know you will. I'll die a very proud man, son, because of you.'

'I'll miss you,' Adam said, the tears now running down his cheeks.

The door opened and the colonel stepped in. 'It's time now, Sam,' he said sadly.

Sam faced him with a brave smile. 'Let's do it!' he said strongly. Nugent went first, then Sam, then Adam. They stepped into the Chamber Room, which was packed with people. Everyone stared at Sam, then immediately looked away. They were ashamed, thought Adam. Ashamed to be here taking part in this nasty little deed. They wouldn't look at Adam.

Monday, the executioner, and his assistant were along the wall next to the chemical room. Two uniformed guards were crowded next to them. Lucas Mann and a deputy warden were near the door. The doctor was busy to the immediate right, adjusting his EKG and trying to appear calm.

And in the center of the room, now surrounded by the various participants, was the chamber, an octagonal-shaped tube with a gleaming fresh coat of silver paint. Its door was open, the fateful wooden chair just waiting, a row of covered windows behind it.

The door to the outside of the room was open, but there was no draft. The room was like a sauna, everyone was drenched with sweat. The two guards took Sam and led him into the chamber. He counted the steps – only five of them from the door to the chamber – and suddenly he was inside, sitting, looking around the men to find Adam. The men's hands moved rapidly.

Adam had stopped just inside the door. He leaned on the wall for strength, his knees spongy and weak. He stared at the people in the room, at the chamber, at the floor, the EKG. It was all so sanitary! The freshly painted walls. The sparkling concrete floors. The doctor with his machines. The clean, sterile little chamber with its glowing luster. The antiseptic smell from the chemical room. Everything so spotless and hygienic. It should've been a clinic where people went to get themselves healed.

What if I vomit on the floor, right here at the feet of the good doctor, what would that do for your disinfected little room, Nugent? How would the manual treat that, Nugent, if I just lost it right here in front of the chamber? Adam clutched his stomach.

Straps on Sam's arms, two of them for each, then two more for the legs, over the shiny new Dickies, then the hideous head brace so he wouldn't hurt himself when the gas hit. There now, all buckled down, and ready for the vapors. All neat and tidy, spotless and germ-free, no blood to be shed. Nothing to pollute this flawless, moral killing.

The guards backed out of the narrow door, proud of their work.

Adam looked at him sitting in there. Their eyes met, and for an instant Sam closed his.

The doctor was next. Nugent said something to him, but Adam couldn't hear the words. He stepped inside and rigged the wire running from the stethoscope. He was quick with his work.

Lucas Mann stepped forward with a sheet of paper. He stood in the door of the chamber. 'Sam, this is the death warrant. I'm required by law to read it to you.'

'Just hurry,' Sam grunted without opening his lips.

Lucas lifted the piece of paper, and read from it: 'Pursuant to a verdict of guilty and a sentence of death returned against you by the Circuit Court of Washington County on February 14, 1981, you are hereby condemned to die by lethal gas in the gas chamber at the Mississippi State Penitentiary at Parchman. May God have mercy on your soul.' Lucas backed away, then reached for the first of two phones mounted on the wall. He called his office to see if there were any miraculous last minute delays. There were none. The second phone was a secured line to the Attorney General's office in Jackson. Again, all systems were go. It was now thirty seconds after midnight, Wednesday, August 8. 'No stays,' he said to Nugent.

The words bounced around the humid room and crashed in from all directions. Adam glanced at his grandfather for the last time. His hands were clenched. His eyes were closed tightly, as if he couldn't look at Adam again. His lips were moving, as if he had just one more quick prayer.

'Any reason why this execution should not proceed?' Nugent asked formally, suddenly craving solid legal advice.

'None,' Lucas said with genuine regret.

Nugent stood in the door of the chamber. 'Any last words, Sam?' he asked.

'Not for you. It's time for Adam to leave.'

'Very well.' Nugent slowly closed the door, its thick rubber gasket preventing noise. Silently, Sam was now locked up, and buckled down. He closed his eyes tightly. Just please hurry.

Adam eased behind Nugent, who was still facing the chamber door. Lucas Mann opened the door to the outside, and both men made a quick exit. Adam glanced back at the room for the last time. The executioner was reaching for a lever. His assistant was inching to the side to catch a glimpse. The two guards were jockeying for position so they could watch the old bastard die. Nugent and the deputy warden and the doctor were crowded along the other wall, all inching closer, heads bobbing up and over, each fearful he might miss something.

The ninety-degree heat outside seemed much cooler. Adam walked to the end of the ambulance and leaned on it for a second.

'Are you all right?' Lucas asked.

'No.'

'Just take it easy.'

'You're not gonna witness it?'

'No. I've seen four. That's enough for me. This one's especially difficult.'

Adam stared at the white door in the center of the brick wall. Three vans were parked nearby. A group of guards smoked and whispered by the vans. 'I'd like to leave,' he said, afraid that he was about to be sick.

'Let's go.' Lucas grabbed his elbow and led him to the first van. He said something to a guard, who jumped into the front seat. Adam and Lucas sat on a bench in the center of it.

Adam knew at that precise moment his grandfather was in the chamber gasping for breath, his lungs seared with burning poison. Just over there, in that little red-brick building, right now, he's sucking it in, trying to swallow as much as possible, hoping to simply float away to a better world.

He began to cry. The van moved around the recreation yards and through the grass in front of the Row. He covered his eyes, and cried for Sam, for his suffering at this moment, for the despicable way he was being forced to die. He looked so pitiful sitting there in his new clothes being tied down like an animal. He cried for Sam and the last nine and a half years he'd spent staring through bars, trying to catch a glimpse of the moon, wondering if anyone out there cared about him. He cried for the whole wretched Cayhall family and their miserable history. And he cried for himself, for his anguish at this moment, for the loss of a loved one, for his failure to stop this madness.

Lucas patted him gently on the shoulder and the van rolled and stopped, then rolled and stopped again. 'I'm sorry,' he said more than once.

'This your car?' Lucas asked, as they stopped outside the gate. The dirt parking lot was filled to capacity. Adam yanked the door handle and stepped out without a word. He could say thanks later.

He sped along the gravel trail, between the rows of cotton, until he came to the main drive. He drove quickly to the front entrance, slowing only briefly as he weaved around two barricades, then stopped at the front gate so a guard could check his trunk. To his left was the swarm of reporters. They were on their feet, waiting anxiously for word from the Row. Mini-cams were ready.

There was no one in his trunk, and he was waved around another barricade, almost hitting a guard who wasn't moving fast enough. He stopped at the highway, and paused to look at the candlelight vigil under way to his right. Hundreds of candles. And a hymn in progress somewhere down the way.

He sped away, past state troopers loitering about, enjoying the break in the action. He sped past cars parked on the shoulders for two miles, and soon Parchman was behind him. He pushed the turbo, and was soon doing ninety.

He headed north for some reason, though he had no intention of going to Memphis. Towns like Tutwiler, Lambert, Marks, Sledge, and Crenshaw flew by. He rolled the windows down and the warm air swirled around the seats. The windshield was peppered with large bugs and insects, the plague of the Delta, he'd learned.

He just drove, with no particular destination. This trip had not been planned. He'd given no thought to where he would go immediately after Sam died, because he never truly believed it would happen. Maybe he'd be in Jackson now, drinking and celebrating with Garner Goodman and Hez Kerry, getting plastered because they'd pulled a rabbit out of the hat. Maybe he'd be at the Row, still on the phone trying desperately to get the details of a last minute stay which would later become permanent. Maybe a lot of things.

He wouldn't dare go to Lee's, because she might actually be there. Their next meeting would be a nasty one, and he preferred to postpone it. He decided to find a decent motel. Spend the night. Try and sleep. Figure things out tomorrow after the sun was up. He raced through dozens of hamlets and towns, none with a room for rent. He slowed considerably. One highway led to another. He was lost but didn't care. How can you be lost when you don't know where you're going? He recognized towns on road signs, turned this way then that way. An all-night convenience store caught his attention on the outskirts of Hernando, not far from Memphis. There were no cars parked in front. A middle-aged lady with jet-black hair was behind the counter, smoking, smacking gum, and talking on the phone. Adam went to the beer cooler and grabbed a six-pack.

'Sorry, hon, can't buy beer after twelve.'

'What?' Adam demanded, reaching into his pocket.

She didn't like his snarl. She carefully laid the phone next to the cash register. 'We can't sell beer here after midnight. It's the law.'

'The law?'

'Yes. The law.'

'Of the State of Mississippi?'

'That's correct,' she said smartly.

'Do you know what I think of the laws of this state right now?'

'No, dear. And I honestly don't care.'

Adam flipped a ten-dollar bill on the counter and carried the beer to his car. She watched him leave, then stuck the cash in her pocket and went back to the phone. Why bother the cops over a six-pack of beer?

He was off again, going south on a two-lane highway, obeying the speed limit and gulping his first beer. Off again in pursuit of a clean room with a free continental breakfast, pool, cable, HBO, kids stay free.

Fifteen minutes to die, fifteen minutes to vent the chamber, ten minutes to wash it down with ammonia.

Spray the lifeless body, deader than hell, according to the young doctor and his EKG. Nugent pointing here and there – get the gas masks, get the gloves, get those damned reporters back on the vans and out of here.

Adam could see Sam in there, head fallen to one side, still trapped under those enormous leather buckles. What color was his skin now? Surely not the pale whiteness of the past nine and a half years. Surely the gas turned his lips purple and his flesh pink. The chamber is now clear, all is safe. Enter the chamber, Nugent says, unbuckle him. Take the knives. Cut off the clothing. Did his bowels loosen? Did his bladder leak? They always do. Be careful. Here, here's the plastic bag. Put the clothes in here. Spray the naked body.

Adam could see the new clothes – the stiff khakis, the oversized shoes, the spotless white socks. Sam had been so proud to wear real clothes again. Now they were rags in a green garbage sack, handled like venom and soon to be burned by a trustee.

Where are the clothes, the blue prison pants and white tee shirt? Get them. Enter the chamber. Dress the corpse. No shoes are necessary. No socks. Hell, he's just going to the funeral home. Let the family worry about dressing him for a decent burial. Now the stretcher. Get him out of there. Into the ambulance.

Adam was near a lake somewhere, over a bridge, through a bottom, the air suddenly damp and cool. Lost again.

FIFTY-TWO

THE FIRST GLINT of sunrise was a pink halo over a hill above Clanton. It strained through the trees, and was soon turning to yellow, then to orange. There were no clouds, nothing but brilliant colors against the dark sky.

There were two unopened beers sitting in the grass. Three empty cans had been tossed against a nearby headstone. The first empty can was still in the car.

The dawn was breaking. Shadows fell toward him from the rows of other gravestones. The sun itself was soon peeking at him from behind the trees.

He'd been there for a couple of hours, though he'd lost track of time. Jackson and Judge Slattery and Monday's hearing were years ago. Sam had died minutes ago. Or was he dead? Had they already done their dirty act? Time was still playing games.

He hadn't found a motel, not that he'd looked very hard. He'd found himself near Clanton, then was drawn here where he'd located the headstone of Anna Gates Cayhall. Now he rested against it. He'd drunk the warm beer and thrown the cans at the largest monument within range. If the cops found him here and took him to jail, he wouldn't care. He'd been in a cell before. 'Yeah, just got out of Parchman,' he'd tell his cell mates, his rap partners. 'Just walked out of death row.' And they'd leave him alone.

Evidently, the cops were occupied elsewhere. The graveyard was secure. Four little red flags had been staked

593

out next to his grandmother's plot. Adam noticed them as the sun rose to the east. Another grave to be dug.

A car door closed somewhere behind him, but he didn't hear it. A figure walked toward him, but he didn't know it. It moved slowly, searching the cemetery.

The snapping of a twig startled Adam. Lee was standing beside him, her hand on her mother's headstone. He looked at her, then looked away.

'What are you doing here?' he asked, too numb to be surprised.

She gently lowered herself first to her knees, then she sat very close to him, her back pressed to her mother's engraved name. She wrapped her arm around his elbow.

'Where the hell have you been, Lee?'

'In treatment.'

'You could've called, dammit.'

'Don't be angry, Adam, please. I need a friend.' She leaned her head on his shoulder.

'I'm not sure I'm your friend, Lee. What you did was terrible.'

'He wanted to see me, didn't he?'

'He did. You, of course, were lost in your own little world, self-absorbed as usual. No thought given to others.'

'Please, Adam, I've been in treatment. You know how weak I am. I need help.'

'Then get it.'

She noticed the two cans of beer, and Adam quickly tossed them away. 'I'm not drinking,' she said, pitifully. Her voice was sad and hollow. Her pretty face was tired and wrinkled.

'I tried to see him,' she said.

'When?'

'Last night. I drove to Parchman. They wouldn't let me in. Said it was too late.'

Adam lowered his head and softened considerably. He would accomplish nothing by cursing her. She was an alcoholic, struggling to overcome demons he hoped he would never meet. And she was his aunt, his beloved Lee.

594

'He asked about you at the very end. He asked me to tell you he loved you, and that he wasn't angry because you didn't come to see him.'

She started crying very quietly. She wiped her cheeks with the backs of her hands, and cried for a long time.

'He went out with a great deal of courage and dignity,' Adam said. 'He was very brave. He said his heart was right with God, and that he hated no one. He was terribly remorseful for the things he'd done. He was champ, Lee, an old fighter who was ready to move on.'

'You know where I've been?' she asked between sniffles, as if she'd heard nothing he said.

'No. Where?'

'I've been to the old home place. I drove there from Parchman last night.'

'Why?'

'Because I wanted to burn it. And it burned beautifully. The house and the weeds around it. One huge fire. All up in smoke.'

'Come on, Lee.'

'It's true. I almost got caught, I think. I might've passed a car on the way out. I'm not worried, though. I bought the place last week. Paid thirteen thousand dollars to the bank. If you own it, then you can burn it, right? You're the lawyer.'

'Are you serious?'

'Go look for yourself. I parked in front of a church a mile away to wait for the fire trucks. They never came. The nearest house is two miles away. No one saw the fire. Drive out and take a look. There's nothing left but the chimney and a pile of ashes.'

'How –'

'Gasoline. Here, smell my hands.' She shoved them under his nose. They bore the acrid, undeniable smell of gasoline.

'But why?'

'I should've done it years ago.'

'That doesn't answer the question. Why?'

595

'Evil things happened there. It was filled with demons and spirits. Now they're gone.'

'So they died with Sam?'

'No, they're not dead. They've gone off to haunt someone else.'

It would be pointless to pursue this discussion, Adam decided quickly. They should leave, maybe return to Memphis where he could get her back into recovery. And maybe therapy. He would stay with her and make sure she got help.

A dirty pickup truck entered the cemetery through the iron gates of the old section, and puttered slowly along the concrete path through the ancient monuments. It stopped at a small utility shed in a corner of the lot. Three black men slowly scooted out and stretched their backs.

'That's Herman,' she said.

'Who?'

'Herman. Don't know his last name. He's been digging graves here for forty years.'

They watched Herman and the other two across the valley of tombstones. They could barely hear their voices as the men deliberately went about their preparations.

Lee stopped the sniffling and crying. The sun was well above the treeline, its rays hitting directly in their faces. It was already warm. 'I'm glad you came,' she said. 'I know it meant a lot to him.'

'I lost, Lee. I failed my client, and now he's dead.'

'You tried your best. No one could save him.'

'Maybe.'

'Don't punish yourself. Your first night in Memphis, you told me it was a long shot. You came close. You put up a good fight. Now it's time to go back to Chicago and get on with the rest of your life.'

'I'm not going back to Chicago.'

'What?'

'I'm changing jobs.'

'But you've only been a lawyer for a year.'

'I'll still be a lawyer. Just a different kind of practice.'

596

'Doing what?'

'Death penalty litigation.'

'That sounds dreadful.'

'Yes, it does. Especially at this moment in my life. But I'll grow into it. I'm not cut out for the big firms.'

'Where will you practice?'

'Jackson. I'll be spending more time at Parchman.'

She rubbed her face and pulled back her hair. 'I guess you know what you're doing,' she said, unable to hide the doubt.

'Don't bet on it.'

Herman was walking around a battered yellow backhoe parked under a shade tree next to the shed. He studied it thoughtfully while another man placed two shovels in its bucket. They stretched again, laughed about something, and kicked the front tires.

'I have an idea,' she said. 'There's a little café north of town. It's called Ralph's. Sam took me –'

'Ralphs?'

'Yeah.'

'Sam's minister was named Ralph. He was with us last night.'

'Sam had a minister?'

'Yes. A good one.'

'Anyway, Sam would take me and Eddie there on our birthdays. Place has been here for a hundred years. We'd eat these huge biscuits and drink hot cocoa. Let's go see if it's open.'

'Now?'

'Yeah.' She was excited and getting to her feet. 'Come on. I'm hungry.'

Adam grabbed the headstone and pulled himself up. He hadn't slept since Monday night, and his legs were heavy and stiff. The beer made him dizzy.

In the distance, an engine started. It echoed unmuffled through the cemetery. Adam froze. Lee turned to see it. Herman was operating the backhoe, blue smoke boiling from the exhaust. His two co-workers were in the front bucket with their feet hanging out. The backhoe lunged in low gear, then started along the drive, very slowly past the rows of graves. It stopped and turned.

It was coming their way.